O F

L O V E

A N D

L I F E

OF LOVE AND LIFE

Three novels selected and condensed
by Reader's Digest

The Reader's Digest Association Limited, London

The Reader's Digest Association Limited
11 Westferry Circus, Canary Wharf, London E14 4HE

www.readersdigest.co.uk

ISBN 0-276-42875-7

For information as to ownership of copyright in the material of
this book, and acknowledgments, see last page.

CONTENTS

Monday's Child
Louise Bagshawe

'Monday's Child is fair of face' goes the old rhyme, but Anna Brown knows that's not always true. For Anna is tall, large-boned and constantly worries about her weight and the size of her nose. What's more, she's in a dead-end script-reading job and saddled with a ghastly boyfriend. But Anna dreams of one day finding that one great script, becoming a producer, winning an Oscar . . . and falling in love with a man who loves her just the way she is.

It happens, right?

Well, it happens to beautiful people . . .

1

'AND SO MOVIES, now more than ever, represent the UK's creativity. And its rich cultural diversity . . .'

I stare at the MC, trying not to seem too bored. It's hard going. I'm tired. It's been a long day at work, and it's not going to end anytime soon. My boss, Kitty Simpson, has been invited to this bash, and naturally she has to show off by taking an assistant. Because it costs £2,000 a head. It's a film industry night for 'charidee', where overpaid actors, directors, agents and producers supposedly raise money for AIDS awareness, but actually just want to see and be seen. The opulence is everywhere: mounds of caviar, circus performers walking around swallowing fire, expensive appetisers, women in dazzling gowns. There's at least twenty grand's worth of out-of-season floral arrangements. You wonder why they don't just write a cheque to the Terrence Higgins Trust and save the overhead, but of course that would be no fun.

'Anna,' Kitty hisses at me. 'I *said* to go fetch my bag.'

'Sorry,' I whisper back.

'You're here to *assist* me. You should be paying attention,' she says, tossing her immaculately styled hair. Tonight she is wearing a long-sleeved, opaque dress with a mandarin collar to hide the wrinkles on her neck; I think it's Armani. She has teamed this with diamond chandelier earrings and an AIDS ribbon, but naturally her AIDS ribbon is a platinum brooch studded with rubies. 'You don't need to just stand there like a huge great sack of potatoes,' she snaps, obviously annoyed. 'Really, you could have at least made an effort. At least *tried* to find a flattering dress. But I suppose there's not much point, is there?' Kitty sighs, losing interest.

I am five eleven. I have huge boobs, a bit of a tummy, strong arms and hands, and an unfortunate beak of a nose. There are some things I like about myself; I've got a decent bottom, not too flabby, and good legs, but I have to cover those up because I'm so tall.

I thought I didn't look too bad tonight, but evidently I was wrong. 'I thought it was an all-right dress,' I mutter. It's navy velvet with sheer sleeves. Comes right down to my flats.

Kitty ignores me. 'My bag? Before I die, please.'

'OK,' I sigh. 'Do you have the cloakroom ticket?'

She shrugs. 'Lost it. Just describe it to them.'

'But that'll take them for ever to find it,' I protest. There are at least a thousand people here. 'And Mark Swan's going to be speaking soon!'

Watching him was going to be the one bright spot in this nightmare of an evening. Somehow they'd actually managed to get Swan, England's hottest director, to give the speech. Mark Swan has won three Oscars for best picture and he's still in his thirties. He's so talented he makes Sam Mendes seem like an amateur. But he's also reclusive, never appears in the press, no parties in Cannes, no photo shoots in *Hello!* magazine. I'm a producer, and I don't understand the fuss they make about directors. But even I want to hear what Mark Swan has to say. (Well, OK, I'm not technically a producer. All I do is read scripts and act as Kitty's general dogsbody. But I work for producers, which is almost the same thing.)

'Just describe it to them,' Kitty says again. 'You know my handbag. It's the black one.'

The black one. Great. 'Could you be a little more—'

'Ssh!' hisses Kitty. 'They're introducing him.'

'. . . third Academy Award for *King Harald* . . . Ladies and gentlemen, Mr Mark Swan.'

I crane my neck towards the stage. But my view is obscured by a fat bloke with a huge bald head. 'Thanks,' Mark Swan says. He's got a rich, sexy baritone and he's very tall. But I can't see what he looks like. 'When you put it like that it sounds impressive.'

A ripple of sycophantic laughter from the crowd.

'You know, the first thing I think when I see these affairs is why couldn't we all just write a cheque?' Swan says. 'How much do those fire-swallowers go for, anyway?'

More laughter, a bit more uncomfortable. I grin and shift in my seat, trying to see. I love the guy already.

'Anna,' Kitty hisses, eyes narrowing. 'Are you deaf?'

I get up reluctantly. 'I'm going, I'm going . . .'

I thread my way through the tables, getting tsk-tsked at when I impede somebody's view of Swan for a second (he is now telling a very politically incorrect joke about a studio head's wife and a pool cleaner), and rush out to the lobby. I really would like to hear this speech. It's a huge opportunity. He doesn't speak, doesn't give interviews . . .

'Yes? Can I help you?' enquires the cloakroom attendant.

'Um, yes. I need to retrieve my boss's handbag.'

'Ticket?'

'She lost it.'

'Then I can't help you.'

'It's a black one,' I say pathetically. She treats this with the scorn it deserves. 'Mine was number three sixty. It might be near that.'

'There are about fifty thousand black bags near three sixty, love.'

'Look,' I say desperately. 'I'm missing Mark Swan's speech—'

'He came by here earlier,' she says, softening. 'Isn't he handsome?'

'I wouldn't know. I'm missing the speech.'

'He is,' she says dreamily. 'Handsome. Tall, dark and handsome.'

'He sounds gorgeous,' I say. 'And I really don't want to miss him. D'you think I could go in there and have a look?'

'Suit yourself,' she says, shrugging.

I plunge into the vast cloakroom, rooting through fur coats (real ones) and leather jackets. All the bags look identical. I spend a good twenty minutes searching hopelessly, all the while imagining Swan being so warm and funny and teasing all the overblown executives.

There aren't that many really good film guys in Britain and I'm missing the best one out there. And, naturally, Kitty will do nothing but yell at me and tell me I've 'lost' her stupid bloody bag.

'Excuse me.' A tall, bearded man in black tie is trying to squeeze past me. 'I didn't expect to see anyone else in here,' he says.

'Oh. I hope it's OK, the other attendant said I could look for my bag.'

'I'm not the attendant, I'm doing the same thing,' he says sympathetically. 'Lost your ticket?'

'My boss lost hers.'

'Millions of black coats,' he says, sighing. 'Why did I choose black?'

'It's a bugger, isn't it?'

'Sure is,' he says, looking down at me, amused. He's very attractive, from what I can see in the gloom. Rugged, muscular. 'How long have you been here?'

'Almost half an hour.' I sigh. 'I've totally missed Mark Swan's speech.'

He pauses. 'I'm afraid you have. Wasn't worth hearing, anyway.'

'He sounded pretty funny when I left,' I tell him. 'Not all puffed up and luvvie like you'd expect. Not even pretentious.'

'Really.'

'Which is strange, considering he's a recluse.'

'Why's that?' he asks, thumbing through the coats.

'Well,' I say, warming to my subject, 'being a recluse is a bit wanky, isn't it? Like you're so important, you have to hide all the time.'

'Maybe he just doesn't want to be hounded,' he says mildly.

I snort. 'Someone should tell him he's not Tom Cruise.'

'I expect he knows,' he says, stroking his beard thoughtfully.

'He sounded funny though. I liked him,' I say. 'But I'll never get to hear him now. I wanted to see what he was like. And now I won't.'

'Found it,' he says triumphantly, pulling a huge and beautifully made black wool coat from the racks. 'What's the bag you're looking for like?'

'It's a Prada clutch. Should be somewhere in the three hundreds. But you get going,' I say. 'No reason both of us should be stuck in this hole.'

'My ex-girlfriend had one of those,' he says. 'Is this it, by any chance?'

It's a miracle. He reached into a pile of bags and unerringly pulled out Kitty's. I quickly open it. Yep, it's hers all right. There are the business cards, the fags.

'Oh, you are brilliant,' I say. 'Thanks so much.'

'Anything to help out a pretty girl,' he says, with a slight bow.

Pretty girl! That's a good one. It must be gloomier in here than I thought.

'Who's in here? You can't all come in here!' It's the cloakroom attendant. 'I take a five-minute break and everybody's—oh,' she says, stopping dead. 'Excuse me! You didn't have to come in here, I'd have found it for you,' she says to him, simpering.

'I lost my ticket,' he apologises.

'I remember *your* coat, Mr Swan,' she says.

I'm so surprised I lose my balance and fall over backwards, upsetting an entire rail of coats.

'Bloody hell!' she roars.

'There now, no harm done,' says Swan, reaching down and pulling me to my feet. I thank God for the gloom now. He can't see my flushed red cheeks. 'That's easily fixed.' He reaches over and pulls up the entire rail, coats and all, with one hand.

'Oh, well,' she says, de-fanged. 'Well.'

'I'm sorry,' I say.

'Be more careful next time,' she snaps. But I'm looking at Swan.

'Relax, it was fun,' he says. 'More fun than the speech.' And he winks at me. 'Nice to meet you. What's your name?'

'Anna. Anna Brown,' I say. 'OK, well, goodbye, Mr Swan.'

'It's Mark,' he says, grinning. 'Bye, Anna.'

'Where the bloody hell have you been?' Kitty asks, snatching her bag from my flustered hand. 'You missed Mark Swan, you know.'

'Ahm—yes.' Oh well. At least she'll never know. Right?

My flatmate Lily is sitting hunched over her computer. Her long legs are revealed in a short, sleek skirt in buttercup leather, showing off her deep golden tan. Her top is a white halter-neck in clingy jersey, and shimmering blonde hair tumbles down her back.

I'm wearing my best summer outfit too. Black jeans, black T-shirt, Doc Martens. Going monochrome is 'really slimming', or so Lily always tells me. So far I don't seem to have shrunk very much. Horizontally or vertically.

My flatmates are both models. Not catwalk, mostly just photo shoots. Lily's five six, and Janet's five seven, but they are both so slim and petite, especially Lily, that they just seem tiny. And I'm just the right height to be a catwalk model and outdo both of them, but that's only going to happen in an alternative universe. When people are feeling kind, they describe me as 'strapping'. I'm a big girl. All over. And then there's my face. I'm the daughter of a handsome father, with masculine Yorkshire features, and a beautiful mother. She's still beautiful now, at fifty. She's also petite, five five, with an elfin bone structure. But I take after Dad. Do I have my mother's slender torso? Nope. Do I have her raven hair? Nope. Do I have her tiny, retroussé nose, so winsome and feminine? I do not. I am mousy-haired, freckled, hearty, strong, and I have a big nose to go with my big face.

Dad always told me I was beautiful, growing up. And I only gradually found out that I wasn't. Being stood up at school by Jack Lafferty, for example, who was supposed to take me to the fourth-year disco, and everybody giggling and laughing. And the next year, at the St John's School dance, the big one, I found out why he'd done it. Fifth years got to celebrate taking their GCSEs with a big dance at the grammar school across town. I spent the previous Saturday afternoon at Supercuts, had a free make-over courtesy of the No. 7 counter at Boots (blue eye shadow was big back then), picked out a dress, a black velvet Laura Ashley thing with a bow on the back. I knew I was tall and had a big nose, but it didn't bother me, not back then. I thought I was beautiful. Princess Diana was tall and had a big nose and people thought she was the most beautiful woman in the world. I hadn't really had too many boyfriends, but I put that down to the fact that they were shy.

Once we got inside that hall, I was so excited, and everybody else seemed to be, all the St John's boys giggling and laughing and whispering, and after five minutes one of them actually came up to me, flanked by a couple of friends. As I looked down at them smirking up at me I felt great. All the Feldstone Comprehensive girls just standing around, and these guys were asking *me*.

'All right?' said the vision. I thought he was a vision, despite his spots. 'D'you wanna dance?' he asked. His friends grinned. I smiled.

'Sure, why not?' I said casually.

'What's your name?'

'Anna,' I said.

'Mine's Gary,' he said. 'And yours can't be Anna. It's got to be Beanstalk,' he added, sniggering. His two friends nudged him, cackling.

'Here, love,' one of them said. 'What's the weather like up there, eh?'

'She should come with lights,' said the other one. 'Warn the low-flying aircraft!'

All three of them laughed heartily, right in my face, and then turned and walked back over to their side of the room as I stood there, stonily, my cheeks burning. I wanted to put a good face on it, I really did, but when I heard some of the girls next to me snigger meanly too, I couldn't take it. I burst into tears, right in front of everybody.

I can still remember running to the loo, through that crowd of girls and slouching aren't-we-cool boys, all giggling and whispering. I didn't go back out. Maybe I should have, maybe I should have gone and found one of my friends and hung out with them defiantly. But I couldn't. I couldn't do anything except crawl inside one of the stalls, sit down on the loo, and cry. I stayed there for four hours, until the coach was ready to leave.

That was the night I learned my lesson. I wasn't pretty, I didn't look anything like Princess Diana. It had been so easy to believe my parents, especially my daddy who always told me I was beautiful and that all the boys would be fighting over me. I believed him right up until the night of that dance.

Never again, though. I adjusted immediately. I shoved all my fancy clothes straight to the back of my wardrobe. I threw away all my high heels and fire-engine-red lipsticks and little tubs of body glitter and shopped for plain tees and basic jeans and khakis; dull, straight-up clothes that nobody would ever notice. When I was older I found a few classic 'don't notice me' dresses and bought four in different colours, and so I go from the office to dinners to the occasional disastrous date, all in clothes expertly designed to conceal me.

I will absolutely never look like Janet or Lily, not even after major plastic surgery, which I can't afford. I've got a Nose Job Fund box, and had a look in there recently. I've saved a massive ninety-eight quid and thirty-four p. There used to be more, but I did take that weekend City Break in Bruges six months ago, when it rained the whole time.

'Anna, what's your date of birth?' Lily asks suddenly.

'Why?' I ask.

'Just for fun,' she persuades. 'It tells you what day of the week you were born.'

'July the 3rd, 1971.'

Lily's long talons peck over the computer. 'Monday!' she says.

Janet looks over at me. Janet is wearing a teeny, body-hugging pale pink dress that looks incredible against her olive skin. 'Monday's child is fair of face,' she says.

Lily sniggers. 'Sorry,' she says. 'It slipped out! Honest!'

'Anna can take a joke, can't you, Anna?' Janet says.

I sigh. 'No problem.'

And it really isn't. I mean, it's not like I haven't heard it before. You get used to it. Being ugly, that is.

I don't deceive myself about my looks. Even my granny stopped saying, 'It's just a phase. You'll see,' when I reached fifteen. I've tried various things. Flat shoes, plain colours. Make-up tips to 'minimise' my nose, shading and highlighting, but nothing helps. It's still huge. It's still there. And just in case I might be tempted to forget about it, I tend to get helpful reminders from male members of the public.

'Bloody 'ell! Packed yer trunk, Nellie?'

That was delivered last week by a drunk teenager as I walked home from Tesco's. I thought it was rather imaginative of him.

'Don't worry, Anna, I think you're, like, totally beautiful,' says Janet.

'Because real beauty is on the inside,' lies Lily. 'And that's what counts.'

'What day were you born, Lily?' I ask, hoping to distract her.

'I'll look it up,' Janet says. She strolls over to the computer, sticking out her perfectly firm, rounded bottom. Janet has a J-Lo fixation. She watches all her videos religiously. She also has an unfortunate tendency to say 'Bling bling' and likes to be called 'Jay-Me', which she prefers to her real name, Janet Meeks.

'Wednesday,' Janet says.

'Wednesday's child is full of woe,' I say, a touch more cheerfully. 'I have to get back to work.' I reach for another paper-bound script. My eyes are watering, but it's Sunday already and I have to get 'coverage' typed up for five more screenplays, all of which will, without a doubt, be as dreadful as the last sixteen I've read this weekend.

'Oh, take a break, Anna. Live a little!' says Janet brightly. Janet works maybe two days a week and makes three times what I do. She looks languidly into the camera for three hours and goes to look-sees and auditions. I type my fingers to the bone all weekend writing coverage for crappy scripts that will never get made, then during the week I run errands, type letters, answer phones, make copies, walk dogs, and generally act as an office slave for a total bitch named Kitty.

Janet and Lily make about forty grand a year. I make sixteen. They are twenty-eight and twenty-three. I am thirty-two.

And yet, and I know this is stupid, I keep thinking things are going to change for me. I mean, I'm in the right industry. It took me four years to find a job as a script reader, and now I have one at a proper production company with fancy Covent Garden offices.

It could happen, right? I could find that one great script I could recommend. I could get made into a development executive like Kitty. I could be a producer and make millions and win an Oscar . . .

Sometimes I think I should try to get a better-paying job somewhere else, but doing what? It wouldn't be in the film business. They pay us bugger all because they know they can. There are forty little Annas out there, fresh-faced from film school, who would kill for my job. I save a bunch of money by paying only £300 a month for my room in this flat. Instead of money I give Lily and Janet all the invitations and tickets that come my way—the movie premieres, the industry parties, the VIP passes to the members-only clubs.

That works out well because I wouldn't bother with those parties anyway. The people who go to them are all varying combinations of rich, beautiful and successful. I'm none of the above, so I just stay home and read more bad scripts.

'We could try a make-over on you,' Janet says, encouragingly.

'It's not all about looks, OK?' I tell her. 'I'm fine like I am!'

'I wonder if Brian thinks that,' Lily says archly.

Brian is my boyfriend. He's always telling me he 'doesn't care' about my looks because 'real beauty is on the inside'. I hear that one a lot. Brian is no prize himself though. He's all skinny and he breaks out from time to time, doing a good impression of a pepperoni pizza. Plus, he's shorter than me—but who isn't? Still, you have to have a boyfriend, don't you? I mean, especially if you're ugly. A boyfriend is great camouflage. He stops people from making pitying comments. So I cling to him.

'Brian likes me for who I am,' I tell Janet defiantly.

'Sure,' she says, brightly. 'Whatever you say.'

The buzzer rings and she leaps to her feet. Lily tears herself away from the mirror above the mantel. They adore the phone, the buzzer, anything. Always expecting something fabulous. And why not? For pretty girls, it mostly is something fabulous.

'Hello?'

'Hi, 's Brian,' Brian's voice slurs.

'Speak of the devil!' says Janet, laughing lightly.

A second later I hear the ping of the lift. Our flat is located above a feminist bookshop in Tottenham Court Road, one of those old Victorian buildings with an ancient, narrow lift. It fits one normal person, or two models, and feels like a coffin without the velvet.

Brian opens the lift door and steps out. He's wearing a white polyester short-sleeved shirt and saggy chinos, but I'm still glad to see him. He's my boyfriend, after all. As in, I have one!

'Hi, honey,' I say, kissing him on the cheek. 'Come in.'

'Hi, Brian,' coo Lily and Janet together, shaking their hair and smoothing their already tight clothes tighter round their bodies.

'Hi,' he says, staring. I do wish he wouldn't drool like that. I mean, I am standing right here.

I cough. 'Are we going out to dinner?'

'I thought you had all that work to do,' says Janet, innocently.

'I can take a break,' I say. 'For you,' I add to Brian.

He looks awkward. 'No, it's not that . . . can we go in your room?'

'No rumpy-pumpy!' says Janet, shaking her finger at him.

Brian giggles. 'It's not that either,' he says. 'I just need some privacy.'

'Come on,' I say, heading towards my 'bedroom'. It's really more of a walk-in closet with a bunk in it, but what can you expect for £300 a month? 'What is it, darling?' I ask, with self-conscious tenderness.

'I have to express myself on our relationship,' Brian says.

Oh God. He's been at the self-help books again.

'Could you do it over dinner?' I ask hopefully. 'We could always go to Pizza Express.' Brian is a touch cheap. 'Dutch treat,' I hasten to reassure him, like it's ever been anything else.

'That wouldn't fit my moral paradigm at this time,' Brian says heavily.

'Sorry, I don't speak weirdo,' I say and instantly regret it.

'Oh yeah. That's just typical,' Brian snaps. 'You've always stood in the way of my self-actualisation!'

I swallow. 'Sorry. What was it you wanted to say?'

'We've been in each other's lives for some time now, and I think we have both gained a lot from the uniqueness of the experience,' he says, offering me a brisk smile.

Hey! Maybe he's going to ask me to move in with him.

17

'I know I have,' I say, smiling back at him encouragingly.

'Of course *you* have,' says Brian as though this were perfectly obvious. 'But my personal boundaries have been trammelled and I'm at a place in my life where I need fresh stimulus.'

I digest this for a second. Then light dawns. 'You're breaking up with me,' I say slowly. I drink him in, all eight and a half stone, lanky ginger hair, pizza face. In short, one of the least attractive men I've ever seen. '*You're* breaking up with *me*.' Oh boy. This is a new depth of humiliation. 'I don't believe this,' I say, trying for incredulity, but my voice wobbles.

'Out of suffering comes strength, Anna,' says Brian wisely.

'You really are a total tosser,' I blurt. 'Just go away, Brian, would you?' But he stays rooted to the spot.

'It's not how you look,' he says virtuously. 'Well, that did have *something* to do with it. Looks are important to me because the body is a reflection of the spirit.' He gestures at my pudgy tummy. 'I think you should work on that. Just a friendly comment.'

'A reflection of the spirit?' I retort. 'Let's hope not, because looking at your face, I guess your spirit has measles.'

He flushes a dull red. 'Mildred says I'm very handsome, *actually*.'

'Who's that? Your new girlfriend?'

He doesn't answer.

'Well, Mildred is either a liar or blind, and if she hasn't mentioned your halitosis, her sense of smell can't be all that great either.' I stand up threateningly. 'Now *get out*.'

I have two and a half stone on him. Brian turns and flees.

'Well,' says Lily sweetly, 'I'm glad he values you for who you are!'

So it's another dull Monday like any other except that I am now boyfriendless. I had the worst boyfriend in the world, and he dumped me.

'Thank *God*,' cries Vanna (her real name) when she hears. Vanna is my best friend. We met back when we were in college together and we've stayed best friends ever since, even though our lives have gone in slightly different directions: me, reader of bad scripts and dogsbody for no money, her, editorial director at one of London's top publishing houses for about a hundred and fifty grand a year; me, now dumped by ugly, bad-breath-reeking loser, her, blissfully married to Rupert, an investment banker, with two small children.

All men adore her. I can't understand why we still get on.

'He was vile, hon.'

'But it was so nice to have a boyfriend,' I say sadly.

'You'll soon get another one. A *better* one. You work at Winning

Productions, after all. Just think of all the talent that walks in there! And I mean talent in the strictly trouser sense,' Vanna adds.

'I don't get much of a chance to socialise at work.'

'You need to try,' Vanna says, ominously. 'You may be letting your best chance slip away. Where else are you supposed to meet your match, eh? A busy, professional woman like you.'

I'm not sure this is an exactly accurate depiction of me, but still.

'A harassed executive,' she continues firmly. 'On the creative side. You have to take this Brian thing as a wake-up call.'

'What do you—'

But when she's in full flow, there's no stopping her. This is one reason she is so successful. Nobody ever dares interrupt.

'A wake-up call that says, "I will not be ignored any more! I will not settle for the dregs in life! I will only go out with *authentically shaggable men* who can think themselves lucky to get a look-in with a hottie like me!" That's your new mantra, darling—*Anna is a hottie!*'

'Very noble,' I said, but at least now I'm laughing.

'I wasn't joking,' she says earnestly. Vanna is totally blind where I am concerned.

Anyway, at least she got me thinking that being shot of Brian wasn't so bad. I mean, I couldn't stand him. Perhaps I could think more about my job, try to make an impression. Get a rise. Something.

'Hi,' I say to Sharon and John, my fellow readers and slaves. Sharon is a pert twenty-two-year-old who is only doing this job as an alternative to waitressing while she hones her acting skills. She has evidently decided that if she flirts with enough male executives here, one of them might get her an agent or something. She would not need a pep talk about looking for romance in the office. Sharon is a pro. Her light brown curls are always bouncy, her freckled, creamy skin always glowing. In summer she favours teensy little dresses; in winter tight trousers and body-skimming jackets. All year round she likes kitten heels and dangly earrings.

John is twenty-eight and regards himself as an utter failure, but unlike me he sees this as a choice. John believes the noble art of the cinema is being bastardised by Hollywood, and only a really serious *auteur* like himself can rescue it. He wants to direct. Surprise. In the meantime, he gets perverse pleasure from reading so many bad scripts and passing on them all. He always wears brown corduroys and an orange or a plum-based print shirt, because he's all about the seventies (except the good bits, like the Wombles). John likes jazz, beat literature and French cinema. He also likes Kitty, who is an utter bitch, which seems to turn him on.

John keeps his job because he is a world-class suck-up and fawner. Sharon keeps her job because the men in the office won't let Kitty fire her. I keep my job because I do all the work.

'How was your weekend?' Sharon asks. 'Meet any hot guys?'

'Not really.'

Sharon looks at me pityingly. '*I* met someone,' she adds, ringlets bouncing, 'at the *Legally Blonde 2* premiere party.'

'Was he handsome?' I ask. 'Sexy? Funny?'

Sharon waves a hand as if to brush away such minor considerations. 'He works for *MGM* in *LA*,' she says triumphantly. It is Sharon's lifelong dream to get to LA and get discovered, so she can be the next Catherine Zeta-Jones. Unfortunately for her Sharon is not talented and only a bit pretty.

'You'd do well there,' I say supportively. 'You're committed. Passionate.'

Sharon's smile broadens. She crosses her long, lean legs under today's white minidress. 'Exactly,' she agrees. 'You can really spot talent, Anna.'

'Do you think I should go to LA?' I ask. Maybe that's what's missing in my career. Maybe I'm just in the wrong place.

Sharon takes a long, assessing look at me. I'm wearing my plain camel cotton skirt and long-sleeved white shirt. It doesn't attract too much attention and I think it's businesslike.

'LA's not for you, is it, really,' she says. 'I'm only being honest. You're doing well here, anyway,' she lies. 'Kitty relies on you.'

'Good morning, team,' Mike Watson says.

We all look up. Oh joy, it's Mike Watson, a development executive, and a total pig. He hates Kitty, but that's about all you can put in the plus column. Mike is a deeply sad man. He loves American slang, working out at the gym and putting women down. Every actress is 'too fat' or 'too old'. Mike has one reader only: Rob Stanford. He's blond, nineteen, and upper class; strictly window-dressing. More importantly, Rob is the nephew of a big agent, Max Stanford, whom Mike sucks up to.

'Hi,' I say. John nods bleakly. Sharon tosses her ringlets and smiles at Mike engagingly.

'Hey, Mike,' she says, in her best breathy little-girl voice. 'Can I get you some iced tea? I know it's your favourite.'

'Thanks, babe,' he says, 'but Rob's already fixed me up.'

'Oh,' says Sharon, crestfallen.

'But you can bring me some biscuits,' he says, grinning.

'Sure thing, Mike,' says Sharon, fluttering her eyelashes.

I think I'm going to be sick.

The phone trills. Sharon jumps on it. 'Winning Productions,' she says. 'Hello, you're with a Winner. What's that? Now? OK. OK, Kitty.

Yes, right away.' She stands up dramatically, giving Mike a nice flash of tanned thigh. 'That's Kitty, she wants us all in her office right away.'

I head into Kitty's interior-designed office. With all the originality of a new burger joint, Kitty has chosen to do up her gorgeous Victorian corner space as a 1950s American diner. She has a non-working soda fountain and posters for James Dean and Rock Hudson movies. And then, of course, there's the Oscar. Kitty once actually won an Oscar for producing Best Foreign Film, *Questa Sera*, back in the seventies, and she's been trading on it ever since. Rumour has it she was shagging the director to get that credit, but I don't believe it. Who on earth would shag Kitty? Other than John, of course. Kitty's scary.

Nobody knows her age. Forty-nine? Fifty-one? She's been Botoxed to death, so she can't frown or smile properly. But she can still yell. She's five foot two and wiry, with the dress sense of Coco Chanel and the warm fluffy personality of Mussolini.

Despite being a pit bull in the office, Kitty is a social butterfly. Put her in a room with a major actor, director or agent, and her personality transforms immediately, superhero-like, to reveal a charming, witty woman, absolutely fascinated by the other person and what they are saying. She takes long, languid lunches at all the right clubs, calls everyone important in her Rolodex twice a month without fail just to catch up. She's a presence on the scene. She's known.

We slide onto the tiny, uncomfortably hard couch (Kitty hates her guests to be comfortable), and wait nervously. This is not like my boss. Normally she comes in, walks into her office and slams the door. Then her mousy, terrified secretary, Claire, brings her the day's call sheet. Then she tells us to prepare for a coverage meeting where she cuts us off and berates us for not finding her the next *Titanic*. After that she usually has me running errands for most of the afternoon, while she lunches with somebody fabulous, and John takes her notes while she's in meetings. Sharon floats about pretending to read more scripts but mostly offering male executives cups of coffee and gossiping in the kitchen. It's a fairly well-honed routine. Why is Kitty calling us in here now? Is one of us going to be sacked?

Kitty walks into her office and slams the door. John looks up at her approvingly, like an adoring dog. And indeed Kitty does look particularly designer-bitch-from-hell today. Yellow Dolce suit with trademark DG buttons, check; Louis Vuitton baguette in spring colours, check; enormous canary-yellow diamond ring flashing ostentatiously, check. Kitty believes in labels. If you can't see who it's by, why bother?

'There are going to be changes around here,' she says dramatically.

I panic. I *am* going to get sacked.

'We're going to raise our game. Find that key project that's out there. Somebody from Winning has to be the first to deliver, and I intend the Kitty Simpson team to be that somebody,' she says. 'It's absolutely vital that we get ourselves noticed.'

'I totally agree,' fawns John. 'You've got such a compelling vision.'

She favours him with a wintry smile. 'Yes,' she muses. 'It needs to be the whole team's vision—the "Kitty Simpson" vision,' she says, drawing a circle in the air with her hand, diamond flashing. 'As I make my mark!'

'As *we* make our mark, you mean,' says Sharon, smiling winsomely.

Kitty's eyes narrow. 'We can start the team effort with you getting us some coffee,' she says. 'You seem to be awfully good at that.'

'Of course,' Sharon says demurely. 'I'll make it for you specially.'

This is obvious code for 'I'll spit in it'.

'Actually, why don't you go, Anna?' says Kitty, after a second.

I walk out gloomily. Of course, Kitty correctly assumes that I will not spit in her coffee. I know I'm far too nice, but I can't help it really. I think it has something to do with being ugly. Non-pretty girls need to be extra sweet and accommodating all the time.

I pile everything onto a tray and head back to Kitty's office. Suddenly, out of nowhere, Rob Stanford materialises. 'Mike's wondering what the "top secret" meeting is all about,' he says.

'Is he?' I ask sweetly. 'If Mike wants to know what the meeting's about, why doesn't he ask Kitty?'

'I'm asking you,' Rob says.

'I can't tell you.' This is perfectly true, as I have no idea myself.

'Well!' he says huffily. 'I won't forget this, you know.'

'I will,' I say. 'Bye, Rob,' and swoop the groaning tray past him with an agility that will do me credit in my future coffee-shop career.

Kitty looks up sharply when I come in. She is tapping her pencil impatiently against her desk. I really don't think she needs any more caffeine.

'Get lost?' she enquires acidly.

'No, Rob Stanford stopped me,' I say, attempting innocence. 'He wanted to know what this meeting was about.'

'Did he indeed,' Kitty hisses darkly. Her heavily lined eyes sweep the three of us. 'For Mike Watson, no doubt. What I am about to tell you remains on this team. Understand?' She takes a sip of her espresso just to draw out the suspense.

'The company is being taken over,' she says. '*Serious* players. Looking to take over our projects. Our people and our talent.'

'Somebody from LA?' asks Sharon, her eyes gleaming now. Visions of being discovered dancing in her head.

'Of course, if any bids *are* made, they're going to look at all the resources of Winning,' says Kitty sternly. 'Bringing in a new, fresh approach. Cutting the dead wood.'

'Winnowing out the chaff,' says John, adoringly.

'And I—we—are not going to be seen as dead wood. I want a *project*. Something big and brash that I can bring to the table. Something with "hit" all over it,' Kitty says. 'Find me something I can package. I want to attach Hugh. Or Catherine. Even Jude, at a pinch. Was there anything in the weekend read?'

We all shake our heads.

'Nothing?' Kitty seems very put out. 'Where is your coverage?'

John and Sharon look sheepish.

'I've done a page of coverage notes,' John blusters.

'For twenty scripts?'

'It was all they deserved, Kitty, I assure you,' he says defensively.

She sighs. 'Get it on my desk. Sharon?'

Sharon blushes. 'My notes were mainly in my head . . .'

'You mean you didn't read any of the scripts,' Kitty says. 'You're a waste of space. You'd better come up with something fast, Sharon. Anna?'

'There was nothing,' I agree. 'But I have two pages on each script. I'll bring them to you.'

'God, no,' says Kitty, losing interest immediately. 'How dull. Just *get* me something, Anna. Find a script for me. There's something in it for the person who does.'

For the first time all day I feel a flicker of something unusual. Hope.

'What would that be?' I ask, trying to sound all casual.

'Advancement,' Kitty says in her most serious voice. 'Your big break.'

Ooh. Why not?

It's not impossible, I think to myself as I sit in my cubicle. I could be the reader that finds that one gem and champions it so eloquently and passionately that they'll *have* to take on my project. And Kitty gets made into a vice-president of production, while I move up to development executive. With a transfer to LA. And readers of my own, and an apartment in a complex with gated security, manicured lawns, and a pool . . .

Maybe not a pool. My tummy has not seen a swimsuit since I was fourteen and it was compulsory. But I could have a nice car.

I look over at Sharon and John. They have already been down to the mail room for their mail. Sharon has actually swiped more scripts than usual—that's not something you see every day.

My phone buzzes.

'Hi.' It's Kitty. 'Come back in. And don't let the others see you.'

Gosh, this is all very exciting today. It's almost like *Wall Street* or something. I shut the door behind me and sit on the couch.

'Now, Anna,' Kitty says, 'you know you're the only one I can trust and that I have *absolute confidence* in you.'

This is news. 'You do?' I ask hopefully.

'Oh, of course. You're my go-to girl,' she says. 'And I want you to know the real skinny.'

I bite my cheeks to stop from saying, 'Sorry, I don't speak American.'

'Great,' I offer weakly.

'The bidder for the company,' she says, 'is *Eli Roth*.'

I sit a bit straighter. 'Eli Roth? Of Red Crest Productions?'

'You know who he is?' demands Kitty, her eyes narrowing. 'How?'

'I read the trades,' I say. How could I not know who Eli Roth is? He founded Red Crest and built it into the West Coast's answer to Miramax. Red Crest are constantly buying out smaller production houses, taking their best talent and projects, and firing everyone else. I can see why Kitty's anxious. We need a hit movie soon, or we're dead.

'Anna.' Kitty snaps her fingers in my face. 'We need to be ready when he comes. I'm relying on you to help me find the right project.'

'OK,' I say. It's not as if I wasn't already looking, is it?

'And I have some good news for you,' Kitty says, lowering her voice to a paranoid whisper. 'This will be a Greta Gordon film.'

I perk up. Greta Gordon. Oscar-winning actress, former Hollywood uber-babe, huge in the eighties. Greta went through a My Drugs Hell and, her career in rags, finally did a stint at the Betty Ford to clean up. And then she quit films, moving to England to be a recluse.

'She wants to get back into films?'

'This is classified,' hisses Kitty, as though she had handed me a folder from MI6. 'But, yes. I've been working on her,' she adds proudly.

It would certainly be big if Greta returned. 'But isn't she a touch old?'

Kitty draws herself up. At her, undetermined, age, she refuses to accept that any woman is too old. 'She's as vibrant and lovely as ever. And she's looking for a lead. A romantic lead. A comedy.'

'Riiiiiiiight,' I say. A romantic comedy lead for a forty-five-year-old former reclusive actress. Well, that should be easy to find, huh? In an industry where thirty equals past it? I want to tell her it's impossible. But instead I amaze myself by saying, 'And then can I have a promotion?'

'What?' barks Kitty.

'If I find you the script, can I be a development executive?'

Kitty stares at me.

'Of course I'd still be working for you,' I reassure her, 'because you would have got promoted. You'd be a vice-president. Out in LA. And you'd need a development girl you can trust.'

Kitty hums. 'You'd need to stay in England,' she says eventually.

Man. She's really agreeing?

'You have expertise in the UK market. It's a good source Eli'd want to keep using,' she says, dreamily. Already he's 'Eli' to her and she's his right-hand woman.

'So, that's a deal?' I say, with a pang of regret for the tan and the hibiscus flowers. 'If I can get you the right script, you'll give me a promotion?'

'Absolutely.' Kitty looks deep into my eyes. 'You have my word on it.'

2

WHY AM I HERE?

I'm standing on the stone steps that lead up to Vanna's porch in leafy Barnes. Vanna has one of those fabulous houses, all Georgian, with grey columns, high yew hedges to shield her from the road, and pebbles all over her drive. Her Land Rover is parked next to Rupert's racing-green Aston Martin, and behind the house is a glorious walled garden.

My finger hovers over the buzzer. I could still run away.

I love Vanna to bits, and I even love coming here, especially on late-summer evenings—when Rupert is away, doing business in New York or Tokyo, and Vanna's two little angels have been packed off to bed by the live-in nanny. We go out into the garden and drink chilled white wine and eat organic strawberries, or whatever I want, really. It's like holidaying in a life you could never afford.

However, I feel totally different about evenings like this one. Rupert is here, and he's an ass. Well meaning, but an ass. And so is some other bloke. His name's Charles; but at least he's gay, so Vanna won't start one of her wretched matchmaking evenings again. I always feel completely out of place with Vanna's brilliant, glittering friends. I so don't want to do this, but Vanna said she was desperate for a fourth, so here I am. I press the button.

'Hi! Darling!' Vanna is there, hugging me. 'Winston! Get down!'

'Hi, Winston,' I say. Winston is a huge and ancient golden retriever who could shed dog hairs for England. Once again, I have somehow forgotten this fact and worn navy, and my neat little sheath dress is now covered in yellow hairs. 'Get down, Winston. Good boy.'

Winston enthusiastically jumps up on me and gives my entire face a huge lick, smudging my mascara and getting dog spit on my lipstick. I think the Koreans have the right idea when it comes to dogs.

Rupert emerges from the kitchen, a martini glass in hand. 'Ha ha ha, great look for you, Anna! Winston, you're such a bad dog,' he adds.

A man appears by Rupert's side. He's five foot four, slender, wiry, and wearing an expensive-looking rather dandified grey suit and a lilac silk tie. He has a neatly clipped goatee beard. And a horrified look on his face. He murmurs something to Rupert.

'Oh, yes, that's Anna,' Rupert says jovially. 'But she scrubs up a lot better than that! Anna, this is Charles Dawson!'

'Excuse me a sec,' I murmur, and flee to the downstairs loo.

Oh hell. It's a trick, isn't it? Vanna has sunk to new depths this time. She *promised* me Charles was gay. Instead, she's trapped me. Again.

Vanna is always trying to matchmake me. She has made my happiness her mission in life, which is fine, but there are other ways to make me happy than to stick me next to a bunch of uptight, self-absorbed wankers, I mean bankers, and make me suffer through an excruciating meal making small talk as they all try to get away.

I dab my face with some wet loo paper and get rid of most of the mascara smudge. I take a deep breath. Face repair, check. I'm wearing my invariable palette: foundation, the slightest bit of brown blusher, mascara and liner. Dress, check. It's navy. It's a shift. It's lined. Discreet string of small white (fake) pearls, check. When you are not pretty, you have different dress requirements from everybody else. Ugly girls want to be wallpaper, invisible. The key is to be appropriate. Dinner with posh friends equals nondescript dress. Nobody gives you a second glance.

I head out of the loo, bracing myself, and instantly run into a small throng of people. Vanna is moving among them, her neat brown cap of hair bouncing jauntily. 'Vanna.' I grab her toned arm. 'What is this?'

'Well, originally it was going to be just the four of us,' she lies weakly, 'but these are all *such nice people* . . .'

Vanna also believes I need a social life. This is a nightmare. I could be at home, ploughing through scripts. Watching paint dry. Anything.

'Charles,' Vanna says, as he passes. 'Come and meet Anna Brown. She'll be sitting next to you at dinner.'

I smile faintly at Charles, who is already wearing that harried, hunted look of a man trapped by Vanna's inexorable will.

'We're best friends,' Vanna tells him.

'Hello,' Charles says, smiling through gritted teeth.

'Charles is a very literary writer,' says Vanna. 'And he has a new novel that he's sending to agents.'

'Yes,' says Charles, visibly preening. 'And you're going to publish it, Vanna! If you're lucky!'

'Would *love* to,' Vanna lies. 'But *unfortunately* our house isn't taking on any literary fiction at the mo'. My hands are tied. *Such* a shame.'

'Hello,' I say back, just to remind him that I am still standing here.

'Vanna and Anna,' Charles says suddenly. 'You practically have the same name. And you look like sisters,' he says, with a stiff little bow.

'Thank you,' says Vanna, which is sweet of her.

'Of course, Vanna is Cinderella,' he adds, with a high-pitched laugh. 'Ha ha ha, just my little joke, Anna!'

I glare at my hostess who in turn is glaring at Charles.

'No offence, you look marvellous,' he says faintly.

'Anna works in the film industry,' says Vanna determinedly. She will force us to like each other if it kills her.

'Oh?' says Charles, slightly more interested.

'Come on, everyone!' Rupert's bass tones boom. He strikes on his beloved little brass gong, which I detest. 'Chop chop! Time for dinner!'

I know what hell will be like. An endless dinner party, just like this. First course, grilled escargots in sickly garlic butter. 'Not fond of snails, Anna?' Rupert says, as he sees me pushing them around my plate.

'I'm on a diet,' I say, 'though they look divine.'

'Good idea,' says Charles, supportively. 'A journey of a thousand miles starts with just one step! Or even of thirty pounds!'

'Have you ever had weight issues, Charles?' asks Priscilla, Rupert's banker colleague who is sitting the other side of him.

'No,' says Charles, admiring her tiny waist. 'I believe in self-discipline. Just like you. Presentation is so important in today's world.'

I can't take it. 'So when are you going to see someone about your bald patch?' I enquire pleasantly. 'It might give you the wrong image, unless you want to be a tonsured monk.'

Charles's face flushes, and Vanna winks at me. As well she might, she got me into this.

'Next course!' Rupert announces, as two waitresses enter and whisk away our plates. 'An *amuse-gueule* of smoked salmon and foie gras.'

'You may find it a bit too fattening on your diet,' Charles says to me, in hushed tones. '*Gras* means fatty in French.'

I want to ask what 'Fuck off, baldie' is in French but content myself with spearing an extra-large chunk and eating it right in front of him.

'You know, Charles,' says Vanna, 'Anna reads scripts for Winning Productions.'

'Never heard of them,' Charles says dismissively.

'Oh, but you must have heard of their movies,' Vanna insists. 'They did that adaptation of *Bleak House* that won all the BAFTAS's.'

Charles has heard of that. He deigns to turn to me properly. 'So you are interested in quality material?' he asks. 'These days the studios are only interested in commercial crap, aren't they?'

Vanna gives me a pleading look, so I swallow hard and merely say politely that perhaps Charles's book could be adapted for the screen.

'Well,' he says, as though considering it. 'It could only be done by a company with real taste and delicate sensitivity.' He looks at me suspiciously. 'Do you have a refined sensibility, Anna?'

'I just evaluate scripts and source material.'

'Oh.' He immediately loses interest in me. 'You don't have the power to green-light? Perhaps I should be talking to your boss. Who is he?'

'Her name's Kitty,' I say, smiling sweetly, 'but she doesn't accept unrecommended projects.'

'This has literary merit to recommend it,' he counters. 'What else does it need? Plus, of course, I can use your name.'

'I'd need to know something about it first,' I say, 'other than its great literary merit. Films have different needs from books. Sometimes what makes a good book doesn't do well on screen . . . We look for a great idea. Something that people will come to see just based on the idea alone. For example *Jurassic Park* or *Fatal Attraction*.'

'Junk! Sounds like the kind of trash Trish writes,' he says.

'Who's Trish?' I ask.

'Trish Evans,' he says. 'My sister's nanny. She writes scripts. Always telling me about her ridiculous ideas.'

'Like what?'

'The last one was about a wedding that goes wrong.'

'Oh,' I say, losing interest myself. Done to death.

'Yes, inane. It's called *Mother of the Bride*,' he snorts. 'She's jealous of her daughter and trying to interfere and control the wedding, and then she falls in love with the groom's uncle.'

I laugh. 'Actually it sounds like fun.' And perfect for Greta Gordon!

'Fun?' he demands crossly. 'It's totally forgettable.'

'You remembered it.'

'My novel—' he begins.

'Charles,' I say, 'what might be a good way to get in touch with your sister's nanny?'

He stiffens. 'I really don't think you should be bothering her,' he says.

'Here's the thing,' I say, determinedly. 'I need to present a mix of ideas to Kitty. If I had something lowbrow, something pulp—'

'Commercial and crass,' he adds.

'Then I could also manage to get her to consider a literary work.'

'So you need to get Trish's work in to smooth the way for mine?'

'Exactly,' I agree.

'I see.' He pulls a thick, gold-embossed business card out of his pocket and writes a number down on it. 'My sister is Lady Cartwright.' Then he lifts his glass of red wine to me in a toast. 'To Anna,' he says, 'whose ship has just come in!'

The rest of the evening passes in a dull blur of conversation and vile food, and by the time the coffee comes I can't wait to get away.

'Wasn't it *wonderful*?' Vanna insists, pressing my arm. She looks so hopeful I think it would be cruel to tell her the truth. 'You and Charles! I hope you two see each other again. He's very suitable. The book's dire, of course, but he's got pots of money,' she promises.

'He's a real catch,' I agree.

'Charles, darling,' says Vanna, grabbing his arm and threading it through mine. 'See Anna into a taxi, won't you?'

'Of course, allow me to take you,' he says graciously, bowing low and practically kissing my hand.

In the taxi on the way home I wonder what I must have done in a previous life to deserve this. On the one hand, Charles is an improvement on Brian. He does not, for example, suggest the cab fare should be my treat, nor does his breath reek of bad fish marinated in old beer. On the other, Charles does not even pretend to be interested in me. He is endlessly entertained by discussing, in no particular order, his own book, his brilliance, and his attractiveness.

'Of course,' he says, as we turn by Leicester Square (almost home, thank God), 'women just don't understand me, Anna. Would you believe I haven't had a steady girlfriend for three years?'

Yes. 'No.'

'It's true,' he says, bitterly. 'They can't cope with the rigours of living with a creative genius. Of course, they don't object to spending my money and staying in my flat uninvited, then claiming to have headaches and so-called woman's trouble.'

'Oh dear,' I say, struggling for composure.

'Woman's trouble doesn't last for two weeks every month, does it?'

'Not typically,' I say. My building is coming up. Hoorah!

'I have so much to offer,' he says, dramatically. 'Yet nobody is prepared to see the real me! Are you seeing anybody?'

'Not right now.'

'No, of course not,' he agrees.

Hey, thanks. 'Well, this is me,' I say gratefully. 'Thanks for the lift.'

'Anna,' he says, as I step out of the taxi. 'I like you. You have a wonderful way of listening. Very feminine, so many women want to talk all the time, banging on about themselves. So maybe I'll give you a call and we can go out? After all, you are a friend of Vanna and Rupert's. We must have something in common.'

'Ahm . . .' Help. How do I get out of this?

'That's settled then!' Charles exults. 'I'll call you. It's a date.'

'Have you heard the news?' Sharon asks, as soon as I get to my cubicle.

I speculate. 'You've read the greatest script ever.'

'No,' says Sharon, shaking her curls as though to wonder how I can be so stupid. Of course, that would mean she'd actually read a script. 'I've got a transfer. I've been promoted.'

My mouth falls open. 'What?' This can't be true, can it? She has only just avoided being fired for the last six months.

'Mike Watson saw my potential,' she says triumphantly. 'I'm now officially working for him as a junior development executive.'

I feel faint. 'But you work for Kitty.' In fact, I am clearly not the only one to be aggrieved. At that moment Kitty storms out of her office, a mini-dynamo clad in circulation-killing Azzedine Alaia.

'What the fuck is this?' she screams, brandishing a memo.

I look round as Mike materialises from nowhere, smiling his big fake smile. 'Is there a prob, Kitty?' he asks coolly.

'Yes, there is,' she snaps, 'actually. There's a memo from Personnel on my desk saying that Sharon reports to you now.'

'That's right,' Mike says. 'I needed somebody else on my team, and you seem well served with these two.' He indicates John and me.

'And you didn't think to ask me?' Kitty demands.

'You're so busy, Kitty,' Mike says smoothly. 'Preparing for the buyout of the company. Eli Roth and all that.'

Kitty shoots a look of loathing at Sharon, who tosses her curls.

'I see you got a promotion, too,' she says to Sharon. 'No need to ask what for!'

'For my talent,' Sharon says blithely. 'Of course.'

'You do realise,' Kitty says to Mike, 'that having sponsored her for that position, your arse is on the line if she fails to deliver? Which she will.'

'My goodness, Kitty,' says Mike. 'Maybe you should have some faith in your team.' But he looks a little less smug. Mike knows that Sharon is about as effective as Cherie Blair's astrologer.

'You two, in my office,' says Kitty to us, and John and I proceed into her office, where she slams the door and screams about disloyalty.

I just sit there. Trying to deal with it. Sharon has just got herself the position I have been slaving to achieve for the last six months, Sharon, a girl who has no brains, no drive and no sense. All she had to do was spill the beans on Kitty's secret to Mike Watson, and there you go.

If I had gone and told Mike about Kitty's knowledge of our impending buyout, what would have happened? Transfer? Promotion? Not bloody likely. He'd have said, 'There's a good girl, Anna,' and smirked at me. Whereas Sharon, he actually promotes. It's all because she's pretty.

Well, I've had it. From now on I vow never to trust a pretty woman again. I hate them all!

Except Vanna, obviously.

'Anna?' Kitty is talking to me. 'Did you come across anything yet?'

I think of Charles Dawson's card. 'Might have done,' I say morosely.

'Well, get to it,' Kitty says intently. 'Now Mike knows, everybody will. There's no time to waste!'

For the record, even though she's not strictly pretty, I also hate Kitty.

'**H**ello? Is that Lady Cartwright?'

'No,' says a voice. Pure Albert Square. 'Her ladyship ain't in.'

'I'm not actually looking for her,' I say. 'I'm trying to get in touch with her nanny, Trish Evans.'

'This is her, innit?' says Trish, her tones as soothing as a cheese grater scraped across a blackboard. 'What do you want?'

This is so obviously a wild-goose chase that I'm about to hang up.

'Are you from Nice Nannies?' Trish continues. 'Because I already told you I ain't switching again. They offered me another four grand to stay.'

'I'm not trying to poach you as a nanny,' I say. 'I met Lady Cartwright's brother the other day.'

'Prick,' she says, loudly and clearly. I can't help wondering where exactly the little Cartwrights are right now.

'Well, he recommended you as a writer,' I lie.

'Did he? Not like him. Thinks he's Charles Dickens.' She snorts. 'What did he say, then?'

'Only that you were writing a movie and I thought maybe we could meet for coffee. My name's Anna, Anna Brown, and I work for a production company. Looking for good scripts.'

'All right,' she concedes. 'I got lunch at one but you'll have to come here. I don't have time to muck about on the tube and that.'

'Give me the address,' I tell her. Well—Lady C lives in Albany, Piccadilly. Just round the corner from me. And a million miles away.

This is totally futile. I'm standing at the entrance of London's grandest rental address. Trish Evans extends a hand. 'Wotcher! There's a coffee place down the street, Cook's got the little ones while I'm on my break.'

I shake, gloomily. Just my luck!

Trish is absolutely, cast-iron, triple-certified gorgeous. Let's run though the list, shall we? Long blonde hair, bleached. Legs that would do credit to an Arabian racehorse. Smooth, pearly skin. Big green eyes. A full, pouty mouth. I want to cry off right here and now. No way Barbie here has written anything remotely interesting.

I look around for a café, and there's Costa Coffee, rising to greet me like an angel of caffeinated mercy. 'We'll just go for a quick coffee and you can tell me all about your writing. I can't promise anything, though,' I hasten to add. 'It's really just to get to know you.'

'You don't need to know me,' she says. 'You just need to read my script, 'cause it's great.'

I smile thinly. 'I'm sure it is.' We sit down at Costa Coffee and order. I get a cappuccino and she gets a plain black decaf. 'Watching your weight, I suppose,' I say glumly.

'I have to,' she says. 'Girl like me. Not much going for me. Dropped out before university. Bunch of crappy jobs, waitressing and temping, then I found being a nanny. That pays well, but I hate it,' she says passionately. 'So I wanna get married. Old-fashioned, right?'

'Why do you hate being a nanny?' I ask. 'If it really pays well?'

'They treat you like a maid. Make you give the kids all this vile stuff they don't want to eat. Macrobiotic. More like macro old bollocks.'

I laugh. 'So you want to marry for money?'

'Maybe you'll read my script and like it and offer me a million pounds,' she says hopefully. 'Then I wouldn't have to.'

'Um. You're not very likely to get a million pounds. You're not all that likely to get any pounds,' I say, and watch her face fall. 'Sorry if I gave you the wrong impression,' and to my surprise I am. I actually like her. 'For what it's worth, I'd like to read your script, but I should tell you, we reject almost every one we read.'

'Why's that, then?' she asks. Genuinely curious.

'Because they're crap.'

'Oh. Fair enough. Well, I'll be OK then because mine's not crap,' she says, reaching into her bag and pulling it out.

'I just think you need to know that everybody believes their script is great,' I tell her, 'and almost everybody's wrong so please don't be too upset if it's not right for us. It might be right for somebody else . . .'

'Look at you,' she says, grinning away. 'Trying to let me down gently and that. I'm not thick, honestly. I was just lazy at school. If you don't like it, no harm done, right? It's hard to even get scripts to readers.'

Amazingly enough I'm in a slightly better mood when I get back to my desk. Trish is an amusing girl. She can't help being stunningly beautiful.

I put her script to one side and make some phone calls, trying to sound very authoritarian.

'Yes, Kitty wants your best stuff. Right away. And nothing like that one you sent me last week about the two circus midgets.'

'Hi. Yes, I heard you have the galleys of *Permanent* in. Any chance you could slip them to us? Kitty's office, care of Anna Brown . . .'

I don't know if it'll work but at least it makes me feel useful. I get a few good responses to the urgency in my voice. When Kitty passes me, she gives me a thumbs up. To my astonishment, she even returns a minute later with a coffee for me. 'Good work,' she hisses, shooting a look of loathing over at Mike's office. 'Keep it up.'

'What's this?' I look up to see Sharon standing by my desk, flicking through Trish's script. '*Mother of the Bride*?' she asks. 'By Trish Evans. When did this come in?'

I snatch it back from her. 'That's mine.'

Sharon extends one hand, her nails glittering with frosted silver polish. 'Actually, it belongs to the company,' she says. 'Hand it over.'

I take it and lock it in my bottom drawer. Sharon scowls.

'I am a development executive now,' Sharon says. 'I'm *senior*.'

'I'm reading this for Kitty,' I say. 'Or do I report to you now?'

Sharon tosses her curls. 'Maybe I'll call Personnel and see if I can arrange it,' she threatens. I take a gulp of coffee.

'Oh, will you?' asks Kitty in icy tones. She has seen this from her office and snuck up behind Sharon, walking as predatorily as a cat.

Sharon jumps out of her skin. 'Oh, hi, Kitty.' She recovers, then looks at Kitty defiantly. 'Maybe you can help me convince Anna that all script submissions are to the agency, and not just to Anna Brown. We work as a team, we all need to share our leads.'

This is so ridiculous that I give a derisory snort. Winning Productions is not a 'team'. It is a hothouse of fear and loathing. And greed.

'That's an excellent idea,' Kitty says smoothly. 'Why don't you run back to Mike's office, gather up copies of everything he's working on and deliver them all to me. Then we'll send you a copy of Anna's discovery.'

Sharon searches in vain for a good response.

'I can't take Mike's things,' she says. 'But I can send you everything *I've* come up with.'

'No, thanks,' says Kitty immediately. 'I don't need any tips on nail-painting or eye-shadow application.'

Sharon flounces off, but not before muttering, 'Oh yes you do.'

'What is that you've got?' demands Kitty. 'Anything good?'

'Doubt it,' I say. 'First try by someone's nanny.'

'Oh. Well. Don't give it to her anyway. And don't just sit there, Anna. Start dialling. Eli Roth will be here *tomorrow*.'

I finally make it home, weighed down with a huge overnight read. All I want is to go down to the offie and pick up a bottle of wine. As I turn the key in the lock, I hear the unmistakable sound of sobbing. It's Janet. She's curled up in floods of tears.

'What's the matter?' I ask.

'It's Gino,' she sobs.

Of course it's Gino. Her Euro-trash boyfriend, an Italian count or something. Inherited a bunch of money from a car-manufacturing daddy, and now dedicates his wastrel life to getting rid of it all as fast as possible. I'm not his biggest fan.

'What's he done now?'

'Du-du-dumped me,' she sobs. 'We were at Brown's and he suddenly says that he thinks it's time to see someone else. And when I asked him why, Gino said that my butt was too big. He said that curves are out . . .'

I look at Janet's incredibly slim form, and her ludicrously high and tight bottom. 'What curves?' I ask. 'You're 34B if you're lucky. That's not curvy.'

'It is for a model,' Janet says. 'I'm huge! I'm a size eight,' she whispers.

'Oh. I see,' I say, trying really hard to be sympathetic.

Because the tough thing is, living with two models I do actually know she's right. Janet is just this side of anorexic looking, which in her world makes her a hefty girl. The more usual look is Lily's, all bony and angular, without an ounce of fat anywhere. And a jerk like Gino trades up with his models like he trades up his watches or his cars.

'Gino's a pig. He was only being spiteful. Look, you stay there,' I tell her, 'and I'll pop out to get us some booze and a Chinese takeaway.'

Janet's eyes round. 'Don't you know how many calories are in that stuff?'

'Chinese people eat it, don't they? And they're all skinny.'

We stay up late drinking Mixed Doubles (rum and Coke for me, gin and tonic for her. I decanted it and told her it was diet) and eating dim sum and shrimp lo mein, which I also told her was diet. Janet eats most of it, and who can blame her? She probably hasn't had a decent meal in five years. Eventually, she hugs me. 'I'm going out,' she announces.

I blink. 'Are you sure? You're a bit merry.'

'I'm fine,' she says. 'Jusht fine. D'you want to come to some clubs?'

I tap my pile of scripts. 'Got work to do.'

'OK, see ya,' she says, wafting out in a trail of Dune and gin.

I look at my watch. Quarter to midnight. The booze is making me sleepy, but I have to read some of these scripts. I make coffee and flick through the first few on the pile. Immediately I feel a headache coming on. Why do people write these things? Pretentious indie flicks, formulaic rom-coms, endless Britflick 'Lock Stock' rip-offs . . .

In desperation, I pick up Trish's script. Idly I read the first page. And the second. And third. And then I slowly put my coffee to one side.

I can't believe it. It's funny, it's fast-paced, the characters are believable. I want to know what happens! I keep reading, keep flipping. It makes me laugh, it's a bit sexy, and sometimes, like the very best comedies, it's touching. Plus, there are no big sets or special effects needed. It could be a film you shot cheaply and made millions on.

This could be it. This could be my chance!

I wake up early, jump out of bed and into the shower. I feel a bit punch-drunk, sure, but a sort of Christmassy feeling is there, shining through the exhaustion, as if I'm about to get a very big and shiny present.

After doing my hair I go into the kitchen, steal some of Lily's vanilla hazelnut coffee, and reread *Mother of the Bride*. At first I'm afraid that maybe it was the booze and the script has turned crap overnight. This happens to script readers the way beer goggles happen to men—you go to bed with a beauty and wake up with an absolute dog.

But not today. It's just as exciting this morning. It actually improves on a second read. I dress hastily, unable to believe my luck. Beige trousers, white T-shirt, my greying sports bra—nobody's going to see my bra, are they, plus it sort of flattens my boobs a bit. When you're as tall and galumphing as me, you don't want a couple of boulders drawing attention, do you? I add a large, cable-knit cardigan that belts round me and hides everything, grab the script and hurry off to the tube.

When I get to the office, Kitty is already there.

'Wow,' I say. 'You look nice.'

She gives me a piercing look, as though 'nice' is totally inadequate.

'Well,' she sniffs, '*some* of us believe in making an effort.'

And how. Kitty has chosen an exquisitely cut, tomato-red dress—looks like Versace—with discreet pearl buttons down the front and perfectly matched red shoes. Her make-up is subtle. She could pass for thirty-five.

'I hope you haven't forgotten that Eli Roth is coming in today,' she says, looking around the half-empty office. 'Everybody else has.'

'I—no,' I say, smoothing down my cardigan in a vain attempt to look more presentable. 'It is only eight thirty.' I have the office all to myself. I can go in and pitch to her, no John or Sharon to try and sabotage me, no filing to get done, no errands to run. It's my chance. 'I think I have something for you,' I tell her.

Kitty's eyes round in a greedy O. 'You do? The script? By the nanny?'

'It's actually pretty good,' I say. 'It could be perfect for Greta, anyway.'

Kitty fairly dances on the balls of her toes. 'What are you waiting for? Get into my office. Where's your coverage?'

'I came in early to write it up, but you're already here, so maybe I could just give it to you in person?'

'Go on,' she says.

'Well, it's a romantic comedy,' I say. '*Mother of the Bride*. The heroine is jealous of her daughter's wedding and unconsciously sabotaging it. But then she falls in love with the groom's uncle. Only he's gone off her because she's been a total prima donna bitch, and then she has to save the wedding and her romance.'

'I don't know,' Kitty says doubtfully. 'I don't think Greta's going to want to play a total bitch. She's America's sweetheart.'

Well, she was, before she was revealed to have done more class A substances than Keith Richards. 'I think she would,' I say deferentially. 'Remember *Starlight* and *Outcasts*? She made her name in those. If she's going to come back, this is funny, it's bitchy, it's poignant . . . It's everything *The First Wives Club* tried to be and wasn't, and that movie was still a hit. Plus,' I move in for the kill, 'there aren't that many great romantic leads for older women actresses.'

'Greta is hardly older,' Kitty says.

'She's older than Kate Hudson,' I say, 'or Natalie Portman. The mother, Elsie, is the only really huge role, so all the rest would be character actors, and there aren't that many locations, it could be shot cheaply. It could be another *Full Monty*,' I say. 'Or *Four Weddings*.'

Kitty presses her bony fingers together. 'Get me coverage,' she says. 'Make it sizzle. Get me something to sell with. Make it appeal to Greta.'

I want to ask if this means I get a promotion, but Kitty's eyes are flinty. 'Hurry up,' she barks. 'We've only got a matter of hours.'

I bring the stapled sheets to her forty minutes later, my fingers stiff from writer's cramp.

'Thanks,' Kitty says, as I hover in front of her desk. She covers her phone receiver with one hand. 'Something else?'

I suppose I was hoping she'd read it through, sit me down while she gets on the phone to Greta Gordon. Something. 'Nothing,' I say.

'Go to Starbucks, fetch me a fat-free frappuccino,' Kitty says, dismissively, and that's it. I honestly don't know why I thought it would be any different. Luck and me just don't go together, do they?

'Don't sulk,' says Kitty acidly as I turn dejectedly towards the door.

I come back from Starbucks in a vile mood. 'Visitor for you in main reception,' mumbles Claire, keeping her voice down, as I hand her Kitty's frappuccino. Kitty likes her secretaries to be seen and not heard.

Visitor? I never get visitors. 'Who is it?'

'Some bloke called Charles Dawson. He says he has that novel you wanted. Shall I send him up?'

'Go ahead,' I say, despondently. I can't very well refuse, can I?

I plaster my professional smile on as Charles steps out of the lift. Oh dear, did he absolutely *have* to wear that three-piece tweed suit with the gold watch on a chain? All he needs is a monocle. People are staring in the corridors, sniggering.

I stride forward with my most businesslike smile and shake Charles's hand with a firm, dry grip. 'Charles, good of you to come,' I say loudly. Maybe I can get people to think he's an eccentric agent. 'Thanks for slipping me this manuscript for a first look.'

'Slipping it to you?' he says, and unfortunately his voice is loud as well as high-pitched. 'I'm hardly doing that. It doesn't have a publisher.'

'We prefer our material fresh,' I say, suppressing the urge to blush. 'Anyway, thanks for dropping by. I'll get right back to you.'

'Helloo,' coos a voice.

Oh great.

'I'm Sharon,' Sharon says, giving him a pearly white smile. She gives me a sidelong glance and extends her slim hand to him.

'Delighted,' Charles drools, eyes popping. 'Oh, delighted.'

'You're bringing a goodie for Anna?' she asks.

This is amazing. She can't get over that I wouldn't give her Trish's script, and now she wants to jump on this just because it's mine.

'I am,' Charles confirms. He puffs out his scrawny chest like a starving pigeon trying to attract a mate, and I almost die of shame.

'Well, thanks, Charles, I'll just take it now,' I say.

'I think not,' says Sharon, lightly but distinctly, smiling away. 'You

37

see,' she adds to Charles, 'I'm senior to her. She just reads material. It's people like me who make the decisions.'

'Is that true?' Charles asks me.

I swallow. 'Well, sort of.' It burns, it really does. I wait for Charles to give her the sodding book.

Charles turns to Sharon, very politely, and says, 'I'm awfully sorry, but I do think I should give it to Anna.'

'And why's that?' she demands, scowling now.

'Because Anna and I have a very special relationship,' Charles says, stoutly.

I smile at him. I can't believe it. He's sticking up for me!

'I didn't know *Anna* had any special relationships with *talent*,' says Sharon, licking the outside of her lips provocatively.

Charles hesitates, but sticks firm. 'No,' he says, 'I promised to give the book to Anna and I must keep my word.'

'*Thank* you, Charles,' I say, triumphantly, swiping the book from him.

'And I'll see you soon,' he says, looking at me hopefully. 'How about tonight? Are you free tonight?'

'Oh, well, if I'd known he was your *boyfriend*,' Sharon says scornfully. 'I thought he was a *real* writer.'

'Charles is a very gifted writer,' I say, because one good turn deserves another. Charles is beaming at me. Sharon storms off. I seize the opportunity. 'Look, Charles, about that date—'

'Seven thirty for eight,' he says, stepping back into the lift.

'But I—'

'No need to say anything, Anna,' Charles says, magnanimously. 'You *deserve* a date. See you tonight!'

Why? Why do I deserve a date? What did I do wrong?

I'm reading Charles's book when Eli Roth arrives on our floor. You can tell it's him by the crackle of electricity that ripples through our normally moribund workspace. I put the manuscript aside, glad of a legitimate distraction. Mind you, it hasn't taken much to distract me from this masterpiece. I've been finding all sorts of things infinitely more interesting, such as arranging my stored emails into folders and tidying up my desk. I want to give him a chance, but it's just so dull.

There's a little knot of people gathering around Roth. I can just about make out a tall bloke in a charcoal-grey suit. Mike Watson is pumping his hand, there's Sharon simpering and flicking her hair about . . .

I glance over at Kitty's office. Magnificently, she has not come out yet. She's waiting for him to come to her. Roth walks over towards her office now, having pressed the flesh, and sticks his head inside. He's about five eleven. Same height as me. This is something I always notice about men—how many of them I tower over in an unattractive fashion. Charles is five four, five five tops. I can't believe he actually *wants* to be seen in public with me. We'll look utterly ridiculous.

Kitty says something to Roth and he steps inside her office. And shuts the door. You have to hand it to Kitty, she's such a smooth operator.

The light on my phone flickers. 'Yes?'

'Anna?' It's Kitty. 'Would you step into my office, please? There's somebody I want you to meet.'

I blink. I can't believe it. Kitty never does things like this. I get up nervously and knock on the door of her office, feeling John's eyes boring jealously into my back.

'Come,' she says.

I open the door just a crack. Roth and Kitty are both sitting on the couch. Kitty looks all relaxed and at ease with the world.

'Eli, I want you to say hi to Anna Brown, one of my readers. Anna's a *great help* to me refining the material I find.'

'Hey,' Roth says.

He's young and powerful-looking. Broad shoulders, nicely defined muscles without being all steroidy, dark Hugo Boss suit, gold Rolex (natch). In fact if you were to conjure up the image of a Hollywood executive, he'd be a perfect match. 'Kitty tells me you're a real asset to her team,' Roth says, looking at me intently.

'Oh—I—yes,' I splutter. 'Thank you, Mr Roth.'

'It's Eli, sugar,' Roth says. 'We don't stand on ceremony at Red Crest.'

Kitty looks at me. Obviously my moment in the sun is over now. That's her 'get out' look.

'Nice to meet you, Mr—Eli,' I say, quickly withdrawing and shutting the door. I walk back to my desk on a high. Kitty introduced me to the boss! I feel a surge of gratitude. She's finally taking me seriously.

Nothing happens after that until lunchtime. I flick through the book (crap, all the way through), type up more notes, and do important office things like playing Free Cell and Spider Solitaire, until finally it's one o'clock and I can buzz Claire. 'Want to go out? Pret a Manger, my treat?'

'All right,' Claire says.

When we get back there's a little Post-it note stuck to my computer. *Meeting at 2 p.m. in conf room 3*, it says.

I check my watch. Fuck it! It's two fifteen right now. When do we ever have afternoon meetings until three? Kitty is always out at some three-martini deal schmoozing somebody famous or powerful. I grab my *Mother* notes and scamper down there.

I open the door as quietly as possible and try to sneak into the room. There are four executives sitting at the table—Kitty, Mike, Carl Smith and Paul Walker. Their readers are all down the other end, with Sharon, who is looking furious at the seating arrangement. And right at the head of the table is Eli Roth.

Carl Smith is in the middle of a presentation, pitching an idea about toys who come to life and go evil and start attacking everybody. He stops, dramatically, as I take the last available seat.

'Afternoon, Anna,' says Mike nastily. 'Glad you could join us.'

'Sorry,' I mutter. 'Lost track of time.'

'Carl, why don't you continue,' Eli says as I blush richly.

'Well, I think this a great paradigm,' Carl says loudly. 'The script charts out like this.' He pulls up a diagram. A diagram! For a movie script! 'The Xs indicate where each plot point conforms to the Hero's Journey mythological structure as invented by Christopher Vogler.'

'It sounds like a fun project,' says Roth, cutting him off. 'But I think it's been done before.'

'Some ancient classic movie,' says Carl defensively.

'No, recently,' Roth says. '*Small Soldiers*.'

Carl looks blank, but clearly he isn't going to say, 'You what?' Instead, he nods and clears his throat. 'Maybe we can translate the elements to a new premise,' he says, sitting down. I glance round the rest of the table. Everybody is looking blank. Of course. This is because they only notice movies that are on at their local multiplex, if then. They don't bother keeping up with what happens in America.

'You guys remember *Small Soldiers*?' asks Roth. Apparently he is thinking the same thing. His eyes scan the room, and I notice that they have lost their friendly look and gone quite sharp.

Everybody looks down. There is a horrible silence.

'Of course we do,' I say, defensively. Somebody's got to say something!

Roth's head comes up and he looks at me. A slight grin plays across his mouth. 'Anna Brown,' he says. 'We met this morning, right?'

'Right,' I mutter, going scarlet.

Roth leans back in his chair. 'Tell me about that movie.'

'It was an Elliott/Rossio thing,' I say. 'Toys that came alive.'

'I don't know those directors,' says Carl sharply.

'They're not directors, they're writers,' I say.

'Oh well, *writers*,' he says scornfully. 'No wonder I haven't heard of them!' He looks smugly around the table for support. A bunch of the executives snigger. And it's true, writers don't have much clout in Hollywood, usually. There are a whole legion of writer jokes: 'Have you heard the one about the blonde? She was so dumb, she went to Hollywood and slept with the writer.'

I go red. Why does he have to be so mean? You can have the biggest star and the biggest budget and if you've got a lousy script you've got a flop. Just look at Arnie in *Last Action Hero.*

'I'm a little surprised,' says Eli Roth evenly, to Carl. 'Anna, you know some of their other movies?'

'Yes,' I say. '*Shrek, Aladdin, The Mask of Zorro*—'

'And *Pirates of the Caribbean*,' Roth finishes for me. 'One of the biggest films of all time.'

People stop sniggering.

'Other ideas?' Roth asks, and the meeting moves on. I sit there, listening to pitch after pitch, and watching the shutters coming down over Roth's eyes. He's obviously not impressed.

'Kitty?' Eli says.

Ooh. I sit up straighter. This will be fascinating. She runs through a couple of bog-standard ideas John offered her and there's a general shaking of heads. Kitty shrugs her bony shoulders. 'I do have one more idea. Something I found myself. It's called *Mother of the Bride.*'

Found herself? What's going on? She refuses to meet my eye.

'It's an interesting premise well executed,' she says confidently, 'and it won't cost much to make.' She's quoting my coverage! 'The movie's about a socialite,' Kitty says, 'who's ruining her own daughter's wedding . . .'

And I just sit there while she tells the story in a nutshell.

'That's interesting,' Eli says. His eyes are sparkling now. 'I haven't seen a good older-lead flick in a long time. Where did you find this?'

Kitty waves one hand airily, her diamond flashing away. 'Personal contacts,' she says. 'I gave it to Anna to write the coverage on.'

Eli glances at me. I sit there, dumbstruck. Should I say something? Kitty's eyes are like chips of ice. 'Right, Anna?' she asks pleasantly.

I nod miserably. 'Right.'

Kitty relaxes perceptibly and flashes me a smile.

'Well, this has got potential,' Roth says. 'Make some copies of the script and the coverage and send it round to everybody, could you?'

'No problem,' Kitty purrs.

She puts her hand on my shoulder as we're walking out of the meeting and squeezes. 'Go straight to my office,' she says. I walk there, sit on the couch and wait, little prickles of adrenaline crawling over my skin like spiders. 'I hope you understand what went on in there,' she says.

'Not really.' I cough. 'I found the script . . .'

Kitty shrugs impatiently. 'We work as a team. I want to get your movie *made*, Anna, and that means it needs the right backing. If Eli thinks it comes from an executive, he'll consider it more carefully.'

'But how will it advance my career?' I say in a small voice.

'Everybody will read your excellent coverage, for a start,' Kitty says. 'Why, even Eli Roth will notice you. I introduced you, didn't I?'

'Yes,' I admit.

'And that was only the start,' Kitty says. 'I'll be making sure you climb up the ladder. We're a team.' She hands me a typed sheet of paper. It's a memo to Personnel asking that I get a rise.

I have to read it three times, I can't quite believe Kitty's done this.

'That's great,' I say, stunned. 'Th-thank you.'

'You're welcome,' she says, smugly. 'Of course, you realise that now you've agreed that I found the script it's very important we stick to that?'

'Oh. Sure.'

'And bring the writer in for a meeting with me,' Kitty says warmly. 'Better still, just give me her phone number. This is going to be a very exciting time for you. You're going to see this project succeed.'

She turns back to her desk, to show the meeting is now over.

I hover at the door.

'Yes?' she says, a little impatiently.

'The rise is great,' I say. 'Wonderful, really, but what about the promotion? I'm still going to get that, aren't I?'

'Absolutely,' Kitty says. 'But right now isn't a good time, not until Eli settles on who he's going to hire. If this project is a success, then the sky's the limit. As long as you and I stick together.'

'OK.'

'I want you to be intimately involved in developing this with me,' she continues. 'Do you have ideas for casting, other than Greta?'

'Oh, sure,' I say, fairly stunned. 'I've got *loads* of ideas. *Masses.*'

'So get me some suggestion lists,' she says. 'Directors, actors, cine-matographers—you know the score.'

I'm glowing with happiness. This is real producer stuff! 'No problem,' I say confidently.

'Get me everything by tomorrow morning. First thing,' she instructs. 'You can take the rest of the afternoon off. Well done.'

Bloody hell. It's a miracle!

I open the door to the flat to find Lily sitting on the floor crosslegged, doing her Tantric yoga thing, chanting loudly.

'Om om om om om om,' says Lily, pretending she hasn't noticed me come in.

'Hi,' I say.

Lily opens one eye. 'Really, Anna, I'm trying to concentrate here. It's very important I clear my mind.'

'Shouldn't take long,' I remark. 'Not much in there to begin with.'

Lily's eyes widen. Honestly, I don't know what's got into me today.

'Don't you have a party to go to or something?' I ask. 'I'm going to watch *EastEnders*.'

'Well, my concentration's shot now anyway,' Lily says, standing up and stretching. 'And, yes, I have tons of invitations, but I'm actually going to stay home and relax too.' She glances at the phone.

'Expecting a call?'

'No!' she snaps. 'Of course not. I don't wait by the phone.'

The door opens and Janet comes in, looking a bit down.

'What's the prob?' says Lily, a look of fake concern on her face.

'My bloody agent,' Janet complains. 'Told me the shoot was for *Heat* but when I got there it was for *Good Housekeeping*, and when they did the close-up shots they told me they didn't need me.'

'Oh my,' says Lily. 'Not needed for close-ups. That *is* bad.'

I really would like to slap Lily sometimes.

'Especially after Gino dumped you,' Lily says. 'That's awful.'

'Hey, Janet,' I say. 'Lily has to stay in and wait for the phone to ring.'

'Nonsense,' says Lily sharply.

'Is it?' I ask innocently. 'Then I'll just jump on the Internet, OK?'

'No, you can't do that,' Lily says at once. 'I'm not waiting in, but I do have a friend who may be calling. Claude Ranier.'

Janet's mouth drops open. 'Not Claude Ranier, the financier? Not Claude Ranier, the one with the huge private yacht?'

'The *Trixabelle*, yes.'

'Not Claude Ranier . . . the one who's ninety years old?' I ask.

I mean, I can't believe it. You know Claude Ranier. Franco-Greek shipping millionaire. He's the old fat bastard who's always in *Hello!* looking like a leathery wrinkled prune, sitting on the deck of his bloody yacht with a bevy of bikini-clad twenty-year-olds.

'He's no such thing,' snaps Lily.

'How old is he then? Sixty?' asks Janet.

'You two are so superficial,' Lily says. 'Claude is fascinating. All that—'

'Money?' I ask.

'Wisdom,' she retorts. 'Age is nothing but a number. I think he's going to invite me to head down to Cannes for the film festival.'

'No way,' says Janet, enviously.

The phone rings and Lily snatches it up. 'Yes?'

43

Her face falls. 'It's for you,' she says, with a disbelieving air.

I take the receiver. 'Hi, Anna,' says a cheery voice. Oh hell. I'd forgotten. 'It's Charles. All ready for the big date? I'll be round there in five minutes. Top buzzer, right?'

'Right,' I agree. There's nothing I can do, is there? 'I'll come down when you buzz.' So much for *EastEnders* and pizza.

'Who was that?' Lily demands. 'Somebody from work, I suppose.'

'It was a date, actually,' I tell her.

'Ooh. Who is it?' asks Janet, encouragingly. 'Somebody special?'

'Don't be stupid,' snaps Lily, still cross. 'You know the kind of person Anna dates. Probably a social worker who lives with his mother.'

'He doesn't work at all,' I tell her.

'There you go. Unemployed. Anna will probably have to pay for dinner,' says Lily viciously.

'Actually, Charles has a private income,' I tell her. 'He owns a flat in Eaton Square. And his sister has a title,' I add, watching Lily sulk.

Lily says, 'Well, he must be mad.'

'At least he isn't senile,' I respond.

'Well!' she says huffily, and storms into her room, banging the door.

'Don't mind Lily,' Janet says supportively. 'She just can't believe you could get a man like that . . . I mean, no offence . . .' She's floundering.

And you know, the sick thing is I do feel a bit of pride. Charles may be a dandy and a midget, but he's better looking than Claude Ranier. And he's loaded. This is the kind of boyfriend that can secure a woman's future, or so Lily and Janet think. And Lily is thoroughly rattled, while Janet is looking at me with admiration for once instead of pity.

And . . . it's nice.

'Aren't you going to get ready?' Janet asks.

'He'll be here any second,' I say airily. 'He can take me as he finds me.'

'Come here.' She leans over me and fusses with my hair.

'Get off,' I say.

The buzzer goes. I head downstairs. It doesn't feel quite like marching to the guillotine the way I'd expected. Maybe this will be fun!

'Hi,' says Charles expansively to me as I emerge from the building. We walk to his car. It's a sleek black Rolls-Royce. Of course, what else?

'Blimey,' Charles says, gesturing at the feminist bookshop. 'Rather you than me.' He hurries to the car and opens the door for me to get in. 'I expect they'll come out and picket me now,' he says, 'holding open a door for a lady. Ha ha ha.'

I try for a dutiful titter as he slides into the driver's seat. At first I thought he'd grown, but looking down discreetly I see it's just stack heels. I feel the familiar clutch of shame in my belly. I'm so bloody huge Charles actually decided to wear *stack heels*.

'So where are we going?' I ask. Trying for enthusiasm.

'I thought we'd go to Mock Turtle,' Charles suggests. '*Fabulous* new fish place off Kensington High Street. Dreadful waiting list, but I got right in,' he adds smugly. 'I know a few people.'

Fish. Ugh. I hate fish. 'Great,' I say uncertainly.

'They do the most wonderful lobsters,' he tells me, steering smoothly through the London traffic. 'Not only can you pick your own, but you can watch as they cook them! You can watch them trying to climb out of the pots. It's awfully funny.' He catches sight of my face. 'You're not one of those liberal loonies, are you, Anna?' he demands.

'I'm not a vegetarian or anything, but . . . cooking them alive . . . I can't watch that,' I say. 'I'm sorry, but I'll be sick.'

He looks over at me, exasperated. 'Bloody hell,' he says. 'I pulled strings to get that reservation.'

'I know a nice Chinese place,' I suggest. 'Very reasonable prices.'

'Reasonable prices?' Charles repeats, as though he doesn't know what I'm talking about. 'Good Lord, no. I know, we'll just pop down to the Savoy. They know me there. We'll get a table.'

And, when we get to the hotel and the car is valet-parked, they do. Charles is welcomed in by discreetly bowing, perfectly dressed staff.

'Good evening, Mr Dawson. I'm afraid your usual table is taken,' says the maître d', 'but we'll make one up for you, of course.'

'That's fine,' says Charles, with the air of one suffering indignity patiently. He turns to me while we wait.

'Have you come here before?'

'Not as such,' I admit.

'I lunch here every day,' he says. 'Wonderful food. Ah, they're ready.'

The waiters sit us at a table for two and leave us menus.

'Mine's wrong,' I say.

Charles looks at me. 'What do you mean?'

'It doesn't have any prices on it,' I say.

Charles blinks. 'My dear girl, of course a lady's menu has no prices. Where have you been eating?'

'Oh,' I say, feeling small.

'Shall I order for both of us?' he says, and a waiter instantly materialises. 'My guest will start with the quails' eggs—they're not on the menu, Anna, but they're divine—and then . . .'

He rattles off a list he obviously knows by heart and I don't say a word. I wouldn't dare.

'There!' Charles finishes proudly. 'That's you all taken care of. Now tell me, Anna, have you been reading my book?'

Oh fuckity fuck. What am I supposed to say? I can't just tell him it sucks like a vacuum cleaner, can I?

'Ahm,' I begin, going bright red.

'Ah, say no more,' says Charles, seeing my reaction. 'Dreadful manners. Excuse me. I should never discuss work with . . . a *beautiful* young woman,' he adds after a pause. 'And I don't want you to think I'm only asking you out for professional reasons. I can see that it might have occurred to you, given . . .' His voice trails off.

'Given what?' I ask.

'Oh, nothing,' he says hastily, looking at his napkin.

Given that I have a nose that would do credit to Gonzo from the *Muppet Show*? And that the only woman taller than me is the Statue of Liberty? 'Why did you ask me out?' I ask him, hoping vainly for a confidence boost.

'Well . . . you were such a good listener,' he says. 'And, you know, you didn't ask *me* out.'

'Excuse me?'

'I don't trust the ones who ask me out,' he says, suddenly, bitterly.

I look at him. He's only five six even in the stacked heels, and the goatee is so neatly trimmed, and he's a bit balding . . . 'Does that happen a lot?' I ask, taking a sip of wine to mask my disbelief.

'All the time,' he says.

'Ah,' I say, mystified. Maybe it's pheromones.

'They want to go to the best restaurants,' he says. 'And they all love the flat. Of course it is a marvellous flat. And then they stay overnight without being asked. Just turn up with overnight cases!' he splutters.

'Maybe some of them are just keen,' I suggest.

He's twirling his wineglass now, his fingers all tight on the stem. 'They aren't keen until somebody tells them about Chester House.'

'Chester House,' I repeat, but the waiter is serving us and he clams up until he's gone. Charles is eating something heavenly smelling and there are a pile of tiny boiled eggs with grey salt by my plate.

'What's that?' I ask.

'Goat's cheese and caramelised onion tart,' he says, without offering me any. 'Try your quails' eggs.'

I pick one up and lower my voice. 'I think their salt's a bit manky.'

'Manky?' asks Charles, horrified. 'That's celery salt. Surely you've had quails' eggs before?'

'Oh yes. Millions of times,' I say, gingerly dipping one in the salt and eating it. It tastes all right. Like a boiled egg, only smaller. I could have boiled my own eggs at home.

'Yes, Chester House,' Charles says significantly. 'They find out I stand to inherit, and then . . . well. You can't get rid of them.'

'I don't know what Chester House is,' I admit.

'It's the family seat. Rather special, I suppose. Eighteenth-century. Nice little park surrounding it. In Gloucestershire.'

Light dawns. Charles is like Mr Darcy from *Pride and Prejudice* and lives in a huge mansion with servants and deer grazing in his grounds.

'But aren't these girls pretty?' I ask.

'Some of them,' he agrees. 'But it doesn't matter. They won't . . .' He looks at me and trails off. 'Or very rarely, anyway. They seem to want to just when I get up enough courage to kick them out.'

'I see,' I say. I'm feeling a bit sorry for him now. He's a pompous ass, and all that, but he deserves better than this.

'Not all girls are like that, you know,' I tell him. 'Can't you find a nice girl with lots of money of her own?'

'D'you have lots of money?' he asks, interested.

'Not a bean,' I say cheerfully, and it's a great weight off my mind. Now I won't have to pretend I know all about vintage champagne and things.

He slumps a bit.

'Still, you didn't ask me out. I asked you,' he reminds me, as though this is a great novelty. 'And you said yes. Did Vanna tell you about Chester House?'

I shake my head.

'Perhaps if I take *you* back to my flat, we can . . .?' he asks hopefully.

'Charles! I only just met you,' I say. 'And I don't want to move in with you. Honestly.'

He smiles broadly at me.

'I like you,' he says. 'How are you fixed for tomorrow night?'

Janet and Lily had waited up. 'How did it go?' asks Janet.

'It was fine,' I say. 'Charles was nice. He wants to go out again.'

'Where did he take you?'

I shrug. 'The Savoy.'

Janet nudges Lily. '*Told* you. Anyway, he's from a really good family. His grandfather was an earl.'

'How do you know that?' I ask.

'Made some phone calls,' Janet says blandly. 'He's got an *enormous* country house. It's *huge*. He's, like, one of the most eligible bachelors.'

'I don't care about all that sort of thing,' I say, and it's mostly true.

'Bullshit,' says Lily, tossing her hair. 'You're so lucky, Anna,' she adds, jealously. 'Anyway, Claude called me. And Claude's *really* loaded.'

'Is Charles really handsome?' Janet asks me, supportively.

I think about him. 'Um, no.'

'See?' Lily demands. 'You're a hypocrite! You tell me I shouldn't see Claude just because of a little thing like age, but you're quite happy to go out with an ugly bastard who's got a country estate worth millions of pounds.' She sounds quite wistful.

'I can't afford to be fussy about looks,' I say defensively. That's the brutal truth, isn't it? You've got to date in your own attractiveness range. Girls like me have to grin and bear it. Charles is pretentious and obnoxious, but I think it's mostly because he's sad and lonely. A defence mechanism. Anyway, why not give him a try? He's better than nothing.

A lot of good marriages have been built that way.

Does that sound cynical? Think about it. You can wait for ever for Prince Charming to come along with the white horse, or you can get out there and try to find yourself someone. Mostly, that seems to mean not being too fussy. If you fuss over every single bloke, you're liable to wind up fifty-five and alone for ever, consoling yourself with some form of small domesticated animal.

No, thanks.

3

THE NEXT MORNING, when I wake up, I still feel jazzed. I emerge from sleep with that great feeling that something wonderful has happened, if only I could remember what it is.

The script. The movie.

I jump out of bed and head for the shower. I'm thinking about actors and directors while I'm brushing my hair. Rachel Weisz, would she be interested? Or Sadie Frost, maybe, for the bride. And unknowns for the male leads, the whole point being that we should do it cheaply . . .

It's so exciting. Kitty actually valuing my opinion. Letting me suggest talent. I carefully pick out an outfit: black low-rise H&M jeans and a little Bon Jovi-style T-shirt from '86 with three-quarter-length sleeves.

I grab my bag and head out of the door, stopping only to drop a two-pound coin into the nose-job box.

John is already hovering by my desk when I step out of the lift.

'Kitty wants to see you,' he says, importantly. 'She needs those casting suggestions from you right away. And she's none too happy about the flowers,' he adds, spitefully.

'Flowers?'

He indicates my desk. I follow his gesture and my mouth drops open. What on earth is that on my desk? There's the hugest, almost obscenely large bunch of roses perched on the corner of my desk, filling my entire cubicle. Yellow and pink roses, twined round with ivy and twigs with berries on them, very designer florist. This has never happened to me before. Girls like Lily and Janet and Vanna get flowers, not girls like me.

Sharon spies me from across the floor and saunters over.

'Got an admirer, Anna?' she asks. 'Better check the card, I suppose you'll find it's printed in Braille.'

'Very funny,' I say, and go over to my desk, fishing around in the huge swathe of blooms for the little envelope. *Thank you for a wonderful evening. Call you tonight. Love, Charles.*

Well. That's certainly very nice of him. He's not so bad, really.

'Charles?' asks Sharon, peering over my shoulder. I instantly shield the card from her.

'None of your business,' I say, blushing.

'Oh, that's too funny,' Sharon says meanly. 'Little and Large! Of course, he's the book guy. Probably just trying to bribe you,' she adds.

'No, he's not,' I say, feeling protective. 'You're just jealous.'

'Oh, yeah, I'm green with envy,' Sharon says. 'I really wish *I* could get roses from a midget.'

'He's not a midget,' I say. 'He's a millionaire.'

Sharon laughs scornfully. 'Anna, you have to stop fantasising! You're not going to bag a millionaire, get over it!'

'And why not?' I ask her. Although I know the answer, don't I?

'Well,' Sharon says, after a pause. 'If you can't figure that out . . .'

'Well, Charles fancies me,' I say defiantly. And I look at my roses and know that it's true, and it feels good, it really does. He's certainly a step up from Brian. Or nothing. Which were my two previous choices.

'It won't last, you know,' Sharon says.

She's probably right. But I don't care if it lasts, I just want to have it for a little bit. Being made a fuss of, just like a normal-height girl with a small nose. I'll call Charles later, he definitely deserves another date.

Kitty sticks her head out of the door. 'Anna, stop mooning over those ridiculous roses and bring your lists in here. And get some coffee. I'm dying of thirst.'

I nod and gather my papers together, then head towards the kitchen. Another fabulous day in the glamorous world of films!

'Yes . . . yes,' Kitty says, approvingly, making notes by the names of various actresses I've suggested for the bride. 'Get on it. Call their agents— no, wait. I'll call the agents. I've got the magic touch with talent, after all,' she says, smugly. 'Greta agreed to do it.'

'Really? That's fantastic news. Oh, well done,' I tell her.

'It was, rather,' Kitty agrees. 'Now, directors.'

I hand her my next list. It's a short one: Roger Michell, who did *Notting Hill* and *Changing Lanes*; Mike Newell, who did *Four Weddings* and *Harry Potter and the Goblet of Fire*; Peter Cattaneo, *The Full Monty*; and the Weitz brothers, *American Wedding* and *About a Boy*.

'Hmm, yes,' she drawls. 'Nice, but mostly unavailable. Who else?'

What does she mean who else? That's it, that's my list!

'There is one other name,' I tell her. 'Though I suppose . . .'

'Who?' Kitty demands.

'Well, Mark Swan.'

She gives a short, barking laugh. 'Don't be ridiculous, Anna! We can't get *Mark Swan*. What are you thinking?'

I don't really know. What *am* I thinking? Mark Swan is known for gritty drama movies. Why would he agree to direct a romantic comedy? Just because I met him in the cloakroom and he was nice. OK, very nice.

'At least let me call his agent,' I hear myself plead.

Kitty shrugs. 'Knock yourself out, darling. Just don't expect anything.'

She's right, of course. Swan's agent, a terribly busy terrier of a woman called Carly Smith, gives me ten seconds before hanging up on me. I should have known, really. Only I can't stop thinking about Mark Swan.

I so want to get this movie made. Eli Roth will want to do it, with Greta on board, but I don't think she'll be enough for financing, not by herself. Roth likes to have studios put up at least half the money, and a studio will want more of a package. A name like Mark Swan would tip it over the edge. For the first time in what you might laughingly call my 'career', I feel I'm close to something.

I check out Kitty's office. She's in there, blinds drawn. She won't miss me if I go out for an hour or two. I pick up my bag from the desk.

'Early lunch?' It's John. Standing by my desk, eyes narrowed.

'No,' I say. 'I'm just going out.'

'Oh, really?' he asks, folding his arms. 'How so?'

I sigh. 'I've got a meeting with Mark Swan about *Mother of the Bride*,' I tell him. 'Be right back!' and I walk towards the lift, leaving John standing there with his mouth open, gaping after me.

By the time the lift doors have closed I'm sweating bullets, of course, but it had to be done. I can't have John running to Kitty. Of course, now I have to actually get to talk to Mark Swan. Which is where I'm headed.

It probably won't be as bad as all that. What are they going to do, throw me off his set? He's only a bloody director, in the end.

'Step back, please.' A beefy man in a windcheater throws one muscled arm against my chest, crushing my boobs under their cotton shirt.

This is maddening. I can see the shoot going on up the heath. And I can't get anywhere near it. I've been standing in the rain in bloody Hampstead for forty minutes. A perfect English summer's day.

'Just ten seconds,' I say.

'You're not on the list.' He looks bored.

'But I'm from Carly Smith's office,' I say, in a burst of inspiration.

He looks at me with pity. 'No, you ain't,' he says, flatly.

No. I ain't. 'OK, OK,' I say, dejectedly. 'I'm going.'

I turn away and walk slowly up the street and head into the newsagent's for a quick fix of something. I grab a *Sun*, a *Mail*, a copy of *Heat*, a family-size pack of Quavers, a Bounty, a Snowflake, a Creme Egg and a Diet Coke and march up to the counter, where a very tall bloke is buying a packet of cigarettes.

'Excuse me.' The *Heat* is slipping out of my grip. 'Can I just put these down while you . . .'

'Sure.' He grabs the *Heat* for me on its inexorable way to the floor. Wow. What a good-looking man. All craggy and masculine in a younger Ted Hughes sort of way.

'Thanks,' I mutter.

'Diet Coke,' he says, amused.

'Excuse me?' I demand again. Bloody cheek! Just because I have some crisps. And a few sweets. I blush bright red.

'Four twenty,' says the checkout girl. I sullenly hand over a fiver.

'I hope you realise you've ruined it now,' I tell him. 'With your *comment*.'

'Oh,' he says. 'You mean . . .' He gestures at my pile of loot.

'Yes,' I say. 'And I hope you know those fags are going to give you cancer. Why don't you think of that when you light up, eh? Try to enjoy them when you're forced to think about the consequences!'

He has the grace to chuckle. 'You're right, I'm sorry. Stress relief?'

'Yup,' I say, pocketing my change. 'I can't get onto the set over there.'

'Johnny Depp fan?' he asks, sympathetically.

'No. Well, yes. Of course. Loved *Pirates of the Caribbean*. His Keith Richards impersonation was spot-on, wasn't it?'

'Sure was.'

'I wanted to speak to the director.' I sigh.

'You an actress?'

'Oh. No. Nothing like that. I work in the film business, I've got a script I wanted him to read. And his agent wasn't interested.'

'So you thought you'd try the direct approach.'

'They won't let me on set, though,' I say. 'You know, Steven Spielberg started his career by sneaking onto the Paramount lot, but they must have had rubbish security back then.'

He stares at me. Gorgeous dark eyes, long lashes, but they are regarding me as though I'm some sort of circus freak. I step back.

'Are you for real?' he asks.

I'm getting a nasty feeling. There's something familiar about him. His voice, his eyes. 'What do you mean, am I for real? You're not with the security, are you? I haven't done anything illegal.'

'You mean you don't recognise me?' he asks.

And then of course I do. With a sickening lurch of horror. I gasp and relax my grip and all the rest of my purchases slither to the floor, and I'm on my knees, face flaming, scrambling to pick them up.

He bends down to help me, not unkindly. I stagger back up.

'No . . . I . . . I didn't. I do now, Mr Swan,' I say, miserably. 'It was the beard. You've shaved your beard,' I cry. Not fair! Why should men be allowed to shave their beards, step out of gloomy cloakrooms and look completely different? 'Um, look, this was obviously a really bad idea. Please just forget about it. OK? Um, goodbye.'

'Wait a minute,' Swan says. 'Don't I know you?'

'Not really,' I mutter.

'Yes, I do. Yes, I do,' he says, insistently. 'Yes, I've got it. You're the cloakroom girl. Aren't you?'

'Yes,' I admit.

'The one with the evil boss with the boring Prada clutch.'

I smile slightly. 'Yes. Er—no. No. I mean, she's not evil. And the bag, I suppose you'd call it classic.'

He steps back. 'I'd call it boring. But at least she isn't a wanky recluse.'

'You know,' I say with dignity, drawing myself up to my full height, 'all you had to say was no, Mr Swan.'

'Mark,' he says. 'And you're Anna Brown. Right?'

I blink with surprise. He remembered? 'That's right.'

'And what company are you with?'

'Winning Productions.'

He looks dubious. 'They did *Midnight Dance*? Couple of years ago.'

'Yes, but we've just got bought out by Red Crest Productions,' I say.

'A big name,' Swan concedes.

I have to do it. I snap open my battered old bag and fish out my *Mother of the Bride* script. 'Here,' I say, shoving it at him. 'Just read the first ten pages. Please?'

'And why do I want to do this?' Swan asks. He makes no move to take the script and it hangs there, limp and pathetic, in my hand.

'Well.' I take a breath, then my words come tumbling out, falling all over themselves. 'It's a good script. Funny. Like nothing you've ever done before, but I thought, you know, he could try something different. It's a romantic comedy for an older actress . . . *Mother of the Bride* . . . she's ruining her daughter's wedding . . . Greta Gordon is attached . . .'

'Is she?' Swan asks, eyes glinting. 'Thought she'd retired.'

'She wants to come back.'

'I'll think about it,' he says, taking the script. 'No promises. Your phone number on here?'

'Yes,' I say, gratefully.

'It really doesn't sound like my kind of story,' he says, gently. 'Don't wait by the phone, Anna.'

'Like Bud Fox in *Wall Street*,' I say, laughing nervously.

Swan grins. 'Yes. I love that scene. Anyway, don't wait like that.' He turns to go out of the shop.

'I'm surprised,' I call after him. '*Wall Street*'s not very arty.'

Swan turns back and lifts his eyebrows. 'Who cares about arty?' he says. 'Don't you think *Star Wars* is the best film ever made?'

'Do you think,' I ask John dreamily when I get back to the office, 'that *Star Wars* is the best film ever made?'

He gives me a look of withering contempt. 'What?' You haven't heard of *Citizen Kane* or *Casablanca*? Or *The Bicycle Thief*?'

'I thought *Star Wars* was brilliant,' I say.

'Yes, well,' sneers John. 'I believe you were the one who said she liked *Speed*. And *Pretty Woman*.'

I want to hug myself. I wonder if Mike Swan liked *Pretty Woman*. I wonder if he likes all my favourite films. Films that aspiring producers aren't supposed to like. You know, *Die Hard*, *Goodfellas*, *Trading Places* . . . There's a real stigma to liking mainstream movies. And I can't get enough of them, while *Citizen Kane* put me to sleep. No, we're all supposed to be like John and be into things that win the Palme d'Or at Cannes and nobody ever goes to see. You know what I call a classic? *Raiders of the Lost Ark*, that's what. I never wish I'd written worthy movies. Instead I wish I'd had the idea for *Shallow Hal*. Or *The Sixth Sense*.

I'd love to write. The best thing about being a scout is reading, getting to sift through scripts. Even though so many of them are so awful. Kitty got the company to pay for me to go to one of those screenwriting workshops once. She wanted me to learn three-act structure and common clichés, so I could give her better coverage. I wasn't supposed to try and write something myself, so I didn't. But you know, sometimes I wonder if what I'd churn out could be any worse than the stuff I have to read.

I figured out long ago that what I love about movies is the stories. You can have a bunch of unknown actors, no special effects, even an ordinary director, and as long as you have a sparkling story it really doesn't matter. You know, *Four Weddings and a Funeral*. Or *Phonebooth*.

And then I pull myself together. Who am I kidding? I'm only Anna Brown. I go back to my slush pile.

'You wouldn't know a good film if it bit you in the arse,' says John. 'Oh, and Kitty wants to see you.'

I go to Kitty's office and knock timidly on her door.

'What's all this I hear about you and Swan?' Kitty barks. 'Did you really have a meeting with him? And if you did, why wasn't I informed? *You* don't take meetings with talent, Anna.'

'It wasn't like that,' I protest hastily. 'I just went up to Hampstead Heath where he's shooting and asked to give him the script.'

'You did *what*? But that's so unprofessional, Anna! How could you?' Her phone buzzes and she presses the speaker button with irritation. 'What the hell is it now, Claire?'

'Phone call for Anna,' Claire's disembodied voice says meekly.

'So bloody what?' snaps Kitty.

'He . . . he says his name is Mark Swan,' says Claire, nervously.

Kitty and I exchange looks. 'I'll just get back to my desk,' I suggest.

'No, you don't,' hisses Kitty, shoving the receiver at me. 'You take it right here. Put him through,' she says to Claire.

I take the receiver, heart pounding, and Kitty picks up an extension, pressing the mute button so she can eavesdrop.

'Anna Brown,' I say.

'All right, Bud Fox,' says Mark Swan's voice, richly baritone and confident, and I can hear the grin in it. 'I want you to buy me twenty thousand shares of Bluestar . . .'

Kitty's eyes are popping out of her head. Clearly she doesn't get it.

'Mr Swan,' I say.

'If we're going to work together, don't you think you should call me Mark?' he says.

'You liked it?' I say. I can't breathe. My insides are melting.

'Very good, Sherlock,' he says. Oh man, he's sexy. 'My agent's having a fit, but I think this might be kind of fun. And I have some space in my schedule for the autumn. Are you developing this project?'

Kitty is making frenzied hand gestures at me.

'No,' I say. 'That's my boss, Kitty Simpson.'

'Well, have her call my assistant Michelle and set something up,' he says. 'And make sure you're in that meeting too, kid.'

Bless him. I love him! 'Whatever you say, boss.'

'I get final cut,' he warns. 'Non-negotiable.'

I look at Kitty, who nods frantically.

'No problem,' I say. 'And thank you so much.'

'Don't thank me,' he says. 'I own you now. I'm going to be working you so hard you're gonna throw up. See you, Bud Fox.'

He hangs up and so do I. Kitty stares at me as if she can't believe it.

'Who the hell is Bud Fox?' she demands.

'*Wall Street*. You know, the movie?'

'Oh,' Kitty says, giving a little tinkling laugh. 'Wretched trashy film. Dear Mark, so ironic,' she says. 'And well done, Anna. Why don't you call the writer—that Trish person. Have her ready to meet her director tomorrow morning. I'll call Eli Roth. And Carly Smith.' She smiles with satisfaction, like a cat, and then admires her canary diamond. 'My movie is really starting to come together.'

I exit her office to find John jumping away back to his desk. Had he actually had his ear pressed up against the door?

'So what happened in there?' he asks, casually.

I favour him with a smile. 'Oh, I was just chatting to Kitty and Mark.'

'Really,' says John, furiously. 'Congratulations.'

I mustn't let him make me any coffee for the foreseeable future.

The phone is ringing as I walk through the door, my arms laden with bags. I have an Indian prawn korma, a family-sized bar of Dairy Milk, a pack of tree-ripened peaches and two bottles of champagne (M&S's own, but it still counts). I don't care, it's a celebration, and Janet and Lily will be on the champagne too (Lily has convinced herself champagne is calorie-free). I also got a six-pack of crisps, all salt and vinegar.

Before I left the office today, Personnel rang and told me my new salary and benefits. I am going to be making thirty grand!

Thirty. Grand. A. Year!

The phone is still ringing, so I drop my bags and pick it up. 'Hello?'

'Anna?'

'Oh, hi, Charles,' I say, with forced enthusiasm. 'Um, thank you for the lovely flowers.'

'I hope they brightened up your morning,' he says, a bit stiffly. But he sounds nervous. I know the feeling. I instantly want to put him at ease.

'They were the perfect start,' I tell him. 'And then I got a rise! I'm assisting on a project now. I can try to get films made.'

'Terrific. So you'll be able to put my novel into production!'

Oh bugger. How the hell am I going to tell him his book sucks? 'I'm still working on the novel,' I lie brightly. 'I want to let it sink in.'

'We're going to go out again this week?' he asks, gingerly.

'Oh, yes, absolutely,' I say, deflating.

I wonder unhappily how long I can wait before I have to shag him. I hate sex. Most women hate sex, don't they? Real women, I mean, not pin-ups like Lily and Janet. It's just so embarrassing. Why do men insist on looking at you even though you've got a bit of a tummy and would prefer to do it in the dark? Everybody pretends sex is so great, but it's dreadful. It's something you have to do to keep your boyfriend, as Brian kept reminding me.

It could be to do with the fact that none of the men I've been out with made me feel excited and edgy like Bruce Willis or Brad Pitt. Or even Mark Swan. But those are fantasy figures, and not very likely to go out with me, are they? The memory of Mark Swan in that shop comes back to me, standing there, all leonine, strong, hugely tall, mountain-craggy.

I shake it off, and remind myself how lucky I am that Charles is talking to me. Hell, Charles is a fantasy date for a girl like me!

'Well,' Charles says. 'I'm having a bit of a house party this weekend. Up in the country. Vanna and Rupert will be there. Loads of people, actually. All staying over. Dancing. Kedgeree and champagne in the morning. Jolly nice to have you there too,' he adds.

The door opens and Lily walks in, going straight into her bedroom.

'Well, I . . . I suppose so,' I say. I can't get out of it, can I?

'Hello?' says a voice. It's Lily, picking up the extension in her bedroom. 'Who is this?'

'Excuse me,' I say coldly. 'Didn't you see I was on the phone?'

'No, sorry,' she lies coolly. 'Sorry to interrupt.'

'That's all right,' says Charles.

'Oooh, is this the *famous* Charles Dawson?' Lily asks. She's dropped her voice an octave to that breathy, sexy smoker's throat thing she does.

'Hi. Ya,' says Charles, warmly. 'Who's this?'

'This is Lily, Anna's flatmate,' says Lily. 'My friend Janet and I live here too. We can't wait to meet you. We've heard so much about you.'

'Oh, well. Come along on Saturday,' Charles says. 'Taking Anna to a house party at Chester House. Plenty of room. Love to have you!'

'They're busy that day,' I say instantly.

'No, we're not,' says Lily, equally instantly, 'and we'd *love* to come.'

'See you all on Saturday night, then,' Charles says, sounding pleased as punch. 'Drinks at seven, dinner at eight. Dancing starts at nine. Black tie, obviously.'

Obviously.

I slam down the phone and march into Lily's room. I am just about to commit physical violence on her when the door opens and Janet comes in. 'Hi,' Lily says. 'Great news! Charles Dawson just invited us to a super house party. I bet there'll be loads of country gents there. Just swimming in money and no idea how to spend it.' She laughs. 'Well, we can help.'

Janet shrugs. 'I don't want to go.' She looks so down. 'They sent me away from a booking today. Told me I had the wrong look. All the other girls were eighteen or nineteen and under a hundred pounds.'

'You really must do something about your weight,' says Lily severely.

'My booker wouldn't take my calls this afternoon,' Janet says, tearily. 'He thinks I'm a failure.'

'Have you considered a face-lift?' Lily asks.

'Oh, shut up, Lily,' I say. 'Janet's only twenty-eight.'

'*Only*,' says Lily, scornfully. 'That's *ancient*.'

'This is so stupid,' I say. 'Janet, you have to come to the party.' The two of them there is my worst nightmare, and now I'm trying to guilt her into coming? 'I need back-up,' I say firmly.

'There are going to be tons of society men there,' says Lily. By this, she means rich.

'And most of them are from *very good families*,' I add temptingly. By that, I mean titled.

'Maybe I'll come,' Janet says. 'If I can lose five pounds by the weekend. I can go on that watermelon diet again.'

'Too much sugar,' Lily says.

'You think a plain fast?' asks Janet, worried. 'To be honest, I've had a rubbish day and I don't think I could take it.'

Lily looks at her pityingly, as if she has no self-control, but backs off when I give her my death stare. I pass her a bottle of champagne.

'Here, open this,' I say. 'Make yourself useful.'

'Oh, champers,' says Lily. 'What are we celebrating?'

'I got a rise,' I say proudly, and tell them all about it. Janet seems genuinely delighted, and Lily pretends to be. Which is about all I can expect. I eat the korma and they both decline (good, there isn't enough to go round), but they agree to eat the peaches. And one and a half bottles of booze later, all three of us are eating salt and vinegar crisps.

It's funny watching Lily struggle with herself over the crisps. She wants another packet. I don't think she's eaten crisps in five years; every time she bites one she looks as if she's having an orgasm.

'Dairy Milk?' I ask, waving the bar under her nose.

Lily looks as though she might faint. But she's a strong-willed girl. 'See you two later,' she says, getting up and draining her champagne. 'I'm going out,' she adds, grabbing her coat.

'Where?' asks Janet.

'Anywhere,' says Lily, slamming the door.

'I'll have some Dairy Milk,' Janet says once the coast is clear. 'It's not like anybody's ever going to hire me again anyway.'

'So, the party,' I say, trying to cheer her up.

'What are you going to wear?' she asks me.

'My black dress with the pearls,' I say.

'You always wear that,' Janet says.

'It's suitable,' I explain. 'Anyway, what are *you* going to wear?' Maybe I can find somebody for Janet. She's a nice girl, under all that beauty.

'I haven't decided,' she says, then fixes me with a stare. 'But I'm taking you shopping on Friday. And to the hairdresser. And we're going to get you made up.'

I feel a flash of anger. 'Give over, Janet. What's the point of that?'

'There's a point,' she says. 'You'll see.'

I shake my head and reach for another packet of crisps.

'Why don't you have another peach instead?' Janet says.

'I can't believe this,' I snap. 'I'm being so nice and sympathetic to you.'

'It's not about beauty,' Janet lies. 'It's about health. You're an executive now. Maybe you should think about changing your diet just a *tiny* bit.'

I put the crisps down sullenly. She's ruined them for me now, anyway. 'But I'll never be skinny,' I say. 'I don't want to eat celery. And drink hot water with lemon in.'

'You could just do a little,' Janet says. 'More peaches fewer crisps.'

'They are delicious, though,' I point out.

'They are,' agrees Janet. 'Tell you what, there are only two packets left. If we have one each we'll have eaten them up and then there won't be any temptation left.'

'It's the healthy thing to do,' I concur.

I wake up the next morning feeling a bit fragile. I stagger into the bath-room and climb into the shower. As the water is sluicing down over me, yesterday comes back to me. The best day ever! I've got Mark Swan. And then there was what Janet said.

As I step out of the shower, swathing myself in my huge bath sheet—I bought it so I'd never have to see any part of my own naked anatomy first thing in the morning—I suddenly decide to do something different.

I actually examine myself. This is too weird. I've spent years not look-ing at myself. In fact, I have elaborate and well-tested avoidance meth-ods. And now here I am, facing the grim truth.

There I am. Am I fat? Depends how you define it. I may not need rein-forced floors to walk on, but there's that big tummy . . . I look at my tall frame, my big, strong hands. You can't see my feet from here, but there's my nose. My skin is really pale. I'm just not very attractive, all round.

Part of me says, well, since you'll never be pretty, you might as well eat whatever you like and dress invisibly. But this morning, there's another part of me that wants things to be a bit different. Because they *are* differ-ent. I've been promoted. Maybe I'll just . . . experiment, I think, guiltily. Guiltily because I'm thinking I could make a change, which is obviously stupid. Anyway, for a laugh, perhaps I'll try to cut back a bit. Just slightly.

'Exciting, innit?' asks Trish, when I arrive to pick her up. She's got her long blonde hair braided into a sleek plait, and she's picked out a silvery shirt with a black pleated skirt and spider-web tights. Next to her, I feel about as feminine as Lennox Lewis.

But Trish is genuinely thrilled. She's doing her patented Tigger impression, bouncing up and down like a child on the way to EuroDisney, making it impossible for me to hate her.

'The deal's not done yet,' I remind her.

'But it will be,' she says with confidence. 'They've got Mark Swan. Did you see *Suspects*? *Great* film. What's he like, then? Is he a moody genius?'

I grin. 'I don't know about moody. But he's a genius all right.'

'That Kitty called me. Came round to see me yesterday an' all.'

I blink. 'What?'

'Yeah, in the afternoon.'

When I was up in Hampstead Heath. What did Kitty mean by that? Going without me? Look, she gave you that rise, I tell myself. No need to be so bloody paranoid.

'She told me all about how she got Greta, and how she's going to be producing,' Trish says, looking sidelong at me under her dark lashes. 'She said she's the one I can trust. You're cool with that?'

'I'm totally cool with it,' I say. 'Kitty's championed the script to Eli Roth, and she attached Greta.' I'm blushing and wondering why I sound like I'm trying to convince myself. I flag down a taxi.

'Jump in,' I tell her. 'Meeting to get to.'

This meeting is obviously going to be big. Kitty is pouting because it's not going to be in her office; Eli Roth has insisted we all take it upstairs to the fourth floor. She is, however, determined to run the show anyway.

'Trish, *darling*,' she says, when I turn up with the writer in tow. 'What an amazing look, that's just fabulous. Eli will absolutely *love*.'

She herself is particularly resplendent today in a fitted suit in yellow wool. She looks like a terrifying, power-mad daisy.

'Greta will be here any minute,' Kitty promises, twitching to look over her shoulder at the lifts. 'And Mark Swan.' I wonder, if they arrive together, whose arse will she kiss first? 'Anna, bring your notes up, would you? And, John, bring my pad.'

'John?' I ask. What the hell is John doing in this meeting?

'Of course, Anna,' says Kitty with the kind of brightness that means if I open my mouth again she will kill me. 'John's on the team too!'

John smiles snidely at me. 'Right away, Kitty,' he says, obsequiously.

I try to smile and take Trish upstairs to Eli Roth's palatial fourth-floor suite. And for the first time, it dawns on me that I might actually be going to get a film made. Because this place seems a million miles from our chaotic little offices downstairs. It just reeks of corporate money.

'So,' Roth says, welcoming us at the door. He smiles at Trish. 'This is the writer,' he says. 'You have a fabulous vision for the piece.'

Trish takes in his even-featured, rather anodyne good looks and grins. 'Should do, shouldn't I?' she asks. 'I bloody thought of it.'

'Absolutely,' Roth says, soothingly. 'And we only have a couple of notes . . .'

My heart sinks. He's going to rip it apart, and it's almost perfect just as it stands. Why do producers do this? Fall in love with a script, buy it and then change everything about it until it's unrecognisable.

Kitty bustles in without knocking, shepherding a woman dressed head to toe in black and wearing dark, wraparound glasses.

'Greta,' says Roth, with a delighted smile. He crosses the room at the speed of light and links his arm in hers, taking her towards the sofa. Kitty scowls. 'What an honour.' He then kisses her hand.

'I'd like a coffee,' says the great lady, distantly.

'Of course,' Roth says. He snaps his fingers. 'Get Ms Gordon a coffee.' Nobody moves.

'Don't just stand there, Anna,' says Kitty. 'You heard Eli, didn't you?'

I am just getting to my feet to go play dogsbody once more when the door opens again and Mark Swan walks through it.

'Sorry I'm late,' he says.

'You're right on time,' Kitty says warmly, darting towards him and thrusting out her jewel-encrusted claw. 'I'm Kitty Simpson, *Mother of the Bride* is my baby,' she says, smiling sweetly. 'This is Trish Evans, who wrote us such a *fabulous* script, of course we have just a few *teeny* changes, and this is the great Greta Gordon, who I'm sure you know . . .'

'We've not met,' says Swan, inclining his head down towards Greta. 'But I've always admired your work.' Gosh, he's tall, isn't he? He has to be at least six five. And so broad-shouldered. He's not pretty, like Eli Roth, but still, powerful. I notice that Trish, me, Kitty, even Greta, have all straightened our shoulders a bit since he walked in here.

'And your script is fantastic,' Swan adds to Trish.

'Great to meet you, Mark,' says Roth, shaking his hand. I can see that Roth doesn't enjoy having Swan tower over him, but he handles it well. 'I love all your movies. Voted for you in the Academy.'

'Thanks very much,' says Swan. He casts a sidelong glance at me, winks. I stare at my shoes, trying not to smile. He winked at me!

Kitty notices. Of course. She never misses a trick.

'You've met Anna, who works for me, and this is John, who also works for me,' she says, smiling. 'Anna was just about to go for coffee, would you like some?'

I blush. I'm being introduced as the dogsbody I am.

'Well, since Anna's completely responsible for getting me to read the script and attach myself,' says Swan, easily enough, 'I think someone should be getting *her* coffee.'

I can't believe he just said that! Oh! I love him.

'That's OK,' I say, going scarlet. But now Eli and Kitty are falling over themselves to agree.

'Ha ha ha, of course,' says Kitty. 'Go and get everybody coffee, John.'

'Right away,' says John, fawningly. 'How do you like it, Mr Swan? I'm such an admirer. Really. Such a pleasure to get your coffee.'

'Black's fine,' says Swan. He looks at me again as if he's barely controlling an impulse to roll his eyes.

I stare at my pad. Am I mental, or is Mark Swan actually trying to bond with me? I can see both Eli and Kitty noticing, and the vibes coming my way aren't exactly appreciative.

'So, the good news is, I ran the package by Paramount this morning,' says Roth briskly, dragging Swan's focus back to him. 'And they're willing to go for it.'

'That's good of them,' says Swan, sarcastically. He's the hottest thing in the UK film industry and he knows it. Of course any studio would jump at the chance to bankroll the next Mark Swan film.

'What I thought would be useful was to get you and Greta together with us, and we can present our vision to Trish,' says Roth. 'The script's too long. You'll need to chop off ten pages. And we should work on a zinger chart. A zinger scene every ten minutes, that's the formula. Ten pages, zinger. Ten pages, zinger,' he repeats, ignoring Trish's horrified face. 'You'll get the hang of it.'

'Elsie needs to be much nicer. And much more attractive,' Greta says. 'Perhaps she should be some sort of model for older women. Highly successful. And a philanthropist,' she muses.

'Coffee,' sings out John. He has returned with a tray laden with cups and saucers and little jugs of milk. 'Get it while it's hot,' he sings.

'I don't know about all them changes to Elsie,' says Trish dubiously. 'She's the whole thing. It'll ruin it.'

'You'll make the changes, Trish,' says Kitty, smiling at her like a crocodile. 'Your job is to execute our vision.'

'But Anna said—'

'Anna's not in charge here. I am,' says Kitty, with soft menace that Trish takes no notice of. Eli Roth clears his throat. 'And Eli, of course.'

'Actually,' Mark Swan says, 'I'm in charge.'

Kitty, Eli and Greta all look over at him.

'Well, of course,' says Kitty placatingly, 'once filming starts, Mark.'

'No. Through the whole thing. Pre-production to final cut.' Swan shrugs. 'I don't work any other way. Any script changes will need to be approved by me; casting, crew hire, everything. I run my movies. Total control, or I don't attach. If you aren't up for that, it's been nice to meet you all and I'll just go home.'

Greta shakes her head, frantically. She has no intention of losing the man who can single-handedly revive her career.

'That's fine with me,' she says instantly. 'You are the maestro!'

'That's right,' Kitty says at once. 'Whatever you say, Mark.' She looks nervously at Roth, who gives a curt nod and a forced smile.

'No problem, no problem,' he says, spreading his manicured hands. 'Trish, let me rephrase. Your job is to execute *Mark's* vision.'

I don't know where to look. The atmosphere in here is as tense as a Florida election. You can almost feel the loathing crackle under the fake smiles pasted on Kitty and Eli's faces. You can almost smell the fear seeping out from Greta Gordon. And Trish is just bewildered and resentful.

The only person who seems completely relaxed about the whole thing is Swan. 'I signed up because I liked Trish's vision,' he says. 'Although why we all toss around the word "vision" is beyond me. It's only a bloody movie.'

Trish cackles with laughter. 'Fuckin' 'ell,' she says. 'You're all right, mate. You're almost normal!'

Swan chuckles. 'Well, cheers.'

'I thought you were a moody genius,' adds Trish. 'But Anna said not. She said you weren't moody, anyway.'

Swan turns round to look at me properly, and I have to force myself not to stare at my shoes.

'Did she?' he says. 'Well, I'm not a genius either, Bud Fox.'

'*Wall Street*,' says Kitty instantly. 'Such a powerful vis— er, movie.'

'The first two-thirds are great,' says Swan. 'Which was your favourite scene?'

Kitty starts to flush. 'Ahm . . .' She looks around helplessly. She hasn't seen the movie.

'You were telling me you loved the scene where Bud Fox walks into Gordon Gekko's office,' I pipe up.

'Yes,' she says, exhaling. 'Love that scene! So funny!'

'Funny?' Swan asks, bemused.

'Kitty thought the underlying satire was really well observed,' I say.

'That's exactly right,' Kitty agrees.

'I see,' says Swan, and I wonder if he's going to wink at me again. Fortunately, he lays off. 'Anyway, I want the lead role, Elsie, to stay as written. I'm surprised you'd want it changed,' he adds to Greta. 'If you're coming back, it shouldn't be with the same cute character you've always played. Elsie's greedy, mean, selfish, pathetic—but that's what gets Oscars.'

'You really think I . . .?' asks Greta, simpering.

'Only if you work really hard at it, and take direction,' says Swan bluntly. 'You've got a bad rep, Greta. I'm the boss on my sets, and I don't like prima donnas. You won't get any special trailers or have somebody to pick out all the red M and Ms. Understand? It'll be written into your contract, and if you throw tantrums, or try to hold up filming, I'll sue.'

Greta looks stunned, but then shakes herself. I can see the little hamster wheel turning in her brain, humming, 'Oscar, Oscar, Oscar.'

'You're in charge, Mark,' she whispers.

Eli Roth and Kitty look impressed. As well they should be.

'Now, you,' Swan says to Trish. 'Same goes for you, sweetheart. I don't want too many changes, but no bitching about the ones I do want. I have final say and if you don't like it we can hire another writer. Fair enough?'

'Not really,' says Trish, grinning. 'But I don't have much choice, do I?'

'None at all,' says Swan, cheerfully. 'And you,' he turns to Eli and Kitty. 'The budget's low. That's OK, I don't care too much about my fee. Labour of love.'

'I admire your passion for the work,' Eli Roth says smoothly.

'But the flip side is I get approval on the lot. And I probably won't want too many suggestions from Red Crest.'

'But, Mark,' says Kitty tremulously, 'surely you'll allow us to sit in on meetings. The producers have to be represented in the process.'

'I don't mind if you come to an occasional meeting,' Swan says.

'I'm sorry, but I have to put my foot down here,' says Eli Roth, a bit anxiously. I can't believe the transformation I'm seeing. Until today I thought Roth was a powerhouse. 'I need to know what's going on.'

Swan pretends to consider it.

'Well,' he says eventually, 'you can send Anna.'

I blink.

'Anna!' Kitty explodes. 'But Anna's just a reader!'

'Anna found me,' Swan says simply, 'and I like her.'

'That was my idea,' says Kitty, instantly.

'No, it wasn't,' says Swan. 'Trying to sneak onto the set is the sort of mental thing only juniors do. It was a ballsy move,' he says, turning to me. 'If you sit in on meetings you can learn something about movies in the real world. It'll make her a better producer,' he says to Kitty.

'She isn't a producer. She's just a reader,' says Kitty, venomously. 'And we don't feel she's ready to move on just yet. I can sit in and report back daily to you, Eli,' she adds deferentially.

'I want Anna,' says Swan.

'Maybe you should take Kitty, Mr Swan,' I say, seeing the fury in my boss's eyes. 'I mean, she won an Oscar,' I bleat.

Swan looks at Kitty and Eli and shrugs. 'I'm about to sign on to do this film for scale. It has to be fun for me. I like Anna, so having her there to rep you guys makes it fun. If you're not cool with that, we can save ourselves a lot of trouble and I'll bugger off so you can call other directors.'

'That's fine, Mark,' says Roth, with a warning look at Kitty who has opened her mouth again. 'We're cool with that.'

'Excellent,' Swan says. 'You three, come over to my hotel at five—47 Park Street.'

Trish and Greta say they'll be there, and I just nod my head.

He stands up and everybody jumps to their feet. Swan goes round the room, shaking hands, starting with Greta. Finally he gets to me.

'Nice seeing you again,' he says, clasping my hand in his giant one.

'See you this afternoon, Mr Swan,' I say, trying to sound businesslike.

'We agreed on Mark,' he reminds me. He gives my hand a gentle squeeze. 'This is gonna be fun,' he says. And then he's gone.

I'm sitting on Eli Roth's couch, twisting my hands nervously in my lap. Even though I've nothing to feel guilty about, I still do. Kitty and Roth really are giving me the third degree.

'And you got this idea how?' Kitty asks acidly.

'I don't know,' I say lamely. 'It just came to me.'

'And you happened to bump into him,' Roth says. He's smiling crisply, but his body language leaves no doubt that he finds me highly suspicious. 'What were you doing again?'

'Just buying some sweets.'

'That figures,' says Kitty, meanly.

'And he agreed to read the script.'

'Yes,' I say. 'Honestly, it was just luck.'

'You're quite sure you had no other *contact* with him?' asks Roth. 'You haven't had . . . *intimacy* with him?'

Intimacy? Not unless you count him catching my copy of *Heat*. Oh, wait a minute, he's speaking American, intimacy means sex.

'Me? And Mark Swan?' I'm so nervous I laugh out loud. The very idea is insane. I mean, Mark Swan could have anyone.

Kitty relaxes a little. 'I suppose that is rather fanciful,' she says, the cow. 'I hardly think Mr Swan would be having a relationship with *Anna*.'

'Just remember, Anna,' Roth says. 'You're not the producer. You've just been delegated, at the director's request, to *report* to the producers.'

'I understand,' I say humbly.

'And you must be clear on your loyalties,' says Roth. He's warning me. 'You work for Red Crest Productions, not Mark Swan. You will account everything you see and hear fully to us.'

'I'll definitely let you know every detail,' I promise. 'I'm hoping for a promotion,' I add, braving Kitty's scowl.

'Well, let's see how you handle this,' Roth says. 'Your future depends on it, Anna.'

John has piled a huge mound of scripts on my desk when I get back to it.

'What's this?'

'The weekend read,' he says.

'But . . .'

The lift doors hiss open and Kitty emerges. 'You'll have your normal duties, Anna, of course,' she says. 'I want you to realise that this whim of

Mark's doesn't change anything—apart from possibly putting our production at risk, trusting somebody so inexperienced.'

I look at the huge pile. 'That's fine,' I say. 'Kitty, can I see you a minute?'

'Thirty seconds,' she says, gesturing to her office.

'Look. I just want to say that I didn't plan this. You can trust me. I want that promotion, and I'm not going to get it from Mark Swan. I'll be your right-hand girl. I'll report everything right back to you.'

Kitty looks at me, and her shoulders relax just a little.

'You know you can trust me, Anna,' she says. 'I gave you the rise.'

'Yes, thanks so much,' I say.

'And I did say you could be promoted when the time is right, so assuming you do a good job for us with Mark . . .' she waves her hand in the air. 'Perhaps after pre-production, then.'

I smile. She's actually putting a time frame on it. She means it!

I float through the rest of the day. I flick through the new scripts (they're all dire) and make a few halfhearted notes. But mostly I'm just watching the clock, waiting for four thirty so I can get out of the office and get down to Park Street. I can't wait. I'll get a chance to thank Mark and sit in on a real pre-production meeting. And prove myself to Kitty.

Everybody in the office is looking at me. You can almost hear them all thinking, *Not Anna*. But it *is* me, it *is* Anna. And I have Mark Swan to thank for it!

Sharon's coming over. 'That was quite a coup you pulled off with Mark Swan,' she says flatteringly. 'The whole office is talking about it.'

'I just bumped into him.'

'And apparently he really likes you.'

'He was very nice,' I admit.

'Does he have a girlfriend?' Sharon asks, casually. Ah. I should have guessed.

'I've got no idea,' I say. 'I expect so. Gorgeous millionaires normally do, don't they?'

'He's not gorgeous,' Sharon says, shocked. 'He's a great big beast. He'd be lucky to get a girlfriend. Of course,' she adds, 'I don't care about things like looks. I'm just attracted to his *talent*.'

'I'm sure he'd be very flattered,' I say.

'Maybe you could find out for me?' wheedles Sharon.

'I'll ask him,' I say reluctantly.

'Mark Swan?' asks Claire, who's been listening in intently. 'Why would you bother with *him* when Eli Roth works right in this very building?' She sighs, dreamily.

'Eli Roth's not available,' Sharon says curtly.

'And how do you know?' asks Claire, bristling.

Sharon tosses her curls confidently. 'I've taken him coffee a couple of times when he's been in to see Mike,' she says.

'So what? So have I,' says Claire.

'Well, he didn't ask me out,' says Sharon. 'So, you know. He's either got a girlfriend or he's gay.'

Claire snorts.

'He didn't ask you out either,' Sharon points out.

'Doesn't mean he won't. Maybe he's working up to it,' Claire retorts. They glare at each other and I grin to myself. Pretty girls! What would it be like, I wonder, to be ignored by a man and actually conclude there was something wrong *with the man*? I'd love to have that self-confidence.

'He's not going to ask you out,' says Sharon, cattily. 'He'd be just as likely to ask Anna.' She laughs. I feel all my happiness draining out. I try to think of Mark Swan and my new career, but I can't. One comment, and I'm back to Anna Brown, the tall, big-boned, big-nosed girl.

A wave of sadness crashes over me. To my horror, I realise tears have started to prickle in my eyes. I may be the story of the day as a future success, but as a woman, I'm still just the office joke. I mean, I know Swan and Roth wouldn't date me, but does it have to be so bloody funny?

'I'm sorry,' says Sharon, catching my expression. 'Of course I didn't mean it like *that*.'

'I just have something in my eye,' I lie. My phone buzzes.

'Anna?' says Charles.

'Oh, hi,' I say.

'How is the most beautiful girl in London?' Charles asks politely.

I smile, despite the tears that are trickling down my cheeks now. I quickly brush them away, although Sharon's already seen them. How does he know to say exactly the right thing when I need it most? I feel a rush of warmth and gratitude.

'How would I know? I've never met Kate Moss,' I joke.

'That bony thing?' Charles says scornfully. 'Looks like a golf club on a diet.'

That one actually makes me laugh.

'Are we going out tonight?' Charles asks hopefully. Well, we weren't, but why not?

'Sure,' I say. 'I'd love to. How about seven thirty?'

'Wonderful. I'll pick you up.'

'No, don't do that,' I say, panicking slightly. I have no wish to expose him to Lily before I have to. Even Janet, who's being so much nicer. 'I'll come to you. What's your address?'

'Forty-eight Eaton Square, flat twelve,' he says.

Eaton Square. Oh yes. 'Right. I'll see you there at seven thirty.'

'Brilliant. I'm really looking forward to it,' he says.

I find I've stopped crying. 'So am I,' I reply.

Forty-seven Park Street is a very discreet hotel a stone's throw from Hyde Park. 'Mark Swan?' I ask nervously.

'Your name, please, madam?'

'Anna Brown,' I say.

He consults a list. 'Somebody will come to get you,' he tells me.

Within a minute a gorgeous, rather shocking young thing has appeared on the stairs. This is exactly the kind of girl who would wind up assisting Mark Swan. She's got the best red hair money can buy, a frighteningly low-cut pair of jeans, and a safety pin through her nose.

'You Anna?' she demands. 'My name's Michelle Ross, I'm Mark's assistant. In the future, you want to talk to him, you can call me. OK?'

Swan has a suite on the fourth floor. When I get there Trish and Greta are already settled on the sofa, sipping drinks. Mark Swan is drinking a Heineken from the bottle.

'Hi,' I say.

Swan glances at his watch. 'You're late.'

I look guiltily at mine. It says five past. 'Sorry, the tube was delayed.'

'Then leave extra time,' Swan says. 'I'm working two projects. I expect you to be exactly on time or early.'

I chuckle at his impression of a stuck-up movie mogul.

'What the fuck is so funny?'

'Oh, nothing,' I say, as it dawns on me he wasn't joking. 'It won't happen again.'

'It'd better not,' he says curtly.

I sit down on an empty chair, blushing. I look reproachfully at Mark, but he just gazes evenly back at me.

I should be angry at the rebuke, but instead I'm feeling something odd. I feel . . . respect. Yes, that's what it is. I wasn't sure at first, it's been so long since I've actually met somebody I respect.

'The reason we're here is for me to give you notes,' he says, looking towards Trish and Greta. 'Greta, I'm going to tell you what I want to see in Elsie. Trish, I'm going to tell you what to rewrite. It's good for you to hear each other's notes, because knowing about the story will help Greta shape her performance, and knowing how I'm gonna direct the lead will help Trish with her rewrites. Everybody with me?'

Greta and Trish nod obediently.

'And why am I here?' I ask him.

Swan glances back at me. 'You're here to listen.'

'I've some great production ideas,' I offer enthusiastically.

He shrugs. 'Well, keep 'em to yourself.'

'So I'm just going to sit here and say nothing?' I ask, my voice rising.

'I see you've got the gist of it,' he says. 'Now, may I proceed?' Swan stares at me for a second, his lip twitching. Then he looks back at the other two women.

'We'll start with Greta,' he says. 'My image of Elsie is . . .'

I stare at my yellow legal pad while he goes on about the character of Elsie. I wish Swan wanted me to contribute something. Frustrated, I doodle words on my pad. 'Master shot', 'complex', 'scared', 'haughty'.

'Yes, yes, I see,' Greta purrs once he's done. 'Fascinating, yes, I can bring all this to the role, I see her in a whole new way now.'

What a suck up. Everybody is staring at me. Oh hell, did I make that slurping noise out loud? I swallow, conspicuously. 'Mintoe,' I say.

'I don't want too many changes,' Swan says to Trish, after looking hard at me for a couple of seconds. 'But I do think you need to work on your second-act pacing, particularly in the scenes with the wedding planner.'

Trish nods. 'D'you think we should have more scenes where Gemma is fighting with the wedding planner?'

'Maybe,' Swan says. 'The dialogue's a bit wooden. I've seen this before. *Father of the Bride* with Steve Martin. This has to be different.'

I bite my lip. No, no, that's all wrong! You don't want to see more of Gemma, the bride. You want to see more of Elsie, her mother.

Swan continues to talk, telling Trish what he wants. This bit of the script does sag, it gets boring in the second act. And Trish keeps giving him her ideas. But I think they're all wrong.

I'd love to say something. I really would. But it's not my script, is it? I jot down a couple of funny lines, like doodling. You know, just what I would put if it *were* my script. But I'm careful to angle my body so she can't see what I'm doing. Everybody thinks they can write, don't they?

'That's great,' Swan says, finally. 'I'll look forward to talking to both of you in a couple of days.'

Trish and Greta both get to their feet. Greta is air-kissing the side of Swan's face, or trying to—even on tiptoe she only comes up to his chin—and Trish shakes his hand. I hang back, waiting politely till they've finished. I feel drained. It was such a triumph to get here, but all I can think of is how frustrating it is not being able to do anything. There's not even any intrigue to report back to Kitty, no plots to go over-budget or anything, no diva-like tantrums from Greta.

I sneak another look at Swan. He's in his element, relaxed, enjoying himself. He focuses totally on the people he's talking to, and his energy and enthusiasm are electric. *Mother of the Bride* is really just an above average, quite funny story that suited the actress Kitty wanted cast. But sitting here, I get the feeling that Mark Swan will mould it into some kind of comedy classic.

I wish it were me he was looking at like that . . .

Oh, don't be ridiculous, Anna! I try to compose myself. Don't want Mark Swan suspecting an idiotic schoolgirl crush or anything.

'See you guys later,' Swan says. 'Michelle'll walk you out.'

It suddenly occurs to me I don't really want to be alone with Swan. I feel vulnerable, exposed. 'OK,' I say briskly. 'That was a very valuable and, er, insightful meeting, and I'll be reporting back to the producers.'

Swan stares at me. I ate a Walnut Whip on the way over here, I hope I haven't got chocolate all round my mouth. Surreptitiously I wipe my lips. But he's still staring. Maybe he needs some arse-kissing, that's what directors like, isn't it? You know the joke—how many directors does it take to change a light bulb? One. He just holds the light bulb and the world revolves around him . . .

'We're so delighted you're on board with this project,' I try.

'God, Anna, do you have to talk like a total wanker?' Swan says.

I blink. 'Excuse me?'

He waves his hand. 'Don't give me that. Just because you work for some producers doesn't mean you have to talk like a Hollywood executive. I liked you because you weren't like all the others.'

'What others?'

'What, you think you're the only one to come looking for me? I get two or three film students a week.'

'Is it the Steven Spielberg story?' I ask, crestfallen. I had thought it a bold and brilliant stroke.

'Yeah,' Swan says. 'Security guards everywhere curse the day that story started making the rounds.'

'So . . . why did you like me?' I ask.

He shrugs. 'I don't know. You took me on over that comment I made about the Diet Coke.' He grins. 'D'you know, I've stopped smoking? Whenever I try to enjoy a nice quiet smoke I keep seeing your face saying every time I light up I'm getting cancer.'

'Ha ha,' I say, triumphantly. 'Now you know how it feels.'

Then I remember who I'm talking to. I have to be careful, this is Mark Swan, as in, *Mark Swan*, all-round film-making god. 'I expect the other film students don't say stuff like that to you,' I offer.

'No. Well, for one they recognise me.'

I blush.

'And for two, then they're dumbstruck. They sometimes ask to sit at my table when I'm in the pub, and if I say yes, they just sit there staring.' He gazes unblinkingly at me. 'But they don't say anything.'

'Like you're in the zoo,' I say, delighted.

'Exactly.' He grins, and then there's a pause. I wrench my gaze away. Shouldn't relish his company like this.

I glance at my watch. 'I'll be off, then.'

'Hold on,' Swan says, and his face turns serious again. 'That meeting. You sat there like a pudding. What's the matter, not glad to be here?'

'Oh,' I say, panicked. He's not going to kick me out, is he? 'No. I was glad to be here. So glad. I loved listening to you,' I say earnestly, then I blush. That came out wrong. I can't let him suspect my admiration.

'But you didn't say anything.'

'You told me to keep my ideas to myself,' I point out.

'That doesn't mean I didn't want to hear from you at all. I didn't ask you to the meeting just so you could be decorative,' he says.

Decorative! Hah. 'But I'm just representing the production company.'

'Not as far as I'm concerned,' Swan says. 'I value your opinion. That's why I asked you there.' He looks at me. 'When we were discussing those wedding-planner scenes you looked like you'd bitten into a lemon, but you didn't say anything.'

'I didn't think it was my place,' I say, blushing.

He smiles. 'But I'm telling you it is. You have a suggestion?'

'Uhm.' I feel rather stupid and exposed, so I blurt it out. 'I don't think those scenes should be about Gemma at all, it's not her story, it should be all about Elsie, and this is where she's really sabotaging the wedding so she could, you know, she could make sure to ask for things that will be impossible. She wants it to be chaos, or for the planner to quit.'

'Hmmm,' he says. 'Go on.'

'But Elsie needs it to sound reasonable. And you want it to be funny. So she needs to make all the outrageous demands with a very uptight little smile. Sounding really . . . saccharine,' I suggest.

He's silent for a beat. I daren't look up at him.

'Can I see that?' He reaches for the yellow pad on which I've doodled my dialogue. Flushing, I move it away.

'Oh, no, that's nothing,' I protest.

'Hand it over,' he says, inexorably, swiping it. I shuffle my feet together while his eyes flicker over it, reading everything I've written.

'Did you come up with these lines?'

'Yes, but I was listening, I swear.'

'Anna. These lines aren't bad. Not at all. That's closer to what I was looking for. The humour, the tone—the whole bit.'

'Oh.' I don't know what to say. I feel a wash of pleasure all over.

'You've a great ear for dialogue,' he says. 'Ever thought about writing?'

'Who? Me? I couldn't be a writer. I'm just an apprentice producer.'

'You're a lot more impressive as a writer,' Swan says.

'You really think I could be a writer?' I ask, delighted.

'What, are you deaf? How many times do I have to say it?'

'Well. Thanks,' I say. 'Thank you *very much*.'

'You're welcome, sweetheart,' he says.

I turn away, spell broken. I had been gazing at him, so full of happiness and gratitude, and of course he's so gorgeous and he's being so nice. But then he said *sweetheart*, and I don't like the teasing. I swallow hard against the sudden lump in my throat. Which is totally ridiculous.

'What happened to that smile?' he asks, grinning. 'Have you got plans for the evening? Maybe you'd like to come out for a drink? Michelle and I usually get a pint about now.'

Oh, absolutely. Love to, so I can sit there while much prettier women come up and fling themselves at him, and skinny Michelle sneers at me. No, no. Mark Swan is far too dangerous to hang out with socially.

'I've got plans,' I say, not looking at him.

'Cancel them,' Swan suggests.

'I've got a date,' I say, with a sudden surge of gratitude to Charles. Yes, I do have a date. Once again, Charles saves me without even knowing it.

'Oh. Who?'

'His name's Charles Dawson,' I say, as brightly as I can manage.

Now Swan does frown slightly. 'Charles Dawson, the one who tipped you off to the script? Trish's employer's brother?'

'How do you know that?'

'I called Trish this afternoon. I make it a rule to get to know the people I work with. It helps me get the best out of them.'

'You think it'll interfere with the movie?' I ask, nervously. 'Him being Lady Cartwright's brother?'

'Oh no,' Swan says. 'Trish quit her job, anyway.'

'She did?' I ask. 'Isn't that a bit risky for her? Nobody knows how the film will do and she's only getting scale.'

'Her film will be a huge hit,' says Swan. 'I'm involved.'

'You're so modest.' I smile.

He shrugs. 'We both know it's the truth.' And of course I do. 'Anyway, you'll find that not risking anything is what you need to be afraid of.'

I look at my watch again. 'If it's OK with you, I really have to go,' I say.

'No problem,' Swan says. 'See you tomorrow. Ten o'clock, sharp.'

'I'll be there,' I say, gratefully. 'Thank you for the chance.' I walk out of the room, trying not to look back at him.

I don't want to feel like this. Just because he's masculine and powerful but still funny and nice, that's no reason to fancy a man, is it?

OK, maybe it is.

But I can never *have* Mark Swan. He's out of my league. That's an excellent reason *not* to fancy him. No point. And the fact that he said lovely things about me maybe being able to write is to do with my career.

I must think about my career.

I must not get a crush on a gorgeous, famous, powerful director.

Note to self. *Do not fall for Mark Swan.*

OK. I'm not going to think about him any more tonight.

4

'COME IN, COME IN,' Charles says, flinging open his door. 'So lovely to see you.' He's beaming from ear to ear. I wait for a compliment, but none comes, which is a bit disappointing, considering how long I spent on this look. Janet helped me with my make-up; she used my neutrals, but she made my eyes really pop. I suppose it does distract from my nose a tiny bit and, more to the point, it at least makes me look put together, sort of elegant. My dress is my nice navy shift with pearls I wore to the dinner at Vanna's, the first time we met. Janet shakes her head over it.

'Makes your arse look huge,' she says, flatteringly. 'Which it isn't. And shows off your stomach,' she adds. 'Meanwhile it flattens your tits and covers your legs.'

'So what?' I demand.

'You should show them off,' Janet says, her beautiful, olive-skinned face serious. 'And you've got no waist in that dress.'

'I've got no waist anyway.'

'We could create one,' Janet says judiciously.

'Who are you, God?' I scoff. 'Look, this is my body. Best thing for it is to wear something conservative.'

'Dowdy.'

'Classic,' I insist.

'Boring,' Janet says pityingly. 'Anna, I am a fashion expert, you know. You're not doing yourself any favours. Don't forget I'm taking you to Harvey Nicks on Friday to tart you up a bit for the dance.'

'Fine, whatever. Just pass me my shoes.'

'If I must,' Janet sniffs, handing over my flat Hobbs pair with the white stitching, which I thought was a great match for navy and pearls. 'They make me want to puke.'

Thus encouraged I set off for Eaton Square in a taxi, even though it was twelve quid. I'm trying not to be intimidated by the fabled flat. It's only a bloody flat. And so here I am. The building is gorgeous. To me it says old, old money that doesn't need to shout about it. No wonder Charles has been plagued by gold-diggers. I feel for him. Lots of men in his position wouldn't object. They'd just pick the sexiest chick and bed down with her, and trade her in ten years later for the next model.

'So this is home,' I say, stepping inside.

'Yes.' He looks around, half embarrassed, half proud. It's insanely gorgeous: red damask wallpaper, prints of hunting scenes, the odd oil here and there, antiques. Books lining the walls, the occasional threadbare Persian rug, deep, worn burgundy leather armchairs. Everything is upper class, lived in, valuable. The sole modern touches are the electronics. He has a huge, flat-screen TV and a sexy-looking, ultra-slim laptop on his desk, which is strewn with bits of paper.

'I'm sorry it's so messy,' he says. 'The char doesn't come till tomorrow.'

'You should see my room,' I lie. I'd hate him to see my room. I wonder what it would be like to live somewhere like this, all the time?

'So this is where you work?' I say, and immediately wish I hadn't.

'Yes, on my book.' He looks over at me. 'Any word on that yet?'

'I'm still reading it. I got a bit distracted by the *Mother of the Bride* thing, and I want to give it all the consideration it's due. It's very complex,' I say, truthfully enough. I was confused after two paragraphs.

'Ah, yes,' says Charles, stoically. 'It is complex, multi-layered. I can see you need time to fully appreciate it.'

'Yes,' I agree, smiling weakly. 'Time. Anyway, it's a lovely flat.'

Charles eyes me nervously. 'I do have a guest room,' he says. 'If you want to stay over?'

'Absolutely not. I hardly know you. I'm not about to move in,' I say indignantly, and then feel bad, because I know that soon I'll have to dump him. I don't fancy him, even though I do like him now. I might tell myself that I'm going out with the poor sod to give him a chance, but in reality

I just like how he treats me and tries to make me feel good about myself.

'Sorry,' Charles says meekly. 'I'm so used to girls wanting that.'

'Not me,' I say breezily. 'I'm a career girl.'

'I know,' he says admiringly. 'I think it's wonderful. Getting promoted and everything,' and I feel even worse. I mustn't use him, like all the other girls. Even if they were using him for money and I'm using him for compliments, it's really the same thing, isn't it? I should say something. Let him know it's not going to work.

'I've been boasting about you to all my friends,' he says. 'They can't wait to meet you this weekend.'

'Oh, yes,' I say. 'Right.' Well, I'm stuck now. I can't break up with him. Not if he's been telling all his friends. I feel a pang of protectiveness. I'd never expose Charles to some of the pain I've been through.

'I'm looking forward to meeting them,' I tell him.

'Are you?' His face lights up. I smile back. I like making him happy, it's the least I can do for all the trouble he takes for me.

'Where are we going to dinner?' I ask.

'Well, here,' he says.

'Here?' I glance around the flat. 'You cooked something?'

'Not exactly,' he admits. 'Bit of a dunce in the old egg-boiling department. I called the caterers. I thought it'd be more romantic to eat here. More intimate.'

I smile but my skin's crawling. I do hope he doesn't mean intimate in the Eli Roth sense. I'm just not ready to have sex with Charles and I don't know if I ever will be.

'Got anything to drink?'

'Of course,' he says, beaming, springing to his feet in his haste to be of service. 'Sherry? G and T? Wine? Scotch? Irish?'

'Gin and tonic would be lovely, thanks,' I say. Charles leaps into action, hurrying to the kitchen (Smeg appliances and Sub-Zero freezer meets terracotta tiles and ancient wooden counter-top) and returning with a beautiful Waterford crystal tumbler filled with ice, slices of lime and a subtly fizzing drink. I take a good hit and start to relax. It's been a long day and the alcohol unknots my muscles. That, plus I realise I won't actually have to endure another restaurant, won't have to see the sidelong glances. What was it Sharon said? Little and Large?

Maybe the flat is better after all. I refuse to think about what happens after dinner. I take another big slug of G&T.

'You've finished, let me get you another,' he says.

I shake my head. 'Don't want to get too tipsy before we start eating.'

'No,' he says, admiringly. 'Very proper. Shall we go in?'

He's so formal. I wonder if my dress is smart enough. 'Where's the butler? No "Dinner is served"?'

'I don't have one,' Charles responds, crestfallen. 'I can get one if you want.'

'I was joking,' I say, aghast. 'Nobody has servants these days.'

He looks a bit sheepish.

'You have servants?'

'Just a couple,' he admits. 'At Chester House. But you know, it's a bare-bones staff,' he excuses himself. 'Just a butler and a couple of maids. And a gardener. And a cook.'

'Oh, well, that's all right then,' I say.

'And my valet,' he admits.

'Charles, that must cost you a fortune.'

'It's a necessity when you live out of town,' he says.

No, it isn't. 'Sure, I understand.'

'No, look, Anna,' he says, reading my expression and pleading his case. 'Don't think I'm just some rich egomaniac with servants.'

That's pretty much exactly what I was thinking, so I start guiltily. 'Hey, it's a free country, right? You can do what you like with your money.'

'They all worked for my father,' he says. 'Except the valet. But he found it hard to get other work and my butler recommended him. And the other staff are too old to just send them packing.'

I soften. 'So you continue to employ the old family retainers?'

'Pretty much,' Charles agrees. I like him for it, I like him immensely.

'What was the valet doing before?'

'Fifteen to twenty for GBH at Strangeways,' Charles says. 'Couldn't get a job after that. But Wilkins knew him, and he's an absolute genius at picking out ties.'

I laugh. 'You know what, Charles, I really like you.'

He glows. 'I like you, too.' He gestures to the dining room. 'Shall we?'

Fortified by my gin and tonic and Charles's dodgy valet, I manage to sit down in his dining room without feeling overwhelmed. I give myself a gold star for that, because, if anything, it's even lovelier than the rest of the place: oak panel walls, a gorgeous table to match; the cutlery is silver and antique, and there are beautiful yellow and white roses arranged in low silver bowls dotted around the room. Candles every-where, and a magnum of champagne chilling in an ice bucket.

'I hope you like it,' Charles says, nervously.

'It's beautiful,' I say, smiling to reassure him.

'I thought we could start with caviar. Do you like caviar?' Charles asks, anxiously. 'Some people hate it.'

'I've never tried it, but I'm sure it's delicious.'

'And then there's roast guinea fowl with stuffing.'

My mouth is watering in a very unladylike manner.

'And there's green tea sorbet, and then pudding is a bitter chocolate tart with ginger ice cream, or you could have cheese and fruit. I had them make up a plate in case you aren't the pudding type.'

I look ruefully down at my ample tummy. 'I am,' I inform him solemnly, 'the pudding type.'

'Champagne, and there's a very nice brandy afterwards . . .'

'Charles,' I say, smiling with genuine warmth, 'this is the nicest thing anyone's ever done for me.' And I kiss him on the cheek.

'Well,' he says, blushing scarlet. He offers me his arm. He actually offers me his arm, but I know how to rise to the moment. I take it, just like Elizabeth Bennet in *Pride and Prejudice* or any of the leading ladies in those old Sunday-afternoon shows, and let him escort me the two feet into the dining room. I think briefly of Lily and Janet and their strings of glamorous escorts. Is this what good-looking girls expect on dates? Men who can't do enough for them, boyfriends desperately eager to please?

It has never happened to me before. During the rare times in my life when I've been attached to a man, I've been the one who needed the approval. I see the same look in Charles's eyes that I've seen in my own. And it gives me an incredible feeling of power, because I can put things right for him the way they weren't put right for me. I can make Charles feel good. I can compliment him, say nice things about him to all his friends, accept what he offers me with enthusiasm. I can protect him from all the snubs, insults and jokes that were levelled at me.

I have a damn good time. The food is insanely delicious; I relax and just enjoy being pampered. Charles isn't the world's wittiest conversationalist but he's not absolutely terrible, either. He talks a good deal about Vanna and Rupert because I know them, to make me feel comfortable, and he asks loads of questions about my work. He's either genuinely interested or a very good actor. Either way, it's nice.

'This has been such a lovely evening,' I tell him.

'Well, it's not over yet,' he says. 'Port? Cognac? Brandy? Something—'

'I can't. I've had way too much. Got to go to work tomorrow.'

'At least have coffee,' he says. 'And petits fours.'

'Mmm,' I say. I should say no but I love petits fours. Some part of me wonders why Charles chose such a heavy meal. Didn't he say to that bony cow back at Vanna's dinner party how much he admired self-discipline? And he made mean cracks about my weight. Yet now we're dating and he's plying me with chocolate tarts and roast potatoes . . .

Something's niggling at me because there's something subtly wrong. 'I think I'll just have the coffee.'

'But you must try at least one,' he says, shoving the silver tray in my direction. All my favourites: brandy snaps, tiny profiteroles . . .

'I'm supposed to be watching my weight,' I say. He looks surprised.

'You're not *hugely* fat,' he says, 'so why not just be who you are?'

'I thought you liked self-discipline,' I remind him.

'Oh. That. Well, that's fine for Priscilla,' he says. 'But you're Anna and I don't need to change anything about you.'

That response should strike me as truly romantic, and I'm not quite sure why it doesn't.

'Maybe just one,' I say, reaching for a brandy snap, because I've had quite enough of analysing things today. 'Thanks,' and I smile at him.

Charles drops me off around eleven, refusing to let me get a taxi home—he says he has to 'escort' me. I spend the journey wondering nervously when he's going to invite himself up for 'coffee', but he doesn't. When he pulls up as close to our building as he can he says, 'May I?' and then, when I nod, he kisses me chastely on the cheek.

'I had a wonderful time,' I tell him, giddy with relief. 'See you Saturday, up at Chester House, OK?'

'Absolutely,' he says warmly. 'Can't wait.' He grabs my large hand in his small one and kisses it.

'What's that for?'

'Oh, nothing,' he says. 'I just think you're the one for me.'

I smile back at him because I'm not quite sure what to say, and maybe he senses it, because he shifts gears, calls out, 'See you Saturday!' cheerfully, and drives off down Tottenham Court Road.

I walk in through the narrow corridor next to the unlit feminist bookshop and wonder what on earth that was all about. He sounded keen, didn't he? Really keen.

In fact, he sounded as if he wanted to marry me.

Janet and Lily are lying on the floor when I come in. There's a huge bottle of champagne empty between them and magazines everywhere.

Lily raises her head. 'I'm just going through some recent shoots with Janet. Trying to show her where she's going wrong. She's getting calls for *catalogue* work,' she says scornfully.

'Whatever pays the bills, right?' I suggest.

'Wrong,' says Lily. 'If you get pigeonholed into that kind of thing you're over. Done. Toast.'

'I turned them down,' Janet says nervously.

'Darling, of course you did,' says Lily. 'I should think so too.'

'Oh, this is so stupid,' I burst out. 'Janet, you're not going to make it onto the Paris catwalks anyway and I bet a few catalogue jobs wouldn't stop you finding work in the glossies.'

'Maybe Anna has a point,' Janet says timidly.

'Oh, really?' says Lily, eyes narrowing. 'She does, does she? You're going to take modelling advice from someone who looks like *that*?' Hey! This is one of my better outfits, actually.

'I could make Anna look all right,' says Janet, protectively.

'No, you couldn't. Don't be ridiculous,' Lily says. 'No offence, Anna.'

I swallow. This is a bit beyond a joke. 'But it is offensive.'

'Excuse me?' she demands, looking up at me. 'I *said*, no offence.'

'I know you say that. Usually after you've said something really mean-spirited,' I reply. I know I've gone bright red, but I don't care.

'Actually, you do do that a lot,' Janet mutters. 'You just said, "Janet, you're twenty-eight, you have to work like a slave to get anybody to book you." And then you said, "No offence."'

Lily flicks her golden hair. 'I'm only saying, Janet, who's the professional here, me or Anna?'

'You are,' says Janet, meekly. She looks at me apologetically. 'Sorry about what I said about making you over.'

'That's OK,' I say, because Janet seems so miserable. 'And you're going to get me some new clothes before the dance at Chester House, right?'

'Right,' she says, perking up. 'I can do wonders for you. You just wait and see.'

I'm getting ready to head out of the door next morning when my mobile trills. 'Anna, where the hell are you?' It's Kitty.

'I was just heading down to Swan Lake.' That's his company.

'I don't think so,' Kitty hisses ominously. 'You must come into the office every morning before you go gallivanting off with Mr Swan. You need to get your instructions and make your report.'

'Um, OK,' I say, placatingly. I can't get Kitty angry. 'I'll be right there.' Oh, bugger. What's the quickest way to the office? The traffic's crawling. And there was a bomb scare at Covent Garden so the tube's out. I feel the panic rising. I'll be late to Swan's. Twice.

There's nothing else for it. I start to run. I make it in fifteen minutes, red-faced and sweating. Kitty's sitting behind her desk, stilettos tapping. She's wearing a scarlet Dolce & Gabbana suit with huge black buttons. Obviously she's in a really bad mood. The more *Dynasty* the outfit, the angrier she is. 'Give me your report from the meeting,' she snaps.

'Well, he gave Trish some notes and discussed the part with Greta.'

'And what else?' she demands, eyes narrowing.

'Nothing.'

'Are you holding out on me?'

'No.'

'Why does he *want* you,' she asks, bitterly. 'You! Of all people!'

'I think he thinks somebody senior would be wasted in those meet-ings, all I do is take notes,' I say, tactfully.

She nods. 'Yes, possibly. Well, anyway, that isn't enough work. I want you to continue with your reading. And I also want you to be Greta's assistant. I want Greta to be made to feel *special* by Red Crest Productions and especially by Kitty Simpson.'

I want to argue but I've got no time. It's already ten thirty. I shudder to think what Mark Swan will say when I show up.

'OK,' I say desperately, 'sure. Whatever you want.'

'I'd better not hear any complaints,' Kitty says viciously. 'And each day as soon as Mark is done with you I want you back here in the office.'

'Of course,' I say. 'Um . . . thanks, Kitty.'

Why? Why am I thanking her for making me be this ageing diva's dogsbody? I'm supposed to be a reader, up for promotion.

'You may go,' Kitty says graciously. I rush out of the door again, pulling out my mobile, tapping in the number as soon as I reach the street. 'Oh, Michelle, hi, this is Anna Brown.'

'From the producers,' says Michelle. There's an ominous touch of triumph in her tone. 'He says you needn't bother to come in today.'

I look at my watch. 'But I was unavoidably delayed.'

'Whatever,' she says. 'He said to say if you called not to bother to come in. I have to go, goodbye now.'

I'm only a few minutes away from Swan Lake anyhow, so I keep walk-ing. What else am I going to do? Although I don't know how I'm going to explain to him . . . OK, here we are. Dean Street. This is it.

And there they are. Swan. Greta. Trish, who sees me and shoots me a sympathetic look. A couple of other people I don't recognise. They're all piling into taxis. I rush forward. 'Mark,' I say. 'Sorry I'm late, but—'

'I don't want you around today,' he says flatly. 'If you can't respect other people's time, Anna, then I've no use for you.'

'But I've got a good excuse.'

'I'm not interested in excuses,' he says. 'I take this stuff seriously and I expect my colleagues to as well.' He starts to climb into a taxi.

'You've got to listen to me!' I protest.

'No, I don't,' he says. 'See you.'

'Oh, fine,' I snap, losing it. 'Don't bother giving Anna ten seconds to see if she's got a reasonable explanation. Ohhh no, just abuse your power and make other people feel terrible when it isn't even their fault.'

And I turn on my heel and walk away, heart pounding. I want to cry. That's it, then. That is the sum total of my Mark Swan adventure. Because he'll call Kitty and she'll be only too delighted to sack me so she can go and hang out with him herself.

'Anna.' I turn. It's Swan.

'Look, I'm sorry I said that, OK?' I tell him tearfully. 'I've—I've had a really bad morning. Just please don't get me sacked because I need the money for rent and things.'

His face softens. 'Tell me what happened.'

'I was on my way to your offices and Kitty rang me,' I said, 'and she made me go into work and I had to leg it because of the tube, you know it was shut down, and she talked to me for a bit and then I had to run to your place . . . I would have got here in bags of time.'

Swan just stands there for a second. Then he holds open the taxi door. 'I'm sorry,' he says. 'You were right. I should have given you a chance to explain. Please hop in. We're going over to the production designers to do some storyboarding. We'll have a talk later. OK?'

'OK,' I mumble.

Greta looks disapprovingly at my red eyes. 'Stop making a scene,' she stage whispers.

Swan leads everybody into the production design offices. 'You guys go on up, I'll be right with you,' he says. 'I need to speak to Anna a second. Look,' he adds, when the lift doors have hissed shut on the rest of them. 'I'm sorry about before. I acted like a total idiot.'

'That's OK,' I say. I'm not really used to important people admitting they were wrong. Or saying sorry.

'I thought, you know, we had a good talk last night. And,' he says, passing his hand over his hair, 'for some reason it really, really angered me when you were late again. I just don't think of you the same way I do the rest of them. You're different. Not so plastic. I think that's why I got so pissed off. I didn't want you to take it for granted.'

'My boss wants me to report to her every morning before I come to you,' I tell him.

He shakes his head. 'Unacceptable. I'll tell her, don't worry.'

I smile gratefully at him. 'Thanks.'

'Forgive me?' he asks.

I nod. I can't help smiling at him. He's so nice.

'OK. I promise not to be a slave-driver any more,' he says. 'Well, not to you, anyway. Still have to keep the actors in line.' And he winks at me.

Oh, my goodness, he is *so* attractive. I look away.

'Well, I'd better be going upstairs,' I say, in a high-pitched voice.

'I'm just going to call my office, you can tell them I'll be right up.'

Greta pats the empty seat at the table next to her as soon as I arrive.

'Sit here, Anna dear,' she purrs. 'Kitty's told me all about you.'

I can imagine. I grit my teeth. Kitty won't like it when Swan calls and tells her I have to go to him first, so I have to be very careful with Greta.

'If there's any way I can assist you,' I say humbly, 'any way at all . . .'

Greta's eyes glint. 'Of course, dear. Got a pen? First of all, I can't stand that filthy swill they serve for coffee in these places,' she says, 'so I want you to run out and find me somewhere that serves a proper cappuccino. And then my dry-cleaning has to be picked up daily. I'll want fresh flowers delivered to wherever we're working, and I need you to pop off to Harrods and pick up my Crème de la Mer order.'

I nod, writing everything down furiously.

'You can start with the coffee,' Greta says.

'OK,' I whisper. Mark Swan walks into the room just as I get up. He raises his eyebrow. 'I'll be right back,' I say hastily. 'I'm just getting Greta's coffee. I'm her assistant,' I add, to his look. 'My boss wants to make sure she's taken care of.'

'Does she, by—' I give him a pleading look. 'Does she,' Swan says, calming down. 'OK. But be back quickly. We're late already.'

'Thanks to you,' Greta says loudly to me.

'A decent cup of coffee is a necessity,' Swan says, judiciously. 'How does everybody take theirs?' He goes round the table, taking orders. I dutifully write them all down, wondering how I'm going to manage to carry them all back. 'And you, Anna?'

'Oh, I don't want one, thanks,' I say. 'I think carrying five is probably my limit. Anyway, I take my coffee plain so whatever they have here is fine.' I notice Greta glaring at me and realise I'm babbling. 'I'll be off, then,' I say brightly.

'You're just getting Greta's coffee,' Swan says. 'You're her assistant, is that right, Greta?'

Greta nods.

'Well, then, somebody has to get Anna's coffee,' he explains. 'So it'd better be me. Anna can get what you need, Greta, and I'll just run out and take care of everybody else's order.'

Greta splutters. 'What? But that's ridiculous.'

'I intended Anna to learn from me,' Swan tells her, easily, but with a touch of steel in his tone. 'So if she's not here, there's not much point in me being here. We can run our errands together. Of course, business will have to wait until I get back, but I don't want to come between you and Kitty Simpson, Greta. Whatever you've worked out is fine with me.'

Greta swallows. 'Well, of course, I don't want to hold up our work *further*,' she says, looking meanly at me. But Swan is having none of it.

'You don't want Anna assisting you, then?' Greta shakes her head. 'Good,' says Swan. 'And Kitty won't complain, as this is your wish. Right?'

'Kitty will be fine,' says Greta.

'Excellent,' says Swan, relaxing, and Greta lowers her eyes. It was a battle of the egos, and he won it, no problem. I know I shouldn't think about it like this, but having him to defend me, it's just so . . .

Well. It's sort of electric. And I mustn't think of it that way.

The next few days are hectic. I go to meetings with Mark Swan, take notes, listen to what he says to the actors, the crew, watch how he slots in our pre-production around the film he's actually shooting. Swan gets me a pass to go on set, so I get to saunter past that security guard, who pretends he doesn't recognise me from before. I stand behind Swan on Hampstead Heath, watch him coaxing performances out of the actors. He's a brilliant director. Implacable, but amazing at getting his actors and crew to do the exact best thing. You can see from the monitor, a shot you'd thought was perfect he'll redo, and then it'll be much better. I trail around after him like a little puppy, and he asks me questions, sharp ones, to make sure I've understood. And when I answer right he nods as if I'm a puppy who's learned to hold up its paw for a piece of cheese.

But I'll tell you something about this process. It's bloody boring. Who the hell wants to stand there in the drizzle, watching a bunch of luvvies flub their lines? Who's really interested in hearing an assistant director go over a bunch of storyboards? I feel guilty, though, I know there are loads of people who'd kill for this chance.

I don't understand. It's quite worrying, in fact. For years I've bitten the bullet of my low-salary, low-prestige job in the hope that one day I'd get my big break, get to make movies, and I'd be rich and fulfilled . . .

'Anna.'

I look up, clutching my notepad. It's Thursday morning and we're standing outside on Wimbledon Common, in drizzling rain.

'Are you . . . yawning?' Swan says to me, eyes narrowing.

'Ahem, ahem,' I say, hastily turning it into a cough. 'No, goodness. Absolutely not. Got a cold,' I say, trying to be perky.

Everybody else on the set is perky, and most of them don't even drink caffeine. It's disgusting really. Health nuts standing about in the rain and rhapsodising over this possible shot and that possible shot and won't this be the *perfect* location for the dog-walking scene . . .

'Mmm,' Swan says, eyes glinting.

Oh crap. Am I in trouble? 'I thought that the pond over there would add some great visuals,' I offer weakly. 'Maybe the dog could chase a duck and pull Elsie into the pond and then her nice dress is ruined.'

'That's funny,' Trish says. 'I like that.'

'And she'd get all pissed off, but the dog wouldn't care. It could just lick her face and ruin her mascara,' I add, thinking of Winston at Vanna's. 'And then she has to go back to the vicarage looking like a total fool.'

'And Mrs Wilkins makes fun of her,' Trish says, getting into it. 'And she's seething. That's fucking great! You're brilliant, Anna.'

I smile at her gratefully and look over at Mark Swan, feeling rescued.

'And this relates to the wedding rehearsal scene how?' asks Swan.

'What?' I ask, nervously.

'We moved on from the dog-walking thing an hour ago. We decided this wasn't a suitable location,' Swan says drily. 'Remember?'

No. 'Oh yes,' I say. 'I remember,' I add confidently. 'The light wasn't any good.'

'Take five, everyone,' Swan says. 'Anna, why don't you just step over here with me a second?'

Oh hell. I paste a suitably radiant smile onto my face, in the manner of an American cheerleader, and walk towards him.

'Anna,' Swan says. 'How would you say you're doing?'

What kind of a question is that? 'I'd say I'm doing *fantastically* well,' I say firmly. 'I've not been late once!'

'That's true,' he concedes.

'I've taken *loads* of notes, I've watched you, and I've reported back to Red Crest. Everybody's happy,' I say. Ha! I don't fold under questioning.

'Everybody except one person.'

'Greta's perfectly fine. I got her that Crème de la Mer she wanted,' I protest. 'She's been very cooperative with you. Maestro.'

'It's not nice to make fun of Greta.'

'I wasn't,' I lie.

'I'm not talking about her anyway. I'm talking about you. You look like me in a marketing meeting. Bored out of your skull.'

'Well, what do you expect?' I protest. 'Standing about here all day, looking at the same boring patch of grass. How can you do it?'

'Anna,' Swan says, gently. 'This is pre-production. You know, checking out locations. It's part of producing a film.'

'I have been paying attention, you know, mostly. I could try to pretend to be more interested if you like. I'm really grateful to you, honestly.'

'It's OK,' he says. 'I'm not angry.'

I breathe out.

'I want you to come back to my house this afternoon,' he says. 'I want to talk to you about something.'

I shake my head. 'I can't. When we don't have pre-production they make me go back to the office.'

Kitty doesn't want me spending any more time with Mark Swan than necessary. As soon as we're done with the day's chores, storyboarding, location scouting, rehearsals, script rewrites, I have to be back in the office. Which is fine with me. It keeps me away from Swan and his gorgeous eyes and his muscular chest. It takes my mind off watching how he controls everything and everybody fawns all over him . . .

He doesn't have a girlfriend, by the way. He told me one morning over coffee, when I caught a particularly obvious fling-herself-at-him from a pneumatic blonde at the production designers. Her name was Susan, and she was working on a storyboard.

'Oh, Mr Swan,' she kept saying breathily, 'this is such an honour.' And then she'd flutter her eyelashes at him and lean forward so he could see her humungous, surely fake, boobs in that low-cut top even better. Do you think a cartoonist needs to come to work in three-inch spike heels? No, neither did I.

I did actually roll my eyes and he caught me doing it.

'Coffee, anyone?' he asked, to cover his laugh, beating a hasty retreat and drawing me aside.

'Sorry about that,' I begin.

'Don't be.' He grins at me. 'It's because of Misty.'

'Misty?'

'My girlfriend.'

I stiffen, I can't help it. Of course Mark Swan would have a girlfriend and of course she'd have a name like Misty. She's American, no doubt, a flawless Heather Locklear clone. (You know the kind of woman: never swears, doesn't drink, eyebrows are always shaped.)

'A model?' I ask cynically.

'An actress,' he says.

'And?' I can see there's more.

'And former cheerleader for the LA Lakers,' he admits.

I knew it.

'Anyway, I broke up with her last month, and there's a bit of'—he's too nice to say 'gold-digging'—'flirting going on,' he says.

'Why did you break up with Misty?'

'She was boring,' he says.

Ho-hum. I wonder how good-looking you'd have to be for Mark Swan not to find you boring? I stare gloomily into my coffee. I don't know why I'm thinking about a man I can't have anyway. I have Charles, and I try to concentrate on him.

'You don't need to worry about Red Crest,' Swan says, jerking me back to the present. 'Let me take care of that right now.'

'You don't understand,' I plead. I really don't want to go to his house. By myself? It's hard enough hanging around him with all these other people. What if I stare at him too long and he catches me? 'You can't stop it, Kitty doesn't like me hanging out with the talent . . .'

He winks at me. 'I know the type, honey. Watch this.'

He flicks open his mobile, punches in a number.

'Kitty Simpson, please. Mark Swan. Oh, hi, Kitty,' he says. 'I'm calling about Anna. She's been talking to me all about your Oscar and your leadership on *Mother of the Bride*. Yes . . .'

I can't stop the grin from spreading all over my face.

'I was wondering, can you send me a memo with your ideas on foreign marketing? Especially in Italy? Since your Oscar was won there . . . That's perfect. I wanted to borrow Anna this afternoon because one of our runners is sick. Any chance? Oh, thanks. I'll look forward to getting your ideas, Kitty. Brilliant. OK, bye.'

He hangs up. 'I think you'll find you won't be in any trouble now.'

'Yes. Thanks.' I look away, because it's just too much. It's so sexy, the way he can snap open a phone and take care of Kitty in five minutes.

'You can go,' he says. Swan waves his rough-skinned hand, dismissing me. 'You're just an extra body on the set, you're worse than useless.' He looks at my crestfallen face. 'Just turn up at my place around half five. I'm having lunch with Rachel Weisz, can't get there before that.'

'Of course.' Rachel Weisz is bloody gorgeous. I try to remember, is she married to anybody? They'd make a perfect power couple . . .

Why am I being so dog in the manger? Why shouldn't he go out with Rachel Weisz. I *have* a boyfriend. My throat thickens, and I swallow hard. 'No problems,' I say. 'I'm going to lunch with my boyfriend.'

'Ah, the millionaire,' Swan jokes.

'That's right,' I reply, tilting my chin up. 'The millionaire.'

I call Charles from my mobile. 'Hi, what are you doing?'

'Me? Just pottering about. How lovely to hear from you.'

'I just wondered if you were free for lunch? I'm buying,' I add quickly. I should have enough money in my account for one lunch at least.

'You certainly aren't,' Charles says, severely. 'I've never let a lady pay for lunch in my life. And of course I want to see you! I'll rustle up a table at the Savoy again, shall I?'

He's so polite. He's such a sweetie. I don't know why I'm close to tears, still. And suddenly it just hurts to be wet and cold and poor and the sound of a lovely lunch in the Savoy served immaculately by career waiters, all warm and cosy, is perfect.

'That's wonderful,' I say gratefully. 'I just need to go home and change. I'll see you there.'

Thank heavens there's a taxi. I hail it and jump in.

I quickly shower and blow-dry my hair, then pull out my navy dress with the pumps again—I know Janet would yell at me, but I don't have time to experiment. This is about looking nice—well, as nice as possible—for Charles. Nothing to do with the fact I'm going to Swan's place later. I twist my hair back in a bun. OK, at least I look businesslike now.

Charles is waiting for me in the dining room when I arrive. I breathe in, trying to relax. And it's not made too hard. There's that buzz that's always around him, the air of money.

'I took the liberty of ordering some champagne,' says Charles, and indeed there's a flute fizzing by my place. 'Hope you don't mind.'

'Not at all,' I say, taking a big slug. Then I remember where I am and sip it instead, delicately as I can.

'Oh, don't mind me,' Charles says. 'Knock it back. You look frazzled.'

Do I? I thought I'd done OK on the old face-repair job.

Halfway through lunch I escape to the sumptuously appointed loos. I stare at myself in the mirror for a long moment.

What am I thinking? Here I am, having lunch with a lovely, kind man who jumped at the chance to take me out, at no notice, to one of the most expensive restaurants in London. I'm being spoilt rotten. Me, Anna, who's never had any attention in her life. And after lunch I'm going to go to a meeting with one of the most powerful directors in the world who apparently wants to mentor me in my career.

Three months ago I was just a grunt reader for Kitty Simpson, desperate to hang on to a spotty oick with halitosis.

So what the hell am I so unhappy about?

I take a deep breath and head back to Charles, forcing myself to smile.

Mark Swan lives in the heart of Notting Hill, in a gorgeous Queen Anne house with a walled garden that puts Vanna's to shame. I've been there before one time, for a script meeting. We walked there from a local restaurant, after lunch, and I got to see the full gamut of women who wanted to attract his attention.

Everywhere he goes people want to be in bed with him. On the one hand you can understand it; a man that powerful, all the film people want to schmooze him. But women seem drawn to him no matter what. They preen whenever he walks into a room. Legs are crossed, toes are pointed, hair is tossed. I think I've seen enough lips tentatively licked this week to last me several lifetimes. There are the fingers laid casually on his jacket sleeve, the light laughter, eyes glancing his way, then away again, all the little tricks. What they used to call 'feminine wiles'. I don't have any of these, so I'm OK. I have just been talking to Greta, reporting back to Kitty and Eli and trying to improve myself, just a little. I go for a jog most mornings, I'm eating salads and diet sandwiches. I'm too busy trailing Swan to eat much anyway. He likes to keep me busy. As well as asking me testing questions on the day's notes, he likes to grill me on movie trivia, which I'm great at, as long as it's about a big budget Hollywood film shot no sooner than '84. He does ask me questions about dull arty films and seems delighted when I don't know any of the answers.

I square my shoulders as I turn in through Swan's cast-iron gate. OK, right. Here we go. I march up his garden path and ring the bell.

'Coming.' Swan wrenches the door open. He's wearing black karate pants, tied at the waist, and . . . that's it. His chest is bare. Bare.

I take a step back, dry-mouthed. Ooh. I love muscular men. His chest hair looks like Sean Connery's. Stop staring. Stop. Staring!

'Oh, I'm so sorry,' says Swan. 'I was working out, lost track of the time. Come in, come in, I'll just get changed.'

'I'll make some coffee, shall I?' I ask. My voice has gone sort of hysterical and squeaky. I hastily beat a retreat to the kitchen.

'Sorry about that,' Swan says, two seconds later. He's pulled on a pair of chinos and a large T-shirt. 'I got carried away. Love martial arts.'

'Were you breaking wood planks with your bare hands?' I joke.

'No, I'm doing bricks now,' Swan says.

'You're breaking bricks with your bare hands?' I ask, looking at him. Swan shrugs. 'It's all technique. Don't look so impressed.'

'I'm not impressed!' I lie. Will I ever be able to get that image out of my mind? And I was doing so well, with the nice lunch and all.

'Have a coffee,' I say, severely. 'Down to business.'

'Mmm, business,' he agrees, eyes glinting again. 'You're looking very . . . professional this afternoon, Anna.'

I stiffen. 'What's wrong with it?'

'Oh, nothing,' he says. 'Except that I feel like I'm about to get a rap on the knuckles with a ruler.'

'You probably need one,' I say haughtily.

'Of course you could do that sexy-secretary thing, you know, unpin that severe bun and shake your long hair loose,' he suggests.

Now I know he's laughing at me.

'It's not nice to make personal remarks,' I tell him.

'Sorry, I know. Only your boyfriend is allowed to flirt with you.'

'That's right. Don't flirt with me,' I say, rather snappily. Then I blink. I mustn't snap at my mentor. But him being flirty with me is the absolute last thing I want. I don't need to be positively tortured.

Swan holds up his hands. 'OK. Let's talk about you learning the business. Your heart's not in it,' he says. 'Why not?'

'I don't understand what you mean,' I say, shaking my head as though puzzled. 'I've been paying careful attention to the film-making process, watching what you've said to the actors, watching you on set . . .'

'Yes,' he agrees, pleasantly enough.

'I have been paying attention, honest,' I plead.

Swan smiles lazily back at me. 'I know that,' he says. 'You're not stupid. You didn't want me to kick you off the pre-production.'

'No,' I say. 'It's fascinating.'

'It is, but obviously not to you.' Swan looks at me intently. 'You only come alive during the script meetings.'

I do love those meetings. Listening to the finished story take shape, watching Trish and Mark work through the characters, beef up the scenes. It must have showed. 'Those are my favourites,' I admit.

'Why is that?' he asks.

'I love the story,' I say honestly. 'I just think the story is funny and poignant and near the knuckle and . . . I love it.'

'But you find discussion about sets tedious.'

'Oh, fuck it,' I say suddenly. I just don't feel like pretending any more. 'It's so bloody boring, I don't know how you do it.'

'What about rehearsing?'

'That's boring too. I wouldn't do it for a million pounds,' I hear myself say dismissively. 'Standing around in the rain watching a bunch of over-paid actors say the same bloody line over and over. How hard can it be, eh? They talk about motivation in the scene—"Mark, what's my motivation here?"' I imitate Greta perfectly.

He laughs softly. 'What would you say?'

'Um, "Your bloody enormous pay cheque"?' I suggest.

Swan's really amused. 'You aren't impressed by the actors' craft?'

'I think they're a bunch of . . .' I stop. 'I expect some of them are really nice,' I say diplomatically. 'And not tossers at all.'

'Very well put,' he says, his face grave. 'So basically what we're saying here is that you only really like the story development stuff?'

'Well, yes. But that's the most important part,' I plead.

'When you were bullshitting me this morning, when I caught you drifting off,' he says, 'no, no need to deny it. You made up that scene where Elsie's dog pulls her into the pond. Right off the top of your head.'

'Yes?' I ask warily.

'Well, that was good stuff.' He takes a drink of coffee. 'And that dialogue you wrote at our first meeting. That was good too.'

'Thanks,' I say, blushing.

'I asked you then if you'd thought about being a screenwriter. Have you?' he asks, looking me right in the eye.

I shrug. 'I don't know . . . I'm just a reader.'

'Could you do better than most of the scripts you read?'

'Oh, fuck yeah,' I say. 'Excuse me,' I add hastily. Nice girls don't say 'fuck' do they? Cheerleaders for the LA Lakers and Rachel Weisz.

'Listen, you're not terrible at producing,' he says. 'You could wind up with an OK career on the conceptual side. You found the right script for the right actress and you went after the right director. That's a big part of it. But all the grunt work of producing, locations, marketing, hiring crew, casting smaller parts, you hate all that stuff.' He looks at me over the top of his coffee mug. 'What's the matter?'

I find I'm gazing at him adoringly again. The irony is, though, that the first time he's actually caught me I wasn't thinking how sexy and hot he is. I was just thinking, nobody has ever talked to me like this. He's taking me seriously. He's listing strengths and weaknesses, as if I was a real movie person, as if I could have a career. It's almost as if he *respects* me.

I don't think I've ever been paid a greater compliment.

'Nothing,' I say. Then I think better of it. 'No, I was just thinking that—'I'm blushing—'it's really kind of you to talk to me like this. Like you believe in me.'

'I do believe in you,' he says, dead serious. 'I saw in you something I haven't seen for a very long time.'

I look at him, asking the question.

'Passion,' he says. 'Passion. Love of movies. Love of stories. Enthusiasm. Most people have love of deals. Not you.'

'Thanks,' I say. I can barely whisper it out. I clear my throat, try to pull myself together. 'I never had a chance till you came along.'

'You always had a chance,' he says. 'Think about this: I didn't just come along, you came to find me.'

There's a moment's pause. I'm staring into his eyes. I force myself to break the look, to wrench my eyes away.

'Doing something tonight? Got another date?'

'Not tonight,' I say, warily. Is he laughing at me?

'Would you like to go for a drink?' He spreads his huge, sunburnt hands. 'No obligation. I want to discuss something with you.'

'Well . . .' It's only 6 p.m. 'I suppose that'd be OK,' I say, insouciantly. But my heart is leaping. What can I say? I can't help it.

He walks me out, down the road and round the corner where there's a small pub called the Queen Adelaide. The barman looks up when we come in. 'All right, Mark?' he says. 'Who's yer ladyfriend?'

'This is the lovely Anna,' Swan says. I stare at him suspiciously for signs of mockery but it doesn't look like there are any. 'Usual, please, Mike,' he says, and the barman pours him a double rye whisky and looks at me.

'Half a cider is fine,' I say.

'Living dangerously,' Swan comments, as he slides some money over the pitted wood.

'I don't want to get too hammered,' I tell him. 'I might lose all my inhibitions and start giving you some home truths.'

He laughs, delighted. 'Shall we sit over there,' Swan suggests, indicating a weatherworn bench.

'Not outside?' The rain has stopped, and now it's a sunny evening, warm and golden.

'I thought we might be more private in here. Some people recognise me, sometimes,' Swan admits, blushing. 'Film students and stuff. Actors. You get a lot of them round here.'

'Yes, it is a fairly pretentious area,' I concede. 'All right then, we'll sit over there to avoid your legions of fans.'

Swan slides into the corner, disappearing comfortably into the gloom, and takes a pull at his rye, instantly relaxing. I can see he feels safe here, protected. People don't bother him.

'I hope you don't think I'm pretentious.'

I don't say anything, just nurse my cider.

'It's OK,' he reassures me. 'You can say anything you like.'

'Sounds like a trap,' I say suspiciously. 'You'll lull me into revealing those home truths and then you'll call up Eli Roth and have me fired.'

'I wouldn't do that,' he says.

'Oh?'

'I'd call my agent and have her do it. I can't stand Eli.' He grins.

'Very funny.'

'Seriously, you can trust me. We're breaking bread together. Or at least booze. That's got to be sacred.'

'All right,' I say, sipping my cider, which is flat. 'I do think you're a bit pretentious, but it goes with the territory. All directors are pretentious. They think the sun shines out of their arses.'

'Don't sit on the fence, Anna,' he says, stretching his hand out on the table. 'Tell me what you really think.'

'Well, it's true,' I say, hotly. 'What is this "A Rob Reiner Film" anyway?'

'The director is the one who's blamed if the film goes wrong, he's the one who makes all the decisions. I think it's fair.'

'You would,' I tell him. 'Directors are so unimportant, I'll never work out why they've got so much power.'

Swan goggles at me. 'You think we're unimportant?'

'Sure. Anyone can coax a performance out of an actor, they just want their egos stroked.'

'So who's important then?' Swan ticks off the names. 'The stars are self-indulgent tossers, the director's a meaningless appendage . . .'

'The writer,' I say triumphantly.

'The writer's the low guy on the totem pole.'

'I know that,' I say indignantly. 'But she shouldn't be. She's written the screenplay, made the story.'

'She,' he says, grinning. 'But a movie's more than a screenplay.'

'I know that too. But the screenplay is the blueprint, isn't it? Film isn't anything more than a story told in pictures. Anybody could make the pictures,' I say hotly. 'But only the person who thinks of the story can make the story. Anybody could act the part, too.'

Swan says, 'I admire your passion.'

'Oh, give over,' I say, scornfully. 'Now you really do sound like an LA executive.'

He laughs, a rich, deep belly laugh that seems to go on and on and sends half the pub staring in our direction. I nudge him. 'Cut that out.'

'I'm sorry,' he says, wiping his eyes. 'I just think you're priceless. And fearless,' he adds, before I can take offence. 'Do you know how long it's been since anybody talked to me like that?' He reaches across the table and takes my hand in his. I look at it, lying there, and for the first time in ages I'm not embarrassed by my too-large, too-utilitarian hands. Inside his large, thick fingers, they seem slender, feminine.

Mark Swan dwarfs me. I understand now, with a sudden shock of recognition, one reason why women react around him the way they do. He's *huge*. It's as if the masculinity of his personality has somehow mani-fested itself physically in his body. There are plenty of tall men around, but Swan is six five and built. His muscles are thick, he's barrel-chested, hairy. He looks as if he's about ready to grab some poor wench by her long plaited hair and drag her off screaming to his cave, though you feel most of them wouldn't be screaming very hard.

I jerk my hand away.

'I think I've discovered your problem,' Swan says, apparently not noticing. 'I couldn't work you out. You seemed to want this badly, your movie, and I thought you were fun,' he says lightly, and I feel a shiver all up my legs and back. 'So I thought I'd give you your break. And once I got you here, you obviously loved movies. But you don't love producing and you never will.'

'So what's my vocation?' I demand.

'You should be a writer. You've got a great feel for story, you're obviously creative. You appreciate good scripts. You think the film is the story. You should write screenplays,' he says simply. 'Last time I mentioned it, it was just a suggestion. Now it's an order.'

I shiver with pleasure. Swan has just recited my secret dream back to me. The dream I've dismissed for about as long as I dismissed the idea of having a solvent boyfriend without acne. But that's happened, so why not this? 'An order?'

He nods. 'After you started riffing on that dog-walking scene I knew for sure. She'd be a good writer. Not right away, but if she worked at it. You owe it to yourself to at least try, Anna.'

I can't help it, I beam at him, and Swan leans back against the wall, his hazel eyes flickering over me.

'When you smile like that your face lights up,' he says.

'Thanks for the suggestion,' I say. 'It's—it's really nice of you.'

'I'm not promising you anything,' he says. 'For all I know you could be rubbish. But just in case you aren't, if you can actually produce a good screenplay . . .' he shrugs. 'I might be able to help you out.'

I don't dare ask what that would mean, but the adrenaline is coursing through my veins. Whatever it means, it's my ticket out. I look at him again, differently. This is *Mark Swan*, I tell myself. Probably the single most powerful man in the British film industry. If he's offering me his help, he's offering me the moon.

'Only if you're good,' he says, sternly. 'You might not be.'

'Thank you,' I say. 'Very much. I appreciate it. You're . . .'

'Don't look at me like that,' he says gently. 'I prefer it when you're telling me to sod off than when you look awe-struck.'

'Awe-struck! I'm not awe-struck. You're just another overpaid loser as far as I'm concerned.'

'Better,' he says. 'Better.' And he reaches out one stubby finger and, grinning, tucks a loose strand of hair back behind my ear.

His touch is electric. Instantly, shamefully, I feel my nipples harden, my stomach liquefy. I can't do this! I can't be like all those other girls. Mark Swan actually likes me. He wants to help me. I'm not going to blow it.

'I should go,' I say, as lightly as I can manage. 'Better get back. Still have a huge weekend read to do.'

'Isn't that what the weekend's for?'

'I have something on this weekend,' I say, thinking of Chester House.

'Well, don't let me keep you from your cup of hot cocoa and your pile of dull scripts,' Swan says. 'See you Monday.'

5

'YOU PROMISED,' JANET SAYS.

'Well, I know, but I've changed my mind,' I tell her. It's Friday afternoon, I've reluctantly come away from the office, and we're standing outside Harvey Nichols.

'Not good enough,' Janet says, spiritedly. 'You *promised* me I could make you over, Anna. You can't tell me you don't want to improve your look, deep down inside. What about all that running? What about all the stuff you've been eating?'

I blush. I was kind of hoping nobody had noticed.

'Now what's the point of taking the weight off and getting healthy if you don't dress to match?'

'Harvey Nichols, I can't afford that. Or the hairdressing.'

'My treat,' Janet says. 'Don't argue. I get staff discount here. Got connections,' she says airily. 'And the hairdressing is for free. Paolo's doing it as a favour to me. I spent ages setting that up. You can't let me down.'

'OK,' I say glumly.

'Come on!' says Janet gaily. And she drags me through the revolving doors. 'OK, waist.' She whips out a little tape and comes at me with it.

'What the hell are you doing?'

'Measuring you,' she says. 'Fit is *everything*. OK, let's try something.' Janet moves through the racks going, 'This one . . . that one . . . this one . . . OK,' she says. 'Off to the changing rooms!'

Bloody hell. There's no escape.

And it's every bit as bad as I'd feared. I try not to look too hard, but you can't help it, can you? It's even worse than the bathroom, because there's a harsh overhead light. And my cellulite . . .

'How are you doing in there?' Janet says.

I pull on one dress without looking at it. At least it's black. And unlike most times I try on stuff, it fits. I step out.

'There. Not bad, for a start. Look at yourself,' Janet says triumphantly, and whisks back the curtain.

I'm amazed. I'm not going to tell you I looked like Kate Winslet at the Oscars, but the dress gives my body a little something. A waist, to be exact. And there's a plunging neckline to show off a bit of cleavage. I stand there open-mouthed. I feel . . . I feel like people wouldn't shout rude things at me any more.

'Skirt hides your tummy, see,' Janet says. 'Until you get it in shape,' she adds hastily. 'Won't be long with all that running. OK. Want to try the trousers? With the jacket. Not that one, the navy one.'

'All right,' I say grudgingly, but I go back inside the changing room, and this time I look at the outfit after I've put it on.

'Hi,' Paolo says forty minutes later. Janet hands her shopping bags to the coat-check girl while I stand there, head down. This hairdresser's is not my sort of place. It smells costly. It looks costly. I'm used to Supercuts.

'I see why you breeng her,' he says to Janet. 'She need 'elp.'

'Don't mind me,' I mutter, but Janet treads on my toe.

'Only you can rescue her, Paolo,' Janet breathes as I yelp.

He preens and runs his fingers through my hair. 'Very thick,' he says. 'Too heavy . . . Revolting spleet ends. No shape. No colour. It ees rat.'

'Mouse,' Janet says.

'Rat, mouse . . . nasty,' he pronounces. 'I can 'elp. Jay-Me, you just leave us. Two, three hours.'

I can't believe somebody else actually called her Jay-Me—wait a second, did he say two to three hours?

'Uh . . . Janet . . .' I say weakly, but it's too late. She's out of the door.

'Now, sweetie,' says Paolo with an evil grin, marching me to a chair. 'You are totally in my hands. Yes?'

'Ready?' he asks.

Ready? I've been ready for the last three hours. The man is a maniac. He has me over in a little chair in the corner, facing a wall. He won't let me see myself in a mirror.

Finally, it's over. 'Yes, I'm ready,' I tell him. Paolo spins me round. For a second I can't quite believe it. Is that me?

My hair—it's gone. Most of it. What's left curls down an inch above my shoulders, and has a feathery, choppy way of swinging about my face. My nose actually looks smaller. I have a fringe, it softens my high forehead, and best of all I can tell that this cut will just fall into place. I can wash it in the morning and it will still be there.

And then there's the colour.

I never realised colour could make such a difference. My hair, my mousy hair, has gone. Now there's a blonde there, shot through with silky highlighted strands in millions of different shades, from spun gold to copper, champagne, lemon, honey . . . It's changed my whole face. My skin doesn't look so pasty any more.

I'm still not pretty. But I look normal now, almost normal.

'I don't know what to say,' I say, and I have tears in my eyes.

Janet arrives to collect me, and after five minutes of air-kissing and mutual backslapping we get to pick up my bags and leave.

'When we get you home I'm going to pack for you,' she says. 'I know exactly what you must take. And I'll do your make-up. Are you going to wear the blue dress for the dancing or the green?'

'The green.'

'Better be the blue,' she says.

I smile gratefully at her. 'OK, the blue. Thanks, Janet. Thanks a lot.'

'All it takes is confidence,' she says. 'And the right fit.'

We walk through the door, and Janet pulls out a case of hers. 'Right. You'll take this . . . and that . . .'

She's packing me as efficiently as an air hostess and has the bag zipped in two minutes flat. It normally takes me at least half a day.

The door bursts open and Lily appears. 'Oh my God!' she squeals. 'Look at *you*! That's too funny.'

'What's funny?' Janet demands. 'She looks fantastic.'

'Well, let's not go too far,' laughs Lily. She's been to the hairdresser too. Her platinum-blonde mane spills down her back. 'But,' she adds, 'it's a *great* improvement, although what wouldn't have been, eh, Anna?'

Instantly I feel all my lovely happiness seep out of me.

'Fuck off, Lily,' snaps Janet. 'She looks great. You really do,' she adds to me. 'Don't let her ruin everything for you.'

'I'm not. I know I—look better,' I say. But it's no good. I'm still the Ugly Sister. It's still a joke to have me turn up with these two in tow.

'Anyway, better go tart myself up. You take off those clothes,' Janet adds sternly. 'I've put your travel outfit on your bed.'

'Thanks, Janet,' I say, and impulsively give her a hug. She's actually turning into a really good friend.

'And then I'll do your make-up,' she adds.

I chuck my jeans and T-shirt in the laundry and change into Janet's choice for the car: flat-fronted, low-cut charcoal-grey trousers and a silk-looking silver shirt. And some slides. I turn in front of my mirror and try to get some of the euphoria back.

OK, I'm still not pretty. But Charles is going to be knocked sideways. And everybody in the office will be really surprised. It'll be great for my career. Like Anna Brown is coming out of her shell. And Mark Swan will be . . . He won't care, obviously. Except he'll think I'm blooming. Professionally.

'Ready?' asks Janet, sticking her head round the door. She's wearing a gorgeous lemon-yellow halter-neck dress that shows off her boobs. 'Now, sit still, this won't take a second,' and then she's all over me, dabbing at my face with little sponges and pencils and brushes and what looks like a pot of lip gloss that's a scary, blood-red colour.

'There,' she says. And when I look, it's wonderful. All very neutral, but painted-on cheekbones and smoky eyes, and red, wet-looking lips. It really doesn't look that bad, apart from my nose. I feel . . . what's the phrase the Americans use? Pulled-together. That's it.

It's seven thirty by the time we're slowed down, looking for the turning into Chester House. Everybody's in a filthy mood. Janet because she's done most of the driving, Lily because she's not in a limo, and me because I'm starving. Suddenly the procurement of food has taken precedence over not wanting to do this.

'You must have missed it,' Lily says petulantly. 'Go back.'

'I bloody haven't missed anything. There haven't been any turnings!'

'What's that?' I say.

Up ahead there's a mini-traffic jam—Land Rovers and Jags trailing back along this tiny little B road with its thick hedges.

'They're turning in,' says Lily, relieved. 'This is it!'

'Look at this drive,' Janet says, and indeed we're through the gateway now and onto a wide, bumpy road, and the cars are streaming down it. On either side rolling grass, gentle hills, copses of oak trees dotted here and there. You can instantly imagine horses and carriages trundling down here for similar parties a couple of hundred years ago.

'He can't own this,' Lily says.

'Apparently he does,' I tell her.

'Look at that,' breathes Janet in awe.

And we do. There's the house. If you can call it that. It's more like an enormous mansion that you go to visit on school trips. A vast edifice of grey stone, complete with spikes and balustrades and statues on the top, like St Peter's in Rome. It's got ivy trailing all over it. It's magnificent.

'I'm glad we did that make-over,' Janet murmurs to herself.

We pull into a driveway at the front of the house, with ushers showing all the cars where to park. I wind my window down for the uniformed man checking the names. 'Anna Brown and guests,' I say.

'Very good, madam,' the man says serenely. He beckons to one of the parking ushers. 'This is Miss Brown's car,' he says, significantly. 'If you'll just follow him, madam,' he adds to Janet.

'Look at this,' says Janet. We have been allocated a parking spot right by the front porch.

The usher springs into action, opening our doors and taking our little cases, but I insist on grabbing them back from him.

'Anna,' says a familiar voice. I turn round to see Charles standing there. He stares at me for a few seconds, blinking. 'Good Lord,' he says. He recovers, reaches towards me, gives me a peck on the cheek, beaming. 'Good of you to come, good of you to come.'

'We wouldn't have missed it,' says Lily huskily, shoving herself forward and thrusting her hand at him, 'for the world. I'm Lily Venus.'

Charles kisses her hand, and she gives a practised, little-girl giggle.

Lily Venus? Her real name's Frutt. Doesn't she realise that if she's going to use a pseudonym it shouldn't sound like a porn star's?

'Delighted,' he says, staring at her awkwardly as Lily licks her lips.

'And this is my other flatmate, Jan—er—Jay-Me,' I say.

'All right!' says Janet in a friendly voice. 'How's it hanging?'

'Yes. Marvellous,' says Charles faintly. 'Shall I show you to your rooms?'

Charles threads his way through the crowd and leads us up a wide, stone staircase, lined with solemn-looking oil portraits of his ancestors.

'Here we are,' he says eventually, after we've been through three corridors and I'm lost. 'The William Suite. I hope that's acceptable?'

'Why is it called that?' asks Lily, peering in at the sumptuous interior.

'Oh, you know. William the Third liked it. Stayed here quite often with one of my predecessors. It's a bit fusty, I'm afraid,' he adds apologetically. 'Anyway, I'll leave you ladies to change. Anna,' he adds, in a low, intent voice as Janet and Lily race into the room in delight, 'you look absolutely sensational.'

'Thanks,' I say, going pink with pleasure.

'Bloody hell,' says Lily, looking around as soon as the door shuts. 'I could get used to this.'

It's like being allowed to walk inside one of those roped-off room exhibits in a palace or a stately home. The walls are hung in a rich yellow damask, there's a vast four-poster, the chairs look Louis Quatorze . . .

We get changed with lightning speed, Janet and Lily because they can't wait to unleash themselves on some unsuspecting duke or other major landowner, and me because if I don't eat soon I'm going to start on wads of loo roll just to stop the gnawing pains in my stomach.

Lily is wearing a slimline strappy number in palest gold silk, with tee-tering matching sandals. Janet has chosen a burnished-copper gown in crushed satin. She's let her raven hair fall loosely and she looks stunning, very Catherine Zeta-Jones in *Zorro*.

I'm wearing the blue dress Janet picked out. It has a silky look to it, a fullish skirt, and a boat neck over three-quarter sleeves. It shows a bit of cleavage and covers my bum and my legs. I look like an ordinary girl with a big nose. But let me tell you something, that's a huge improvement! I resolve to try not to look too much at the other two. Anyway, if we don't get downstairs soon I may just eat them.

Cocktails are finished, and people are being ushered into the dining hall. Charles is there, waiting and hovering.

'Ah, ladies,' he says. 'You all look absolutely incredible.'

'Fuck me, who's this?' asks a man standing next to him. Despite the upper-class accent and the black tie he looks like a huge oaf. 'Charles, you lucky sod. You're not seeing all three of them, are you?'

'Shut up, William,' says Charles loudly.

'Please excuse my friend,' he says to us. 'Jay-Me and Lily, this is William Lyons. And Anna is my girlfriend,' he adds, with a touch of pro-prietary pride.

'We're not seeing anyone,' says Lily.

And suddenly there is a throng of black-tie men all trying to get closer to Lily and Janet. Charles and I are shoved aside, but not before I've heard one of the yahoos say to his mate, 'Fancy a bit of rough?'

'Mmm, yeah,' says the other one. 'Good for a tumble, at least.'

I suddenly feel a burst of anger. Poor Lily, she's got no idea.

I push my way back to them. 'Excuse me.' The crowd melts—they have to, I'm a woman—and I thread my arms through both of the girls'. 'I think we should go in to dinner now,' I say.

'Let me go!' hisses Janet, outraged. 'You've got yours!'

Some of the men hear her and chuckle to themselves, which makes me even angrier. I drag the two of them into the hall. It's easy. I've got thirty pounds on both of them.

'She's right,' whispers Lily to Janet. 'Always leave them wanting more.'

I examine the seating plan for their places. 'You're on table four and you're on nine,' I say to them in turn. 'And look, find me after dinner. I really need to have a word with both of you.'

Charles and I are sitting together on table one. It's the most enormous dining hall with a huge vaulted ceiling. I can imagine long medieval trestle tables with benches in here, but today there are round tables, covered in white linen. Little fairy lights and chiffon drapery have been pinned to the walls, giving the whole room a sort of Snow Queen feel.

'Just a little party,' Charles says modestly, at my open mouth. 'I was thinking about something special for my birthday. Maybe you could help? Plan it with me. You know. As the hostess.'

'I . . . maybe,' I say. 'This is amazing, Charles.'

'Well, you look divine,' he says. 'The dress, and the . . . the . . .' He waves his hand at me and I feel a little thrill of pleasure. Then he puts his hand gently on my upper thigh and squeezes it.

I half choke on my champagne. Urghh . . .

'Caviar, ma'am?' asks a waiter.

'Oh! Yes, thanks,' I say, jumping, so Charles is forced to dislodge his hand. What's wrong with me? He was only putting his hand on my thigh. He's sweet, isn't he? Free from any obvious deformities? No perversions? Enormous mansion, millions of pounds?

So why do I feel like bolting as fast as I can leg it?

Dinner is delicious, and I'm just wolfing down my main course when the man on my other side speaks. 'Hello,' he says. 'I'm Ed Dawson.'

'Anna Brown,' I say, shaking his hand. He's about my age, with brown hair and hazelnut eyes. A bit skinny for my taste but a nice smile.

'So I gather Charlie's lucky enough to have you as a girlfriend?'

'I—well . . .' I become aware Charles is listening in. 'Yes,' I say lamely.

'That's fantastic,' he says warmly. 'I'm his cousin. We've been hoping for ages he'll find someone nice. He usually dates such slappers.'

'Um, well. We . . . we have fun,' I say.

'I was just wondering,' he says, awkwardly. 'The young ladies you came in with . . . Obviously they have boyfriends . . .?'

'Actually, no,' I say, 'but they're both very nice girls.'

'Of course,' says Ed. 'They look . . . *very* nice.'

'You mustn't judge them by their looks,' I say hotly. 'Just because they're beautiful, they're not people's toys.'

'Gosh, no,' he says humbly. 'Of course not.'

'They've got their own brains and . . . careers and things.'

'What do they do?'

'They're . . . models,' I say reluctantly, 'but they take it very seriously and . . . manage their own money.'

'That's excellent,' he says. 'Tell me about the blonde girl.'

'That's Lily,' I say. 'Lily Frutt—er, Venus.'

'Lily Frutt-Venus,' he says, reverentially.

'Just Venus,' I correct myself. 'And the brunette is called Janet, but she likes to be called Jay-Me.'

'Why's that?' he asks.

'Just because,' I say, and then Charles leans over to ask me something and Ed turns to his other side..

Dinner proceeds just fine after that. Charles doesn't put his hand on my thigh again, just makes small talk. 'Have you come to a decision on the book?' he asks.

Oh help. I asked John for his report too, just to be certain, I mean it's more his type of thing. Theoretically. Only it wasn't. *Total bullshit*, I think it began. *No potential whatsoever.*

'Well,' I say carefully. 'My reader thought your manuscript was very different, Charles.'

This is the worst book I have ever read, went the conclusion.

'So?' Charles says eagerly. 'Are you putting it into production? '

My mouth goes dry. Suddenly I remember how Vanna handled it.

'I don't think it's right for film,' I say carefully, 'because it's so complex, so varied. Film would butcher it!'

'I see,' says Charles. His face falls. And now I feel horrible. All mean and nasty, when he's tried to be so nice to me.

'Charles,' I whisper, but he shakes his head.

'Come on, everybody,' he says loudly as the waiters whisk away the plates. 'Shall we dance?'

The dancing is pretty awful. Charles dances the upper-class shuffle with me. This involves putting your arm round a girl's waist, then lifting one foot and putting it down in exactly the same spot, and repeating with the other foot. Sort of marching in place. When we finally break for a while, I think it must be 3 a.m but it's only been an hour.

'Must go and check on people,' says Charles. 'Host, you know. OK?'

'Oh, of course,' I say, gratefully. 'I'll be at the bar.'

I rush off to get myself some more champagne and find Ed standing there, looking longingly after Lily.

'You could always ask her to dance,' I say.

'What's the point,' he responds, gloomily.

Lily glances our way and waves at me. A second later she's broken off from a throng of men and is teetering towards me on her high heels.

'What shall I do?' asks Ed, panicked.

'Champers!' says Lily loudly, snapping her fingers at the barman. 'Anna,' she says ingratiatingly, 'wonderful party. All the boys tell me Charles is very taken with you.'

'He is,' agrees Ed.

'He thinks you might even be the one, apparently.'

After the book thing, I doubt it. 'Don't be silly. I've only just started—'

'No, it's true. You see, Charles is tired of pretty girls,' Lily explains to Ed, with a sigh.

'Then why is he going out with Anna?' responds Ed, chivalrously.

Lily gives her breathy giggle. 'You're so funny. And you are?'

'Ed Dawson,' he says eagerly. 'Lovely to meet you. Lily, isn't it?'

Janet bounces up to us in a froth of bronze silk. 'Top party,' she says.

'And you must be the lovely Jay-Me. I'm Ed,' he says.

'Yeah,' she says, going red with pleasure. 'Right on!'

'So, Ed,' starts Lily. Here it comes. The patented Lily Frutt Inquisition. 'Dawson,' she says. 'Same name as Charles. Coincidence?'

'Not entirely,' he says, diffidently. 'I'm his cousin. Second cousin.'

'And what do you do?'

'I work on a farm,' he says.

Lily pulls a tiny face. 'How interesting,' she says distantly. 'And I suppose that must be hard if you have a big place to run? Like this one?'

'Oh no,' says Ed. 'I live in a small flat in Bath.'

'You own it?' she asks brightly.

'Rent,' he says. 'And it's daylight robbery. Of course Bath is—'

'Excuse me,' says Lily, cutting him off with a cold smile. 'I must get back to my dance partners. Nice to meet you, anyway.'

And she sets down her crystal flute and marches off instantly. That's actually not the worst I've seen her. Once we were in a club and a guy comes up and asks her to dance. She says, 'What kind of car do you drive?' He says, 'Ford Fiesta.' She turned her back on him.

Ed stares miserably into his champagne. Janet and I exchange looks. 'I've always wanted to go to Bath,' Janet says warmly.

'Really?' Ed asks.

'Would you like to tell me about . . . farming?' she says, kindly.

Some of the humiliation clears from Ed's face. 'We could go and find some chairs,' he says. 'And they're serving sorbet in the next room.'

'I'd love a sorbet,' says Janet. She smiles at him. She seems to like him. I'm relieved, and suddenly exhausted.

I scope out the room. Oh yeah, there's Charles . . . surrounded by girls. I walk over to him.

'Hi,' I wave.

He sees me through the crowd and extricates himself. He looks hunted. 'Anna,' he says with relief. 'This is Anna,' he says to the crowd. 'My girlfriend,' he adds firmly.

Damn. This is ridiculous. I like Charles but . . .

I know I should be sensible. I'm a girl without many romantic prospects. And here's a nice guy with a huge fortune and he's actually interested in me.

But I look at the goatee and the platform shoes and I just know . . .

There's no spark. At all. I just can't spend the rest of my life with this man. I'll tell him, I promise myself. I'll tell him tomorrow.

I wake up not quite sure where I am. I blink and clear my head. Right, I'm at Chester House. Blearily I haul myself out of bed. No chance of waking the two Sleeping Beauties, they're both crashed out in their party frocks and full make-up.

As I step into the bath, I look regretfully around me at the beautiful house (the bathroom has antique Chinese wallpaper), the view outside the window—lush grass, terraced lawns, even some deer grazing in the background. I must be mad.

But I just can't do it to him.

Poor sod. He's been mucked about by women after his great country pile all his life. I can't do the same thing, can I? Go on dating him, just because he's loaded? We've nothing in common, except that we're both part of life's rejects' club.

I put on make-up and unzip my case. Janet has packed everything, bless her. The morning outfit is the black dress I first tried on. I've just managed to zip myself up the back when there's a quiet knock on our door. It's Charles. 'Are you decent?' he hisses.

I nod. 'The other two are asleep.'

He fidgets a bit. 'Can you come out for a walk?' He looks totally despondent. 'I'll understand if you don't want to.'

'No, no,' I say hastily. 'I'd love to come for a walk.'

Charles leads me down a flight of back stairs. 'We won't go through the kitchen,' he says. 'Bit of a zoo in there. Lots of people never even went to bed. We'll just slip out here.' He opens a little side door and it's a really beautiful day, already warm. He leads me along gravel paths lined with lavender bushes, down the terraced steps of his lawn, past huge stone urns covered with trailing roses.

'Nobody can see us now,' he says breathlessly.

'That's great,' I say nervously. He isn't going to make a move, is he?

'Anna,' he says suddenly, 'my life is shit.'

I glance behind us at the grey stone mansion. 'Um . . .'

'You don't need to lie about the book,' he says plaintively. 'Vanna got drunk last night and told me I have no talent. I thought it was amazing. I thought it was a masterpiece. It took me ages to write.'

'You had great discipline,' I say weakly. 'Just because she—we—didn't care for it . . .'

He shakes his head. 'It's rubbish. Like everything else I do,' he says, unhappily. 'Everything I try goes bad. I went into the stock market and lost half a million. I bought a racehorse and it never won. I tried to be a lawyer once . . .' shakes his head. 'Stupid exams. I'm nothing, am I? I'm just a useless failure. And people are all so horrible to me. All the time.'

'You know, when I met you,' I say carefully, 'you were a bit . . . stand-offish and stuck-up. But you've got a lot better since then,' I add.

'It's only because people laugh at me,' he says pathetically. 'If I don't stand up for myself they all laugh.'

'So . . . you're striking first,' I ask. 'In the stuck-up stakes?'

He looks at me, smiles weakly, and nods.

'And girls?' I ask relentlessly. 'You were mean about how I looked.'

'Same thing, if you look like me. All those pretty girls. At first I believed them,' he says bitterly. 'But they were always just laughing. I can't help it if I'm a bit short. You're so different from them, Anna. You didn't know about Chester House. You've got your own life. A real career,' he adds, admiringly. 'More than I've got. I want you to help me find something to do—just to help me,' he adds, sadly. 'If I didn't have you I wouldn't have anything.'

I open my mouth. Now's the time. To bravely break up with him.

'You're the one good thing in my life,' he says, and to my horror breaks into sobs.

Pants! 'Don't—don't cry,' I say, pleadingly, fishing around for a tissue.

'I'm so lucky to have you,' he goes on. 'If you left me I don't know what I'd do.'

What can I say?

'Don't worry,' I tell him with a forced smile. 'I'm not going anywhere.'

Back in the kitchen there are indeed loads of people, and to my amazement two of them are Lily and Janet. They've pulled themselves together in record time. Lily is wearing sexy white jeans and a clingy pink sweater, and Janet has on a red skirt and matching silky top. They are both nursing Alka-Seltzers. And sitting with blokes!

OK. The fog lifts. Nothing but men would persuade them to get up this early. Janet is curled up with Ed on a cushioned window seat, and Lily's sitting on the lap of someone I haven't met yet. He's younger than her usual type. Very handsome, dark and intense. And there are Vanna and Rupert; I didn't see them last night.

'Anna,' Vanna says, looking absolutely thrilled. 'You two lovebirds been out for a romantic tryst?'

'Yes,' says Charles smugly. 'In the orchard.'

Everybody goes 'Oooh'. My skin prickles with embarrassment.

'Love the new haircut,' says Rupert loudly. 'You look a much better filly like that. Have you lost weight? Bloody good job. Ow, Vanna! Mind your damn foot, it's on my toe!'

'Vanna, have you met my flatmates?'

'We've been introduced,' Vanna says, which means she doesn't think much of them. Vanna doesn't value modelling as a career.

'I hope you slept well, Anna,' says Lily, warmly. 'We don't want you too tired on the way back. Anna's a top movie executive,' she announces to the room. 'She needs to be fresh! For her business.'

I blink. Apparently I have travelled into another dimension, where Lily is nice and sings my praises to everybody.

And then it dawns on me. Charles still has his arm round me. Vanna and Janet are beaming at him. A few of the Sloaney girls curled round their coffee cups are casting death stares in my direction.

They all have me married off already.

'Who's this?' I ask Lily, desperate to change the subject.

'I'm Henry,' he says, extending a firm hand. 'Nice to meet you.'

'Henry's going to be my boyfriend,' Lily purrs.

'Only if you're very lucky,' Henry says sternly. 'And play your cards right. And know how to iron a shirt properly.'

Everybody laughs while I just blink. Nobody talks to Lily like that, even for a joke! But she doesn't seem to mind. She's tracing her fingers across his chest.

'Henry's in property,' she says. 'It's a very exciting field.'

'Deathly dull, actually,' Henry says. 'But a family tradition.' He shrugs.

'That's Henry Marsh,' Lily tells me, with a sly nod.

Oh, I get it. Henry Marsh. Must be of Marsh and Strutter, one of the biggest estate agents in the country. Trust Lily to pick up a property mogul for herself. But she really seems taken with him.

'Men are from Marsh, women are from Venus,' says Ed.

'Oh, her real name's not Venus,' Henry says stoutly. 'That was a load of old bollocks. It's Frutt.'

Lily nods meekly. Bloody hell, I really like Henry.

On the drive back, I don't have to say much, luckily. Janet does ask me about Charles, but all she really wants to do is talk about Ed. And Lily is equally taken with Henry. All that's required of me is to drive home.

'They've got offices everywhere. They're *the* people to see in Chelsea. Henry's probably got lots of properties himself.'

'Ed said he'd like to take me to the theatre. He's coming down to London. On Tuesday, actually. We're going out to dinner.'

'I don't know how you can go out with him, Janet,' says Lily airily. 'He's obviously totally skint.'

'At least he's not ninety,' I say. 'He's young and . . . pleasant.'

'Well, pleasant doesn't pay the rent.' Lily examines her nails as I join the M25. 'Now Henry, he's young and gorgeous. As well as loaded.'

'When are you seeing him again?'

'Probably Saturday,' says Lily. 'If I decide to let him take me out.'

'He seemed to have a pretty good handle on you,' I say. 'Maybe you'd better not try your normal routine.'

'What do you mean?' she asks innocently.

'Oh, you know. Keeping him waiting for twenty minutes,' I say. 'Vetoing all his restaurant suggestions. I don't think he's going to take it.'

'He'll take whatever I give him,' Lily says, shrugging. 'And he'll like it.'

'Whatever, Lily *Frutt*,' I retort.

'Shut up,' she says. 'And before you take relationship advice from *her*, Janet, I do hope you've noticed she bagged herself the richest guy.'

'I know,' says Janet loyally. 'I think it's fantastic.'

I sigh. I wish I did.

6

I HAVE A LOT OF TIME to think about that over the next couple of weeks. Mark Swan is called to LA to edit his last movie, and I'm back at the office, trawling through scripts once again.

I don't care. On the first Thursday a courier package arrives for me from Hollywood. It's from Swan. *Final Draft*—scriptwriting software. This stuff costs a bomb. There's a note in with the package, unsigned. It says, 'Make it good.'

I hug the package to myself, letting the emotions wash over me. This seems more romantic than any bunch of roses or box of truffles . . .

Of course, he didn't mean it that way. But he does mean me to be a writer. I glance at the pile of useless scripts on my desk.

I can do better. I'm sure of it. Mark Swan believes in me, and so do I.

Let's see. I start playing with ideas almost immediately. A comedy, definitely. I like those best. Something cheap to make. High-concept. But cheap, and unusual. How about a ghost? I like ghosts . . .

Sharon slinks over to me. 'You know, I've been waiting for your call.'

'Oh?' I pretend not to know what she's talking about.

'Mark Swan. Whether he has a new girlfriend yet.'

'Oh, that. Well, I didn't ask him.'

'And why not?' she demands. 'That's very selfish of you, Anna.'

'I feel awkward asking him personal questions,' I say. 'But you've no chance,' I tell her. 'Everybody wants him.'

'So?' she snaps.

'So what does he want another reasonably pretty girl from the film business chucking herself in his path for?'

Sharon pulls back her shoulders and shoves her not-very-impressive tits in my direction. 'Who wouldn't want to get with *this*?' she hisses.

'Mark Swan for one,' I say, giggling. She's so ridiculous!

'You are quite simply jealous,' snarls Sharon furiously.

'You don't even know him,' I say. 'You've never *met* the guy, for heaven's sake. The only thing about him that appeals to you is that he's rich and powerful.'

Sharon laughs bitterly. 'Oh yes, and you're such a bloody saint! What could it be about Charles Dawson that makes you want to go out with him? It couldn't possibly be all that money, could it?'

I shudder inwardly. 'Goodbye, Sharon,' I say, picking up my script and ostentatiously opening it in front of my face.

She makes me think, though. Lily said it before—I'm dating Charles because he's loaded. And it stings. All the more because I'm not being fair to the guy. I look at the cool cardboard box of software on my desk. I have a career going now, I have my dreams. I don't want to use Charles Dawson just because I'm afraid of winding up alone. I'm going to have to break up with him. And it makes me sad.

'What's the matter with you?' Lily says, as I walk morosely through our front door. I ignore her. I go to my tiny desk, slide the software into my laptop. I've already got the idea. A ghost story . . . a caper . . .

I flex my fingers, and start typing.

It feels really good. I write the first scene, then the next, then the next. I stop to read it over, love it, and write some more. It's as if I can't stop! By the time the phone rings, I've written fifteen pages.

'Hello, sweetie,' says Charles. 'How was your day?'

A fresh wave of guilt breaks over me. 'Oh, fine. Look, do you think we could go out for dinner? I'd like to talk to you.' I know I'm doing the right thing. Of course he'll be sad, but he'll thank me for it later. On the other hand I'm sad right now, and I wonder if I'll be thanking myself . . .

'Hello,' says Charles. 'You look absolutely marvellous.'

'Thanks,' I say. I've dressed really carefully. I'm wearing my most chic dressy dress, a pale yellow silk thing with an A-line skirt. I'm going to dump the guy. At least I can try to make him look good. Right?

'Let's have champagne,' he says.

'We're not celebrating, are we?' I ask, anxiously.

'Every day with you is a celebration, Anna,' he says. Oh, this is a disaster. How am I supposed to break up with him? Please don't say things like that. I've had absolutely no practice at being the dumper. I am a lifelong dump-ee. It started with Robby Caldwell in the fourth form. I think his parting shot was 'You're fat and ugly'. Charles doesn't deserve the unwanted open-heart surgery without anaesthesia that men apparently think it's OK to practise on women.

Quick, change the subject. 'I'm really enjoying being back in the office,' I lie brightly. 'Away from Mark Swan for a bit. Getting lots of work done. I thought I might write a script.'

'Oh yes?' Charles says, warmly. 'You're a star, Anna. You have to give me some career advice. I'm bloody useless, can't do anything.'

That takes care of the starter course; I rabbit on inanely, between telling Charles he isn't useless, he just hasn't found the right job yet. The wine we've moved on to also helps. I am convinced that without alcohol the entire planet would come crashing to a halt. Charles is so genuinely pleased for me. I really like the guy. It's such a shame I'd rather chew my own foot off and swallow it whole than think of his hands on my boobs.

Eventually we are halfway through our main course and I still haven't said a thing. I take one more big, fortifying gulp of wine and plunge right into it. 'Look, Charles, we need to talk.'

He looks perplexed. 'We are talking, aren't we?'

'About us, I mean. I think you're a fantastic person, but I don't think we're right for each other.'

He looks amazed. 'Do you mean romantically?'

'Yes,' I say gently.

'But why?' he asks, bewildered. 'We get on OK, don't we?'

'Oh, absolutely,' I say, agreeing with him. 'I think you're great.'

'I know I was a bit bloody at first,' he says, apologetically, 'but I thought you'd forgiven me.'

'Oh. I have. Totally.'

'Then what is it?'

Arrrgh! 'I think you're a wonderful friend and I really enjoy your company,' I say. 'But there just isn't that spark between us.'

'Oh,' he says, sounding relieved. 'I know *that*. That's not a problem.'

'Um . . . how exactly isn't it a problem?'

'Oh, you know,' Charles says airily. 'That goes away. Everyone says so. You have passion for a few years, then it wears off, and you're left with friendship. Long-term success is about getting on with the other person. Seeing eye to eye.'

'I think I need that passion, though.'

'You don't,' he says, sighing heavily. 'You need to not be lonely. To spend time with a person you like. Otherwise, life's bloody awful.'

What he says makes sense. It sounds completely reasonable. So why do I still feel like I want to run away?

'How many girls do you know who have followed passion, only to be completely miserable within six months?'

I think of Janet, chasing Gino. And others. 'Maybe one or two.'

'And old married couples. How passionate are they?'

Well, I can't visualise Mum and Dad rattling the bedposts.

'Not very,' I say. 'But don't you think people should at least start out with passion? Then they mellow as they get older.'

'Yes, ideally,' Charles concedes. 'But look, we're just skipping that stage. I don't fancy you,' he says earnestly.

'Oh. Well, thanks.' That explains a lot. All the delicious food, for one thing. What was it he said about my dieting? 'Why not just be who you are?' I suddenly understand why it rankled when he told me he liked me for my personality—it meant he *didn't* like me for my looks.

I don't want much. I know what I look like. Logically I shouldn't expect anything in that department. But the fact is, the thought that Charles is completely indifferent to me *does* hurt.

On the other hand, if I insist on waiting for a man who actually wants me, I'll be waiting for ever, won't I? Waiting alone.

'It wouldn't be difficult to *learn* to fancy you, Anna,' he offers. 'The more we get to know each other, I mean. You look so much better since you had your hair changed. At the ball, you looked almost pretty.'

He's so sincere it's hard to be cross.

'And I know you don't fancy me, but, you know. Dark room, couple of bottles of champagne, we'd be OK,' he says heartily. 'I bet you'd be a great mother. And I could be a good husband. Supporting your career. Providing you with nice things.'

'I don't care about that.'

'I know,' he says, smiling. 'It's one of the main reasons I like you so much. But we could be so happy together. Close friends. We could have a nice family and lots of money. I can give you anything you want.'

For the life of me I can't think of a good reason to say no. It may be a little out there, but he's sounding awfully practical.

'And you say you want to write films? I can support you while you do that,' he offers earnestly. 'You'd never have to be a struggling writer. You can live in comfort with me for as long as it takes to be successful.'

I smile at him. What a gorgeous thing to say.

'It would be a terrific wedding,' he says, encouraged.

I blink. 'Wedding?'

'Of course wedding,' he says. 'You could plan it, anything you wanted. Perhaps your friends could be the bridesmaids. Janice and Lila.'

'Janet and Lily.'

'Right,' he says, making a dismissive little gesture with his hands. I beam at him. Ha! I introduce Charles to two younger models and he doesn't even register their names.

I drift off for a few seconds into fantasy—a warm stone village church, its porch wreathed in flowers, white and yellow, I think, a huge cream-coloured marquee on the lawn, the chink of champagne glasses . . .

Ooh. It *is* a nice picture. I never thought I'd get married. Not unless it was to some utter loser in the Brian mode who'd offer me a shitty register office ceremony where you don't even get to wear a dress. 'Are you for real?' I ask. 'You want to marry me?'

'I'm not joking, Anna. I'm serious about you. You're the one,' he says, reaching out and taking my hand. 'You're clever, you're ambitious, you don't want me for my money, you're nice, you're interesting.'

'Charles, I—I don't know what to say.' I'm flattered, but no. No, thank you. It's an honour, but I can't. That's what I should say, and yet I don't.

'Then don't say anything,' Charles suggests. 'Think about it. It's all I've done since I met you. You probably need more than one night.'

'I can't make any promises,' I tell him.

'You mull it over, and you'll realise I'm right. We're trained to think of love and marriage as decisions to make with the heart, but they're too important for that. They're decisions we should make with our heads.'

I look at him, longingly.

It's been so bad, you know. Being lonely all this time. Dating losers that treated me like rubbish, just so I had someone to go out with. Wanting and hoping to look different, and waking up every morning in the same tall awkward body with the same big-nosed face.

I thought that maybe now, when my career's going better, I'd stop caring about romance. I'd just give up on it and find fulfilment in my job. But for some reason that hasn't worked at all. I still want love. And the wine and gloom in the restaurant are softening Charles. Like he said, a couple of bottles of champagne, turn down the lights . . . That song from *Four Weddings* starts playing in my head: the one about getting married and not being lonely any more.

I want that. Not to be lonely any more. And I can actually have it. I look at Charles Dawson and I feel a huge wave of gratitude, real gratitude, and I think, gosh, I *love* you, I love you for rescuing me.

'No need for that,' I hear myself say. 'I'd love to marry you, Charles. Thanks very much.' And I reach across and kiss him on the lips.

'Oh God,' he says, eyes blinking owlishly. 'Oh God. Really? That's— that's *fantastic*. We're going to be *so happy*.'

'I know we are,' I agree, and take another huge gulp of wine.

Charles pays the bill and then pours me into a taxi.

'D'you want to go home?' he asks.

I shake my head. If we're going to be married I'm going to have to sleep with him, so I might as well get it over with, I think. 'Let's go back to your place,' I suggest, lowering my voice.

He smiles at me. 'Sure.' And kisses my hand reassuringly.

When we get to his building he over tips the driver and offers me his arm to go inside, which could be out of chivalry but could also be a cunning plan just to keep me upright. I stagger inside the flat and he takes me straight into his bedroom, which is just as I expected: cosy, with cream linens and bookshelves, and not a bit sexy.

'I'll just go and freshen up,' I say brightly. He's got a little en suite bathroom. I sluice out my mouth with spearmint Listerine and peel off my clothes, grit my teeth and open the door, trying not to be too frightened.

'Coming, ready or not,' I say brightly, stepping forward seductively, but the room's pitch dark and I catch my foot on the end of his rug, which slips, sending me tumbling to the ground.

'Hell, are you all right?' asks Charles, from somewhere ahead of me.

'Fine,' I say, feeling like a total prat.

'Let me get the light,' he says.

'Oh no, don't do that,' I beg. Heaven forbid. I don't know which is less appetising, the thought of being seen naked, or the idea of having to

111

gaze on Charles as nature intended. He's so short, especially compared to me. And I feel sure he's got a really bony chest.

'No problem,' Charles says, sounding relieved. 'Come straight ahead. Yes . . . yes . . . there you go,' as I reach the duvet.

I crawl into the bed. Charles reaches for me, his bony (and yes, it is bony) arm snaking round my plump waist. 'Don't worry,' he says, reassuringly. 'It'll be OK.'

And he does his best, fiddling here and stroking there, and it's not as bad as I'd expected. But it is kind of embarrassing and the only thing I want to do is get it over with. After he's done he turns me round so we're spooning and kisses the top of my shoulder, and then he falls asleep. It doesn't take long before my body untenses and I've dropped off myself.

'Wakey-wakey.'

I blink. I'm not sure where I am. And then I remember. Charles's face is looming above me. 'What time is it?'

'Nine fifteen,' he says.

'Oh, bloody hell, I'm late.' I jump out of bed and race to his little en suite bathroom with lightning speed.

'Couldn't you take the morning off?' he asks, standing outside and knocking gently on the door. I open it a crack.

'I can't. I have to get back home to get some new clothes and everything,' I wail. 'It's going to be half ten by the time I get in.'

'Say you're meeting a writer,' he suggests. 'It's true, at least technically. I want to go shopping with you.'

I blink. 'Shopping? What for?'

'Well, we are getting married,' Charles says reasonably. 'Don't you think we should get you a ring?'

'Afternoon,' I say, happily, tucking a strand of hair behind my ear. 'Beautiful day, don't you think? Not too hot, just perfect,' I add, waving my left hand insouciantly around. It's 2 p.m. and I'm just back in the office. I told Kitty I was doing some scouting work for Mark Swan. I'll have to spend an afternoon typing up totally fictitious location reports, but it's completely worth it. Charles spent all morning with me in jewellery shops, and now I'm flinging my hands around like a TV evangelist hoping somebody will ask me about the fantastic rock on my finger . . .

'What the fuck is that?' asks Sharon, suddenly.

She noticed! 'This?' I ask casually. 'Oh, this is my engagement ring.'

'My God,' she says, her face draining of blood. 'It is real?' She snatches up my hand, gasping. 'No way, Anna. No way!'

'What's all this?' Kitty asks, emerging from her office and taking my hand from Sharon. 'Pretty. Is it Butler and Wilson?' My ring is gorgeous. A glittery ruby, pigeon's blood red, with diamonds on each side.

'No,' I mutter. 'It's real. Charles and I got it at Garrard's.'

'Who's Charles?'

'The book guy,' Sharon informs her. 'Turns out he's Anna's boyfriend.'

'It's nice, if a little ostentatious,' sniffs Kitty. 'Congratulations.' Then a light comes into her eyes. 'Shall I tell Mark you don't want to work with him any more?'

'What?' I ask, panicking. 'Why?'

'Well, you won't need to now, will you, dear?' she says. Kitty's eyes are beady little slits. She sounds as sexist as my granddad.

'I'll still be working, Kitty,' I say, firmly. 'I want to make movies.'

Charles has two dozen blood-red roses delivered to my desk in the afternoon, provoking long-drawn-out sighs of sheer envy from most of the girls in the office, and he calls to say he's booked us in to the Ivy for dinner because it's nice and close to my work. And asks if 'Jane and Lucy' can join us. I decline on their behalf.

'We'll have to tell everyone,' he says enthusiastically. 'I thought we'd start with your friends. After your parents, of course.'

Mum and Dad! With a guilty start, I realise I had forgotten about them. Of course I must tell them. 'What about your parents?'

'Both dead. If they were alive I wouldn't have Chester House. But I've got you now,' he says, delightedly. 'You'll be my family.'

'Course I will,' I say, loyally.

'I want to put the announcement in the papers. And we must have a party. Vanna will be thrilled. Maybe you two can plan it together,' Charles says. 'Vanna's wonderful at parties. We want to make it really big with loads of guests. All your friends.'

'Right,' I repeat. All my friends? Who are they? Janet and Vanna, basically. Lily and Sharon, possibly. Claire Edwards. And, um, that's it.

Oh, except Mark Swan. A chill runs through me at the thought of inviting him, somehow. Probably because it's not a good idea to mix business and personal.

Yeah. That must be it.

'So we'll go and see your parents on Sunday, for lunch?'

'Oh. Yes. Absolutely,' I say, trying to sound more enthusiastic. 'You put the announcement in the papers, then.'

'I will. Do warn your parents, they'll want to cut it out and keep it,' Charles says. 'Day after tomorrow. Toodle-pip.'

'Toodle-pip,' I say, dutifully. Toodle-pip? I'm going to have to get used to that. I have a sudden vision of myself in ten years, a great strapping country matron with a ruddy, weather-beaten face, saying things like 'down the hatch' and 'chin-chin' and stuff.

That's pretty depressing, so I look down at my ruby and diamonds to cheer myself up. It works. They're so bright and sparkly it's like wearing a firework.

The phone rings again. I expect Charles, but it's Vanna. She doesn't actually say any words but I can tell it's her by the high-pitched squeal of delight that starts at a note only dogs can hear and rises from there.

'Daaaarling,' Vanna shrieks when the squealing has tailed off. 'You're brilliant! Incredible! Fantastic! Spectacular! Amazing!'

'You make me sound like I've just acquired super-powers,' I say.

'But you have,' Vanna cries. 'X-ray vision is nothing compared to the power to obtain vast estates with a single syllable! "Yes,"' she sighs. '"I do." Well, that's three syllables but who's counting? I'm so *proud* of you, Anna. I'm coming over.'

'I'm still at work.'

'I'll pick you up. It's almost five thirty now.'

I glance towards Kitty's office. She's in there with Eli Roth, the two of them probably discussing my made-up location reports. Normally I hang around the office till six or later, but with my luck, Roth will come out here in his sharp suit and ask me too many penetrating questions and I'll get caught. 'Yes, come over,' I hiss to Vanna. 'Quick as you can.'

Vanna arrives ten minutes later in a cloud of glory. Or it could be Chanel No. 19. It's hard to tell, frankly. She struts out of the lift looking amazing in something tight and black, possibly Azzedine Alaia. She's so formidable she makes Kitty look like Anthea Turner.

I quickly gather up a few scripts for cover but, possibly scenting a rival, Kitty has emerged from her office. Bugger. And Eli Roth's right behind her. Kitty is staring coldly at Vanna as though she's a half-dead bird some nasty cat has dragged in. 'Can I help you?' Kitty asks her.

Vanna does not flinch. She returns Kitty's stare with an equally icy gaze. 'I don't think so. I have a meeting with Anna.'

'Oh, really,' says Kitty, giving a little laugh for Eli Roth's benefit. 'Another of her friends being entertained during office hours?'

'I am a friend of Anna's, yes,' says Vanna smoothly. 'Who isn't in London?' I splutter, but manage to turn it into a little cough. 'But I'm seeing her on business now.'

'What are you guys meeting about?' asks Roth.

'Books,' says Vanna. 'She's looking for new properties to adapt. Right?'

'Right,' I say meekly.

'Oh dear,' say Kitty, superciliously. 'Another unpublished author. You really must stop this, Anna, it's a waste of company time.'

'I'm not an unpublished author,' Vanna says. 'I'm not an author at all. I'm the editorial director of Artemis Books. Of course, if Winning isn't interested in discussing any of our titles—'

'It's Red Crest now,' says Eli Roth, elbowing Kitty to one side. She stands there blushing as he hurries to repair the damage, smiling at Vanna with a full-wattage LA beam. 'You must be Vanessa Cabot.'

'That's me,' Vanna says coolly.

'I make it my business to know the names of all the players,' Roth says. 'So you're going to give Anna first look at some of your stuff?'

'Of course. I heard she was working with Mark Swan.'

'News travels fast,' Roth says. He slaps me heartily on the shoulder. 'Well done, Anna. Best get off to your meeting.' He looks over at Kitty rather crossly, and she, in turn, shoots me a nasty death stare. I shiver, but Vanna is smiling and dragging me away to Costa Coffee. Thank God.

'You could have been a bit nicer,' I protest.

Vanna gestures impatiently. 'Darling, no, I couldn't. She was challenging me and therefore you. She has to do that, of course, because she's so scared of you.'

I laugh out loud. Luckily I haven't yet had a sip of my fat-free, taste-free cappuccino. It would have gone everywhere.

'You're so blind sometimes,' Vanna sighs. 'Imagine if you were—what's her name?—Kitty. You're a woman of a certain age in an industry that only values youth. Your company just got bought out, and the only person with a viable script going is a young girl who works for you, so you steal the credit, but the young girl attaches a major director all by herself and is his preferred partner from the producing team. What has this Kitty done? Nothing. And she knows her boss probably knows it.'

'She told Roth that she found it.'

Vanna snorts. 'And you don't think he knows the truth? He knows. He's not dumb. The only reason he hasn't started firing people yet is he's figuring out the most cost-effective way to do it.'

'But Kitty won an Oscar.'

'What for?'

'Best Foreign Film.'

'Doesn't count,' says Vanna dismissively—and somewhat accurately. 'He won't fire you, because you've found him something, got it off the ground. But he won't give you much pay or credit either, unless you stand up for yourself.'

'But why not?'

'Because he doesn't have to,' Vanna says simply. 'But who cares about bloody business? Let me see the rock! Ooh. A ruby.' She pulls my hand closer to her eyes, scrutinising the stones carefully. 'Darling, that is stunning. Very attractive. And tasteful.'

'He does have good taste,' I concede. 'But don't you think we're going to look kind of silly?'

'Silly? What do you mean, the height difference? Don't be ridiculous,' Vanna scoffs. 'Nobody ever thinks millions of pounds are silly. Everybody will be green with envy. Everybody. All those years of people saying cruel—' she pauses, not wanting to give anything away, like I didn't know already—'of people wondering why you weren't married yet and now this! You couldn't have *done* any better.'

I smile weakly at her. 'It is kind of amazing.'

'And he treats you well? Not tight with his money?'

'Oh no, he's very generous,' I say, looking at my huge sparkler.

'And he makes you feel good? Supportive of your career?'

'That too,' I say. 'Even when I let him down about the book.' And now I'm going to write, is Charles being resentful? Not even slightly.

'So he's the perfect boyfriend,' Vanna says, triumphantly.

'Yes, I know. I—I'm really thrilled,' I tell her. I suddenly feel overcome with tiredness and have to smother a yawn.

'You go home and get your beauty sleep,' Vanna says, putting a note on the table. 'You'll need your strength. We have a huge engagement party to plan.' She drops me home before rushing back to leafy Barnes to break the news to Rupert.

I paste a big, hearty smile on my face as I fling open the door. Janet is flicking through *Heat* with her headphones on, and Lily is drawling on the phone to someone or other. 'Hi!' I say, gamely. 'Big news!'

They ignore me.

'Big news!' I repeat enthusiastically.

'Do you mind?' Lily hisses.

Janet looks over at me, fingers on her headphones. 'Waiting for tonight,' she warbles tunelessly. 'When you would be here in my arms—'

'I got engaged!' I shout. Loudly.

That does the trick (subtlety has never been Lily's strong suit). She says quickly, 'Call you later, baby, *ciao bella*,' and hangs up. 'What?'

Janet slides the headphones off her ears. 'What?'

'I've. Got. Engaged.' I thrust my hand towards them waggling it wildly, and little bursts of light sparkle all over the room.

'Oh. My. God,' says Janet.

'No. Way,' says Lily.

We must stop speaking in Morse code!

'Yes way, actually,' I say, proudly. 'Charles proposed. And I accepted!'

Janet screams. 'Aaaargh! Aaaaargh!' She leaps up from her chair and jumps up and down like a mad yet gorgeous baboon.

'I don't believe it,' Lily says faintly. 'Chester House. Eaton Square. Congratulations. Let me see the ring,' she manages with a forced smile. I have to give it to her, though, she's at least making an effort.

I thrust it forward a bit further.

'That is nice,' says Lily, seizing on it. She holds it up to her eyes. 'Princess-cut ruby, about four carats, translucent, two trillion-cut diamonds, two carats apiece, cut is very good, colour's a D . . .'

'What does that mean?' I ask innocently.

Lily swallows drily. 'Retail? About thirty grand,' she says.

Thirty thousand pounds? I feel sick. Charles didn't let me see the price tags when we were choosing the ring.

'I think it's wonderful. Congratulations, hon,' Janet says.

'Yes, well done,' says Lily. She forces another smile. 'Congrats.'

I'm touched, at least she's being civil.

'I expect you'll have one of these soon,' I say. 'From Henry.'

'Yes,' Lily says. She gives herself a little shake. 'No doubt. And he's loaded,' she adds, more to herself than me. But her heart doesn't seem to be in it. 'Good night, guys,' she says, and goes into her room, shutting the door quietly.

Janet hugs me, oblivious to Lily and her moods. 'This is so brilliant, Anna. Tell me everything, you've got to tell me everything. Did he go down on one knee? Was it totally romantic?'

No. And no.

'It was more just a conversation, but it was really nice,' I say, sounding defensive, but I can't seem to stop myself. 'Anyway, I'm actually pretty tired too so I'm going to turn in as well. See you tomorrow.'

I shut the door to my closet-sized bedroom and feel my racing heartbeat slow down. Thank God that's over; nobody else left to tell, besides Mum and Dad. Just before I sleep I look in the direction of my ring for some sparkly reassurance, but it's gloomy and I can't see it glitter.

There is one more person I have to mention it to, I think as I drift off. Mark Swan.

I wake up in the morning feeling a bit disorientated.

'Morning,' says Lily brightly as I emerge. 'It's the bride-to-be!'

I start, then it comes back to me.

'You can have the shower now, and use some of my Aveda shampoo, if you want,' she offers, with very uncharacteristic generosity.

'Are you feeling OK?' I ask, gingerly. Lily marks the level of her cosmetics on her bottles with wipe-off magic marker. I got my own back, though. Diluted them with water. And once I decanted her entire bottle of Perlier bubble bath and replaced it with Safeway's own and she never knew the difference.

'Of course,' she says briskly. 'You know me, share and share alike.' She smiles at me winsomely. Obviously Lily has slept on it and is terrified that what's mine might not be hers. But she needn't have worried. She can come and spend a year in one of Charles's many guest bedrooms for all I care. I want to clutch on to everything familiar, even Lily.

'Have you told your parents?'

No. Let me do that now. I dial their number, just wanting to get it over with, and feel a huge sense of relief when I get the answering machine.

'Hi, Mum and Dad, it's me,' I say redundantly. 'Anna. Anyway, I've wonderful news, I'm getting married. His name's Charles Dawson and he's a'—what?—'a writer. I don't want to tell you this on the answering machine,' I lie, 'but he's keen on putting the announcement in the papers, so I had to be sure you'd hear it from me. He's very nice, you'll like him. Call you later, bye!'

I hang up, making a mental note to ring them properly tonight.

'Let's go shopping for wedding dresses!' Lily suggests.

I start. 'I can't. Got work.' I think about my ghost comedy. I can't wait to get back to work on it. Get into the second act.

'Well, it's your choice,' she says reluctantly. 'If you will insist on slaving away for peanuts when there's no need to.'

'Women need to work, Lily,' I tell her severely. 'We need our own independence and careers.'

'Good God, why?' she asks.

I think about giving her a passionate answer then decide it's not worth it. Thank God I *do* have work to think about, or I'd be going nuts. Oh, yes, I am a professional woman. And, just as an aside. Not that it's really important. Mark Swan is back today. I'm leaving the office to work with him again. And it's such a great *professional* opportunity.

'Morning, Anna,' says Michelle coolly. 'Good to see you again.'

I doubt it. 'Is he about?' I say. 'Did he have a good holiday?'

'Going to Hollywood to battle the studios is hardly a holiday,' corrects Michelle. 'Coffee?'

'No, thanks,' I say, erring on the side of caution.

'Suit yourself,' says Michelle, icily. 'He's in a meeting.' She nods at the closed door.

I cast around for something to read, but there's only this week's *Variety* and I read that ages ago.

'What's that?' Michelle asks suddenly. She's pointing at my ring.

'My engagement ring,' I say, wishing to twist it out of sight. Why?

'Ooh, it is stunning,' she says, in a markedly more friendly voice. Then she pauses and a shadow crosses her face. 'Who . . . who's it from?'

'His name's Charles and he's really nice,' I say. My standard answer.

'Oh!' she says, brightening. 'Well, that's great! Congratulations. Sure you don't want that coffee? We've got herbal tea and all. Even some PG Tips,' she offers, generously. I instantly get the impression that she would no longer be spitting in it.

'That's OK.'

'Let me buzz Mark for you,' she says, smiling full wattage at me. She goes back to her desk and presses the buzzer before I can stop her.

'What is it?' asks his disembodied voice, a bit tetchily.

'Anna Brown's here.'

'Yeah?' He sounds pleased to hear it. 'Great, I'll be right with her.'

'And she's engaged!' says Michelle, loudly.

'What?'

'*Engaged*,' Michelle repeats. 'To be married. You should come and see the ring!'

There's a pause and I find I'm blushing.

'That's great,' Swan says, politely. 'As soon as I've finished I'll be out there to admire it. No more interruptions, please.'

'You didn't need to do that,' I tell her, but Michelle shakes her head.

'Wonderful news like that, he's gonna want to know straight away,' she says. 'You madly in love?'

'Oh . . . yeah, sure.'

'He's loaded, ain't he?'

'How do you know?'

She points at the ring.

'Well, yes. But I didn't marry him for that.'

'Course not,' she says indignantly. 'Country gent, is he?'

'You can't tell that from the ring.'

'I knew it,' she says with satisfaction. 'Don't know, just seems your type. Country gent. Getting away from it all.'

But it's not, I want to tell her. Not me at all. I'm London. I'm crowded tubes and *Loot* and drooling over overpriced flats. And most of all I'm walking around Soho, dreaming about writing movies. I'm Mark Swan's world, at least in my dreams.

Then the door opens. I jump to my feet. Swan is shaking hands with another man in a suit. 'Thanks,' he says to Swan. 'Good to see you. Good day, miss,' says the guy to Michelle. She simpers.

'See you soon, Mr Giallo,' she says.

Not . . . not Frank Giallo? He's one of the most powerful men in Hollywood. After David Geffen and Steven Spielberg, this bloke is *it*.

And here he is, courting Mark Swan.

I feel slightly faint. Swan catches my eye. He glances at me neutrally, his eyes flickering to my ring, then sees the expressions of awe and sheer terror crossing my face, and his body relaxes slightly, as though he's thinking better of something.

'Hold on a second, Frank,' Swan says, stopping him. 'Here's somebody I want you to meet. Anna Brown, this is Frank Giallo.'

'How do you do . . . sir,' I say, dry-mouthed.

'Sir!' says Giallo, pumping my hand and chuckling. 'Love those English accents. Too cute. You can call me Frank, honey.'

'Anna's a talented producer, but she's going to start writing scripts,' Swan says, grinning.

'That right?' says Giallo to me. 'Are you any good?'

'If she is,' Swan says, 'I'm going to messenger her script over to you and you're going to read it.'

'Are you attached, Mark?' asks Giallo, cannily.

'Don't pass it down to some shitty vice-president either,' says Swan, not answering the question.

'Oh, that's OK,' I say, because my face has gone so red it makes a becoming match for my ruby. 'You don't need to do that, Mr . . . Frank.'

'Mr Frank!' says Giallo, delighted. 'Listen, sugar, if you have powerful friends and they pull strings for you, don't say no. I'll be reading the first thing of yours I see because Mark Swan recommended you. If you've impressed him,' he shrugs, 'that impresses me. See?'

'Yes,' I manage. 'I—thank you,' I say.

Giallo grins. 'She's learning, Mark. It's been good to meet you, Anna,' he says, to let me know he remembers my name. And then he wishes us a good day and I watch the lift swallow him up.

'I can't believe you just did that,' I say.

'Why not?' Swan asks easily. He reaches round and grabs his coat. 'Ready? We're meeting Trish again this morning.'

'Oh.' I swallow hard, try to get my act together. 'Yes.'

He doesn't pay any attention to me all morning. Not to my ring. Not to my haircut. Trish sits there and complains as he demands more changes, and I sit there taking notes for Kitty and Eli, but I'm doing it on autopilot. I'm miles away. Trying to process what just happened.

I mean, I knew he was big. And popular. But power . . . I don't think I'd realised exactly how much power he had. Or thought he would flex those muscles for me. In thirty seconds, he just turned my whole life upside-down. Now screenwriting is more than a dream. A studio head's going to read it. People can spend ten, fifteen years trying to break into Hollywood and never get a chance like that.

And Mark Swan got it for me in ten seconds.

'That was good work,' Mark says to Trish. 'Lunch?'

'Can't,' she says. 'Got lunch with Peter, my boyfriend. You go with Anna, have a good time.'

'Anna. Yes.' Swan turns to look at me, without much enthusiasm. 'Well,' he says, after a pause. 'I suppose we'd better go out to lunch.'

'OK,' I say, feeling hunted. I was so longing to see him, to tell him about my script, to tell him what I've done with his gift. But now the moment is here I just want to run away.

I don't want to talk about Charles and me with him.

'How about Eduardo's?'

'I don't know it.'

'Little tapas place in Holland Park. Not very fancy,' says Swan. 'I suppose you're only eating the best now, huh?' he adds, nodding at my ring.

'Who, me? McDonald's is my idea of fancy. You know me.'

'Not all that well, perhaps,' he says. What does he mean by that? 'Eduardo's it is.'

'Fine,' I say. 'As long as you don't order off the menu for me,' I add with a touch of my old spirit. 'Why do men always do that and think it's sexy? It's not. It's aggravating.'

Swan looks at me and his mouth twitches very slightly. 'I promise you can order for yourself.'

Eduardo's is, as promised, not very fancy. It has small tables covered with oil-proof laminated cloths, the tables are all crowded together, and the place is heaving. I love it immediately. The delicious scent of Spanish cooking is everywhere, everybody is stuffing their faces and having a good time. Plus, nobody looks at Swan.

A waiter swoops down on us, grinning, bearing four or five platters of little hot, delicious things. 'Señor Mark,' he says. 'Ow good to see you! Here you go.' He lays them out for us, steaming plates of tortillas, little grilled sardines, some herby sausage things, some pitted, marinated olives, and fried jalapeño peppers stuffed with cheese.

I scowl at Swan.

'*Gracias*,' he says to the waiter.

'I get the rest of it. And your wine. Señorita,' he nods to me.

'I thought I told you I hate people ordering for me,' I snap. 'God, you're such an egomaniac control freak, Mark Swan!' The stress of this meal is mounting by the second.

He picks up an olive, admires its glossy skin, and puts it in his mouth.

'Aren't you even going to answer me?' I demand, furiously.

'These aren't for you, sugar britches,' he says. 'These are for me.'

Oh. I sit back in my seat, feeling like a total idiot.

'Your paella, señor,' says the waiter, arriving with more food. 'Your cold meats . . . your fried artichokes . . .' The little dishes are placed down in a seemingly never-ending stream. 'And, miss, for you?' he asks.

I shake my head. 'I'll share some of his.'

'Very good,' the waiter says, putting down a large carafe of red.

'Sorry,' I mutter.

'Who said you could share mine?' Swan asks lightly, picking up a sardine and crunching it in his mouth. He pours a glass of wine for himself. 'I wouldn't want to intrude on your culinary decision-making.'

'You love making me sweat, don't you?'

'Mmm,' he says, winking at me. 'You make it so easy.'

He's so gorgeous. So tanned and huge and self-confident. And the way he's mocking me, so lightly . . . I swallow hard against the overwhelming wash of desire that rips through me. Don't be bloody stupid, Anna, I tell myself. I reach for the little dishes, helping myself to food, pouring the wine, anything to distract myself.

'Thank you for what you did,' I say. 'In the office today. And, you know, thank you for the *Final Draft*.'

He nods, acknowledging this gracefully. 'Always happy to help out a friend. You're still planning to use it, then?'

I blink. 'What do you mean?'

'You're going to try to write? Not quit your job?'

'Bloody hell,' I say. 'Why does everybody keep asking me that? Why would *you* ask me that?'

'Hey.' He holds up his hands. 'Just checking you're not being pushed into something you might not want to do any more.'

'Why wouldn't I want to write? You said I had talent.'

'You think you can write a good screenplay?'

'Oh, absolutely.' I smile at him, back on solid ground. Movies. My career. 'It's a great premise. I'm almost halfway through it already.'

'Tell me,' Swan says. Not a request. His dark eyes are holding mine, assessingly. As if he is about to weigh my talent in the balance. The man who can make or break me. I realise he holds my future in his hands.

'It's not a very arty film,' I begin. 'It's just a little comedy really and—'

He holds up a hand. 'Stop. You don't begin with an excuse. You have a story to tell, tell it.'

'OK,' I reply. Suppressing a wild urge to say, 'Yes, sir.' He's speaking with such authority, it's insane.

'And,' he adds, with a grin, 'don't start out saying what cross it is.'

'What?'

'"This is *Gladiator* meets *Pretty Woman*,"' he quotes.

'That sounds quite good, actually.'

'Doesn't it? Might have to do that one myself.' We smile at each other and I feel relieved. Despite all the teasing, and the massive help, he's seemed a bit cold. And I've been so ungrateful and snappy. I love it when he smiles at me. It feels like it used to. I value his friendship.

'Go on,' he orders.

'All right.' I swallow nervously. 'It's called *Mrs Watkins*.'

'Shit title.'

'I know, I have to think of something better. Anyway, it's about these two antique dealers who go around ripping off housewives buying their antiques for nothing. And one day they buy this Welsh dresser from this old lady. They take it away but it's haunted. And the ghost is making their lives miserable so they try to return it. But the old lady's moved, and they can't sell it or dump it so they have to drive round the country looking for her . . .' I daren't look at him.

'And hilarity ensues?' he asks, deadpan.

I sigh. He hates it. I might have known. 'Yes, hilarity ensues,' I admit, feeling about as hilarious as Eeyore on a particularly gloomy day.

He doesn't say anything, so I push my food around my plate, glumly.

Swan reaches out and puts a calloused fingertip under my chin, tilting my head up so I have to look at him.

'Anna, that's not bad,' he says.

I start. 'Really?'

He nods. 'It's an old-fashioned caper. It's fresh, it's funny—at least as a premise. You have a long way to go before anybody buys it, but I'd be at least interested, based on the pitch.'

'Thank you,' I say.

'Don't thank me,' Swan says, sipping his wine. 'Just finish the script. Make me proud.'

My throat thickens. I so badly want to make him proud. 'I will.'

'That's if you've got time, of course.'

'What?'

'Well,' he says, looking me over. 'You've got to spy on me for Red Crest. And of course you'll be spending a lot of time with your new interest.'

'My what?' I ask, blinking.

Swan raises a craggy eyebrow. 'Your fiancé. Don't tell me you've forgotten about him already?'

'Oh.' I start. 'Of course not.'

'It's a very nice ring,' he says cordially.

'Thank you.'

There's a long pause. I eat a giant olive to fill it. It's absolutely delicious, but it tastes like ashes in my mouth. I don't want to discuss Charles with him. Because Charles and me is too private, I tell myself.

'Do you want to know who it is?'

'I already know who it is,' he says. 'Charles Dawson.'

There's another pause. He disapproves, I think nervously. Why do I suddenly feel like crying? I blink it back, furiously.

'Aren't you going to congratulate me?' I ask, and hope I'm not sounding too whiny and shrill.

'No,' Swan says. 'I'm going to wish you joy. That's from a Jane Austen adaptation I directed in college. They used to wish the women joy. Only the men were congratulated, because they had been lucky enough to win the hand of the woman.'

I try not to stare at him. 'That's very . . . chivalrous.'

'I'm old-fashioned in many ways,' Swan says, and looks away.

'Many . . .' I can't stop myself, it's like worrying a tooth. 'Many people have been, you know, congratulating me because Charles is well off.'

'What does that have to do with anything?' he says, and looks at me, and now his eyes are narrowed.

'Nothing,' I say hastily. 'That's what I'm trying to tell you. Nothing. I'm not going to become a rich country lady.'

'So, you're not marrying the guy for his money?'

'I would never do that!' I say, angrily. And this time I really am angry. My eyes are flashing. I can't stand it that Swan would say that to me. I don't care when other people suggest it, but him? 'Never! Never.'

There's another horrible pause, then he says, 'I believe you, Anna.' And signals for the waiter, who is at our table in less than five seconds with a bill. 'I've got to get over to the editing suite,' he says as we emerge from the restaurant. 'Can I drop you at Red Crest?'

'No need,' I tell him. 'I'll make my own way.'

Swan nods and hails a taxi. He drives off without looking back.

When I get back to the office I fling myself into my work. Which is to say I type up some bullshit about our 'working lunch'. That gives me an hour or two to work on my script. It's the only thing that eases the stress. The second act is flowing now. My fingers hammer over the keyboard, and when I finally take the floppy disk out I exhale. At least that's something done today.

Next I bite the bullet and call my parents. They're delighted, Dad blustering on about how lucky Charles is, and my mother giving me the third degree about his money; honestly, she's worse than Lily. I make an appointment to take Charles round tonight. Best to get it over with.

'Anna.' It's Claire, looming over me.

'Here it is,' I sigh, holding out the ring for her inspection.

'Yes, it's really nice,' she says, awkwardly. 'Really nice. But actually, can you go upstairs?'

'Upstairs?' I stare at her. 'What for? I have to work,' I say severely.

'Eli Roth wants to see you,' Claire says, apologetically.

I feel a shiver of apprehension. 'Why?' I whisper.

She shakes her head miserably. Obviously terrified to say anything.

'OK,' I say, nervously. 'I'll be right there.' Is there anything I need to take off my computer? I wrote my script on a floppy, thank God, I think, as I slip the disk into my pocket.

'I'm so sorry,' Claire mutters, 'but you have to go up right now and I have to escort you. Otherwise . . .' She jerks her head behind her and I see two security guards standing in the corridor.

You don't need a degree in office politics to figure this one out.

'I'm getting fired?' I say wonderingly.

'Please, Anna,' pleads Claire, unhappily. 'Are you coming?'

'No, I don't think so,' I say. I stand up and pull my bag out from under my desk.

'But you have to,' says Claire, almost crying.

'No, I don't,' I tell her. 'They're going to sack me for something. Whatever it is, it isn't fair. I'm the only one in this whole office who's done anything worthwhile for ages.'

'But what shall I tell Mr Roth?' wails Claire.

'Tell him he can stick his lecture up his arse,' I suggest. 'You have my home number. No hard feelings, OK?'

'OK,' snuffles Claire, looking at me admiringly. As, I notice, are all the people working within range. But nobody says 'Well done' or 'You tell 'em' or even 'Goodbye, Anna'. They all want to keep their jobs. I pick up my handbag and head for the lifts.

'Where the hell do you think you're going?'

It's Kitty. Like a vampire, she has moved at the speed of light, yet silently, from her office doorway to block my path. There's a light of real malice in her eyes. So much for my being her go-to girl. But somehow I'm not in the least surprised.

'I'm going home,' I say simply. 'See you.'

'You can't get out of this, Anna,' she pronounces. 'You're going to be terminated whether you pretend to be off sick or not.'

'I never said I was sick. I said I was going home,' I tell her.

'Aren't you even curious as to *why* you're being fired?' she hisses.

'Not really, no,' I say. 'It's some line of bullshit you and Eli Roth have concocted so you can steal the credit for *Mother of the Bride*.'

'That's my project. I found the script. And you agreed to that publicly,' Kitty reminds me. 'You're being fired,' she adds loudly, 'because you gave me a set of fabricated location reports yesterday. You weren't at those locations!'

I suppose she must have a spy who reported seeing me with Charles.

'That's true, I made them up,' I say. 'But taking a half-day off is hardly a sacking offence when I'm the sole person in this office to have come up with a viable project in the last six months.'

'You had very little to do with this film. Really nothing.'

'I found the script and the director,' I say.

'You provided a bit of coverage and Mark Swan would have attached anyway. He did it for the script, not for you,' Kitty snarls.

'You're just jealous,' I tell her. 'Jealous I can find good scripts, jealous Mark Swan likes me, and now you're jealous I'm getting married,' I say, suddenly understanding that it's true.

'Don't think Mark Swan will protect you!' snaps Kitty. 'He's under contract now. We've got him,' she adds, viciously. 'He can't just walk away to save the hide of the sixty-foot woman. Yes, that's right, get lost,' she shrieks, as I punch the button and step into the lift. 'Don't you have to go and ravage Tokyo or something?'

'Don't you have to go and get some Botox shots?' I retort. 'Bye, Kitty. Enjoy being an old maid,' I say loudly, and have the satisfaction of watching the look on her face before the doors mercifully hiss shut.

I make it out into the sunny streets of Soho before I break down. Mostly because my devastation is mixed with shame. I threw the same kinds of insults at Kitty that everybody throws at me, insults to do with her face and body and lack of a man, when really I should only have insulted her bitter, selfish, vengeful personality. But I knew instinctively what would hurt, and I used it.

Lily's sitting on the couch when I get in, brushing her waterfall of platinum hair with one hand and holding the phone to her ear with the other.

'Yes,' she says, giggling flirtatiously. 'Absolutely, darling!' She looks over at me with disappointment. 'Actually, she just walked in.' She holds out the receiver to me, giggling snapped off as if someone had flicked a switch. 'It's for you,' she says crossly. 'It's Charles.'

What's she doing giggling with Charles? I stare at her suspiciously.

'Hello, darling,' he says. 'Having a nice day?'

'Not really,' I say. 'I just got fired.'

'No!' says Charles, outraged. 'What are they, morons?'

He's so supportive, I think. 'That's very nice,' I say. 'We've got dinner with my parents tonight, if you're free.'

'Free? Absolutely,' he says, gleefully. 'What time?'

'Eight.'

'I'll pick you up at six. Five thirty, as you're not working.'

'I don't want to go to dinner with my parents,' I cry. 'I want to stay home and get drunk.'

'That's not good for you, darling.'

'Who sodding cares?' I say, then feel bad. It's not his fault, is it?

'Does this mean that you won't be working with that Mark Swan chappie any more?' says Charles.

Oh.

'Hello, are you still there?'

'Yes. Yes, I'm here,' I say, faintly. Of course, it does mean that, doesn't it? It doesn't mean I'll never see him again. I try to calm myself. He said I was his friend. Of course we'll see each other in the future.

'You should keep up your links with him,' says Charles, judiciously. 'Why don't you invite him to the engagement party, darling?'

'Sure,' I hear myself say. 'I'll ask him.'

'I wouldn't worry,' Charles says. 'You'll have a new job in no time. And if you don't, well, you don't bloody need one, to be quite honest.'

'Thanks . . . darling.'

'Pick you up at five thirty, then,' Charles says, merrily.

Charles arrives in the Rolls bang on time and we head off to Surrey. He doesn't ask me about being fired, which is great, because I don't want to talk about it. All he wants to do is discuss wedding plans.

'. . . and I know a marvellous chappie who can get orange blossom, even out of season . . . The cake . . . I was thinking of traditional, maybe six tiers, and two flavours, tiers of white chocolate with fresh raspberry sauce and then lemon with puréed strawberries . . . You'll love our vicar. He's so nice and gives such short sermons . . .'

He goes on and on.

'Look, darling,' I say eventually, as we're pulling in to my parents' village. 'Maybe we should go for something a bit simpler.'

He looks at me in horror. 'What? Simpler? Why?'

'It's just that I'll be looking for another job,' I extemporise. 'And that's going to take absolutely ages. And I have to finish off my script. I don't know if I could do justice to this kind of really fancy wedding.'

'Don't worry about that, sweetie,' Charles says reassuringly. 'You can leave the whole thing up to me.'

'I . . . OK.'

'Your career's important to you, so it's important to me,' he says supportively. 'Is this your parents'?'

I look up at our house. It's a three-bedroom semi with pebbledash and concrete, a neat little garden lawn and an amusing gnome baring his bottom. I have always been fiercely ashamed of the gnome baring his bottom, but now I stare at Charles accusingly, just daring him to feel the same way. 'Yep. Home sweet home,' I say challengingly.

His jaw's set firm; not a sniffle of a sneer. 'Lovely,' he says, bravely.

Mum and Dad react just as I'd expected. Dad, who's tall and strong, looks a bit askance at Charles's height, but I glare at him and he backs off. And Mum is fawning even before she's figured out what he's worth. I can see the relief written all over her face. Very flattering.

My mother serves roast lamb with traditional overdone vegetables and Charles makes polite conversation. He compliments the cooking. He compliments the lawn. He compliments the gnome baring his bottom. And then he asks for a second helping of mushy broccoli. He's being a complete star.

'We're thinking of having the wedding at Chester House, if you give your permission, of course,' he says, tactfully. 'The bride is usually married from her parents' house, and that would be *wonderful*, but we do have rather a lot of guests. It's purely logistical . . .'

'What's Chester House?' Dad asks.

'That's Charles's house in the country,' I say.

My mother pauses, her eyes fairly glazing over with pleasure. 'But I thought you lived in London, Charles?' she asks, a bit too eagerly.

'I've got a flat there. Comes in useful,' Charles says.

'It's in Eaton Square, Mum,' I say, as she's about to ask herself.

'Ooh,' says my mother, going almost catatonic.

By the time we manage to get out, and Charles is driving me back in the darkness, I'm well aware exactly how happy I have just made my beloved parents. And Charles isn't even being a dick about their middle-classness or anything, he's saying how great they are, and can he send a limo to ferry them to the engagement party . . .

My mother said, 'You're the luckiest girl in the whole world!'

And I know I am. There's no doubt about it.

7

I WAKE UP LATE. I glance at the clock, and, horrified, swing my feet out of bed. Fuck it, it's half nine, I'm late for—

And then I remember. There is no work. I've been fired.

I groan miserably and head into the kitchen to make myself some coffee. Janet emerges from her bedroom, her hair all sexily mussy.

'Hi. Lily told me,' she says. 'I'm so sorry.'

'That's OK,' I say, even though it isn't. 'I expect I'll get another job.' A wave of fear crashes over me. I found the script and attached Swan, but I can't prove that, can I? And no doubt Kitty's been busy on the phones, making my name mud.

'I'm sure you will. You've had a brilliant career,' Janet lies, kindly. 'And you've got that director bloke. He'll help you.'

I look at her. 'Janet, that's brilliant! Of course he will. He'll help me.' I gulp a quick swig of coffee and pick up the phone.

'Mark Swan's office,' Michelle says.

'Hi, Michelle, it's Anna. Look, is he there?'

There's a brief pause, and then Swan's voice on the line. Rough, impatient. 'Anna? What's up?'

'I got fired yesterday,' I say.

'Really? Why?'

'Over nothing. Over making up some location reports for Kitty. I was out . . .' I trail off. 'Out shopping for a ring.'

'I see.'

'It's still not fair,' I say tearfully. 'And she knows it. I found the script, I found you—nobody does anything at that shitty company.'

'So why don't you complain to the boss?'

'Eli Roth? He was in on it. He wanted me fired.' I pause. 'Come to think of it, I don't know why. Kitty was jealous, but Eli . . .'

'Eli didn't care about you,' Swan says, shortly. 'He cared about me. I've signed on for the movie now. I can't quit without damaging my reputation, maybe lawsuits. So because I insisted on having you around, he thought it'd be a great time to flex his muscles. Crack the whip on the maverick director.'

'What are you going to do about it?' I ask, momentarily distracted.

'Something. I haven't figured out what yet. But it will cost him.'

'Can you get me my job back?'

'Did you make up the reports?'

'Yes.'

'Then, no, not really.'

My cheeks burn. 'You've got power,' I accuse.

'Ah, but I only use it for good,' Swan says.

'Very funny.' I breathe in. 'But I don't need a job, do I?'

'I gather not.'

'No, I don't mean Charles,' I say, blushing. 'I mean, my script's almost done. You'll read it and you'll help me sell it, right?'

'I'll read it,' he says. 'But this is just a first draft, Anna. It'll take a lot of work to get that script ready to show anybody. And no, I'm not going to help you sell it.'

'Why?' I demand. My voice has gone all shrill. And I'm close to tears. 'Why won't you help me? Everybody listens to you!'

'Because you've got to make it on your own,' he says. 'I thought you knew the film business better than to think your first attempt at a script is going to be perfect.'

'I thought you'd be supportive,' I snap.

'I am being supportive,' he says. 'You just can't see it.'

I swallow hard. 'OK,' I say, feeling defeated. 'OK.'

'Got to go,' Swan says, sounding distracted. 'Important call from the studio. Talk later, OK?'

Janet is watching me from the couch. 'So he wasn't much help then?'

I burst into tears and she comes over and hugs me. 'He's so powerful,' I sob into her shoulder. 'And he could have helped me . . . but he said I wasn't good enough . . . He won't help me get an agent. And I need one to sell my script. Nobody will take me on.'

'Why wouldn't they? Isn't your script good?'

'You don't understand,' I wail. 'The script's great, but I'm thirty-two, I don't even look the part. These days writers have to be young. And chic.'

Janet pulls back, hands me a Kleenex. I blow obediently. 'Have you forgotten how I made you look for the ball?' she says. 'I can make you look sharp.' She snaps her fingers. 'You already have the hair.'

It's true. My hair still looks good from the fabulous cut Paolo gave me.

'But clothes are so expensive,' I say. I *want* to believe it, but . . .

Janet raises one beautifully tapered eyebrow. 'Anna,' she says patiently, 'how much have you got in your bank account?'

I think. 'About one and a half grand.'

'Then let's spend it.'

I gawp at her. 'Are you insane?'

'Are you?' she retorts. 'Maybe you've forgotten but you *are* marrying one of the richest men in England. You want to get that new job, don't you? You want to look like a film-biz person?'

I nod.

'Then don't argue with Jay-Me,' she insists. 'Follow me!'

We take a taxi to New Bond Street, Janet's personal Mecca. Crammed to the gills with scary designer clothes and shoe shops.

'That'd be perfect on you . . . Ideal for covering the upper arms . . . Red's very smart with cream. It's the new navy . . .'

'But, Janet,' I wail. 'Look at these prices. At this rate I'll only be able to buy three things.'

'Oh, bloody hell, all right,' says Janet. 'No Voyage, then. No Donna. But I'm thinking H and M, I'm thinking . . . ah, here we are. Banana Republic. First stop. Now,' she says, pausing in front of the revolving doors, 'you have to agree to put yourself entirely in my hands.'

'Whatever you say, Trinny,' I tell her.

Janet tosses her sleek black hair. 'Those two? Amateurs,' she says.

I may have mentioned before that I absolutely hate shopping. And I hated it this time too. I don't look in the mirrors. I don't really have a chance to. As soon as I pull anything on, Janet says, 'Yes, OK,' and snatches it from me, or, 'No. Gross!' and removes it from the cubicle. In fact I'm bending over and struggling in and out of clothes so much it's quite a workout. I get dragged from store to store, getting more red-faced and tousle-haired each time, until I just can't take it any more.

'Please,' I beg. 'Haven't we got enough now?'

Janet considers.

'Water,' I croak. 'I need water.'

'Well,' she concedes. 'The bags are a *bit* heavy, I suppose.' Heavy? Arnold Schwarzenegger would have trouble hauling them around. Janet couldn't possibly carry them, so yours truly, being a strapping lass, has to strain and grunt her way into each successive shop like a pit pony hauling a cart full of coal. 'We'd better get a taxi,' she adds judiciously.

Twenty minutes later we're home. I've had a shower and washed my hair, and now Janet's blow-drying it. My new haul of clothes is laid out around the room, and Janet has my make-up bag next to her.

'If you're going to cheer me up with a make-over why can't we use your cosmetics? You've got all the good stuff.'

'This isn't a make-over,' Janet says, authoritatively. 'This is about changing your life. We have to use what you've got so you can do the same. I know how you feel about how you look, but it's all in your head. If you could just see that.'

'Please don't tell me beauty comes from the inside,' I sigh.

'I'm not saying that. You're never going to be petite or pretty, in a conventional way, but you don't have to be pretty to be sexy, Anna. You've got a sort of fire about you. And you have great skin, and you're tall, and you have lovely eyes and hair.'

'And Gonzo's nose.'

'Your nose is *distinguished*.'

'I'm going to get it fixed,' I say fiercely. 'Soon as I've married.'

'Don't do that,' Janet says in horror. 'You'll take all the character out of your face.'

'I don't *want* character. I want to be *pretty*.'

'Why?' Janet asks. I look at her sharply but she doesn't seem to be joking. 'Every other girl is like that. You look different.'

'I look like a bloke,' I say despairingly. 'All huge and tall and strong.'

Janet laughs. 'You look nothing like a bloke. You're more feminine than you think. Let me show you, OK? Are you looking?'

'I'm looking, I'm looking.' She's laying the contents of my make-up bag out in front of me.

'Sponges.'

'Check.'

'Foundation.'

'Check.'

'Stop saying check and pay attention!'

'Sorry,' I say meekly. 'I'm grateful, really I am.'

'So, blusher, mascara, lip gloss, eyeliner. Lose the black, too heavy for you. Go with a light brown. Picks out the blue in your eyes.'

'Wouldn't blue do that?'

'Blue? Hell, no,' Janet says, severely. 'Do you want to look like Bananarama from the eighties? First we start with moisturiser. It should contain a sun screen.'

'You what?'

'Doesn't give you spots,' Janet says, dabbing some on. 'Next, concealer. This goes under foundation not over it. That gives a more even look,' she says, dabbing my long-lasting Max Factor under my eyes. All of a sudden I do look a bit less tired. 'And then foundation: you sweep up and away, up and away, blend it in at the hairline.'

She gives a practical demonstration. I watch her in the mirror. OK, well, yes, I can see my face is smoothing out a bit. Fair enough.

'Next, do your blusher. You dab some on the apples of the cheeks, here, and sweep a touch under the jawline and I'd go on top of the forehead for you. There,' she says, satisfied. 'You following, Anna?'

'Yes,' I say. 'I am, actually.'

It's really quite impressive. I turn my face from side to side. My cheekbones sort of stand out more, and my face looks slimmer. And I have this rosy glow, and all my eye-shadow bags have gone.

'And the eyes,' she says, moving on. 'You've got great eyes, don't overdo them. Just this light brown shadow or a nude, one shade, just on the lid, super-simple. And you've quite dark lashes. I wouldn't ever wear mascara in the day. For evening just a coat on the upper lashes only, like this . . .' She swipes. 'Makes them look even bigger. See?'

'Yes. Gosh, you're really good at this,' I say.

'So that just leaves lips. Yours are very sexy,' she says. Is that actually a note of envy in her voice? 'Very full. For day, what you do is basically nothing. You dab on a bit of Vaseline or a clear gloss at the most.'

She demonstrates. Suddenly I actually notice my lips. They *are* quite big and soft. Who'd have thought it?

'For night you can use a nude colour, make sure it tends more to pinks than browns. Then perfume. You want a signature perfume.' She reaches behind me and before I can stop her, sprays me with something from a white flowery bottle.

'Get off—what is that?' I sniff. It's sort of light and floral.

'Anais Anais,' says Janet.

'That stuff?' I protest. 'That's so uncool.'

'It's a gorgeous perfume. Totally floral. Very feminine. And that's what you are, Anna, you are very feminine. Don't be such a snob,' Janet says firmly. 'Do you think Charles will know what the smell is? No, he'll just think Anna smells like a lovely bunch of flowers.'

'OK,' I say humbly. I keep staring at myself in the mirror. Is that me? Truly? I look like a new person. And there isn't even any shading around my nose. I've got big eyes and rosy cheeks and glossy, sexy lips, and OK, I'm still not pretty, or even normal, but I don't think I look ugly either. I look—what's the word—striking. Yeah. Striking.

'Not bad, huh?' demands Janet with a certain amount of pride.

'It's really great,' I tell her. 'Thanks.'

'You haven't seen the clothes yet,' she says, excitedly. 'Come on!'

'All right,' I say, forcing some enthusiasm. 'Let's go!'

Janet looks at me shrewdly. 'It's amazing,' she says. 'I make you over twice, you look incredible both times, and you *still* don't trust me. What's that weepy look on your face for?'

'I'm just thinking you can't make a silk purse out of a sow's ear.'

'Man,' Janet says. 'You really do have problems. You're not a sow's ear. How can you walk around thinking of yourself like this?'

'Because other people think of me like that,' I mutter.

'Oh, excuse me,' Janet says with heavy sarcasm, 'and you are the girl marrying one of the most eligible bachelors in England?'

I want to burst right out and tell her. Charles doesn't fancy me. Nobody fancies me. But I keep quiet. It wouldn't be fair to him to say anything. 'I suppose,' I say. 'But love is blind, you know that.'

Janet purses her lips. 'Girlfriend, I think *you're* blind. OK. First thing, try on this,' she flings me some Zara flat-fronted trousers, 'and this.' A very ordinary-looking cream jumper from H&M.

Reluctantly I step into the trousers. They fit very well, at least they're comfortable. But the sweater . . .

'I can't.' I look at it despairingly. 'Why did you pick this? It's all fitted and it's got a V neck.'

'Because it's fitted and it's got a V neck.'

'But that will show my boobs,' I point out.

'Exactly,' says Janet, triumphantly. 'Now put it on.'

I pull it over my head. I'm still turned away from the mirror; she isn't going to reveal the full horror to me yet.

'Now we accessorise,' says Janet. 'Put on this,' she chucks me the chunky leather wristwatch she bought me, 'and this,' the gorgeous Coach handbag she made me buy, and you have no idea how much it was, 'and slip your feet into these.'

I stare at them. 'What are they? I didn't buy those.'

'Shoes. Pied a Terre. I bought them, they're a present.'

'But . . .' I struggle with myself. 'Janet, that's so lovely of you, but I can't possibly wear those. Those are *heels*,' I explain. 'Kitten heels.'

'Yeah. So?'

'Um, I'm five eleven,' I say. 'If you hadn't noticed.'

'Anna,' Janet says patiently. 'You're not going to shrink, you know. There's no point always wearing flats and slumping your shoulders like you do, trying to be smaller. Flats don't do anything for you. No, don't start crying,' Janet says. She rushes forward with a Kleenex. 'If you bloody well ruin that make-up job I'll kill you.'

'Sorry,' I sniffle.

'These are only an inch, maybe less, but what they do for your legs is . . . well.' She steps back and looks at me, satisfied. 'Turn round and look in the mirror. You'll see.'

I turn round. And look. And blink.

Who is that? I mean, I know it's me. But it's not. I don't have a tall, confident pose, and shapely hips, and attractive arms and delicate wrists—the watch makes my useful, thick wrists look small in comparison. And the low-slung trousers fit me perfectly, and they shave off inches everywhere. And the heels . . . the heels are sort of forcing me to stand up straighter, which makes me look about eight pounds lighter. The top shows off my cleavage, but it's thick cotton, and it doesn't look slutty, just . . . womanly. OK, not delicate, but womanly. And polished.

I gasp in delight. 'I can't believe it. I look great.'

'I know you can't believe it,' Janet says. 'That was always your problem, Anna.'

I examine myself again. Instead of hefty, I'm seeing myself as strong; instead of gigantic, I'm seeing myself as tall; instead of thickset, I'm seeing myself as curvy. I *do* have a waist. The flat front of the trousers is hiding my tummy, you don't even notice it. And my boobs look impressive instead of slutty. They fit the rest of my body.

'Don't just stand there preening,' says Janet triumphantly. 'Take that lot off. We've more to get to. Lots more.'

It's incredible. Almost everything she's picked, I love. It's an autumnal fantasy of black, cream, red and beige.

'Everything mixes. Try that burgundy leather skirt with the knee-high boots. And the fishnets,' she says.

'I can't wear . . . OK. I'll try them.' I thought she'd lost it when she showed me the fishnets, but the amazing thing is, they don't look tarty, they look pulled-together, a bit Manhattan, even. They show off my legs, which aren't bad, in a sexy way. Wow. I look so film-business.

I could ask for an agent anywhere dressed like this. I could walk right into William Morris and . . .

'I told you,' Janet says, as if she can read my mind. 'I told you. This can change your life. I know you think it's only clothes, and it's really superficial, but when you look the best you can, it helps. It just helps.'

'Thanks, Janet,' I say, giving her a hug. 'Thanks so much.'

I manage to kill a whole afternoon playing with my clothes. Mixing them up. Trying on all my new accessories. Everything looks great.

Then I walk determinedly over to my desk and boot up my laptop and start writing. The script pours out of me. I feel so confident now, like nothing can stop me. I write and write until finally, that's it, the end of the third act. I'm done. Screw Kitty and Eli. And screw Mark bloody Swan, too, I tell myself mutinously. I don't need any of them. I'm a screenwriter now. I can do this!

I pick up the phone, hesitate for a moment, then dial the first number.

The phone buzzes just as I'm on my way out of the door.

'Brown,' I say snappily. Wow, this new me is something else!

'Anna? Is that you?'

'Hi, Charles. Darling,' I add.

'Darling.' I can hear the pleasure in his voice. 'Are you quite sure you don't have any extra guests for the engagement party? It's tonight, remember. At Vanna's.'

'Oh. Oh, yes.' I'd forgotten all about it. 'No, just Janet and Lily.'

'You never gave me the address of your friend Mr Swan.'

I feel perverse relief. 'Oh, no need to ask him,' I say.

'But I found it out,' Charles continues. 'And I asked him. He accepted.'

Did he? 'That's great,' I say. 'I can't wait to introduce you.'

I've got that green dress I bought with Janet first time around, the one I didn't wear to the ball. Well, who cares what Mark Swan does, I think. I've got my green dress. I'm going to look *fantastic*.

I look at my watch. My first interview's in twenty minutes and I've got another one half an hour later. And then one more tomorrow morning. It was amazing how easy it was to get people to see me. I just called a couple of the big agencies, and mentioned my script, and how I've been working with Mark Swan, and they all asked me to come in!

'Gotta go. Don't want to be late. I'll see you tonight, sweetie.'

I will not think about Mark Swan. I will not think about Mark Swan. I repeat this in my head like a mantra as I turn into Soho Square. He thinks I'm not good enough. He won't back up my script. All that encouraging my hopes and dreams, and now he's pulling away . . . It hurts. It does. More than it should. But it's a blessing in disguise, I think to myself. I was, just possibly—so ridiculous—just starting to develop the *tiniest* crush on him. And I'm going to be married. So it's a good job that I've been sacked and he's not helping me any more.

OK. The Gryphon Agency, Inc. Here we are. I push through the revolving doors, a new spring in my step. The receptionist is gorgeous, but this time I'm not intimidated. 'Hi.' I smile at her confidently. 'Anna Brown, here for an interview with Paul Fallon?'

She glances at her sheet. 'Oh, yeah, he's expecting you. You can go right in,' she says.

Wow. This is brilliant. I open the door, step inside.

'Anna Brown,' Fallon says warmly, getting up out from behind his desk to greet me. 'So good to finally meet you,' he says.

'And you,' I say. 'I'm a big fan,' I lie. We smile Cheshire cat smiles at each other and he gestures me to take a seat. Man! This is so easy. I'll be represented here by the end of the day.

'So, I've heard all about your great work on *Mother of the Bride*.'

'Well,' I say confidently, exhaling and stretching out my legs. 'It was a great script. I knew as soon as I found it that I could—'

'How did you attach Mark Swan?' he asks, cutting me off.

'I found him and asked him to read the script.'

'Just like that?' he asks, sounding disappointed. 'Didn't you have some kind of special connection with him?'

'No,' I say. 'I bumped into him in a newsagent's and I didn't even recognise him at first.'

'So you didn't know him from before? Film school?'

'I didn't go to film school. But I did get him to read the script. I think I found a good story.' I pull my script out of my bag. 'In fact, Mr Fallon, that's what got me interested in writing my own scripts, because I was good at story. Mark pointed that out. What I've written is a comedy—'

'Anna, let me put my cards on the table,' says Fallon briskly. 'I'm sure you're a great writer, but scripts aren't exactly in short supply. Unless you can bring something spectacular to the table?' He looks at me expectantly. 'Mark Swan,' he explains impatiently. 'You have to use your relationship with him. We hear that you're friends.'

'You hear from where?'

'You've been seen around,' he says. 'Now, obviously, we here at Gryphon *love* Mark and we *adore* his vision. Do you have influence with him? Can you attach him to this script?'

'But the script's good enough by itself!' I say mulishly.

'With Mark Swan, sure. Without him . . .' Fallon spreads his hands. 'It's been nice to meet you.'

I stand up and walk out. I don't know how I have the guts to do it, really. The old Anna would have cried. I feel upset, but I'll be damned if I'm going to let this bastard see that. I get outside, half choking on fury and hurt. Oh well, I've another interview coming up, after all.

A sudden, nasty thought hits me. I walk into the little park in Soho Square, perch myself on the edge of one of the benches and pull out my mobile. The other agency's name is Westin.

'Hi there. Can I speak to . . .' What was his name? 'Richard Hatherley, please. This is Anna Brown, his four p.m. Yeah, thanks.'

Hatherley comes on fast. 'Anna,' he says. 'Not calling to cancel on me, I hope?'

'Oh, I don't think so,' I tell him. 'I just want to be sure we're on the same page. You are interviewing me about my script, aren't you?'

'Absolutely,' he says, enthusiastically. 'That's exactly what we're interested in, Anna. Can't wait to read it.'

'Phew,' I exclaim. 'For a moment I thought you might only be interested because you thought I had some influence with Mark Swan.'

There's a long pause.

'You mean you *don't* have any influence with Mark Swan?'

My heart sinks. 'No, none. I've had a falling-out with him, actually.'

'A falling-out? How do you "fall out" with an A-list director?' Hatherley demands. 'He's the only reason we wanted to speak to you. How do you "fall out" with someone like that?' The jovial, fatherly tone has disappeared and he's snapping at me. It reminds me vastly of Kitty.

'Very simple,' I say, seeing red. 'You tell him to fuck off. Like this. *Fuck off!*' I yell, then press the red button. It's not the same as slamming the receiver down, though, is it?

OK. I think it's safe to say they won't be reading my script.

When I was in college, do you know what I wanted? To be a millionaire by the time I was thirty. Vice-president of a Hollywood studio. But instead, I'm thirty-two and an unemployed script reader.

My script feels thin and pathetic inside my handbag. I thought the agents wanted to see my work. But they only wanted to get to Mark.

Despite my new, cool clothes, my eyes fill with tears, but I can't afford to cry, not now. For one thing, it'll ruin my fabulous make-up job. For another, I have to get myself over to Vanna's for the engagement party. I can't let Charles see me all upset at that. And Mark Swan will be there. No way am I going to let Swan feel any pity for me. If I want to cry, I can do it tomorrow.

Vanna's place is already packed by the time I get there. Cars are stacked three deep in her driveway, there are blokes outside rigging outdoor lights and caterers coming and going. I thread my way into the hallway past them. 'Vanna? Vanna?'

Rupert comes lumbering up, followed by Winston. I reach down with a pre-emptive ear scratch before he can ruin my make-up again.

'Upstairs, slapping on the old war paint,' he says. 'Who are you? We haven't been introduced.'

'Rupert.' I wave frantically at him. 'It's me, Anna.'

'Anna. Anna?' he says, astonished. He comes closer, peers at me. 'Anna! By God, it is, too. I didn't recognise you.'

'Oh,' I say, feeling pleased.

'You look *terrific*,' he says, sounding amazed. 'I say, did you have a nose job?'

I grit my teeth. 'No, Rupert, I did not have a nose job.'

'Because it looks a bit smaller,' he says charmingly. 'And that's a very flattering outfit. You should wear dresses more often, Anna! That way, people won't assume you're a lesbian.'

'Top tip, Rupert,' I say. 'Thanks.' I look round desperately for Charles, but he hasn't got here yet. A mature person would handle this whole situation with Zen-like calm found deep from within. On the other hand, I'm going to handle it with alcohol. 'Pass the champagne, would you?'

I'm sipping away as Vanna appears in the entranceway to the kitchen and blinks. 'Anna? Is that you? I don't believe it,' she says.

I don't know whether I should be flattered or annoyed by all this incredulity.

'I didn't look *that* bad before,' I mutter. 'Did I?'

'No, it's not that,' she lies blatantly. 'But now you look *delicious*, darling! Have you had some . . .' Her voice trails off. I lift an eyebrow.

'*Work* done?' she hisses. 'Botox? Collagen lip injections?'

'Nope.'

'Well, that's fabulous. So this is all you,' Vanna says, warmly. 'You should have done this years ago. Did you use a personal shopper?'

'Sort of.' I explain to her about Janet.

'I'll have to reassess your friend. She's done a simply marvellous job. Oh, Charles! Angel,' Vanna adds. I go bright red and spin round to see Charles standing there, clutching two huge bouquets of roses.

'Ladies,' says Charles. He's wearing his stack heels and a dark suit. 'These are for you, Vanna, to thank you for throwing the party.' He hands her a vast bouquet of yellow and pink roses. 'And, Anna, my dear, these are for you.' He passes me an equally ginormous bouquet of crimson-red roses. 'To thank you again for agreeing to become my bride.'

'I didn't bring you anything,' I say, as Vanna beckons her housekeeper over to whisk away the flowers and stick them in water. 'I'm sorry . . .'

'You're giving me the ultimate gift,' Charles says, bowing stiffly. 'Your hand in marriage.'

I hug him and reach for my champagne glass again. The first guests are drifting in through the door, and the party's about to start.

'Let's go and stand next to Vanna and welcome everybody in together,' I suggest. Charles smiles up at me gratefully. I thread my arm ostentatiously through his. Dear Charles, he's so sweet. I am absolutely not going to be ashamed to be seen at his side.

'Do you like my new dress?' I ask him. 'My make-up? I had it all done specially for tonight.'

'Oh, yes,' he says, giving me a cursory glance. 'You look very nice.'

I tell myself it doesn't matter. Men don't have an eye for these things, everyone knows that.

Mark Swan doesn't show up.

It's a fabulous party. One of Vanna's best. Everybody seems to be having an incredible time. There are three different kinds of champagne, a string quartet out in the garden, and all the trees are strung with fairy lights, and candles in glass jars are strategically dotted around the lawn. Vanna's catered a huge buffet with every kind of delicious food imaginable. I don't seem to have much appetite, though. I'm picking away at smoked chicken, sitting at the top table with Charles and Vanna and Rupert, and generally watching everybody else have a fabulous time.

Is it just me, or is it really dull showing everybody your engagement ring every five seconds? It's like going to university and being asked over and over again what A levels you did. I'm so sick of extending my hand and simpering. I know, I know, I must sound like a total grouch. And I *want* to be better at this. Happier. I don't know what's wrong with me.

I do enjoy Lily and Janet, though. They've turned up with Ed and Henry. Janet's all over Ed while Lily is trying to do her princess act on Henry. And Ed, who's rather scruffily dressed, is very solicitous, constantly fetching things, mostly for Lily, as Henry doesn't seem to be asking how high when she says jump. Lily's pretending to be all stiff and cold, but she actually looks happier than I've seen her for ages.

'Darling.' I turn to Charles. 'Would you excuse me just a moment? I'd like to go and have a chat with Lily and Janet.'

'Of course, poppet,' he says, turning back to Rupert.

'Hi, guys,' I say.

'Anna, congrats,' says Henry, shaking my hand warmly.

'Charles is a lucky man,' Ed says. 'Let's have a look then. Ahm, yes,' he says, examining the ring. 'Pretty.'

'I wouldn't need something that big,' Janet says eagerly. I wince for her, but Ed doesn't seem to have noticed.

'Oh, yes, I prefer smaller stones, myself,' he says.

'I bet you do,' mutters Lily with a warning look at Janet.

'Tell you what, Dawson, let's go and talk to Charles, leave the girls by themselves for a few minutes,' says Henry to Ed.

'Anna, you look awesome,' says Janet. 'Charles was knocked off his feet, wasn't he? Blown away?'

'Um, absolutely. But never mind about me,' I say. 'What about you girls? You look like you're in love.'

Janet sighs blissfully. 'I totally am.'

'And the whole world knows it,' Lily tells her, shortly. 'You're not going to get whatever costume jewellery Ed can afford acting like that.'

'Am I being too keen?' Janet asks humbly.

'I've seen limpets less clingy than you,' Lily says witheringly. 'But you really can't go out with him. He's too poor.'

'No, he's not,' say Janet and I together. Mild-mannered Janet's bristling, so: 'Tell me about Henry,' I say, to ease the tension. 'You look like you're quite keen on him.'

'I'm not keen on men, they're keen on me.'

'But you have to admit, he's not bad looking.'

Lily relaxes slightly, sighs. 'He is gorgeous,' she concedes. 'Even though he's very arrogant. He wouldn't fetch my drink,' she pouts.

'That's because you changed your mind three times.'

'A woman has a right to change her mind,' Lily insists, tossing her hair. 'Anyway, Ed got it for me.'

'He's very chivalrous,' Janet says.

I look at Janet staring adoringly after Ed and suddenly feel a painful clench around my heart. But Charles is a good man who wants to take care of me for the rest of my life, and if I hold out for some stupid, romantic notion of true love . . . It's just that I think I look pretty damn good in my new clothes. And I wish my man felt the same.

And then I see him. Standing in the kitchen doorway, a large present in his hand. Looking for someone. For me.

He came. Three hours late, but he came. I square my shoulders, shake out my hair. The green dress Janet picked is ruched at the bodice, it looks rather Georgian, empire-waisted, draping skirt, and my make-up is the same as it was this afternoon; I just freshened it. And I'm wearing Anais Anais . . . But why would he notice? Charles didn't.

I take a deep breath. I'm only doing this to take his gift and be polite, I tell myself. And after tonight I probably won't see the guy again.

'Hello, Mark,' I say, in what I hope is a suitably patronising tone.

'Anna,' he says. He stands there clutching his gift and looks me up and down. 'Anna,' he repeats.

'That's my name, don't wear it out,' I joke.

'You look stunning,' he says.

I melt just slightly but try to freeze myself back over. Swan looks pretty stunning himself. In honour of the occasion, he has decided to wear a suit. It's dark, charcoal grey, with a pale blue shirt. Totally out of character, but he looks good in it.

'Thanks,' I mutter. I catch sight of our reflection in Vanna's glass door. Tall though I am, he dwarfs me.

'This is for you,' he says, awkwardly, shoving the gift at me.

'Thank you, you needn't have bothered,' I say neutrally. *You certainly didn't bother to help submit my script* hangs in the air.

'I can see you're consumed with curiosity as to what it is,' Swan says
drily, 'so let me put you out of your misery. It's a Sony Vaio.'

'The souped-up laptop?'

He nods. 'You can load the *Final Draft* I gave you right onto it and
start rewriting your movie.'

'How do you know it needs rewriting?'

'How do you know it doesn't?' he asks, patiently.

I pull myself together. 'Very kind of you,' I say dully. 'You shouldn't
have. It's far too generous a gift.'

Swan shrugs. 'I've got a lot of money. As, I suppose, do you.' He
makes a gesture at the party raging expensively all around us.

'This is my friend's house,' I tell him. 'And yes, Charles is rich, but so
what, that's not my money.'

He grins. 'Wives all say that, until the divorce courts.'

Oh! He's so arrogant, standing there, looking down at me. The awk-
wardness has gone and he's back to his old, self-confident self. 'Speaking
from experience?' I snap, seeing red. 'Bitter because you have to pay her
alimony?'

'Not at all.' His tone's pleasant enough, but a shutter comes down
over his eyes. 'I was glad to give Maryann what she asked for. In fact I
gave her more.'

'Well, aren't you Mr Perfect,' I retort. 'I know you probably find it a
wild and crazy idea, but some of us want to make our own money.' I
thrust the gift box back at him. 'Maybe you should take this back.'

'Are you still sulking because I wouldn't help you submit your script?'

'I'll never get an agent now,' I cry. 'I can't make it on my own, I'll
always be seen just as a short cut to *you*. And you won't even *help* me.'

Swan looks at me. 'Anna,' he says. 'You need to think about this.
You're just being pathetic.'

'Pathetic?' I demand furiously. How dare he? Something snaps inside
me. Mark Swan, standing there, looking so gorgeous, so disdainful. I
step forward, hand raised to slap him round the face, but his own hand
darts out, lightning quick, and catches mine.

'You shouldn't resort to physical violence,' he says softly, and he's
looking at me like . . . like . . .

We're close, his chest is inches from mine, his head, his weather-
beaten, craggy face, and that sexy, kind, laughing mouth . . .

I feel my own lips part, involuntarily. My heart is racing. His eyes are
flickering down over my face . . .

'Don't look at me like that,' I manage.

'But I want to,' he says, still softly.

I sway on my feet a little, I feel almost faint. He lets me go and I take a step back. It can't mean what I think it does. Can it?

'Darling.'

I give a little shriek and spin round. 'Charles! You scared me.'

'Sorry, poppet,' he says. 'I missed you. She has to mingle, I suppose,' he says jovially to Swan. He looks at me expectantly.

'Charles, this is Mark Swan,' I mutter. 'He was my former . . . colleague. Mark, this is Charles Dawson, my fiancé.'

'Congratulations,' says Swan neutrally to Charles. I see him stand there, drinking Charles in. Charles is looking up at him, rather hostile.

'Thank you,' he says. 'You must be very upset that Anna's been fired, having had the good fortune to work with her.'

Dear Charles. Trying to protect me. He slips a slender arm round my waist possessively.

'I think Anna can do bigger and better things,' Swan says, politely. He pauses, then adds, 'And how long have you known Anna?'

Charles smiles. 'Whirlwind romance, wasn't it, darling?'

'Yes,' I agree miserably.

'That's very nice, to have passion for someone like that,' says Swan, and looks me right in the eye. I feel dizzy. I swallow.

Don't be so stupid, says the voice in my head. *This is Mark Swan. He could have anybody he wants.*

'Indeed,' Charles agrees. 'Anna's the one for me, aren't you, darling?'

Both men look at me. 'Oh, yes,' I agree. 'I definitely am.'

'It was very good to meet you, Charles,' says Swan. 'You're a lucky man. I have to go. Goodbye, Anna.' He puts his gift box down on the kitchen table, turns round and walks out, without looking back at me.

Charles pulls me closer. 'Want to go back to my place?'

So not. 'Sure,' I say, turning to him and smiling weakly.

Afterwards, sitting up in bed, Charles has a bony arm round my shoulder. 'Thought it went brilliantly, didn't you?' he says. 'Everybody was there. And all so pleased for us, darling. We must get on with planning the wedding.'

'I know, but I told you, I'm just a bit busy and—'

'Come down tomorrow,' he says, turning to me and pleading. 'Just one morning won't hurt. I want to show you my ideas.'

I can't say no to those puppy-dog eyes. 'All right,' I say. I try to force some enthusiasm. 'Sounds like fun.'

He's as good as his word. We wake up at seven, go into the kitchen for a quick breakfast, then he takes a shower, drives me home.

'Quick as I can, I promise,' I say. 'I just need a shower and change.'

'Hello, you two,' Lily purrs. 'Back from your lovers' tryst? Anna, I'm jealous.' She smiles. 'Come and sit next to me, Charles,' she suggests, patting the couch beside her. 'Anna won't be a mo'.'

Charles looks hunted, but I nod at him.

'So, tell me about Henry,' Lily suggests. 'His family's very rich, aren't they? The Marshes?'

'Oh, ya,' says Charles, and I watch Lily relax and beam with approval. 'Harriet and Fred Marsh are absolutely rolling in it, but you needn't worry, it hasn't spoilt Henry a bit.'

'Oh, no,' breathes Lily, as I grab my towel and clothes. 'It doesn't worry me. I don't object . . .'

It ought to annoy me as I step into the shower and baste myself, soaping all over just to feel clean, to shake the nasty feeling of last night away. But somehow it doesn't. All I do is sigh and think, Poor Lily.

But with Charles hovering, there's no time to pore over Lily and her many mental problems. I towel off, duck into my closet-cum-bedroom, and choose another Janet-approved outfit. Red A-line skirt, cream scoop-neck cotton jumper with red trim. I check myself out. Apart from my wet hair, I look wonderful.

'Tah-dah,' I say, emerging from my bedroom and doing a twirl for Charles, who's just sitting there gazing at Lily.

'Oh. Right,' he says, wrenching his gaze away. 'You're ready,' he notes, barely glancing at my outfit. 'We'll be off then.'

I'm bloody glad when we finally pull in to Chester House's long, bumpy drive. For one thing I need the loo. For another, Charles has spent almost the entire journey alternating between in-depth post-mortems of the engagement party and in-depth predictions for the wedding. I'm hiding behind a huge pair of Ray-Bans so he can't see the total lack of interest in my eyes as I watch the glorious English countryside slip by. And concentrate on not thinking about Mark Swan.

I'll admit it. It's something of a losing battle.

I keep replaying that moment in my head. His hand, catching my wrist. The firm set of his jaw, his sexy mouth, the way he looked at me.

But no. No. I mean, he already had every opportunity to say something to me . . . And, anyway, why would he? I mean really?

'Here we are,' Charles says.

We're served tea and homemade scones by Mrs Milchen, Charles's venerable housekeeper.

'I always said it were about time Mr Charles got himself a young lady, didn't I, Mr Charles?' she says, beaming.

'You did, Mrs Milchen,' says Charles, jovially. Mrs Milchen hugs him; Charles's butler and dodgy valet—blimey, the guy looks as if he eats puppies raw for breakfast—seem equally pleased. And he's so relaxed around them, they obviously like him.

He's such a nice bloke, I think. I completely understand now why he was so nasty the first night, at Vanna's. Women just using him. No self-esteem. Hey, I can relate. He squeezes my hand and gives me that grateful look, and I feel something constricting my heart like a band.

Pull yourself together, Anna.

'Let's go through into the blue drawing room—I've got some stuff in there,' he says, beaming. We adjourn into the said blue drawing room, which is indeed painted in a gorgeous Wedgwood blue. On an antique oak coffee table there are about twelve huge folders, laid open. I can see charts and lists, magazine pictures, glossy brochures.

'Charles!' I exclaim. 'How much planning have you done?'

'Oh, just the odd bit here and there,' he says, modestly. 'Shall we start with the menu ideas? Or the flowers? Or shall we pick a marquee?'

I sit beside him and try to pick and choose. It's the fairytale, he's offering me everything. It would give Charles and Di a run for their money. Or Madonna and Guy, come to that. It's just about everything I've ever dreamed of in a wedding. Except the groom.

After that, he insists I stay for lunch. I endure more delighted fussing and clucking from Mrs Milchen, then finally manage to persuade Charles to run me to the station.

'Call me soon, OK?'

'You got it,' I tell him, kissing him hastily. I have to get away from him. I have to do some serious thinking.

I buy a couple of magazines in the station W.H. Smith's. *Cosmo* and *Company* and . . . *Heat*. I pick up the magazine, hold it in my fingers.

I can't help it. The memory of Mark Swan, reaching out and grabbing my copy. The way I felt when he called me, in Kitty's office. The pub. My hand looking . . . delicate, in his. My engagement party, and all I wanted in the whole world was . . . to have him kiss me . . .

'Love.' I blink. The woman at the till is scowling at me.

'Sorry, I was miles away,' I mutter. I hand over some money and run for the shelter of the train.

It's no good, I think to myself. I'm in love with Mark Swan. I need to see him, I need to tell him . . . and I need to tell Charles. I shudder at the thought. Poor, poor Charles. He doesn't deserve to be hurt . . .

But I'm going to do it today. I can't marry him, because I want to marry Mark Swan, and that's all there is to it. I just love Mark.

I jump in a cab and give the driver Mark's office address. I don't know what I'm going to say. I only know I want him and I'm going to risk everything to tell him.

I burst through the front doors of Swan Lake Productions. The burly man on reception tries to challenge me, but I quell him with a look.

'I'm Anna Brown from *Mother of the Bride*,' I say imperiously. 'And I want to speak to Mark.'

'Wait a second,' he says severely, and turns away from me, mumbling into his phone. 'Michelle says you can go up,' he grunts.

I jump into the lift and ride it up to the first floor, breathing deeply, trying to calm myself.

The lift doors hiss open. Michelle's sitting there, wearing a drop-dead gorgeous scoop-neck body-hugging short black number.

'Anna,' she says coolly. 'Bit of a surprise to see you here.'

'I have to see Mark,' I say. My eyes are sparkling.

Michelle pauses. 'Is it about business?'

'No, it's definitely not about business,' I say. 'I need to tell him something, something personal. Is he here?'

Michelle's eyes narrow and she looks at me, consideringly. 'No, he's not here but he should be back soon. This . . . this about your love life?' she asks casually.

I smile at her, trying to warm her up to me. 'Yes, it is, actually.'

'Well,' she says, giving me a smile that doesn't reach her eyes, 'I'm sure he'll be delighted to hear how everything's going with your fiancé.'

'As a matter of fact—'

'You know, because we're so happy together,' she says, looking me dead in the eye. 'Since we started going out.'

My mouth opens. 'What? You and Mark? But you weren't going out.'

'Not till he asked me, no,' says Michelle. 'But we've loads in common. I want to be a director too. And we work out together. Mark loves women with good bodies,' she says with heavy emphasis.

I'm trembling. I try to steady myself. But I daren't speak because my voice is going to wobble and she'll know.

'He told me he really liked you,' Michelle says. 'You and I'll have to go out, Anna. Get to know each other. Maybe swap a few wedding ideas.'

'He asked you to . . . to marry him?'

'Not yet,' Michelle says. 'But I think it's coming. Fingers crossed, eh?'

'I'd better be going,' I manage. 'Just, just give him my love and . . . and ask him to let me know where I can send the wedding invitation.'

'Just send it to Notting Hill,' Michelle says, smiling at me like a crocodile. 'It's really nice of you. We'd *love* to come.'

8

I DON'T KNOW HOW I manage to get home, but I do it somehow. I get on the tube like a zombie. I feel so bereft and so stupid. Of course I misread him. What was I thinking? Of course Mark Swan would want a girl like Michelle, she's so slender, so pretty, young and hard-bodied, interested in sodding directing.

At least, I tell myself, I haven't ruined anything. I haven't said anything to Charles *or* Mark. I can still get married, still have a companion.

I open our door. And stop dead.

Janet is sprawled over the sofa, shaking with sobs. There's a huge bottle of gin right next to her. I rush right over and put my arms round her. 'What happened?'

'Ish my agent,' she says. 'He shays he doeshn't want me any more.'

'Stay there,' I say. I pick up the gin bottle and empty it down the sink. Then I run downstairs and out to the Boots across the road, and pick up some Shapers sandwiches and some fizzy mineral water with elderflower. Then I race back up to our flat.

Janet's exactly where I left her. I put some ice in a tall glass and pour the elderflower water over it. 'Drink this,' I say.

Janet takes a sip then pushes it away. 'Ish sweet, I can't drink thish,' she wails. 'I'm *fat*, thash why I've got sacked. Fat an' old.'

'It's diet,' I say. 'No calories. Now drink!' I force her to drink four huge glasses of water until she rebels. Then she manages to eat two low-cal prawn sandwiches. Eventually she seems to calm down a little bit, the water works, she's not so drunk.

'OK,' I say. 'Tell me what happened.'

'I called Marcel about this gig,' she says tearfully. '*Harpers and Queen*. It was my first big national shoot for a while. But when I called in, Marcel said they'd decided to go with Laura Boynton. D'you know her?' she asks, pathetically. 'She's nineteen. She's so hot right now.'

'That's only one shoot,' I say sympathetically.

'But Marcel said he couldn't be my agent any more. He told me the agency've got a new policy and they only represent girls over twenty-three if they're exceptional.'

'Oh, Janet,' I say, hugging her.

'He said, "To be honest, you've been living on borrowed time, Jay-Me. Maybe you should think about retiring. Or try one of the specialist agencies for older women,"' she wails. 'It was so *humiliating*.'

I pass her some Kleenex. 'OK, look,' I say, when there's a ten-second break in her crying. 'Look, Janet. You are incredibly beautiful. If you don't fit into the model mould any more, so what?'

'I'll have to live on the streets,' Janet says. 'I'll starve. There aren't any charities to help old models,' she adds plaintively.

'I don't think Help the Aged starts at twenty-eight, no.'

'I suppose I could get married. D'you think Ed would still be interested?' she asks hopefully. 'Even if I'm not a model any more?'

'I'm sure he would, but I wouldn't bring up marriage,' I say hastily. 'You haven't actually dated for a month yet. But why does that have to be your only option? You're a clever girl. You've got personality.'

Janet sighs. 'I've never done anything else.'

'Do you have any qualifications?'

'Oh. Those. Yes. I've nine GCSEs and two A levels.'

'That's great!' I say enthusiastically. 'What are the A levels in?'

'Pottery and art history.'

'OK,' I say, carefully. 'Well, we'll think of something. You can start a new career. I bet you can be really successful and make loads of money. How much money do you have right now?'

'I don't like to look at my bank statements,' she says.

'Maybe we should start. Why don't you get them?'

Janet gets up a bit unsteadily, goes into her room, and comes back with a sheaf of unopened Barclays statements and credit card bills.

'OK, open the newest statement and see what it says.'

Nervously, she rips it open. 'Oh, that's not so bad,' she says. 'Five thousand and thirty-eight pounds and sixty-two pence.'

'There you go. You'll be fine while we find you a new career.'

'What does OD mean?' she asks.

'Overdrawn,' I say. 'Does it say OD by that figure?'

'Yes,' she says, miserably. 'I thought something was wrong when I went to the ATM machine last week and it ate my card.'

'It did what?' I ask in horror. 'How have you been managing?'

'These!' Janet says brightly. She fishes her purse out of her bag and shows me a dazzling array of credit cards in gold and platinum.

'Janet,' I say. 'You must have . . . at least fifteen. And on this one'—I tap an Arsenal FC card, and Janet hates football—'you owe three and a half grand. It's maxed out.'

'But I only have to pay twenty-nine pounds,' Janet says brightly. 'See? It's easy. You only pay a bit. I get cash advances from the newest cards and pay off the old ones with them! I've loads of space.' She picks up a gold Visa card. 'My limit's six thousand on this one.'

Poor Janet, she's clueless. She's got no idea what she's got herself into.

'Um, can I have that calculator?' I ask. She passes it over, and I tap in the figures. 'OK. And now can I have your purse?'

She passes it over. 'What are you doing?'

I take it into the kitchen. 'Nothing,' I say.

'*Nooo!*' Janet shrieks. She rushes into the kitchen as I start cutting up all her credit cards, arms flailing at me. 'I need those!'

'I'm leaving you this one,' I say. I hand her back the gold Visa with the six-grand limit.

'What the hell did you do that for?' she yells.

'Janet,' I say, 'you owe these people twenty-one thousand pounds.'

She blinks.

'Your monthly minimum payments come to eight hundred pounds.'

'So, I'll have paid them all off in two years,' Janet says defensively.

'No. That's just the interest. You could pay eight hundred pounds a month for your whole life and you'd still owe the same amount.'

'But . . . but that's robbery,' Janet says faintly. 'They're just thieves.'

'And with the bank overdraft, that's twenty-six grand. With rent of seven hundred a month, you need to find one and a half grand every month after taxes and that doesn't include any bills or food,' I say.

'I don't . . .' Janet says. Her eyes are tearing up. 'How can this be happening? Oh my God, Anna. What the hell am I going to do?'

'I'll figure something out.' What the hell. At least this is distracting me from my own pain. I do what I can. I call some debt services and negotiate a lowered interest rate, and get Janet on a payment plan. Same thing with her bank. They won't give her any more overdraft, but they have stopped threatening legal action.

'It's a start,' I say.

'What about the rent?' she asks unhappily. 'I can't pay! You know what Lily's like.'

Yes, I do. 'Maybe you could get somewhere cheaper,' I suggest.

'But I wouldn't be with you two,' Janet says. 'You're my friends. And this is Zone One.'

'I don't think you can live in Zone One any more,' I say gently.

'Oh my God,' says Janet, starting to cry again. 'I've been dumped because I'm too old and too fat, and now I'll never make any money again and I'll have to live in Neasden!'

'We need to find you a job,' I say. 'And maybe you could borrow some money from your parents. Don't worry. We'll fix it all.'

'You know, you're really amazing, Anna,' says Janet wistfully. 'I wish I was like you.'

She wishes she was like me? That's good for a laugh.

'But you're gorgeous,' I say, self-consciously.

'You look pretty good too, these days,' Janet says. 'And you're so clever and funny and everybody likes you. If you're clever and make a lot of money you can make yourself beautiful. But if you're beautiful and not clever you can't really do anything.'

Lily comes home at 3 p.m. after a successful *Company* shoot. I'd like to say she's sympathetic and understanding. But I'd also like to be able to do the splits. Neither seems particularly likely right now.

'But I don't understand,' she says, screwing up her face in mock concern. 'Why did Marcel say that? Oh, he only mentioned your age? Not your weight problem? Older women agency, I suppose you could *try*,' she says. 'I don't think you can rely on them accepting you, to be quite honest. Maybe if you went on a fast. For two weeks.'

'Lily, pack it in,' I say quietly.

'It's partly your fault, Anna,' says Lily to me severely. 'You've changed Janet. You've been making her eat chocolate and crisps. And you've got her going out with this Ed loser.'

'He's not a loser!' Janet says fiercely.

'He doesn't have any money,' Lily says. 'And now you've got no job, who's going to look after you? Huh?'

'Maybe she can look after herself,' I say. 'Janet's going to be moving out. She's had some financial troubles and she can't make the rent.'

'What?' Lily snaps. 'It's due next week. You have to give notice.'

'I didn't know,' Janet says humbly. 'I'll look for somewhere else right away.'

'That's not good enough!' Lily screeches. 'You *owe* me that money!'

'But I've no money. The cash machine ate my card.'

Hearing this, Lily pauses for a second, going rather pale. Then her eyes narrow. 'Well,' she says. 'You can pay me in assets, can't you?' Lily marches into Janet's room and flings open her wardrobe. 'Look at all these clothes! You've got your Dolce, your Chloe, your Voyage, your Armani.'

'Leave those alone!' Janet says in horror.

'Lily, be reasonable,' I plead. 'We're friends. Be supportive . . .'

'Supportive?' Lily shrieks. 'What are these?' she demands, holding up the most exquisite pair of pale green high heels. 'These are bloody

Patrick Cox, that's what. And she's got eight pairs of Manolos! Why should *my* debts go begging?'

'They won't fit you,' I say hastily. 'Janet's a different size to you.'

'I'll say,' agrees Lily spitefully.

Janet breathes a sigh of relief.

'But that's not the only thing you've got. What about handbags? Louis Vuitton. I quite like that one. Fendi baguette. So yesterday. Chanel . . . you don't have any, I'll take this Coach one and the Louis Vuitton . . . and these Kate Spades,' she adds triumphantly, loading her arms with all Janet's handbags.

Janet starts to cry again.

'Don't be so wet,' says Lily. 'I've left you the Fendi baguette, though personally I wouldn't be seen dead with it. And I'll have that DKNY you're using right now,' she says, reaching for it.

I smack her hand.

'Ow!' Lily yelps.

'Leave those alone,' I say. 'I'll pay her rent for next month and you can consider this your month's notice.'

'Anna, you can't,' says Janet tremulously.

'I'll expect it on the 1st,' Lily says coolly.

'No need to wait that long,' I say, reaching for my coat. 'I'm taking Janet out to dinner and then I'll come back with both our rent money. And it's one month's notice from me too. I'm leaving as well.'

I take Janet round to Bella Pasta. 'I can't possibly,' she protests. 'All the complex carbs! Pasta's refined flour.'

'You can eat now if you're not going to be a model any more. Perhaps you'll go up to a size ten. You'll still be skinny. However little you eat you'll never look like Lily.'

'Why was she so horrible?' Janet asks.

'I don't know,' I say. I order a couple of Diet Cokes and a grilled chicken salad for me. 'But it's a chance for you. A fresh start. And maybe you should think about your wardrobe, you know. You could sell a few things on Ebay and raise quite a bit.'

'Yes,' Janet says thoughtfully. 'That is a good idea.'

Suddenly I have a brilliant thought. 'Ooh. Janet. You were quite good at art history weren't you?'

'I got an A at A level in that one,' she says proudly.

'Maybe you could do something in art,' I say, 'And after you call your parents you should call Ed.'

'But I don't want to tell him,' she says pathetically. 'He won't fancy me any more.'

'Of course he will,' I say. 'But you don't need a man to take care of you, you know. You can actually make some money of your own.'

When we get home Lily has gone out, leaving a huge pile of bills on the coffee table with what we owe marked in red. I write out a cheque and leave it on her bed.

'I think I'm going to bed early,' Janet says weepily. For a second I panic. I want to stop her; after all, if I'm looking after Janet I won't have to think about myself.

'That's fine,' I say. 'You get some rest.'

I sit by myself on the couch and try to take stock.

OK, I'm fired. I've spent all the money I have in the world. After the clothes, that rent cheque wiped me out. I can't get another job because Mark Swan's shadow is looming over me everywhere I go. I'm in love with a man who's already got a girlfriend.

And I'm engaged to a multimillionaire who's devoted to me.

I look down at my ring. It glitters beautifully in the twilight.

Then I pick up the phone and call Chester House.

'Miss Anna, how nice to hear from you,' Mrs Milchen says. 'But Mr Charles ain't here. He went back to London this afternoon, miss.'

I pick up my bag and ride our coffin-lift down to the street, hail a taxi, wondering what the hell I'm doing. No job, no flat, and now no man? But I know what I have to do. I don't love him. And knowing now that I can love someone, really love them, I'd rather be alone than settle.

I pay the taxi, climb out onto the pavement. It's a cool autumn night and I press the bell. I shiver, but mostly, I think, not from the cold.

'Hello?' comes Charles's disembodied voice.

'Charles, it's me,' I say, teeth chattering. 'Can I come up?'

There's a pause, and instantly I know he knows.

'No problem,' he says dully. 'Come up.'

'And I suppose I can't change your mind?' Charles asks, stiffly, when I've finished. He hasn't burst into tears, but I can see the pain in his face.

I feel sick. I don't give pain to other people. 'I'm so sorry.'

'This other chap isn't available. You might end up with nobody.'

'I know.'

'And you'd rather be with nobody than with me, I see,' says Charles, and now his eyes do fill with tears.

'It's not like that,' I say desperately. 'It's just that I thought I could do without being in love, but I can't.'

'I see.' Meaning he doesn't.

'Charles, women have always used you,' I say passionately. 'And you're better than that. You don't deserve to be used for your money. *Or your good nature, which is what I'd have been doing if I'd stayed.'*

'You've every right to hold out for better,' Charles says bravely.

'It's not better, it's just different,' I say. 'Look, has it ever occurred to you that you deserve better too?'

'I don't want better, I want you,' he says.

'No, you don't,' I tell him. 'And that's the problem. You don't find me at all attractive.'

'But what does that matter, when I loved your personality?'

'Charles, you didn't,' I cry. 'You loved the idea of being married, having a wife who wasn't after your money, having a family life. You know what your biggest compliment to me was? That I was a good listener. You were just lonely. But there's someone out there for you, someone really nice, who you can also love. Not like me.'

He takes this in but doesn't respond for a moment.

'So what will you do?' he asks, eventually.

I shrug. 'Go back to Mum and Dad's for a bit. I have to, I've no money.'

'I can give you some money.'

I squeeze his hand. 'Thanks, Charles, but no. Although that's really sweet of you.'

'Sweet,' he says bitterly. 'I don't want to be bloody *sweet*.'

'I can find you someone,' I promise.

'But they'll still be after my money,' he says.

'Not the right girl. You'll . . . you'll just know.'

'And what about you, Anna?' he asks. 'What about you finding the right man? This Swan chappie. You have to tell him.'

'Don't be silly, I'll never say anything. He's got Michelle. She's much prettier than I am.'

'That doesn't matter,' he says. 'You look fine.'

'You never fancied me,' I point out.

'Not as such,' Charles admits. 'But he did. I saw it in his eyes. Don't you think I can tell when another chap's after my woman?'

That makes me feel awful again. 'I'm so . . .'

'I know, I know,' he says briskly. I can see he's still hurting, but he's pulled himself together. 'Not your fault. You never wanted to be with me and I talked you into it. I don't regret that, you know,' he says fiercely. 'I still think we could have been happy. And I had to ask.'

'I understand.'

'Which is exactly why you need to see him,' he says. 'You risk only a little . . .' he pauses. 'Perhaps a little embarrassment, shall we say, if you ask him. I had to ask you, Anna. I had to try. Be brave. Tell him.'

I sleep late the next morning. Exhausted and drained, I finally stagger into the living room at about eleven, to find Janet, in much better shape.

'I called my parents,' she said. 'They said they could lend me a thousand. And I called a few of those agencies. The catalogue ones. And I took my portfolio in to Elegance and they said they could get me work starting tomorrow.'

'That's great,' I say, with a sigh of relief. 'That's great, Janet.'

'I mean, a job's a job, right? And Ed was really nice to me. Even though I got sacked. Actually, he said he'd come round later. We're going out.'

'See? I knew he'd be like that,' I tell her.

That evening, when the buzzer sounds, Janet leaps to answer it.

'Come on up,' she says. 'It's him,' she says.

'Oh, yes,' says Lily, 'the boyfriend with no cash.'

There's a quiet knock on the door and there he is.

'Hi,' Janet says, smiling hugely. 'Come on in.'

Ed enters. He's wearing cords and a dark blue shirt that's a bit frayed. His wardrobe could do with a bit of updating and so could his hair. But he has a nice smile.

'Wow, you look awesome, babes,' he says to Janet, giving her a huge kiss on the cheek. 'Brought you some flowers,' he adds, producing some wilting chrysanthemums. They probably cost him all of three quid.

'Thanks so much,' says Janet, smiling and taking them.

'Hello, Anna,' he says. 'You look marvellous too. How nice to see you. And . . . Lily,' he adds, staring at her. He goes pink in the face.

Lily is wearing a string-mesh vest with a nude silk lining that makes her look like a slave girl in chains, coupled with a pair of the shortest, tightest crotch-hugging white mini-shorts this side of an arrest for indecent exposure. 'Hi,' she says, without interest.

'So you'll be seeing Henry soon?' Ed asks her. 'He's a decent chap.'

'Very,' Lily agrees.

'How do you know Henry?' Janet asks.

'Met him through Charles,' Ed says. 'Brave man. Went into the Marines for a couple of years. Rumours of gallantry in Bosnia. Good egg.'

'Yes,' Lily says sweetly. 'As good as gold,' she adds, looking at me significantly. 'Actually, he's coming by this evening too.'

'Great!' says Ed. 'Maybe we could all go out together.'

'Do you know,' Lily says coldly, 'I'm not sure Henry and I would be quite your speed, Ed.'

'No,' says Janet hastily. 'Let's do that some other time. OK?'

'Oh. Yah. Sure,' says Ed, rebuffed. 'Whatever you say.'

'There are lots of great restaurants round here that are *very* reasonable,' Janet says earnestly. 'There's Mr Chow's Sun Fun Palace, there's Pizza Nation, there's Freddy's Fried Chicken.'

Lily snorts. Ed is looking at Janet as if she's started speaking Swahili.

'Or we can find somewhere cheaper,' says Janet, a bit desperately.

Lily's humming under her breath. I realise it's 'Hey, Big Spender'. Luckily, Ed seems totally oblivious.

'OK, you two, have fun!' I say brightly, pushing them out of the door, then I round on Lily. 'I don't know why you have to be so mean.'

Lily widens her cornflower-blue eyes. 'Mean? I'm just trying to help.'

The buzzer goes again. 'Oh, hi, darling,' Lily purrs. 'Come on up.'

Another knock on the door and Henry arrives. He's wearing an immaculate suit and carrying a bunch of dark red roses.

'Hi, Henry,' Lily purrs. 'Flowers? For me? How adorable. Let me just go and stick them in some water and repair my face. Kiss kiss.'

Henry comes over to me and offers me a kiss on the cheek. 'Anna, great to see you,' he says. 'How did you like the party? Charles never stopped going on about you.'

'Yes, well. He's a great guy,' I say guiltily.

'Where's your other friend? Janet, isn't it?'

'That's right,' I tell him. 'She just left on a date, actually. With Ed.'

'Great bloke,' says Henry. 'They should have come out with us. Course, it would have had to be somewhere fairly plain. And I don't think Ed's used to that.'

'Doesn't he like exotic food?'

'No, I mean, price-wise. I know a bunch of great places to eat around here, but they're not exactly first-class. Not what Ed Dawson's used to.'

'Oh?' I ask, moving a bit closer to the edge of my seat.

'He rarely goes to any restaurants where there are prices on the woman's menu, if you know what I mean,' says Henry, smiling. 'Got more cash than most Third World nations, that lad.'

'Ed?' I ask. 'But isn't he a younger cousin? And rents his place?'

'Oh, yeah, no family money to speak of,' Henry says. 'But he's a stockbroker. A brilliant one. Made his first million while he was still at school. Retired when he was thirty, bought a farm, potters about on it for fun. And he's renting that flat because his manor house is being rewired.'

I check to see if he's joking, but he isn't. 'But his clothes?' I protest.

'Oh, yes.' Henry grins. 'Scarecrow chic? He has absolutely no idea how to dress. Ed's a very astute art collector, but apparently doesn't know the name of a single good tailor. Maybe Janet can sort him out.'

'Really,' I say, trying not to grin back. 'How fascinating.'

'Now, I have to be more discerning,' Henry says. 'Find good suits on sale, wear them until they fall to pieces.'

'So you're not quite as flush as Ed?' I ask, then blush. 'I'm sorry, obviously that's none of my business.'

'God, no,' says Henry. 'Poor as the proverbial church mouse.'

'But don't you work for your family's estate agency?'

'I do,' he says. 'But I'm not very good at it. Don't make all that much. I'm thinking about trying to do something else. I have to stay there, though, just to pay off my credit-card bills.' He sighs.

'But your family . . .'

'They're just cousins,' he says. 'I'll have to find something proper to do for a career eventually. I can't really go on like this at my age.'

'What do you like doing?'

'Music,' he says, blushing slightly. 'I used to play the cello a bit. Of course, that doesn't pay the bills either. I tell you, I'm quite pleasantly surprised a girl like Lily would go out with me. Most girls in her position seem to look for something a bit more substantial.'

Lily sticks her head out of the door. 'Ready!' she says brightly.

'D'you like Moroccan?' Henry asks.

'Love it,' Lily says, flouncing out of the bathroom and pirouetting for his approval. 'Where did you have in mind? Momo's?'

'I was thinking more of Dhelirious,' he says. 'It's a funky little dive off Earl's Court. Great atmosphere, great food.'

'A little dive?' Lily asks, her voice strained. Then she gives a sexy little wriggle and beams at him. 'But that's so *adventurous* of you! Don't you think it's *adventurous* of him, Anna?'

'Absolutely,' I say. 'In fact, the whole evening should be a real adventure for you, Lily.'

They walk out, Henry sliding his thumb into the small of her back, and Lily giving a pleasurable little shudder at the touch. Henry's quite different to all the old goats she goes out with. I wonder what the fireworks are going to be like when she finds out just how different.

I pick up the receiver and call my parents. Oh great, another slap in the face; they're on holiday for a week. I could get the spare key off Mrs Watley, the next-door neighbour, but that would involve having to sit in her doily-filled 'front parlour' and have my life dissected for forty-five minutes. And I can't be bothered. So I'll have to gut it out here for another week. What the hell, I've paid the damn rent.

I'm alone in the flat. I make a cup of coffee and think calmly about what to do. First, there's housekeeping. I call Vanna, explain I can't marry Charles. She's wonderfully sympathetic, offers to come round (no, thanks), offers to send back all the engagement gifts (yes, please).

'Don't worry about a thing, darling,' she says.

'Thanks. I'm really grateful. And I'm sorry you spent all that money.'

'Don't be! It was a great party and anyway I've got pots of it. Speaking of which, would you like some? Just to tide you over.'

Oh dear, I'm going to cry again. 'That's OK,' I say.

'Well, consider coming to work for me. I can always use an extra assistant. Good pay, no coffee-making. I'll teach you the business.'

'That's really kind of you. But no, I don't think so. At least, not yet.'

I hang up on her feeling really grateful. OK, I may not have a place to live, a job, or a man, but at least I've got friends. Vanna and Janet. And Charles. His words from last night come back to me. I can't tell Mark Swan. I can't face him. It's time to see if I can hack it or not. On my own.

I've got my friends. And I believe in myself.

I open up my ancient laptop, take a deep breath, and type: FADE IN.

9

THE ATMOSPHERE IN THE FLAT has been poisonous lately. Ever since Lily discovered how stinking rich Ed is, she's been too jealous to speak to Janet. A procession of new, and thankfully vile, potential flatmates are forever traipsing round our rooms, I'm trying to rewrite and not think about Mark (yeah, right), and now Henry and Lily have stormed back in, slamming doors and fighting.

'Remind me again,' Lily bellows. 'Why the fuck am I dating you?'

I try to hide myself behind the *Evening Standard*.

Henry follows her into the flat and closes the door. 'I have no idea,' he says, quite calmly. 'But don't feel under any obligation to continue. Excuse us,' he adds apologetically to me.

'Oh, don't mind me,' I say, pretending to be busy reading. I wouldn't miss this for anything.

'Why would he mind you? When he doesn't even mind me?' Lily spits. 'I arrive at the bloody restaurant and he's leaving!'

'You were thirty-five minutes late.'

'Traffic,' Lily snaps. 'Ever heard of it?'

Henry sighs. 'I told you, if you were late you should call my mobile.'

'I forgot,' screeches Lily. 'You should have waited for me! You're a sexist pig!'

'Oh, really?' Henry demands coolly. 'This is the third time this week you've turned up late for a date. Are you in the habit of doing this?'

Absolutely.

'Of course not,' spits Lily. 'And anyway, I'm worth it.'

'Not to me, darling,' says Henry. 'Goodbye.'

Lily stands rooted to the spot as he turns and walks towards the door. Then she springs, like a cat, grabbing him by the shoulders. 'Do you think you can talk to me like that?' she demands. 'I'm Lily Venus! Who the hell do you think you are?'

'Somebody who's not interested in a spoilt little girl playing head games and doing it badly,' Henry says.

'I'm the best thing you've ever had,' Lily hisses.

'You're not even in the top fifty per cent,' says Henry. 'I'm amazed I actually stuck it out this long, in fact. Histrionics don't do it for me.'

Lily pauses, trying to think of a good riposte. 'You're poor,' she says finally, with deadly venom. 'A scrub like you can't afford a girl like me.'

Henry shakes his head. 'Lily,' he says, 'you're never going to get a man until you stop talking like a high-priced hooker.'

Ouch.

'I could get anyone I wanted tomorrow,' Lily snaps.

Henry walks over to her and kisses her lightly on the mouth. Lily is completely shocked, too shocked to do anything. It's very sexy, actually.

'Well,' Henry says, licking the taste of her off his lips, 'good luck with that, baby.' And then he really does turn and walk out of the door.

Lily and I both stay completely still, listening to his footsteps disappear down the stairs. 'He'll be back,' says Lily.

'He won't, you know,' I say. 'Maybe you should go after him.'

'Me? Run after some poor chump with holes in his shoes?' Lily laughs savagely. 'I don't think so, darling. I'm a *diva*.' She laughs bitterly. 'Think of it! Me, getting dumped by a poor person!'

'Diva is just a politically correct word for a spoilt bitch, Lily,' I say. 'Clearly you really like the guy. Why don't you just apologise and start over? Chasing rich guys hasn't worked out for you, has it? You've gone from one rich guy to the next, and none of them proposed. And you finally find a man you like, someone who won't put up with your shit, which is exactly what you need—'

'So what?' she says. 'The only reason I haven't hooked up with a man properly is because *I* wasn't ready to. As soon as I set my mind to it'—

she snaps her elegant, fire-engine-red talons—'I'll have anybody I like reeled in. Not like you, letting Charles get away.'

'Suit yourself.' It's funny. Looking at her, I just feel pity.

Janet comes back in the next morning after a catalogue shoot and I tell her the whole Henry story.

'Ed will be sorry,' she says. 'He thinks Henry's wonderful.'

'How's it going with you two?'

'Oh.' Janet flushes. 'Actually, really great. He's asked me to meet his parents next week. And he offered to pay off all my debts. I was so surprised when I found out he had money.'

'What did you say?'

'I told him no.' She looks sideways at me. 'Was that stupid? I like Ed, but I want to do it myself.'

'I think that's wonderful.'

'But I don't want to do the catalogues for ever. Ed had a suggestion; he said I could go to work in a gallery. I could sell art. You know, for one of the big dealers.' She blushes again. 'He said I was so pretty that everybody would want to buy from me.'

I stare at her. 'But that's brilliant. You'd be great at it. He's right!'

'Ed knows some people. He said he'd get me a few interviews.'

'So will you move into his place?'

Janet shakes her head, shyly. 'I found another flatshare. In Camberwell. I thought I should have a place of my own.' She looks at me nervously. 'Do you think I'm being mental like Lily says?'

'Never mind about Lily, she's just jealous.' I hug Janet.

Janet scribbles her new number on a piece of paper for me. 'And what about you? Where are you going?'

'I'm moving back with my parents. Till I can get another job. Or . . .' She looks at me quizzically.

'Or, you know, until my script sells,' I say. I feel stupid, but there it is.

Janet hugs me back. 'I bet you'll be a wonderful writer.'

'Thanks. You've always believed in me,' I say.

'Everyone who knows you believes in you, Anna,' Janet says. 'You just needed to believe in yourself.'

Two days later I'm out of there. My mum drives her Ford Fiesta all the way to London, to pick me up. When I get home darling Dad has made me tea and Marmite toast. My parents have cleaned my old room and put fresh flowers in a milk jug by my bed. Dad tells me I did exactly the right thing (though Mum does look a bit disconsolate) and I have to wait for it to be exactly right. It's an incredible weight off my mind. I unpack all my nice clothes, put my scripts on a bookshelf, take out my laptop. I start reworking my script. After all, there's nothing else to do.

I settle back into my old life. I'm writing every day, going for walks round the village with our ancient dog, Rover, just to clear my head. Walking is supposed to do that. Funny, mine's just as muddled, wrapped up in a blanket of cotton wool and pain.

I'm making plans to move back to London. I'll borrow some money from my parents, put a security deposit on somewhere cheap, and then find a flatshare near a tube. I need a job, an actual job that pays.

It's all incredibly depressing and I only have one remedy against it. Working on my script. I've grown up now, the hard way. I know I'm not going to get Mark Swan to help me, I know Frank Giallo isn't gagging to read it. In fact, the odds against it getting noticed and read are tremendous. But I keep writing it.

It's the only dream I have left.

'Anna,' my mother says anxiously when I come back from my lunchtime stroll, 'you've had a phone call. There's a message on the answering machine from somebody called Jamie, but it sounds like a girl.'

'Jay-Me,' I say, excited. Oh man, it's good to hear from Janet!

'She seems a bit upset,' says my mother.

My heart somersaults. When Mum says somebody is 'a bit upset' there has usually been screaming and wailing you could hear in Scotland. I rush to the answer machine, press the button.

'Anna,' sobs Janet's disembodied voice. 'Ed . . . left . . . Lily . . .' She's crying, really bawling, so bad I can't make it out. I run upstairs, retrieve her mobile number. Nothing but voicemail. So then I try our flat.

'Hello?' It's Lily.

'Hi,' I say. 'What's going on? Is Janet OK? I need to speak to her.'

'Oh, Janet,' says Lily, with more ice in her tone than usual. 'She's left. Moved out. You can get her on her cellphone.'

I have a sinking feeling. 'Lily,' I say slowly, 'what happened?'

'She thinks she owns Ed after four dates,' Lily snaps. 'They didn't exactly have a relationship. They hadn't pledged their undying love.'

'Ed broke up with her?'

'That's right,' Lily says. 'He met somebody else, and as it turns out, Janet couldn't be objective about it. She's very immature.'

Poor Janet, oh poor, poor Janet. I know she truly loved Ed. And Ed was so nice, and then he just dumps her?

'Do you have any idea who the new girl is?' I ask.

'Well, of course I do,' Lily snaps. 'It's me.'

Oh hell. I can just see it. Ed, so nice, diffident, just starting to really like Janet. But he always had that thing for Lily. Staring at her like a dog slavering over a steak. 'And Henry?'

'He had his chance and he blew it,' she says.

'Lily,' I say, 'you've got problems. I have to go.'

I hang up and dial Janet's cellphone again, but I still get her voice-mail. I look at the clock by my bedside: 2 p.m. I don't want to think about any of these disasters, mine, Janet's, Henry's. But I have to. I can't let things stand like this. Hastily I pack up a little overnight case.

I catch the high-speed train into Paddington and get a cab to the flat. I let myself in with a spare set of keys I forgot to give back to Lily, then call Janet at her new number.

'Hi, how's it at home?' she asks, without enthusiasm. God, she sounds so down. As if she's talking through a blanket of fog.

'Never mind about that. I need a place to stay. Just for a week while I sort myself out.'

'But you're with your parents.'

'Not any more,' I tell her. 'I need to be in London. Job-hunting. I'm desperate. Please?'

Janet is momentarily shocked out of her depression. She didn't expect a cry for help. 'Sure,' she says. 'It's pretty grotty,' she warns me.

I scribble down the address, call another cab, and I'm over there in half an hour. Janet opens the door. She looks wrecked. Her lovely olive skin has gone sallow, her eyes are red and puffy from crying. 'What happened?' she asks.

'I can't face living at home any more,' I tell her, part truthfully. 'And I'm about to have a huge row with Lily and I need your help.'

'Why are you going to have a huge row with Lily?'

'Because she's stolen some of my money,' I lie, easily enough. Definitely getting better at that. 'She won't give back my deposit. And I need back-up from you.'

'No way,' Janet recoils. 'I can't go and see her again. Ever. Besides, he might be there. He's been calling here . . . my cellphone.'

'Oh?' I perk up. 'What's he been saying?'

'I don't take his messages,' Janet says, trying to look dignified.

'But you can't let Lily steal my money,' I plead. 'I need my deposit back. And you can say I didn't wreck my room.'

'Is that what she's saying?' asks Janet. 'She's such a cow.'

'And Ed's not in London,' I lie. 'He's staying in the country with his parents. Lily told me. Please, let me call her and arrange something.'

Janet wavers. 'Well, let me just go and have a shower and put something on,' she says.

I call Lily when Janet's safely in the shower. 'I need to come round and return the spare keys. I took them home with me by mistake.'

'Oh. All right, I suppose.'

'Is Ed with you?' I ask.

'Yes,' she says. 'Why?'

'Well, I should say hello to both of you. You know, as a couple. Ed and Charles are cousins. We're going to be seeing a lot of each other if this works out for you. Charles and I are thinking of getting back together,' I extemporise. 'So will he be there with you later? About half an hour? I'd like to say hi. Maybe Charles will be with me, I'm not sure.'

'Oh, yes. Charles is such a sweetie,' says Lily smoothly. 'Of course, *do* come over, I think a family get-together would be lovely.'

We take the tube down to Tottenham Court Road and get out and walk. Janet wants to bottle out, but I keep telling her I need her as my witness, to get the money back. We knock on the door.

Lily opens it. I shove Janet inside.

'What the hell are you doing here?' Lily sneers at Janet. She's wearing a slinky little black dress and is made up to the nth degree. Ed, on the other hand, is perching nervously on the end of our couch in a Hugo Boss suit. It looks bloody awful on him. I've seen startled racehorses that look more comfortable than Ed does now.

When he sees Janet, it's hard to say which of them looks more horrified. Janet gives a strangled cry and makes for the door. But I'm blocking it. 'Ed,' I say. 'What the hell are you doing? You broke up with Janet in order to date a woman who is only interested in your money.'

'Please don't,' says Janet, starting to cry.

'How dare you,' shrieks Lily. 'I love Ed for himself! Get out!'

'That's not true,' I say, looking at Ed. 'She wanted nothing to do with you back when she thought you were poor, and she tried to talk Janet out of dating you. But Janet stayed true.'

'Rubbish!' squeals Lily. 'That's complete nonsense.'

'How could you dump somebody that cared about you like that?' I demand. 'Ed, how could you?'

Ed shoots to his feet. When Janet starts to cry properly he can't help himself. He bounds over to her, grabbing her hands. 'Please,' he says desperately. 'Janet, don't, don't . . .'

'It's all a bloody stunt, she'll get over it,' Lily snarls. 'Let her go.'

'I can't,' Ed says, miserably. 'I'm sorry, Lily. I—I love her. I tried to call you,' he says to the sobbing Janet. 'I tried to find you. I was so sorry . . .

it was just a moment's madness . . . when you caught us kissing . . .'

'Madness?'

'Yes,' he says. 'Lily had . . . her cardigan slipped and I . . .'

'Slipped, right,' I snort.

'You're actually falling for this?' Lily yells. 'I can't believe you! You need me, Ed! You wanted me!'

'I wanted you,' he admits. 'But needed you . . .' He turns Janet's face towards him and kisses down the salty tracks on her cheeks.

'Well,' says Lily. 'I hope you're happy, Anna, ruining my life like that.'

'I haven't,' I say to her. 'You're in love with Henry. You're just afraid. You were horrible to Janet when her modelling career went wrong because you think it's going to happen to you, soon.'

'No, it isn't!' she shrieks. 'Shut up!'

'And you don't think you can do anything else,' I continue, relentlessly. 'You think that as soon as your beauty's gone it's all over for you. That's why you're looking so desperately for rich guys you don't even care about. Because you think your looks are all you're worth.'

'Liar!' Lily half screams. And then she bursts into tears, sobbing, great heaving, wrenching sobs that make Janet's waterworks look totally unimpressive. Janet comes over to hug her, horrified.

Ed says quietly, 'Excuse me,' and withdraws into the hallway. I hope he isn't about to bail.

'You—you don't know what it's like,' Lily shudders. 'You've got no idea what it's like to think about your looks every single day.'

I smile faintly. 'Actually, you'd be surprised.'

'Every line,' Lily says. 'Every hair, every tiny wrinkle . . . I use all the products but it doesn't help. It's easy for you, you've got a degree,' she sobs. 'I've got no qualifications. All I know is modelling.'

'So become a scout. Start an agency,' I suggest. 'You know what it takes, you know the photographers, the ad executives.'

Lily's sobs calm down just a little. 'Do—do you really think I could?'

'You'd be great at it,' Janet encourages her. 'You could always tell which girls would make it and which wouldn't. You knew I wouldn't.'

Lily looks at her shoes. 'Sorry for being such a bitch,' she says. It's almost inaudible, but it'll do.

Ed walks back into the room.

'I just called Henry,' he says. 'He's on his way over.'

'Oh God,' Lily says, panicking. 'No. I can't see him. I can't. What can I say to him?'

'Sorry?' suggests Ed. 'That's what I said to him. Took it quite well. Good chap, Henry.'

'You know,' I tell Lily, 'you've got to start by getting some courage up. You've got to see Henry and tell him the truth. Just apologise and explain why you did it. You'll feel better.'

'I'll do that,' she says. 'Thanks, Anna. You made me face up to some things.'

'It'll be OK,' I say. And for her, I think it will.

Ed and Janet leave, but Lily wants me to stay, so I sit with her curled on the couch and hug her while she cries.

'And what about you?' Lily asks, blowing her nose loudly.

'I don't understand.'

'Oh yes you do,' says Lily, her reddened, still-lovely eyes narrowing shrewdly. 'You broke up with Charles over that Mark Swan man and he still has no idea you want to go out with him.'

'That's different,' I say. 'He's got someone else, Henry doesn't.'

'Is he married?'

'Not yet.'

'Then you should still tell him.'

I shake my head. 'You should see his girlfriend.'

'I don't know if you've noticed, Anna,' says Lily patiently, 'but since Janet made you over you've been looking different. Better. You know, men could fancy you,' she says, encouragingly. I can't even be cross; Lily isn't going to change her whole personality in five minutes, and at least now she means well. 'I bet he was interested in you. On some level you know he was, or it wouldn't hurt. Women always know.'

I look at her with new eyes.

'I'm not as stupid as I look,' Lily says.

'You're not stupid, you're . . . you're canny,' I tell her. 'But you know, he had a long time to say something to me. And he never did.'

'All that time he thought you were going out with Charles.'

That's true.

'Just call him,' Lily says, shoving the phone at me. 'Otherwise you'll spend the rest of your life wondering.'

There's a knock on the door. 'Hi, Henry,' I say, opening the door before Lily can respond. He's got a wild look in his eyes, and glances from me to Lily. 'I was just leaving,' I reassure him. 'See you guys later.'

I walk out of the door and close it on Henry folding Lily into his arms.

She's right. I mean, what do I have to lose? Nothing important. Hope. Self-esteem. Face. But still. I will always, always wonder.

I'm going to Swan Lake Productions. If I'm going to do this it's got to be right. Whether he says yes or no, I have to see him. Even if Michelle's there. Especially if Michelle's there. I don't want to go behind her back.

I almost want to smile. If this goes wrong, and let's face it, it's going to, it will be the single most awful, embarrassing moment of my life. It'll be worse than that bloody school dance.

But somehow it doesn't matter. I feel so much lighter, so much freer. This will finish it, one way or the other.

I enter Swan Lake. The security guard is snoring behind his desk, so I slip quietly into the lift, ride up to Mark's floor, feeling sick.

'What the fuck do you want?' snaps Michelle. 'You're not on the list. Did that moron downstairs let you up again? I'm going to get him fired.'

She's wearing a simple white T-shirt and jeans, and even with my smart little outfit (shirt dress, kitten heels, chunky amber necklace) and my killer haircut and pro make-up she knocks me for six.

'I snuck up,' I say. 'I want to see Mark.'

'Not without an appointment,' Michelle says stiffly.

'I want to see him because I'm in love with him and I want to tell him that,' I blurt out.

She laughs, a fierce, hostile laugh. 'I *knew* it,' she says. 'Knew you were just like all the others. And you with a fiancé!'

I show her my bare left hand. 'I broke up with him. I need to tell Mark. I know you're going out with him. But I want him to break up with you and be with me,' I say.

'Do you realise how stupid you sound?' she demands. 'Just leave! Don't make me call security. I won't tell him how you embarrassed yourself, it happens to lots of women around Mark.'

I look at her, long and hard. Something in her voice. It's . . . it's *panicky*. She keeps glancing at Mark's inner office. And then it hits me, in an overwhelming burst of sheer joy. 'And you're one of them! Aren't you? He's not going out with you, he never was. I should have known.'

'What the hell do you know about it?' Michelle asks, her young face crumpling. Her eyes fill with tears. 'He could have gone out with me! He would have, eventually. If it hadn't been for *you*,' she hisses.

'What do you mean?'

'Why can't you just go away?' she asks, and then she starts crying. 'You don't know what it's like, sitting here day after day. Booking lunch places for all the little girlfriends, and then he meets you, and you don't even want him, you're with somebody else.'

I fish out a Kleenex from my bag. 'I'm sorry,' I say.

'You had to take two men,' she says, sobbing. 'You couldn't leave any for anybody else, even people that love them . . .'

I walk awkwardly towards her and rub her on the back. Is that how

165

she sees me, some sort of femme fatale? 'I honestly love him,' I tell her.

'I know,' she mutters.

The door opens and Swan is standing there. He looks at me with my arm round Michelle. 'Anna,' he says. 'What the hell's going on?'

Michelle looks at me, her expression hunted.

'Michelle just found out her . . . auntie died,' I say.

Swan looks at the two of us again. 'OK,' he says. 'Why don't you take the rest of the day off, Michelle. I can get the phones.'

Michelle nods, grabs her bag and exits without looking back.

'You'd better come in,' he says to me.

I walk in behind him, sit down on one of his couches. Swan sits down opposite me. I glance over towards his desk, and see something familiar. It's the boxed Sony Vaio he bought me as an engagement gift, still in its wrapping paper. 'You got it back then,' I say.

He nods.

'I split up with Charles,' I try.

'So I gathered,' Swan says drily. 'From your friend Vanna.'

'Aren't you going to say anything?' I ask, desperately, when he doesn't add anything. 'Aren't you going to ask me how, or why?'

'Why should I?' he demands. 'You expect to just walk back in here, Anna, and have me fawning all over you? Why should I care what you do with your life?'

I stand up. 'You're . . . you're right. I'm sorry, this was a huge mistake.'

So that's it. I turn on my heels, I don't want to cry in front of him.

A large hand comes down on my shoulder. Swan spins me back round. Forces me to look up at him towering over me.

'Where the hell do you think you're going?' he asks. 'You're not walking out on me again, Anna Brown.'

'Mark . . .' I say. I can hardly breathe.

'You were going to marry someone else,' he says. 'Somebody you didn't even love. And then you finally break up with him, and what happens? You don't even call. What was it, Anna? Still throwing that tantrum because I wouldn't help you hamstring your own career? Your script wasn't ready. You weren't ready.'

'I thought you didn't care about me,' I mutter.

'Didn't care? Damn, you're frustrating,' he says, shaking his craggy head. 'I'm the one who started you writing. I'm the one who got you to do what you really loved. You'd think you would have trusted me, but no. Because I wasn't going to send you out there with something half-baked, I don't care.'

I look at him, not daring to hope. Trying not to hope.

'You only see what you want to see,' he says, bitterly. He lets me go and moves away. 'And when you break up, and I think maybe . . .'

'Maybe what?'

'But you don't even give me the courtesy of a phone call. As soon as I wouldn't help your so-called career, you didn't care about me any more.'

I think of Michelle. Poor Michelle. I can't tell him the truth.

'It wasn't that. I didn't think you'd want me,' I mutter.

Swan blinks. The rage is gone from his face. He looks *astonished*. 'Excuse me?' he demands. 'Why the hell would you think that?'

I make a gesture at my face, at my nose. 'Men don't fancy me.'

'The hell they don't,' Swan says.

'But my nose . . .'

'Is beautiful,' he says. 'Like the rest of you.'

'Give over,' I say scornfully. 'I'm tall and strong and—'

'You're not tall from where I'm standing. And anyway, what's wrong with tall? I'm tall. Should I be offended?' Swan asks, with just a touch of humour. 'And stop fishing for compliments.'

'What?'

'Oh, you know how lovely you are,' he says. 'Those breasts . . .'

I blush.

'Those legs. Those eyes. Your hair. You look even prettier since you started showing it off.'

'I didn't think you'd noticed.'

'I notice everything.'

'But I'm not thin . . .'

'So what?' he says. 'I can't stand that anorexic look. You're gorgeous.'

'Maybe if I got a nose job . . .'

'Over my dead body,' he says. 'You've got an interesting face, not like all those two-dimensional bimbos.'

'You fancied me?' I ask. Pathetic, I know. But I can't help myself. 'You're not joking?'

'Are you delusional?' He moves towards me again, stands right next to me. Looking me over, head to toe. A sweeping look, full of intent. 'I hate the word fancy,' he says softly. 'I don't fancy you, I *want* you.'

I go all liquid. Instantly.

'I liked how you looked, but I didn't want you because of that. I fell for you because of . . . I don't know. Your sense of humour. Your fearlessness. Your intelligence.'

'Really?' I whisper.

'Because you're just Anna,' he says. 'You're not like anyone else. You're . . . Anna.'

'I'm in love with you,' I say.

'I know that,' he says. 'But I thought you didn't. Or you knew it, but didn't care. Is that why you came here today?'

I nod.

'Not to ask me for help with your career?'

I shake my head. 'I don't want your help. I'm rewriting. I want to make it on my own.'

He chuckles. 'Not a chance, baby. I'm going to pull strings like you wouldn't believe.' He looks down at me, and gently kisses me on the mouth. His lips just brushing against mine, just a feathery, electric touch. A wave of wanting crashes all through me.

'Will you go out with me?' I whisper.

Swan gathers me into his arms. My weight is nothing to him. 'I'd much rather stay in with you,' he says. 'What are your plans?'

'For when?'

'For the next sixty years,' he says. 'We can start with that.'

And then he kisses me again.

LOUISE BAGSHAWE

Louise Bagshawe has never been afraid of starting new chapters in her life. After graduating from Oxford University, where she was Young Poet of the Year in 1989 and former President of the Rock Society, her love of music took her into the record business. At only twenty-three, however, Louise decided that that was not the industry for her and wrote her first novel. Since then, she has never looked back. *Monday's Child* is her eighth best seller and she has also written several screenplays.

Her writing and involvement in the film industry took Louise to live and work in Los Angeles, but another new chapter began when she met a New Yorker. 'I met Anthony on a blind date at the British Museum—he'd flown over from New York especially for it,' she told me. 'The moment I met him, I felt as though I'd known him for years.' The couple are now married and work together, buying and renting property in New York. 'My husband values houses so he is the expert. Our dream is that by the time we are thirty-five we will have enough rental income to retire and never have to work again.'

Besides being an up-and-coming property mogul, Louise has recently become a mother—her son Caius is eleven months old—and she is also writing her next novel, *Tuesday's Child*. 'It stars a girl who is a bit of a tomboy with no social graces—the flaw in each girl in the series is linked to the rhyme.

I usually write as early in the morning as possible, while Caius is still asleep. I love being a mum, but I never fully realised how horrendously exhausting it is. I adore having Caius on my lap and reading to him and I love it when he crawls round the room trying to kiss our poor fat pug, who waddles away as fast as she can—which isn't very fast!'

I asked Louise, who has just turned thirty-three, how she felt about getting older and whether her experience of the publishing and film industries have led her to believe that writers have to be young and chic to succeed? 'The good news is that the older you get, the less you care about ageing. I was depressed when I turned nineteen because it was my last year of being a teenager. Now I say, roll on fifty! My mother told me once that every stage of life has its own pleasures and if you cling too hard to one stage you miss the fun of the next. And with writing, talent is the *only* thing that counts. I just heard today from a lady who sold her first screenplay at fifty-two years old!'

So what is next for Louise Bagshawe? 'I loved living in L.A,' she told me, 'as it's far more laid back than New York. But neither of them are a patch on England. I can't wait to return home and we are planning to come back to the UK to live just as soon as my second baby, due in November, is big enough. I am counting the minutes.'

Jane Eastgate

The
Alphabet
Sisters

Happy birthday

80

Carrie

MONICA
McINERNEY

Anna, Bett and Carrie Quinlan used to be known as the Alphabet Sisters, childhood singing stars who performed in shows up and down the Clare Valley, Australia. But that was years ago, before they stopped talking to one another and split up for good.

Now Lola, their feisty grandmother, has summoned them home for her eightieth birthday . . . to make a shock announcement that will change their lives for ever.

CHAPTER ONE

London, England

'YOUR SISTER IS MARRIED to your ex-fiancé?' Jessica's voice rose to such a pitch Bett Quinlan half expected the light bulbs to explode. 'We've worked together for nearly two years and you tell me this now?'

Bett knew right then she had made a big mistake. 'It didn't ever really come up until now.'

'Something like that doesn't need to come up. That's something you tell people within minutes of meeting. "Hi, my name's Bett, short for Elizabeth. I work as a journalist in a record company and my sister is married to my ex-husband."'

'Ex-fiancé,' Bett corrected. She tried to backtrack. 'Look, forget I mentioned it. I'm fine about it. She's fine about it. He's fine about it. It's not a big deal.' Liar, liar.

'Of course it's a big deal. It's a huge deal. And they'll both be at your grandmother's party? No wonder you're feeling sick about it.'

'I'm not feeling sick about it. I said I was a bit nervous about going home for it, not sick.'

'Tomato, tomayto. Oh, Bett, you poor thing. Which sister was it? The older one or the younger one?'

'The younger one. Carrie.' Bett felt like the words were being squeezed out of her.

'And what happened? Were they having an affair behind your back? You came home from work early one day and caught them at it in your marital—sorry, engagement—bed?'

'No, it wasn't like that.' Bett stood up. She'd definitely made a mistake. That afternoon at work she'd decided to invite her friend and

173

colleague Jessica back for dinner to tell her the whole story. She'd hoped it would help make this trip back to Australia easier. Prepare her for people's reactions again, like a dress rehearsal. But it wasn't helping at all. She ran her fingers through her dark curls. 'Can I get you a coffee? Another glass of wine?'

'No, thanks. Don't change the subject. Did you go to the wedding?'

Bett sat down again. 'I didn't, no.'

'Well, no, of course you didn't. It would have been too humiliating.'

She blinked at Jessica's bluntness.

'So who was the bridesmaid? Your older sister? Anna?'

'No, she wasn't there either.'

Jessica frowned. 'Neither of her sisters were there? What? Did it cause some huge fight between the three of you?'

In a nutshell, yes. 'It was a bit like that.'

'And you haven't spoken to either of your sisters since the wedding?'

'No.' Bett shifted uncomfortably in her seat. 'Not for three years.'

'Your grandmother's party will be the first time you've seen your sisters in *three* years?' At Bett's nod, Jessica gave a low whistle. 'No wonder you went so weird when that fax from your grandmother arrived.'

'I didn't go weird.'

'Yes, you did. Have you got any photos of your sister and your fiancé together?'

'Why? Don't you believe me?'

'Of course I do. I just need to get the whole picture of it in my head, so I can give you all the advice you need.'

'I'd rather you didn't—'

'Please, Bett. You know how much I love looking at photos.'

That much was true. Jessica was the only person Bett had ever met who genuinely enjoyed looking at other people's holiday photos.

'Thanks, anyway, but—'

'Bett, come on. You've told me half of it. I may as well see the rest.'

Bett gave in, picking up the small photo album lying on top of a bookcase. The only photos in it were those her parents and Lola had sent.

As Jessica gleefully started turning the pages, Bett picked up a music magazine, trying to pretend she wasn't watching her friend as she pored over each photo. She wondered how her sisters would have reacted in the same situation. Anna would have given Jessica a haughty stare and chilled her into silence. Carrie would have tossed her blonde head and told her laughingly to mind her own business. But not Bett. Thirty-two years old and she still hadn't learned how to stand up for herself.

'Is that your mum and dad?'

Bett glanced at a photo of her parents, arm in arm in front of the main motel building, wearing matching Santa hats, squinting into the sunshine. They'd sent it in their Christmas card the previous year. 'That's right.'

Jessica read the sign behind them. 'The Valley View Motel. Is that where you grew up?'

'We moved around a lot when we were younger, but that's where they are now.'

Jessica nodded and turned the page. 'And this is Lola? The old lady wearing too much make-up?'

Bett didn't even have to look at the photo. 'That's her.'

'Would you look at those eyebrows! They're like caterpillars on a trampoline. She was your nanny, did you tell me?'

'Sort of.' Lola had certainly minded them as children. With their parents so occupied running the motels, it was Lola, their father's mother, who had practically brought up Bett and her two sisters—but she was more a combination of etiquette teacher, boot-camp mistress and musical director than nanny.

'Is she wearing fancy dress in this next photo?'

Bett glanced over. It was a picture of Lola beside her seventy-ninth birthday cake, nearly twelve months earlier. She was wearing a gaudily patterned kaftan, dangling earrings and several beaded necklaces. Nothing too out of the ordinary. 'No, that's just her.'

Jessica kept flicking the pages, and then stopped suddenly. Bett tensed, knowing she had reached Carrie and Matthew's wedding photo. Bett had wanted to throw it away the day she received it, but had stopped herself. She hadn't wanted her grandmother to be right. It was Lola who had sent the photo to her, enclosing a brief note: *You'll probably get all dramatic and rip this up but I knew you'd want to see it.*

'This is them?' Jessica asked.

'That's them.'

Jessica studied it closely. 'Carrie's very pretty, isn't she? And he's a bit of a looker too, your Matthew. Nice perm.'

At least Jessica hadn't said what people usually said when they remarked how pretty Carrie was: 'You don't look at all alike, do you?' As for her other remark . . .

'He's not my Matthew. And it wasn't a perm. He's got naturally wavy hair.'

Jessica grinned. 'Just seeing if you would defend him.' She turned the page and gave a hoot of laughter. 'I've been dying to see proof of the Alphabet Sisters. Look at you with that mad head of curls.'

Bett tugged self-consciously at that same head of curls, now at least slightly less mad. Lola had sent her that photo, too. It had arrived with just a scrawled note, subtle as ever. *Remember the good times with your sisters as well.* It had been taken at a country show in outback South Australia more than twenty years previously, at one of the Alphabet Sisters' earliest singing performances. Anna had been thirteen, Bett eleven and Carrie eight.

Jessica was inspecting it very closely. 'You were a bit of a porker back then, weren't you?'

The smile disappeared. 'Well, that was nicely put, Jess, thanks.'

Jessica was unabashed. 'I always believe in calling a spade a spade. And you were a plump little thing. Look at that little belly and those rosy-red cheeks.'

Bett didn't need to look. That little belly and those rosy-red cheeks had never gone too far away.

Jessica was taking in every detail, the flicked fringes, the matching dresses, the bad make-up—all Lola's handiwork. She glanced up at Bett. 'You're not very alike, are you? Even apart from the appalling eye make-up and the different hair colours. Unless they're wigs?'

'No, all our own work, I'm afraid.' Anna had straight black hair, Bett's was dark brown and Carrie's dark blonde. She presumed her sisters' hair colours hadn't changed in three years. She'd find out soon enough. In less than two weeks, in fact. Her stomach gave a lurch.

The fax from Lola in South Australia had arrived at Bett's office out of the blue, just the one line. If Bett didn't come home for her eightieth birthday party, she would never talk to her again.

Bett had rung her immediately. 'Lola, don't do this to me, please,' she'd said, straight to the point as soon as her grandmother answered. 'You know what it'll be like.'

'Elizabeth Quinlan, stop being such a baby. You're scared of seeing your sisters. So what? I'm nearly eighty and I could die any moment. Now, hang up, book your ticket and get here as soon as you can. I've got something I want you to do.'

Lola had obviously taken her extra-strength bossy tablets that day. 'I can't drop everything just like that, Lola. I've got a life here now.'

'And you've got a grandmother in Australia who has missed you very, very badly and wants to see you again.' Her voice had softened. 'Please, Bett. Come home. For me.'

In the end Bett had compromised. Yes, she would come back for the party, but it would be a lightning trip. She'd arrive in South Australia on the day and leave as soon as possible afterwards.

Lola hadn't been pleased. 'But I need you here for longer than that.'

'I can't, Lola. I've got a life here,' she'd repeated firmly.

Beside her, Jessica was going through the album again. 'It's a tricky one, that's for sure. Your first meeting with your sisters and the happy couple in three years, not to mention the added tension of a party.' She shut the album with a snap. 'I'd say it's going to be ferocious.'

Sydney, Australia

ANNA QUINLAN KNEW that less than a mile away the waters of Sydney Harbour were probably glinting in the sun, to a soundtrack of ferry horns, gull cries and tourist-guide commentaries. She'd been trapped inside this coffin of a recording studio for three hours now, trying to get the voice right for a range of kitchen sponges.

She peered through the glass of the studio window again, counting to ten as she caught sight of the client. He looked like a suit-wearing spotty child who surely couldn't have driven himself to the studio today. She snapped back to attention as Bob, the producer/technician, pressed the button on the intercom so his voice came into her headphones.

'Anna, Henry feels you are really getting there, but he wonders whether you could combine the laugh in your voice from that first take with the kind of bubbling tone you did on the one before that.'

Henry leaned towards the microphone. 'Yes, loved that bubbly sound, Anna. Just perfect for our demographic. You don't mind, do you?'

Mind? Mind that she had spent three hours saying one sentence in dozens of different voices? Mind that the preschooler in the suit had tried to describe the mind-set of a kitchen sponge to her? 'It's determined, it's energetic, it's fun . . .'

No, it's not, Henry, she'd thought. It's a square of detergent-soaked sponge with a scouring pad on one side. It isn't Russell Crowe.

She bit her tongue. Whatever you do, Anna, keep cool, keep smiling. She'd learned that lesson after years of unsuccessful auditions for parts. No one wanted a moody actress.

Anna looked at Bob for help and some of her frustration must have shown on her face. He spoke again, surreptitiously inclining his head towards the client. 'Anna, perhaps if you visualised yourself in the sink, getting psyched up to help clear all those dirty dishes. And there's one particularly greasy pot that's going to need special energy, but you know it will be worth it to scrub like mad until every spot is gone.' Another barely noticeable nod at the client. 'Whenever you're ready. Tape's running.'

It worked a treat. Staring through the glass, seeing her sharp bobbed hair and immaculate make-up reflected back at her, Anna imagined Henry evolving into a dirty saucepan. She imagined herself as the sponge, leaping out of nowhere and scouring his face until every spot and blackhead had disappeared. She leaned towards the microphone. 'Let me at it! I'm the clean machine!'

Henry's pimply face broke into a huge smile. 'That's it. Perfect.'

Anna had just leaned down to pick up her bag when his voice came in again. 'But would you be able to do it one more time? I think it needs just a touch more softness.'

An hour later Anna was driving out of the studio car park. The voice of the sponge was now lodged in her head and she knew from experience it would stay there for the next few days. Last month her voice had varied between a kitten stuck up a tree (for a cat food commercial), a warm-hearted nurse (health insurance) and a cake waiting to be iced.

Her seven-year-old daughter, Ellen, loved it. Lying sleepily in bed listening to a good-night story, she'd pick and choose the voices. 'Mum, can you read this one like the Zoomer Broom?' The Zoomer Broom featured in a TV commercial where the ordinary household broom metamorphosed into something Harry Potter could have used for Quidditch, babbling nonsensically all the while. Ellen's other favourite was a gurgly underwater voice.

Anna parked in the street across from the hospital, ten minutes late. Hurrying towards the lift, she composed her face, already hearing the disapproving tones from her neighbour, who had grudgingly agreed to collect Ellen after school and bring her here to the clinic for her latest appointment. The lift door opened and Anna spied her little daughter in the distance, chatting to one of the staff. In the dozens of hospital visits since Ellen's accident, she had got to know all the nurses very well. Anna tensed, as she always did when she remembered the trauma of those first months. She decided it was time Ellen had a good spoiling: she'd give her whatever she wanted for dinner, let her watch whatever video she wanted, and then read her all the stories she wanted, as well.

But by nine o'clock Anna's patience was wearing thin. Ellen still wouldn't settle. She stood in the doorway of the living room now, tears on her face. 'Is Dad home yet?'

Anna kept her voice mild with effort. 'No, darling, he's not.'

'Where is he?'

'At work, I think.' She didn't have a clue where Glenn was. He didn't ring and tell her any more.

'Can you read me another story, then?'

'Sweetheart, you've had enough stories. It's time to sleep.'

'I can't sleep. I'm scared again. I keep remembering.'

The doctor's voice came into Anna's mind. 'There will be some post-traumatic stress and recurring fear, but it's important you learn to listen without making too much of it. Children are very skilled at knowing which buttons to press.' She pulled herself up out of the deep sofa. 'All right, Ellie. You hop back into bed and pick another story. I'll be there in a moment.'

By the time Anna got to the bedroom, Ellen had changed her mind. 'Can I hear Really-Great-Gran's tape?'

The tape had arrived from Lola more than two years earlier, with a note to Anna attached. *This is for you to play to Ellen. I'm still having no part of this nonsense between you and your sisters but I'm not losing a great-granddaughter because of it.*

Anna put the tape in, then lay on the bed beside Ellen, stroking her dark hair back from her face as Lola's Irish-accented voice filled the room. 'Hello, Ellen. This is your great-grandmother speaking. Now, my little dote, I've been giving a lot of thought to what you should call me and I think I've come up with the best solution. Your scoundrel of a mother started calling me Lola when she was just a child and her two sisters followed suit, but you need a different name for me, I think. And not just Great-Grandmother. I'm much better than great. So, my darling, I would like you to call me Really-Great-Gran from now on. OK?'

There was a pause on the tape.

'Are you listening, Ellen?' Lola asked.

'Yes,' Ellen answered sleepily beside Anna.

The voice on the tape continued. 'Good girl. And are you happy with that? Happy to call me Really-Great-Gran?'

'Yes, Really-Great-Gran,' Ellen answered in the pause. She knew this ritual off by heart.

'Good girl. Now, I'm going to tell you a few stories about your mother and your grandfather, but first I'm going to sing you one or two of my favourite songs. So settle back and relax.'

Relax? Anna bit her lip as Lola started warbling 'Don't Sit Under the Apple Tree' in her falsetto voice. The last thing Lola's voice would make you do is relax. She could clear a room in seconds. Ellen didn't seem to mind. Her lids were getting heavier by the second, her lips mouthing the words along with her great-grandmother. Anna smiled, remembering the song. It was one of the first ones Lola had taught Anna and her sisters. There'd been a row over who got to sing the high notes.

Lola reached a shrieking crescendo, then paused on the tape, as if expecting her performance to be followed by rapturous applause. 'One of my favourites, Ellen. As is this one. Sing along with me, darling.'

As Lola embarked on 'The Good Ship Lollipop' Anna glanced down. Ellen was fast asleep.

Back in the living room, Anna poured herself a glass of wine and pressed the TV remote control. She stared at the screen, trying to pick up the plot of the thriller, fighting the desolate feeling inside her that seemed to be rising closer to the surface each day. One phrase kept occurring to her. *I'm lonely*. Lonely. Yet she had friends in Sydney, didn't she? Not any more. They had all slipped away the past year or so, like extras in a film, Anna thought. She couldn't blame them. Who would want to be around to see how she and Glenn treated each other?

She put down the glass and rubbed her face with her hands. She wanted to talk to her sisters again. She wanted to tell them both how awful things had become with Glenn, especially since Ellen's accident.

She could ring her mother or father at the motel, but she'd never really confided in either of them. She could ring Lola, but lately those calls hadn't been having the calming effect they used to. For the first year or two after the Big Fight, Lola had been understanding, trying to see each of their points of view. But understanding had turned to exasperation and then, for the past six months, there had been silence on the subject.

A scream on the TV made Anna jump. A young blonde detective was being chased down a dark street by two men. 'Oh, shush, would you,' Anna said aloud. She pressed OFF and put the remote control on the shelf under the coffee table. As she did she noticed the mail in a pile beneath the free local newspaper. How many times had she asked Glenn not to leave the mail there?

She flicked through the bundle: bills, advertising material—and a thick cream envelope. She turned it over, recognising the handwriting immediately. How long had that been there? She checked the date— more than two weeks old. Puzzled, she tore it open. It was an invitation. She read it again. No, not an invitation. A summons.

Clare Valley, South Australia

LOLA QUINLAN TURNED her gaze away from the vineyards visible through the window of the Valley View Motel dining room and back to the table where her youngest granddaughter was sulkily folding serviettes.

'Carrie, are you ignoring me?'

The younger woman kept her head down as Lola came closer.

'That's fine, but don't frown like that, darling. It's very bad for the skin. If you're going to sulk, at least try doing those exercises I showed you, the ones that firm your chin. See, like this.' Lola started grimacing, stretching her lips sideways, then into a tight pout. 'A little alarming for any passers-by, but that's the price we pay for endless beauty, isn't it?'

Carrie started to smile.

'That's more like it,' Lola said. She leaned over and kissed her grand-daughter on the top of the head. At five foot nine, her posture still excellent, Lola towered over Carrie. 'I still love you, you know.'

'If you really loved me, you wouldn't have—'

'Yes, I would have.' Lola collected her handbag. 'Will you be staying on for dinner?'

'No, I'll go home, I think.'

'How are those renovations going?'

Carrie and her husband had bought an old farmhouse several miles south of the Valley View Motel the year before. 'Fine. Slowly.'

Lola was watching her. 'And how is Matthew, Carrie?'

Carrie turned back to the serviettes. 'He's fine. Up to his eyes in sheep manure and vet magazines as usual.'

'You're getting on all right, are you?'

'Yes, thanks.'

'Really?'

Lola was like a human sniffer dog, Carrie thought, still not looking up. 'Really. It's a bed of roses, in fact.'

'Rubbish. No marriage is a bed of roses. That at least was one of the positive things about Edward dying so young. We might have missed out on the good times, but we missed out on some of the bad, boring times as well.' Lola was amazed, as always, at how easily the lies about her husband tripped off her tongue. 'Tell me, do you ever get bored with Matthew, Carrie?'

'Tell me, do you ever think you're overstepping the mark with your questions, Lola?'

'Oh, good Lord, yes. But people are usually so shocked, they've answered before they've had time to think twice. Do you know what I found out in the charity shop this morning? That Mrs Kennedy is stepping out with her son-in-law's father. Having a grand old time, she told me.'

Carrie felt a rush of combined affection and annoyance, her usual reaction to Lola's behaviour. 'That's the only reason you're still working in that charity shop, isn't it? It's nothing to do with helping the poor.'

Lola made an elegant gesture with her hand. 'If people choose to tell me things, there's nothing I can do about it. I see it as my gift to society: helping people unburden themselves of their problems. Now, then, I must be off. I'm going to call on your mother in the kitchen and beg some afternoon tea. I really do have the perfect set-up for an old lady, don't I? A son and daughter-in-law with their own motel and restaurant and a granddaughter who is the sweetest in the world.' Lola gave Carrie another kiss, then swept out of the room, leaving a faint trace of expensive perfume behind her.

Alone in the dining room, Carrie worked quietly until she had folded the last of the serviettes. One hundred paper swans surrounded her. This time in two days the room would be transformed for a wedding reception, the paper swans swimming elegantly up and down the rows of long tables. She sat back and flicked at one of the paper swans with a finger. It toppled, falling against the swan beside it. Within moments a whole row of them had fallen, domino-style. She could have jumped up and stopped them, but instead watched idly as the last dozen or so flipped onto the unswept floor.

She didn't care. At that moment she was sick of it all. She was sick of her job. She was sick of the motel. She was feeling especially sick about her grandmother wanting to throw a huge party for her eightieth birthday and insisting that Bett and Anna attend.

'But why, Lola? Why now? It'll ruin everything,' Carrie had said that morning.

'I've given you all three years to sort it out and you haven't even got to the starting gate. So I'm taking charge once and for all.'

Scooping up the paper swans now and ignoring the state of some of their wings, Carrie replayed the conversation yet again.

'You wouldn't be happy with a nice family dinner, you and me and Mum and Dad?' Carrie had suggested hopefully.

'Of course not. I could die any day and I want to go out with a bang. And I want Anna and Bett to see the explosion. Besides, I've got something important I want the three of you to do for me.'

'Important? What's wrong? Lola, you're not sick, are you?'

'Don't pry, Carrie. I want to talk to the three of you about it once I have you all in the same room together again.'

The three of them. The three of them who hadn't spoken to each other for years, let alone been in the same room. Or the same town. Or the same country even. And whose fault was it? Hers. Who did everyone blame? Her.

But now it had all changed, hadn't it? The reason none of them had spoken to each other in that time no longer existed. Which would make this reunion of Lola's even more hideous and humiliating and horrible than it might have been.

CHAPTER TWO

A WEEK BEFORE HER FLIGHT back to Australia, Bett walked into the record company's office in the centre of London, took off her raincoat, sat down and slowly, rhythmically, banged her head against the pile of papers on her desk.

'Great new move,' Jessica said, wandering over. 'Can't see it taking off in the clubs though.'

Bett looked up, her head still on the desk. 'You should have seen this one, Jess, heard the things he was saying.'

Sprawled on the sofa in the plush Kensington hotel room, the young pop singer had fixed Bett Quinlan with a sincere blue gaze and tossed his head so a lock of blond hair shimmered across his forehead. 'I want to grow with my music but stay close to my beginnings. Most of all, I want to keep it real.'

'Where are our consciences, Jess?' Bett asked now in mock despair. 'We're sending young men to their deaths, armed with nothing but microphones.'

'Rubbish. We're sending them on their way to fame and fortune. You child performers are all the same, pining after more innocent times, when all it took to put on a good show was a few matching outfits and a tinny backing track.'

'Yes, hilarious.' Bett sat up and switched on her computer. Jessica hadn't stopped teasing her about the Alphabet Sisters or the situation with her sisters since the night in Bett's flat. 'I thought you'd promised to leave me alone about all of that.'

'No, I promised to help toughen you up about all of that. Anyway, I can't leave you alone. I have to give you another assignment. Karl phoned from Spain. He wants to work you to the bone till you leave on Friday. Said he must have been off his head giving you that week off to go to your granny's party.' Jessica put the folder on the desk beside her. 'It's this new band from West London he's signed. He wants you to whip up a quick article for the in-store mags.'

'But I can't write about them. I haven't seen them play live yet.'

'That's because they haven't played live yet. Don't even know if they can play live. They probably never will play live. Here, have a look.'

Bett took the biogs and photo. Five children in heavy eye make-up sneered at her. If they were hers she'd tell them to wash that muck off their faces and go and do their homework.

Bett pretended to weep as she opened a new document on her computer screen. As she wrote she started speaking the words aloud in a dull monotone, finding it hard to concentrate. More to the point, finding it hard to care about the sulky-faced brats who she knew had been chosen for their looks rather than any musical talent. She stared out of the window instead, suddenly filled with gloom.

She'd been working in the press office of this small but very successful record company for two and a half years, writing media releases and puff pieces for record-store magazines, as well as training their artists in interview techniques. At the start it had been a dream job, a combination of her love for music and for writing. But lately it had started to wear her down. She'd been feeling the same way about London, even though she had loved it when she first arrived.

The night before she'd been working late. It had been past nine o'clock when she left to catch the tube home and then do the fifteen-minute walk from the station to her basement flat in Camden Town. She was tired, hungry and cold by the time her street was finally in sight. And five steps from her door when she realised she'd left her keys at work.

'In you go, then, love.' The locksmith had taken less than ten seconds to open her door. It had, however, taken him nearly two hours to arrive. Bett was frozen.

'Thanks,' she'd said, through icy-cold lips, handing over fifty pounds.

'Now, love, far be it from me to put myself out of a job, but have you thought about leaving a spare key with friends or family?'

She'd nodded, smiled politely. She'd spent the time waiting for him thinking just that, before realising with a dull aching feeling that not only did she have no family here, but no friends close by either.

She blinked now and dragged her attention back to the computer in front of her. Everything was peachy, wasn't it? She had a great job, she was living in the epicentre of the music industry, she'd never been happier. Not only that, she was about to fly home to Australia, to see Lola and her parents for a week. And yes, all right, Anna and Glenn and Carrie and Matthew would be there, but she was a grown woman and she'd cope. And it would be great to see her niece, Ellen, again too, wouldn't it? Yes. Exactly. She shut her eyes, then opened them again quickly, staring at the computer screen. A new, frightening thought had appeared in large letters in her head.

She didn't want to do this any more. It wasn't about music, it was about packaging. Karl had said as much to her a month ago, on one of his fleeting visits to the office. 'Just a licence to print money, Bett. Stop taking it so seriously. Pop singers, disposable music, remember?'

She looked out of the window at the rain and thought of the Christmas just past. She had celebrated with Jessica and her family at their home in Suffolk, keeping her voice bright and cheery on the phone to her parents and Lola in South Australia. She'd felt miserable inside.

She recalled the words of the travel agent earlier that week. 'It's such a long way to travel for seven days. Are you sure you can't stay longer?'

Her words to Lola the day she'd received the fax flashed into her mind. What had she said? That she couldn't go back to Australia because she had a life here in London? What she had wasn't a life. Not the sort of life she wanted, anyway.

Bett stared over at Jessica, amazed at what she was about to say, and even more amazed by how sure she felt about it. Do it, she thought. Quickly. Before you change your mind.

'Jessica, can you give me Karl's mobile number?'

The other woman glanced up. 'You're going to ring him? That's taking your life in your hands. Why would you want to do that?'

Do it, Bett. Be brave. Go home for good. Bett swallowed. 'I think I'm about to resign.'

In Sydney, Anna Quinlan was finishing her packing. She looked up as her daughter came into the room holding a framed photograph.

'Should I bring this, Mum?'

Anna took the photo. It was the two of them, taken twelve months previously, both smiling at the camera, Ellie's perfect six-year-old face upturned. 'Why do you want to take it, Ellie?'

'So I can show Really-Great-Gran what I used to look like. In case she decides she doesn't like me like this.'

'Ellie, Lola doesn't need to see that. She loves you whatever you look like.'

Ellie's voice became small. 'What if she calls me names, though?'

'Oh, Ellie, she won't. Don't think things like that.' Anna tried to keep her voice steady. It kept happening—just when Anna thought she had things running smoothly, out of the blue there'd be a question like this. Or a loud child's voice in the supermarket like there had been yesterday.

'Mummy, what's wrong with that girl's face?'

'Shh, don't stare.'

Anna had coolly answered the child. 'It's a scar. My daughter was attacked by a dog last year.' She was half tempted to carry a photo album with her. 'See,' she'd say at times like that, 'she was perfect when she was born. But then I took her to the park one afternoon and someone had a Rottweiler on the loose and the dog thought my little girl was a toy. And by the time I could drag her away from him his teeth had torn half her face.'

Anna smoothed back her daughter's hair. 'Ellie, your dad and I and your Really-Great-Gran and your gran and your grandpa love you no matter what you look like.'

'My aunties too?'

Anna's voice didn't change. 'Your aunties too. All of us, no matter what you look like, what you're wearing, how messy your hair is and how bad you smell, OK?'

That brought a glimmer of a smile. 'Even if I smell really bad and haven't brushed my hair for a year?'

'Two years even. Now, put that away and let's finish your packing.'

Ellie put her hands on her hips. 'I have finished. Can we run through our checklist?'

Our checklist? There was something about that solemn little voice and face of hers, that always went straight to Anna's core. She barely noticed Ellie's scar any more. She was aware of it—how could she not be?—but it didn't change the essence of Ellen.

Except Glenn hadn't been able to see it that way. In his eyes, things had changed for ever and it was all Anna's fault.

'I'm not the first man to feel like this, Anna. This happens to lots of marriages after a child trauma like this. I read it on the web.'

Her voice had grown icy. 'You've been researching reasons to back up why you're having an affair? Why you're walking out on us?'

'I'm not walking out on you.'

'Shall we look up the web for other ways to put it, then? Key "selfish" and "immature" into a search engine and see what websites turn up?'

'Anna, you're not making this easy.'

Ellen had heard them fighting, Anna knew that. Ellen also knew Anna and Glenn were sleeping in separate rooms. And that her father wasn't home every night. Anna wanted to tell Ellen it wasn't her fault. He still loves you, Ellie, I know he does, she thought. It's me he doesn't love any more. It's me he blames.

Perhaps things would have been different if they'd been on steady ground before Ellen was attacked. But the foundations had been eroding for years, gaps and holes slowly appearing. Fights about his work taking up too much time. Snide remarks about her great acting career ending up in sound-recording booths. Even digs about her appearance. She'd put on a few pounds a year or two after they married, nothing too serious, so she'd thought. Until Glenn had brought home gym brochures, made pointed remarks about people letting themselves go.

'Me?' she'd said, good-humoured at first. 'Glenn, are you joking? All my clothes still fit, don't they?' Size ten at that. 'I thought you'd like to see me a bit more curvy.'

He hadn't smiled. 'I just want you to look your best.'

And that phrase had been the key, she'd discovered. He loved her, wanted her, but only when she looked her best.

Ellie's arrival had soothed things on one level. Glenn had shifted his attention onto her, showering his daughter with gifts and love, while he withdrew the same things from Anna. Their fights became less regular, the mood shifting from tension to indifference. He had been only mildly interested to hear about the fight between her and her sisters—he'd never met Matthew and had never got on with Bett or Carrie. His attention had turned to work, while she kept her days busy with Ellen and the voice-over jobs.

Until the day in the park changed things for the worse. The long days in hospital were followed by nights of tension at home. Glenn turned further away from her, to his job—and to Julie. Anna was sure of the timing. The late nights working with his PA had only started after Ellen had been attacked. Likewise, the weekends away at supposed conferences, business trips . . .

'Mum? The list?'

Anna focused back on Ellen. 'Ready when you are. Books?'

A nod from Ellen.

'Clothes? Teddies? Puzzles?'

More nods.

'Sounds good to me. You have enough for two weeks?'

Another solemn nod.

She and Ellen had been back to the motel twice in the past three years, timing their two-week visits for when Carrie and Matthew were away on holiday. Ellen had enjoyed every minute, trailing behind Lola most of the time.

'I really like it at the motel. It's peaceful.'

'Peaceful?'

Ellen shuffled, wouldn't look at her. 'No one picks on me there.'

Anna's breath caught. She knew that life in Sydney had been hard for Ellen since the attack. Yesterday's remark in the supermarket hadn't been the first. She crouched down and brushed her daughter's hair away from her face, looking into her eyes. 'Has it been that bad?'

There was a little pause, the smallest of nods and then Ellen started to cry, noiselessly. Anna took her into her arms and held her tight, feeling her daughter's body shuddering against hers. 'Ellie, it's all right, it's fine, it's all right,' she said over and over again. Ellen's tears didn't stop. As Anna rocked back and forth, soothing her, kissing the top of her head, another part of her mind switched into decision-making mode.

Could they stay on after Lola's birthday party? For a month or two? Longer, even? There were good schools in the Valley. Of course, her work could be a problem. She doubted there'd be much demand for a voice-over artist in the Clare Valley. But perhaps she could rearrange her schedule, fly up to Sydney for a day or two a week. Or stop work altogether for a while, living off the money that Glenn, regularly, guiltily, was putting into her bank account. As for coping with seeing Carrie and Matthew every day, well, she'd face that when she had to.

Ellen's sobs had now turned into breathy gulps. Anna stood up, lifting Ellen onto her hip as if she were a toddler. 'I've got a good idea.' Holding her tight with one arm, she reached up into the wardrobe with the other and pulled out a bigger suitcase. 'We might stay away a bit longer than two weeks.'

In the ladies' powder room of the Valley View Motel, Carrie stared at her reflection in the mirror. She cleared her throat. 'Bett and Anna, there's something you should know. Matthew and I have separated. And I'm not going to go into the reasons but, yes, I think it's for good.'

No, too apologetic. And maybe it would be better if she broke the news to them one by one. 'Anna, I want you to know something important. Matthew and I have decided to separate.'

Not bad. But then Anna would be the easiest to tell. Carrie took a breath. 'Bett, I don't want you to gloat but I've got some news for you.'

She was interrupted by a knock at the door. 'Carrie?'

Carrie blushed, embarrassed. How long had her mother been outside? She didn't answer, stood stock-still.

Another brisk knock. 'Carrie, did I hear you talking to yourself in there? Can you come and give me a hand moving these tables? Carrie?' The door handle rattled. 'Are you all right?'

Oh, perfectly all right. Couldn't be better. One final glare, a smoothing of her hair and she unlocked the door. 'Sorry, Mum. I'm coming.'

As petite as Carrie, Geraldine Quinlan was dressed in her usual trim skirt, crisp shirt and sensible shoes. Her hair was as no-nonsense as the rest of her—short, dark, neat.

She gave her daughter a speculative look. 'Is everything all right?'

'Everything's fine, Mum. Thanks.'

'Are you sure?' There was a pause. 'You're not feeling nauseous or . . .'

'No, it's not that,' Carrie said, colouring. Several months back, her mother had caught her reading pregnancy magazines at reception. She hadn't said anything, but there had been a quick exchange of smiles.

Geraldine gave her a similar smile now. 'That's a shame.'

'Mmm,' Carrie said, trying to sound upbeat. If her mother only knew how non-existent that possibility was. She gave a fake laugh. 'No, the only thing making me feel sick is the idea of Lola's birthday party.'

'You're not alone there.' Geraldine's lips tightened. 'I tried to explain to her that events like this need proper organisation, that neither you nor Jim and I can just drop everything. But of course that was like water off a duck's back.'

'I bet it was.' Carrie had actually been talking about the idea of Anna and Bett coming back making her feel sick, not the party itself. 'Still, I suppose it's not every day she turns eighty.'

'No, thank God.' Geraldine glanced at her wristwatch, a functional one bought purely for timekeeping. 'So, can you come and help me move these tables? And I wouldn't mind your help with the new computer program. I still can't make head nor tail of it.'

'Of course.'

In the forecourt of the motel one week later, Len the local butcher slammed the door of his delivery van. 'All set for old Mrs Quinlan's hooley tonight, Jim? Sure you don't want me to DJ again?'

Jim Quinlan remembered the last time Len had DJed at a motel function, when he'd played 'Islands in the Stream' seven times in one night. 'Not this time, Len. No, thanks. You just come along as our guest and enjoy yourself.'

'It's going to be some party, by all accounts.' Len gave a throaty laugh. 'The Alphabet Sisters together again. What I'd give to be a fly on the wall at that first meeting.'

Jim kept his face expressionless. It seemed the entire population of the Valley was hoping to be a fly on the wall at this reunion of his three daughters. 'Good to know my family's providing so much entertainment, Len. I would have thought you'd have plenty of things to keep you busy.'

Len was unabashed. 'Girls will be girls, won't they, Jim? No need to watch soaps with them around the place.'

The phone rang, the sound echoing across the forecourt. Jim knew

Geraldine was at the reception desk and would answer it, but Len didn't. 'Better run, Len. See you tonight. And thanks for the meat.'

Geraldine winked over at her husband as he came in through the front door, rolling his eyes. She concentrated on keeping the warm, friendly tone to her voice. 'That's no problem at all, Mr Lawrence. And you're still happy with that room? Very good. Thank you very much.'

This Richard Lawrence in Room Two was turning out to be the perfect guest, she thought as she hung up. Extending his stay week by week, keeping to himself, and so polite. Such a charming English accent too. Geraldine was mildly curious what he was up to—some sort of writing project, she'd gathered, after seeing the computer and the papers spread round his room when she delivered his breakfast. But she wouldn't dream of asking him for any details about it. Not like some people . . .

She carefully typed the information into the computer on the desk beside her. Carrie had been very persuasive, insisting that it really was very efficient and of course Geraldine would be able to master it. She tentatively pressed SAVE and gave a satisfied sigh, just as a blue station wagon pulled up outside.

A casually dressed man with dark hair leapt out of the driver's seat, reached into the back for a pile of newspapers, then took the steps two at a time and came inside. 'Mrs Quinlan? Your copies of the *Valley Times*, hot off the press. Will I leave them here?'

'Yes, thank you.' He wasn't the usual newspaper delivery man, but he did look vaguely familiar. 'Where's Pat?'

'He had a bit of an accident last night.'

'Not again. Is he all right?'

'Nothing two weeks in a drying-out clinic won't fix.'

'Who are you talking about?'

They both turned. Lola had come in behind them.

'Pat the delivery man from the newspaper office.'

Lola nodded, giving the new arrival a good close look. His hair was a bit long but she liked those laughter lines around his eyes. 'Well, you're certainly far better looking than poor old Pat. You've taken over from him permanently, have you?'

The man laughed. 'No, I'm double-jobbing. I usually do the photographs, but we've divided up his round between us today.'

She peered at him. 'I know you, don't I?'

'I know you, too, I think. From the charity shop. Lola, isn't it?'

'Cheeky monkey. It's Mrs Quinlan to you.'

A hint of a smile again and a glance at both women. 'It's just there are two Mrs Quinlans here. I didn't want to confuse myself.'

Lola clapped her hands. 'Marvellous. A man with a bit of wit about him. Are you married?'

Geraldine interrupted, exasperation in her voice. 'Lola, would you leave the poor man alone? And would you both excuse me, I need to make a few calls before the girls get here.'

'Of course, my dear.' Lola stared at the man, eyes narrowed. 'I have it now. It's Daniel Hilder, isn't it?'

'You've got a very good memory.'

She batted her eyelashes in an exaggerated way. 'I never forget a good-looking face. And I remember you taking those photos when we re-opened the charity shop a few years ago.'

'Lola, please?' Geraldine stood with her hand on the phone and a pained expression.

'We're just leaving, aren't we, Daniel?' Lola took him by the arm and steered him outside. 'Now, what are you doing back in the Valley again? I'm sure someone told me you moved away.'

'I've been in Melbourne the past few years, but I came back six months ago. My mother's still living here and she hasn't been too well recently.'

'You were in Melbourne?' Lola remembered then exactly who he was and why she knew his name. Her smile stretched even wider. 'Well, you're a good kind boy to come and see your mother. Tell me, would you be a good kind boy to me too? I need a little hand in my room with something. Your newspaper deliveries can wait a moment, surely?'

Daniel looked amused. 'Of course they can. Lead the way.'

Geraldine watched, shaking her head, as her mother-in-law led Daniel across the forecourt, talking all the while. God help him, Geraldine thought as she reached for the phone.

'There it is, there it is,' Ellen shrieked. 'There, up on the hill.'

Anna pulled the hire car onto the side of the road and looked out of the opposite window. 'I can't see anything. Are you sure?'

Ellen was laughing now. 'Mum, you're looking the wrong way.'

Anna looked down at her feet. 'No, nothing here.' Then she looked up. 'No, nothing there either. Ellie, your eyesight must be much better than mine.'

'*Muuum.*' Ellie leaned over, placed a little hand on either side of Anna's face and turned it in the right direction. 'See, there.'

'It does look a bit familiar. What does that sign say?'

'It says The Valley View Motel. Vacan . . .' Ellen struggled with the word at first. 'Vacancies. Restaurant and Bar. Function room available. What's function?'

'Another word for a party.'

'Is that where Really-Great-Gran's birthday party will be tonight?'

'I think so.' Anna gazed at the motel. Built in the 1970s, it was a perfect example of the architecture of the time: a series of building blocks, placed clunk-clunk-clunk beside one another on the hillside just north of Clare, the largest town in the Clare Valley. There were fifteen guest rooms, one row of seven facing another row of eight, with the extra room the linen store. Linking the two lines of rooms was the small bar, a tiny reception area, a medium-sized restaurant and kitchen and a large function room. Anna had always thought the motel would make the perfect setting for a retro drama series, right down to the brown carpets, white plastic bathrooms, nylon curtains and orange bedspreads.

'Mum, *come on.*' Ellen was tugging at her arm. 'We're not going to park here, are we?'

'You're sure you're ready? Sure you want to go there?' Anna teased.

Ellen considered the question seriously. 'I am feeling a little bit shy. I haven't seen them for a long time, have I?'

Anna knew exactly how Ellen felt. She was nervous about seeing her sisters again too, she realised. Three years on she still felt caught in the middle—trying to make peace between Carrie and Bett, she'd managed beautifully to make things worse. 'Nothing to be frightened of here, Ellie. They're your family, remember?'

Her cheery tone convinced Ellen, but it did nothing for herself. She wished she felt fresher. It had been only a two-hour flight from Sydney to Adelaide, and then the same length drive from the airport to here. The long straight highway from Adelaide to Clare cut through flat plains and wide yellow paddocks, slowly giving way to the curving roads of the valley with vineyards and tree-covered hills on either side. But she still felt drained. It must be the tension of coming home, she thought. Or the aftermath of emotion from that morning's spat with Glenn. He'd made a point of being there to say goodbye to Ellen.

'You know I'll cry myself to sleep every night while you're away,' he'd said, as he picked the little girl up in a hug. He was so broad it took nothing out of him. Ellen could have been two, not seven.

'Me too,' Ellen had giggled, as Glenn tickled her. She had thrown back her head, laughing, completely unselfconscious with him.

'And don't forget to do me lots of drawings. And to breathe in lots of that country air.' He had done some mock deep breaths, making Ellen laugh even more. 'And you won't forget you're my favourite daughter, will you?'

Ellen shook her head.

'And not only that,' Glenn continued. 'But the best daughter in—'

'—the whole wide world!' Ellen had finished it for him, as she always did.

Anna had received no such attention. She and Glenn had spoken quickly, coldly to each other. She'd been deliberately vague about how long they might be away. He had reminded her of the possibility he'd need to go to Singapore for business, if the office expansion ended up going ahead. She had pretended she had forgotten all about it, knowing it would annoy him. Ellen hadn't noticed a thing—she hoped. She had been too busy waving until her father was long out of sight.

Anna tried to block out those thoughts and smiled across at her daughter now. 'Ready, sweetheart?'

'I'm ready, sweetheart,' Ellen replied, grinning at her own cheekiness. 'But we can't go yet.'

'Why not?'

'You have to look at yourself in the mirror first. That's what you always do.'

Anna laughed. Indeed she did. 'You don't miss a trick, do you, Miss Ellen?' She ostentatiously checked her face in the rearview mirror, wrinkling her nose, baring her teeth, playing up to Ellen's laughs beside her. Then she took a deep breath and started the car.

Anna and Ellen walked through the reception area into the kitchen, surprising her mother who had been wrestling with something in the walk-in freezer. There was a brief hug, then Geraldine turned to Ellen, bending down, giving her a quick hug and kiss.

'Well, aren't you both looking great. Ellen, you must have grown three feet since we saw you last.' Geraldine straightened up, put her hands on her hips and stepped back.

That was the physical contact over for the visit, Anna thought. She knew it wasn't her mother's fault she wasn't a tactile person, but it had been hard at times to be her affection-craving daughter. Anna showered Ellen with hugs and cuddles, more than the child wanted sometimes. Ellen pressed close against her now, still shy, her hair forming a curtain over the right side of her face. It wasn't the first time Geraldine had seen the scar. She had come to Sydney after the accident happened, to lend a hand, much to Anna's surprise. But it was the first time she'd seen her granddaughter in months.

Geraldine busied herself in the kitchen again, passing on news over her shoulder. Anna and her sisters had always laughed at their mother's conversational style. She had to be doing something while she asked questions or relayed information, be it mopping the floor or preparing meals for guests. She'd had the same approach to mothering, in fact—fitting it in around her other, more pressing tasks.

'Carrie will be back in a moment. She's gone into town to collect the last of the flower displays for the party. Bett's flying in today too, of course. Insisted on driving herself up from Adelaide. Lola is around somewhere. I'm surprised she didn't hear the car coming in. Your father had to make a quick trip to the bottle depot this morning but he said he'd be back as soon as he could—'

'He's here now, in fact.'

They both spun round at the sound of his voice. He'd come in through the back door. 'Hello, Anna, and aren't you looking beautiful?'

'Dad! Full of charm as usual,' she said, smiling at him.

'No, just telling the truth. You took after your mother, luckily,' he said with a wink in Geraldine's direction.

Anna was amazed to see her mother get soft-eyed at the praise. Honestly, what were the two of them like? She waited and, sure enough, her father dropped a kiss on her mother's head as he went past her.

'You should be glad your parents get on so well,' Glenn had said in their early days, when she'd tried to explain how excluded she and her sisters had felt. 'Mine fought all the time. Your parents are unusual, though. Business partnerships and marriages don't tend to last.' But her parents had loved working together, making decisions together. Anna had childhood memories of lying in bed at night, hearing her parents come in from locking up the motel, listening to the murmurs of conversations as they talked over their day, planned for tomorrow. That's what she'd wanted, thought she had, when she met Glenn.

Anna reached up to give her father a quick kiss on the cheek, followed by a warm, close hug. He was tall, like Lola and herself, but chubby, not thin, his square, open face red from too much sunshine. She watched intently again as he got down on his haunches to be at eye level with Ellen.

'And welcome to you, Miss Ellen. And aren't you looking beautiful as well? All set for the party tonight?'

Ellen nodded shyly again, struck dumb by the attention.

Jim tousled Ellen's hair. 'Good girl. It's great to have you both home again.'

Ellen stared at him. 'It's not really home. My home is in Sydney.'

Jim gave a roar of laughter. 'You can't call a big city like that home, darling. Home is where the heart is. Isn't that right, Geraldine?'

'That's right, Jim.'

'But isn't my heart in my body all the time?' Ellen asked Anna, looking confused. 'Not just when I'm at home?'

'Grandpa's teasing you, Ellie. Don't mind him.'

'Best advice I've heard all day,' an Irish voice behind them said. 'Hello, my darlings. The birthday girl is here.' It was Lola, dressed in a pink trouser suit, with a small pink rose pinned in her white hair.

'Lola! Happy birthday!' Anna found herself rushing to meet Lola as if she was a child again herself. Now she knew for sure she was home. Lola turned from her hug with Anna, then leaned down with melodramatic groans to Ellen's height, took her face between both hands and then kissed her extravagantly on both cheeks. 'That scar is fading so quickly there must be a miracle at work.'

Anna relaxed. Trust Lola to bring it into the open. Ellen didn't seem to mind, she noticed. She was nodding. 'It is going a bit, I think, Really-Great-Gran.'

Lola gave a shout of laughter and kissed Ellen again. 'You're still calling me Really-Great-Gran, you dear little pet.'

Ellen looked delighted with herself. 'I listen to that tape a lot.'

'You're a little girl with wonderful taste. I know it in my bones.' Lola stood up with another groan. 'Creaking and feeble as those bones might be. It's time for a tour, my dear Ellen. And may I introduce your tour leader for the day. Myself, your Really-Great-Gran.'

Ellen beamed up at her. 'But can I call you Lola, now, Really-Great-Gran? Like Mum does? Now I'm here?'

'You can call me all the names under the sun, my little darling,' Lola said, and swept out of the room with her.

Anna looked out of the kitchen window now and saw Lola and Ellen walking by the back fence. On one side was bushland, on the other the start of the motel grounds, with a strip of bright green lawn, flowers and bedding plants, all her father's work. As she watched, a tubby white sheep trotted up behind Lola and Ellen. Her parents had bought it the year before, to help keep the grass down. Anna saw Ellen's reaction, a shriek and then a push against her great-grandmother, looking for a shield. As her hands clenched, Anna felt her mother's eyes on her and gave an embarrassed smile.

'Sheep have fairly blunt teeth,' Geraldine said. 'She'll be all right with Bumper. Besides, Bumper is so besotted with Lola she only has to whisper a word and he behaves.'

The sheep was now on one side of Lola, Ellen on the other. Lola had a hand on each of their heads and was inclining her head towards one and then another. Lola's voice filtered in. 'Can you feel his lovely soft wool,

Ellen? Sheep have lanolin in their wool. If you ever meet a shearer, ask to shake his hand. You'll never feel softer skin in all your life. Now, let's go and say hello to the chickens. They're a bad-tempered bunch. We won't worry about shaking their claws today.'

Anna turned from the window, a smile on her face. At that moment the kitchen door opened and Carrie walked in, carrying a large bundle of long brown twigs.

Anna's stomach gave a leap and the smile froze. 'Carrie. Hello.'

Carrie stopped short. 'Hello, Anna.'

Anna swallowed, kept a smile on her face. 'You look well.'

'So do you. Have you been here long?'

'About half an hour.'

'How was the trip?'

'Fine, thanks.' Anna forged ahead. 'All set for tonight?'

'Just about, thanks.'

They were standing like two store dummies, stiff and awkward. She tried again. 'Do you need any help?'

Carrie paused. 'No, thanks. Everything's under control.' She glanced around. 'Where's Glenn?'

'He couldn't make it. Work.'

'Oh. And Ellen?'

Lola had seen Carrie's car arrive. She flung open the door with a flourish, talking loudly to Ellen, deliberately interrupting. 'And here we are back in the kitchen. Oh, and look who's here, your Auntie Carrie. Carrie, you remember our beautiful Ellen?'

Carrie turned, and after a flicker of something passed over her face she bent down to her niece, who had gone straight over to Anna. 'Hello, Ellen. It's great to see you again. Did you have a nice trip?'

The little girl nodded, her face pressed against Anna's side.

'She's gorgeous, isn't she?' Lola said proudly. She glanced around, judging the mood. It was like Iceland in here. Time for some defrosting. 'Carrie, don't tell me that pile of twigs over there is for my party, is it? Are we having a bonfire tonight?'

'They're for the flower displays,' Carrie said sulkily. 'You told me you wanted a bush theme.'

'Did I?' Lola asked. 'Good heavens. Was I drunk?'

At Adelaide airport, Bett was walking up to the car-hire desk. A young man in a badly fitting suit smiled at her. 'Can I help you, madam?'

She smiled back. 'I've booked a car, thanks,' she said, handing over the paperwork. As he started pressing keys on the computer, she saw her rumpled, baggy-eyed reflection in the mirror behind him. Was it too late to find a gym and lose a stone? she wondered. She turned side on, sucked in her stomach as hard as she could and nearly fell over in the process.

'Is everything all right, madam?'

'Fine. Just doing some after-flight exercises.'

He looked a little suspicious. 'Your keys, madam. Car number fifteen.'

Pulling her case behind her, she stopped at the airport door, struck by the high temperature now she was outside the air-conditioned building. It felt like someone had opened an enormous oven nearby.

Bett looked around for a phone box and spied one in the car park. She'd promised Lola she'd call and let her know she was on her way. The phone box was no cooler, the receiver hot to touch. She stared at the phone. Of course she could handle this. Hadn't she been out in the world for the past three years, surviving in Melbourne, Dublin and London?

She dialled. A cross-sounding voice answered. 'Valley View Motel.'

It was Carrie. Bett hung up immediately.

'**H**ello? Hello?' Carrie waited a moment, then hung up. People were so rude. At least the ringing phone had got her out of the kitchen, though, before she exploded at her grandmother in front of everyone. Did Lola have any idea how hard it had been for the florist to find all those twigs?

She waited a moment to see if the caller rang back, but the phone stayed quiet. It had probably been another one of Lola's elderly friends.

'It's not just going to be a room full of old people reminiscing, is it, Lola?' Carrie had asked her several days before. 'There seem to be a lot of croaky old voices ringing up.'

'All human life will be represented, Carrie, my dear. There'll be some reminiscing, some entertainment, a little bit of this, a little bit of that.'

'A little bit of what?'

'It's a surprise.'

'Lola, please. You're the one who is supposed to get a surprise at your party, not us. What are you planning?'

'Carrie, how many times do I have to ask you to please treat me with adoration and respect? I'm not telling. All you have to do is set up the room exactly as I've outlined, follow the running order we have discussed and then leave the rest to me.'

'You're not going to tell me why Frank from the electrical shop was here yesterday, are you? Or what was in that box I saw him carrying in?'

'No, I'm not.'

'Have you finished your table plans yet, then? Are you still expecting sixty people?'

'More like seventy now, I think. Oh, and I also invited that quiet Englishman who's staying in Room Two. He said he'd be delighted to attend. Have you spoken to him? He has the most beautiful manners.'

Right then Carrie didn't care if that Englishman was the most well-mannered man in history. 'Lola, you have to tell me these things. What are we supposed to feed these extra people?'

'Oh, they won't mind if they have to share their meals.'

Carrie had given in and started to laugh. It had been funny then, but it wasn't funny now. Nothing was funny now. She took her pulse, felt her heart beating fast. And no wonder, all the pressure she was under. She heard laughing and looked out in time to see Lola, Anna and Ellen head over to Anna's favourite room, number seven. She fought off a little feeling of hurt, picked up her car keys and scribbled a note to her mother. She was going back into town for a long, slow cup of coffee.

'**A**t last, at last, at last.' Lola held Bett tight in another hug, then stepped back to look at her again, a wide smile on her face. 'You had me worried sick. I thought I'd have to start the party without you.'

Bett was surprised to find herself fighting tears. 'As if I'd let the birthday girl down.' Another hug. 'Let me look at you.' Bett took a step back, still holding Lola's hands. She'd felt bones under Lola's pink clothing. 'You've lost weight, Lola.'

Lola was looking at her just as closely. 'So have you. Not too much, thank God. I wouldn't know you without your curves.'

Bett glanced around her. 'Are the—'

'—others here? No darling. I poisoned them all this morning. I decided it would make for a much more peaceful life if you and I had the place to ourselves.'

The sound of the front door opening halted any more questions. Bett looked up as her mother and father came towards her. 'Bett! Welcome home!' She was enfolded in hugs from another two sets of arms.

An hour later, her head was spinning with news of the motel, of the Valley, of the party that night. There had been no sign of Anna or Carrie yet, and no mention of them.

Grasping a break in the conversation, Lola stood up with a groan loud enough to make them all look at her, then crossed to Bett and tucked her hand into her arm. 'Now, come on, Bett, I'll help you unpack. I've organised Room Six for you, your favourite.'

Lola and the three girls had been sleeping in the motel rooms rather than the manager's quarters ever since the family had first moved in, fifteen years before. It had been Lola's idea. She'd decided it was better to use the rooms during quiet times, rather than have them lie idle.

As they walked out into the sunshine, Bett noticed quite a few rooms had a car parked in front of them. 'It's busy enough for this time of year.'

'Not bad, actually. Carrie has been working hard. Mostly one-nighters, though Room Two has been here for two weeks now. An English fellow. He's coming along tonight, actually. He's researching a book and I'm dying to find out more about it.'

With a flourish, Lola produced the key to number six. 'Here you are, darling. All yours once again. Now, be sure to make yourself at home. If your luck holds and we don't get many guests, you might be able to stay put the whole time you're here. You do have neighbours, though.'

'Neighbours?'

The door to number seven beside them opened and Anna and Ellen came out. Bett's stomach flipped as she saw them for the first time in years. Anna looked as fresh and elegant as ever, wearing a white shift dress that showed off her toned, brown body. Ellen was in a pale blue sundress, holding a straw hat.

Lola coughed politely. 'Anna Quinlan, may I introduce your sister, Bett Quinlan. Bett Quinlan, this is Anna, your older sister.'

'Hello, Anna.'

'Hello, Bett.'

'And this is Ellen,' Lola continued. 'You remember Ellen.'

Bett looked down at the little girl, glancing at the scar on her cheek. Keeping a big smile on her face, she leaned down. 'Hello, Ellen.'

Ellen pressed close against Anna and wouldn't look up.

'Ellen, this is Bett, your auntie. My sister.'

Ellen still didn't look at her. Anna gave Bett a tight smile, a half shrug, as if to apologise.

Bett looked behind her, waiting for Glenn to emerge as well. Anna noticed.

'He's not here,' she said. 'He wasn't able to get away.'

Bett relaxed slightly. 'Oh. I see.'

Anna spoke again, her voice measured. 'So how was your flight?'

'Fine. Long. But I had a night's stopover in Singapore, so I'm not too exhausted. And you? Did you drive down or fly?'

'We flew, early this morning.'

'Mum,' Ellen's voice was little more than a whisper, as she started pulling at her mother's hand.

Anna leaned down, stroking her daughter's hair from her face. 'You're hungry, I know. Come on, darling. We'll go and see what Grandma has for you. See you later, Bett.'

'Yes, see you, Anna. See you, Ellen.'

As they walked away, Lola sighed. 'If that was the best you and Anna could do, then God knows what you'll do with Carrie. It's been the world's most ridiculous feud. Over Matthew, of all people.'

'It wasn't just over Matthew. It was . . . all sorts of things.' Bett wasn't ready for this. She tried to find the words. 'Maybe we were unnaturally close all our lives, you know, with the three of us moving so much and the whole Alphabet Sisters thing.'

'So now you're blaming me?'

'Lola, of course I'm not blaming you. I loved the Alphabet Sisters, until—' She stopped short. Was that actually the truth? She grabbed her grandmother's arm. 'Can we please not talk about it right now? Can you and I go inside and talk about normal things, like the party tonight or—'

'In a moment.' Lola had heard the sound of a car coming up the driveway. 'Carrie has just arrived back and I want you to meet her.'

'No.' To her own astonishment, Bett leapt inside her room and shut the door.

A second later it opened and Lola came in. 'What happened to you in London? Don't tell me you were about to hide under the bed?' Bett had spent hours of her childhood under the bed. 'I'm sure you weren't this cowardly before you went away.'

'I wasn't. And I wasn't this cowardly while I *was* away.'

'So you admit that you're being cowardly now? Listen Bett, you're one of my dearest girls in the world. Come and meet another of my dearest girls. Her name's Carrie and she's your sister.'

At first there were fifty yards between them. Then forty. Thirty.

'Good afternoon, Carrie,' Lola called as they reached ten yards.

'Hello, Lola.'

'Carrie, may I introduce your sister?'

'Stop it, Lola,' Bett muttered. She forced herself to look directly at Carrie, taking in the blonde curls, the petite figure, dressed in jeans and T-shirt, an inch of flat brown belly showing, casual, stylish, neat. In her own mind she ballooned to Michelin Man proportions, her skirt and T-shirt turning super size . . .

Lola interrupted her train of thought. 'Say hello, girls.'

'Hello, Carrie.'

'Hello, Bett. How was your flight?'

'Good, thanks. Long.' She swallowed. 'How is—' she couldn't say Matthew's name. She tried again. 'How is work?'

A look of relief crossed Carrie's face, Bett was sure of it. Perhaps Carrie didn't want to talk about Matthew yet either.

'Fine. We're busy enough for this time of year.'

Then there seemed to be nothing else to say. 'I'd better finish getting ready for the party, then,' Carrie said briskly.

'Do you need any help?' Bett forced out the words.

'No.' Carrie answered too quickly.

'Are you sure about that, Carrie?' Lola's voice was firm.

'It's under control, thanks, Lola. See you, Bett.'

'See you, Carrie.' They stood silently as Carrie walked through the back door of the kitchen.

'Well, that went OK,' Bett said, once she was out of sight.

'Gloriously. All those years of rancour swept away in one easy and honest conversation.'

'Sarcasm is the lowest form of wit, Lola. You taught us that yourself,' Bett said, stung. She thought it had gone OK. A wave of tiredness and emotion hit her as they walked back to her motel room. 'Not that anyone in this family seems to care enough about my life to have even asked what I've been doing in London the past few years.'

Lola surprised her with a burst of laughter and a kiss on her cheek. 'I promise we will talk about you, my dear Bettsie. But don't rush things.'

Bett grinned. 'You're a fine one to talk. The woman who's summoned us all home like this, forced it to a head.'

'I had to.' Lola decided there was no harm in dropping another hint. 'I need the three of you to do something for me.'

Bett stopped at the door to her room. This was the second time Lola had referred to something needing to be done for her. 'Lola, what is it? You're not sick or anything, are you?'

'Right now, because you are here, I feel one hundred per cent. Patience, Bett. All will be revealed in time. Now, come and unpack.'

As she opened her case, Bett glanced at Lola. 'I thought Anna looked well. And Ellen is very sweet.'

'Anna doesn't look well. She looks exhausted. And unhappy. Something's wrong there. And Ellen is a bag of nerves. That scar is fading but not as quickly as it should be. The city air is no good for that child. Now, have you had any thoughts about work yet?'

Bett laughed. 'Lola, I've just arrived.'

'It's just I had a fascinating conversation with Rebecca Carter last week. You remember Rebecca?'

'Of course.' She and Rebecca had worked side by side as reporters on the *Valley Times* for two years.

'She's editor now, imagine. She was so interested to hear you were coming back home and looking for work locally.'

'But I'm not.'

'Of course you are. You'll see her at the party and you can have a good talk about it with her. So, then, show me what you're wearing tonight.'

Bett took out the dress and held it against herself. She'd found it in a vintage shop in London.

'Beautiful. Try it on for me.'

Bett did as she was told. The style was sleeveless and simple, the fabric a rich red brocade, swirls of colour picked out with gold thread here and there.

Lola asked her to turn around, inspecting her from all sides. 'I think that back seam could do with taking in, to stop the skirt flaring so much. Would you like me to do it for you?'

Bett took it off and handed it over without argument. If she didn't agree, Lola was just as likely to come running after her at the party with a needle and thread.

'I'll drop it back in a little while.' She held her granddaughter tight against her for a moment. 'I really am very, very happy to see you.'

'I'm very, very happy to see you too. I've got something for you, by the way.' Bett reached down into her handbag. She had searched the stalls at Camden market until she had found what she wanted. She watched as Lola opened the blue velvet box. Inside was a pair of earrings and a matching necklace, made from extravagantly coloured glass beads.

Lola looked up, eyes wide. 'Bett, they're beautiful. I love them. Thank you.' Bett was enveloped in another hug, and then spoken to sternly. 'Now, leave your unpacking for the time being, climb into bed and have a quick nap. You've bags under your eyes big enough to take shopping.'

Bett did as she was told, peeping up at Lola from under the sheets, the white cotton pulled up to her nose. 'Thanks, Granny.'

'Don't you Granny me, you bold girl.' With that, Lola pulled the curtains, turned out the light and shut the door firmly behind her.

Lola walked two doors down and let herself into her own room. Number four had always been her favourite, with its view over the vine-covered hills. She went straight to her CD player and put on a Glenn Miller collection, then sat down and shut her eyes. She always played Glenn Miller when she needed cheering up. What had she expected? That the girls would only have to glance at each other and all the troubles of the past would melt away?

She still found it hard to believe this rift between the girls had lasted so long. And even harder to believe that it had been caused by Matthew, of all people.

'The three girls had a terrible cat fight over him, I believe,' Len the butcher, the town gossip, had said to her just after it had happened.

Lola remembered suggesting he shouldn't believe everything he heard. A cat fight, indeed. But afterwards the term had quite appealed to her. Her granddaughters weren't unlike a trio of cats. Anna, the eldest, like a Siamese, all sleek and sophisticated. Carrie, the youngest, still in her kitten stage, even though she was nearly thirty. Sweet as can be one minute, hissing and spitting the next. As for Bett, her middle darling— Lola softened at the very thought of her. Bett reminded her of a lost stray sometimes, needing lots of affection but then repaying it in spades.

For weeks now she'd been thinking of nothing else but this reunion. She was sure the other ladies in the charity shop were sick of hearing about the girls, and especially about their days as the Alphabet Sisters.

'Was it a serious thing?' Mrs Shaw had asked. 'Like the Andrews Sisters? Proper tours and recording contracts?'

'Oh, good heavens, no,' Lola had answered. 'I started it more as a way of keeping the three of them occupied, to tell you the truth.'

It had been her idea to take on the role of minding Anna, Bett and Carrie while Jim and Geraldine got on with the running of the motels. She'd been concerned how little attention the girls were getting from their parents. They weren't neglected, but too many late nights and too much roaming around unchecked hadn't been good for them.

The arrangement had suited everyone. Lola had been so busy trying to find her feet in Australia when Jim was a child that she'd never had the luxury of enjoying being a mother. They had been very close, and still were, but being a grandmother was more carefree, more fun. Watching her granddaughters running around outside in the sunshine, or even hearing them call to each other in their Australian accents, had made Lola feel settled here in Australia, she'd realised.

But she had also discovered that three strong-minded, intelligent little girls needed more than dolls and puzzle books to keep them stimulated. She started to teach them Irish songs she'd known since she was a child, picking out the tunes on the old piano that took up a corner of the dining room in the motel they were living in at the time.

She'd been surprised at how quickly they'd taken to it. Anna's voice had been distinctive even back then, deep and melodic. Carrie's voice had matched her looks, sweet and instantly appealing. But it was Bett who shone musically, quickly displaying not just an ear for harmonies but a real talent at the piano. When they'd moved to a new motel the following year, the first thing they'd bought was a good-quality piano. It had been with them ever since.

It wasn't the piano, though, but three dresses that had marked the start of the Alphabet Sisters. Lola still couldn't think of the day she brought home that first trio of dresses without laughing. Anna had been twelve at the time, Bett ten, Carrie seven. The dresses were of green and red gingham, with tight bodices and flared skirts. They had been made for little girls of fifteen, thirteen and eleven, but Lola folded and pinned each of them, then lined the three girls up, eyes shut, in front of the mirror in her bedroom and then told them to take a look.

Anna was appalled. Bett was horrified. Carrie was quite pleased.

'We look like we should be in *Little House on the Prairie*,' Anna said in a disgusted voice.

Bett was just as alarmed. 'We look like we should be in a dustbin.'

'I think we look nice,' Carrie said. She was happily admiring herself in the mirror. 'Who did they belong to?'

'I asked the lady in the charity shop, and it was quite some story. They apparently belonged to a famous trio of child conjurers called the Okey Dokey Gals, who toured the world with their pet camel and a small grey-faced cat.'

'How did their dresses end up in a charity shop?' Bett challenged.

'It was a tragic story and one for another day. What do you think of them?'

Anna was not happy. 'They'd be perfect for a country-and-western singing group called the Yukky Pukky Gals.'

Lola was actually pleased. 'Do you think you look like a singing act?'

Anna nodded. 'We look like those poor kids you see forced on to talent shows on the TV.'

Carrie brightened. 'I'd like to be on one of those shows.'

'Would you, Carrie?' Lola smiled, feeling like a fisherman slowly bringing in a catch. 'That's good. Because I've entered the three of you in a competition the local TV station is running. The winners get to perform at the agricultural show next month. All proceeds to charity.'

Anna groaned. 'Lola, no way. I'd die of embarrassment. Who sings in public with their sisters?'

'There is a long and honourable tradition of family singing groups. The von Trapps, the Partridge Family, the Osmonds. And now there's—'

'The Quinlan Sisters,' Carrie called out.

Bett wasn't impressed. 'It's not very catchy.'

'Anna, Bett and Carrie?' Lola suggested.

Carrie pouted. 'Why am I always last?'

'Because you're the thickest,' Anna said. Carrie pinched her. 'Ow! Lola, Carrie pinched me.'

'Only because she got there before me. Carrie, you are always last because your two older sisters are preparing the way for you, in the way flower girls prepare the way for a beautiful bride.'

Anna and Bett rolled their eyes. Carrie looked happier.

Lola clapped her hands. 'I have it. Anna, Bett and Carrie, the ABC Girls. No, let's make it catchier. The Alphabet Sisters. Perfect for TV.'

Lola laughed out loud now, alone in the motel room, as she remembered their first TV appearance. Over the years the girls had got used to singing on TV, but that first time they had been overawed by the lights, the cables and the cameras, not to mention the excitable hostess. Their harmonies had disappeared, their carefully rehearsed hand movements had looked more like violent twitches.

Lola felt a sudden welling of tears in her eyes, as the tension she'd been feeling for the past few weeks drained out of her. She'd been waiting and worrying for something to go wrong. For Anna to call and say she wasn't going to be able to make it. For Bett to say she had decided to stay in London.

Had her girls any idea at all how much she had missed them? she wondered. She wasn't fanciful enough to think that things would ever return to the glory days of the Alphabet Sisters. All the dressing up and the attempts to get them to rehearse their songs, and those early-morning drives to this show or that country TV station. And of course the fights over who got to sit in the front of the car, or whose favourite song would be sung first, or which order they would stand in. But for every fight there had been a funny moment, even if Lola had to pretend to be cross with them, to try to keep some control at least. Some chance. As the past three years had shown, she had no control over them at all.

There had been a moment a year ago when she'd thought the feud was about to be over. The terrible time when Ellen was attacked by that dog. Bett and Carrie had been shocked when she'd told them and Lola knew for a fact that they had both contacted Anna in the days afterwards. Bett had written, and Carrie had rung and left a message with Glenn. But nothing more had come of it. Which was when she'd realised she was going to have to try another way . . .

Oh, if only this had all happened years ago, when her bones weren't as creaky, when her mind was faster. 'You are nearly eighty,' her doctor had said at the last visit, when Lola admitted she needed an afternoon nap some days. 'Though you're in remarkably good nick, I'll give you that.'

'That'll be the gin,' Lola said. 'I'm preserving myself.'

'Good Irish blood, probably, and all that hard work over the years. Are you still doing those stretching exercises twice a day?'

Lola nodded. 'I'm so agile I could get a job in a Bangkok nightclub.'

The doctor had nearly choked. 'Lola, you get worse every visit and you know it. Don't get too stressed about anything. Try to take things easy, enjoy yourself. You deserve it.'

Lola put a finger on each temple and gently massaged. She had been treading on thin ice today, she knew. But it was so hard to be patient. Every day she was so conscious of time ticking away from her. The idea of turning eighty had hit her with a terrible shock and propelled her into making these plans, getting the girls back together.

Her birthday party was just hours away and Lola was in no mood to have them edging around each other the whole time, the way they had been so far today. How much further could she push them? She looked over at the portable bookcase and writing desk in the corner of the room. Jim had made it specially for her, so she could wheel it from room to room and feel immediately at home. The folder containing her special project was tucked well out of the way on the third shelf. Should she take it out now? Would they be angry with her? Or would they guess the whole purpose of it was to keep them together for as long as possible? Get them working closely together again? She didn't mind if they did guess. But, no, it was too soon. Besides, she wanted to reveal it in front of as large an audience as possible.

What could the girls work on together in the meantime? The food was prepared and the room was arranged, so there was nothing to be done there. Then she thought of the large pile of twigs Carrie would soon be putting into vases. Or not, perhaps . . . She picked up the phone and dialled the florist shop in town.

An hour later Lola was standing in the function room with ten newly emptied vases, eight bunches of freshly delivered flowers and three stony-faced granddaughters. Carrie had been summoned from the office, Anna from the kitchen, Bett out of her bed.

Lola gave them her most winning smile. 'I know I'm the very devil for changing my mind at the last minute, but seeing the three of you together again reminded me of that Christmas you strung up mistletoe and pine cones all over the motel for me . . .'

Bett stared at her blankly. Perhaps it was jetlag, but she couldn't remember ever doing Christmas decorations for Lola. It had always been Geraldine in charge of the decorations.

'And I realised it would be the icing on my birthday cake to see your flower decorations at my party tonight,' Lola continued. She patted each of them on the cheek. 'So will you get to work? And no hard feelings about the bush theme, Carrie? I'm sure we'll find a use for those twigs.'

Half an hour later, eavesdropping from outside, Lola was forced to admit her plan hadn't worked. It was more dysfunction than function room in there. No laughing and joking together as they merrily arranged the flowers. Just several frosty exchanges.

'Please don't put that vase there, Anna,' she heard Carrie say in an overly polite voice.

'Why not? I think it looks good.'

'All the arrangements are to go on the side tables.'

'But you'll hardly see them once you're sitting down.'

'I've given it a lot of thought over the past weeks and decided that is the most practical place for them.' Carrie was speaking in a steely tone.

Outside, Lola winced. The underlying message being that Anna had no right to just march in and do what she liked . . .

There was silence for a minute or two, then she heard Bett's voice. 'Are there any more vases?'

'I'll get them for you.' Carrie, her voice still stiff.

'That's all right. I can get them.'

'They're in the cupboard under the bar.'

'Yes, I know.'

After Bett came back there'd been more silence, broken only by the sound of vases being moved and stalks being snipped. As she walked into the room, Lola wasn't quite sure what to try next. The flowers were beautiful. Much nicer than the twigs had been. 'Oh, well done, girls.' There was no response. She ambled over to the piano, lifted the lid and experimentally ran her fingers up and down, playing one or two chords.

'Do you remember this one, Anna?' she said loudly. She thumped out the beginning notes of 'Don't Sit Under the Apple Tree'.

Anna shook her head.

'Poor Anna. Your memory gone and you still so young. Bett, your turn. What about this?' She played a swirly introduction to 'Danny Boy'.

Bett glanced over. 'I can't place it, Lola, sorry.'

'Too much smog in London, darling. Your brain cells need a shake-up. Carrie, what about you? What's this one?' She played the introduction to 'My Favourite Things'.

'I'm not sure,' Carrie said, not looking up.

Lola was shocked by a surge of anger. She stood up and clapped her hands. 'Right, you little buggers.'

Three startled faces turned to her. Lola rarely swore. 'I want to speak to the three of you. Over here, now.'

She gave them a moment to get closer, then glared at them, genuinely cross. 'I know I should be more patient with you. I know you are probably jetlagged, Bett, and you must be tired too, Anna. But, I'm sorry, I've been waiting three years for this, wanting this feud to be over every single day and I can't wait any longer to get it all sorted.' She pointed a long, varnished fingertip at her middle granddaughter. 'Bett Quinlan, tell me the truth. How do you feel right now?'

Bett coloured, transported straight back to being a ten-year-old. 'I really don't want to play this, Lola.'

'Play it, Bett. How do you feel right now?'

'Lola . . .'

It was a game she had played with them when they were children. Some trick she'd picked up at a drama class or from some TV documentary. Back then she'd had a magic wand that she would point at them. The truth stick, she called it. She said it saved time. Point and talk. How are you? What's wrong? How do you feel and why? They had to answer. Back then the answers had been simple. 'I'm cross because Mum told me off.' 'I'm mad because the other two got more ice cream than me.'

Lola turned away from Bett. 'All right, then. Carrie, I'll start with you.'

A long pause and then a low voice. 'I'm cross because you keep changing your mind about the decorations.'

It wasn't what Lola had hoped to hear, but it was a start. 'The customer's always right, Carrie, remember. Anna, what about you?'

Anna glared at her. 'I'm furious because I am thirty-four years old and you are treating me like a child.'

'You're all behaving like children so I'm going to treat you like children. Thank you, Anna. Bett?'

Bett hesitated. 'I'm upset because I hate this.'

'Do you really?' Lola said a silent thanks. Now she was getting somewhere. Say it, Bett, she urged. Say how much you have hated fighting with your sisters. 'What do you hate exactly?'

Bett lifted her head, a picture of defiant misery. 'You telling us off. And this truth stick business. I've always hated it.'

Lola put down the imaginary stick. It had been a last-ditch effort in any case. 'Very well. I'll try some straight talking instead. You see, I've always had the idea that you might have missed each other during the past three years. And then I had the even more obviously ridiculous idea that all it would take for you to become friends again was to get you together to talk about it.'

No response.

'No? Then it seems I have got it all wrong. Such a shame. However, as has always been my wont, I am going to try to make the best of a bad situation.' She glared at them. 'So, my little brat-faced princesses—'

Bett suddenly had to bite back a smile. Lola hadn't called them brat-faced princesses in years.

'Do you think it would be possible for the three of you to put this ridiculous fight behind you for a short time? Because I want to enjoy my party and I certainly won't if I have to see your sulky faces all night long. Or all week long. And possibly beyond that. In fact, let's say definitely beyond that.'

She ignored their looks of surprise and clapped her hands again. 'From now on, there is to be conversation between you, do you hear me? I want some smiles too. While you are all living and working here, I want peace and conviviality between you. There is to be no mention whatsoever of the events of three years ago.' She turned to Carrie. 'I know this will be hardest on you, Carrie. But I'd like you to keep Matthew away from here for the time being. Tell him I'm sorry, but that's the way it has to be.'

Carrie swallowed hard. If Lola only knew how easy it was going to be. She'd long ago banned Matthew from coming to the party. She nodded.

'Now, there's still plenty to be organised. Carrie, ask your sisters to help you.' She was almost at the door when she remembered something else. 'One last thing.'

They turned to her as one, like a chorus line, waiting.

She gave them a beautiful smile. 'Thank you all for being here. You've made an old lady very happy.'

CHAPTER THREE

THE FUNCTION ROOM was a mass of fairy lights. There were ten round tables, each set with white linen, sparkling glasses and gleaming cutlery. Irish music played quietly in the background, overlaid with conversations from the seventy guests. Young waitresses in white shirts and black skirts were circulating with trays, collecting empty champagne glasses.

At the door, Carrie glanced at her watch, then across the room at her oldest sister. She had stiffly asked for her help that afternoon, and just as stiffly Anna had agreed. 'Are you ready?' she mouthed.

'Ready,' Anna mouthed back.

Carrie signalled over to her other sister in the far corner by the speaker system. At Bett's nod, Carrie turned the room lights on and off and on again to get everyone's attention, then turned them off once more, leaving a spotlight over the main door. The room went quiet. Anna turned on the microphone. 'Please will you stand and welcome the belle of tonight's ball, the reason we're all here, the woman who is celebrating her eightieth birthday this very day—Lola Quinlan!'

Lola swept in to the sound of The Kinks's 'Lola'. She stood in the doorway for full dramatic effect, then gazed around the function room with pride and glee. The girls had done themselves and her proud.

Bett watched now as Lola moved from table to table, greeting every guest in person, having a word here or a word there. Across the room, Carrie glanced down at the running sheet in front of her. So far so good. Guests to be greeted in person at front door. Tick. Champagne to be circulated by waiting staff. Tick. In the past two days Lola had gone into a kind of white heat. 'What do you think about playing "I Do Like To Be Beside the Seaside" as the waitresses bring out the prawn cocktails?' 'Do you think it's too late to ask everyone to come in costume?'

Carrie had finally put a stop to it. 'Lola, it's not a Broadway production.'

'Do you think it's like a Broadway production? Really? Which parts?'

It wasn't supposed to be a compliment, Carrie stopped herself from saying. 'From what you've deigned to tell me, you already seem to have a lot of different activities throughout the night. People will want to talk to each other and eat. You need to let a bit of it happen of its own accord.'

To her surprise, Lola had agreed, taking the pen and swiping it through several items on the run-down. She had kept in two items, though—one dubbed S and the other SS.

'What do they stand for?' Carrie asked.

'Surprise and then Super Surprise.'

'I don't like surprises. Tell me.'

'You'll find out when you need to find out,' Lola had said grandly.

Which wouldn't be long now, Carrie thought with some relief.

Two hours later it was ten minutes to Item Seven, the first of Lola's surprises. The starters and main courses had been served—prawn cocktails, followed by Wiener schnitzels served with chips and salad. There had been three spot prizes, also Lola's idea. The lucky winners had received bottles of Lola's favourite gin. Dessert was to follow after the next set of speeches. There was a choice of fruit salad and ice cream or homemade chocolate pudding.

Carrie and Lola had argued about that as well. 'You can have any food you like, you know. Something special if you want.'

'I like your mother's menus. Plain, nourishing . . .'

Boring, Carrie didn't say out loud. The motel food had long been a sore point between Carrie and her mother. Geraldine had her favourites and had never seen any reason to change them.

Carrie caught Lola's eye across the function room. 'Ten minutes,' she mouthed, holding up both hands, fingers spread wide, for clarity. Lola nodded, sending her a beaming smile, before returning to her conversation with the neighbour on the table she was currently sitting at. She'd arranged the seating so there was a vacant seat at every table. 'That way I can move around all night, talk to everyone.'

She'd explained her reasoning to Carrie at one of their pre-party meetings. 'Don't you think it's silly to have me at a head table with your mother on one side and your father on the other? I can talk to them every day. I'm going to share myself around all night long. And I'd love it if you girls would do the same thing.'

The table-swapping seemed to be working well. Anna and Ellen had already moved to a table on the opposite side of the room. Carrie could see them both, Anna, with Ellen on her knee, talking to the lady from the chemist shop. Anna looked very glamorous, Carrie thought, in an elegant midnight-blue dress set off with a dramatic pair of earrings. Ellen was all in pink, with a sweet matching hat.

On the other side of the room she could see Bett, laughing at something the parish priest was saying. She was wearing a vintage dress. Stunning material, Carrie admitted, but she knew in her heart that her own outfit was the most eye-catching. It was a deceptively simple, long gold dress, with a matching gold silk wrap. She'd woven little silk flowers through her hair and taken a long time over her make-up.

'You look like a model,' Len from the butcher shop had said admiringly when he'd arrived with his wife. Then he'd fixed her with a beady eye. 'Matthew not here yet?'

She'd told the almost-truth. 'He's away up north on a sheep station, for the final part of his vet's training. Fantastic experience. It's just a shame it's so remote. Lola understood, of course.' She could tell by his eagerness to get away that he was dying to pass the news to everyone in the room. Good, it would save her having to do it.

Looking at Bett again, Carrie noticed she had lost a bit of weight while she'd been away in London, but she was still—well, not chubby any more, but certainly not thin. Guiltily, Carrie realised she was relieved. She had a feeling Matthew preferred slender girls. She'd asked him one night as they were going to bed, in the early days, when she'd gone through a period of guilt and uncertainty.

'Matthew, did you think Bett had a better body than me?'

He'd seemed uncomfortable. 'Carrie, I'm not answering that question.'

'Then you must have,' she'd said sulkily. 'Well, you should go back to her then, shouldn't you?' She had glanced up at him under her lashes. He hadn't been sure whether she was joking or not, she knew that. She had stood up, walked across the bedroom in her extremely lacy and sexy underwear. She had discovered early on that Matthew liked sexy underwear. At the door she'd stood and relished the look on his face as he took in her body. 'I'll ring Bett, will I? See if she'll come back to you?'

Matthew was lying on the bed. 'Come here, Carrie.'

'Why?'

'You know why.'

'What will you do if I do come over?' From the look in his eye, she had a very good idea exactly what he had in mind . . .

She shook the memory away. There was a time and a place for sexual fantasies and her grandmother's eightieth birthday probably wasn't it.

What would Matthew be doing now? She tried to picture him on the sheep station, 200 miles away. The job offer had come out of the blue six months earlier, a perfect practical application of all he'd been learning in his latest course in veterinary farm management.

She suddenly wished he was at the party. That she could go across to him, whisper something funny or sexy in his ear, make it all right again, the way they used to do. Until . . . She realised she was staring over at Bett when her sister caught her eye. She flushed and looked away.

Bett looked away too, embarrassed to have been caught staring at Carrie. There was no doubt about it, her younger sister looked stunning. She had been proud of her own outfit, until she had seen herself beside Carrie and Anna. The whole family had been summoned to Lola's room for one quick drink together before the party. Her father had made a toast. 'We'll do this again publicly, but cheers to you, Lola, a wonderful mother, mother-in-law, grandmother and great-grandmother.'

Lola had called Bett back as they were all leaving her room. 'You look marvellous, darling.'

In her room Bett had thought that the now-mended dress did look good, the vintage brocade such an unusual design. But one glance at Anna and Carrie and her spirits had plummeted again. 'Do you think?'

'Darling, I say you look wonderful and you do. The colours are glorious and your hair is shining. I just want that glint back in your eyes that I haven't seen since you got here.'

'Sorry, Lola. Sorry to be so stupid on your birthday.'

'That's my girl.' She had pinched Bett's cheek. 'Now, your turn to shower me with compliments. Do I look a picture?'

Bett had taken in Lola's outfit in all its glory. She was wearing a long purple taffeta skirt, a gold shimmering tunic, at least five necklaces, including her new one from Bett, and surprisingly tasteful make-up. 'You look sensational. Like you belong in Hollywood.'

'The very words I wanted to hear. Thank you, darling. Now go and have a good time. And by the way, you're sitting next to the Englishman from Room Two. Did I tell you he was a journalist too? Imagine that. You'll have lots in common to talk about.'

Bett had groaned, not in the mood for matchmaking. 'Lola, what have you done?'

'Whatever I like. It's my birthday, remember.'

Sure enough, when Bett got to her table there was a man sitting next to her. He was perhaps ten years older than her, lean, solemn-faced, wearing glasses. He was dressed in a casual suit. He smiled at her, a surprising, beautiful smile that lit up his face. 'Quite a party,' he said.

Bett smiled back. 'She's quite a woman.'

'Have you known her long?'

'All my life. She's my grandmother.' She held out her hand. 'I'm Elizabeth Quinlan, known as Bett.'

'Richard Lawrence.' They shook hands.

'You're English? Is that a London accent?'

'It is, yes.'

'I'm just back from there. Only this morning in fact.'

'All that way for a party? You *are* a social creature.'

Bett laughed. She noticed then he had very sparkly eyes behind his glasses. 'I didn't have a choice, believe me. And you're on holiday here, are you?'

'Well, a working holiday, I supp—'

A slap on her back nearly sent Bett flying into the table. 'Bett Quinlan, great to see you again, love.'

Her other neighbour had arrived, a man who had done the landscaping around the motel and knew the family well. He'd immediately launched into a conversation that hadn't let up through the first course. Out of the corner of her eye Bett had noticed Richard Lawrence being interrogated by his other neighbour, one of the local councillors. She'd heard snatches, something about doing research for a writing project. She'd been about to ask him more about it when Lola had wafted past her and whispered that it was time to move tables. 'Circulate, darling.'

Bett found the move between tables difficult, being intensely aware of people looking at her and talking about her. But then she'd found herself sitting beside the parish priest, who had surprised her with his rapid-fire joke delivery. She hadn't laughed so much in ages, and three glasses of local shiraz had helped things along beautifully, too. To make things even more pleasant, one of her favourite dishes had been on offer for the main course: lovely crispy Wiener schnitzel, served with a pile of fat chips and salad.

Three tables away, Anna smiled up at the young waitress as she collected her plate. 'Thanks very much. That was delicious.'

The girl frowned. 'Why didn't you eat any of it, then? It looks like you hardly touched it.'

Anna tried not to laugh. 'I'm just not very hungry,' she said politely. She knew from experience that her mother would have called on her pool of casual waitresses for tonight—local schoolgirls, young mothers, anyone needing a bit of part-time work.

The girl looked a little uncertain. 'Will I bother bringing you a dessert then, if you're not very hungry?'

'Just a small one would be great, thanks,' Anna said. 'And one for my daughter. She'll be back in a moment.' Lola had come over and swept Ellen away a few minutes before. 'I want to show her off,' she'd said brightly. Ellen had gone off happily with her.

Alone at her table for a moment, Anna looked round the room. Lola, hand in hand with Ellen, was moving regally from table to table. Her parents were standing nearby, chatting to another couple. Her father's arm was casually resting on her mother's back. Bett was still sitting two tables away, laughing at something the man beside her was saying. A possible suitor? Anna caught herself thinking. Then the man moved and Anna saw he was wearing a priest's collar. Perhaps not.

Anna finally spotted Carrie, too, shining in her golden dress on the other side of the room. Her sister had become very skilled at running events like this, it seemed. Not surprising, really. Carrie had always had that confidence with people, the ability to charm them so effortlessly.

'Hello, love. Are you enjoying yourself?'

Anna turned and smiled up at her father. 'Dad, hello. Sit down.' She patted the chair beside her. 'It's a great night, isn't it? Carrie's done a very good job.'

'She has. She's doing wonders around the place, in fact. Your mother and I will wake up one day and Carrie and Matthew will have taken over while we were sleeping.'

It was funny to see how naturally her father referred to Carrie and Matthew as a couple. She shouldn't have been surprised, she supposed.

He'd had three years to get used to them both. 'It's all that good training you gave us as kids.'

'I'm so glad to have you home again,' Jim said simply. 'We missed you, you know. You and Bett.'

'It's good to be back, Dad.'

'Hi, Grandpa.' Ellen popped her head in between the two of them and then climbed onto her grandfather's lap. 'Can you do that trick where you take the coin from your ear and then put it in my ear?'

'That's not a trick, Ellie. I really do keep coins in my ear. It's much safer than the banks.'

'*Grandpa*,' Ellen said, shooting Anna a glance. 'He's joking, Mum, isn't he?'

'Oh, no, Ellen. Your grandpa has a fortune in his ears.'

'Show me, Grandpa?'

He checked his watch, then touched the end of Ellen's nose. 'A little later, sweetheart. I just have to make a quick announcement about the birthday girl, but I'll be back as soon as I can.' He stood up and made a show of straightening his tie. 'My moment of fame has come at last.'

Ellen watched him go, then turned to Anna. 'Mum, Grandpa is Lola's son, isn't he?'

'That's right.'

'They're both a little bit mad, aren't they?'

Anna burst out laughing. 'Yes, Ellie, they are.'

Bett said goodbye to the priest and moved back to her original table, carrying her fourth glass of red wine. She'd hardly have believed it possible, but she was almost enjoying herself. It seemed she just needed to keep herself mildly drunk and surrounded by a crowd and she would get on just fine. She smiled at Richard as she sat down beside him.

He picked up a bottle of wine and went to top up her glass. 'May I?' he asked. She accepted, impressed by his good manners.

Richard raised his voice over the sound of the Irish folk tunes. 'Lola told me all four generations of her family would be here tonight. Is that right? She seemed very happy about it.'

'That's right,' Bett said, hoping he wasn't about to ask her to introduce him to everyone. She was enjoying him too much herself. She was guiltily pleased when she noticed her father had started making his way to the microphone to introduce Lola's speech. 'Excuse me,' she said to Richard. He nodded and turned towards the front of the room too.

She wriggled around to get a better view of her father and then nearly leapt out of her seat as a sharp pain ricocheted through her right thigh.

She moved and another sharp pain shot into her bottom. Bloody hell, had she sat on a spider? She lifted up her bottom an inch, lowered it and nearly shot out of her seat as the pain struck again. She couldn't get up now, make a scene, not during Lola's big moment.

Her father was making his introduction. 'Once again, I give you my mother and the birthday girl herself, Lola Quinlan.'

The lights came on and in the front of the room was Lola, pulling back a curtain to reveal a large white screen. The guests shifted expectantly.

Lola waited until she had every last person's attention. 'Thank you, my darling Jim. Before I move on to the next important event of the night, I'd like to properly introduce my family to you all.' Lola pointed them all out, one by one. 'My son, Jim, and his wife, Geraldine, who have been so good and kind to me over the years, even when I was driving them mad.'

'Never,' Jim called across. Geraldine smiled stiffly.

'And my granddaughters. Anna, put your hand up, darling, would you? Anna's home from her successful acting life in Sydney for a little while with her daughter, my dear great-granddaughter, Ellen, who has just turned seven and is adorable.' Bett noticed Ellen was pressed against Anna, her hair hiding her scar.

'And at the table next to Anna and Ellen is my middle granddaughter, Elizabeth, known of course as Bett . . .' Bett self-consciously raised her hand as Lola continued, 'who has left behind her glamorous life in London to come home and spend time with me.'

She turned and gestured towards Carrie, who was standing by the door. 'And, of course, my dear Carrie, there in the golden dress with the golden hair, who not only keeps me young on a daily basis, but has pulled out all the stops for tonight. Thank you, Carrie darling.'

Lola waited for the applause to come to an end before she spoke again. 'When we were first planning this evening's entertainment, I learned that a tradition these days is to have a little slide show ready to surprise the guest of honour. Carrie suggested it and I turned her down immediately, not wanting to be embarrassed by photos of myself that I thought had long disappeared. But then I thought about it some more, and I decided, yes, perhaps it would be good, especially if I got to choose the slides.

'So I went ahead and prepared a little slide show of some of my favourite moments and I'd like to share them with you. Please forgive my indulgence as I reminisce a little about the past eighty years.'

A lilting Irish song started playing as slide after slide came up on the screen, with captions of the year and the place underneath. There was

Lola as a child beside an enormous oak tree in front of her big family house in Ireland, standing with her parents behind her, the only child. As a young woman at a gala party, in Dublin. On her wedding day, Edward serious-faced, Lola almost a child bride. A photograph of them on the boat to Australia in the late 1930s, then several of Lola with a baby, Jim, on their own. Bett heard whispers at the tables around her. 'She was widowed very young, wasn't she?' 'Tragic, wasn't it? Her with a young son, too.'

Bett was fascinated. She hadn't realised that Lola had those photographs from Ireland, or so many from her early days in Australia. Lola had rarely spoken about those days in any detail. Bett had visited Lola's house in Ireland, taken photos of it and tried—but failed—to find anyone who remembered Lola and her family from years before. She'd like to have looked more closely at the slide, but it had flashed past too quickly. She'd have to ask Lola about it another time.

The next slides were of Lola and Jim in the different guesthouses and motels they had gone on to manage all round Australia. They had moved dozens of times over the early years. Geraldine and then the three girls started appearing on screen. There was a wonderful photo of Lola in her mid-fifties on holiday in Tasmania, looking like a film star. Another of her in her late sixties, behind the counter of the charity shop here in the Valley, the year she had announced herself officially retired from motel work. One from her seventieth birthday party in the middle of the vineyard in front of the motel on a glorious summer day, like today. The day that she had signed over all the ownership to Jim and Geraldine. Bett remembered it clearly. Lola hadn't listened to any arguments. 'I don't want money for it. It's yours to do what you like with, as long as there's always a room and a ready supply of gin for me.'

Bett relaxed as the screen went white again. Thank God Lola hadn't included any slides of the Alphabet Sisters. She knew there were dozens of hideously embarrassing photographs from their various performances all over the country, none of which Bett ever wanted to see again. Lola usually pulled them out at any occasion. Who'd have thought she'd have respected their privacy like that tonight?

Lola's voice sounded out over the room again. 'It's been a long and eventful life, and one of the most special parts of it has been not just the joy of having three granddaughters but having three immensely talented, performing granddaughters. So I'd also like to take this opportunity to share with you some of the finest moments from their years performing as the Alphabet Sisters. Music please, maestro.'

The room filled with the sound of Perry Como singing 'The Alphabet

Song'. Bett covered her face with her hands as one photo after the other of the Alphabet Sisters in an array of outfits flashed up onto the screen.

Hearing the laughter around her, Bett made a gap in one hand and peered through. It was getting worse. Why had they reached their performing peak when puff-ball skirts, fluffy hair and fluorescent colours had seemed fashionable? As Perry continued crooning in the background, working his way through the alphabet one more time, she covered her face again, praying for the song to finish.

At their table Anna and Ellen were in gales of laughter. Over dinner, Ellen had been solemnly informing the lady sitting next to her that her mother and aunties had once been famous singers. Behind her, Anna had been vigorously shaking her head, smilingly denying everything. Five seconds of these slides had been the proof. And the dresses! They were even worse than Anna remembered.

On her lap, Ellen was in fits of giggles. 'I hope you're not laughing at me?' Anna said mock sternly.

'You all look so silly,' Ellen whispered back. 'And look at Auntie Bett's hair.'

Oh, poor Bett, Anna thought, as another slide flashed up showing Bett with her mouth caught wide open in mid-song, her mad brown curls dancing around her head.

By the door, Carrie was enjoying every moment of the surprise slide show. She'd been taken aback at first, but was now revelling in the memories. She had loved every moment of the Alphabet Sisters. The dressing up, the singing, the applause . . . and she'd never minded any of the dresses they'd had to wear.

The lights finally came on again, and Lola moved back in front of the screen. 'Some wonderful memories there for me, as I'm sure you'd agree. The days working with my little Alphabet Sisters were among the happiest of my life, and ones that I had thought, sadly but inevitably, had come to an end.'

And not a moment too soon, Bett thought. But Lola's next words had her sitting upright again.

'Then something wonderful happened. My darling granddaughters agreed to the most wonderful birthday present a grandmother could ask for. I would like to share it with you all tonight.'

Oh no, Bett thought. She glanced at Anna, and at Carrie. Did they have any idea about this wonderful birthday present? It didn't look like it. Anna shot her a questioning glance. Bett shook her head, signalled that she had no idea either.

At the side of the room, Carrie was looking down at the running order. She seemed just as puzzled. Bett turned round. At the back of the room Frank from the electrical shop had moved back by the slide projector and was as alert as a gun dog, waiting for Lola's signals.

The room lights went out once again, leaving a spotlight on Lola.

Her voice was assured. 'For the past ten years, I have been working on what I regard as my life's project. And I have this man to thank.'

The spotlight went out. On the screen behind her was a large photo of a man in uniform.

'The American general, Douglas MacArthur,' Lola said. 'One of the heroes of World War Two, famous for a wartime speech that galvanised hearts and minds all over the free world. Yes, indeed. "I shall return," General MacArthur promised, not just to his men in the Philippines but to all the Allied forces. It became the war cry of the Pacific campaign.'

Two older people near Bett nodded and whispered to each other. They obviously remembered it, even if it was news to her.

Another slide came up. General MacArthur standing on a platform at a small railway station, his elegantly dressed wife beside him, their small son between them.

Lola's voice filled the room. 'And where did he say those momentous words? In London? No. In Washington? No. Perhaps even in Sydney? No. General MacArthur said those words on the 20th of March, 1942, on the platform of the Terowie railway station. Yes, the little town of Terowie, South Australia, just sixty miles from here, as he travelled by train from Alice Springs to Adelaide. What an event for the people of that tiny place, I've always thought, with the war and worries swirling all around them. It touched me deeply. Some years ago I started imagining and thinking and putting down ideas, and before I knew what was happening my thoughts had become a short story, which became a longer story, which became a musical. Yes, I, Lola Quinlan, in the twilight of my years, found that I had written a musical.'

Lola took a big, dramatic breath and paused. 'For many months it languished in my bottom drawer. Until I shyly showed it to my three granddaughters, as we reminisced about the wonderful days of the Alphabet Sisters—'

Bett shot Anna a glance. Anna looked over at Carrie. They'd done no such thing.

'And, to my great joy, they offered there and then to mount a fully staged, complete musical in the Valley for everyone to enjoy, with all proceeds going to the Valley Ambulance Fund.'

The party-goers started clapping, some of them a little uncertainly. Lola reached into a bag beside her and pulled out a bundle of leaflets.

She started moving from table to table, handing them out to everyone in the room. She reached Bett and handed her one with a big smile. Bett scanned it.

Many Happy Returns
A Musical for all the Family

Written by Lola Quinlan

To be performed by

The Alphabet Sisters
and the people of the Clare Valley

Clare Town Hall, March 20

Bookings: Valley View Motel

All proceeds to the Buy a New Ambulance Fund

Bett had to grab her grandmother's arm as Lola started to move away. 'Wait! What in God's name is all this about?'

Lola lowered her voice. 'Darling, don't blaspheme, especially on my birthday.'

'I'm serious.'

She patted Bett on the head. 'In a moment, darling.' She glided off.

Carrie came up to her next, looking put out. 'Is this a joke, Lola?'

Lola was unperturbed. 'Is the musical a joke? Well, it certainly has some hilarious moments, but it has a serious side to it as well.' She sailed past her too.

Anna came up behind her and helped herself to a leaflet, a smile fixed on her face. 'You've put us in an embarrassing situation tonight, Lola.'

'Really? I thought you all looked very nice.'

'You know we can't do this. You should at least have asked us.'

'But you might have said no.'

'Of course we'd have said no. Lola, you have to call this off.'

'But everyone looks so interested.'

Anna glanced around. The people in the room did appear interested, with just about everyone reading the information. On the other side of the room she saw two of the waitresses giving Bett their contact details. In another corner Carrie was surrounded by a small group of people.

A petite woman came over to Lola and Anna, clutching the leaflet. 'Will you be holding open auditions, Lola?'

Anna recovered, finding a confident smile somewhere. 'We haven't talked through all the details yet. Still a few grey areas to discuss.'

Across the room, as the waitresses moved away, Bett picked up the leaflet, reading the details again.

Richard Lawrence was watching her closely. He looked amused. 'Pardon me for enquiring, but are you slightly surprised about this?'

Her head shot up. Slightly? Overwhelmingly. But that wasn't something to admit to a complete stranger. She gave a light laugh. 'Oh, that's Lola for you. Always springing little surprises on us. She really is something else.' She moved back in her chair and yelped out loud as the worst pain yet shot into her bottom. 'Excuse me, will you?' She nearly shouted the words.

She moved through the room and practically ran into the ladies, which was blessedly empty, and started to unzip her dress. As she did so there was a tearing sound.

'Oh shit,' she said loudly. She locked herself into a cubicle and took the dress off completely. She heard another little ripping sound as the old material tore even more.

Something glistened in the seam of the material. She looked closely. They weren't spider eyes, but industrial-sized staples, their ends as sharp as needles. She groaned. She couldn't put the ripped dress on again, unless she wanted to treat the entire gathering to the lovely sight of her large black-undie-clad bum. And she couldn't run down to her room in her camisole, tights and shoes. Shit, shit, shit. She heard someone come in and tensed. She peered under the door.

She recognised the gold strappy sandals. It was Carrie. She'd rather be here all night than ask Carrie for help.

Then the reality hit her. She could well be in here all night if she didn't ask Carrie.

'Carrie?' Her voice was small. 'Carrie?' A bit louder.

'Bett?' She sounded surprised. 'What's the matter? Are you sick?'

'I'm fine. It's just, I've, uhm, ripped my dress. Lola mended it for me but she seems to have used a stapler rather than needle and thread.'

'Come out, let me see.'

To Bett's relief, Carrie wasn't triumphant or sneering. 'Oh, hell. I thought she'd stopped doing that. It's an upholsterer's one she got at the charity shop. I caught her stapling the curtains in her room last year.'

'I thought a spider had bitten me, that I'd sat on a whole nest of them.'

Carrie grinned, then the two of them worked to pick them out of the dress. There were more than twenty.

'Did you know anything about this musical?' Bett asked, as she clambered back into the dress again.

'Not a word. Had she said anything to you, in any of her letters?'

221

So Carrie had known that Lola wrote regularly to Bett. She shook her head. 'It's ridiculous of course. There's no way we can do it.'

'Of course we can't. I don't know what she was thinking.'

There was silence for a moment and then a loud blast of music came from outside. Carrie started. 'I'd better get out there. It's the last spot prize before we sing "Happy Birthday". Look, what about wearing this?' She took the gold wrap from her shoulders and in a deft movement tied it round Bett's waist. She twisted the fabric, tucked it here and there and then tied a loose knot in the side so that the shimmering material fell in folds. 'What do you think?'

Bett stepped back and looked in the full-length mirror. The gold wrap folded over the brocade as though it was meant to be there. 'It looks like a designer did it. Thanks a lot, Carrie.'

'You're welcome, Bett.'

It was the longest conversation they'd had in three years.

CHAPTER FOUR

THE MAGPIES WERE CALLING into the sharp blue sky. Bumper the sheep was giving plaintive little bleats. The glass bottles were rattling as Jim Quinlan carried the first of the crates out to the bottle bank behind the kitchen. In bed in room number six, Bett groaned at all the noise. What time had she gone to bed? Three or four? She peered at her bedside clock. Nine thirty. Whose bright idea had it been to have this emergency meeting about the musical at ten? And whose bright idea had it been to finish the evening with cocktails? Hers on both counts, she realised.

The night before, Lola had collared her on the dance floor. 'Isn't that Carrie's wrap? What a nice touch. You're getting on so well already.'

Bett didn't take the bait. 'We still can't do it, Lola.'

'Can't do the musical? Of course you can. You have to have more confidence in your own abilities, Bett.'

'It's not about confidence, it's about not being asked, about wondering whether any of us actually want to do this.'

'So if Anna and Carrie agree, you will too?'

'Lola, stop this.'

'Bett, I'm ashamed of you. Telling an old woman off on her birthday. We'll discuss it tomorrow when I give you the script.'

'You actually have written a script?'

'Of course. What did you think I'd done, scribbled a few notes on the back of a shopping list?'

Bett remembered an Alphabet Sisters performance that hadn't been too far from that. She'd been about to remind Lola when her grandmother glided off, cornering another man for a dance.

The party had continued for several more hours, with the DJ playing a mixture of Irish jigs, fifties dance tracks and old-style tunes. Bett had two waltzes with Richard. As they turned around the floor the second time, she noticed him laughing at something over her shoulder.

She turned in time to see Lola lift her skirt and give a little high kick.

'Is your grandmother always as entertaining as this?' Richard asked.

She shook her head. 'She's quite low-key tonight, actually.'

He laughed. 'I enjoyed all those photos of you and your sisters in your performing days. You weren't tempted to do a surprise performance for Lola tonight?' he asked as they waltzed past Lola once again.

'No. We broke up too many years ago for that.'

Another twirl. 'And why was that? You didn't want to make a career of it?'

She gave the answer she always did. Not true, but true enough. 'We were getting a bit old to be wearing matching dresses.'

Lola came up to them both. 'You're getting on. Good, good. I was sure you would. Bett's a journalist too, Richard. Did I tell you?'

'You did, Lola.'

'Richard is here researching a book, aren't you, Richard?'

'Really? What's it about?' Bett was glad to change the subject.

Lola waved her question away. 'Oh, plenty of time to hear about that tomorrow. Come on, Dicky, come and dance with me again.' And off they had gone.

Bett turned over in bed again. The slide show came to mind, and with it a niggling thought that had occurred to her during the party. One of the photos had surprised her, but between the debacle with the dress and then the rest of the party . . . And now her poor brain was so drenched in alcohol it wouldn't come back to her.

She lay there hugging her pillow as another party memory returned. Rebecca Carter, her fellow reporter on the paper three years ago, had arrived late. She was tall, willowy, her hair in a stylish blonde ponytail. She'd headed straight for Bett, hugged her, poured them both a glass of wine, then made an offer. 'The woman who took over from you is about to have a baby and I need a part-time reporter to cover for her maternity leave. The job's yours, if you're interested.'

Bett had needed to shout over the noise of the music. 'I'm only home for a week or two. I'll probably be going on to Melbourne or Sydney.'

'Lola said you'd be staying here, though. Surely you've been yearning for the simple country lifestyle? Come on, Bett. Think about it.'

They'd talked about it over another glass of wine and a cocktail or two. Had she agreed to take the job or not? She really couldn't remember. Turning the pillow over to the cool side, Bett shut her eyes and gave another long, low groan.

Anna was first to arrive in the dining room. She'd left Ellen in the kitchen with Geraldine, helping to clear the guests' breakfast trays. She took a seat at the window. In the morning sunlight, the curving rows of vines across the road were a lush, glowing green against the dark soil.

'Morning.' It was Carrie.

'Morning.'

Carrie poured a coffee and took a seat. 'Huge night, wasn't it?'

'You did a great job organising the party. It all went so smoothly.'

Carrie coloured. 'Thanks.'

Anna decided to ask the question she'd been wanting to ask since she arrived. 'Before Lola gets here, I have to ask you something. Was Matthew OK about not coming last night?'

'He was fine,' Carrie said briskly. 'He's working up north at the moment, anyway. On a sheep station. It saved him a long trip.'

'Oh. Good.' Anna waited, but it seemed Carrie had nothing more to say about him.

'Morning.' They turned. It was Bett, hair bedraggled. 'Has it been called off yet?'

'Any minute now,' Anna said.

The three of them sat in silence, then the door opened again. Richard Lawrence stood there. 'Good morning. Am I too late for breakfast? I'm afraid I forgot to put my order out last night.'

Carrie stood up. 'It doesn't matter. We'll make something for you.'

Bett noticed that Anna was waiting to be introduced. 'Richard, this is the oldest of us, Anna Quinlan, actress and mother of one. Anna, this is Richard Lawrence from London. He's a journalist staying here at the motel while he researches a book he's writing.'

'Hello, Anna.' Richard gave her his lovely smile. 'I must say I'm thinking of throwing all that research away in exchange for another audience with your grandmother. Much more material there, I think.'

'You can do the musical instead of us while you're at it,' Anna said.

He seemed surprised. 'You're not going to do it?'

'Of course they're going to do it.' Lola swept in behind him, dressed in a turquoise kaftan top over white trousers. 'Dicky, dear, how are you? Marvellous dances we shared last night. You've a fine pair of hips on you.'

Bett was too hung over to protest at Lola's boldness for once. She just wanted to go back to bed.

Carrie took Richard into the kitchen and handed him over to her mother, then came back and shut the door. 'So then, Lola, what's the best way to call this whole thing off?'

'Call it off? Why would we want to do that?'

'We can't do it, Lola,' Bett said.

'Why not?'

'Because we won't be here to do it,' Anna said patiently.

'You won't? Where will you be?'

'Well, Ellen and I are going back to Sydney, of course.' This wasn't the moment to mention she'd been thinking about staying on.

'Why?'

'Because it's where we live. Where I work. Where Ellen goes to school.'

Lola noticed Glenn wasn't mentioned. She turned her attention to Carrie. 'What about you, Carrie? I'd have thought you'd have leapt at a chance to get back on the stage.'

'I'm very busy with the motel,' she said quickly.

'Bett, what about you? Didn't you tell me in one of your letters how much you've missed playing the piano? And you're staying here in the Valley, aren't you?'

Bett's head was throbbing now. 'I don't know for sure.'

'What about the job Rebecca offered you at the newspaper?'

'How do you know about that?'

'I told you. I had a word with her in the street last week. And I saw her talking to you last night.'

'Shall we just get a town crier to shout out everyone's secrets and be done with it?' Bett said crossly.

Lola wondered if her judgment was failing. She'd thought they'd leap at it. This called for plan B. 'Very well, then. There's something else I need to tell you. The other reason I brought you all back here.'

Three heads shot up. They'd been waiting for this.

Lola paused dramatically. 'I was at the doctor's last week. She's worried about me.' It was true that the doctor was worried that Lola was drinking too much gin. She'd promised her she'd cut back after the party.

'Worried about what?' Bett asked the question for all of them.

She had their attention. Good. Now, use it. 'The fact that I am a very elderly lady and that my time on this earth is fast running out.'

'Your doctor actually said that to you?' Carrie exclaimed.

'She didn't put it exactly like that. But all I'm saying is, who knows how long I might be here?' That was true enough, she thought—who knew how long any of them would be around? 'And it would mean so much to me if the three of you staged the musical,' Lola continued in her most cajoling voice. 'Anna, the local schools are very good, you know. And, Bett, Rebecca tells me the job she's offering is part-time and for six months, which would suit you well. Plenty of time for rehearsals. And you, Carrie, well, of course we'll all lend a hand with the motel. So surely you'll be able to make time to learn your lines for the lead role.'

'The lead?'

Lola gave a light laugh. 'I keep forgetting you haven't read the script. Yes, I'd thought of you for the lead, Carrie. You as musical director, Bett, unless you would like to get up on stage again? No, I thought not. And, Anna, I actually saw you as the director of the production. We'd change the billing, to read "Written by Lola Quinlan, Directed by Anna Quinlan, Music by Bett Quinlan, Starring Carrie Quinlan". Oh, I can see the programmes now.' A calculated pause followed, before she lowered her voice. 'Of course, once you've all read it you might have your own ideas.'

Bett knew at that moment how sheep felt when they were being nosed into a pen by a collie.

'So you have actually finished it?' Anna was still suspicious.

'Indeed I have,' Lola said proudly. 'Seven main characters, a chorus, lots of minor characters. You'd be able to involve half the Valley if you wanted. There are even one or two parts for children. I was thinking of Ellen if you think she is up to it. And I've even written in a cameo for the Alphabet Sisters. Imagine. That was sheer indulgence on my part. You might decide to take that out.'

'We haven't decided anything.' Anna spoke for them all.

'Of course you haven't. You have to read it first.' Lola reached into the bag beside her. 'So here you are, your reading copies, hot off the press. Mind you, by the looks of the three of you, you might want to wait until those hangovers have passed.' She finished handing out the folders. 'So will we meet here tonight to see what you think?'

The scripts were nearly an inch thick. 'Tonight?' Anna squeaked.

'It's not as if we can drop everything, Lola. I've got a motel to run,' Carrie added.

Bett said nothing. She just wanted someone to carry her to her bed.

'Very well, then,' Lola said. 'Will we say tomorrow afternoon? Splendid.'

Later that day, Lola made her way to the kitchen. Lunch had been served some hours before and the preparations for dinner were still to be done. It was her favourite time in the motel. The large silver table in the middle of the kitchen was cleared and shining. Geraldine was in the office sorting accounts. Lola had just helped herself to a cup of tea and the remains of last night's chocolate dessert when her son walked in.

'You look well set up. Geraldine not here?'

Lola made a show of looking under her saucer. 'I can't see her, no.'

Jim grinned. 'I never learn, do I? Ask an obvious question—'

'—Get a clever answer. Sit down, Jimmy, and talk to your old mother.'

Lola loved these moments, enjoying the energy that buzzed off her fine, strong son. Sunny-natured he was, through some stroke of luck. God knows his father had been anything but sunny-natured.

Jim made himself a cup of tea. 'Can I get you anything else?'

'I've had exactly as much as I want, darling, thank you.' Lola leaned back and smiled. 'You've never regretted going into the motel business with me, have you? Resented all that moving around?'

'Of course I have. My entire childhood spent in kitchens and bars, never knowing how long I'd be able to call one place home.'

Lola always enjoyed it when Jim teased her. 'That's right. And don't forget you were chained to the sink since you were barely able to walk.'

'Exactly. Do you know I was the only boy in any of my schools who had dishpan hands?'

'And don't forget I always used to drag you out of those schools, just as you started to make friends.'

'Not to mention ruining any chance I had of being a professional footy player. Remember that time we moved motels three weeks before the final? The move after that was the best one we ever made, of course.'

'Was it? Why?'

Jim laughed. 'It was where I met Geraldine.'

'Of course.' Geraldine had been working in the kitchen of that next motel, training as a cook. When Lola and Jim had moved on again, two years later, Geraldine had come with them, as his wife, and already pregnant with Anna.

Lola often wondered if Jim had ever noticed that she and Geraldine couldn't bear one another. Oh, they were polite on the surface—with all of them living in such close proximity, there had to be good manners. But in the early days, Lola had seriously considered moving to another motel, leaving Geraldine and Jim to their own devices. But then the girls had come along and Lola had quite simply fallen in love with them. Since then she'd made a pact with herself to keep things fine between her and Geraldine. Jim was devoted to her, but she was too much of a cold fish, in Lola's opinion. Buttoned up. More interested in Jim and the motel than her daughters. It always hurt Lola to see the three girls trying to get Geraldine's attention and usually failing. It had been another reason for her to shower them with attention.

Lola reached into her bag, took out a folder and passed it to her son. 'For me?'

'For you. For you and Geraldine, in fact.'

'What is it?'

'Have a look and tell me what you see.'

'Tickets.' He opened them. 'First-class train tickets.' There were two sets, one for a two-night trip on the legendary *Ghan* from Adelaide through the desert centre of Australia to Darwin. The other for the *Indian Pacific*, a four-day journey from Sydney across the Nullarbor Plain to Perth. In another folder were plane tickets for their connecting flights. 'All in the name of Jim and Geraldine Quinlan.'

Lola loved these sorts of moments. 'And now look at the dates.'

'Departing from Adelaide next week? And not coming back for a month? Lola, we can't take these.'

'Of course you can. I insist.' She held up her hand to quell his protest. 'I'll run the place while you're away. And don't tell me I can't because I was doing it long before you even had a notion. And I've got the girls to help me now. I've been in touch with Geraldine's standby cook and she said she'd love the work.'

'Have you asked the girls about this? No, don't answer that one. And presumably you're going to tell me these tickets are nonrefundable?'

Lola nodded happily.

'And you've got the rest of your argument all worked out too, I suppose. That we haven't had a holiday in years and this is the best chance to do it.'

'That's right.'

Jim was grinning. 'So I'd better go straight to Geraldine and tell her to start packing, is that it?'

'In a nutshell. Come here, darling.' She reached up and gave him a big kiss on the forehead. 'Thank you, Jimmy. You always were such an obedient boy.'

In her room the next day, Bett finished unpacking the contents of her suitcase. She'd checked the bookings register and it looked as though she'd have this room for the next few nights. That had always been the drawback of sleeping in the motel rooms, having to pack up quickly and do a hasty but thorough cleaning job when real guests turned up.

When they were in their mid-teens, their father had presented each of them with a large box on wheels. The boxes were perfect for storing or transporting their clothes, pictures, vases, posters—all the things they liked to bring into the rooms to make them their own. Lola had called them their personality boxes, after seeing them lined up side by side one afternoon, when they'd needed to move out of their rooms. Anna's had been full of make-up samples, a gold-framed mirror, a theatre magazine, a book of tips on stagecraft and a length of fake fur that she had taken to wearing wrapped dramatically round her shoulders. Bett's box of tricks had held a smaller box crammed with music cassettes, a portable tape player, a bundle of imported pop magazines, sheet music for the piano. Carrie, animal-mad at the time, had stored her two cloth mice toys, a book of horse tales and three packets of plastic farmyard animals.

Bett had to force the wardrobe door shut. There was only just enough room for the shirts, skirts and dresses she had brought on the plane with her. The rest of her things were coming by ship. She'd slowly put together a whole new wardrobe over the past three years, having taken hardly any of her belongings when she'd left the Valley.

It had turned out to be a good thing, in a way. Being forced to start from scratch, on a very small budget, she'd had to buy most of her clothes at vintage shops and secondhand clothing stores around Dublin and London. She'd smiled at the irony. After years of protesting about being forced to wear vintage clothes as the Alphabet Sisters costumes, she'd voluntarily started going out and buying them for herself.

Bett put away her empty suitcase and checked the time. Nearly three o'clock. She'd better hurry. Time for the first production meeting, as Lola was calling it. A get-out-of-this-if-we-can meeting, Bett was calling it. She peered into the kitchen as she went past. Geraldine was back at the stove, Jim at the table with Ellen on his knee. They were poring over a map of Australia and a pile of travel brochures.

Bett had been taken aback at the news of her parents' holiday. 'It's a practical decision, Bett,' Lola had said to her that morning. 'Your poor parents haven't been away properly in years. With the three of you home to lend a hand this is the perfect opportunity for them to go.'

'But we've all just got here.'

'And you'll see plenty of them when they get back.' She had pulled Bett close, planted a big kiss on her forehead, then lowered her voice. 'I've done it deliberately, so I can have you girls all to myself.'

Anna, Carrie and Lola were already in the function room when she arrived. Anna was explaining to Lola that it might be better if she left them alone. 'We want to talk about it on our own, Lola. In case—'

'You hurt my feelings?' At Anna's guilty nod, Lola laughed. 'No, talk away among yourselves and I'll look forward to hearing what you've got to say.' She gave them a cheery wave. She'd been in earlier and opened all the windows, knowing their voices would float out. She'd even taken a chair out to the back. Silly things, as if she was going to let them talk about her musical without her hearing.

The sisters pulled their chairs round a table in the centre of the room, the scripts and a plunger of coffee in front of them. Bett shot Anna and Carrie a look. Anna was as sleekly turned out as ever—designer clothes, dramatic silver jewellery, all thin lines and sharp hair. Carrie looked like she was on her way to film a shampoo ad, with bouncy blonde hair and trim body, in hipster jeans and tight-fitting T-shirt. Bett tucked her unruly hair behind her ears and tugged at her waisted jeans.

'So,' Anna said, taking charge. The mood was tense. 'Have you both read it?'

Carrie and Bett nodded.

'And what did you think?'

Neither Bett nor Carrie spoke, both looking down at their scripts. Anna waited a moment. Still nothing. Then she leaned forward and spoke, her voice very low and very firm. 'I don't know whether Lola spent ten years or ten minutes on this, but I think we owe it to her at least to talk about it. You both know as well as I do how good she was to us. Right now putting on a musical is the last thing I want to do, to be perfectly honest. But the sooner we talk about it, and decide whether we do it or not, the sooner this meeting's over.'

Bett stared at her script some more. The worst thing about Anna was that apart from being so bossy she was also so often maddeningly right.

'I'm not asking you to do it for me,' Anna continued. 'I'm asking you to do it for Lola. It would make her very happy.'

Carrie looked up then. 'It's easy for you to say. She's been driving me and Mum bananas the past few months.'

'She's been driving Mum bananas for more than thirty years, Carrie, and you know it.' She poured herself some coffee. 'So then.' She tapped the script in a businesslike manner. 'What did you both think of it?'

'It was certainly different,' Bett offered.

She noticed quick answering grins from Carrie and Anna, before their shutters came down again. Different—the word used in the Valley for anything out of the ordinary, a polite way of saying appalling.

'Let me rephrase that,' Bett said. 'I think it's the maddest piece of musical theatre I have ever read.'

Anna's lip twitched. 'I'd agree with that. Carrie?'

Carrie still looked a little sulky. 'If you ask me it's like she took all her favourite pieces from all her favourite musicals, flung them into a blender with a few lines of dialogue and this is what came out.'

Outside, Lola was weighing up whether to be hurt by anything she'd heard. After a moment's reflection, she decided not to be. She smiled serenely. Good girl, Carrie. That was exactly what she had done.

Bett turned to Anna. 'Could you actually work out what was going on?'

'I think so. It's set in Terowie, in wartime, where the villagers get wind that General Douglas MacArthur is coming through on a train—'

'Cue three verses of "Chattanooga Choo Choo",' Bett recalled.

'—and a big row breaks out between two rivals in the local Country Women's Association over who will organise the welcoming party at the railway station. Which develops into a full-scale row—amazingly like the fight scene from *West Side Story*. And of course the son of one rival and the daughter of the other are secretly in love.'

'And just happen to be called Romeo and Juliet, those two common names in 1940s Australia,' Carrie said.

Lola bristled. They might well have been common names in Terowie. How were the girls to know? She listened closely as Anna, Bett and Carrie took it in turns relating the story. They might have been laughing at her musical, but at least it meant they were talking about something.

'. . . And they all live happily ever after, including the couple. Cue "Happy Talk" from *South Pacific*.' Anna leaned back elegantly in her chair.

'Has Lola made up all the General MacArthur business?' Bett asked.

'No, it's true,' Carrie said. 'I checked on the Internet this morning. He did stop in Terowie and that is where he made that famous speech. But I don't think any of that other stuff happened.'

'No, I'd hardly imagine Mrs MacArthur singing "My Favourite Things" to her scared little son in that first scene, when they're flying in from the Philippines,' Anna said.

'And I don't reckon the Terowie villagers came out every day, gazed at their cornfields and sang "Oh, What a Beautiful Morning",' Bett added, fighting another smile.

'There were some good bits, though, didn't you think?' Carrie said. 'I loved the scene where the couple are dancing around the local football oval, singing "I Am Sixteen Going on Seventeen".'

Anna raised an eyebrow. 'You mean the scene that is a direct lift from *The Sound of Music*?'

'Well, that was always my favourite scene in the film, too,' Carrie said defensively. 'And I also liked that scene the night of the first MacArthur's visit, when the lead actress sings "I Could Have Danced All Night" from *My Fair Lady*.'

Bett knew that song well. It had been Carrie's most popular solo moment in the Alphabet Sisters' days.

'But I don't think it works when the next day she sings "I Like To Be in America",' Anna said. 'Not when she's been going on about how much she loves the Australian countryside and that Romeo.'

'But that's the whole thing,' Carrie said passionately. 'She thinks she loves Romeo, but she's torn between her simple life in the country and the pursuit of her dreams.'

Anna stared at her. 'You've really lived this, Carrie, haven't you?'

'Well, I can see what Lola's trying to say,' Carrie said blushing. 'And I think that song is perfect there.'

That song, which just happened to be Carrie's second-favourite song from the Alphabet Sisters' days, Bett thought. She'd just realised what Lola had done.

Anna's tone was now extremely businesslike. 'And what did you both think of the Alphabet Sisters' cameo in the second act?'

Bett's smile disappeared. 'I crossed it out.'

'I did too,' Carrie said.

'Fine. I'll cross it out too.' Anna patted her script. 'Here's what I think. It's completely mad, of course, but it could be done. That's if Lola is actually serious about doing it.'

Lola popped her head up over the window ledge. 'I'm quite serious.'

They all jumped. Anna frowned. 'Lola, this is supposed to be private.'

'Don't be ridiculous. You must have known I'd have been eavesdropping outside. Now, what did you all think of it?'

'It's actually very good,' Anna said.

'Don't sound so surprised,' Lola said.

'I really enjoyed it,' Bett said.

'I knew you would.'

'There's definitely something in there for everybody,' Carrie said.

'That was my whole intention. So it could work?'

'Well, yes,' Anna said. 'But it would need a hall.'

'I've booked it.' She waved the flier at them. 'For March the 20th. It's the anniversary of General MacArthur's visit. Perfect, don't you think?'

'That's so soon. What about sets? Costumes?'

'Len the butcher said he'd be happy to help. He's not a bad carpenter. I've been tucking bits and pieces away for costumes from the charity shop for the past few months.'

'And what about a band?'

Lola gestured grandly at Bett. 'Who needs a band when we've got Bett? You could use the piano here for rehearsals and we could move it to the town hall for the show. Though there are lots of talented musicians in the Valley if you wanted more than piano.'

Bett was going through the song list. Lola had looked after her too. She had chosen many of her favourites.

Anna was leafing through the script again. When she first left drama school in Sydney, she'd joined a musical theatre group that put on mini musicals for corporate functions. That was how she had met Glenn. He'd been organising the Real Estate Association Christmas party. She'd picked up all sorts of tricks and tips for staging a show on a budget. Lola's script was surprisingly good, but she could see where a little cutting here and there would help it . . .

Lola was now all eagerness and excitement. 'I thought you could put an ad in the paper calling for auditions. I've got some wording for it here, look.' She waved another bit of paper at them.

Bett wasn't convinced. 'It's still very tight time-wise.'

Anna took a diary out of her bag. 'Not if we got moving with the auditions, then started rehearsals twice a week. Carrie, would this room be available?'

'I'd have to check the bookings, but it's usually free on week nights. But hold on a moment. Are you all going to stay in the Valley? Here in the motel?' Carrie looked from Anna to Bett. This was moving too quickly for her. 'What about your work, Anna? And Glenn?'

Anna's face was expressionless. 'If we did decide to do the musical, I could juggle work. Go up to Sydney for two days a week. Ellen could come with me.' She didn't mention Glenn.

'No, Ellen couldn't, actually.' Lola gave a guilty smile. 'She'll be in school here. I spoke to the principal today. She's a friend of mine. She said they can certainly find a place for her.'

Carrie turned to her other sister, fighting a feeling of panic. It was one thing hiding Matthew's absence from her sisters for days, but for weeks? 'And you, Bett? What about your work?'

Lola stepped in again. 'She's accepted a part-time job at the *Valley Times*. Haven't you, Bett?'

Bett stared at Lola in amazement. She'd only phoned Rebecca that afternoon. She'd decided to accept the job first and worry later about living so close to Carrie and Matthew.

The mobile beside Anna started vibrating. She checked the number. 'Excuse me,' she said, walking outside to answer the call. 'Glenn?'

'Anna, hello. How are things? How's Ellen?'

233

'Fine. How are you?' So stiff, so awkward with each other.

'Fine, fine. Big news. The Singapore trip is on. I leave in two days.'

'I see. How long will you be away for?'

'Three weeks to begin with. But it's only eight hours' flight from Sydney. I'll be back and forth. I'll still ring Ellen every night, of course. In fact, I'm thinking about getting her a mobile.'

'A mobile? She's only seven years old, Glenn.'

'I like the idea of her having one anyway. To keep her safe.'

One more dig at her failure as a parent. Anna felt very tired, even as she realised he'd just helped her to make the final decision. 'As it turns out, Glenn, that works out well. We're going to stay here in the Valley for a month or so.'

His anger came down the line like a sonic wave. 'Without discussing it with me? At least I told you the Singapore trip was on the cards. What if I hadn't been going there? When was I going to get to see Ellen?'

She walked further away from the motel building, her voice low, the anger only just controlled. 'When would you want to see Ellen? In between nights at Julie's house? In between work trips?'

'Anna, I love her. She's my daughter. You know I see her as much as I can. And just because I'm not with her every hour of the day doesn't mean I'm not thinking about her. What are you going to do about her schooling? Your work?'

Anna had to sit down on a bench, her chest tight with anger. 'I don't know yet. We're still sorting it out.' There was a long pause and then she had to ask. 'Is Julie going to Singapore?'

He tried to bluster through it. 'Well, she's my senior assistant and it's a big deal to set up a brand-new office. I couldn't do it on my own.'

'Is Julie going as your lover as well as your assistant, Glenn?' Anna's voice was smooth. She wanted the truth.

'Julie's coming with me, yes.'

So it was still happening. 'Look, Glenn, I can't talk now. I'll ring you tomorrow.'

She hung up and sat for a moment with her eyes shut, waiting for her breathing to calm. Then she used all the years of drama-school training to put a smile on her face as she walked back into the function room. 'That's all sorted. Glenn's got to go to Singapore for a while, so the timing couldn't have been better. Ellen and I can definitely stay.'

Still outside, leaning in through the window, Lola gazed at her three granddaughters. 'So, have you made a decision? Will you do it?'

Anna looked at Bett, who looked at Carrie, who looked back at Anna. Then they all turned to Lola. 'We'll do it.'

In the function room a week later, Bett was practising songs on the piano for the following night's auditions. Jim and Geraldine had left for their holiday that morning and Bett was on reception duty. She'd already interrupted her piano-playing twice to welcome guests and give out room keys. Carrie had been in the bar earlier, serving rounds of drinks to a small group of people. It was now dark in there. Bett assumed Carrie had closed it all up and gone home for the night.

She finished playing 'Oh, What a Beautiful Morning', walked to the window and stared out into the car park. Being back in the Valley again was sparking memories. Not just about Matthew and the terrible fight with Anna and Carrie, but everything that had happened afterwards.

The morning after the fight, she'd got up at dawn, packed one small bag, filled her car with petrol and started driving. From a roadside motel en route to Melbourne she'd phoned the *Valley Times* office and taken leave without pay until further notice. She'd called a friend from journalism college now based in Melbourne and explained what had happened. By nightfall, she was set up in her friend's spare room.

The next three months had passed in a kind of frenzy. With too much time on her hands, she'd started drinking too much. She had found some freelance work with city newspapers, started falling in and out of bars with a fluid, rowdy gang of reporters. One night, watching a band in a new club, she had bumped into an old work colleague from home. He'd bought her a drink, then another one. The vodka fuelled her confidence, helped her pretend to be carefree, as they swapped stories of newspaper life, keeping it light, fun.

It got later, and the band finished playing. They went on to a late-night bar for more vodka, and then she found herself back in his flat. She remembered getting upset, even crying a little about something. Had it been about Carrie and Matthew? The fight with Anna? He had taken her in his arms and given her a sympathetic hug and that's when the evening had changed. She was the one who'd made it happen. Insisted on it. She wanted to kiss him, to rid herself of memories of Matthew, to behave in a way she'd never behaved.

When she woke the next morning, wild and reckless Bett was long gone, leaving ashamed and hung over Bett lying naked beside him. She lifted his arm from her waist, moved away, trying not to make any noise. She didn't leave a note. It was a big city. They'd never see each other again.

Back home she'd taken to her bed. By nightfall she'd been desperate to talk to someone about it. Too shy to tell her flatmate, unable to ring her sisters, she'd called Lola and told her everything.

Lola had been nonjudgmental. 'Perhaps it was better that it was someone you knew, not a stranger. Do you want to see him again?'

'Of course I don't. How could I face him?' Then she'd started crying. 'I don't do things like that, Lola. I don't know what's happening to me.'

'Bett, it was a one-night stand, not a mass murder. Keep it in perspective. Millions of people have those every day. For now, get into your pyjamas, go to bed and have an early night. Don't have a drink. And calm down.'

Then, a few days later a postcard arrived, addressed to Bett, with one line in the centre: *Go and live overseas.*

She phoned Lola immediately.

'I've been pushing you to go for years. The money is burning a hole in my pocket.'

Lola had given each of the girls a return airfare to the place of their choice for their twenty-fifth birthday. Anna had gone to America for an acting course. Glenn had followed her out and proposed to her as they took a horse and carriage ride round Central Park. Carrie had headed off on a round-Asia trip, which then turned into a year away. But between study and work, Bett had never found time to leave Australia.

'I can't take it from you, Lola. You can't afford it.'

'Darling, you haven't the faintest idea whether I am poorhouse material or a rich old lady. Just take the money and run.'

And so it had happened. Bett finally agreed to accept the fare and, two weeks after that conversation, found herself in Dublin.

With an Irish passport, courtesy of Lola, she set off looking for work in newspapers, before realising she could combine music and writing by getting a job behind the bar in one of Dublin's many music venues and writing the occasional review of the gigs for newspapers.

She found a flatshare, sharing a four-storey red-brick terraced house with young students and walking to work through the fruit markets. She started living a strange upside-down life, working in the night, sleeping in the day, seeing as many as ten live bands a week in the venues she worked in. Just as the late nights started to lose their appeal, a chance conversation with Karl over the bar, while one of his early signings played to an empty room, led to a move to London and the job in his record company. She'd felt brave, adventurous, free . . .

But then she had started to miss things. She would find herself longing for conversations with Anna—and even with Carrie.

There'd been only one communication between them in the three years, when Lola had told her about Ellen being attacked. Bett had been shocked by the news. That same night she sent Anna a card, brief, to the point, telling her how sad she was to hear about Ellen. She heard nothing back. After that, there hadn't been another opportunity. Not until the excuse of the eightieth birthday party had arrived.

Images of Anna and Carrie came to mind now. Things weren't as she'd expected with them. Anna wasn't as snooty or as aloof as the imaginary Anna she had been carrying in her mind through the years. And Carrie wasn't as smug or self-satisfied as she'd expected either. In fact, they both seemed . . . what? Bett wondered. A little troubled?

In the kitchen of her house, Carrie glanced up at the clock. Nearly ten o'clock. He should be here any moment. She checked her appearance again, smoothed down her dress, straightened the knives and forks on the table. She was nervous, she realised. Of her own husband.

Of her estranged husband, to be accurate.

She went out onto the verandah. The paddocks all around the house were dark for as far as she could see. In the daytime she liked the peace and quiet. In the night time, without Matthew, it gave her the creeps. It was a hot evening, but she still shivered.

She longed for a return of the days when the very sight of the house would give her a lift. She and Matthew had agreed on everything—they wanted an old-style stone house, with a verandah, open fireplaces, and perhaps an acre or two of land. And they wanted at least three bedrooms.

'Four,' she'd said.

'You want three children?' he'd laughed.

'At least,' she'd said airily. 'And as soon as possible.'

'Not too soon.'

She should have picked up the hints then, shouldn't she? But no, she'd chosen to go on making plans, picking out nursery colours before they even had a nursery, let alone a baby . . .

They'd found this house by accident. One weekend they'd gone for a drive and taken one of the dirt roads to the south of the town, winding up between the vineyards. A hand-painted FOR SALE sign at the end of the track led them up to an old stone house. The house had almost everything they had been looking for—the original stonework, the verandah, the slate floors. They'd made an offer the next day. Two months later they'd moved in.

Carrie forced herself to stay outside now, waiting for the sound of his car. He'd been surprised at her call that afternoon, she knew that. No wonder, considering what she had shouted at him last time they had spoken, several weeks ago now. 'It's over, Matthew. Can't you see that?'

He'd sounded exhausted on the phone, but he'd agreed to make the long drive home, to hear what it was she had to say.

It was after midnight by the time he finally arrived. She'd worn a track in the verandah from her pacing and was a little drunk from the red wine she'd been sipping. She greeted him, offered him a beer, then led the way into their living room.

'So how was work today?' she asked cheerily, even though the sight of him—exhausted, his clothes covered in dust—gave her the answer.

He ran his fingers through his hair. She knew the gesture well. It meant he was tired and it also meant he was feeling impatient. 'Can we cut to the chase here, Carrie? What did you want to talk about?'

He was angry, too. And she supposed he had every right to be. She'd kicked him out of the house after all. Hung up on him each time he'd called. She decided to tell him the truth. 'It's about Bett.'

He ran his fingers through his hair again.

'She's staying on in the Valley. She's taken a job at the local paper.'

'Has she? Good on her.'

'So how does it make you feel?'

'About her job? Carrie, it's got nothing to do with me.'

'I don't mean about her job. I mean, how do you feel about Bett being close by again?'

'Carrie, I feel what I felt when you asked me about Bett six months ago. A year ago. I can't keep telling you.'

'I don't believe you.'

He raised his voice at her then. 'Because you don't want to believe me. It's like banging my head against a brick wall, and I'm sick of it, Carrie.' He sighed. 'Listen, may I have a shower? Can we talk about it after that?'

She turned her back, shrugged. She saw in the reflection in the window that he stood and looked at her for a few moments, before he went to the bathroom. She took her drink out onto the verandah, waited for him to join her. Twenty minutes later she was still waiting.

She got to her feet and walked into their bedroom and found him asleep on top of the bed, half undressed. It seemed he hadn't even got to the shower, simply lain down on their bed and fallen asleep. She felt a ripple of guilt looking down at him, at the boyish face asleep on the pillow, the fair hair tousled, dirty.

'Matthew?'

She lay down on the bed and touched his back. No response. She ran her hand down his side and he flinched. She waited, tried again. He muttered something, moved away, lying on his front, out of reach.

'Forget it, then,' she said crossly. When had this happened? The two of them who had barely been able to keep their hands off each other since the first night they met. How had she made such a mess of things?

She fought back tears, fanning angry feelings instead. If it hadn't been for Lola, the way she had started talking incessantly about how much she missed the three of them, she'd never have been in this position. Lola had never said it, but Carrie knew what was beneath it all—it was all Carrie's fault, for stealing Matthew from Bett. If she had never done that, they would all be living happily ever after, wouldn't they? She hadn't been able to get the guilty feelings out of her mind, at the same time that Matthew's work started taking him away for stretches at a time. When he was home, they seemed to fight. And not just about having a baby. Finally, in a fit of temper two months earlier, she had said they needed a trial separation.

He'd been shocked. 'Why?'

'Because it's not right. We shouldn't have got together. You should have stayed with Bett.'

'Carrie, we've been through this. I fell in love with you. It would have been wrong for me to stay with her.'

'Maybe it wouldn't have. Maybe that's what you should have done.'

At the back of her mind were Bett and Anna's voices. 'We told you so.' She couldn't bear it. What a horrible, awful, unfair mess, she thought, curling into a ball on the edge of the bed.

Beside her Matthew gave a loud snore. It was all she could do not to smother him with her pillow.

In her room at the motel, Anna was lying on her bed with Ellen tucked in beside her, fast asleep. Anna's eyes were wide open as she stared into space. Her skin felt clammy, her stomach was churning, she felt exhausted but unable to sleep.

She'd had another fight with Glenn on the phone that evening. More guilt, more blaming, more heated words, all in hushed tones so that Ellen, in the bath, couldn't hear. She'd come out wrapped in a towel, and asked, 'Is that Daddy?' At Anna's nod, she'd reached for the phone and settled herself on the bed, chattering away to him as if things were perfectly normal with them all. And then the worst of it. 'Will you say hello to Julie for me too?' Anna had nearly been sick. Ellen was friendly enough with her father's lover to send her messages.

When Ellen had handed back the phone, Anna had barely been able to speak to him, only keeping her voice civil because she knew Ellen was listening to every word. Afterwards, she'd wanted to throw the mobile across the room, hoping to see it smash, the parts fly into all corners. On the verge of doing that, in sight of Ellen or not, it had started ringing again. Not Glenn this time, but her booking agent, Roz. She apologised for ringing so late, but explained that a big job had come up from one of her past clients.

'They've specifically asked for you. It's a good gig, Anna. You could do it in your sleep.' It was the voice-over for three teenage sex-education videos. 'Top rates, a few days' work, maximum. Can you do it?'

Anna had massaged her temple with her spare hand. She'd promised Ellen they would have a long break together. But this job would pay well. She wouldn't need Glenn's money for a while. 'Of course I can.'

CHAPTER FIVE

BETT TRIED OUT her new swivel chair again, giving it a spin and ending up facing Rebecca's office across the corridor.

She'd had a long meeting with Rebecca that morning. Apart from wanting her to write general news and feature stories, Rebecca also wanted her to write the editorial for a new project, a twelve-page supplement on the Valley's tourist attractions, sponsored by the tourism commission. 'They've asked for lots of colour, all the sights and smells and tastes, so I want you and the photographer to actually try everything out.'

'You want me to do it? The new girl?' It was a dream assignment.

Rebecca laughed. 'Yes, I know. I'd rather be doing it myself. Let me tell you, being editor's not all it's cracked up to be.'

Bett had returned to her desk, for the first time in months feeling buoyed and enthusiastic about a writing project. She'd started drawing up a list of subjects: the wine-tasting tours, the gourmet cooking course in one of the Clare Valley's grand country homes, the overnight sleeping-under-the-stars experience at the Valley's oldest sheep station, the guided historical walk along the path of the old railway line . . .

She had picked up the phone to dial one of the tour operators when a voice behind her had made her jump. 'Bett Quinlan, as I live and breathe.' It was Neil, the sports reporter who'd been with the paper since it started. 'It's great to see you. Welcome back.'

She stood and hugged him. 'Great to see you too, Neil.'

'I've been hearing all about your grandmother's musical. Don't suppose you've got a part for an old fellow like me?' He burst into the first line of 'The Sound of Music'.

'Auditions are on tonight. Why don't you come along?'

Rebecca came out of her office. 'I'm thinking about coming along myself. I wouldn't want to miss the chance of seeing some of the locals auditioning. Much better than watching those reality shows on telly. Now then, Hildie's just come in, the photographer you'll be doing the tourism supplement with.' She poked her head into one of the side rooms and called out. 'Hildie, come and meet our new reporter.' Then she lowered her voice. 'You might remember him, actually. It was before my time, but he used to work here before he went to Melbourne for a few years. I snapped him up when he came back last year.' She smiled over Bett's head at the new arrival.

'Bett Quinlan, from London, I'd like you to meet Daniel Hilder.'

Bett turned and felt the colour run from her face. Her one-night stand had just walked into the office.

In the gym at the country club, Anna looked up at the clock. She'd only been on the treadmill for ten minutes and she was already breathless after just a few days away from exercise. She could almost hear her personal trainer's voice: *A little every day keeps age and fat away.* Too bad. She could do nothing about her age and it wasn't as if she needed to lose weight at the moment. If anything, she needed to put some on.

'Hello, Anna.'

She turned. It was Richard Lawrence, dressed in shorts and a T-shirt, a towel over his shoulder. It was the first time she'd seen him since the day after Lola's party. He looked quite like an athlete. Lean and spare.

'Richard, how are you?' She reached forward and turned off the treadmill, gradually adjusting her steps as the belt slowed.

Richard smiled. 'I'm well, thank you. I didn't realise you liked to work out here too.'

'Occasionally. But I'm not in the mood this morning. I think I'll try the natural air approach and walk back to the motel instead.'

'Do you mind if I join you? I've been hoping to have the chance to talk to you again.'

She stood in front of him, a towel in her hands. Years ago she had decided to get it out into the open when men made approaches to her like this. 'Really, Richard, you're being very forward. Are you trying to pick me up?'

'I don't know yet,' he said calmly. 'You're certainly very beautiful, and I like that spark in your eye, but I like to be able to have a conversation with my lovers, not just look at them. So it's probably too early to tell.'

To both their surprise, she burst out laughing. 'That is the best answer I have ever heard. What about your workout?'

He grinned. 'We could walk the long way back, couldn't we?'

At seven twenty that evening, the function room was filled to capacity. The plan was for Lola to welcome everyone, briefly sketch the musical, then pass it over to Anna, who would run the auditions. 'It's your baby, now,' Lola had told the girls that afternoon. 'I've done my bit. I want to enjoy it at the end, when all the hard work has been done.'

'You're not going to sit in on every rehearsal, making comments?' Anna asked.

'Me, make comments? What do you take me for? No, I'm leaving it all to you and spending the time with Ellen instead.'

Lola hadn't been surprised when Ellen had said she didn't want to be in the musical. She'd noticed how self-conscious the little girl was. 'Excellent news, Ellen,' she'd said cheerfully. 'That means you and I can keep each other company while the others get on with the hard work.'

Lola made her way to the front of the room now. She waited dramatically for the chatter to stop, then gave a little bow. 'Thank you all for coming. It's the most wonderful turn-out. You may have heard this is my life's work, something I have been planning for nearly ten years . . .'

Bett gazed around the room as Lola gave a précis of the storyline. A late arrival coming in the door caught her eye. Richard Lawrence. She wasn't surprised to see him. He'd been curious about the musical since Lola's party. She brought her attention back to Lola's speech.

'. . . So you'll see it's the age-old story of family against family, young love thwarted, a town pulling together against the odds, the tyranny and ferociousness of war, all to a soundtrack of lots of marvellous old songs from everyone's favourite musicals.' There was a burst of applause, then Lola held up her hand again. 'So now, over to my granddaughter Anna.'

Anna moved forward, all glamour and poise. 'Good evening, everyone, and thanks for coming. We'll have a warm-up or two, and then we'll hear you do your individual pieces.'

In Room Seven, Lola was sitting on the side of Ellen's bed, telling stories about the girls' childhood. 'I called it my Collection of Cries, Ellen. I had a whole row of jars and as soon as I'd hear your mother cry, or Bett, or Carrie, I'd sneak up behind them and capture their cries in the jar, then put the lid on. It was marvellous. They'd stop crying immediately.'

Ellen was giggling. 'And have you still got all the jars?'

Lola sadly shook her head. 'No. Unfortunately three bold little girls opened all the lids one afternoon. You've never heard such a racket. Five years' worth of tears and tantrums released in a moment.'

Ellen moved further down in her bed. 'Can you tell me another story?'

'Yes, but not tonight. It's past all good great-granddaughters' bedtimes.'

'But wait, Lola. I've got another question.'

Lola waited. She was well used to these delaying tactics. 'One more question, then.'

'Why have you got a funny voice?'

'What do you mean a funny voice?'

'You talk differently to other people. You talk like this: "It's past all good great-granddaughters' bedtimes".'

Lola laughed out loud. Ellen had just perfectly mimicked her Irish accent. She was definitely Anna's daughter. 'That, my love, is called an Irish accent, not a funny voice.'

'I like it.'

'Good. I'll keep it, then.' She kissed Ellen's forehead. 'Night night, sweetheart. Sleep well. And I'm three doors down if there's anything you need.'

'Night night, Lola.' Ellen's voice was barely audible.

Letting herself back into her own room, Lola felt suddenly exhausted. She'd have liked to sit and watch every moment of the auditions. She'd have liked to sit in on every production meeting, too, and paint the sets. But she didn't have the energy for it any more. She was in better nick than most eighty-year-olds, there was no doubt about it, but it was all downhill from here and she didn't like it one bit.

She opened the bar fridge and mixed herself a gin and tonic. She'd have a little read, a little think, a little drink and then a good night's sleep. She was longing for her bed, in fact. They didn't warn you of that in the growing-old books, did they?

She took a sip of gin and moved to turn on the TV, then changed her mind, preferring her own thoughts. She'd been remembering a lot from her childhood recently, ever since she had gone through the few photos she had, picking them out so Frank from the electrical shop could turn them into slides for her. He'd dropped the originals back that afternoon, and come in for a chat. He was off to Ireland himself in a few months and did she want him to call at her old house and take photos?

She'd patted him on the hand. 'Kind Frank, thank you but no. Bett did that for me when she was there a few years ago.' Not that Lola had ever looked closely at the photos Bett had sent. It wasn't as if they had meant anything to her. All the same, she'd sent Bett a note, thanking her for going to all the trouble of taking them.

She took another sip of her drink and turned to her crossword. She'd finish the last few clues, then go to bed. As she reached for her pen and reading glasses, there was a crackle and a fizzing sound and the ceiling light went out. She had a spare light bulb in the wardrobe. She stood up and felt the desk chair. Yes, it was sturdy enough and the ceilings were so low, she'd easily be able to reach.

She took a scarf off the end of her bed to unscrew the hot bulb. Opening the wardrobe door to give herself something to hang on to, she climbed up onto the chair. As she did, the chair shook slightly. She turned to grasp the wardrobe door but misjudged the distance. The chair tilted and she felt herself falling, then her head knocked sharply against the wardrobe door and she fell to the floor.

The break was over and everyone was milling back from the bar. At their table, the three sisters were flicking through the forms.

Bett glanced down her list. Many of the names had enthusiastic ticks beside them. 'What did you think, Anna?' She was quite surprised how easy it had been tonight to make conversation with her sisters.

Anna moved her hand and sighed heavily. Her sheet of paper was blank, apart from a few doodles. She flicked through the forms again. 'Have we heard this Daniel Hilder audition? He filled out a form and he'd be the right age for the Jack-the-Lad character, wouldn't he?'

Bett stiffened. 'Daniel Hilder's here?'

'The photographer?' Carrie looked up. 'I didn't see him. Will I go and ask him to audition?'

'No.' Bett spoke louder than she intended.

Anna looked surprised. 'You don't want him to audition?'

'No, I mean I'll go and ask him.' Bett stood up, taking her glass of wine with her. She did a circuit of the room, then spotted him walking in from the bar, a drink in hand. 'Daniel?'

He turned, and at that moment someone behind her stepped back suddenly, bumping her elbow and sending her glass of red wine flying. She stood there with red wine dripping from her chin to her knees.

For a split-second she was tempted to run out of the room. Then she had a brainwave. 'I'm going to ignore the fact that even happened,' she said coolly.

'Are you?' He seemed surprised. 'All right, then. So will I.'

She tried to ignore a glint of amusement in his eye. 'I was wondering whether you wanted to audition, because if you do there's still time.'

He nodded, but didn't answer.

'Well?'

He smiled. 'I'm sorry, Bett. I really am trying to ignore that little accident, but it's a bit hard when you've got wine dripping down your chin.'

She clung desperately to her new cool persona. 'Well, we can't have that.' She reached for a serviette and wiped the wine away. 'Would you like to audition? I noticed you'd put your name down.'

'I got called out for an hour,' he said. 'And missed my slot.'

She opened her mouth, needing to say something about their night together, trying to find the words for it, when a voice behind her said, 'Hi, Daniel. I'm Carrie. I don't think we've met.'

'Hello, Carrie.'

Carrie looked from one to the other. 'So are you two ready to get down to it?'

Bett blushed. She didn't look at Daniel. 'Pardon?'

'The audition?'

Yes, the audition. 'Of course.'

Bett followed Carrie and Daniel to the piano, surprised the candles on the tables weren't melting from the heat coming off her face.

Anna was businesslike. 'OK, Bett, Daniel, when you're ready.'

Bett stared at the sheet music. Hands poised over the piano, she glanced up at Daniel, nodded and played the first note.

A loud shrieking filled the room. They all turned. Ellen was in the doorway, dressed in her pyjamas, tears pouring down her cheeks.

'Mummy, Lola's dead.'

Bett pressed her cheek against the wall of the hospital corridor, feeling the coolness as she spoke into the public phone. 'No, you don't need to come back, Dad. She's in hospital. It's all under control.'

'Are you sure? We can catch a flight and be there in a few hours.'

'Seriously, you don't need to. She's a bit shocked, but it's just a broken wrist and a bad cut on her forehead. She wasn't even unconscious when Ellen found her. It's just Ellen got such a fright.'

Nothing compared to what Ellen's words had done to the rest of them. The auditions had been forgotten as Bett, Anna and Carrie ran to Lola's room. The first sight was the worst, seeing Lola sprawled across the floor, the chair upended beside her, her left wrist bent at an angle.

Anna reached for her right wrist to feel the pulse, then nearly leapt out of her skin as Lola spoke. 'Hello, darling.'

'You're not dead?'

'Not unless heaven looks like the motel.'

Bett was on the floor beside her in seconds, gently touching her. 'Are you hurt? What happened?'

'The stupid light bulb. I told your father to buy better quality ones.'

'Lola, we've told you not to change those bulbs,' Anna said crossly. 'You're too old to be climbing up on chairs.'

Lola rallied. 'One minute you're crying because you think I'm dead, the next minute you're telling me off.'

Bett got up and called for an ambulance and Carrie stayed with Lola while Anna moved to the door, asking the crowd that had gathered to please move back. 'She's fine, she'll be fine. She's not dead at all.'

'Mummy?' A familiar little voice came from the back of the group. Anna turned as Richard Lawrence came into view, holding Ellen by the hand.

He brought her forward. 'I found her crying in the function room.'

Anna pulled the little girl into her arms. 'Ellie, I'm so sorry to leave you behind.' In the rush to find Lola after Ellen's announcement they had run straight past her. 'You're such a good girl, you might have saved your great-grandmother's life, do you know that?'

Bett saw headlights approaching and crouched down beside Lola again. She gently took her good hand. 'The ambulance is here.'

It wasn't the ambulance but an ordinary station wagon. Daniel Hilder got out and walked over. 'I thought it might be better if I took Lola to the hospital. The ambulance could be a while yet.'

'You see how important this musical is?' Lola said. 'I told you this Valley needs another ambulance.'

'Lola, are you sure you're OK to move?' Bett asked.

'I'm fine. It's just my sore head and this stupid wrist.' She was shaking.

Carrie was on one side of her, Bett on the other. Bett turned to Daniel. 'We'll accept, if you don't mind. Carrie, you and I go in with her. Anna, you'd better stay here with Ellen. Lola, can you stand?'

Daniel stepped forward. 'I'll carry you to the car, Lola, if you need it.'

'So kind of you, Daniel,' Lola managed to be gracious. 'But I'll walk. Where's my little Ellen?' Ellen came forward and Lola touched her on the cheek. 'Thank you, my little darling, for doing exactly the right thing.'

Ellen's face filled with pride. After that it had been all action, getting Lola to the hospital, into the waiting room. Daniel Hilder had been there, helping, then he had gone before Bett had a chance to thank him.

On the phone, Jim Quinlan sounded relieved. 'You're sure you don't need us there, Bett?'

'I'm sure, Dad. Lola's sleeping now. I'll call you in the morning.'

Bett made her way towards the exit, where Carrie was speaking to Matthew on her mobile phone.

'Bett?'

She turned. It was Daniel.

'Is everything OK? Is Lola all right?'

She nodded. 'She's going to be fine.' Nearly two hours had passed since they had arrived, the time speeding past in a flurry of doctors' visits and X-rays, before Lola was finally settled into a small ward. 'Have you been waiting all this time?'

'I didn't mind. I had a book with me. I thought you and your sister might need a lift back to the motel.'

She gave him a big, grateful smile. 'Thank you.'

At the motel, Anna tucked the sheet round Ellen's shoulders. The child was nearly asleep, stirring now and again to ask another question. 'Lola will be all right, Mum, won't she?'

Anna stroked Ellen's forehead. 'Of course she will, Ellie. She'll be back home before we know it.'

Ellen's eyelids fluttered, then closed, and in seconds her breathing was slow, measured.

As Anna came out of the room, she jumped as a figure appeared in front of her. It was Richard. She noticed the bar and function room were already in darkness.

He came closer. 'I hope you don't mind, I wanted to do something, so I closed up for you. I know where all the light switches are.'

'Thank you,' she said, surprised and touched.

'And Lola will be all right?'

Anna nodded. 'I'm sure she will. It's us who nearly died of the shock.'

Richard looked concerned. 'Anna, can I make you a cup of tea? I know my way round the kitchen, I think.'

'Thanks, Richard. That would be really kind of you.'

'**F**usspot.'

Anna grinned. 'Lola, I'm not a fusspot. I'm doing what the doctor told us to do, checking on you all the time.'

'Much ado about nothing, if you ask me.'

'Taming of the shrew, more like it.'

Anna stood by Lola's bed, looking down at her grandmother, sitting up against the pillows, her arm in a sling made from a wildly patterned silk scarf. Her bed jacket was a bright yellow satin. There were bunches of flowers all over the room—they'd been arriving all day as word got round that Lola was out of hospital and back at the motel.

Anna gently tucked the sheet in around her grandmother. 'Are you sure I can't get you anything before I go to rehearsals?'

'I'm fine, darling. Now, off you go.'

Anna had been gone only a minute or two before Carrie knocked lightly on the door and came in. 'Is everything all right, Lola?'

'I couldn't be happier, darling. All this spoiling, it's marvellous.' She patted the bed. 'Now, enough about me. Let me interrogate you for a quick minute. Are you coping with all the motel business while your parents are away? Do you need any extra help?'

'Everything's fine. No problems at all.' Carrie was enjoying it, in fact. It was giving her the opportunity to try out a few things.

'And how are things with Matthew?'

'They're fine,' she lied smoothly, picking up one of the Get Well cards on Lola's bedside table, concentrating fiercely on the greeting inside. 'He sends his love. Says he would have brought you a bunch of grapes if he'd been here.'

'If he'd been allowed to be here, you mean. Carrie, I've been thinking about the ban and I've decided it can be lifted. I think it would be all right now if he visited here again. I'll leave it up to you to arrange it. The sooner the better, I think.'

Carrie turned away before Lola saw her expression.

Lola had just gone back to her crossword after Carrie's departure when there was another knock. A dark curly head poked round the door. 'Lola? Are you OK?'

Lola smiled at her. 'Bett, darling, shouldn't you be at the rehearsal?'

'I'm on my way. I got delayed with a late arrival at reception. I just wanted to check if you needed anything or if you wanted to come up and watch. We've actually got a pretty good cast lined up.'

Lola was leaning back against her pillows, content. 'I can hardly wait until opening night. Tell me, Bett, are you ready to see Matthew yet?'

'Haven't you got a little bell you can ring to warn me you're bringing up something personal?'

'Do you want to see him? I think you should. Get it over and done with. It will clear the air between you and Carrie.'

'Carrie and I are fine.' They weren't, actually. Things may have been thawing between her and Anna, but they were still covered in snow with Carrie. She kissed her grandmother. 'You know, you're lucky I love you so much or I'd call you an interfering, meddlesome old bag.'

Lola laughed and returned to her crossword.

That night, Carrie was in the office when she heard a knock at the door. It was Bett. Carrie was surprised. So far they had done their best to avoid being alone together. 'Is everything all right? Lola's OK?'

'She's fine. Watching TV, complaining that her gin and tonic levels are down.' Bett hesitated. 'I wanted to talk to you about something else.'

'Oh. Come in.'

Bett took a seat and tried to feel her way. 'It's about Matthew.'

Carrie stiffened.

Bett couldn't help noticing. 'Carrie, I need to see him.'

'What do you mean "need"?'

'I think the three of us need to get together. Maybe Lola was right at the start to ask you to keep him away, but I'm staying on and, with the musical and everything, I think it's important.'

'You've been talking to Lola, haven't you?'

'Yes. But it's what I want, too.' Couldn't Carrie even meet her halfway?

'He's away for work,' Carrie said shortly.

'Then when he's back at the weekend.'

'He doesn't come back every weekend.'

'Well, on a weekend he does come back.'

Carrie was looking down again. 'I'll think about it.'

'I don't get it,' Bett whispered to Anna several minutes later. On the way back to her room, Bett had seen Anna's light on, and on the spur of the moment knocked gently on her door. Anna had seemed surprised, but beckoned her in, her finger on her lips. Ellen was asleep in the single bed. 'What does Carrie think I'm going to do, hurl myself at him when I see him? Manacle myself to his legs? It's like she doesn't want me anywhere near him, in case I try to steal him back or something.'

'And you wouldn't, would you?'

'Wouldn't what?'

'Try to steal him back.'

'Sorry?'

'You wouldn't want him back, would you?'

Bett tensed. 'I don't know.' A pause. 'I'm not sure how I'll react until I see him.' She looked away. She didn't want to spoil this new fragile friendship with Anna. 'I mean it. That's why I need to see him.' She rushed to change the subject. 'So how did Ellie enjoy school today?' The little girl had started at the local school that week.

Anna hesitated, then accepted the change of topic. 'Fine. It takes time to settle in, though. You remember what it's like, arriving at a new school in the middle of term.'

Bett nodded. The tension was back between them. What should she do now? Try to break through it again? Ask about Glenn, when he was one of the main reasons she and Anna hadn't spoken in three years? 'How's Glenn, Anna?' The words came out sounding half chewed.

'He's fine,' Anna answered.

Bett knew her well enough to know that was the most Anna would say about it tonight. She watched as Anna went to the fridge, took out a bottle of wine and reached for the corkscrew. She looked amazing—the sleek straight hair, the perfect make-up, the thin, tanned body. And that cool poise she had. It suddenly seemed important to Bett to compliment Anna, to let her know how great she looked, to be the first to start building bridges. As Anna came over to the bed with the opened bottle and two glasses, she smiled up at her. 'Anna, you really are amazing.'

Anna's brow creased. 'Pardon me?'

'You look incredible. The perfect figure, perfect clothes, perfect hair, perfect skin, the perfect marriage, gorgeous little daughter, all so effortlessly.' Bett laughed, pleased with how it was all sounding. 'I'm sure the day will come when we're reading about the Anna Quinlan range of home and beauty products.'

To Bett's amazement, Anna wasn't amused. And she certainly didn't take it as a compliment. 'You think it comes easily? Effortlessly?' Her voice was still low but her eyes were furious. 'You think I am skinny by accident? No, Bett. It's called discipline. Think my hair looks like this naturally? No, it costs a fortune once a month. And my perfect marriage?' Anna took a breath, 'Oh, yes, Bett, it is so perfect that I am—'

'Mummy?'

Anna put down the wine and moved swiftly over to Ellen, talking gently, stroking her forehead until she settled again. When all was quiet, she moved silently back.

Bett stood up, her voice a whisper. 'I'll go. I'm sorry to interrupt—'

'Please don't go yet.' Anna looked very tired all of a sudden.

They sat awkwardly for a moment, neither of them speaking. Bett shifted on the bed, wanting to apologise. She took a breath. 'Anna, I'm sorry for what I said about the way you look. I meant it as a compliment, really. It just came out wrong.' In front of her eyes, tension slipped out of Anna's body, the tight look round her mouth disappeared.

Anna gave an embarrassed smile. 'I'm sorry for snapping at you. I'm just really tired, I think.' She stood up, retrieved the wine and poured two glasses, passing one to Bett. They sat in silence for a moment, before Anna spoke again. 'So London was good? And Dublin?'

'It was, yes.' There it was, three years summed up in one sentence.

Another pause and then Anna spoke again. 'Bett, can I ask you something personal . . . Did you meet anyone in Dublin or London? Any men, I mean?'

Bett shook her head. The sad truth was she hadn't met anyone she liked, or anyone who had liked her, either. She decided to keep her answer light. 'No. Destined to stay on the shelf, I suppose.'

'I'm sure you'll meet someone. Maybe even a nice country boy.'

Bett laughed softly, exhilarated by the pleasure of talking to Anna again. 'That'd be ironic! I spend three years in Dublin and London and all the time my dream man is waiting in my home town.' She'd been joking, but someone came to mind. 'Do you know who is nice? Richard, the Englishman here at the motel. I sat next to him at Lola's party and he's good company. And have you seen when he smiles? It's like a transformation. Should I ask him out for a drink, do you think? Tonight, even?'

'I think he's out.'

'No, he's not. I saw him go into his room earlier.' Bett stood up. 'I think I'll ask him if he wants to go into town and have a drink with me.'

'No, Bett.'

'Why not?'

'I think there's a motorbike rally on in town. The pubs are jammed.'

'Oh. Well, perhaps I'll have an early night.' She hesitated, then leaned over and kissed Anna. 'Thanks. It was very good to talk to you again.'.

'I liked talking to you too.'

Bett let herself out, quietly closing the door. Anna sat down on her bed and breathed a slow sigh of relief.

In his room, Richard typed one more paragraph, then pressed the SAVE button on his laptop computer. Good, he'd managed to get a lot done and still leave himself time to get ready.

As he stretched he looked with pleasure at the growing pile of paper beside him. It had been a good idea to come here. He was easily imagining his characters in the same landscape more than 150 years earlier. The Clare Valley was like a wilder version of Tuscany, he'd decided. Rolling hills, vineyards, olive groves, old stone buildings and that incredible wide blue sky, day after day. He'd explored the villages and soaked up the scenery—the wooded hills, the gum trees silhouetted against the sky and the willow trees edging the dry creek beds.

He said another silent thanks to his aunt, who had died a year earlier, leaving Richard and his two sisters more than £30,000 in her will. The money had come through six weeks after he had split with his long-term girlfriend, a reporter on the same newspaper. It had spurred him on to get out of journalism and make a real attempt at writing a novel.

He'd spent a month in Sydney before deciding to base himself in the Clare Valley. He'd found the Valley View Motel on the Internet. It hadn't quite lived up to its name, he thought with a grin. More Part of a Hill

View than Valley View. But he hadn't expected to uncover such fascinating research material from the local history group. Or to come
across such a character as Lola Quinlan. And he certainly hadn't
expected to meet anyone so beautiful, or so fragile, or so entertaining
as Lola's granddaughter.

There was a knock at the door. He opened it and smiled. 'Hello.' He
turned and gestured extravagantly towards the small table set with a
bottle of wine and two glasses. 'Please, come in.'

Anna smiled. 'Thank you. I'd love to.'

Out at the farmhouse, Carrie was lying in the middle of the double bed,
wide awake. After she'd got back from work, she'd scrubbed the whole
house and cleaned out the fridge. But she still wasn't tired and she still
couldn't get her conversations with Bett and Matthew out of her head,
knowing now that they both wanted to see each other.

From her position on the bed, she noticed a T-shirt had fallen
between the wardrobe and the dressing table. She hadn't noticed it
before. She was over to it in a moment. It was one of Matthew's.

She didn't think twice. She stripped off her nightie and pulled his
T-shirt over her head, breathing in his smell, feeling the cotton against
her skin, trying to imagine how he felt when she hugged him.

It made her feel a bit better.

Anna let herself quietly back into her room. She went straight over to
Ellen and kissed her gently. The little girl was still fast asleep.

She walked into the bathroom and started taking off her make-up.
What an unusual man. He hadn't made a pass at her or made her feel at
all uncomfortable. They had just enjoyed a glass of wine and talked. The
same way they had talked so easily the night of Lola's accident, when he
had made her a cup of tea. He was just so interested in everything, in
what she did for a living, in what had happened to Ellen, in how long
her parents had owned the motel.

'Are you a detective?' she'd asked him.

'No, I'm not. I'm a journalist trying to become a novelist.'

'In my experience, people don't ask so many questions unless they're
after something.'

He had laughed. 'Why are you so suspicious? I'm interested because
I'm interested in people, especially people with such beautiful voices.'

She had blushed.

'I've also discovered there's nothing to fuel the imagination like
hearing other people's stories,' he said. 'So it's not so much curiosity as

cannibalism. I'm feeding off you so I can write my own book.'

'Oh, in that case, that's fine.'

He'd understood completely when she had slipped away several times to check on Ellen, a few rooms away.

'Everything all right?' he'd asked each time.

'She's fast asleep,' she'd been able to answer.

'So you can stay a bit longer?' At her nod, he'd poured her more wine. Anna was enjoying the gentle atmosphere. 'Are you really writing a book or is that a cover story for something much more sinister?'

'I'm really writing a book. Trying to write a book, at least,' he'd said. 'And this is the perfect place to do it. The scenery is beautiful. All the people I've met seem very interesting.' He paused. 'One in particular.'

'Really?' A look had passed between them. 'That's good.'

She smiled as she finished taking off her make-up and moved quietly back into the bedroom. She'd been flirting with him, she realised. And not only that, she'd enjoyed every minute of it.

CHAPTER SIX

SITTING ON A COMFORTABLE CHAIR in front of her room the following morning, Lola closed her eyes in the sunshine, feeling like a tired old cat snoring on a windowsill. A tired, satisfied old cat, at least. Broken wrist and banged head aside, things were going well. She'd managed to get the musical underway, send Geraldine and Jim off on holiday, and get the girls working together in the motel. There was the little matter of getting Matthew back on the scene, getting the reunion out of the way, but that day was drawing closer, Lola knew.

So now what should she do with herself? The best way to keep the mind alert was to keep it occupied. She needed another project, something else to do. This morning she'd been reading her new copy of *Ireland's Treasures*, the magazine sent airmail to her each week, hoping that might spark some idea. There was a fascinating article about the Lisdoonvarna Matchmaking Festival in County Clare. An annual event, when bachelor farmers would come down from the hills and meet young ladies in the genteel surroundings of tea dances and elegant lunches. So civilised. Perhaps she could suggest to Geraldine and Jim that they start up something similar here in the Valley. There were already plenty of connections between the town of Clare and County Clare in Ireland. They already exported wine from Australia to Ireland. Perhaps Ireland could ship over a few dozen bachelors in return?

She put down the magazine as Richard Lawrence walked towards her, dressed in shorts and a T-shirt. Lola waved and beckoned him over. He was quite the fitness fan, it seemed. Back from the gym again. Just like Anna. It had been good to see him and Bett chatting away at the party. They had a lot in common—journalism, London . . .

'Morning, Richard,' she said as he came closer.

'Good morning, Lola.'

'It does the heart good to see a fit young man like yourself.'

'Young man?' He grinned. 'Don't make me worry about your eyesight now, will you?'

'Oh, you're just a child in my eyes. Tell me, will you pop in a little later? I've a bottle of gin that I need help opening. Around four? Perfect.'

She waved him off as a blue station wagon came up the drive. Lola watched as Daniel Hilder climbed out with a load of newspapers. Bett had chosen her one-night stand well, she thought with a wicked smile. He certainly wasn't fashion-catalogue handsome, but a pair of laughing eyes took a man a very long way, she'd always thought.

Bett came into view, pushing the cleaning cart. Lola watched as she took out the master key and let herself into one of the rooms. Dear girl, it was so good to have her home again. She had been so rocked by the business with Matthew. In Lola's opinion, it had been a narrow escape. She had always felt Carrie and Matthew made a better pair than Bett and Matthew. She had held her tongue on the matter, though.

Moments later Daniel Hilder stepped lightly down the front steps and climbed back into his car. In a few minutes he would drive right past her room, on to the next delivery. She re-read a quote from the magazine article. 'It's a simple process. We interview all the single men and then we interview all the single women. It's a matter of getting to know people, assessing their suitability before we bring them together.'

She started to smile. The Valley View Motel Matchmaking Festival might not have the same ring as Lisdoonvarna, but the principles were the same, surely? Her smile broadened.

Rising as swiftly as her old bones would allow, she moved inside, picked up the cane she used for walking and knocked a painting off the wall, wincing as it crashed to the floor. As the sound of a car started up, she returned to the doorway, waving madly with her good arm.

Daniel slowed the car to a stop beside her, wound down the window and smiled. 'Lola, hello. You're looking very well again.'

'Pulling the devil by the tail, as we say at home. Daniel, a painting has fallen off the wall. Could you spare a moment, do you think?'

She smiled to herself as he turned off the engine. This might be even more fun than writing the musical.

The next day, Bett was driving back to the *Valley Times* office with Daniel. They'd spent the afternoon following one of the Valley's young winemakers around his small winery, as he showed them the process from grape to bottle. At the end of the session, Daniel had handed over the digital camera and watched as she flicked through his shots. They were very good, a bit quirky. Rebecca would be pleased.

Bett was pleased with herself, too. So far today she'd managed to stay quite composed in Daniel's company. Even better, she'd had several conversations with him without turning bright red.

Daniel's mobile rang and he pulled over to take the call. Bett took the opportunity to have a good look at him. He was probably thirty-five or thirty-six by now, she guessed. She thought she remembered him celebrating his thirtieth birthday just after she'd first joined the *Valley Times*. He'd had a girlfriend at the time. One of the high-school teachers, if memory served her right. And she had been going out with Matthew.

Back then, she'd always found him easy to work with. It had been the same today. Bett had interviewed the winemaker while Daniel strolled the property taking photographs, like a normal journalist and photographer team. The only difference being they'd had a night of wild sex three years ago and not mentioned it since.

He finished the call, from one of the other reporters on the paper setting up a photo shoot for the next day. 'Sorry about that,' he said.

'No problem. Daniel, before you start the car, I think there's something we need—'

'Is it about that night in Melbourne, by any chance?'

'Yes. Yes, it is.' Was that squeak really her voice?

'I wondered which of us would bring it up first.' He started the car and began to drive. 'Bett, it's all right. I'm a grown man. I got over it.'

'You got over it?' Had it been that bad?

'Of course,' he said. 'It wasn't the first time and it won't be the last.'

That he had a one-night stand? She was feeling worse, not better. 'I thought I had to mention it, in case . . .' she trailed off. *In case you were thinking that I was an old slapper.* She couldn't say it.

They were coming into the town now. 'Bett, it's OK. I got the message in Melbourne. So please don't feel awkward working with me.'

What message? She hadn't left him a message.

His phone rang again and he answered it without pulling over. 'Hi, Rebecca . . . About five minutes away . . . No worries. I'll drop Bett at the office and head out there.' He turned to her. 'Sorry, Bett. That fire out at the old quarry has flared up again. Rebecca wants me to go straight there.'

'Of course.' They were silent as Daniel drove up the main street. He pulled in behind a tree sending out splashes of shade onto the roadside.

'See you later, then.'

'Yes, see you.' She got out of the car so quickly she nearly tripped.

Lola took a long sip of her gin and tonic and pointed the remote control at the CD player. She did love singing along with those old show tunes. But now it was break over and time to get back to work.

She had drawn up a shortlist of suitors. Just the two names. Then drawn up a list of their attributes. She'd done that too, based on her interviews, formal and informal, over the past little while. They were similar in some ways. Both seemed very kind, with good senses of humour and glints in their eyes. They both had a bit of life experience behind them, too—always a good thing. They'd both lived in the city, but had chosen to be in the country for the time being—also a good thing.

Now all she had to do was make her final choice. She read the lists again. It was close, certainly, but she was veering towards the one on the left. Yes, she decided firmly. He was the one.

Operation Richard and Bett.

At home in the farmhouse two nights later, Carrie poured a glass of wine and moved from the living room to the bedroom, then back into the kitchen, trying to decide where to do it. She finally settled on the kitchen. She pulled a chair up to the wooden table, reached into her bag and took out the magazine. She'd seen it in the newsagents in town that morning, its glaring coverline talking directly to her—*How To Save Your Marriage.* She'd bought a whole selection of other items to pad all around it—pens and writing pads, even a *Your Garden* magazine—so the woman behind the counter wouldn't guess.

She skimmed past the perfume ads, the fashion pages and the eligible bachelors until she reached the *How to Save Your Marriage* article. She skim-read the introduction to the article. *Do you feel the gloss has gone out of your relationship?* Not just the gloss. *Don't know where it went wrong?* She shifted uncomfortably. *Then try this exercise to get in touch with your feelings. Sit quietly, and recall the early days of your relationship. Think about everything that first attracted you to him, and him to you. Remember your first touch, your first kiss, the first time you made love. Let the memories wash over you. Let go of any anger you may feel now. Let go of any hurts or misunderstandings. Take your mind back to your early days, remembering the wonderful first moments of attraction.*

Carrie moved the chair further back from the table, shut her eyes and concentrated. She opened an eye, and read the last line again. *Take your mind back to your early days, remembering the wonderful first moments of attraction.* That she could do, at least. It had been the first night she met him, when she got home from her overseas trip. At first, in all the fuss of arriving, her luggage everywhere, the talk and the chat with her parents and Lola, he'd just been Bett's fiancé—medium height, sandy brown curls. Solid-looking. But later, in the pub where Bett had insisted on taking her, something had happened between them.

Jetlagged, exhilarated to be home, she remembered being in teasing form. 'Normally, Matt, I'd have got to know you slowly, vetted you to make sure you were good for my sister, but I'll just have to do a crash course now. Should I check him out, Bett?'

'Go right ahead,' Bett had said, laughing at her.

She patted him down, commenting all the while. 'Yes, fine shoulders, a lovely broad chest and oh, yes, a flat stomach too.' Bett was enjoying it, Carrie thought. 'And he's got terrific legs, Bett, hasn't he?' Did her hands brush against his thigh deliberately? 'Yes, he'll do very well.'

All laughter and joking, standing there arms round one another, Bett in front of them. But as she sat down, just for a moment there was an exchange of glances between her and Matthew. The laughter had gone out of his eyes and there was a flash of desire. She saw it. She felt the same thing. A tiny spark, the quickest of flickers between them.

Except she remembered it the next day.

In the first few weeks the tension between her and Matthew masqueraded as simple teasing between a brother-in-law- and sister-in-law-to-be, encouraged by the whole family. But it was more serious than that, even from the start. With Matthew it was as if all her senses had sprung to attention. At a family picnic, when Anna, Glenn and Ellen were home one weekend, they all piled into one car. Bett was driving. In the back, Carrie needed to sit on Matthew's knee, Anna, Glenn and Ellen squeezed in beside them, Lola in the passenger seat in front. Had any of them noticed the effect the physical contact had on her and on Matthew? The touch was like exquisite pain to Carrie, feeling his thighs beneath her, the brush of his hand against her bare arm.

He slowly moved his left arm so it was almost round her waist. Just as slowly, she lowered her hand so it was on top of his arm.

Everyone's attention was on three-year-old Ellen, delirious with too much soft drink and attention, squealing each time they turned a corner, their bodies moving from side to side with the momentum. Carrie felt a slow burning between her and Matthew with each motion. When they arrived back at the motel, she climbed out quickly. There was just a glance between them, loaded with meaning. But he's Bett's fiancé, she told herself.

Remember your first kiss . . .

It happened the day he drove her to the agricultural college with him. She'd been trying to decide whether to do a course, and it was Bett who suggested she make the trip with Matthew. She was aware of dressing more carefully, choosing the pale blue dress that looked good against her brown skin and blonde hair.

They drove for an hour perhaps, not even halfway there, the teasing conversation rippling between them. Feeling hot, she had wound the window down. An insect had blown in, right at her face.

'Oww,' she said. 'Something flew into my eye.'

He pulled over right away, their car the only one on the long straight road. He unbuckled his seat belt, leaned across. 'Let me see.'

His hand was on her face, his face closer than it had ever been. There was a moment when all the tension between them seemed to tighten and contract until they were no longer apart but lips on lips, bodies pressed as close as possible.

She pulled back first, reluctantly, eyes wide. 'We can't. I'm sorry.'

He made a noise somewhere between a laugh and a sigh. 'I am too.'

'We should keep driving.'

They did, silently for ten minutes, and then his hand came off the steering wheel and crossed the seat, meeting hers. His voice was soft. 'Carrie, I have never felt about anyone the way I feel about you.'

She understood what he meant.

'I don't feel about Bett the way I feel about you.'

'It's wrong. You're Bett's fiancé.' It was hard to say, when the touch of his hand was sending what felt like sparkling explosions into her bloodstream. She placed his hand on her thigh, and heard the little intake of breath. She thought of Bett, and then consciously, forcibly, blanked her out. This wasn't about Matthew and Bett any more. It was about the two of them and what was happening here.

'You feel it too, don't you?'

She nodded.

'We need to talk about this.'

Ahead there was a sign pointing to a camping ground just off the main road. He turned in. The park was sheltered, too early in the morning, even on a hot day, for anyone to be there. He got out. She got out after him. They stood against the railing, looking down into the dry creek bed, not speaking, the only sound the crackle of wind through the peeling bark on the gum trees. The sun was hot on her skin.

She touched his arm and he flinched as though it had burnt him. But the movement had set the tension buzzing between them again. She felt her own body respond, felt her breasts strain against her clothes, wanting to touch him again. This had to be right, Bett or no Bett.

He moved first, running a hand gently from the shoulder strap of her dress down her arm. She closed her eyes, feeling every nerve-ending in her skin respond. She didn't move, just breathed in deeply, as he traced the neckline, his hand brushing against her breasts.

And then she did the same to him, ran her hand down the length of his arm, then his other arm, touching the skin, feeling the little hairs. It became a slow, intense trade of pleasure, taking it in turns, not speaking. He moved towards her, touching her dress, tracing her breasts through the material. It was all she could do not to push herself against him.

Staring into his eyes, she was intensely aware of all the sensations around her, the heat of the sun, the slightest of breezes, the hum of insects. She touched his body again, running her hand over his stomach, over the denim of his jeans, watching the response in his eyes.

'We can't. We have to stop this,' she whispered.

'I know,' he said, shutting his eyes.

The sound of a car behind them called a halt. It was a family, a man and woman with three small children, parking just yards from them, and immediately unloading chairs and barbecue equipment.

'Lovely day for it,' the man called out.

'Sure is,' Matthew answered.

They returned to the car and sat for a few moments, before Matthew started the engine and headed back onto the main road. She wasn't surprised when he pulled into a side road a few miles down and turned to her again. Some reason had come into her mind by then—the shock of nearly being caught, the shock of realising she had been about to have sex with Bett's fiancé. And the shock that she still wanted to.

Another hot, deep kiss until she pulled away first. 'What about Bett?' she whispered again, barely able to speak.

'I don't know what to do about Bett,' he answered.

For four weeks they resisted it, trying not to spend time with each other. But it was like a fever, an addiction. The tension between them increased. There were phone calls, three, sometimes four, a day.

Lola noticed something, Carrie knew. And perhaps Bett suspected something. She tried not to spend too much time with her sister, needing to keep the distance. She had one awkward conversation with Matthew about her.

'Are you still sleeping with her?'

Matthew looked uncomfortable. 'I can't. I want it to be you.'

It made her feel better, for herself, even while she felt sorry for Bett. It just seemed out of their control, as though it was destined.

Then, the night before they were due to go to the agricultural college again, Matthew rang her. 'I've made a decision, Carrie. I'm going to break it off with Bett. I can't live like this, feeling one thing with you, talking about the wedding with her, feeling like I'm lying.'

'Are you sure?'

'If you are.'

Remember the first time you made love . . .

That conversation had been the turning point. The next morning he collected her from the motel as usual. Bett had left for the newspaper office early. Carrie was glad of it.

They barely spoke as he drove, but she found herself unable to take her eyes off his hands on the steering wheel, feeling the lightness of her own dress against her thighs. He turned into the forest clearing they had first visited five weeks earlier. There was no one else there. The air was as hot and still, the sky as cloudless. They climbed out of the car. He took her by the hand and they started the slow, erotic dance again, his hand tracing her body, her hand tracing his, no words being spoken until they were both faint with desire. 'Are you sure?' he whispered.

She nodded.

From that moment they wouldn't have cared if there had been rows of cars around them. He slowly undid the buttons of her dress and she unbuttoned his shirt and jeans. He kissed her deeply, his hands holding her body tight against his. They moved up against a table and had fast, passionate sex, both of them still partly clothed, their hard, fast breaths and moans the only noise around.

Carrie knew she shouldn't have done it. She knew it the moment they had finished, the moment the tension passed and the two of them were holding each other close, his head against hers. But then he held her even tighter, whispered, 'Thank you,' and she felt that it had been the right thing. And that they would be able to face Bett together. Which was exactly what they did that night. Matthew called her, arranged to meet in the motel. They had both broken the news to her . . .

Remember your wedding day.

Quiet, without fuss, everyone trying to ignore the fact Anna and Bett weren't there.

Think back to the early days of married life.

The passion lasted between them for nearly two years. Longer than most, from what Carrie could gather from talking to her friends. One girlfriend said that once their three kids had come along she and her husband had both lost interest. 'Honestly, if he wants to go off and have a mistress, it's fine with me. Between the kids and work, I haven't got time for sex.' The same friend, a little later that evening and a lot drunker, had gone further. 'Has Matthew ever compared you and Bett? You know, said anything about what you were both like in bed? Haven't you ever been curious, Carrie?'

Of course she had been. But she'd told her friend to mind her own business and tried not to think of it again herself. And there had been plenty of consolation in their lovemaking—surely it hadn't been like this for Matthew and Bett, or he would never have left her.

Can you pinpoint when things started going wrong?

Easily. When Carrie started feeling guilty about the marriage. Started noticing more things wrong with Matthew. Started picking on him, deliberately wanting him to fight with her, to prove that he loved her. Except it had backfired, hadn't it? She'd picked on him so much he'd been glad to leave.

Are you sure things are as bad as you think?

She realised she was crying, and roughly wiped away a tear. They were, but she wished they weren't. She missed him, really missed him.

Sometimes it can be as simple as sitting down and talking about things. Don't be afraid to be the first person to say sorry.

Sorry? To who, though? Matthew? Bett? Anna? Lola? What was she supposed to do—hire a stadium and make a PA announcement? Get it over in one fell swoop? Stupid magazine. Didn't they realise things were never that simple?

In Anna's room the following night, Lola and Ellen sat side by side on the single bed, both wearing dressing gowns. They had towels wrapped as turbans on their heads and their feet were soaking in basins filled with steaming, fragrant water.

'So, Madame Lola, you'd like which treatment today?' Anna said in an excellent French accent.

'The full works, thank you. I'd like to look twenty years younger.'

'No problem at all, even if it will involve a little plastic surgery. And you, little madam, what would you like done? The full treatment?'

Ellen nodded. 'I would like to look twenty years older, please.'

Lola hooted with laughter. 'We'll meet in the middle yet.'

Anna gently tucked in the turbans around both their faces. 'What I shall be doing today is applying my finest products in the most gentle way, giving you both the full pampering treatment. So sit back, relax, and let Anna of the Magic Fingers do her best work.'

She had applied the first of the creams to their faces when there was a knock at the door. Bett poked her head in. 'Anna, message from—Good God, what is this? A cult meeting?'

Lola and Ellen looked out at her through faces covered in cream, their eyes panda-like. 'We're seeking eternal youth and beauty, as supplied by Anna of the Magic Fingers,' Lola said. 'Would you like to join us?'

'I'd need a full construction team, not Anna of the Magic Fingers.' She sat on Anna's bed so she had a full view of the proceedings. 'A message from Len for you, Anna, to say that the set designs are nearly finished.' She picked up a magazine from the bedside table.

'All those years of cutting up chops have finally come into their own,' Lola said.

'Enough talking, thank you, Madame Lola,' Anna said. 'You are supposed to be relaxing.'

There was quiet for a little while and then Ellen spoke up. 'Mum, is it true that Lola was raised by the fairies in Ireland?'

'Of course I was, Ellen,' Lola murmured.

'Lola, tell Ellen the truth.'

Lola crossed her feet in the water bath and gazed across at Ellen. 'Once upon a time . . .' Then she stopped. 'I can't tell a story and have a facial at the same time. Bett, can you tell it for me?'

'Of course.' Bett put down the magazine. 'Your great-grandmother was born in Ireland, Ellie, on the other side of the world. Her father was a businessman, and her mother was a very elegant lady and they lived in a beautiful big old house with a long drive leading up to it, surrounded by fields with black-faced sheep.'

'Did you have a pet sheep when you were a little girl, Lola?'

'Hundreds of them, Ellie.'

Bett continued. 'Lola went to boarding school, where they taught her to be a fine lady, and how to ride horses and arrange flowers. And then in the school holidays she would come home and have parties and at one of these parties she was introduced to a handsome young man called Edward. Before six months had passed, Lola and Edward were engaged to be married. How am I going so far, Lola?'

Lola's eyes were shut. 'Perfect, darling. Keep going.'

'Edward's father had business interests in Australia, and to Lola's great excitement, he suggested that Lola and Edward spend a year in Australia. Within four months of their wedding the two of them were living in Melbourne. Edward's job was to keep an eye on the wool and crops that were being produced on his father's farms, and, while he did that, Lola stayed in Melbourne, making the house beautiful.'

Anna stopped applying the second cream, waiting for Bett to tell the next bit of the story.

'Around this time World War Two broke out and Edward, your great-grandfather, volunteered to join the Australian Army. He trained to be a soldier, only getting to see Lola once every few months, before he was sent away with the rest of the troops. And then something very sad happened. Edward was killed on the very first day of fighting.'

'He was killed?'

Lola had told the lie so many times the words came easily. 'That's right, Ellie. The soldiers told me afterwards he had been very brave. That I should be proud of him.' Far better than the truth—that her husband had not been a brave soldier but a weak, bullying drunk.

Bett took over again. 'And two days after Lola got word of that, Ellie, she discovered that she was having a baby. And that was James, your grandfather.' She had always found it so heartbreaking that Edward had died without knowing he was going to be a father.

Beside her, Anna was quiet. She always imagined Lola, so young, away from her family and her own country, discovering she was not just a widow, but about to become a mother too.

'Why didn't you go back to Ireland, Lola?' Ellen asked.

'I wasn't well enough to travel and it was wartime. There were no ships available for passengers like me. And by the time the war was over I had started up the guesthouse, and Jim was nearly ready for school. So we decided to stay.'

Ellen seemed to take all that in. 'Have you ever been back to Ireland?'

'No, I haven't. My own family are gone now and it's too far away for a creaking old woman like myself.'

'But I visited Lola's house when I was in Ireland, Ellie,' Bett said.

Anna looked over. She hadn't known that.

'And were there still sheep and ponies and parties?' Ellen asked.

'None that I saw, but there might have been some behind the walls.'

'What did it look like?' Anna asked.

Bett remembered the day she had gone across to Galway on a day trip from Dublin. She had rung Lola the night before to get directions, surprising her. 'Would there be family left that I could speak to?'

'Oh, no, Bett. The family would be long gone,' Lola had said.

The house had been different to what Bett had imagined, much smaller, the drive not as curvy as she remembered Lola telling them. The front entrance has been spoilt by a clump of pine trees, she thought. She had taken a roll of photos and sent them to Lola, who had seemed grateful, but not all that interested. As she described it to Anna and Ellen now, the thought that had been niggling at the back of her mind since the slide show at Lola's party came back. It was about the trees.

'Lola, that slide you showed at the party, that was of your house, wasn't it?'

'It was.'

'And what tree was out the front?'

'A huge oak tree.'

Bett clapped her hand to her forehead. 'I can't believe it. How stupid was I? You know how I got so lost that day I went looking for your house, trying to follow your directions? That weekend I went to Galway to see if I could find anyone who remembered you and Edward? The house I went to had pine trees out the front, not an oak tree. No wonder I couldn't find anyone who knew you. I was at the wrong house, wasn't I?'

'Yes, Bett, you were,' Lola said honestly.

'Oh, Bett, you silly sausage,' Ellen said.

The three of them burst out laughing. Bett turned to Lola. 'Why didn't you tell me when I sent you those photos, Lola?'

'I didn't want to embarrass you.'

She clapped her hand to her forehead again. 'Idiot. Sorry, Lola.'

'It doesn't matter at all, Bett.' Time to change the subject, Lola thought. 'So that brings you up to date, Ellie. Time now to concentrate on the beauty treatments.' She leaned back and shut her eyes, glad of the silence. She had always hated lying, even though sometimes it had to be done. She especially hated lying to Bett.

The next day, it was Bett's turn to walk Ellen to school. She waited in front of the motel as Ellen ran over to say goodbye to Bumper the sheep. She'd already taken ten minutes to say goodbye to Lola and Carrie. It was probably as well Anna had left early that morning for her voice-over work in Sydney, or they would have been delayed another twenty minutes while she said goodbye to her.

'Ready?' she called as the little girl ran over to her, her school bag bumping on her back, one sock already down at her shoes. Ellen had been going to the new school for nearly two weeks, and the goodbye routine each morning seemed to take longer every day.

Ellen nodded and reached for Bett's hand.

It was a beautiful summer morning, the front gardens in the main road lush with growth, the air crisp, the sky already a deep blue. As they walked, Bett started singing 'Oh, What a Beautiful Morning'. 'There you are, Ellen. A little taste of the Alphabet Sisters for you.'

'Did you and my mum and Auntie Carrie really travel all around the country singing?'

'We did, indeed. And sometimes we'd even dance a little bit. Would you like to be up on stage?'

Ellen shook her head. 'No. I don't really like people looking at me.'

'I don't like it all that much either.' They walked on a little way, swinging their hands. Bett pointed out a tall gum tree with a fork in the middle. 'See that tree, Ellie? Your mum got stuck up one like that one day when she was a bit older than you.'

Ellen laughed. 'Tell me another thing about my mum.'

'She borrowed all Lola's make-up once, and made the three of us up. We were all even younger than you, covered in lipstick and eye shadow.'

'I borrowed Mum's lipstick once. And Julie let me use some of hers once too.'

'Julie?'

'Dad's friend. She's really nice to me.'

'Your dad's friend?'

Ellen nodded. 'She keeps his secrets too.'

Bett stopped. 'Sorry, Ellie, who is Julie?'

'She works with Dad. In his office.'

Bett got it then. God, for a minute it had sounded like this Julie was Glenn's girlfriend or something. 'Julie is Glenn's secretary?'

Ellen nodded again. 'He's in Singapore with her. Mum doesn't like it.'

'No, well, she must be missing your dad.'

'I miss him too. But he rings me every night.'

'Does he? Oh, that's good,' Bett said, keeping her tone neutral. Ellen didn't need to know what she thought of Glenn. They reached the school gates and Bett knelt down in front of her niece, checking her shoelaces were tied and the ribbon was straight in her hair.

'There, you're perfect. So, have fun and I'll see you after school, OK?' She gave Ellen a big hug and watched as she ran off.

It suited Bett to walk her niece to school and then get into work early. To be efficient, she told herself. To be hard at work by the time Daniel Hilder arrived, was the truth. Rebecca had picked up something and challenged her about it the day before.

'We're old friends, aren't we?' Rebecca asked.

'Sure.'

'Can I ask you a favour, then? Go easy on Daniel. Be nicer to him.'

'I am nice to him.'

'Bett, you're not. You go all stiff and weird. And he changes when you're around as well. I don't know what's between the two of you, but he could do with a bit of support.'

'Is something wrong? He's living with his girlfriend, isn't he? Someone he met in Melbourne?'

'No, they split up months ago, I think. He came back on his own.' Rebecca was looking intently at her. 'What's going on? Did you and Hildie go out together years back? Have a messy break-up?'

'No.' If she concentrated she could keep the blush from rising. 'No, we didn't. I was going out with Matthew when Daniel was here before.'

'Ah yes, you and Matthew. I never did get to the bottom of all of that business.' Rebecca's phone rang. She grinned. 'Saved by the bell, Bett. I'll keep that interrogation for another time.'

In Sydney that afternoon, Anna was speaking in a low, measured voice. 'Take the condom carefully in one hand and slide it over the erect penis.'

Bob's voice came into her headphones. 'Sorry, Anna. Can you do that last bit again? Problem with the tape there.'

Anna stepped close to the mike again. 'I suppose you think this is funny, Bob? How come we managed to do the entire section about childbirth without any problems but we've had to do this bit how many times now? Three?'

'It's that husky voice. You know it drives me crazy.' He grinned through the glass at her. 'OK, half-hour break, I think. You're starting to sound a bit breathless, or perhaps that's wishful thinking on my part.'

'Very funny.'

'See you back here at three for the joys of teenage pregnancy.'

Outside the sound booth, Anna made a coffee and took it onto the little balcony. She leaned her head against the warm brick wall and shut her eyes. Once upon a time she would have dismissed anyone who said emotional problems had an effect on a person's health. Now she wasn't so sure. She was either tired all the time and wanting to sleep, or so wired she couldn't sleep at all. And she was getting short of breath now and again. She'd been noticing it more in the past week or two.

On her way to the airport in Adelaide the previous day she'd seen a sign for a medical clinic. No appointments necessary. On the spur of the moment she'd gone in.

The doctor was in his mid-sixties, she guessed. Red-faced, cheerful. She'd run through her symptoms. Feeling tired. Feeling short of breath. Loss of appetite.

'Could you be pregnant?'

She and Glenn hadn't had sex in months. 'No, no chance.'

'I see your home address is Sydney? But you're living here? Can you tell me a little of what's going on in your life?'

The doctor started smiling sympathetically midway through Anna's reply. 'I think we've found our answer. Your daughter's accident alone could be the cause of this. You would have unleashed enough adrenaline that day to fuel you for a year. Do you get a tight feeling across your chest, as if it's hard to breathe. Yes? And any nausea?'

She nodded. 'All of those things.'

'It sounds to me like you are having panic attacks. Also known as anxiety attacks. It happens when a person is especially stressed. You subconsciously hold your breath, so then your lungs have to work twice as hard, and your heart as well, which explains the breathlessness. And loss of appetite is often another sign of stress.' He glanced at Anna. 'You're very thin already. You really do need to make time to eat.'

He checked her blood pressure, her eyes, her tongue. All fine. 'And your age is on your side, too. Thirty-four? Prime of life. Tell me, can you take life a bit easier?'

Anna laughed and decided not to mention the fact she was in the middle of producing a full-scale amateur musical. 'Not really.'

She made a follow-up appointment for a few weeks' time. But the doctor was reassuring. 'Slow down, Anna,' he said. 'Don't forget to enjoy life while you're rushing through it.'

Now, on the balcony, Anna had a sudden urge to ring Ellen. She took out her mobile and switched it on. She'd had it turned off during the recording. It beeped, telling her she had two messages.

'Anna, hello, this is Mrs Harold from Ellen's school. Would you please come and collect Ellen? She's very upset and I think it's best if she goes home for the rest of the day. Can you call me as soon as possible?'

The second message was also from her. 'Anna, Mrs Harold again. Can you call me as soon as you get this message?'

Anna checked the time. Both calls had been left in the last fifteen minutes. She pressed the speed dial on her mobile and didn't bother with greetings when Mrs Harold answered.

'It's Anna, Ellen Green's mother, Mrs Harold. Is she sick? Hurt?'

'Hello, Anna. No, it's just there's been an incident in the playground.'

A rush of panic up her back again. 'Not another dog?'

'Nothing like that,' the voice soothed. 'But it would be better if we talk about it face to face. Ellen is here in the office with us. Could you come in as soon as possible?'

'I'm sorry, I can't. I'm in Sydney. For work.' Anna waited for the disapproval, the change in tone, and was amazed when it didn't come.

'Is there anyone else who could collect her? One of your sisters? Lola?'

Anna gave a little prayer of thanks for small towns. 'I'm sure one of them can. I'll give them a call now. May I talk to Ellen first?'

The woman's voice was lowered. 'She's fallen asleep. It might be best not to wake her.'

'Of course. Right. I'll call home straight away.'

Ten minutes later it was all sorted. Bett had been back at the motel for lunch and had answered the phone. 'Of course, I'll go and get Ellen now. I'll ring you as soon as I get back.'

Anna felt the phone vibrate against her leg just as she was voicing the segment about the different methods of pregnancy testing. It was her turn to stop the tape. 'Sorry, Bob. I'll be right back.'

She answered the phone outside. 'Bett? Is she all right?'

Bett's voice was low. 'No, she's really upset. Crying a lot. She's with Lola at the moment. She's trying to put her back to sleep.'

'What happened?'

'The kids were picking on her. A gang of them.'

'What were they doing?'

Bett paused. 'Calling her scarface.'

Anna had never felt such rage. 'That's it, I'm taking her out of school. Can you tell her I'll be home tonight, as soon as I can get a flight, but she's not to worry, she'll never have to go back there again.'

'Lola said—'

'I don't care what Lola said. She's my child, Bett, and she's not going back to that school again. Put Lola on.'

A minute went past, then Lola's Irish voice came on the line. 'She's sleeping now, Anna. Poor little mite. She was very upset.'

'Of course she was. And she's not going back there again, Lola. I'm getting a flight tonight, and she'll stay home with me tomorrow.'

'I thought you'd say that. But what about your work? Didn't you say it was three days' worth? You don't have to rush back. We'll spoil her rotten tonight and then tomorrow I'll take her to school myself.'

'Lola, didn't you hear me? She's not going back to that school.'

'It's the best thing to do. She has to face her fears. They are seven-year-old children, Anna. They don't know they're being cruel. It's just

268

the way kids are. She needs to go back to show them they haven't won.'

'It's not a matter of winning or losing. I just don't want her to be hurt any more. She's not going back, Lola. I'll be home as soon as I can, no matter what you say.'

'Anna, I know you're upset but please don't talk to me in that way. Stay there. Bett and I are here with Ellen. She'll be fine tonight. I think you're wrong but if you don't want her to go to school tomorrow, then that's fine, she won't. I'll keep her here with me. But don't cancel your trip, or rush home yet. You said this job was an important one.'

The tension was draining from her. 'It is.'

'Then finish it. And I will watch over Ellen like she has never been watched over before, I promise. I'll get her to ring you if she wakes up. And you can ring her again tomorrow. All day long if you want.'

Anna realised she was right. 'I'm sorry, Lola.'

'That's all right, darling.'

The following morning Lola let Ellen sleep in. If she had been her child, the little girl would definitely have been back at school the next day. But Anna had insisted. So a day off it was. Ellen seemed bright enough, Lola thought, watching her playing, but there was a tight quality about her. Tension, imminent tears.

Anna arrived home late that afternoon, driving at great speed into the car park. Ellen had been listening out for her. Lola watched with interest as she changed moods in an instant. One moment she had been playing very happily with her dolls, then, at the sound of Anna's car, she started crying and ran out to her mother, wailing at the top of her voice. 'Mummy, Mummy.'

Anna pulled her tight and held her close, the two of them staying like that for some time. They ate dinner together, Ellen still weepy, needing to be fed like a toddler. The evening before she had used a knife and fork without any problem, Lola recalled. She nearly needed to tape her mouth shut to keep the comments in.

Once Ellen was in bed, a tortuous enough exercise, with more tears and tantrums, Lola made a pot of tea and took it into the bar, where Anna was alone, curled up in one of the big chairs, looking at the television, but in a dazed way. She was still a picture, Lola thought, but so slender these days, fragile even. 'Anna, darling, some tea?'

Anna smiled gratefully. 'You've come to lecture me, haven't you? Tell me where I'm going wrong with Ellen. What a bad mother I am. That I've made the wrong decision taking her out of school.'

'I think you're a wonderful mother. I think Ellen is a wonderful child.

But there might be other ways to approach this situation. You can't keep taking her out of situations each time they get tricky for her. So you take her out of this school, move her to a new one and the same thing happens there. Then what? You take her out of there as well? Try another school? She'll get through this, Anna, she will. But you need to help her, make her brave. You can't protect her all the time.'

Anna opened her mouth, wanting to tell Lola everything—about Glenn, about their marriage being over, about the hundreds of things she wanted to protect Ellen from—but the words stuck in her throat.

Lola was watching, waiting, then moved over to her. 'I am an interfering old woman, Anna, but I think I am right. I think Ellen has to go back to school and face them. And I think you should go in with her and sit down and tell every one of those children what happened to Ellen. Show them the photos. Let them ask Ellen questions.'

'What good will that do?'

'I think it will help them understand. Trust me, Anna. It'll be for the best, you wait and see.'

'All right,' Anna's voice was low.

'Are you sure you're up to the rehearsals tonight?'

Anna smiled, a little shakily. 'You know yourself. The show must go on.'

Lola rang her friend the principal the next morning. They had a long discussion and set a time and date. She found a letter and some photos she had received from Anna several months after Ellen was attacked, showing what good progress she had made. Lola rang Frank in the electrical shop and asked him to make up several more slides. Then she sat down with Anna and Ellen and put her suggestion to them.

Three mornings later, Anna stood in front of a classroom of seven-year-olds, more nervous than she had ever been on stage or in a recording studio. The teacher hushed the children, then introduced her.

'This is Anna, Ellen Green's mother. She wants to talk to you about what happened to Ellen and I'd like you all to listen and watch closely.'

Anna showed a slide of Ellen before the attack, then explained what had happened with the dog on the day in the park. She showed slides of Ellen in the hospital, straight after the attack. Several of the children gasped. She showed another slide of a close-up of the wound. She showed slides from the next month or two, as Ellen went through surgery, stitches, plastic surgery, in and out of hospital.

'That's why Ellen has the scar on her face. It's a sign that she survived a horrible attack from a very large dog, and I am so glad she did, because she is very precious to me, and to her father, and to her aunties, and grandparents and great-grandmother. I wanted to tell you this today so that you will understand and I hope you will be kind to her. She is a very nice little girl.' Anna's voice cracked slightly.

The teacher went outside and fetched Ellen, who had been waiting there with Lola. They had explained to her exactly what Anna would tell them, and that she would come in afterwards.

The teacher smiled at her, then turned to the class. 'So then, children, any questions for Ellen or her mother?'

A little boy held up his hand. 'What happened to the dog?'

Anna answered truthfully. 'It had to be put down. That means the vet had to give it an injection to make it die, in case it did something to another child, something even worse.'

That satisfied the little boy. Another boy put up his hand. 'Will she always have that scar on her face?'

'We're doing laser treatment on it at the moment.'

'Laser? Like in *Star Wars*?'

'Not quite, but they shine a special light, a laser beam, onto Ellen's face to break down the scar tissue bit by bit. So when she's older hopefully it won't be so obvious.'

'Is Ellen scared of dogs now?'

To Anna's surprise, Ellen answered. 'Not all dogs. Just big dogs.'

'So you can't have pets, then?'

'I've got a sheep called Bumper Baa. My Really-Great-Gran gave it to me. It's got lanolin in its wool which makes your hands soft.'

The teacher was trying not to smile. 'Bumper Baa? That's a very good name for a sheep, Ellen.'

'It's my Really-Great-Gran's idea. She's outside, but she told me she'd have her ear pressed against the door so she could hear everything we're saying. She's very old, but I heard my grandfather say she still has hearing like a bat. And my grandmother said, "Yes, an old bat".'

They all clearly heard Lola's laughter through the door.

Anna was waiting at the school gates at the end of the day. She stood back a little from the other school mums, though she knew they were watching her and probably knew who she was. The principal had sent out a note to all the parents, explaining that Anna would be giving a talk, and why, and asking for their support.

The bell went and the children came streaming out. Ellen finally appeared, on her own. Anna searched her face for tears. Nothing. 'Hi, Ellie. How was the rest of the day?' She kept her tone breezy and light.

'Good, thanks.'

'Lunch was good?'

Ellen nodded. 'But I'm still hungry. Can I please have an ice cream when we get home?'

'I think you can today.' No mention of the talk that morning. Anna decided not to push it either.

They were nearly at the car when a little girl ran over, her mother a few yards behind. 'Ellen, can you ask your mum now?'

Anna stopped. 'Ask me what?'

The little girl spoke before Ellen. 'Ellen and I were wondering if I could come and play at the motel and see the sheep one night?'

Ellen looked up at her. 'I can show Hannah round, Mum, can't I? Patrick and Samuel wanted to come too, but I said I thought they would have to wait their turn. That was the right thing to say, wasn't it?'

Anna leaned down and tucked Ellen's hair behind her ears, smiling at her. 'That was the perfect thing to say.'

Hand in hand they walked over to talk to Hannah's mother.

CHAPTER SEVEN

'SO HOW ARE REHEARSALS going?' Daniel asked.

Bett and Daniel were in the car on their way back from Martindale Hall, a nineteenth-century Georgian-style house.

'Good,' she lied. No, they weren't. The way things were going there was more chance of Lola appearing on the cover of *Vogue* than her musical being ready for its gala premiere in mid-March. 'Actually, no, they're not. You might have had a lucky escape.'

'I don't know. I'd like to have got up on stage again, as it happens.'

'Again?'

'You're not the only child performer in this car, you know.'

'You were a child performer?'

He nodded. 'Briefly. As a twelve-year-old. I had my own band.'

She saw that glint in his eye again. 'Really? What were you called?'

'Promise you won't laugh?'

'No.'

'We were called Dangerous.'

She smiled. 'Talk about scary. Did you get many gigs?'

'One. It was on a TV show. A talent quest.'

'Did you do a cover or an original?'

'Bett, I was an alternative artist. An original, of course.'

'Would you sing it for me now?'

'No.'

'It's a shame videos weren't invented back then.'

'They were, actually.'

'But you're going to tell me you've lost it, aren't you?'

'No, it's at my mother's house.'

'I really would like to see it.'

He hesitated, then grinned. 'All right. Have we got time now?'

'Now?'

They were a few miles south of the Valley town of Sevenhill. 'My mother's house is over there.'

It was a big old stone house, with a verandah running round all four sides. They walked up a path of flagstones, well-cut grass to the left, a well-tended vegetable patch on the right. Bett noticed corn, tomatoes, watermelon, the leaves lush and green, the fruit hanging heavy.

He opened the door and she followed him inside to the living room. It was a bright, cheery area, full of feminine touches. Daniel switched on the overhead fans, sending a cool breeze through the warm room.

'You're sure you want to see this?'

'If you're sure you want to share it.'

'I bet I'll regret it, but, yes.' He smiled. 'I'll get the tape.'

While he was gone she studied a photo on the television, an old black and white shot of a man and a woman with a baby. Daniel's parents, she guessed. His mother was very elegant.

He returned with the tape. 'Unfortunately I was able to lay my hands on it straight away.'

Bett put down the photo, hoping he hadn't minded her looking. 'Are you an only child?'

'No, I've got a younger sister. Christine. She's away studying in New Zealand at the moment.'

She'd liked to have asked more questions, but he was now crouched in front of the television and video recorder. She looked at his long back, lean under the T-shirt, and had to blink away a clear memory of kissing it.

He pressed PLAY and then PAUSE so that a shimmery stilled image appeared on the screen. 'You realise I'm only doing this in the interests of fairness.'

She took a seat on the sofa and nodded. 'I understand. The "I show you mine and you show me yours" principle.' In light of their Melbourne meeting, it suddenly felt like the wrong thing to have said.

His lips twitched. 'That's right.' He stood up and leaned against the door frame behind her and pointed the remote control.

It was a low-budget TV talent show from the early 1980s. Dangerous were on third, after a dreamy-looking harpist playing a Scottish air. The host introduced the group with mock fear.

She recognised Daniel immediately, a smaller version of himself, with black kohl round his eyes, black lipstick, spiky hair and ripped clothes. Skinny white arms poked out of his torn T-shirt and he'd perfected a good snarl that obviously amused the director. There were at least six close-ups of Daniel pulling a face at the camera.

She was still laughing when Daniel pressed PAUSE. 'So did you win?'

'No, and to this day, I don't know why. I think we were much better than the harpist.'

'You're lucky Lola hasn't seen this. She'd have written a part in the musical especially for you. You beat the Alphabet Sisters hands down.'

'Oh, I don't know. What was it you won? Third prize in the Miss Indooroopilly Talent Quest of 1978? Even though you were the only entrants?'

'Lola told you about that as well?'

'No, you told me. That night in Melbourne.'

'I did?'

He gave her a long, thoughtful look. 'Bett, do you actually remember much of that night?'

She'd spent three years trying to forget it. 'Um, yes, some of it.'

A pause. 'Do you mind telling me which parts?'

'I remember meeting you at the club . . . going to the bar. And then to your flat, talking, and then, um, going to bed with you . . .'

A glimmer of a smile. 'Good.'

Something about the way he was looking at her made her want to tell him the truth. 'But mostly I remember waking up and being so embarrassed at my behaviour I crept away as quickly as I could.'

'Embarrassed? Why? I enjoyed it. All of it.' He gave a slight shrug. 'That's why I was disappointed that you'd gone when I woke up. I went back to the bar where we met a couple of times, but I didn't see you there again. I was going to ring the motel here, to see if they had a number. But I thought because of all the problems with your sister and your fiancé that might be a bit awkward.'

She cringed inside. Had she shut up for a single moment all night?

'And then I figured if you'd wanted to see me again, you would have left a note. Look, as I said the other day, I was disappointed, but I got over it. I don't want you to feel awkward about this.'

'That's what you meant last week when you said you'd got over it?'

He looked puzzled. 'What did you think I meant?'

'That you'd got over the night. Got over how terrible it was. And then you said that it wasn't the first time and it wouldn't be the last time. I thought you were talking about having one-night stands.'

He threw back his head and laughed. 'Oh, yes. Danger Hilder rides again. No, Bett. I actually don't make a habit of one-night stands. Not that we were a real one-night stand, anyway, were we? Don't one-night stands have to be between strangers?'

'I'm not too sure of the official definition. I haven't made a habit of them either.'

'No?' His eyes sparkled. 'You're very good at them, for a novice.'

'You're one to talk.' She couldn't believe they were joking about this.

His phone beeped and he checked the text message. 'I don't know why I thought country papers would be quieter than city ones. We'd better get back.'

Lola lay back further against her pillow and yawned delicately. 'It's a terrible thing, but since I've turned eighty I seem to be feeling tired earlier each night.'

'Is it your arm? Do you need any painkillers?' Bett turned from the wardrobe where she was hanging up Lola's clothes. The three of them had been taking turns dressing and minding Lola since she had broken her wrist. Tonight Bett was on duty. Carrie was on a night off. Anna had gone to Adelaide again to collect the last of the costumes. Ellen was already tucked up in Bett's room for the night.

'Not at all. It's not giving me any bother at all. You're the ones it's bothering, having to come in here every morning and night to dress me. And don't think I'm not noticing that you're trying to change the clothes I wear, because I am.'

Bett smiled innocently.

'What do you think of that Richard Lawrence, Bett?'

Bett didn't blink at the change in subject. 'He seems nice.' He seemed very nice, actually. But she still hadn't invited him out for that drink. Life seemed to have become too busy, between the musical, and work in the motel, and the assignments with Daniel around the Valley . . .

'He has an excellent sense of humour, you know.'

'He seems to have, yes.'

'I wish I'd known at your age that a sense of humour is worth far more than a bulging wallet or a bulging—'

'Stop it, Lola.'

'Truly, a shared sense of humour is all you need to get you through.'

'Did Edward make you laugh?'

'No.'

'Why did you marry him, then?'

'Things were different in my day. And especially with my family.'

'It was an arranged marriage, do you mean?' Lola had never been so forthcoming.

'A suitable marriage would probably be the correct term.' Lola wasn't in the mood to talk any more about that right now. She yawned widely, covering her mouth in a mannerly way. 'As a matter of fact, Richard was asking about you today.'

'Was he?'

Actually, he hadn't been. Lola hadn't seen him today. 'Yes, he asked me if you were single. He also said he thought you had the most beautiful eyes he'd seen.'

'What?'

'And the creamiest skin. Is that how he put it? No, sorry, he said milky-white skin.'

'Richard said that? How would he know what my skin is like?'

'He mentioned how much he enjoyed your company at my party.'

'Did he?'

In Lola's experience, nothing made someone more attractive than to think they found you attractive. And Richard may well have thought all those things about Bett. Perhaps he was too shy to mention them.

A knock at the door. Richard poked his head round. 'I'm ready when you are, Lola. Oh, good evening, Bett.'

'Hello, Richard.' Her smile was very broad.

Lola yawned extravagantly. 'I'm so sorry, Richard, but I just seem to be overcome with tiredness this evening. And so suddenly.' She turned to Bett. 'Richard was saying today how curious he was about the whole MacArthur story and kindly invited me out for a meal so he could pick my brains.' Another yawn. 'Richard, my dear Bett knows the story as well as I do. Bett, would you mind taking my place as Richard's dinner guest tonight? Richard, I promise you she's sparkling company.'

Richard handled it all very smoothly. 'It would be my pleasure, of course. But I wouldn't like to deprive you of a night out, Lola. We can reschedule for another night when you're not so tired, if you like.'

'I seem to be tired every night these days.'

Bett glared at her. It was only tonight she'd been complaining of this tiredness. 'I can't go out, Lola. I'm minding Ellen.'

'Is she asleep yet?'

Bett shook her head.

'Then bring her in to me and I'll mind her myself. We'll both be asleep before eight o'clock, I should think.'

Five minutes later Ellen had been transferred into the double bed beside Lola. Bett had hurried back to her room, changed into a new skirt, run a brush through her curls and applied some lip gloss.

She poked her head into Lola's room. 'You're not up to anything, are you?'

'How could I be? I'm too tired. I look tired, don't I, Ellen?'

Ellen was propped up with several pillows, in imitation of Lola. 'Yes, you look very, very tired.'

That sounded suspiciously rehearsed to Bett. 'Well, good night, then.'

'Have fun,' Lola called.

'Have fun,' Ellen echoed.

Lola waited until Bett had definitely gone, then brought out a packet of chocolate éclairs from under her pillow, pointed the remote control at the TV and grinned at her great-granddaughter. 'Make yourself comfy, Ellen. You're going to love this.'

As the opening credits of *Mary Poppins* came up, Lola smiled to herself. *Operation Richard and Bett*, we have lift off.

Richard had made the dinner booking at Lorikeet Hill, a small restaurant south of the town. The food was delicious, the Irish music playing in the background soothing. The wine relaxed Bett's mood and loosened her tongue. Richard seemed genuinely interested in so many things. Not just the General MacArthur story, but in Lola, Anna, Carrie, herself—all of them.

He refilled her glass. 'So you went to journalism college a couple of years after you left high school, and Anna went to drama school around the same time?'

She nodded. 'That's right. Anna always said that the Alphabet Sisters had given her the edge. Not many people have spent six years touring the country by the time they're nineteen.'

'And she met her husband in Sydney?'

'That's right.' She pulled a face. 'Unfortunately.'

'You don't like him?'

'Sorry, that was very childish.' And alcohol-induced, she realised. Bett tried to find the words. 'If Glenn was an animal, he'd be a bear. If he was a vehicle, he'd be a bulldozer. But he adores Anna, and I suppose that's all that matters at the end of the day.'

'He adores Anna?'

'He idolises her. Worships the ground she walks on.'

Richard was looking at her closely. 'And how long since you've seen Glenn and Anna together?'

'It's been a while, actually. More than three years,' she admitted.

As the waiter came up and removed their plates, Bett realised how much she'd been talking. He must have been a skilled journalist, she guessed. She should be taking tips from him, not spilling her soul. She waited until the waiter left before she spoke again. 'You're not about to write an unauthorised biography of the Alphabet Sisters, are you? I don't know if there's enough scandal for a book.'

'Oh, I don't know about that.'

She caught something in his tone and narrowed her eyes.

'May I ask exactly what you've been told?'

'That you had been engaged to a man here in Clare but then he met your younger sister and fell in love with her instead. And that there was a row between you and Anna and Carrie, and that you hadn't spoken to, or seen each other from then until Lola's party.'

'Well, that's it in a nutshell, I suppose.'

'It must have been terrible for you when your fiancé left you for your sister.'

Bett blinked. 'Yes. Yes, it was.'

The waiter came then with their main courses. Bett was glad of the interruption, taking the opportunity to steer the conversation back to safer ground. They spoke about the musical, about Lola, and then Richard moved on to the Alphabet Sisters again.

'So why did it come to an end?'

Bett thought about it. She could wave it away. Or she could tell the truth. 'Because of me. I refused to do it any more.'

'Why?'

Because of their awful final performance at the local music society Christmas show. 'It's a long story.'

'Tell me,' he said.

She took a sip of her wine, gathered her thoughts, then started to talk.

They'd been too old for it, really—Anna eighteen, Bett sixteen, Carrie nearly fourteen. The three of them had stood in age order, as always. Lola had gone all out on their outfits, dressing each of them in red satin, with a green tinsel hat. In the mirror, Bett had been aware that her dress was tighter on her than Carrie's and Anna's were, but Lola had just hugged her, told her she was gorgeous and sent the three of them out onto the stage.

Midway through 'Sisters', their opening number, Bett looked out into the audience and noticed the three cool boys of the town. Her heart gave a leap, as she veered from self-consciousness to excitement. She looked away, then looked back. The three of them were actually looking at her, concentrating on her for once, not Anna, not Carrie. She had a rush of confidence, stood straighter, sang louder, smiled wider.

Then one of them shouted, 'Piggy in the Middle.'

She noticed neighbours leaning in and asking what he'd said and then stifling a laugh. The three boys kept it up as a sort of chant, under their breaths. Then the people in the front of the hall heard and began mouthing the words. Bett tried to keep singing, knowing her cheeks were fiery red, feeling as though her skin was about to burst. Anna hadn't noticed or, if she had, hadn't cared. Carrie had probably been too busy revelling in the fact she was attracting most of the admiring glances.

Somehow Bett got through the other three songs. But she was in tears when they came off stage. Lola was waiting. 'They're just stupid, silly boys, Bett. Ignore them, do you hear me?'

In Lola's arms, Bett was almost comforted. Then from behind her came Carrie's voice. 'Maybe you could lose a bit of weight, Bett, if you don't mind me saying. We probably would look better if we were all the same sort of size.'

Her tears stopped abruptly. She felt as though iced water had been flung over her. She turned to her other sister. 'And what do you think, Anna? Do you think I should lose weight?'

Anna gave a shrug. 'Carrie's got a point, yes. But it's your choice how you look.'

There had been three more performances booked after the Christmas one, but Bett refused to do them. Lola tried talking sense. Anna tried to apologise. Carrie was sent in, pleading, eyes filling with tears. But it was too late for Bett. She was never going to perform with her sisters again.

Anna didn't mind too much. She'd already set her heart on getting into drama school and treated the Alphabet Sisters as a joke by this stage. But Carrie was very upset.

'I didn't call you Piggy in the Middle, it was those boys. But you are behaving like a pig now. A selfish pig. And I'll get you back for this, I promise.'

Bett didn't tell Richard this, but the truth was that her sisters' lack of support had hurt far more than the taunts. From that moment on it seemed as though Anna and Carrie had been set adrift from her, into a world of romance, dates, boys and confidence. Bett had felt like Cinderella and Bessie Bunter rolled into one—overweight, unhappy, finding pleasure only in food and books and her piano.

'And that was the end of it,' she said to Richard. 'We just stopped.'

He had been listening closely. 'They always say it's the people closest to you who know how to hurt you the most. Is that why you think Carrie made a play for Matthew? To get you back for something that had happened years before?'

'I'm sorry?'

'You said that Carrie told you she was going to get you back for it one day. And then years later she broke up your engagement and married your fiancé. Do you think it was connected?'

Was he mad? Carrie and Matthew had fallen genuinely in love. Bett had always known that. She'd seen how they were with each other. It had been an almost instant attraction.

She stared at him as she realised what she'd just admitted to herself. Behind his glasses, Richard was assessing her closely. Kindly, but still closely. She decided then she'd had enough of talking about herself.

'No, I don't think it was connected at all. In fact, I'm sure it wasn't. So, enough about me.' She was pleased with how firm her voice sounded. 'This book of yours, Richard. It's set in the 1850s, did you say?'

Anna had a very productive trip to Adelaide, collecting the final props and costumes from different fancy-dress shops around the city. It had surprised her how much she was enjoying the musical. Not just the rehearsals, but all the production side as well.

She glanced at the dashboard clock as she drove through Auburn, the town that marked the start of the Clare Valley. She was making good time. She noticed her hands on the steering wheel. They were actually quite relaxed, not gripping it like it was a lifeline.

She'd tried to explain exactly that to the doctor that morning, when she'd called in to the surgery for her follow-up appointment. She'd expected to get the cheerful older man again, not this serious-faced woman, who looked less than twenty-five.

'I don't like the sound of that breathlessness. How many weeks now?'

'A month, maybe two. It's probably just panic attacks,' Anna had said to her. 'I've been stressed, but things are getting much better at home.' Not just with her sisters, either. She'd even managed to have a normal phone conversation with Glenn in Singapore.

'Anna, I'd like you to have a scan. Just to ease all our minds.'

'Is that necessary? It's just I've got a lot on, and it means coming down to the city again. I live two hours away.' She gave the doctor the look which usually stopped people in their tracks.

'I think it's very necessary, to put my mind at rest as much as yours.' The young doctor made several phone calls, while Anna sat fidgeting.

At last, the young woman put down the phone and smiled. 'We can get you in at the end of next week. They've had a cancellation.'

Anna checked her diary. It was two days after the musical. She'd be down in Adelaide anyway returning the costumes. 'Fine. Thanks.'

As she walked back out to the car she'd checked her phone messages. There was just one, from Lola, asking her to call.

Lola was laughing. 'You should know that Ellen's invited everyone in her class to the motel for her birthday party and they've all accepted.'

'But it's not her birthday for months.'

'I don't think she specified a date. She seemed more interested in out-lining what the food and entertainment would be. Prawn cocktails, hide-and-seek in the motel rooms and rides on Bumper's back featured quite prominently, I believe.'

Anna had been laughing by then. 'Oh, Lola. Can you sort it out for me?'

'Sort it out? What's there to sort out? I'm going to take lessons from her.'

Anna rang off and grinned again at the thought of it. Being in the Valley had been so good for Ellen. She had noticed her daughter grow-ing more confident every day. Happier. More relaxed.

As she got closer to Clare, driving through the vineyards, Anna started thinking of someone who made *her* feel happy and relaxed. Richard. She thought of the late-night glasses of wine and conversations they'd shared. He was so interested and courteous.

He had turned on the small TV in his room and made her sit with him until one of her ads came on. They hadn't had to wait long. He sat in silence as the ad played. Afterwards he took her hands and kissed her on each cheek. 'You were marvellous, darling. Such a combination of pathos and urgency. It was a truly bravura performance.'

The ad was for brake fluid and she had been the voice of the car. She'd inclined her head, accepting the praise, trying not to laugh. 'I do actually think that was one of my best moments.'

She smiled now, remembering the teasing. He'd told her more about his life in London. He'd talked about the three-year relationship he'd had with a fellow reporter, until she had ended it the year before. And so she had told him about Glenn, and Glenn and Julie, and Glenn and Julie and Singapore.

She felt warm, good, thinking about him. And the more time she spent with him, the sexier she was finding him, too. They'd arranged to meet for a glass of wine when she got home tonight. He was taking Lola out to dinner, he'd told her the night before, but expected to be home by eleven. It was half past ten. She couldn't wait to see him.

Bett and Richard stood in the motel car park.

'Thanks, Richard. That was a lovely night.'

'You're welcome, Bett. I enjoyed it too.'

She wondered whether she should invite him in for a glass of wine. But there was no spark between them, she'd realised. She liked him, enjoyed talking to him, even if she had told him too much. But that was all.

'Well, good night.'

'Good night.'

Inside her room, she went into the bathroom and stared at herself in the mirror, not liking what she saw. She decided to have a shower, needing to wash away some troubling thoughts. She turned the shower tap on full blast, wanting to fill the room with steam. As she went back out to the bedroom area to get her dressing gown, she heard a car pull up next door. Anna arriving home from her trip to Adelaide, she guessed. Bett undressed, stepped under the streaming water and shut her eyes.

After carrying the costumes into her room, Anna simply turned off the light again, shut the door after her and walked five doors down. She knocked lightly, two little taps.

He answered immediately. 'Anna, welcome back.' His smile was as warm as his voice.

'Hello, Richard.' She took in every detail of him.

'Anna? Are you all right?'

'I'm fine.' She was more than fine. She was happy, she realised. She was home at the motel. She knew Ellen was safe in Lola's room. There had been a note on Anna's bed in Ellen's best handwriting. 'I love you Mummy', with a picture of Bumper the sheep and the two of them in bright colours. Anna felt light after months of heaviness. She spoke softly, but surely. 'Richard, I know I should be coy. And that we should spend more time together first, and get to know each other better. But I don't want to wait that long. I want to go to bed with you.'

'Right now?'

'Yes.' She faltered slightly.

'Will you at least give me time to make the bed?'

She smiled. 'No, I won't.'

'Never mind, then. We'll have to manage.' He took her by the hand and drew her inside his room.

By the time dawn came, Bett still wasn't asleep. It was a combination of the wine she'd drunk and the conversation with Richard, she decided. It seemed to have unleashed memories she'd kept well locked away for more than three years. Uncomfortable memories.

The motel room felt very claustrophobic. She pulled on track suit pants, a light windcheater, laced on her sneakers and crept out of her room as the sun was coming up. She headed north past the vineyards, where the early autumn colours were appearing on the leaves.

Walking usually soothed her. She'd been walking for an hour a day most days, since the year after she had first started working on the *Valley Times*. Lola had got her started, in her usual blunt way. She had come into Bett's room one afternoon, pulled a chair beside the bed Bett was lying on and looked very serious. 'Bett, we need to talk.'

'About what?'

'Do you remember that Piggy in the Middle jibe that upset you so much all those years ago?'

Bett had put down the bag of crisps she was holding. 'Yes.'

'You might want to be careful or someone will call you that again.' She ignored Bett's shocked expression. 'I'm not the body police, but I don't like to see someone letting themselves go, and that's what you're doing. You have two choices, Bett. Do something about your weight, or stay as you are and decide not to let it bother you.'

'It does bother me. But I'm useless in a gym or those aerobics classes.'

'What are those two things hanging off your waist there?'

'They're my legs.'

'And what can they do?'

'Hold me up. Walk.'

'Walk. Exactly. From today I want you walking an hour a day, in rain or shine, fog or mist. Or, more likely, seeing as it's summer, in blazing sunshine day after day.'

So she had started it, walking for an hour every day, along the dusty roads at the back of the valley. Three months later Bett had summoned up the courage to go clothes shopping. She'd dropped only a size, but her body shape was different, firmer.

She'd met Matthew not long afterwards. He had moved to the Valley as a junior vet, while he was studying at the nearby agricultural college. She had interviewed him on his second day for a feature on new arrivals in the town. When he mentioned he didn't know anyone locally yet, she'd invited him for a drink up at the motel bar. Her father had poured him beers and asked him lots of questions, while Bett sat beside him, joining in, enjoying the fact it was her, not Anna or Carrie for once, sitting beside a good-looking man on these bar stools. Carrie had been on her overseas trip at the time. Anna was in Sydney.

The next weekend she and Matthew met again, this time in one of the three pubs in town. She felt relaxed with him. They met again the weekend after that.

He'd kissed her on their fifth date. By the seventh date it had progressed to his hands touching her body. She'd decided six weeks into the relationship that she was going to sleep with him. On a weekend away, two months after they'd met, they'd had sex for the first time. It had been nice. Not earth-shattering, not painful, not even especially passionate, but comfortable. She was still self-conscious, not liking to make love in full light, feeling a bit awkward in the sexy underwear he started buying her. But the relief she felt outweighed any of that. Because the truth was she had been a virgin when she started going out with Matthew. At twenty-eight years old. She hadn't told Matthew, and he hadn't guessed, either.

They fell into an easy-going relationship—meeting for drinks once or twice a week, dinner one night a week, after which she would usually go back to the house he was sharing in town. Sometimes they would make love, sometimes they wouldn't. Then, five months later, out of the blue, Matthew asked her to marry him. They were on their way back from a friend's wedding. During the wedding reception, the two of them had been teased, been asked when their big day would be. 'A wedding begets a wedding, you two, remember.'

On the drive back to Clare, Matthew stopped the car, took her hands. 'Bett, do you want to get married? You and me?'

She felt a warm, comforting feeling. She wasn't a failure, someone loved her enough to want to marry her. They drove straight to the motel to tell her parents and Lola. That night, Carrie happened to ring from her travels and they told her the news too.

But had it felt like it was something they both were destined to do, couldn't live without doing? No. If anything, the pressure came from people around them, their friends, who were all busily planning their weddings and buying their first houses.

They didn't rush into any wedding planning. They set a date, booked the church for a year's time, but, mostly, life settled down—Bett with her work at the newspaper, Matthew with his work and his study, both living separately. The fact that they were engaged was a nice link between them, but nothing life-changing. Again that thought: comforting. Which had started to feel like boring.

Bett recalled coming at the subject in a roundabout way during a phone conversation with Anna. 'Did you ever have doubts about Glenn before you married him, Anna?'

Anna got to the point immediately. 'Why, are you having second thoughts about Matthew?'

'No.' A pause. 'But with Glenn, for example, do you ever, um, I don't know, find yourself sitting there wondering what to say next?'

'No, I don't think so.' Anna laughed. 'If we're not talking, we're usually fighting about something, so communication isn't usually the issue. Have you run out of things to say to Matthew?'

Bett had, but she'd hedged around it. 'Maybe we've just been too tired to talk. Things have been pretty busy work-wise for both of us.'

'But you must have things in common you can talk about, even if you are tired. Do you like the same things? The same sort of music or books?'

Bett grimaced. She and Matthew couldn't be further apart in their musical tastes and Matthew didn't read much, either, apart from veterinary magazines, whereas Bett always had two or three books on the go.

'Um, no, not really.'

'Does he make you laugh?'

She had to think. 'Sometimes,' she said to Anna.

'What about his work?'

It had been interesting enough to begin with. But she had never been that keen on animals. Carrie was the animal fiend in their house, the one who collected photos of dogs and horses.

Bett remembered thinking that the music Matthew listened to was the same sort of music Carrie had liked. That she wasn't a reader either. That even the way he looked was more to Carrie's taste than Bett's.

She and Anna had talked about it some more, before Bett deliberately moved the conversation on to other matters. Four days later, she got a letter from Sydney.

Dear Bett,

I've been thinking a lot about our phone call last night, and rather than ring again, I decided to write to you.

What seemed to be coming loud and clear through everything you were saying is that you have serious doubts about marrying Matthew. So, can I ask you a very blunt question? Why are you marrying him? I'm not too sure you love him, but do you even like him all that much? It worried me when you said that you and he don't have all that much in common.

While I'm on the subject, why does Matthew want to marry you? Is he interested in you, as Bett, rather than as a woman he can marry? It just sounds to me as though the pair of you have drifted into something and don't know how to drift out of it again.

If you are still reading this, then you are probably thinking I should mind my own business. But you are my sister and I love you dearly. It would be a lot less messy to get out of this engagement than it would be to get out of a marriage. It sounds like the two of you get on OK, and maybe you would make better friends than lovers, or better acquaintances than husband and wife.

I'll shut up now. I just wanted to say that I hope you'll think about this carefully. It wouldn't be the end of the world if you called it off.

Never forget how much I love you.

Anna xxx

Anna had come back to the Valley not long after to see Carrie, but Bett hadn't mentioned the letter or her doubts to her again. There'd been so much fuss about Carrie's return that it had been easy to avoid the subject. Bett had loved the novelty of having a boyfriend to show to Carrie. She'd enjoyed the feeling of going to the pub with them that first night, watching as Carrie jokingly road-tested him for her. She hadn't minded at all when the two of them often became the three of them, Carrie joining them for dinner, drinks in the pub. When Carrie was around, Matthew seemed to have lots more to talk about. It was Bett who had suggested Carrie go to the agricultural college with Matthew and sit in on some lectures, when she'd seemed so interested in his vet stories. Bett had a clear memory of that day. *Matthew and Carrie should be together, not Matthew and me.* She had actually thought that.

She stopped walking, alone on the path, the early-morning air crisp around her, cool against her skin. Her memory jumped to the night Matthew had told her about Carrie.

Fury, hurt and anger had propelled her through the next few months. Then the ticket overseas had turned out to be a lifeline. It had been a chance to leave the mess that was her life in the Clare Valley, her relationship with her sisters, far behind her.

It had been frightening, but it had been a chance to be herself, to stop measuring herself against Anna and Carrie. Except she hadn't been able to leave them behind, had she? All the memories had come with her.

And they were still there.

Out at the farmhouse, Carrie pointed the remote control at the television and turned down the volume. Lola had insisted she take the night off from the motel. 'You've been working too hard, darling. Have a break. Prepare yourself for the musical, with lots of relaxing, lots of good food, lots of snuggling up to Matthew.'

Some chance of that. She was too stressed to relax, there was no food in the house and the only snuggling she'd been doing was with the sofa cushions. She'd spent all afternoon watching imported American confrontational chat shows. The programme credits came up, with a contact number if you needed a family matter sorted out.

If only it were that easy. What would the producers do? Make them talk about their true feelings? Insist they were honest? Carrie could almost hear herself telling Matthew how sorry she was for all the fighting. How much she missed him. How she wanted to give it another go.

She sat upright. She did. That was exactly how she felt. But what would Matthew say if she asked him to come home again?

She realised there was only one way to find out.

CHAPTER EIGHT

ANNA RAN HER HANDS down Richard's body, stretching herself so she was full length against him, skin against skin. He smiled into her eyes, leaned forward, kissed her on the lips again. There was just a white cotton sheet covering them, the one lamp throwing a soft light into the room. She felt wrapped in warmth, in compliments, in his admiration. She loved the touch of his fingers on her body, his lips on hers, the sound of his voice telling her stories, asking her questions, showing interest in her like she hadn't felt in years.

Anna had never had this with Glenn, simple lying under the sheet together, talking, their bodies entangled, the memory of lovemaking fresh on their skin and in their minds, the promise of more to come in the stroking of fingers on bodies, the look in each other's eyes. She felt reckless, like a teenager again, staying out late, comforted by the thought of Ellen safe with Lola.

Richard had just told her some of the conversation from his dinner with Bett several nights before. She was struck equally by his gentleness and his curiosity, as if he was trying to understand her, and her sisters, and the feud between them.

'I can understand why Carrie and Bett might have fought, but why did you and Bett fight about it all?'

'Oh, not just me and Bett. Me and Carrie too.' She smiled. 'We were

never a family to do things by halves. I fought with her straight after I'd
fought with Bett, actually.'

'Tell me about it.'

'You really want to hear?'

'I do. I love hearing you talk.'

Anna had been in Clare on a quick weekend visit, while Glenn had
taken Ellen to visit his parents in Queensland. She was in her room
when Bett burst in, wild-eyed, her mop of curls more unruly than usual.
She spilled out the story in moments, before Anna sat her down and
made her go through it again, slowly.

Bett took a deep breath. 'Matthew had something urgent he needed to
talk to me about. So we met here, in the bar. I thought it would be about
a job move or something about work, but no . . .' A pause, as Anna
could see Bett was trying not to lose control. 'No, he said he needed to
call off our wedding.' Bett told Anna that she had scarcely mouthed the
word 'Why?' before Matthew had delivered the answer. 'He said:
"Because I've fallen in love with Carrie."'

And then into the bar walked Carrie. A glance between her and
Matthew, Bett said, and she had known. Carrie felt the same way.

'You should have seen them, Anna. The two of them sitting there,
holding hands, telling me how hard it was for them, for *them*. Carrie
kept going on about how they had tried to fight it, but it had been too
strong, too *passionate*, between them to ignore.'

Anna winced. 'I can't believe Carrie would do this. And what is
Matthew playing at? Creeping from your bed to Carrie's?'

Bett shifted uncomfortably. 'Matthew and I . . . hadn't actually
been . . . well, not for a while. I don't know, there hadn't been time.'

Hadn't been time? Anna was puzzled. Wasn't sex something you made
time for—especially when you were in the first flush of love? 'Bett, things
really hadn't been OK with you and Matthew before this, had they?'

'Of course they had,' Bett said quickly. 'Things were perfectly fine,
until this.'

Anna frowned. 'Really? You don't remember calling me about him?'

There was no answer.

'Bettsie,' Anna used the pet name, 'come on. Remember our phone
call? The letter I wrote that you never acknowledged? You know you
weren't feeling sure about Matthew. You told me as much. Maybe this
was the chance to have told him.'

There was still no answer.

'Oh, Bett, please.' Anna gave a quick laugh. 'Don't deny it. You must be the only journalist in the world who makes a habit of changing the facts to suit yourself.'

'You're one to talk. You're hardly broadcasting from the Palace of Truth yourself.'

Anna stopped laughing. 'And what is that supposed to mean?'

Bett lifted her chin. 'You and Glenn.'

'What about me and Glenn?'

'Why do you stick with him? Do you really love him? Does he love you? Or is it because of Ellen? Or your social standing?'

'Sisters who come seeking help shouldn't turn into complete and utter bitches.'

'Bitch? Excuse me? I have been completely humiliated and you turn on me.' She stood up, her eyes blazing. 'Fine. Brilliant. Off you go to Carrie, then. Tell her how delighted you are. Tell her what a wonderful success she has made of her life. The two of you again, Miss Perfect and Miss Even More Bloody Perfect. No need to worry about me cluttering up your perfect space again. Enjoying life up there in the ivory tower, are you, Anna? Good. Great. You're welcome to it, though I'm sure Carrie and Matthew will enjoy popping in for a visit now and again, if they pass muster, don't spoil your décor.'

Anna only just held her temper in check. 'Stop it, Bett. You're upset. You're not seeing things clearly. Calm down, for God's sake. I told you I'm on your side.'

'You are not. You never have been. It's only ever been about you. We saw through it, though. No one likes Glenn. I mean, all right, marry for money if you have to, but couldn't you have picked someone who was a little more like a human being?'

'That's enough.' Anna was now furious herself.

'Good thing Ellen is so pretty, I suppose, though God help the poor girl if she ever puts on a gram of excess weight. I can see it, you'll have her down at the Kiddy Gym. Like mummy, like daughter.'

Anna's fury rose like a geyser. 'I wanted to help but you're beyond it, Bett. Forget it. Go. Good riddance. You're on your own now.'

Bett stared at her coldly. 'Maybe I have been for years, Anna. I wish I could say it's been a pleasure being your sister but quite frankly it hasn't.' She walked out, slamming the door behind her.

Anna barely had time to catch her breath when the phone on the bedside cabinet rang. It was Carrie.

'Annie?' She only called her Annie when she was upset. 'I need to talk to you. Are you alone?'

Anna noticed then that her hands were shaking. 'Yes. Bett's just left.'

'Can we talk to you? Will you come to my room?'

So 'they' had become 'we' already. A united team. Quelling her angry feelings towards Bett, trying to be calm, Anna went straight to Carrie's room. Inside, Carrie and Matthew were sitting side by side on the bed. Carrie was crying. Beside her Matthew had his arm around her shoulder, stroking her awkwardly, looking embarrassed.

'So it's true,' she said, looking at them both.

Two nods, Matthew a little shamefaced, Carrie defiant. 'We couldn't help it, could we, Matthew? It just happened.'

Anna looked from one to the other. 'And you're sure?'

Matthew nodded.

Carrie looked at him and nodded too. 'We are. Hurting Bett was the last thing, the very last thing, I ever wanted to do.'

Anna had suddenly had enough. 'All right, Carrie. You don't have to lay it on too thick.'

The crying stopped. 'What do you mean by that?'

Anna put it to her straight. 'You know you and Bett have circled each other for years. I'm not saying you deliberately made Matthew fall in love with you, but be honest with me if not with yourself. At the start was there not a bit of playing with fire, flirting, to annoy Bett?'

'Are you saying I deliberately made this happen?'

'Subconsciously, maybe. I don't think you thought it would come to this though, no.'

Carrie's lower lip was quivering. 'Yes, you are. That's exactly what you're saying. That I made this happen to hurt Bett.'

Anna laughed. She couldn't help herself. Carrie looked like a sulky five-year-old.

Carrie turned stony-faced. 'It's not funny. You've always taken Bett's side. It's always been the two of you, ganging up on me.'

'What?'

'You know it has been. You both always hated me tagging along behind you, getting in the way.'

'Carrie, what are you talking about? Stop behaving like a child.'

'That's it exactly. You've been saying that to me for years. Well, Matthew and I have made an adult decision. We love one another and it's none of your business. And if this is what it took for you and Bett to see I'm not a child any more, then I'm glad it happened.'

'Sorry, Carrie, can I get this clear—you're glad you've broken up Bett's engagement? I hope to God you're joking because if you're not you are a much sadder case than I already thought.'

Matthew leaned forward then. 'I have to step in here, Anna.'

Anna didn't look at him. 'Shut up, Matthew. Mind your own business.'

Carrie gasped. 'Don't you dare talk to Matthew like that.'

Anna was beyond reason now. 'What? I should keep it sweet with him in case he gets sick of you and wants to make a play for me? He's going for the hat-trick, is he?'

Now both Matthew and Carrie looked outraged. 'That was uncalled for, Anna.'

Inside, Anna knew it was exactly that. But the pair of them, sitting there, all smug and wound round each other, had suddenly annoyed the hell out of her.

'I apologise for that remark. But I don't apologise for anything else I said, Carrie. You're a self-centred, selfish little—'

'I don't care what you think of me, actually.' Carrie's lip quivered. 'Come on, Matthew. This is pointless. Let's go.'

'You can't go,' Anna had said, suddenly exhausted. 'You're in your room. I'm the one who has to go. And I'm happy to, believe me. Goodbye, Carrie. Goodbye, Matthew. Good luck whatever happens to you both in the future, but I don't want anything to do with it.'

'Good. I don't want you to have anything to do with us either.'

And with that Anna had slammed the door.

Richard shook his head in amazement. 'And where was Lola in all this? I can't imagine her sitting back and letting it happen.'

'No, she didn't.'

There had been a family conference, Geraldine and Jim, Anna and Lola, with a number of phone calls made to Carrie on her mobile phone. She had left the motel and gone to stay with Matthew in his mother's house. Bett had left too. Got in her car the next morning and just driven away. She had phoned Lola to tell her she was safe, that she was in Melbourne, and had then turned off her mobile.

Jim Quinlan had been sure it would all blow over. Lola had put him right. 'Darling, you haven't noticed any of this going on, have you?'

'Noticed what?'

Lola had shaken her head. 'Geraldine, what about you?'

Anna remembered her mother looking a little uncomfortable. 'It's been so busy here, Lola, I thought they were all getting on so well.'

'They were,' Lola had laughed. 'Just in the wrong combination.'

They'd all agreed what to do next. The wedding would have to be called off, the church booking cancelled, any engagement presents returned and word carefully put around a few key information-brokers in the town. Lola volunteered to do it all.

Anna had left the Valley the following day, still furious with Bett and Carrie. 'They've shown their true colours, Lola—Bett lives in fantasy land and Carrie is a selfish little cow, and I don't care if I never speak to either of them again.'

One month later she was still cross, and she'd heard nothing from Carrie or from Bett, who had now decided to stay in Melbourne. The one-month silence between them grew to two, then to twelve.

Anna heard via Lola that Bett had gone travelling overseas. Carrie married Matthew, a very small affair in Adelaide—neither Anna nor Bett was invited. Lola attended with Geraldine and Jim, and sent a photograph of the couple to both Anna and Bett.

Anna put the photo away and turned all her attention to Glenn, Ellen and work, returning home to the motel just once a year, timing it to coincide with Matthew and Carrie's annual holiday away. One year became two, became three years, when the attack on Ellen happened, and took precedence over everything else.

'And that's how things were,' she said to Richard. 'Until Lola's party.'

'You've been through a lot lately, haven't you?' he said.

She lay looking into his eyes. 'Yes. Yes, I have, I think.'

She felt the touch of his fingers on her arm, on her bare skin. 'Too much to go through on your own. I wish I'd known you then. I'd like to have helped.'

She moved closer, moulding her body against his, feeling an answering reaction from him. 'You're helping me now,' she said.

At that moment, in the vet's quarters of the Red Hills sheep station, Carrie was kissing Matthew's chest.

'Carrie . . .' he murmured.

'Shh,' she said. 'I told you, I'm tired of talking.'

'We have to talk.'

'Matthew, if you say another word I'm getting back in my car and driving home.' Once she'd made her decision it had been simple. She loved Matthew and she was going to fight for him. She'd changed her clothes, packed a bag and driven for two hours without stopping. He'd been in his quarters when she knocked on the door. She'd given him no chance to protest, no explanations, just moved into his arms and started kissing him. It had taken him only a second to respond.

'I've missed you so badly.' His voice was nearly hoarse.

She held herself a little away from him. 'And you don't regret marrying me?'

'No, I don't.'

'You don't want to go back to Bett?'

'No.' He pulled her close. 'Carrie, can you shut up about Bett for one minute and come here so I can . . .' He finished what he was going to do in a whisper in her ear.

The phone rang as Bett was passing reception. It was her turn to mind the bar and the phone. Carrie was on a night off and Anna had said she wanted an early night. Ellen was in with Lola again. She'd decided her favourite sleeping place was her great grandmother's double bed. Bett had checked on the pair of them a little while before. They'd both been asleep, books strewn on the bed around them.

Bett picked up the phone. 'Valley View Motel.'

'Hello, could I speak to one of your guests please.' The caller had a well-bred English accent. 'Mr Richard Lawrence.'

'Certainly, sir. I'll put you through to his room.'

She tried it and got the engaged tone. 'Can I take a message? I'm afraid I can't get through at the moment.'

'I've been trying for the past two hours and it's been constantly engaged. And his mobile is turned off too. Would it be possible for someone to knock on his door in case he's accidentally left the phone off the hook? I need to check something with him urgently.'

'Of course. Who can I tell him is calling?'

'Please tell him it's Charlie. It's about the filming.'

Bett walked over to Richard's room and knocked softly at the door. 'Richard, I'm sorry to disturb you. There's an urgent phone call.'

She heard moaning.

'Richard?'

Another kind of deep sigh.

Good God, was he all right? 'Richard?' She tried the handle. The door swung open just as Richard and Anna reached orgasm together.

Bett was back at the reception desk in record time. 'Hello? Um, Richard is a bit tied up at the moment. Can I take your number and get him to call you back?'

'Damn.' He sighed. 'Could I speak to Lola, then?'

How did he know Lola? 'She's asleep, I'm afraid.'

'I'll just have to leave a message, then. Can you tell Richard we need to change the filming arrangements? Can he have everything set up for the day after tomorrow rather than next week? He'll know what I mean. And could he ring me as soon as possible to confirm?'

She took his details and tucked the note in her pocket. There was no way she was going to go back to Richard's room with the message. Not yet, anyway. She was completely shocked. How long had this been going on between them? What about Glenn?

She was in the kitchen making up the breakfast trays for the morning when she heard the door open behind her.

'Bett?' It was Anna. 'I think we need to talk.'

Bett didn't turn round. 'Anna, you don't have to explain anything. What you do is your own business.' Bett picked up the next order form—one cereal, bacon and eggs, eggs hard not runny, underlined five times. And honey, not marmalade please. Also underlined.

'Bett, I want to explain.'

Bett picked through the box of preserves, searching for a little sachet of honey. 'You don't need to.'

'I still want to explain. I don't want this to cause another rift between us.' She hesitated. 'I know you were a bit interested in Richard.'

Bett kept busy with the tray.

'Please put down that bloody honey and listen to me.'

Bett turned. Anna was dressed in a silk dressing-gown. Bett was struck by how tired and fragile she looked. 'So how long has this been going on between you?'

'Not long. A week or two.'

'And what about Glenn?'

'Glenn and I have been over for a long time, Bett. He's having an affair.'

'He's *what*?'

Anna walked over, shut the kitchen door and started talking.

Forty minutes later, Bett was holding her crying sister close against her. 'Oh, Anna, I'm so sorry for you. I didn't realise it had been so bad. Why didn't you tell us?'

'When? How? We weren't talking.'

'But what about telling Lola? I can't believe you've been through all this on your own.'

'It was pride. I knew if I told Lola, she'd tell you and Carrie. And I decided I could bear the life, the silences with him, more than I could bear the two of you telling me that I shouldn't have married him.'

'Does Ellen understand what's going on?'

'Some of it. She's picked up the tension, and the fact he's away so much. Even though he'd try and get back in time to take Ellie to school most mornings.' Glenn would come in, freshly showered from Julie's bathroom, to be sitting there in the kitchen when Ellen woke up, for all the world the perfect father. 'That's the only good thing. He adores her at least. And she adores him. And he's wonderful with her.' It was a simple fact. 'It's the two of us . . .' She stopped, started crying again. 'It's been a horrible, awful, lonely mess, Bett . . .'

Bett held her close until the tears stopped. 'And this thing with Richard?' she asked softly.

'I don't know. All I know is that he is kind and he listens to me and he makes me laugh. It's what I need now. Do you understand?'

Bett thought of her night with Daniel three years ago. 'Yes, I do.'

'I'm sorry. I should have told you the night you were going to ask Richard for a drink. Told you that he and I were becoming friends.'

'I don't mind at all. Really, I don't.' She smiled. 'But you might want to think about locking the door from now on.'

Anna hugged Bett close again, then took a step back. 'Bett, I'm so sick of having secrets from each other. Please, can't you and Carrie sort things out too? Have you talked to her about Matthew yet?'

Bett shook her head, wary again.

'Please, Bett. You have to. She thinks you're still in love with him, I'm sure of it. You need to—'

The door opened behind them. It was Richard. 'I'm sorry to interrupt. I'll come back—'

Bett was relieved. She moved away from Anna. 'It's fine, really.'

He looked uncomfortable. 'Bett, I must apologise. I'm sorry if that put you in an embarrassing position.'

Her lip twitched. Actually it had been him in the embarrassing position. 'It's fine, Richard. And I'm very sorry for barging in on you like that.' She took out the note from her pocket. 'I had a message for you. Someone called Charlie rang to tell you the filming will have to take place the day after tomorrow not next week.'

'The day after tomorrow?'

Bett nodded.

'Is something wrong?' Anna asked him.

He smiled awkwardly. 'I think there's something I'd better tell you.'

As she drove into the Clare Valley that night, Carrie knew that everything had changed for the better. She loved Matthew and she knew he loved her. He had actually cried in her arms.

'Carrie, I stopped loving Bett when I met you. I don't know any more if that was what I felt for Bett. We got on well, but—'

'But she loved you so much. She was so upset when you split up.'

'I know. I'm so sorry, but I couldn't do anything about it.'

They had talked about the past few months, about the fighting and the separation.

295

'It was other things too.' She paused, then forged ahead. 'You stopped talking about having a baby.'

He had held her close. 'Carrie, I didn't think we could afford to have a baby yet. I want one as much as you do, but I'm not qualified yet. I tried to explain that's how I felt, but I couldn't get through to you.'

Carrie recalled heated conversations, which generally ended in her storming out. That was what he had been trying to tell her, she realised guiltily. She'd heard 'I don't want a baby', when what he had been saying was 'I don't want a baby yet'.

That morning over breakfast he had agreed to come back to the Valley to meet Bett. He would come the day after tomorrow. Carrie kept driving, straight to the motel. It was after ten but she was determined to speak to Bett that night, to arrange a time and place for the meeting.

All the motel lights were on. She was surprised to find both her sisters in the office. Bett was finishing a call just as Carrie walked in.

'Carrie, you're back early. That's great. Can you—'

'In a moment, Bett.' She couldn't let herself be distracted. 'I'm sorry to get right to the point but we need to talk about something.'

'In a minute, Carrie. Something's come up. We need to ring—'

'It's important.' Her tone surprised them both. 'Matthew is coming back to the Valley and he wants to see you. And I want him to see you. Do you still want to see him?'

Bett blinked at her. 'Sure. Yes. Fine. Can we worry about him later, though?' She thrust a list of phone numbers at her sister. 'We've got a musical emergency on our hands.'

By eleven o'clock the following morning the cast and a hastily assembled crew were in the Clare Town Hall. The piano had been transported from the motel in the back of a refrigerated truck, sandwiched between twenty boxes of ice cream.

Richard was worried. 'It's not a full-scale documentary, Anna. It's just a short segment. Maybe only a few minutes long. I'm worried you're going to too much trouble.'

Anna lowered her voice. 'I think your friend Charlie is doing me a favour, actually. Everyone's pulling together because of the filming. We'd never have got everything done by opening night otherwise.'

Anna and Bett had known nothing about Charlie Wentworth's plans to film a rehearsal of Lola's musical. He was travelling round Australia making films for cable television, and Richard had put him in touch with Lola, who had agreed to the filming on condition that his visit was a surprise for her granddaughters.

Lola, her arm still in its sling, was watching all the activity from a chair to the side of the stage. It was an excellent vantage point. In a corner of the hall, three of the ladies from the charity shop were organising the costumes onto racks. Bett was at the piano, frowning a lot but otherwise looking in control of her little band of musicians, who had been summoned straight from the high school, still in their uniforms. Len was moving set panels. As Lola watched, Daniel Hilder arrived and started helping him. Up on the stage, Carrie was practising her solo dance scene, striking quite an elegant pose. One thing puzzled Lola. Anna's behaviour with Richard Lawrence. Were eyes deceiving her or was there a lot of flirting going on there? Little hand touches. Glances.

She made her way over to Bett and sat down on the piano stool beside her. 'Hello, darling.'

'Hello, Lola,' Bett smiled distractedly. Some of the songs weren't working, now that she had seen them performed on stage. The tempo or the length was wrong.

'Bett, can we have a word about Richard Lawrence?'

'Mmm?' Bett had her pen in her mouth, sheet music in one hand and was trying out a chord with the other.

Lola lowered her voice. 'Have you and he had another dinner or a drink or anything since the night I was so tired?'

'Me and Richard?' Bett took the pen out of her mouth. 'Oh no, Lola. Richard's having an affair with Anna. Anna and Glenn's marriage has broken up, too, by the way. Months ago. He's been having an affair with his PA. I only found out last night. Sorry. I know Anna would have told you too but all this took over.'

Lola didn't even blink. 'Oh. I see. Well, I'll leave you to it, then.' She returned to her chair. Anna and Richard. Who would have thought? She turned slightly so she could see them, standing on the edge of the stage. Anna was smiling at something he was saying. His expression was courteous. Mindful. And very affectionate. Still waters ran deep, as the saying went. As for the break-up with Glenn—was she surprised? Not particularly, she realised. She actually quite liked Glenn, with his bristling energy and booming voice. He'd always been so good with Ellen, too. But perhaps Anna was better off with a gentle man.

Len's voice sounded through the hall. 'That's it, Daniel. No, sorry, a bit to the left. Now right. Forward. Forward. No, back again. To tell you the truth, I think it might be upside-down.'

Lola watched as Daniel Hilder and Len stood in front of one of the Terowie Railway Station set panels and determined that, yes, it was indeed upside-down. They carefully lowered it to the floor again. Lola put on her glasses and took the opportunity to assess Daniel one more time. He was good-humoured, that much was obvious. And patient. He could do with a haircut, though. But that casual, unstructured look was quite the fashion, according to a TV show she'd seen the night before. Yes, he'd do fine. A worthy second choice.

Operation Bett and Daniel sounded so much better, anyway.

Charlie arrived at half past nine in the morning, sweeping into the town hall with his film crew. He was as flamboyant as Richard was quiet, long hair tied back in a ponytail, hugely amused by everything and everyone. 'Anna, it's a pleasure. I've heard great things about you. And Bett, I'm charmed. And you must be Carrie, is that right? But where is the magnificent Lola, whose phone calls have been entertaining me so hugely these past few days?'

'I'm right here.' They turned round. Lola was dressed in a brightly coloured combination of a long red satin overshirt, wide-legged paisley trousers, glittering costume jewellery, teased white hair and bright red lipstick. Her wrap was of gold lamé. She had wound a coloured ribbon round her walking cane.

Charlie bowed deeply. 'Lola, this is an honour. I don't suppose you could do that entrance for me again? On film this time?'

She gave him her most dazzling smile. 'Darling, I'll come somersaulting in, if you want me to.'

An hour later Anna had nearly chewed her bottom lip to pieces. It had taken three takes to get 'My Favourite Things' right. The train stalled midway across the stage in the first verse of 'Chattanooga Choo Choo'. General MacArthur forgot his lines and said 'I might return' instead of 'I shall return'.

But Charlie was delighted. He strode into the centre of the hall and clapped his hands. 'Wonderful job, everyone, just wonderful. If we can have the three granddaughters up here singing "Sisters" together, we'll be done for the day.'

Bett turned from the piano. Carrie stopped in the middle of the stage. On the hall floor Anna stepped forward. 'Sorry, Charlie, that's not part of the show.'

'But it's in the script.' He waved his copy.

Anna noticed he had Lola's original version. 'No, we took it out.'

Charlie frowned. 'But that's the charm of the story. I had the whole thing edited in my head. Shots of Terowie, the MacArthur plaque at the railway station, snippets from the musical, an interview with Lola, the three of you singing, finishing up with Lola coming in proudly behind you.'

Lola stepped forward. 'Would you want me to be smiling, Charlie, or would you prefer I had a tear in my eye?'

'We'll try both, Lola, I think. So you'll do it, girls? Terrific.' He didn't give them a chance to protest, turning to call to the cast and his crew. 'OK, everyone. Thanks for a great morning's work. We'll have a break and be back in twenty minutes with the three sisters on stage together.'

Bett sat at the piano, fighting a rush of memory and self-consciousness. Back with the three sisters on stage together? She couldn't do it.

'Bett?'

She turned. Anna and Carrie had come up to the piano. Anna seemed exhilarated after the filming. 'What do you think? Will we do it?'

'No,' Bett said. She said it to Anna, trying not to look at Carrie.

Anna noticed that a member of the cast was standing nearby. She spoke loudly and deliberately. 'Let's go backstage, then, will we? See if we can remember all the words.'

They followed her into the long dressing-room behind the stage. Anna checked that they had it to themselves, then turned to Bett again. 'This isn't because of that Piggy in the Middle business, is it? Bett, that was more than fifteen years ago, for God's sake. Carrie apologised to you. I apologised to you. Can't you leave it all behind?'

Bett felt a ripple of anger inside her. 'It's not always so simple, Anna.'

'Of course it is. Is it really going to kill you to get up on stage again? You know how much it would mean to Lola.'

There was only silence from Bett and Carrie.

Anna lost her temper. 'Fine. Brilliant. More silences. Well, I've had enough of it, do you hear me? All this tiptoeing around each other. I'm going to start talking about all the things the three of us have managed to avoid so beautifully the past month.' She was having trouble getting her breath and had to pause for a moment. 'I hereby put it on the record that I hated that stupid fight we had. I hated the fact you both came running to me to try to fix it and I ruined it. Do you think I liked not talking to you both? Liked having my marriage crumble around my ears and not having anyone to talk about it with, or—'

'Marriage crumble?' Carrie was shocked into speech. 'But Glenn worships you.'

'No, he doesn't, Carrie. Glenn and I are getting divorced. And in the new spirit of openness, here's another piece of news. I'm having an affair with Richard Lawrence and loving every minute of it.'

Carrie turned to Bett. 'Did you know about all this?' At Bett's nod, she lost her temper too. 'Of course you did. Fine. Perfect. The two of you, ganging up on me again, like you always have.'

'What? What are you talking about?' Bett was furious now as well. 'It was never me and Anna. I was always the one who was left behind.'

'Stop changing the facts to suit yourself, Bett,' Anna snapped. 'You did it with Matthew three years ago but I'm not going to let you do it again now.'

Carrie tensed. 'What do you mean she did it with Matthew?'

'Changed the facts. Didn't you, Bett? I've been trying to talk to you about this since we got here. You know exactly what I'm talking about. It's time we brought all of this business out in the open so we can—'

'I've been trying,' Carrie interrupted. 'I've asked Matthew to come and see Bett.'

'It's not just about seeing Matthew again, Carrie. Is it, Bett? It goes back further than that.'

Bett's face was burning. 'This is the wrong way to do things, Anna.'

'Then what is the right way? Because I don't know any more. All I know is we were lucky to have each other and now it's all ruined.'

'It's not ruined.' Bett stared at Anna, remembering all her sister had been through with Glenn and Ellen. On her own, because Bett had been too proud to admit the truth to Carrie. She took a breath. 'I'll tell her.'

Carrie was looking back and forth between the two of them. 'What? Tell me what?'

'I didn't want to marry Matthew, Carrie.'

Carrie went still. 'I don't believe you.'

'It's the truth. I'd been talking to Anna about it. Telling her things weren't going well with us.'

Carrie looked at Anna. Anna nodded. 'What do you mean "weren't going well"?'

Bett wavered. 'I'd realised we weren't suited to one another.'

Carrie seemed genuinely shocked. 'Then why did you get engaged?'

Bett told the truth. 'Because I thought that once I had a fiancé everything would be all right.'

'So were you ever in love with him?'

She paused. 'No, I don't think I was.'

'But you were so upset when . . . when he fell in love with me.'

'I was hurt. Of course I was. And shocked. But I was just as upset with you. And then with Anna as well. It was the way you both reacted. You, Carrie, as if it was your right. You didn't even seem surprised that Matthew would have fallen in love with you.' The words were pouring out of Bett now. 'And you, Anna. When I came to you, all I wanted was your sympathy. And you just stood there, all cool and collected, making me feel like I had made a mess of everything yet again.'

'I didn't, Bett. I just wanted you to admit that you'd been having doubts about him. But you just lost your temper and started attacking me.'

'I couldn't help it.' She felt tears in her eyes and roughly wiped them away. 'It just seemed like final proof I'd never be as good as either of you.'

'But how did you think it was for me, Bett?' Carrie said passionately. 'You wouldn't listen to us, even though we wanted to try and explain. And when I went to you, Anna, you just spoke to me as if I was a child, like you always had.'

'I couldn't win, could I?' Anna said. 'Caught between you, yet again. I told Bett she should admit the truth, to you and to Matthew, and she just flew off the handle. And then you flew off the handle too, Carrie. And I thought, well, to hell with the pair of you.'

'So did I,' Carrie said. 'That's exactly what I thought. To hell with the pair of you. I wanted to live my own life.'

'Me too,' Bett said. 'That's what I wanted to do. As far away as I could.'

'So why didn't you come back, though? Why did you stay away?'

Bett hesitated. 'Because once I'd got over the shock and got through the first few months in Melbourne, I realised I liked being away from you both. I liked the freedom. I liked being just me, not Bett, sister of Anna, or Bett, sister of Carrie.'

'I felt like that too,' Anna said suddenly. 'To begin with, anyway. But do you still feel like that? Now?' Anna looked very serious.

Bett shook her head. 'I haven't felt like that for a long time. I got so lonely without you both. Once I'd proved to myself I could live away from you'—her voice wavered—'I missed you both so much. And then Ellen was attacked, and, Anna, this is a terrible thing to say, but one part of me was glad, because it was a reason to write to you. So I did. But then I didn't hear back so I thought you didn't want contact again.'

'Me too,' Carrie said. 'I wanted to go to Sydney, but Lola and Mum got in first. I rang and talked to Glenn, left a message. But then I didn't hear anything either.'

'I couldn't contact either of you. I'm sorry. I didn't have any room for anyone but Ellen. I was so angry with myself for letting it happen, at Glenn for blaming me. I couldn't handle anyone else. I'm sorry.'

There was silence and then Carrie spoke. 'I think you both should know that Matthew and I have been separated for a while.'

'*What*?' Anna and Bett spoke in unison.

'Everything went bad for a while. We only decided to get back together yesterday.'

'Oh, Carrie, why?' Anna asked.

'Misunderstandings about things. And I got guilty. I thought I was being punished for taking Matthew away from Bett.' She wasn't looking at either of them. 'And I wasn't sure if Matthew was over Bett.'

'Carrie, he was. I'm sure he was.' Bett had seen the wedding photo. She knew Matthew had never looked at her the way he looked at Carrie. 'I'm sorry for not telling you before, Carrie. And I'm sorry that you had to go through everything on your own, Anna.' She was embarrassed to feel her eyes filling with tears. 'It had just gone on for so long, and even though I wanted to I just didn't know how to fix it.'

'It doesn't matter now, does it?' Anna asked. 'We're talking again. And we'll keep talking, won't we? No matter what?'

Bett and Carrie nodded, then they all moved towards each other, into a long, warm hug. After a moment, Carrie stepped back.

'Do you want to meet Matthew again, Bett? He's here. He came down this morning. He's outside. Will I get him?'

Bett hesitated, then nodded.

Anna waited until she was gone before she spoke. 'Do you want me to go, to leave the three of you alone?'

Bett shook her head. 'No, all for one, one for all, don't you think?'

'I'm glad you told her, Bett. I'm sorry I had to force it.'

'I'm glad you did.'

They heard noises from the hall, as the camera crew finished its break. They heard a faint hum of traffic from the main street. A car door shutting. Footsteps and the glass door opening. Bett turned and there he was, with Carrie a few feet behind.

'Hello, Bett. Hello, Anna.'

'Hello, Matthew,' they said in unison.

Bett took in every detail of his appearance. The sandy hair, the curls now cropped short. The square, kind face. The stocky body. It was like looking at someone she had been at school with years before.

He looked uncomfortable. 'How are things, Bett?'

'They're fine. It's good to see you again.' And it was. Nothing more and nothing less.

'You too.' Matthew gave an embarrassed laugh, looking from one to the other. 'Bett, I'm sorry for what happened. With me and Carrie. For hurting you like that.'

For one moment she was tempted to tell him the truth. That she had gone out with him for all the wrong reasons. Then she looked at Carrie, standing proudly beside him. 'It's fine, Matthew.'

He didn't seem convinced. 'If Lola was here she would probably use her truth stick, I suppose. Make us all say how we're really feeling.'

'You know about the truth stick?' Anna asked.

Matthew nodded. 'Not that Lola ever used the truth stick on me. It was more a family thing, wasn't it? Very handy sometimes, she said.'

'It was, yes,' Anna said. She turned to Bett. 'If Lola was pointing the truth stick at you now, what would you say, Bett?'

Bett answered honestly. 'I would say I'm feeling a bit uncomfortable but I'm also very relieved to finally see Carrie and Matthew together. And I think they make a good pair. And I'm so sorry it's taken this long for me to tell you and Carrie how I felt. And you, Anna?'

'I'd probably say I've been feeling sick about all of this for years. And I'm glad it's over and I hope we won't ever have a fight like this again.'

Carrie was gripping Matthew's hand. 'And I would say I'm sorry for any hurt we caused you, Bett. And you, Anna. And I hope you forgive us.'

'And I would say about bloody time.'

It was Lola, standing in the doorway. 'That's the thing about swear words,' she said, smiling broadly. 'Use them sparingly and they always have much more impact, don't you think? So, all set to do the "Sisters" song for Charlie?'

Oh hell, Bett thought. She'd forgotten all about that. 'I'm sorry, Lola, but I can't do it. I've forgotten the words.'

'If she has, then so have I,' Anna said.

'Me too,' Carrie added.

'Oh, I'm sure it'll come back to you once you get started. It's that one about the mister coming between the sisters. No? Then it's just as well I brought these.'

She passed over three sheets of lyrics. They were cornered. 'Come on, then. Charlie and his cameraman are waiting. He was just saying again how this is going to be the centrepiece of his segment.' Complete lies, of course. Charlie had no interest or intention of using any of this footage of the Alphabet Sisters. He had staged that little scene earlier purely as a favour to Lola. She had explained the whole situation to him on the phone the day before and he had been highly amused and happy to oblige. And, by the looks of things, it had worked.

'Come on then, girls.' She started shooing them in front of her, one by one. Then she stopped. 'And you, too, Matthew. I've had the very amusing idea of using you as well.'

Half an hour later, Charlie strolled over to where Lola was sitting, watching all the action. She took his hand and smiled up at him. 'Thank you, Charlie, darling. You're quite an actor yourself.'

He bowed deeply. 'A pleasure to be of service. You never know, I may end up using the footage yet. They were rather good, weren't they? Some wonderful harmonies.'

'Once they stopped laughing, yes, they were. That was always their problem. They didn't take it seriously enough.'

'Matthew was a good sport, to stand there like that while they sang that "Sisters" song around him.'

Not so much a good sport as terrified of what might happen if he didn't do as he was told, more like. 'Wasn't he just?'

In bed that night, Jim and Geraldine were talking about their holiday and their homecoming a few hours earlier.

Geraldine took off her glasses and reached out to turn off the bedside light. 'The girls seem to be getting on very well again, don't they?'

'Remarkably well. I was sure there would have been at least one row or something while we were away, but it seems not. Perhaps that's all it ever needed, just getting them back under the same roof again.' He chuckled. 'I take my hat off to Lola.'

Jim didn't see Geraldine's expression. 'They're grown girls. I knew they'd sort it out eventually themselves.'

'Of course. Good night, darling.'

'Good night, Jim.'

He put his arm round his wife and shut his eyes.

CHAPTER NINE

BETT WOKE UP with just the slightest hint of a hangover. She and Anna and Carrie had stayed up talking and drinking red wine until very late. Richard, Matthew and Lola had joined in at first, before stealing away one by one, leaving the three girls on their own.

Another time, after that much wine, Bett might have woken with a headache, a sense of the dreads. But not this morning. She could remember every word, every joke, every laugh they had shared, even though it had been nearly 2 a.m. by the time they went to bed, practically pouring a giggling Carrie into the taxi they had called.

Bett stretched, enjoying the feel in her muscles. She had a glorious, light feeling inside her, that things were going to be OK again. She hadn't felt so good in years.

She checked the time. Eight o'clock. She'd better get up and get ready. She had two more assignments with Daniel that day, and they'd arranged to meet at the office at nine thirty. She chose her favourite dark green shirt and vintage skirt, and some Italian shoes.

'You look smart, Bett,' her father said as she walked into the kitchen for a coffee. 'Have you got something special on today?'

'No. Just doing a couple of stories for that tourism project.'

'With Daniel?' Lola piped up from her chair.

'Yes, actually.'

'Marvellous!' Lola beamed.

Lola didn't have to have looked quite so delighted, Bett thought as she walked into the newspaper office half an hour later. Her grandmother's face had lit up as if Bett had said she was heading off to elope to Gretna Green. She and Daniel just got on well.

Their first stop was Sevenhill Cellars, the Valley's oldest winery.

'We've a few minutes before they're expecting us,' Daniel said, glancing at his watch. 'Do you mind if we take the scenic route? The light's good today for a shot I want to take over the hills.'

'No, I don't mind at all.'

Daniel turned the car off the main road onto the bumpy dirt road.

Her reply echoed in her mind as she watched him stop and start the car at different spots along the road, choosing scenes where the sunlight filtered through clumps of gum trees, sending dappled light onto the rows of vines. No, she didn't mind at all seeing him concentrate on finding the best picture; she didn't mind at all if they got to spend a bit more time in the car together, talking and laughing.

The realisation came on slowly and surely throughout the day. She was acutely aware of him walking close behind her as they were taken on a tour of the cool stone winery building, breathing in the rich smells of the wooden barrels of wine around them. She noticed his manner with the people he was photographing, how quickly he put them at ease.

They drove back into Clare in the early afternoon. The sight of his lean, brown hands on the steering wheel was beginning to have quite an effect on her. The way he tapped his long fingers gently in time to the music on the radio. As they stopped at an intersection, she nearly leapt out of her seat when he reached over suddenly to catch a brochure that kept sliding back and forth along the dashboard.

He sent her a puzzled look. 'Bett, are you sure you're OK today? You seem a bit distracted.'

'Do I? Am I? Sorry. I must be coming down with something.'

Opening night arrived. The last tickets had been sold that morning. Lola stood, dressed in full splendour, at the front door of the town hall. Her floor-length orange taffeta skirt clashed with the purple tunic, which clashed with the gold wrap. It all clashed with her make-up. She had a rose and a fabric butterfly pinned in her hair, and nearly rattled as she walked from all the jewellery.

Beside Lola, in a much more low-key outfit, but with just as bright a smile, was Ellen. She'd been put in charge of handing out programmes as people came in and greeted everyone who passed her with the same message. 'Good evening. Enjoy the show, won't you?'

Backstage, Anna was checking on costumes, make-up and sets. She was glad and relieved to feel the adrenaline coursing through her, giving her the energy and buzz she had always loved before a performance. She'd had a very bad night's sleep, tired but unable to sleep, feeling the tightness across her chest again. Perhaps that scan the young doctor had mentioned was a good thing, she'd thought as she lay there in the dark, thinking the worst. She'd confided in Richard, and been comforted by his matter-of-factness.

'It's probably asthma, by the sound of things. But the doctor's right. It's just as well to get it checked out. When is the test?'

In Adelaide, two days after the musical, she'd told him, when she was returning the costumes. She'd been surprised by his next words.

'Would you let me come with you? I'd like to take you somewhere really splendid for lunch. To celebrate the musical. And to celebrate you and—' he had stopped there. 'Well, just to celebrate.'

She had been very touched. 'I'd love that,' she'd said.

At the edge of the room, leafing through her music for the tenth time, Bett was loving this part of the evening, all the excitement before the show began. Carrie was beside the mirror, applying make-up to all the cast members. Lola's ladies from the charity shop were making last-minute adjustments to the costumes. She tucked the music under her arm and went up onto the stage, nervous and excited. She peered through a gap in the curtains into the hall. It was nearly full and there was a warm, bubbling noise of conversation.

Bett made her way down the side stairs and out into the little musical pit they had set up at the foot of the stage. The young members of her band were already seated: a sax player, a guitarist and a drummer. She greeted them warmly, noticing their flushed cheeks, their bright eyes. She took her seat and nodded, and they began playing the first of the introductory tunes, Glenn Miller's 'In the Mood'. Looking up from the keyboard, her fingers so familiar with the notes, she spied Rebecca in the audience, with a gang of people from the newspaper. Daniel was at the end of the row. He winked at her as she caught his eye.

The noise in the hall changed as Lola started making her way to the stage through the centre aisle. She climbed the stairs, then paused dramatically in the middle of the stage, just as Bett finished the last notes of Vera Lynn's 'We'll Meet Again'.

'Ladies and gentlemen, boys and girls, thank you all very much for coming tonight.' She gestured flamboyantly. 'Welcome to the world premiere of *Many Happy Returns*!'

At the interval, Anna went out to the hall to say a quick hello to Richard and Lola. She couldn't get near her grandmother. Lola was standing in the middle of an admiring crowd, holding court.

Anna smiled as Richard came up to her. 'So? What do you think?'

'It's wonderful.'

'Wonderful?' Anna pulled a face. 'I don't know about that.' She lowered her voice. 'The train got stuck. The dancing wasn't in formation—'

He caught her hand and squeezed it in his. 'And it's still wonderful. Look at the mood. Everyone's having a great time.'

She grinned. 'They are, aren't they?'

Back at the piano, five minutes before the end of interval, Bett felt a touch on her arm. It was Daniel. 'Congratulations. It's hilarious.'

'Hilarious? It's supposed to be serious drama.'

'Sorry. Of course it is. That's what I meant to say. It's hugely dramatic.'

'Careful. We have an audience participation spot, and I have connections with the director.' The bell sounded to indicate the end of the interval. 'Are you staying on for the party?'

'If that's OK. I wasn't sure.'

'You were last-minute crew and nearly cast. Of course you should be there.' She wanted him to be there.

He smiled. 'Great. I'll see you later, then.'

In bed that night Lola stretched one leg, then the other, did her facial exercises, then gave up. She didn't want to do exercises. She wanted to just lie there and grin all night long. She wanted to savour every minute, rewind it all, relive it second by second, from Bett's music, to Anna's direction, to Carrie's singing and dancing. Had she ever felt as proud in the Alphabet Sisters days as she had that evening, standing there on stage with her three girls, her son, Jim, and granddaughter, Ellen, smiling up from the audience at her? Even Geraldine had been smiling and had actually hugged her afterwards.

And had she ever felt as good as she had at the party afterwards? All those people coming up, showering her with praise, firing questions. Were they going to stage it again? What about a tour? Had she thought about sending the script to a professional company? What about next year's project? She had laughed them all away, insisting tonight was no night for future plans, it was for savouring a triumph.

But lying there, she did have a thought. Richard had put it in her mind, with all his research into English convicts and Irish servant girls coming to the Clare Valley in the 1850s. What a marvellous storyline that would make. She could follow just one of them, or no, perhaps two, even three sisters, on their journey . . .

Lola sat up and reached for the notebook on her bedside table.

Forty-eight hours later Bett was sitting beside a campfire near a clutch of gum trees, experiencing first-hand the Drover's Experience. This would be the final article for the tourism supplement.

She had a notebook filled with quotes from the drover himself, craggy-faced, brown-skinned, laconic. The perfect face for a man with his job. 'Straight out of Central Casting,' Daniel had whispered earlier as he set up shots of Fergie with his sheep.

They'd eaten dinner by the campfire—damper bread, billy tea, stew in a pot—exactly as the tourist groups would enjoy it in the months ahead. Their tents would be pitched in a circle round the campfire too, logs acting as seats, under the night sky. Tonight there were just the three tents, one for Fergie, a long way back from the main camp site—'I snore,' he'd explained succinctly—and one each for Bett and Daniel.

Fergie had told Bett some of the tales he'd be sharing with the tourists. He knew the whole story of the area, from its Aboriginal history to the early pioneer days.

Bett put her notebook away. 'This isn't for the article, but tell me, do you ever get sick of sheep?'

Fergie laughed. 'No. If I do, I get a whole fresh bunch every spring, remember. That's the wonder of nature.'

Daniel came back to the campfire. He'd been taking photos from a distance as the final light faded around them. 'I'll take a few more in the morning, Fergie, if that's OK.'

'I'll be up at five, Dan, with my best smile on.' He pulled an exaggerated face and they both laughed. 'Early to bed for me, anyway. You'll sort out the fire, won't you? Good night to you both.'

Bett stretched out her legs towards the fire, alone for a moment while Daniel went to his tent to put away the camera equipment. Her mobile rang, the noise incongruous in the surroundings. She read the name on the display. 'Lola? Is everything all right?'

'Everything's fine, darling. Your parents are in the bar with a couple of guests, swapping stories about train journeys. Carrie is home with Matthew and little Ellen is staying over with them for the night. Anna is in Adelaide returning the costumes. Richard's gone with her for the trip. Do you suppose they'll be staying in separate rooms tonight?'

'You're too old to be thinking things like that.'

'What is the tent situation like there, darling?'

'We have one each, Lola.'

'Really?' A pause. 'You know that if it gets cold, the best way to warm up is through body heat?'

'I'll tell Fergie that, will I?' She had discovered earlier that Lola and Fergie knew each other from some years back. 'That will be a surprise for him in the middle of the night. A little visit from me.'

Lola laughed. 'Good night, darling. Have a nice night.'

Bett glanced up as Daniel came back to the fire. He nodded to the phone. 'Everything all right?' He took a seat on the log next to her.

'Everything's fine.'

There was a long pause before he spoke again. 'So are you going to stay on in the Valley, now the musical is over?'

'I don't know yet. I'll see what happens.' She took up a stick and poked at the embers, watching sparks fly into the air. 'Did you get some good shots today?'

'I think so. A good subject always helps.'

'It's not just that. You're a very good photographer.'

'Thank you.'

'Is it what you always wanted to do? When you were growing up?'

'Always. I had a box brownie as a teenager.' He threw more wood into the fire. 'What about you? Did you always want to be a journalist?'

'No. It was a choice between something to do with music and something to do with writing, and writing won. Now I love being a journalist.'

'You do, don't you? What about it, exactly?'

She thought about it for a moment. 'I like watching something happen and turning it into a sentence or a story. Capturing it.'

'And you don't miss the music? You can't do both?'

'I tried. When I was in London, I wrote about music and bands but it wasn't for me in the end.'

He reached down to the bottle of wine. 'More?'

'Yes, please.'

The sounds around them became distinct. The slow glug of the wine into her glass. A quiet crackle from the flames in front of them. A bird far off in the trees. Faint rustling noises and low bleats from the sheep.

'So was it hard to leave London?'

She shook her head, remembering the day she'd decided to resign. 'Once I'd decided, it was the simplest thing in the world. I knew this was where I wanted to be.'

'It's easier for women in lots of ways, don't you think?'

'What's easier?'

'Life. Decisions.' He waved an arm. 'Women seem to know how to do it. That was one of the first things I noticed about you, how confident and alive you are, how comfortable you are in your own skin.'

'No, I'm not.' Bett was astonished. 'You should have looked closer.'

He gave a soft laugh. 'I was probably too busy worrying about my own appearance.'

'But men don't get worried about what people think of them, do they? I mean, I haven't got any brothers, but I thought you all knew exactly what you wanted, how to act, how to—'

'Of course we don't. I can't speak for the entire male population, but I get scared and worried about things. That I'll make a mess of something, misread a situation . . . I'm scared now, for example.'

'Of what?'

He hesitated. 'Of what you'd do if I asked you if I could kiss you.'

She blinked. 'You want to kiss me?'

'I've wanted to kiss you for weeks.'

'Why haven't you?'

'In case you slapped me. Told me to go away.'

'Oh,' she said. A warm glow had started deep inside her. 'And how were you planning on going about it?'

'I was thinking of coming over and sitting beside you, and perhaps putting one hand on your cheek. And I was probably going to lean down and kiss you. That was when I was worried that you might slap me.'

'I see.' She thought about it for a moment. 'I don't think I would.'

'Should I check?'

She nodded.

He moved towards her. Her breath caught at the touch of his lips against hers, soft, exploring. She felt the touch of his hand on her face.

'Aphrodisiac qualities, those campfires, I've always found.'

They both jumped at the voice. It was Fergie, coming out of his tent. They separated, embarrassed, and stared into the fire again until Fergie returned from the tree he was visiting. He gave them a cheery wave from the opening of his tent.

A moment passed, and then they turned back to one another. This time she met his lips halfway. They kissed, long, slow kisses that tasted like red wine. He kissed her eyelids and the lobes of her ears and the side of her neck. She kissed the side of his face, the corners of his lips. He pulled her in against his body as they both stood up.

A huge sneeze from Fergie's tent resounded in the air. She could feel Daniel laughing, even as she laughed herself.

'The cry of the wildebeest,' he whispered, kissing her again. He moved his hand down her body. Without realising it she started to tense.

He pulled away. 'Do you want me to stop?'

She shook her head. 'I'm just a bit nervous.'

'Of me?'

She shook her head again. 'Maybe not nervous. Maybe self-conscious.'

'But you're perfect. And I should know. I've been staring at every inch of you for weeks. I could draw you from memory. This curve here,' he brushed her thigh. 'The curve of your arm.' He touched her arm. 'Your breast.' Her breathing faltered as he slowly stroked her breast.

Somehow they moved from the campfire to his tent, to the sleeping-bag on the ground, as warm, flickering shadows from the fire played against the canvas. She loved the feeling of his hands on her body, and she loved the feel of him, lean and silky to touch. Was there touch memory, she wondered. Did her body remember what it had felt like to have Daniel against her that night? Because it was responding now as though it couldn't wait to repeat the experience . . .

Bett woke as sunlight was coming into the tent. She felt stirring beside her and turned towards Daniel.

'Good morning.' His voice was soft.

She smiled. 'Hello.'

'Did you have a good night's sleep?'

He knew full well she hadn't. Nor had he. They had been making love most of the night. 'Not really. To be honest, I'm a bit worried.'

She felt him tense. 'What about?'

'My article. Do you suppose I can promise this experience for every woman doing this camping trip?'

He relaxed. 'I could have a word with Fergie. It might be a handy sideline if I lose interest in the photography.'

She laughed, closing her eyes as she felt his fingertips brush her bare skin. His voice was quiet. 'So if you were writing an article about what happened last night, what would you write?'

She thought for a moment. '"Reporter Bett Quinlan announced that she was a bit embarrassed to be waking up naked with Daniel Hilder but said she didn't regret a second of the previous evening's shenanigans.'''

'Shenanigans?'

'Shenanigans. Your turn.'

'"Photographer Daniel Hilder today admitted that he had fancied local reporter Bett Quinlan for some time." Have I got the tone right?'

'Yes. Yes, that's very good.'

'"When questioned, he said that he had always been a sucker for a shock of brown hair and a pair of cheeky eyes, and Ms Quinlan was endowed with both." Am I still getting it right?'

Bett's head was on his chest, her eyes closed as he stroked her skin. 'It's very good.'

'"When asked about his future plans, Mr Hilder gave another insouciant shrug and said, 'It's up to Ms Quinlan, really.' The press corps then gathered around Ms Quinlan seeking her reaction."'

She could feel his fingers down her back now. '"Ms Quinlan responded to reporters' questions by first checking what the time was?"'

Daniel lifted his wrist. 'Six thirty.'

'"And then wondering aloud if it would be possible for Daniel Hilder to make love to her once more before they left the tent that morning."'

He moved closer, his fingers caressing her body. It seemed it was yes.

It was early afternoon by the time they arrived at the Valley View Motel. Daniel pulled into the drive in front of the reception area and turned off the ignition. 'Can I see you tonight?' he asked.

'I'd love to. Let me just check in with everyone, make sure nothing's happened while I've been gone.'

'I'll ring you about six?'

'Perfect.' She waited on the steps of the motel until he had driven away, then turned. She felt like she was radiating happiness. 'Hello?' she called as she came into reception. There was no answer. She checked the bar. It was empty too. 'Hello? Where is everybody?' She went outside and heard her name being called.

'Bett?' It was Carrie, coming from Lola's room. She was crying.

'Cancer?'

Bett looked at the faces in front of her. Lola was ashen. Carrie's eyes were swollen. Her mother and father were holding hands.

Jim Quinlan repeated what Anna had phoned and told them. She had called from the hospital. 'She had an MRI scan this morning. There's a very large tumour in her lungs. They admitted her straight away.'

Bett stared at him. 'But . . . she hasn't had any symptoms.'

'She has. It's just they were mistaken for other things. Stress. Exhaustion. Anxiety attacks. And she's always been so thin, so even the weight loss wasn't too out of the ordinary.'

'But what made her have the scan? Why didn't she tell us?'

'A young doctor in Adelaide arranged it.' Jim's voice was dull. 'She didn't want to worry anyone, she said.'

Bett tried to take in everything as her father kept talking. It was as if the world was slightly off kilter. She wanted to blink, to start again, to get out of Daniel's car, come in the door and see Lola reading in the bar, Carrie in the office, Anna and Ellen playing Scrabble.

Someone was missing. 'Where's Ellen?'

'She's in her room playing. Anna spoke to her on the phone but she's asked us not to tell Ellen too much yet.'

'So can we go to Anna? Ellen, all of us? Now?'

Geraldine shook her head. 'Anna said there was no need to come down tonight. They're giving her sleeping tablets. She'd be asleep before we got there. Richard's with her in the hospital. They're starting radiation treatment first thing in the morning.'

'So it's treatable? So she's going to be all right?' Bett looked around again, knowing she hadn't been the first to ask that question.

No one would answer her.

Time started moving at a different pace, as though they were in slow motion, in a bubble of their own. Anna's treatment started immediately, a team of people working with her—a specialist, a doctor, nurses. Geraldine and Bett were the first to go to Adelaide to be with her. Richard returned to Clare. They took it in turns talking to Anna's doctors, getting test results, phoning back to the motel. Anna spent most of every day in bed, already exhausted from the X-rays, the scans, the drugs, the shock. Bett and her mother sat beside her, talking a little, watching her while she slept. Bett couldn't reconcile this frail-looking Anna with the woman who had been smiling up onstage just a few days before. She was still bright and cheerful at first. But the mask dropped when the two of them were alone after Geraldine had left the room to get coffee.

Anna reached for Bett's hand. 'I'm scared, Bettsie. I'm really scared.'

'We all are, sweetheart. But we'll know more soon, won't we?'

'I don't know. The specialist said I could be in here for weeks. What about Ellen? Who'll look after her if I'm in here for that long?'

Bett squeezed Anna's hand. 'All of us. We're fighting over who gets to look after her. Don't worry about Ellen.'

'Will you ring Glenn?'

Bett called him in Singapore that night. She could hear the shock in his voice. 'I'll come back as soon as I can. What about the hospital? Is it the best one? Money's no problem, Bett.'

She could tell he was truly concerned. It made it easier to put her anger towards him aside. Did some love survive at the bottom of all failed marriages? she wondered. 'It's a very good hospital. They're doing every test, every scan. We can't get near her for doctors and nurses.'

'What does Ellen know?'

'She knows Anna is in hospital, that she'll be home soon.' Lola had sat with Ellen and explained that Anna wasn't feeling very well, that there was a germ in her body the doctors were trying to get rid of and that fighting the germ sometimes made Anna very tired. They would bring her down to visit Anna very soon. In the meantime, Ellen was talking to Anna twice, sometimes three times a day on the phone.

'And will Anna be home soon?'

Bett had told him the truth. 'We don't know.'

Lola and Carrie came down several days later, bringing Ellen with them. They'd told her the truth—that Anna needed to stay longer in hospital while the doctors did more tests on her. Ellen seemed to take it all quite calmly. As Lola said, she was used to hospitals.

Bett drove her mother back to the motel. She had seen Geraldine walking down the corridor with Anna the previous night. All around them were other families, some of them in even worse situations. Geraldine had held herself erect, composed. She'd helped Anna get back into bed, hadn't flinched when Anna's gown had lifted slightly and they had seen just how thin she was.

But an hour later Bett had gone in search of a cup of tea. She had been about to turn on the light in one of the side sitting rooms when she had seen a figure in one of the armchairs in the corner of the room. It was Geraldine, staring out of the window, crying softly.

Bett had hesitated, about to go in and comfort her, but her mother had noticed her and had stood up immediately, briskly wiping away the tears. 'A cup of tea, Bett? Let me get one for you?'

Neither of them mentioned her tears.

Anna put her hand on Lola's arm. 'Lola, I'm so scared.' They were alone in Anna's room.

Lola took both Anna's hands in hers. 'Darling, of course you are. You don't know what's going to happen. That's always scary.'

'What's going to happen to Ellen if I don't get better? How is she going to cope without a mother?'

'Anna, you mustn't think like that. And you must never worry about Ellen. She'll never be on her own, I promise you that.'

There was a knock at the door. It was Glenn, straight from the airport.

Lola stood up and moved aside immediately. As she shut the door she saw him reach down and take Anna in his arms.

Outside, in the waiting room, Carrie railed at Lola.

'It's his fault. This wouldn't have happened if it wasn't for him. I read all about it on the Internet. Stress can cause cancer and that'—she searched for the insult—'that bastard caused her so much stress and pain. How can you even let him stay here, Lola?' She had ignored the concern he was showing, the offers of financial help, the offer—gently declined by Anna—to move her to a private hospital in Sydney.

'It's not Glenn's fault. It's no one's fault, Carrie. It's just happened. We can't waste time blaming someone, fighting among ourselves. We have to think of Anna.'

Carrie was with Anna when the specialist came to talk to her, two weeks after she'd been admitted to the hospital. Coolly, succinctly, he explained the situation. It was a very aggressive tumour. They had discovered some secondaries, but so far they were confined. Surgery wasn't an option at this stage. There was more treatment to try: more radiation, some new drugs.

'And if the new drugs don't work?' Anna's voice was as calm as his. Beside her, Carrie was tightly holding her hand.

His tone softened. 'Then we're looking at a palliative-care situation.'

Bett arrived back at the hospital several days later. She was shocked at the change in Anna, who was sitting up in the bed, pillows propped all around her, like a tiny bird in a white nest. She was even thinner and her skin seemed to be changing in texture and colour. Her breathing was changing too, becoming more laboured.

She managed a big smile, though. 'Hello, Bett. You've come to admire my new nose jewellery?' Anna had two plastic clips in her nostrils, carrying oxygen into her system. She wasn't able to breathe properly without it any more.

Bett managed a grin too. 'It's very fetching. Does it come in a range of colours?'

'Horrible clear and even more horrible white, I think. I did tell them white wasn't my colour but they can be very obstinate in here.'

Bett sat in the chair beside the bed and took Anna's hand. 'Can I get you anything? Do you want the radio on? Any tapes?'

Anna shook her head. 'Tell me about Ellen this week.' Ellen came down to the hospital three days every week.

Bett told her the latest stories. Ellen had invited two of her friends over to play after school. They had been rehearsing their own mini musical, for when Mum came home.

'She'd better hurry it up, then.'

'What do you mean?'

'I've made a decision, Bett.' Her voice became serious as she explained what the specialist had told her that afternoon. That there was still another course of treatment ahead of her. Still in the experimental stages. 'I agreed, Bett. What did I have to lose?'

'But isn't it dangerous?'

'What? Might it kill me?' She laughed softly at the expression on Bett's face. 'I can joke about it, Bett. It's me who's dying of cancer.'

'You're not dying of cancer. There's still lots of things they can try.' Bett was shocked by a sudden flare of temper. 'Don't be so bloody passive about it. Fight it.'

Anna was calm. 'You don't think I am? You really think I want to bow out here and now, slip off, leave all this? Bett, I hate every tiny thing of it. Being pumped full of this drug and that drug, getting X-rayed, feeling my lungs trying so hard. All my life I was never conscious of what my body was doing to keep me alive, and now it's as if I can hear every cog turning, every cell doing its job. Of course I hate this. I see a sunrise, or a bird or the smallest beautiful thing and I treasure it and I want it for ever and I can't have it. I might not have any of it for much longer.'

'What would you like? If we could get you anything, make anything happen for you before you went?' Bett stumbled on the word.

'It's not the obvious things. It's not seeing Ellen walk up the aisle, or holding my first granddaughter. It's the ordinary things. I want mornings in a coffee shop with her when she's about twenty-five. I want more drunken nights with you and Carrie. And I want to hear all those stories again about your misadventures. Please, Bett, tell me the one about you falling off the treadmill again. I love that story.'

'You're very cruel.'

A smile, vivid in the pale, thin face. 'I know. Shall I start you off? Once upon a time, you were in a gym and . . .'

'The new drugs haven't worked. It's spread even further.' Geraldine spoke as soon as she walked into the kitchen two weeks later.

Jim, Lola and Bett stopped what they were doing. They had known

Geraldine was talking to Carrie, who'd been in with Anna for the previous two days. They had known that crucial X-rays were taking place that morning. All day each of them had kept busy, filling the hours.

Geraldine spoke as if she was reading from a list, her voice expressionless, her eyes distant. 'The radiation hasn't worked either. It's spread into her lymph nodes. And her spine.'

A few weeks ago Bett hadn't known what a lymph node was. 'Did Carrie talk to Anna's specialist? About what Anna's decided to do?'

A nod. 'He said that if that was Anna's decision, he fully supported it. He told Carrie afterwards that he felt it was the right option.'

Anna had made her decision three days before. If the latest, more intrusive attempts to stop the cancer hadn't worked, she was going to stop all the radiation, the scans, the invasive procedures.

Jim spoke. 'So she's coming home?'

Geraldine nodded. She didn't need to spell it out. Anna was coming home to die.

CHAPTER TEN

HER FAVOURITE ROOM in the motel was prepared. They hung bright curtains in the windows. Lola chose a colourful bedspread and a new rug for the floor. Ellen picked fresh flowers and put them in vases. Lola had tried to explain to her that Anna was still very sick, but Ellen hadn't seemed to take it in. She'd been too excited by the fact that her mother was coming home. Jim went to the garden centre and bought plants and trees in pots, arranging them outside the room, to give Anna something green and restful to look at from bed. Bett scoured every surface, washed the windows, wiped down the walls.

She smiled at Richard as he carried a box of Anna's favourite books into the room. She was helping him arrange them on a shelf when he spoke, his voice low.

'I should leave, Bett. This is a time for close family.'

She was struck by the deep sadness in his expression. 'No, it's not, Richard. It's a time for anyone who loves Anna to be close to her.' She touched his arm. 'I know it's been very hard on you. When things had only just started between you. But you make her very happy.'

'I'd like to have made her happier. For longer.'

Bett blinked away tears. 'So would we,' she answered softly.

Anna arrived home the next day in the car with Carrie and Geraldine. She'd travelled in a nest of pillows, fragile from the treatment and the illness. She was even thinner, her face even more gaunt.

She had to be helped into the room. The oxygen came everywhere with her, pushed on a small trolley beside her. Her voice was changing, becoming weaker, but she was still bright, interested.

'Ellie, did you do those drawings for me? They're gorgeous.' She leaned and kissed her daughter, who was clinging tightly to her hand. 'And all the flowers. And look at that bedspread. It's beautiful, everyone. Thank you very much.'

As Anna was settled, Ellen skipped around, unable to stay in one place, running up to her mother, hugging her, then running away again. She sidled up to Bett, as she stood outside Anna's room.

'My mum is very sick, isn't she?'

Bett stroked her hair. 'She is, Ellie. She's very sick.'

'When she gets better, Daddy, Mum and I are going to go on a holiday.'

'Did Daddy say that?'

She nodded. 'He said maybe he would even take us to Disneyland.'

'That'll be fun,' Bett said, keeping her voice bright. She knew what Glenn had been trying to do. She also knew Anna wouldn't be going with them.

The days fell into a pattern. Anna had more energy in the mornings. She could sit and talk with one or other of them, eat a little, before needing to go back to bed again. Now and then she managed to go for a short walk, or would let them push her in a wheelchair, in the cool of the morning, or after dusk, when the heat of the day had passed. The palliative-care nurses visited twice a day and monitored her pain. They showed Bett, Carrie and their mother how to measure the morphine, answered their questions, calmed and soothed them.

Anna slept a great deal. When she was feeling strong enough, she came into the kitchen in a brightly coloured silk dressing-gown and sat in a corner, watching all the activity around her. Ellen continued going to school, but ran in each afternoon, with a new drawing, or a love note, which Anna would exclaim over and put into her pocket.

When Anna was too tired to get up, they all took turns spending time with her in her room. Geraldine was there the most, tidying the room, counting the tablets, straightening the curtains or just sitting quietly by

Anna's bed. She seemed to know when Anna was feeling any pain, when she needed more oxygen, what she might like to drink or eat, almost by instinct. No one remarked on it, but everyone noticed.

'Can I get you anything, love?'

Anna looked up from the bed. Ellen was tucked in beside her, asleep. The two of them had been watching cartoons together. 'No thanks, Dad.'

'A cola? A squash? A rainbow drink?'

'A rainbow drink? Now you're talking. Not for me, but for Ellie when she wakes up.'

'You're not thirsty at all? Or hungry?'

She shook her head. Her appetite had almost gone now.

He turned to go to the bar to make Ellen's drink when she called after him. 'Dad, can you make Ellie's drink later?'

'Of course. Is there something else you want done instead?'

'Would you just sit here with me for a while?'

He sat down in the chair beside her bed, taking her hand in both of his. 'Of course, sweetheart. For as long as you like.'

Lola carefully draped the scarf over Anna's bedspread, then stepped back and looked critically at it. 'It will do for the moment. I've got my eye on a rather nice pink one down at the charity shop. I think I'll put in a bid for that and bring that home for you as well.'

Anna smiled up at her. 'I love you, Lola.'

Lola stopped still. She gazed down at Anna, then gently, slowly lifted her hand and stroked the soft cheek. 'Not as much as I love you.'

'Do you believe in heaven, Bett?'

'I want to. I want to know that you are going somewhere special, somewhere that you'll love, and that you'll get a good spot ready for us when we arrive.'

'I will, I promise. Sun or shade?' She was trying hard to sound bright.

'A bit of both, I think.'

'Bett, will you do something for me?' Her voice was getting weaker.

'Anything.'

Anna reached under her pillow and took something out. 'Would you look after these for me?'

It was an envelope, filled with pieces of folded paper. 'What are they?'

'They're birthday cards for Ellen. Little notes. Until she turns twenty-one. I was going to ask Glenn to give them to her, but I'd love you to do it instead. If you don't mind.'

319

'If I don't mind?' She had a lump in her throat. 'I'd be honoured.'

'And you'll help him look after her, won't you? Even if it's hard some-times. I know you and him haven't always—'

'Of course I will. We both love her dearly, Anna. You know that.'

'And, Bett, will you tell her about me? Please? I don't know how much she'll remember.'

Bett blinked away tears, so used to them now she barely noticed them. 'Of course I will. I'll tell her how beautiful and how kind and how brave—'

Anna's smile was frail but full of mischief. 'Well, you don't have to get too carried away.'

Richard moved the chair in close to Anna's bedside and reached into the box beside him. 'I've Jane Austen or Seamus Heaney or—'

'Don't read to me. Talk to me instead.'

'What about?'

'Anything you like.'

'Anything I like? Then in that case I want to talk about you.'

Anna didn't speak, just kept looking at him.

He started, haltingly. 'I want to talk about how unfair this is. And how much I wish this wasn't happening. But that would all be about me, not about you.' His face was very sad. 'I'd liked to have made you so happy, Anna. I'd liked to have gone travelling with you. I'd liked to have got to know Ellen. For the three of us to have got to know each other.' He paused. 'I'm sorry, it's about me again, not you. What *I* would have liked. But it's the truth. All I would have wanted was to be with you. Making love, drinking wine and talking all night. Telling you how much I loved you, every day, until you got tired of hearing it.'

Tears formed in her eyes. 'I wouldn't have got tired of hearing that.'

He didn't say anything more then, just picked up her hand and pressed a kiss against her palm.

Carrie learned she was pregnant a week after Anna was brought home from Adelaide. Bett was in the room with her when she told Anna. 'It's still early, only a few weeks. But I wanted to tell you.'

'Carrie, that's fantastic news.' Anna's smile was almost luminous now. 'That lucky little baby. If you get morning sickness, dry bread is sup-posed to be good, but only if someone brings it to you. Is Matthew being good?'

'He's great. It's apparently not even the size of a clothes peg yet, but he keeps telling me he can feel the baby moving.'

'Oh, that's sweet.' She shut her eyes.

Bett moved closer to her. 'Anna? Are you in pain?' They had given her morphine an hour before, but they could give her more if she needed it.

Anna opened her eyes. 'No, I was just remembering when I was pregnant with Ellen. It's a wonderful time, Carrie. Write it all down, so you'll remember it. You'll tell yourself there's plenty of time to do that, because there's no way you'll forget something like this, it's so amazing. But then an even more amazing thing will happen, and then another, layer on layer of them.' She looked from one to the other. 'You'll make sure Ellen gets to see her cousin a lot, won't you? You'll go up to Sydney or ask Glenn to fly Ellen down here?'

Carrie hadn't dared ask. 'She'll stay with Glenn after . . .'

'After I'm not here.' The smile again. 'I'm lucky in a way. He loves her so dearly and she loves him just as much. But I've asked him to make sure Ellen spends as much time as she likes here with all of you.'

'She can live with us if she wants to. I'll adopt her.'

'I will too,' Bett said.

Anna gave another gentle laugh. 'Then will you both help him look after her for me?'

Carrie's eyes filled with tears. 'We will, Anna, we promise.'

Bett reached for their hands and held them tightly. 'I'm so sorry for taking three years away from all of us. For taking so long to tell the truth about Matthew. If I had done it earlier—'

'It wasn't just you, Bett. It was just as much my fault.' Carrie was as upset. 'I should have tried to—'

'Stop it.' Anna sat up a little, her voice surprisingly strong. 'Don't waste all this time wishing that you'd done this or done that. Please. It's what happened.'

Carrie managed a smile. 'You were always so bossy, you know that.'

Anna's head was back on her pillow. 'I'm the oldest. I'm allowed to be. And soon Bett will be the oldest so you have to let her boss you.'

She didn't get any further. Bett and Carrie were crying too hard.

A week later, Bett and Daniel walked down the tree-lined road behind the motel. Since Anna had come home Daniel had called by every few days, dropping in for just a few minutes with flowers for Anna or a bottle of wine for the rest of them. Each time he had invited Bett to go for a walk or a drive with him, or for a meal in one of the local restaurants. The first few times she had said no.

'Go, Bett,' Lola had finally insisted. 'You have to have some time for yourself. Otherwise you'll have nothing left to give her.'

'But what if . . .'

'Take the mobile and I will ring you if there is any change.'

From then on she started walking with Daniel several times a week, out on the quiet back roads behind the motel, or along the walking track that followed the path of the old railway line through the Valley. The walks began to mean a great deal to her, brief breaks from the slow heartbreak of seeing Anna fade away a little more each day.

That morning Anna had been sleeping, with Geraldine and Lola by her bedside, when Daniel had come to collect Bett. As they started walking he put his arm around her, holding her tightly.

'She's not even dead yet, and I miss her, Dan. And sometimes I go into the room and she's asleep and I think, oh, she's died, as if it will be some simple thing like that. But I know it won't be. And I can't bear that she's suffering. But the thing is, I just don't want her to leave us.'

Her tears came in a flood. He took her in his arms and held her close for a long time.

Glenn came to stay at the motel full time. He and Richard circled each other for a day or two, before there was a silent acceptance of each other. They took their turns at Anna's bedside.

Walking past the kitchen one afternoon, Bett heard Glenn's low tones, followed by her parents'. Glenn saw her passing and beckoned her in.

'Bett, I was just explaining to your parents that Ellen's going to come to Singapore with me after . . .' his voice seemed to catch. 'Afterwards. But you'll always be her family as well. I want you to know that. I want her to come here as often as she can, I want you to feel you can all come and see her as much as possible. No matter where we are.'

Bett needed to bring everything out into the open. This was no time for secrets. 'Will your girlfriend be all right with her?'

She saw her parents' heads shoot up. She would have to explain it to them later.

'Julie and Ellen get on very well,' he said simply. 'And she knows that, for me, Ellen will always come first.'

Bett knew he meant it. 'Thank you, Glenn.'

Then Geraldine spoke, her voice very soft. 'Ellen needs to know that it's not going to be long now. We need to tell her. Prepare her.'

There was a pause before Glenn spoke again. 'Anna and I talked about it last night. She's asked me not to tell Ellen in front of her. She said that it would be too hard for them both.'

Bett had never seen Glenn look so vulnerable. 'Do you want me to be with her when you tell her?'

He nodded. She could see he was now fighting tears too. 'Yes, please.'

The moment came the following afternoon. Ellen had spent the morning lying on the bed beside Anna, chatting away as normal. When the palliative-care nurses arrived, she'd only gone a little way away, sitting outside Anna's room, drawing with chalk on the footpath. She was still there when Glenn and Bett went to find her.

Hand in hand the three of them walked over to a bench overlooking the vineyards. Ellen clambered up onto her father's knee, waiting, as if she knew something important was happening. Glenn cleared his throat. 'Ellie, we have to tell you something very sad about your mum.'

'I already know.'

'You know?'

'She's not going to get better, is she?' Her voice was matter-of-fact.

Glenn and Bett exchanged glances. 'How did you know that?'

'I heard the ladies talking about her. They said they thought she might not have more than a few weeks to live.'

Bett took her niece's hand then. 'Ellie, do you know what that means?'

Ellen nodded. 'It means she's going to die.'

Another shared glance. Bett could see Glenn was struggling.

'And do you know what that means?'

Ellen shook her head.

Bett tried to find the right words. 'It means that this time we have with her now is very special, Ellie, because after your mum dies—' She lost her way for a moment. 'Ellie, after she dies that means we won't be able to see her any more.'

Ellen looked puzzled. 'But she doesn't go anywhere, does she? Doesn't she just stay in the bed even after she dies? And we keep on visiting her?'

'No, Ellie. It means she's going to go away from us.'

'But where is she going to go? Why can't I keep seeing her?'

Glenn held Ellen tight against him, pressed his face against her hair, tried to hide his tears. 'I don't know, Ellie. I don't know.'

Anna's funeral took place on a perfect autumn day. The sky was blue. The air was crisp and clear. The rows of vines around the church and the cemetery were vivid reds, browns and oranges.

The church was crowded. The service was simple, the readings and music beautiful. Lola had produced a sheet of paper the day after Anna died. It was a list of the songs she wanted played, the readings she loved. She had dictated it to her grandmother several weeks before.

After the funeral mass, after the time in the cemetery, everyone came back to the motel. The mood was dull, subdued. There was talk, but not a great deal. Cups of tea. Sandwiches. Bett felt removed from everything. She kept expecting to turn and see Anna with her glossy dark hair and tall, straight back. She wanted to hear her voice.

She saw her father pouring tea. He looked ten years older. Her mother was on the other side of the room, her face like a mask. Carrie was standing with Matthew. Richard was in conversation with the local priest and Glenn was holding Ellen.

'Bett?' Daniel came up behind her. 'Is there anything I can do?'

In that moment it seemed to hit her. There was nothing he could do. There was nothing anyone could do. He opened his arms and she moved soundlessly into them.

Glenn and Ellen left a week later. The departure was heartbreaking for all of them. An hour before they were due to leave, Ellen disappeared. Bett found her tucked up behind the shed at the back of the motel, holding tightly to Bumper.

'Ellie, you need to go, sweetheart. Daddy's nearly ready.'

Ellen wouldn't look at her. 'I want to stay here.'

'You can come back here whenever you like.'

'I want to be here now.'

Glenn came up behind her and took in the situation. He got down to Ellen's level. 'Ellie, I promise you can come back very soon. I want you to come home with me for a while first, though. I need your help.'

She shook her head.

Bett realised this was a moment for father and daughter. She slipped silently away, back to where Lola and her parents and Carrie and Matthew were waiting. Ten minutes later Glenn and Ellen came towards them, hand in hand. Ellen was subdued. She said goodbye to each of them very solemnly and hugged them round the neck.

Richard left three days later. Bett had gone for a drink with him the evening before. He was as sad these days as they were. He was going back to London, where he'd been offered work at his old newspaper.

'Will you keep in touch with us?'

'If you'd like me to.'

'We'd like it very much.'

They all hugged him goodbye as well.

'Enjoy your stay, won't you?'

It was six weeks after Anna's death. Bett was at reception, checking in some late-night guests. She had handed them their room key, explained how to order breakfast, where the dining room was and the opening hours for the bar. She'd felt like a fake the entire time, as she smiled and tried to talk normally to them.

She closed the registration book and found the day's mail lying underneath it: bills, circulars and several cards in pale cream envelopes. Word of Anna's death had filtered through to her acting friends, advertisers she'd worked for in Sydney, clients, neighbours and mothers of Ellen's friends. The cards had come in a rush the first few weeks. Even now, they were still arriving in twos and threes each day. Bett opened them automatically, reading the messages, simple and heartfelt. 'We are thinking of you in your great sorrow.' 'She was a beautiful woman, we will miss her very much.'

Bett noticed the airmail sticker on the final envelope as she slit it open. This one had an Irish postmark.

Dear Lola,

I write this tentatively, hoping that you are the same Lola Quinlan, originally from Leixcraig House, Kildare, Ireland, who I knew more than sixty years ago.

I saw a programme called 'Did You Know?' on the Discovery channel last week, featuring you and a musical you had written on General MacArthur. Would you be the same woman who married my brother Edward and then emigrated to Australia with him just before the war?

I am sad to write that Edward died five years ago, leaving behind no family. After he left Australia he continued to travel, spending some years in America, before returning to Ireland and the family home in Kildare. He died at home, aged 78. May he rest in peace.

Edward never explained the whole story of your separation but I wish you no ill will, Lola. If you find it in yourself to contact me, I would be pleased to hear from you.

Yours truly,

Margaret Hegarty (née Quinlan)

Bett walked as if she was in a dream, through the motel, out to the yard, along the row of rooms until she reached Lola's door. She knocked once, twice. A soft voice called her in.

Lola was at her writing desk. 'Bett? More cards? People are very kind.'

Bett couldn't speak.

Lola was puzzled. 'Bett? Are you all right?'

She handed the letter over to Lola without a word. She watched as Lola started to read, watched Lola's hand creep up to her neck. Heard as if from a long way away Lola say softly, 'Oh, dear God.'

Bett found her voice. 'So Edward didn't die during the war.'

Lola looked up. Her hand was still at her neck. 'No, Bett, he didn't.'

Bett wasn't angry or upset. Not yet. She just needed to understand. 'So who was Dad's father?'

'It was Edward. He didn't know that I was pregnant when I left him.'

'You left him?'

'I had to. If I had stayed with him I—'

'You would have given Dad a father.' Bett was stunned. Confused. 'Lola, I don't understand. We had a grandfather all this time . . .'

'I'm sorry, Bett.'

'Sorry for what? For leaving him? Or for not telling us the truth?'

'Only for not telling the truth. I couldn't stay with him. He was not a good man. And I didn't realise it until we were married and here in Australia.'

'But why say he was dead? Why not say you had left him?'

'Because this was the 1940s, Bett. Because a month after I left him I discovered I was pregnant. I was a young woman in a new country at wartime. A widow was respectable.'

'But I can't understand why you didn't ever tell us the truth.'

'How could I? Tell Jim that the father he thought was long dead was in fact very much alive? And then what? Try to find him? Trawl every bar in the country? The truth is, Bett, I didn't ever want to see him again. I didn't know what would happen if he found out he had a son.'

Bett took back the letter, trying to make sense of everything she was hearing. She read the address. 'She's writing from Kildare. Is that where Edward was from? Where you were from?'

Lola nodded.

'That day I went to take photos. You sent me to the wrong place.'

Lola was very calm. 'I had to.'

'Why? Because you thought I'd find out the truth? Find him?'

'I panicked, I admit it. I was worried that you would go to the right house and possibly even find Edward living there. And I didn't want you to have that shock.' Lola glanced down at the letter again. 'But it seems he was dead by then. You wouldn't have met him.'

'This will devastate Dad, you know that.'

'Only if he finds out.'

'You're not going to tell him? Show him that letter?'

'No. There's no point now. What he knows is enough. It was my decision years ago and it's one I've stuck with, even if it has been difficult.'

'But how can I keep a secret like that from my own father? From Mum? And Carrie? Ellen? Don't you see they have to know?'

'No, I don't.'

'You'd let this continue? You, who spent your entire life telling us to face our fears and tell the truth? Can't you see this changes everything?'

'It changes nothing, Bett. I am the same person, you are the same person, all the things we have done or said to each other are the same.'

Bett stared at her. 'I think you're wrong.'

She left the room and returned to the reception desk, where she updated the booking register and set out the last of the breakfast trays. She sent her parents to bed and closed down the rest of the motel herself, switching off the lights one after the other. Finally, she walked across the car park to her room. She opened the door quietly and then nearly leapt out of her skin as she saw Lola sitting in the armchair.

'You won't do this to me, Bett. I won't have it. I won't have you walk out on me like that, or ignore me, or stop talking to me. Do you hear me?'

Bett had never seen Lola so angry. 'I'm not ignoring you. I'm trying to take it in. I can't hear something like that and just let it wash over me.'

'Of course you can. That's exactly what you have to do. Let it wash over you, let it soak into you, and then get on with it. Nothing has changed, Bett. I still want you to face your fears and tell the truth. Even if your fear is that the family is ruined and that you hate and despise me. So tell me now. How do you feel?'

Lola didn't need to mention a truth stick. Bett could feel it being pointed at her without being told.

'I'm shocked.' Bett hesitated. 'And disappointed.'

'Why?'

'Because the grandmother I idolised was lying to me for years.'

'A little melodramatic, perhaps, but all right, accepted. What else?'

'I'm sad, Lola.' The truth burst out of her. 'Sad, sad, sad. And I can't take any more bad things.'

'Yes, you can. And you'll take a lot more before you're dead yourself. There'll be more deaths, more disappointments, more people will let you down. Perhaps I was wrong. There was a time, when your father was small, when things were very hard, when it would have been easier to go back to Ireland. But I wanted freedom and I wanted adventure. I was trapped in my family, Bett. It was rules and regulations and expectations, and it was suffocating me. Marrying Edward and going to Australia had seemed like a lifeline. But I knew within weeks that I'd made an even bigger mistake. He wasn't what I thought he was.'

'What I can't understand is why you didn't tell us the truth.'

'I've wanted to. For years. But I wasn't sure who to tell or how to tell it. And the lies became real to me. I began to think of Edward as dead. Began to think fondly of him in a certain way. I started pretending I was a brave young widow and so I had to become a brave young widow.'

'But it wasn't true.'

'No, it wasn't. And I can't force you to forgive me. But I can ask you to use your imagination, the imagination I have done my best to feed over the years. I want you to imagine yourself in my place, to see how it might have been for me. Don't disappoint me.'

'You've disappointed me.'

'No. What I've done is show you one more bit of truth about me. And that is something you would rather not see. You've disappointed me because I would prefer you were the perfect understanding grand-daughter just as you would prefer me to be the perfect faultless grand-mother. I'm not perfect. I never have been. I never will be.'

'You were perfect. You were the most wonderful grandmother.' Bett started to cry. 'You still are the most wonderful grandmother.' She found herself in Lola's arms. 'I'm sorry, I'm so sorry. It was your life. You had to do what you had to do. Of course I know that. But it's one more hurt, Lola. One more person gone, one more thing changing.'

'You wouldn't have liked him.' Lola held Bett close. 'We don't always get what we want. I wanted a good husband, not a drunken bully. I wanted lots of things I didn't get. I also got things that I never wanted or expected.'

'Like Anna dying.'

'Anna dying. But also the life I've had with all of you. Because the real truth is that I have never loved anyone in my life like I love your father and the three of you, and now Ellen too. You have all been the most wonderful thing that ever came to me. More than I ever imagined I would have. Some things we can make happen, other things happen to us. We just have to keep going, whatever happens.'

'I just want Anna back, Lola.'

'We all want her back, darling. All of us.'

Bett cried then as if it was the first time since Anna died. Lola held her tight until Bett's breathing calmed. 'I'm so sorry, Lola.'

'It's all right.' She kissed Bett's forehead.

'I won't tell Dad or Mum or Carrie. It's not for me to tell them.'

'You can if you want to. It's up to you.'

'What good would it do?' Bett hesitated. 'Are you going to write back to Edward's sister?'

Lola shook her head. 'I think it's best that I don't.' She took Bett's face between her hands. 'I'm sorry I hurt you. You are very precious to me. I want you to know that. I'm glad it's you who found out.'

Bett mirrored the action, her hands against Lola's soft, powdered skin. 'I'm glad it was me, too.'

EPILOGUE

ANNA'S GRAVE was on the high side of the cemetery, overlooking a sweep of vineyards. It was a cool, crisp May day, the air fresh. They parked their cars at the bottom of the hill, walked up past the other graves, gravel and fallen gum leaves crunching under their feet. Everything they needed was now packed neatly into two baskets.

Glenn, Matthew and Jim carried the chairs, arranging them round the gravestone, looking out over the hills. Geraldine and Bett laid the fold-up table with a tablecloth, champagne glasses and the plates of food.

Once everything was organised, Lola stood up. 'Now, we have to do exactly as she says.' Leaning on her stick, she started reading aloud from a piece of paper, written in her own hand. Anna had dictated the words to her three weeks before she died.

'"First of all, pour champagne and orange juice and drink a joyful toast to each other and to me." The champagne is a gift from Richard, by the way.' Richard wrote to Lola every month or so. He was still at the newspaper, but he'd started working on the novel again, he'd told her.

Anna had left exact instructions on how they were to mark the first anniversary of her death. It was like a mini play, filled with stage directions, a cast list ('my family'), what props they'd need, and the setting: her graveside at lunchtime.

'Is this joyful?' Ellen asked, moving her glass of juice vigorously from side to side.

'I'd say that's more enthusiastic than joyful,' Bett said, stepping out of the way as drops of juice flew through the air. 'Slow it down a little, Ellie.' She turned in time to see Carrie juggling her baby daughter on one hip, a bottle in one hand, a glass in the other. 'Carrie, do you want me to take her?'

She pulled a face. 'Would you, Bett? Just for a second?'

Bett took her niece, moving her head back as a little hand made a grab for one of her earrings. She'd been christened Delia Anna. 'Her name had to start with the letter D, didn't it?' Carrie had said. 'We had A for Anna, B for Bett, C for Carrie and then a jump to E for Ellen. This way she's a bridge between us. She joins us all up again.'

'Ready, everyone? You all have your glasses?' Lola called out the toast. 'To us and to Anna.'

'To us and to Anna,' they echoed.

'And now to the food,' Lola said.

'It's a bit hard to know where to start, isn't it?' Jim said.

'Are we allowed to top up the glasses, Lola?' Glenn asked.

Lola checked Anna's instructions. 'She didn't say, but as the matriarch, I'll make the decision. Of course you can. Have as much as you like.'

'Will I give Mum a glass of champagne?' Ellen asked. 'She liked champagne, Dad, didn't she?'

'She sure did.' He poured a glass and Ellen put it on the gravestone.

'I was talking to her last night,' Ellen said as she came back and settled herself on her father's knee. 'I asked her how things were and told her about how Dad and I are going to Disneyland next week.'

'And did she say anything back?' Bett asked, keeping her tone light.

Ellen gave her a pitying look. 'No, of course not. I say her bits for her. Like when we do plays at school, and I play more than one part.'

Lola peered up into the sky. The blue was nearly gone, darker clouds coming in their direction. 'I think it's time for another message for all of us.' She unfolded the last piece of paper and started reading.

To my darling family,

If it is possible for me to be watching you today, I promise you I will be. If you notice some champagne missing from your glasses, that will be me who has taken it, too. All I want to say is that I love you all very much, and thank you for all you did for me, and for my beautiful Ellen, during my life. I have been very, very lucky. Thank you for being so obedient today and don't worry, I'm not going to make you come back here year after year. It's up to each of you how you remember me from now on, but please keep eating your favourite things and drinking champagne, even if I'm not there to boss you around.

With all my love,
Anna

Lola held up her glass. 'Another toast, I think. Just to Anna.'

'Just to Anna,' they all echoed.

One year later

BETT LOOKED UP as the screen door snapped shut. 'Is everything all right?'

'It's fine,' Daniel said. 'They'll be here soon.'

It wasn't a formal lunch, just a barbecue and some salads. Everything was ready to go, the barbecue coals heating, the table already set in the garden. They'd been lucky with the weather, blue and clear, with no sign of the rain they'd had the previous year. Bett checked the time. There was still an hour before Ellen was going to ring from Singapore. Everyone was sure to be there by then. Bett had promised Ellen, and Glenn, that she would be able to say hello to them all, even if she wasn't with them on the actual date of Anna's second anniversary.

Two years on, Bett had realised that it wasn't the date that made them think of Anna, in any case. Thoughts of her flowed freely between all of them, no matter where they were or when it was. There were memories and conversations that made them sad, memories that made them laugh. It helped them all when Ellen came to stay, or when they went to visit her and Glenn in Singapore. It was as Lola had said. Anna's life and Anna's death had become a part of them all.

Bett shifted up a little so Daniel could sit on the swing seat beside her. They both put their feet up on the verandah rail. Daniel went back to the book he'd been reading when the phone had rung. She returned to hers.

They had moved into this house together nearly a year before. It was a stone cottage in the hills behind the motel, on the northern edge of Clare. The town was on one side, paddocks and vineyards on the other.

'Bett?'

'Mmm.'

'What about Fred?'

Bett gave it some thought. 'No, I don't think so.'

'Flossy?'

'If we have a pony instead of a baby, sure.' She turned. 'Daniel, the name doesn't really have to start with an F.'

'Yes, it does. I love the idea of it.' He put down the battered copy of *1001 Names for Your Baby*. 'And we have to get in quick, before Carrie and Matthew have another one, and we get stuck with G.'

Bett laughed. 'Can we get the wedding out of the way before we worry about the baby's name? I'm not even pregnant. Anyway, what if we can't have children?'

'Then we'll get lots of pets and treat them like our children.'

She smiled and went back to her book. She was on the second to last page when he spoke again.

'Bett, how do you feel about having eleven children? Or eleven pets?'

'Pardon?'

'I've just worked it out mathematically. If you and Carrie spend the next eleven years having a baby a year, you and I will end up with Z. Isn't that great? I've always liked the name Zelda, or Zephaniah if it's a boy.'

'That's a lovely offer, Dan, but no, I don't think so.' Bett stood up as

Carrie and Matthew's car turned off the main road and started up the dirt road to their cottage. She could already see Lola waving majestically from the back seat. Not far behind them she saw her parents' car.

Daniel stood beside her, his arm across her back. He leaned down and brushed his lips against her ear. 'Xanthes? Wilhelmina?'

She started to laugh. 'No, Dan.'

'Violet? Ursula? Thomasina? Please, Bett, can't we have a Thomasina? You'd grow to love her, I know you would. And Saxon. And Rhiannon . . .'

She turned in his arms. 'All this time we've known each other and I never realised you knew your alphabet backwards.'

'I can juggle a bit too. I could teach the children. We could go on the road, pick up where the Alphabet Sisters left off. All of us juggling together. Little Olaf, and Nero and Magenta. Leopold. Klaus . . .'

Carrie and Matthew's car came to a halt at the end of their garden.

Bett looked up at Daniel and smiled. 'Have you finished?'

'Nearly,' he said, a sparkle in his eyes. 'Jefferson. Indigo . . .'

She was laughing as she walked down the steps to greet her family.

MONICA McINERNEY

Meeting up with Monica McInerney in a restaurant beneath a bookshop, close to London's Piccadilly Circus, turned out to be the perfect rendezvous. Ever since she was a child the author says she has surrounded herself with books. 'I've usually got several on the go. My mother was a librarian, and one of my earliest memories is of her standing, with a baby on her hip and one of my sisters beside her, reading a book. When we were children, we belonged to a library service in Australia. Books used to be delivered by train to our local station, where my father was the station master, and I remember the excitement, once a month, when we'd go down there to collect the brown-paper parcels containing our books. Of course my mother had to package them all up again a few weeks later. Can you imagine!'

Monica grew up in the Clare Valley, South Australia—the setting for *The Alphabet Sisters*—part of a close-knit family of seven children. It's clear that her happy childhood as one of a crowd provided her with much inspiration. 'I wrote my first book at the age of eight, and when we were kids we used to make up our own plays. I love exploring the relationships and layers in a family. I write loads of background material about what my characters were like as kids, so that I know them all really well before I actually start writing the book. I know how they're going to react to each other and how they'll cope with the juggling act of being a member of a family.'

As her name suggests, the author has Irish roots, so was the flamboyant eighty-year-old Lola in her novel based upon one of her forebears? 'Lola isn't really just one person. My mother's mother was called Maude. I never met her, but I've heard so many stories about her. I know she was theatrical and independent and rolled her own cigarettes! My own mother is only sixty-five, but she's like Lola in the way she treats her grandchildren. She has a sparky relationship with them. I think for me Lola is what every eighty-year-old should be like. She has the freedom to do as she pleases and a family who loves her; she's got loads of energy and just a little wickedness!'

Monica McInerney met her Irish husband John fourteen years ago at a party in Melbourne, where he was working as a journalist and she as a book publicist. With family in Ireland and Australia, they divide their time between the two countries, and Monica, who became a novelist in 2001, wrote *The Alphabet Sisters* in Dublin. 'In the room where I write, I have a window that looks down on the street. There's not a blade of grass outside so I have two window boxes and that's my view, but in my head I'm smelling the air of the Clare Valley and seeing the hills and vines and just living that life. It's probably why I've been able to throw away the packing cases for a year or two!'

The author is now busy writing her next book, set in Cornwall and Australia, and entitled, perhaps with tongue in cheek, *Ten Thousand Suitcases*.

Anne Jenkins

ANTHONY CAPELLA
The Food of Love

The recipe of love

Take one American girl with honey-coloured skin

and freckles like orange-red flakes of chilli on

her shoulders.

Fill her with flavours, with basil and tomatoes and

pine nuts and parsley.

Warm her gently with your hands for several

hours, turning occasionally, and serve with wine and

laughter, straight from the dish.

Antipasto

'An Italian meal is a lively sequence of sensations in which the crisp alternates with the soft and yielding, the pungent with the bland, the variable with the staple, the elaborate with the simple . . .'

MARCELLA HAZAN,
The Essentials of Classic Italian Cooking

IN A LITTLE SIDE STREET off the Viale Glorioso, in Rome's Trastevere, there is a bar known to those who frequent it simply as Gennaro's. It is, to look at, not much of a bar, being the approximate size and shape of a one-car garage, but the passing tourist would note that there is room outside for two small tables and an assortment of plastic chairs that catch the sun in the morning, while the passing coffee-lover would note that there is room inside on the stained zinc counter for a vast, gleaming Gaggia 6000, the Harley-Davidson of espresso machines. There is also room, just, behind the stained zinc counter for Gennaro, widely regarded as the best *barista* in all Rome.

Which was why, one fine spring morning, twenty-eight-year-old Tommaso Massi and his friends Vincent and Sisto were standing at the bar, drinking *ristretti*, arguing about love, waiting for the *cornetti* to arrive from the bakery, and generally passing the time with Gennaro before jumping on their Vespas to go off to the various restaurants around the city that employed them. A *ristretto* is made with the same amount of ground coffee as an ordinary espresso but half the amount of water, and since Gennaro's espressos were themselves not ordinary at all but pure liquid adrenaline, and since the three young men were all of an excitable temperament, the conversation was an animated one.

The unusual strength of Gennaro's *ristretti* was the result of his honing the Gaggia's twin grinding burrs to razor sharpness, packing the basket with the resulting powder until it was as hard as cement, then building up a head of pressure in the huge machine and waiting until the dial showed eighty pounds per square inch before finally allowing the water to blast into the packed coffee. What came from the spout after that was barely a liquid at all, a red-brown ooze like honey dripping off the end of a butter knife, with a chestnut-coloured *crema* and a sweet oily tang that required no sugar, only a gulp of *acqua minerale* and a bite of a sugar-dusted *cornetto*, if only the bakery had delivered them. Gennaro's goal was to get the Gaggia up to a hundred PSI, way off the gauge, and make a *ristretto* so thick you could spread it like jam. Tommaso was privately convinced that even to attempt this feat was to run the risk of the Gaggia exploding and taking them all with it, but he respected his friend's ambition and said nothing.

The conversation that morning was about love, but it was also about football. Vincent, who had recently become engaged, was being scolded by Sisto, to whom the idea of restricting yourself to just one woman seemed crazy.

'Today you might think you have found the best woman in the world, but tomorrow'—Sisto flicked his fingers under his chin—'who knows?'

'Look,' Vincent explained patiently, or as patiently as he was capable of, 'how long have you been a Lazio supporter?'

'All my life, idiot.'

'But Roma are . . .' Vincent hesitated. He wanted to say 'a better team', but there was no point in turning a friendly discussion about women into a deadly fight. 'Doing better,' he said diplomatically.

'This season. So far. What of it?'

'Yet you don't start supporting Roma.'

'*E un altro paio di maniche, cazzo.* That's another thing altogether, you dick. You can't switch teams.'

'Exactly. And why not? Because you have made your choice, and you are loyal to it.' Vincent turned to Gennaro triumphantly and ordered another *ristretto*.

Tommaso, who until now had taken no part in the argument, murmured, 'The real reason Vincent and Lucia got engaged is that she said she'd stop sleeping with him if they didn't.'

Vincent shrugged. 'It's true. Lucia wants to be a virgin when we marry, just like her mother. So we had to stop sleeping together until we got engaged.'

Vincent's statement, apparently illogical, drew no comment from his friends. In a country where literal, fervent Catholicism was only a generation away, everyone knew there were as many grades of virginity in girls as there were in olive oil—which, of course, is divided into extra virgin, superfine virgin, extrafine virgin, and so on, before finally reaching a level of promiscuity so unthinkable that it is labelled merely as 'pure', and is thus fit only for export and lighting fires.

'But at least I'm getting it now,' he added. 'I'm sleeping with the most beautiful girl in Rome, who adores me, and we're going to be married and have our own place. What could be better than that?'

'Tommaso gets it too,' Sisto pointed out. 'And he isn't getting married.'

'Tommaso sleeps with tourists.'

Tommaso shrugged modestly. 'Hey, can I help it if beautiful foreign girls throw themselves at me?'

This amiable conversation was interrupted by the arrival of the *cornetti*, a tray of tiny sugared croissants, which in turn called for a final *caffè* before work. While Gennaro flushed the pipes of his beloved Gaggia in readiness, Tommaso received a sharp nudge in the ribs from Sisto, who nodded significantly towards the window.

Coming down the street was a girl. Her sunglasses were tucked up on the top of her head amid a bohemian swirl of blonde hair, which, together with her calf-length jeans, single-strap backpack and simple T-shirt, marked her out immediately as a foreigner even before one took in the guidebook entitled *Forty Significant Frescoes of the High Renaissance* that she was holding open in one hand.

'Psst! *Biondina! Bona!*' Sisto called. 'Hey! Blondie! Gorgeous!'

Tommaso cuffed him. 'That isn't the way, idiot. Just act friendly.'

'She's coming over,' Vincent noted.

The girl crossed the street and paused next to the bar, apparently oblivious of the admiring stares of the three young men. Then she pulled out a chair, put her backpack on the table and sat down.

'Definitely a foreigner,' Vincent said sadly. Because every Italian knows that to sit down to drink coffee is bad for the digestion and will cost three times as much as you'd pay at the bar. 'You wait. She'll ask for a cappuccino.'

Gennaro, watching the pressure gauge of the Gaggia intently, snorted dismissively. No proper *barista* would dream of serving cappuccino after 10 a.m, any more than a chef would offer cornflakes for lunch.

'*Buon giorno*,' the girl called through the open door. She had a nice voice, Tommaso thought. He smiled at her encouragingly. Beside him, Vincent and Sisto were doing exactly the same. Only Gennaro, behind the zinc counter, maintained a suspicious frown.

'*Giorno*,' he muttered darkly.

'*Latte macchiato, per favore, lungo e ben caldo.*'

There was a pause while the *barista* thought about this. Although the young woman had spoken in Italian, she had revealed her origins as much by what she had ordered as by her accent. *Latte macchiato*—milk with just a splash of coffee—but served in a *lungo* or large cup, and *ben caldo*, hot, so that it could be drunk slowly instead of being thrown down the throat in a couple of quick gulps in the proper manner. She was indisputably American. However, nothing she had ordered actually offended propriety—she had not asked for decaff, or skimmed milk, or hazelnut syrup—so he shrugged and reached for the twin baskets of the Gaggia, while the three young men tried to look as handsome as possible.

The girl ignored them. She pulled a map out of her pack and, with a perplexed expression, compared it with a page in her guidebook. A *telefonino* rang in her backpack; she took that out, too, and proceeded to have a conversation that those inside could not overhear. When Gennaro finally judged his *macchiato* worthy of being served, there was a scuffle to be the one to deliver it to the girl's table, which Tommaso won. He placed one of Gennaro's little *cornetti* on the saucer and presented it to the girl with a smile and a muttered, 'On the house.' But the girl was engrossed in her call, and her smile of thanks was all too brief.

In fact, Laura Patterson was deeply troubled, or as troubled as it is possible for a twenty-two-year-old American girl to be in Rome on a fine spring morning, which was why she was glad to discover that it was her Italian friend Carlotta who was calling. Carlotta worked for a magazine called *Stozzi* in Milan. She was also part of the reason that Laura had come to Italy, having been a very good college friend back home.

'*Pronto.*' In Italy it is customary to answer the phone by snapping 'Ready!', for reasons which are now obscure.

'Laura. It's me. What are you up to?'

'Oh—hi, Carlotta. Well, I was looking for Santa Cecilia, as it happens. She's in possession of some rather fine frescoes by Cavallini. But it seems Santa Cecilia doesn't want to be found, so I'm having coffee instead.'

Carlotta ignored this nonsense and cut straight to the reason for her call. 'And last night? How was your date?'

'Ah. Well, it was fine,' Laura said in a voice that made it clear that it hadn't really been fine at all. 'Paolo was perfectly nice, and he knew a lot about architecture'—at the other end of the phone, Carlotta snorted derisively—'and he took me to a restaurant near the Villa Borghese.'

'What were you wearing?'

'Um—the red top and the black trousers.'

'Jacket?'

'No jacket. It's warm down here.'

There was an audible sigh at the other end. Carlotta, like all Italian women, thought that anyone who committed offences against fashion had only themselves to blame for whatever calamities subsequently befell them. 'Did you wear sneakers?' she demanded suspiciously.

'Of course I didn't wear sneakers. Anyway, the meal was good. I had squid pasta and a really nice lamb thing.'

'What happened afterwards?' Carlotta asked impatiently.

'Ah. Afterwards, we went for a walk round the Giardino del Lago, and that's when he jumped me. Literally, because unfortunately there was a slight discrepancy in our respective heights, which meant he actually had to propel himself off the ground. Then after that, of course, he was trying to get me into bed—well, not bed exactly, since he still lives with his parents, but he was certainly trying to get me into the bushes. And before you say anything, I really don't think wearing a jacket would have made much difference.'

Another sigh. 'Are you going to see him again?'

'No. Honestly, Carlotta, I think I've had it with Italian men. They're all so ridiculously oversexed and, well, just *clumsy*. I think I'm going to have to go back to dating Americans for a while.'

Carlotta was horrified. '*Cara*, coming to Rome and dating Americans would be like going to the Piazza di Spagna and eating at McDonald's.'

'A few of us did that the other day,' Laura admitted. 'It was kind of fun.'

There was an exasperated tut at the other end. 'Imagine what a waste your year in Italy will have been if the only men you've dated are people you could have met back home.'

'Imagine what a waste it'll have been if the only people I've dated are frustrated Italian rapists who still live with their mothers,' Laura retorted.

'You're just meeting the wrong people. Look at *my* last boyfriend. Filippo was a sensational lover. Considerate, inventive, passionate—'

'And currently, I think you said, working in a restaurant in a ski resort, precise whereabouts unknown.'

'True, but it was great while it lasted. That's the thing about chefs. They know how to use their hands. It's all that chopping and slicing they do. It makes them dextrous.'

'I have to admit,' Laura said wistfully, 'dextrous would be a nice change.'

'Then, *cara*, you simply have to make sure your dates can cook before you agree to go out with them,' Carlotta said decisively.

Laura laughed. She had a remarkably dirty laugh, and the sound permeated into the interior of Gennaro's bar, causing the young men inside to glance up appreciatively from their *cornetti*. 'And I suppose, being a chef, he had a great sense of timing?'

'Exactly. And he never rushed. You know how we Italians like to eat—at least a dozen courses.'

'But all of them very small ones,' Laura teased.

'Yes, but believe me, by the end you can't eat another thing.'

Even as Laura continued to joke, a part of her couldn't help admitting her friend might have a point. Someone creative, who understood taste, and texture, who knew how to combine ingredients for the purpose of sensual pleasure . . . if only she could meet someone like that.

'There you are, then,' Carlotta was saying. 'It shouldn't be hard. Rome's full of restaurants. It stands to reason it must be full of chefs as well.'

By the time Laura rang off she had half-jokingly, half-seriously promised her friend that from now on she was definitely only going to date men who knew their béarnaise from their béchamel.

Tommaso had made up his mind he was going to speak to the American girl. Who could resist a laugh like that? As Vincent had said, he had an excellent track record with female tourists, who seemed to melt when they saw his big-featured, handsome head with its shock of corkscrew ringlets. Not that Roman girls didn't melt as well, but Roman girls had a tendency to want him to meet their parents afterwards.

He waited for the right moment. The American girl stayed on the phone, occasionally sipping slowly at her *macchiato*—no wonder she'd wanted it hot—until Tommaso realised that he was going to have to go. He would already be late getting to the restaurant. He slapped a few coins on the counter and waved a farewell to Gennaro. His *motorino* was parked outside, next to the girl's table, and he lingered for a last moment as he crouched down to unlock it.

'No more Italians, then. Not unless they can cook,' she was saying. 'From now on, I don't date anyone who isn't in the *Good Food Guide*.'

Tommaso's ears pricked up.

She scooped the final frothy globs of *latte* out of her cup and licked them off her finger. 'My God, this coffee is fantastic. Hold on. Yes?'

Unable to stop himself, Tommaso had tapped her on her shoulder. 'I'm sorry to interrupt your call,' he began in his best English. 'I just wanted to tell you that your beauty has broken my heart.'

She smiled appreciatively, if a little warily, and tried to sound polite as she replied, '*Vatte a fa' 'n giro, a fessa 'e mammata,*' words that her first Italian date had told her to use whenever she was paid a compliment.

Tommaso's face fell. 'OK, OK,' he said, backing off and throwing his leg across the scooter.

Laura watched him go, then turned her attention back to Carlotta.

'Who was that?' her friend wanted to know.

'Just some guy.'

'Laura,' her friend said carefully, 'what do you think you said to him?'

Which was how Laura discovered that she had actually been telling the young men of Rome in perfect idiomatic Italian to piss off back up the orifices of their mothers from which they were delivered.

'Oh,' Laura said. 'Oh dear. That's a shame. He was quite cute, too. But it doesn't really matter, does it? Because from now on I'm holding out for someone who can cook.'

Primo

'Once the general and commonsense principles of menu planning become clear, the choices remaining before us are an infinite number of agreeable and workable combinations . . .'

MARCELLA HAZAN,
The Essentials of Classic Italian Cooking

IT WAS A WEEK before Tommaso saw the girl again. He had gone to Gigliemi, the great food shop near the Piazza Venezia, to pick up some supplies for the restaurant. Earlier there had been a phone call to say that a hunter had driven in from the countryside that morning, his Fiat full of tender young *lepre*—baby hares, the first of the season. Tommaso had been instructed to be quick, so he walked straight through to the back, shouldered the box that Adriano gave him with only the briefest of pauses to discuss Adriano's family, his uncle's marriage and his second cousin's business, and was hurrying out again when a movement in the corner of his eye caught his attention. It was a girl. She was reaching up to the top shelf for a packet of pasta, exposing a band of taut stomach.

A keen aficionado of female beauty, Tommaso muttered, '*Fosse a' Madonna!*' under his breath and swung the box down again. '*Momento,*' he called to her. He reached up for the packet and handed it to her with a smile. '*Prego.*' Then he realised he'd seen her somewhere before.

She smiled. '*Grazie, faccia di culo.*' Thank you, assface.

Of course—he remembered now. The girl from Gennaro's. He also remembered her saying that she was only going to sleep with—well, date, but it was famously the same thing with American girls—someone who could cook, and if she was buying her own pasta, the chances were that she hadn't yet found that someone. It was his opportunity, and he took it.

'*Spaghetti*,' he said, glancing at the packet in her hand. 'And what are you cooking it with? What sauce?'

'Well—I thought perhaps bolognese.'

His look of bewilderment was not feigned. 'But you can't,' he objected.

'Why not?'

'First, because you're not in Bologna,' he pointed out reasonably. 'And secondly, because what you have in your hand is *spaghetti*.'

'Yes. Spaghetti bolognese.' She saw his expression. 'Not a good idea?'

'It's just impossible,' Tommaso explained. '*Ragù bolognese* is a sauce for *tagliatelle* or *gnocchi*, or possibly *tortellini*. We eat *spaghetti all'amatriciana*, with a sauce of *guanciale*, which is the pig's'—he ran his finger down her cheek, a touch so fleeting she was hardly aware it had happened—'this part of the pig's face. We fry it in olive oil with a little chilli, some tomatoes and of course some grated *pecorino romano*, hard cheese. Or if you don't want *spaghetti* you could have *bucatoni*, or *calcioni*, or *fettuccine*, or *pappardelle*, or *tagliolini*, or *rigatoni*, or *linguine*, or *garganelli*, or *tonnarelli*, or *fusilli*, or *conchiglie*, or *vermicelli*, or *maccheroni*, but'—he held up a warning finger—'each of them demands a different kind of sauce. For example, an oily sauce goes with dried pasta, but a butter sauce goes better with fresh. Take *fusilli*.' He held up a packet to show her. 'The spiral fins carry the biggest amount of sauce relative to the surface area, you see? But it only works with a thick, heavy sauce that can cling to the grooves. *Conchiglie*, on the other hand, is like a shell, so it holds a thin, liquid sauce inside it perfectly.'

'Are you a cook?' she asked, understanding dawning in her eyes.

'I am a chef, yes, at one of Rome's best restaurants,' he said proudly.

She hesitated. 'Can I ask you—what would *you* make if you were me? I don't do a lot of cooking, but my father's flown in for a few days and I'd love to cook him something Roman.'

'If I were you . . .' Tommaso thought hard. Then his eyes fell on the box of baby hares. 'I would cook *pasta con sugo di lepre*: pappardelle with hare sauce,' he said triumphantly.

'Is it easy?'

'It's fantastically simple. You cook the hare in onion and garlic for a little while, then add some red wine, cloves, cinnamon, and that's it.'

'And I can buy the meat here?' she asked.

'No,' he said. 'They only supply delicacies like hare to those they know well. But for you—' He went over to his box, took out a hare and presented it to her proudly on the flat of his hand. 'It's a gift. So that you will never make bolognese sauce again.'

She seemed to recoil a little. 'Don't they sell them skinned?'

'Ah, skinning it is easy,' he said happily. 'It will take you two minutes.' He called to the assistant for a paper bag.

'And is it—gutted?' she asked doubtfully.

'Of course not,' he said, sounding a little offended. 'Gigliemi wouldn't sell a hare with the best bits removed.' He dropped it in the bag and swung it round to close it. 'Here,' he said, pressing it into her hand. 'And—here.' He took out a pencil with a flourish and wrote his mobile phone number on the bag. 'If you need any help with the recipe, any help at all, just call me. My name is Tommaso Massi and I will be delighted to assist you.' He swept the box of hares up onto his shoulder before she could ask him about the recipe in any more detail.

'Well, thank you. I'll do that. If I need help, that is.'

'*Ciao*, then.'

'*Ciao*. For now.'

Ciao for now! He liked that, it had a good sound. And the way she was looking at him—he had definitely made an impression.

He had, indeed, made an impression.

He's nice, Laura thought. Like a character from a Michelangelo drawing, with his big extravagant features and his hands waving in the air all the time like that. And, ah, undeniably easy on the eye. But he didn't hit on me, which is refreshing. And he's a chef. How weird is that? Carlotta and I had that joke about me going out with a chef, and then here one is.

Serendipity?

It was only when this internal reverie had finally played itself out, that she realised she was walking along the Via Aracceli with a smile on her face and a paper bag in her hand containing a dead baby hare.

Tommaso strapped the box of hares onto the back of his Piaggio and sped off through the traffic. *Uanema*, he was late.

He took the Via Aurelia past the Vatican, his little scooter chugging up the hill towards Montespaccato, weaving expertly through the endless traffic jams and holdups. Finally he came to a part of the city that was higher, cooler and calmer.

He parked the Piaggio round the back of a large white building, making sure that it was precisely in line with all the other scooters, then carried the box of hares shoulder-high through a pair of double doors into a vast room full of steam and heat. There was no sign outside the big white building to announce it, but this was the kitchen of Templi, one of the most famous gourmet restaurants in the world.

ANTHONY CAPELLA

Tommaso took the box of hares over to the head chef, Karl, who wordlessly picked up one of the dead animals to inspect it, sniffing its mouth and anus for decay before pronouncing himself satisfied with a nod. Only then did he say, 'You're late.'

'Traffic. An overturned lorry on the Ponte Garibaldi.'

'And one of the hares is missing. I ordered a dozen.'

'That's right. There was one that wasn't quite dead. Suddenly it jumped out and ran back to its mother. Through the traffic. Do you know the extraordinary thing? It was just as we were going past the Vatican. And they say the Holy Father is in residence. Perhaps it was a miracle. Yes, a miracle, that's it.'

He was just warming to his theme when Karl, with a faint sigh, said, 'Go and help with the glasses, Tommaso.' He nodded towards the sink, where the bottle-washer, Amélie, was working her way through a mountain of glass.

Tommaso reached for a pair of polishing gloves. The glassware at Templi was all lead crystal, and there was never a single speck of lint or dust on it, let alone a smear. Every single one was polished by hand.

There are three kinds of restaurant in Rome. There are the local *trattorie* and *osterie*, most of which serve only *cucina romana*, Roman cooking. It is a tradition firmly rooted in the ingredients available from the markets and slaughterhouses, with no part of the animal wasted. Then there is *cucina creativa*, the cuisine that takes that tradition and experiments with it. Many ordinary Romans remain deeply suspicious of experimentation, not to mention the increased prices that go with it.

And thirdly there is *cucina gourmet*—the awkward collision of French and Italian indicating that the concept doesn't quite fit comfortably in this region. The ordinary Roman loves his food with a passion but, however wealthy he is, he will probably pass his entire life without setting foot in one of the handful of Michelin-starred establishments dotted around the Eternal City. Many major American and European corporations have their local headquarters nearby, however, which means there is a small but steady demand for an international style of cooking.

Standing at the very apex of these restaurants is Templi, the three-star establishment of Alain Dufrais, the great Swiss chef and internationally acknowledged master of nouvelle cuisine.

Polishing glasses is boring work, particularly when you are in love. Tommaso relieved the tedium by whistling to get the attention of his friend Bruno, who was making *zabaione* nearby.

'*Ueh*, Bruno. *Psst*. I'm in love.'

'That's good,' Bruno said. He was concentrating on his zabaglione, which he was making in a traditional, round-bottomed copper pot, directly over a flame. 'But nothing new. You were in love yesterday.'

'This is someone else. An American girl. Blonde and very cute.'

Bruno grunted.

'*Ueh*, Bruno. How do you make *sugo di lepre*?'

This question, being about food rather than about women, did make Bruno glance up briefly. He was not good-looking like his friend Tommaso, being thickset, heavy and slightly awkward. His eyes, which tended to shy away from direct contact with others, only really settled when he was visualising something to do with cooking, as he did now. 'Well, you fry the hare with some *pancetta*,' he began.

'*Pancetta!*' Tommaso clasped his forehead. 'I knew I'd forgotten something.'

'Then you remove the hare and *pancetta* and you soften some onions and garlic, very gently. Add a bottle of red Sangiovese, some cinnamon, cloves, rosemary and plenty of thyme and then you put the hare back and simmer it for at least two hours, until it starts to collapse into the sauce, which becomes so sticky it coats the pasta like glue.'

'Two hours!' Tommaso couldn't remember if he'd actually told the girl to cook it for that long.

'And, of course, just before serving you remove all the bones.'

'Shit!'

'Why do you ask?'

'Damn!'

'Tell me what happened,' Bruno said gently. He spooned the zabaglione into ramekins and slid them into the fridge. They were to form part of a complex assemblage of warm and cold, consisting of a fresh peach *gelato*, just starting to thaw; then zabaglione made with Barolo wine, slightly chilled; then a warm froth of more zabaglione, a thicker one this time, made with the yolks of goose eggs and rich, sherry-like Marsala; and finally a topping of crisp fried mint leaves and freshly roasted espresso beans, arranged like the petals and seeds of a flower on top of the other ingredients.

When Tommaso had finished explaining, Bruno said neutrally, 'So you gave her a hare. That was romantic of you.'

'It was, wasn't it?'

'Other men give flowers. But you, Tommaso, give dead animals. Dead *baby* animals. To an American.'

'You think the hare might have been a mistake?'

Bruno shrugged.

'She did ask me how to gut it,' Tommaso said, remembering. 'I thought

347

that was strange. I mean, women know how to gut game, don't they?'

'Maybe not Americans.'

Tommaso smacked his fist into his palm. 'Shit! Shit! Shit! The hare *was* a mistake. I should have given her some *tortellini*. Even an idiot can cook *tortellini*. Even *I* can cook *tortellini*.'

'Why don't you call her and give her the right recipe?'

'I don't have her number. I gave her mine and told her to ring me if she had any problems.'

'Well, if she does call you, at least it'll prove she isn't in the mortuary with a hare bone stuck in her throat.'

A faint pinging sound came from beyond the swing doors that led to the restaurant. Someone had just struck a glass, softly, with a knife.

'You'd better go,' Bruno said gently.

'Shit!' Tommaso raced to get into his uniform. Black trousers, white shirt, black tie, black jacket. Franciscus, the maître d', didn't like to be kept waiting.

When Tommaso told Laura he was a chef, he wasn't exactly telling the truth. Tommaso wasn't a chef, or a *sous-chef*, or even a *commis chef*. Tommaso was a waiter, a very junior waiter—a waiter so lowly that even Amélie the bottle-washer was allowed to give him orders.

The ritual that was about to take place in the restaurant was the same one that took place on the first day of every month. It was time to fill Templi's *libro prenotazioni*, the reservations book.

While the waiting staff stood in a semicircle, three or four vast bags of post were emptied onto a round table. Each letter was opened and handed to Franciscus, who perused the contents, gave a curt nod or shake of his head, and passed it to one of the two waiters to his left. One of these put the rejections into a rubbish sack while the other wrote the names of those accepted into a leather-bound reservations book. Tommaso's job was to take the full sacks and replace them with empty ones.

It is not enough, of course, to telephone Templi and simply ask for a reservation. Even if you could find the number, which is ex-directory, the waiter who answers the phone would explain to you very politely that, due to excessive demand, reservations are only accepted in writing, on the first day of each month, for the period three months in advance. Even so, there are more applicants than places, and thus a great deal of care has to be taken when writing your letter to make sure you are one of the lucky ones.

It is rumoured, for example, that it helps to give some indication when you write that you are the sort of person by whom the legendary pushed through the swing doors, a gust of raucous laughter or a bellow of conversation came too, which Bruno only noticed because it gradually affected the mood of the chef—something to which the members of the kitchen brigade were as finely attuned as gorillas are said to be attuned to the emotions of their dominant silverback.

To begin with, Alain Dufrais raised his head, puzzled, and listened intently before going back to his work without comment. A few minutes later, however, a waiter came in, bringing with him a cheer from the dining room. Dufrais stopped what he was doing and walked over to the waiter. 'What is that?' he asked quietly.

'Table two. A birthday party.'

'How many people?'

'Twelve.'

Alain started to walk away. Then, as another waiter entered, followed by another bellow of raucous conversation, he abruptly changed his mind. Straightening his hat, he marched out into the restaurant.

In the dining room, the birthday party had fallen silent—not because they were aware of the approaching storm, but because one of their number had just tapped on the table with his knife. As the hubbub subsided, he wiped his mouth with his napkin and got to his feet, grinning from ear to ear. Umberto, the father of Federica, whose twenty-first birthday celebration this was, intended to make a speech.

'My friends,' he began.

The Swiss chef stalked towards him, his towering height magnified still more by his immaculate chef's hat, tall as a guardsman's bearskin.

Umberto, not at all put out, turned to greet him. 'Hello,' he cried happily. 'This is fantastic, really fantastic. Isn't it, everybody?'

Alain took in the table with a single glance. He saw the unfinished food in front of Umberto, the row of corks that testified to too many bottles of good red wine consumed. A hush fell across the room.

'You are leaving,' Alain said curtly. 'Now. All of you. Get out.' He turned on his heel and walked back to the kitchen.

Someone laughed, thinking it was a joke, but the laughter died on his lips when he realised that the chef was serious. A platoon of waiters, mobilised by Franciscus, was advancing courteously but with unmistakable determination towards the offending table. Umberto opened his mouth to protest but his daughter pulled at his sleeve, her face pink with embarrassment.

Slowly, in stunned surprise, the group rose from their places and departed, each one escorted outside by a waiter.

The disruption meant that the lunchtime service rolled straight over into the evening one. All afternoon the chefs sliced and chopped and stirred and seasoned without a break, desperately trying to restore the kitchen—and the mood of their chef—to its normal equilibrium. By eight o'clock, calm once again reigned at Templi. The first diners of the evening were eating their *amuse-gueules* and sipping *mûre royale* as they perused the menu in an atmosphere of studious rapture, trying to choose between *rôti* of quail stuffed with wild mushrooms, potato strings *au jus* with truffles, or rib-eye of lamb *en persillade* with a *cassoulet* of pole beans and thyme-infused olive oil.

It did not help, therefore, when a mobile phone somewhere began to play the 1970s Deep Purple anthem 'Smoke on the Water'.

The moment he heard it, Tommaso knew that it was his. He had been so busy thinking about the American girl that he had not, in fact, turned off his *telefonino* upon entering the premises, in accordance with the standing instruction to all staff. Failure to comply with this rule was cause for instant dismissal.

The ringing was coming from the staff coat cupboard. Tommaso had to act quickly. Hurling himself into its depths, he pulled his phone from the jacket where he had left it and pressed the answer button. 'One moment,' he whispered into it. Simultaneously, he patted the coat pockets until he located another *telefonino*, one that *had* been switched off. Slipping his own phone into his pocket, he emerged from the cupboard with the second phone held triumphantly aloft.

'This is the one,' he said to Franciscus. As the maître d' took the phone, placed it on the floor and calmly ground it under his heel, Tommaso slipped away into the garden.

'*Si?*' he said as soon as he was alone.

'Hello,' a girl's voice said hesitantly on the other end. It was the American. 'It's Laura Patterson—we met earlier? In the delicatessen.'

'Of course. How are you, Laura?'

'Well, I'm fine, but I'm not so certain about the hare sauce. I'm not sure I quite understood what you told me.'

In fact, Laura was at that very moment staring at a mound of steaming yellow *pappardelle*, perched on top of which was a whole, almost raw, baby hare. She had managed to skin and gut it, which had not been easy for either her or the hare, although it had to be said that of the two of them the hare seemed to have come off worst in the encounter.

'I guess I'm having a bad hare day,' she joked nervously.

'What?'

'Um—never mind. Terrible joke. Is there anything I can do?'

'Did you remember the *pancetta*?' Tommaso asked sternly.

'*Pancetta*? Oh. I don't think so.'

'And how long did you cook it for?'

'Um—about twenty minutes.'

Tommaso scratched his head. Passing on a recipe was one thing, but rescuing a recipe gone wrong was way beyond his limited culinary skills. He began to walk rapidly towards the kitchen. Bruno would know what to do.

He would have handed the phone over to his friend but for the sudden recollection that his chances of seducing Laura depended on maintaining the pretence that he could cook. Tugging Bruno's sleeve, he pulled him into the most hidden recesses of the *pâtissier*'s corner and pointed to the mobile phone tucked against his own ear.

'So you have the hare, which you have cooked for twenty minutes, and the *pappardelle*, which you have cooked for—what?' he said.

'Fifteen,' Laura said.

'Fifteen,' Tommaso repeated, looking at Bruno significantly.

Bruno winced. 'Fresh pasta,' he murmured.

'You'll need to cook another lot of *pappardelle*,' Tommaso told Laura.

'But not yet,' Bruno added hastily. 'First we need to deal with this hare. Does she have a frying pan?'

'Is there a frying pan?' Tommaso asked.

Laura, at the other end, said, 'Yes.'

'Yes,' Tommaso relayed to his friend. Laura looked at her phone, a little puzzled. Either there was an echo, or Tommaso was repeating everything she said to him.

Bruno nodded. 'Good. Now let's take a look at what's in her fridge. We won't be able to do proper *sugo di lepre*, not if she wants to eat before midnight, but we may be able to do something similar.' He picked up a lemon and began to dice the zest into tiny pieces with a paring knife as he talked Tommaso, and by extension Laura, through the preparation of a simple meat sauce. He had always been able to do two things at once if they were associated with food. It was only when it was nothing to do with cooking that he became all fingers and thumbs again.

It was midnight before the two young men left Templi. They had a nightcap at a small bar before walking home through the warm, quiet streets to the tiny apartment they shared in Trastevere.

Tommaso had stored Laura's number in his phone when she called. As they walked he dialled it.

'Hey, Laura, it's Tommaso. How was your meal?'

'Oh, hi, Tommaso. It was wonderful. I can't thank you enough. That thing with the hare and the tomatoes was just inspired,' Laura said. 'Though I guess my sauce wasn't as good as *you'd* do it.'

Tommaso grinned at Bruno. 'You know, I'd like to cook something for you, Laura. Properly, I mean.'

'Really?'

'What are you doing tomorrow night?'

Laura paused. She didn't want to appear too keen, but that hare really had been delicious. 'Nothing much,' she said.

Tommaso ended the call and let out a whoop that echoed down the narrow street. 'She wants me to cook for her!'

'Fantastic,' Bruno said drily. 'I will be interested to see what you decide to serve.'

'Well, I thought you might give me some advice there, my old friend.'

'*Hai voluto la bicicletta . . .*' Bruno shrugged.

'Aw, come on. You know I'd do the same for you.'

'You could hardly do the same for me,' Bruno pointed out, 'seeing as how you can't cook.'

'You know what I mean.'

They walked on for a few moments. Bruno said carefully, 'Just so I'm clear, what are you asking me for?'

'Just to come up with some ideas. Something so fantastic, so sumptuous and sexy that it will make Laura, the beautiful Laura, swoon with love and fall into bed with me.'

Bruno thought about this. 'But which?' he said at last. 'Because, you know, to make someone horny and to make someone fall in love are two very different things.'

'How so, philosopher?'

'If you want to make someone cry,' Bruno said slowly, 'you give them an onion to chop. But if you want them to feel sad, you cook them the dish their mother used to cook for them when they were small. You see the difference?'

Tommaso shrugged.

'And to make someone horny,' Bruno continued, 'well, that's harder than crying, but certainly not impossible. Seafood, of course, has aphrodisiac qualities. Perhaps some *carciofini*—baby artichokes cooked with mint, pulled apart with the fingers and dipped in soft, melted butter. Wine, obviously. And then, to finish, a burst of sugar, so that you feel full of energy and happiness . . . but that's only one side of the story. If you wanted someone to fall in love with you, you would cook them something very different, something perfectly simple but intense. Something that shows you understand their very soul.'

'Such as?'

'Well, that's the difficulty. You'd have to really know the person concerned: their history, their background. You would have to have tasted them, to know whether their own flesh is sweet or savoury, salty or bland. In short, you would have to love them, and even then you might not truly know them well enough to cook a dish that would capture their heart.'

'*Parla come t'ha fatto mammeta*,' Tommaso said, laughing. 'This is too much thinking for me. Just get her into my bed and your cooking will have done all that I ask of it.'

'My cooking? I thought I was just providing a few ideas.'

'Ah.' Tommaso looked a bit shamefaced. 'It's just that—think how terrible it would be if I ruined your wonderful menu. You'd be unhappy, and then I'd be unhappy, and then I wouldn't be able to make Laura happy. Besides,' he added craftily, 'how often do you get the chance to try out your dishes on a real live American?'

'That's true,' Bruno said sombrely. 'I'm just a factory worker in a production line up there at Templi. Every day I make Alain's pastries, Alain's *dolci*, Alain's famous crème caramel with the baked vanilla pod in the centre—even when I could do something better, he doesn't want it. And as for Roman ideas . . .' He mimicked the chef's Swiss accent, '"We don't want any of those peasant recipes here, thank you." It's Michelin, Michelin, Michelin. *Foie gras*, white truffles, champagne sauce. And—'

'So you'll do it?' Tommaso said quickly, having heard his friend make this particular speech many times before. 'You'll cook something fantastic I can pretend to Laura I prepared myself?'

Bruno laughed and punched his friend lightly on the arm. 'Of course. I'll get you your *bicicletta*. Just make sure you know how to pedal it, OK?'

Laura phoned Carlotta the next morning and told her the news. 'I've found a chef. And, *cara*, he's so good-looking. Like a Michelangelo. He gave me a pasta recipe already and talked me through how to cook it. And I'm going round tonight for him to cook for me—'

'*Lentamente*, Laura. Slow down. You're going to his apartment? On the first date?'

'Well, yes. Where else would he cook for me?'

'Are you going to sleep with him?'

'Of course not. I've only met him once.'

355

'If you go to his apartment, he'll think you're going to sleep with him,' Carlotta said flatly.

'He didn't seem like that.'

'*Siamo in Italia*, Laura. We're in Italy. Trust me, he thinks you're going to sleep with him.'

It was Bruno's morning off, and he spent most of it at the Mercato di San Cosimato, Trastevere's main food market, looking for ingredients for Tommaso's great meal of seduction. He had no menu at this stage, and no plan. He simply walked around, seeing what was available and letting an idea of the seasonal delicacies sink into his mind. The *carciofini* were good at the moment, particularly the *romagnolo*, a variety of artichoke exclusive to the region, so sweet and tender it could even be eaten raw. *Puntarelle*, a local bitter chicory, would make a heavenly salad. In the *Vini e Olio* he found a rare Torre Ercolana, a wine that combined Merlot with the local Cesanese grape. The latter had been paired with the flavours of Roman cuisine for over a thousand years; they went together like an old married couple. There was spring lamb in abundance, and he was able to track down some good *abbacchio*—suckling lamb that had been slaughtered even before it had tasted grass.

From opportunities like these, he began to fashion a menu, letting the theme develop in his mind. A Roman meal, yes, but more than that. A springtime feast, in which every morsel spoke of resurgence and renewal. He bought a bottle of oil that came from a tiny estate he knew of, a fresh pressing whose green, youthful flavours tasted like a bowl of olives just off the tree. He hesitated before a stall full of fat white asparagus from Bassano del Grappa, on the banks of the fast-flowing river Brenta. It was outrageously expensive, but worth it for such quality, he decided, as the stallholder wrapped a dozen of the pale fronds in damp paper and handed it to Bruno with a flourish like a bouquet of the finest flowers.

At the end of his tour of the market he came across an old man sitting in a deck chair, snoozing. At his feet was a creased old carrier bag. Bruno crouched down and opened the bag carefully. Inside, like eggs in a nest of straw, were half a dozen *ricotte*. The old man opened his eyes.

'All from my own animals,' he said proudly. 'And made by my wife.'

Bruno eased one of the cheeses to the surface and inhaled. Instantly he was transported to the tiny pastures of the Castelli Romani, the hilly countryside around Rome. He didn't really need any more food, but the ricotta was so perfect that he knew he would find a place for it somewhere in his meal, perhaps served as a dessert with a dusting of cinnamon and a dab of sweet honey.

He was on his way to the pasta shop across the square when he saw the girl again. Bruno stopped, his heart in his mouth. He had no idea who she was, but he had seen her half a dozen times over the last few weeks, wandering round Trastevere, particularly here in the market, where she seemed to stare longingly at the stalls piled high with dozens of different vegetables: *radicchio*, *cime di rapa*, cardoons, *bruscandoli*—the little green hop shoots that appeared in the market for a few weeks in spring; *borragine*, *barba di frate*, even *lampascione*—wild hyacinth bulbs. He had never seen her buy anything, though. Once he had been close enough to see that her carrier bag contained a jar of Skippy peanut butter, from a shop on the other side of the market that sold imported food. He deduced that she was American or Australian, and was homesick sometimes for the tastes of her own country. But the way she looked so hungrily at the unfamiliar vegetables made him long to cook them for her, to show her what she was missing. Once he had got as far as walking up to her and saying, 'Buon giorno,' but when she turned to him, those wonderful grey eyes lighting up as she waited to see what he would say, he lost his nerve and pretended he needed to reach past her for some tomatoes. 'Scusi,' he had mumbled, and she had stood back to let him pass.

Today she was wearing a white halter top. He stood and drank in the way her shoulders were dotted with orange-red freckles beneath the swirl of blonde hair, like a scattering of chilli flakes. For a moment, with the clarity of hallucination, he could almost taste her in his mind, imagining on his palate the salty smoothness of her honey-coloured skin. I *will* talk to her, he thought.

His mind made up, he started towards her, but he was just a moment too late. The girl had turned and walked away. Bruno watched her go.

On the other side of the market was a row of tiny shops, each barely larger than a doorway—a minuscule hardware shop, a pharmacy, a shop selling nothing but olive oil and another selling lingerie, all packed into about ten yards of street. The girl stood in front of the display of lingerie for a moment, then pulled open the door and walked inside.

Bruno stopped short. What are you doing, you fool? he cursed himself. She already has a boyfriend. A lover, in fact. Why else would she be buying lingerie? He turned, heartsick, and went back to his shopping.

Laura loved to walk around Trastevere, the district where she was staying. According to the guidebooks it was a slightly seedy place, a working-class enclave in the heart of the Eternal City, but she loved the down-at-heel vibrancy of the cobbled lanes, barely wide enough to accommodate the Romans' miniaturised cars.

One day soon after her arrival she had found herself passing a little shop. The window display was barely larger than a closet, but it held more than a dozen sets of the most beautiful underwear Laura had ever seen. There were delicate floral camisoles edged with lace, as fine as that for any wedding dress; sassy low-slung hipsters; black suspender belts; creamy silk basques. At the time she had dragged herself away from the shop without entering, but now, preparing for her date, she found herself standing outside it once again. Carlotta's words rang in her head: *Trust me, he thinks you're going to sleep with him.*

A little light-headed, she opened the door and stepped inside.

'I'm going to teach you how to chop,' Bruno told Tommaso. 'That way, when she arrives you'll look as if you're doing the cooking.'

'Sure,' Tommaso said confidently. Bruno took an apple and placed it on the work surface. Then he unrolled his canvas knife bag.

'You should start with this one.' He passed Tommaso a small Global. 'It's Japanese. Made of vanadium steel.' Bruno poured a little olive oil onto a carborundum stone. 'First, I'll show you how to sharpen it.'

After five minutes of sharpening, Tommaso was bored. 'It must be ready now.'

'Nearly.' When he was satisfied, Bruno took out a diamond steel. 'And now we hone it.'

It was several more minutes before Bruno allowed his friend to start on the apple. 'You use the heel of the knife for thicker objects, the point for finer work,' he instructed. 'Work across the apple at an angle, like so. Don't wait for the first slice to fall before you move on to the next one. And keep your fingertips tucked in. This blade can slice through a pig's trotters, so your little digits won't be much of an obstacle.'

While Tommaso practised chopping, Bruno baked *tozzetti*, hazelnut biscuits. The *dolce*, after so much rich food, was to be a straightforward one—the ricotta, with honey and a sprinkling of cinnamon, and a glass of *vin santo*, sweet white wine, into which the *tozzetti* would be dipped.

He had decided to serve the asparagus with a warm *zabaione* sauce; not the complex version he prepared in the restaurant but a simple, sensual froth of egg yolk and white wine. What he hadn't yet told Tommaso was that finishing the zabaglione would have to be done at the last moment, just before it was served. Learning to use a knife was the easy part. His friend was also going to have to learn how to use a double boiler.

By the end of the day, Tommaso was still struggling with the concept of the double boiler. Time after time he started to whip up the egg yolks, only for the froth to collapse into a sticky mess.

'You're being too brutal,' Bruno told him. 'Here. Move the elbow as well as the wrist. Like this.'

Tommaso tried again. This time he was too energetic and the mixture flew off the end of his whisk.

'I can't do this,' Tommaso said, wearily putting down the whisk.

'It's necessary. Now, one more time—'

'Ah, but it isn't necessary, is it? Not really,' Tommaso said craftily. 'After all, we'll be sitting at the table, so what's to stop me from pretending to come in here and whip the zabaglione, while really you do it?'

Bruno thought about it. 'But where would I be?'

'In here, of course. Laura needn't know. Then, when it's all plated, you could just creep out.'

'Well, OK then,' Bruno said reluctantly. It certainly had to be easier than teaching Tommaso how to cook.

At eight o'clock Laura found the address Tommaso had given her, a dingy door beside a scooter shop. She rang the bell.

Tommaso's face appeared high above her head. 'Come up,' he shouted. 'It's open.'

She stepped into a dark courtyard and trudged up endless flights of stairs. At the top, the door was open, and she stepped inside.

The apartment was tiny and by no means smart, a nest of four little rooms festooned with old film posters and pictures of seventies rock stars. But the view took her breath away. Red-tiled rooftop after red-tiled rooftop stretched away below her, a chaotic jumble of houses, apartments and churches all crammed together, tumbling down towards the Tiber. Beyond the river, the palaces and churches of old Rome were floodlit islands amid the darkness of the surrounding buildings.

'Wow,' she said reverently.

The window gave onto a sloped roof, which had been adapted into a makeshift and rather lethal-looking balcony by the addition of two battered armchairs and a few pots of herbs, scattered among a thicket of television aerials. Tommaso was getting out of one of the chairs to greet her, impossibly beautiful, his sculptured face crowned by an explosion of curly ringlets as thick as the twists in a telephone cord.

'Hi,' he said. 'How are you, Laura?'

'I'm great.' Even better than the view, however, was the smell emanating from the kitchen, which almost knocked her off her feet. 'My God,' she breathed. 'What is *that*?'

'Dinner,' he said simply.

'It smells'—she inhaled deeply—'*fantastic.*'

'It's pretty good,' he said modestly. 'Needs another twenty minutes.'

'Twenty minutes!' She wasn't sure she could wait that long. She wanted to taste it now, right now.

'Sure. Don't worry. It will be even better if we have to wait a little. The anticipation will be part of the pleasure.' He ran one hand down her back as he kissed her cheek in greeting.

Laura gave a tiny, secret shiver. Carlotta had been right.

After a glass of *prosecco*, Laura was completely relaxed. Tommaso was an excellent host—at least he was once she had persuaded him to turn off the atrocious music he had playing in the background.

'You don't like the Ramones?' he said, surprised. 'But they're American.'

'So's Mariah Carey,' she pointed out. It seemed strange that someone whose taste in food was so highly developed could be completely deficient in musical taste.

With the Ramones ushered politely out of the apartment, they chatted happily as Tommaso sliced tiny spring vegetables for *pinzimonio*, a dip of olive oil, vinegar, salt and pepper.

'When did you learn to do that?' she asked, watching Tommaso's knife dance over the chopping board.

'Oh, it's easy. And,' he added, more truthfully, 'I had a good teacher.'

The wonderful smells from the oven were making Laura's mouth water. 'So what are we eating tonight?'

'Here.' He handed her a menu with a flourish and a bow, like a waiter.

She looked at the card and read: *Antipasto: verdure in pinzimonio. Primo: spaghetti all'amatriciana. Secondo: abbacchio alla cacciatora. Contorni: carciofi alla romana, asparagi con zabaione. Dolci: ricotta dolce; vin santo, biscotti.* 'My God. We'll never eat all that.'

'*Quanto basta.* Just enough. They are very small amounts, just enough to waken the palate. Not like American steaks, which sit on the stomach and make you—' He mimed exhaustion.

There was the sound of a door closing. 'Who's that?' Laura asked.

'Just my room-mate. Don't worry, he's going out.'

'Is he a chef as well?'

'Bruno? Not exactly. That is, he's a trainee. Just a bottle-washer, really. Now, shall we eat?'

Laura had never eaten food like this before. No: she had never eaten before. It was as if these flavours had always existed, had always been there in her imagination, but now she was tasting them properly for the very first time. Each course was more intense than the last. The spaghetti was coated in a thick sauce of meat and wine, rich, pungent and sticky. The lamb, by contrast, was pink and sweet, so tender it seemed to dissolve in her mouth. It was served without vegetables, but afterwards Tommaso brought the first of the *contorni* to the table: a whole artichoke, slathered in warm olive oil and lemon juice and sprinkled with chopped mint. Laura licked every drop of oil off her fingers, amazed by the intensity of the flavour. Her stomach kept telling her that it was full, stretched to bursting point, but her appetite kept telling her she could take a little more, just another mouthful, until she felt quite dizzy with the excessiveness of it all.

Tommaso left her while he went to finish the asparagus. After a few minutes, missing his company, Laura decided she'd go and help. She piled up the dirty plates and carried them towards the kitchen.

'Tommaso? I'll wash these while you're doing that.' She pushed the door, which didn't open.

'Sorry,' Tommaso called from within. 'It's, uh, stuck. It does that sometimes.'

She rattled the door handle. 'Want me to push it from this side?'

'No, I'll sort it in a minute.'

For a confused moment Laura thought she heard voices murmuring behind the door, but it was only Tommaso breaking into song.

At last the door opened and Tommaso came out, holding a platter from which emanated the most amazing aroma. 'Fixed it. Tell you what, why don't you take this to the table?'

A few minutes later they were eating the asparagus. It was breathtakingly good. The stalks, nestled in their foamy sauce of beaten egg yolk and wine, were so tender at the tip that she could almost suck the plump heads off, but got progressively firmer as she chewed down towards the crisp base.

'Tommaso,' she said rapturously, 'I have to tell you—'

'I know,' he said, smiling at her, and she felt her whole body bathed in a languorous, sensual glow.

In the kitchen, Bruno carried the pans over to the sink and carefully, so that they wouldn't make any sound, lowered them into the water.

'So what are you doing in Rome?' he heard Tommaso say.

'I wrote an essay on art history for a competition,' a girl answered. 'The winner got to come to Rome for a whole year. It's sort of like a scholarship.'

There was something about her voice that made Bruno think of *dolci*, of meringues and sweet *zabaione* and peaches bubbling as they poached in wine. Unable to help himself, he listened for just a moment longer.

'But you can have some fun as well?'

'Are you kidding? Art history is fun.' Bruno, imagining Tommaso's expression, smiled. 'No, really,' the girl was saying. 'I mean, I guess you're used to it. You can go and look at a Caravaggio every day if you want to, but for me it's the chance of a lifetime.'

'Caravaggio?'

'You don't know Caravaggio?' The girl sounded surprised.

Tommaso said quickly, 'Sì. Of course. All Romans know Caravaggio. Which is your favourite?'

'Well, it's hard to choose one—'

'Of course.'

'—but if I absolutely had to, it would probably be *The Fortune Teller*, in the Musei Capitolini.'

Hands in the sink, Bruno nodded. It was his favourite, too.

'If I were a painter,' Tomasso said reverently, 'I would only paint you, Laura. Then all my pictures would be beautiful.'

Bruno's smile broadened. When it came to the art of seduction there was no one to match Tommaso. Drying his hands, he tiptoed to the door that led out of the apartment.

Eventually even the ricotta lay in crumbs on its plate. Tommaso carried the *biscotti* and *vin santo* to the battered old sofa.

'I've drunk so much already,' Laura murmured.

'In Rome we have a saying: "*Anni, amori e bicchieri di vino, nun se contano mai.*"'

'"Years, lovers and glasses of wine; these things must not be counted,"' she translated.

'Exactly.' He dipped one of the biscuits in the golden liquid and held it gently to her lips. She hesitated, then opened her mouth. The sweet, raisiny taste suffused her taste buds. She closed her eyes ecstatically. 'My God, that's beautiful.'

'*Sei bellissima,*' he murmured. 'Like you, Laura.' Now he dipped two of his own fingers in the wine. Again, she hesitated for just a moment, then allowed him to slide them into her mouth. She licked the sticky, honeyed wine off him until every morsel of sweetness was gone. A few drops fell on her neck and he kissed them off greedily.

He unwrapped her slowly, peeling off her clothes as if he were pulling the leaves off an artichoke, kissing her between each layer. This is exactly what I hoped for, she thought. Who would have believed it? Carlotta, of course. Carlotta was right all along.

Secondo

'When there has been time to relish and consume the first course, to salute its passing with wine and to regroup the taste buds, the second course comes to the table. If one is ordering in a restaurant—one that caters to Italians, not to tourists—the choice of a second course is made after the first course has been eaten. This doesn't mean that one has made no plans, but that one waits to confirm them, to make sure that original intentions and current inclinations coincide . . .'

MARCELLA HAZAN,
The Essentials of Classic Italian Cooking

THE NEXT MORNING, Vincent, Sisto and the other early customers at Gennaro's were greatly entertained to see Tommaso running across the road towards the bar, still wet from the shower and naked except for a towel round his waist.

'*Due cappuccini, Gennaro, presto per favore,*' he shouted.

From Tommaso's broad grin it was clear that he had a good reason to be in a hurry, and his friends knew what it was likely to be. They greeted him with a round of applause.

Pausing only to grab a couple of *cornetti*, Tommaso bore the two cups of coffee back across the street, dodging traffic. A Fiat van hooted at him, but although he shouted a ritual Roman insult back, his mind was already on other things.

Laura came back into the bedroom from the shower, wrapped in a towel, her skin wet and glistening in the early-morning sunlight and her hair plastered back across her head.

'You're beautiful,' Tommaso said sincerely. '*Sei bellissima,* Laura.' He picked up a little digital camera from a table. 'Smile?' She smiled and he pressed the button. 'Now, come back to bed.' He patted the space beside him, where the tray of breakfast waited invitingly.

She got back into bed and put her arms round him. He took a little froth from his cappuccino and flicked it onto the end of her adorable nose. She laughed, so he took her cup from her and, placing it carefully on the floor, turned to kiss her. After a moment's hesitation she wriggled into his arms, kissing him urgently, pushing back at him along the length of her body.

Laura had to run to get to her first lecture, but she managed to find time to phone Carlotta on the way. The first question her friend asked, of course, was: 'So?'

'Uh—I went a little further than I'd intended,' Laura admitted.

Carlotta's second question: 'And? What did he cook?' She was, after all, an Italian.

As Laura described the menu, item by item, and tried to do justice to the taste and flavour of each, there was a series of gasps and hisses at the other end of the phone.

'White asparagus? From Brenta? With *zabaione*? My God, Laura, that's a fantastic dish. I've only had it once, and I still remember it.'

'That was the high point,' Laura admitted.

'*Cara*, I'm so jealous. Maybe I'll have to come down and visit. What's he cooking next time?'

'He didn't say. Anyway, I've got to go. I'm at my lecture and I'm late.'

The college campus was housed in a Renaissance villa set in a garden of pine trees on the Janiculum Hill. As Laura had guessed, the lecture she was meant to be at had already started, and she took a seat next to her room-mate Judith in the seminar room as unobtrusively as possible.

'So,' Kim Fellowes, the lecturer, was saying, 'the High Renaissance. A period of just thirty years, between 1490 and the sack of Rome in 1520, during which the patronage of a Pope and the talents of just a few dozen artists created the greatest flowering of genius the world has ever seen. Good morning, Laura. You look as if you've come hotfoot from a Bramante chapel or a Bernini fountain, so you can be the first to tell us what you have seen of the High Renaissance so far.'

Laura thought quickly as she sorted out her books. 'Well,' she said, 'I've been to the Sistine Chapel, obviously, and seen the Raphaels in the Vatican, and some of Michelangelo's architecture—'

'*Momento*. Who is this Michael Angelo, please?' Kim interrupted.

'Oh. Er, sorry.' In her haste she had pronounced it the American way. 'I meant *Michelangelo*.' This time she pronounced it as he did, in Italian.

Kim Fellowes was an American, but he had lived in Rome for so long that he was, as he said, almost a native; the staff at the university referred to him simply as *il dottore*. It was to be regretted, he told the students, that his book on the Renaissance had had to be written in English rather than Italian, thanks to the dictates of a publisher eager for a commercial best seller. And a best seller it had inevitably become; he kept the reviews, carefully laminated to protect them from greasy finger-prints, on his desk for the students to examine. It had been acclaimed as that rare thing: a work that combined the erudition of a scholar with the sensitivity of a true artist. Everything about Kim proclaimed his perfect taste, from the gorgeous linen shirts he wore, to his pale seersucker jacket, and the straw Panama that kept the fierce Italian sun off his finely featured face when outdoors. Laura was overawed by his sensitivity and intelligence, and did everything she could to impress him.

'And what did you think of the Sistine Chapel?' he was saying.

She hesitated. But she couldn't bear not to tell him what she had really thought. 'I thought it was a barn.'

The other students laughed. 'A barn?' Kim Fellowes repeated questioningly, knitting his fingers together and placing them on his knee.

'Yes. I mean, it's beautifully painted and everything, but the paintings are so high that you have to look upwards all the time, and the room is so big and rectangular . . .' She trailed off, certain she was about to be ridiculed. To her surprise, though, Kim was nodding approvingly.

'Laura is absolutely right. The Sistine Chapel,' he said, looking round at the students to make sure they all understood him, 'is considered by many experts, including myself, to be the embodiment of all the worst excesses of the Renaissance. The colours are gaudy, the design overpowering and the conception unharmonious. It was commissioned purely as a status symbol by a nouveau-riche philistine who destroyed some rather fine Peruginos in the process. Michelangelo Buonarroti himself didn't want to touch it, which is why we will be studying his drawings instead. Now then, who can tell me what *contrapposto* is?'

'That man is such an asshole,' grumbled one of Laura's fellow students as they packed up their books after the seminar.

'He knows what he's talking about,' Laura retorted. She was feeling a little guilty: for the first time she had found her attention wandering during Kim's seminar, remembering the feel of Tommaso's kisses.

'As he keeps reminding us,' the other student said sourly. 'Anyone want pizza?'

'Where?' Judith asked.

'The mortuary?' This was their name for the marble-lined pizzeria down the road. 'One o'clock?'

'OK. See you there. Laura?'

'Uh—yes. I guess so.'

Laura had been surprised by her fellow students. For her, coming to Rome had been the chance of a lifetime, an adventure made even more attractive by her mother's insistence that it was (a) academically a waste of time and (b) perilously unhygienic, a consequence of the Italians' notorious inability to wash their hands after visiting the bathroom.

She had landed at Fiumicino airport just a few days before the first semester began. Accompanying her were a backpack crammed with art books and two small suitcases, all she had been allowed to bring. As the letter of acceptance from the Anglo-American University in Rome had breezily informed her, 'Closet space is cramped in even the grandest Roman apartments—and believe us, yours won't come into that category.'

Before she could get to her suitcases, though, there was the small matter of Passport Control. Like Passport Control halls the world over, the one at Fiumicino contained two separate areas: one for locals and one for everyone else. A series of zigzags painted on the floor, culminating in a yellow line in front of each little booth, indicated where you were meant to form an orderly queue before stepping up to present your papers. That was the theory, at any rate. In practice, only one booth in the entire place was open. Crammed into the tiny interior were three young men in elaborate uniforms, complete with military hats tilted at jaunty angles, while in front of them surged a great sea of travellers of different nationalities.

From her position at the side of the mob, Laura was able to see a young woman wearing tight cutoffs and a very brief top, which highlighted the small tattoo high up on one shoulder, leaning up against the booth chewing gum while the three men flirted with her under the pretext of examining her passport. Eventually the young woman was allowed to pass, though it was not until her impressively pert behind was completely out of sight that the young men were able to drag their attention back to the job in hand.

When Laura finally had her own turn at the booth, she laid her passport on the ledge and tried her very first 'Buon giorno'.

The official glanced at the photograph, then back at Laura.

'Good afternoon,' he said in perfect English. 'Where will you be staying in Rome?'

'At the Residencia Magdalena. It's in Trastevere.'

'Bene. I will come and meet you there on Saturday night. We will go out on a date.'

Laura's mouth dropped open. Then she laughed.

'No, why not?' he insisted, sounding a little hurt. 'It will be fun.'

'Scusi.' This was one of the other officials, reaching over and picking up her passport. He was wearing a more extravagant uniform than his colleague so presumably he was the more senior. He examined her passport minutely, turning it this way and that.

'Is there is a problem?' Laura asked.

'*Si*. The problem,' he announced gravely, 'is that you are so much more beautiful than your photograph. I should like very much to take you out to dinner.'

A very short nun pushed her way to the front of the booth and started haranguing the men in a shrill voice.

'Enjoy your stay, Laura Patterson,' the first official said, unperturbed, as he stamped her passport. '*Prego*.'

When Laura found the minibus that was to take her to where she was staying, the girl with the small tattoo was already sitting in it, surrounded by a vast pile of luggage. It soon became apparent that this was Laura's room-mate, Judith. It also became clear that Judith's interest in Michelangelo and Raphael was rather less than her interest in Versace, Prada and Valentino. She was majoring in Fashion Psychology.

After they had settled in—the letter had been right, by American standards the apartment was minuscule—they set off to explore Rome, armed only with bottles of water and identical copies of the Lonely Planet guidebook. It was hot, and both women wore shorts. The reaction was extraordinary. Cars sounded their horns like huntsmen sighting prey. Young men on scooters—even those with girlfriends on the back, impossibly beautiful Italian girls with cascading black tresses and perfect burnt-umber skin—slowed down alongside them to call '*Ueh, biondine!*' appreciatively, muttering rapid-fire suggestions.

'Do you get the feeling we might be underdressed?' Laura said.

The next day had been Orientation Day. The first to stand up to address the assembled students was Casey Novak, the president of the grandly titled Student Government. Casey smiled brightly as she gave the assembled newbies the benefit of her own six months' experience.

'The food here is nice, if a little oily,' she told them, 'but be careful what you eat—many restaurants have really gross stuff on the menu, like wild songbirds or veal. Everything is shut between two thirty and five for siesta, and on Mondays and Thursdays most shops are closed all day, which is a real pain but you get used to it. What else?' she mused. 'Well, CNN is on channel sixteen. MTV is on twenty-three. There's a good American music radio station called Centro Suono. Italian music is truly awful, by the way, but not as bad as Italian TV. They use the same two voices to dub every American show—a guy with a butch voice and a girl who's supposed to sound like a sex kitten, which is weird when you're watching *Friends*—which, incidentally, is on every Thursday evening.'

By the time Casey sat down, Laura felt a bit like a moon-colonist—safe as long as she stayed inside her airtight capsule with the other colonists, but surrounded by a deadly atmosphere outside.

The next person to stand up was the elegant figure of *il dottore*. '*Benvenuti a Roma, la città eterna,*' he began. He spoke in fluent Italian for a minute or so, then switched to English. 'Welcome to the birthplace of Western civilisation. I promise that you are about to have the most extraordinary year of your life.'

This was more like it. Laura listened intently as Kim Fellowes told them which art galleries had ruined their treasures with restoration, and which were closed all day Monday. He told them which galleries had introduced half-hour time limits on viewing, which famous sights were ghastly, and which were exquisite.

'If I could say just one thing to you about your year in Italy,' he concluded, 'it would be this. You are here not only to study the Renaissance but to live it. This is the only city in the world where Renaissance masterpieces are *housed* in Renaissance masterpieces, where the drinking fountains, the bridges, the churches, even the city walls, were designed by the likes of Michelangelo Buonarroti and Bernini. To walk the streets, to eat in a restaurant, to have a conversation with a taxi driver about his football team or to buy fruit at a market stall is to be part of a living work of Renaissance genius. Open yourself to Rome, and Rome will open herself to you.'

'Oh, I almost forgot,' Casey said, standing up as Kim Fellowes sat down. 'The main place we hang out is an Irish bar, the Druid's Den. And there's a baseball team that plays every Sunday.'

The cheer that greeted this remark seemed to indicate that the majority of Laura's fellow students found Irish bars and baseball a rather more enticing prospect than Bernini fountains.

Little by little, Laura's days and nights fell into a routine—lectures and seminars in the morning, art galleries or language lessons in the afternoon, CNN or pizza in the evenings. Friday nights saw her at the Druid's Den with the other students, drinking Bud and watching American or British sports on TV. Occasionally they might go to one of the little restaurants in Trastevere, and even more occasionally she might have a date with an Italian, each romantic disaster being subsequently relayed by phone to Carlotta in Milan. Then, quite by chance, she wandered into a little bar off the Viale Glorioso, and Rome—noisy, impetuous, colourful, chaotic—decided to reach out and haul her into the dance.

The pizzas were cooked in the Roman fashion: thin slivers of dough, as crisp as poppadoms, slathered with a sauce of fresh tomatoes, mozzarella and basil. Traditionally, a Roman pizza is cooked for the length of time that the cook can hold his breath, and these had been fired to perfection in the wood-burning oven at the front of the restaurant, making them hard underneath but leaving the sauce still liquid.

'This isn't a pizza, it's a pancake,' a student called Rick muttered. 'Do the words "deep" and "pan" mean nothing to these people?'

The boys had all ordered side salads. Laura almost told them that in Italy you had the salad afterwards, but thought better of it.

A mobile phone rang. It took Laura a few moments to work out that it was hers, since for some reason it was now playing the Cream classic 'Sunshine of Your Love'. Then she realised Tommaso must have changed it while she'd been in the shower.

'*Pronto?*' she said cautiously.

It was Tommaso. 'Laura! Do you like your new ring tone?'

'Thank you. I love it.'

'I just can't stop thinking about last night,' he said dreamily.

She lowered her voice. 'Me too.'

'I don't think I've ever had a night quite like that before.'

'Me neither.' She remembered the taste of that *zabaione*. 'It was fantastic.' She blushed a little.

'When can I see you again?'

'Well, I guess I'm free on Saturday.'

He sighed. 'Unfortunately Saturday is our busiest night. But I can get Sunday off.'

'OK. Would you like to go to a movie?'

'No, I'd like to cook for you,' Tommaso said. 'Something really special.'

Just the sound of his voice was enough to make her blush again. 'OK. I'll look forward to it. *Ciao*, Tommaso.'

'*Ciao* for now, Laura.'

'Seafood,' Tommaso hissed.

'What?' Bruno asked. He was busy making a series of tiny meringues stuffed with soft chestnut paste and nuggets of chopped fresh pistachio.

'Next time, we'll give Laura *frutti di mare*.' Tommaso, who was in the middle of service, pushed a pile of dirty bowls into the sink and dashed back to the pass, where a neat line of plated dishes waited to be carried into the restaurant. 'It will make her horny,' he called gleefully as he spun out of the kitchen doors into the restaurant, a tray held over his head in one hand like the swirl of a matador's cape.

Although the centre of Rome is only twelve miles from the sea, the excitements of the city have always tended to distract its inhabitants from the pleasures of the coast. Eels from the Tiber are a traditional

Roman delicacy—pan-cooked with soft onions, garlic, chilli, tomatoes and white wine—but a much more common dish is *baccalà*, preserved salt-cured cod, which is fried in thin strips, then simmered in a tomato sauce flavoured with anchovies, pine nuts and raisins. For really good, fresh fish you are better off heading either up or down the coast, towards Civitavecchia to the north or Gaeta to the south.

'I don't understand,' Tommaso said when Bruno explained all this to him the next day. 'Am I meant to go all the way to Civitavecchia just to bring back some fish?'

'I thought perhaps, instead of bringing the seafood to Laura, you could take Laura to the seafood,' Bruno suggested.

Tommaso's brow furrowed. 'How will that work?'

'You could borrow Gennaro's van and drive her to the sea. You could even do some surfing, if you go far enough. Then you just build a charcoal grill on the beach.'

Tommaso looked a little shifty. 'But that will mean I have to cook.'

'Yes, but grilled fish?'

'My grilled fish,' Tommaso said sadly, 'won't be as good as *your* grilled fish. You have to come too.' He brightened. 'I know. I'll pretend to be giving you instructions, so it'll look as though you're preparing the fish under my guidance.' Tommaso nodded enthusiastically. He rather liked the idea of talking to Bruno like a chef. After all, he'd watched enough of them over the years, giving their underlings hell. 'And, ah, afterwards . . . well, you'll just have to go for a walk or something.'

'I'm not sure—' Bruno began.

'Oh, come on,' Tommaso said impatiently. 'What else are you doing this weekend? Nothing. Besides, Laura's got a room-mate, another American. I'll get her to come along too. It'll be a double date. You just have to pretend that I'm the one who can cook. How big a deal is that?'

There were two very good reasons why Bruno agreed to go to the sea with Tommaso.

Years ago, when he had first come to Rome, he had been forced to take the only restaurant job open to someone without qualifications: a waiter. He had been terrible at it. Distracted by the food coming out of the kitchen, he forgot which table was which and mixed up the bills. Only the quick-thinking of another young waiter, who saw what was going on and sorted the problems out before anyone else noticed, prevented him from being fired on his first day. That waiter was Tommaso. Taking Bruno under his wing, Tommaso taught him the rudiments of the job and covered for him when Bruno drifted off into one of his culinary-inspired daydreams. He showed Bruno how to magic half-full bottles of wine away at the end of the shift, and how to pocket enough food from the kitchen to keep from being hungry on their rare days off. In return, Bruno cooked the stolen food for them both. Tommaso needed to take only one mouthful to realise his new friend had talent. It was Tommaso who pushed Bruno into attending catering school to get the all-important qualifications, Tommaso who let him stay in his apartment and cook instead of paying rent. By the time Bruno graduated—he came top of his year—Tommaso was still a junior waiter, happily wasting his time flirting with pretty foreign guests. But Tommaso was as loyal to his friends as he was fickle to his women. He knew through his network of contacts where the best job openings were, and always made sure that Bruno was working in the best place. Bruno owed Tommaso a great deal, and he found it very hard to refuse him anything.

The second reason was even simpler. He rarely got a chance to cook really good fish.

On the other side of the city, Umberto Erfolini, the Italian who had been forcibly ejected from Templi, paid a visit to an impressive house in a quiet suburb. He walked into the entrance hall, where two large men patted him down before they nodded him through towards the study.

In the study, the man in the chair put down his cigar and stood up. Umberto, who was only five foot eight, towered over him. 'Umberto. My old friend,' the man said, reaching up to kiss Umberto on both cheeks, 'how are you? And how is my beautiful goddaughter?'

'Federica's well, Teo. Well, but a little upset.'

'Upset?' Teodoro asked, concern flitting across his face. 'Why?'

'I took her to a restaurant to celebrate her twenty-first birthday, a fancy foreign place.' He shrugged. 'I know. What was I thinking of? But I thought it would be an interesting experience for us. It was a restaurant called Templi, up in Montespaccato.'

'And?' Teodoro prompted gently.

'Well, it *was* an experience. But a humiliating one.' As Umberto explained, the expression on the other man's face darkened.

'Truly, Umberto, this does require our attention, and I want to thank you for bringing it to my notice. But be patient.'

They had agreed to meet at Gennaro's before setting off. This was partly because it was necessary to fortify themselves for the trip with several coffees, but also because Gennaro had removed the fuel pump from the old van's engine to see if it would improve the performance of his

Gaggia, and they had to wait while it was returned to the vehicle.

It was the football season, and all of Rome seemed to be wearing either the yellow and purple colours of Roma or the blue and white of Lazio. The fans—or *tifosi*, meaning, literally, those afflicted by typhus—had festooned their team's colours from every car window and balcony. In Gennaro's bar there was much hilarity because Sisto had lost a bet with Vincent and, as a penalty, had been forced to wear the colours of the hated *Romanisti* for a day.

'What he doesn't know is that I've got the Lazio strip on underneath,' Sisto confided to Bruno.

Bruno wasn't listening. He had just seen two girls walking down the street towards them. They were carrying backpacks and rolled-up towels, and each of them was holding a bottle of water. One of them was a typical Tommaso girl—pretty, curvaceous and tanned, with a mass of dyed blonde hair and a small tattoo. And the other—he simply couldn't believe it—was *the* girl, the girl with the freckled shoulders he had seen so many times around Trastevere. His whole body quivered like a plucked string.

'Ah,' said Tommaso. 'Excellent. Here are the girls.'

The two girls were coming into the bar. Bruno wanted to kiss his friend. For once everything had worked out perfectly.

His exultation was quickly followed by a spasm of terror. What if she didn't like him? What if he was so tongue-tied that he never got the chance to impress her? But then he relaxed. He would be cooking, which meant he wouldn't get nervous—he was never nervous when he cooked.

The two girls had come into the bar with a flurry of *buon giorno*s. Vincent and Sisto were staring open-mouthed at Tommaso's girl. Bruno, his heart pounding, waited to be introduced to her room-mate.

Sisto whispered to Bruno. 'My God but you're a lucky bastard.'

'I know,' Bruno said. He still couldn't believe it himself.

'Bruno, this is Laura,' Tommaso said as he did the introductions. 'Laura, Bruno; Judith, Bruno.'

'Hello, Laura,' Bruno said. Then he turned towards his girl, holding out his hand with an awkward smile on his face. He wondered if she would remember him from the market. 'Hello, Judith,' he said softly.

The girl laughed. 'No. I'm Laura. *She's* Judith.' She pointed at the girl with the tattoo.

'Hey, Bruno,' the other girl said. 'Nice to meet you.'

He was still staring at the first girl. 'You can't be.'

'I can't?'

'I mean—' Bruno desperately tried to salvage the situation. 'Right. So you're Laura. And she's Judith. And you're going out with Tommaso. Well, of course you are. You're Laura. For a second there, I was confused. You see, I've seen you before. In the market. Do you remember?'

'I'm afraid not,' Laura said, looking puzzled.

Bruno stopped, his face burning red. She didn't remember him. He was looking more of an idiot with every word he said.

'What is *wrong* with you?' Tommaso hissed as they loaded up the van with borrowed surfboards and wet suits.

Bruno shrugged. Now that the embarrassment had worn off, there was the awful realisation that he was actually helping Tommaso in his seduction of Laura. As they drove out towards the coast, Bruno found himself staring miserably at the floor of the van.

They parked on a long strand of beach just below the harbour at Santa Marinella, unloaded the boards and ran straight into the water. The others were still in the sea an hour or so later when Bruno came out to begin the preparations for supper. First he made a fire pit on the beach, which he filled with charcoal and aromatic vine prunings from a sack he had brought with him in the van. Then he went in search of the menu.

On the harbour front there was a long, low wooden building, unprepossessing from the outside, its function given away only by the rows of fishing boats tied up next to it, their decks still littered with glittering nuggets of ice, discarded crab shells, rolled-up nets and other fishing paraphernalia. In the shade, an ancient fisherman sat and worked his way methodically through a pile of *totani*—flying squid—beating each one with a wooden club to tenderise it.

Bruno stepped inside, his heart quickening. Now *this* is a fish market, he thought to himself, as his eyes adjusted to the gloomy interior.

Piles of fish rose on either side of him in the half-darkness, and the pungent stink of fish guts assaulted his nostrils. On his left hung a whole tuna, its side notched to the spine to show the quality of the flesh. On his right, a pile of huge *pesce spada*, swordfish, lay tumbled together in a crate, their swords protruding lethally to catch the legs of unwary passers-by. And on a long marble slab in front of him, on a heap of crushed ice dotted with lemons, were the shellfish and smaller fry. There were *riccio di mare*—sea urchins—in abundance, and oysters too, but there were also more exotic delicacies—*polpi*, octopus; *datteri di mare*, sea dates; and *granchi*, soft-shelled spider crabs, still alive and kept in a bucket. Bruno also recognised *tartufo di mare*, the so-called sea truffle, and, right at the back, an even greater prize: a heap of gleaming *cicale*.

Cicale are a cross between a small lobster and a large prawn, with long front claws. Traditionally they are eaten on the harbour front, fresh from the boat. First their backs are split open. Then they are marinated for an hour or so in olive oil, breadcrumbs, salt and plenty of black pepper, before being grilled over very hot embers. When you have pulled them from the embers with your fingers, you must spread the charred butterfly-shaped shell open and suck in the meat '*col bacio*'—'with a kiss'—leaving you with a glistening moustache of smoky olive oil, greasy fingers and a tingling tongue from licking the last peppery crevices of the shell.

Bruno asked politely if he could handle some of the produce. The old man in charge of the display waved him on. He would have expected nothing less. Bruno raised a *cicala* to his nose and sniffed. It smelt of ozone, seaweed, salt water and that indefinable reek of ocean coldness that flavours all the freshest seafood. He nodded. It was perfect.

Bruno bought a sea bass, as many *cicale* as he could afford, some oysters, a few *tartufi*, some clams, a double handful of spider crabs and one of the squid he had seen the fisherman beating outside.

Bruno walked back into the sunshine, which was turning redder now that the sun was low in the sky, and wandered down the shoreline to where Gennaro's old van was parked. The others were still in the sea. He stood for a moment, gazing at Laura, her sleek figure outlined in a wet suit as she clambered over the waves with her board. As he watched he saw her put an arm round Tommaso and pull him towards her for a kiss. Bruno flinched, and turned his attention back to the meal.

This is for Laura, he told himself. *From me to her, even if she never knows.*

He spread a tarpaulin, found a stone to use as a chopping board and set to work. He had brought garlic, courgettes, fennel and potatoes with him from Rome, and now he busied himself peeling and chopping. After a few moments his mind drifted into the semiautomatic trance that cooking always seemed to induce in him, looking up only when the long shadows of the others fell across what he was doing.

'Ah, Tommaso, you're here. It's nearly ready for you to start cooking,' he said respectfully.

Laura squatted down next to Bruno to look at his haul. 'It's all so beautiful,' she breathed, picking up a clam shell in which red shaded through to orange, like a sunset.

Bruno glanced at her hair—wet, tangled from the sea and crusted with salt. Her face, too, was daubed with Apache-streaks of dried salt under each eye, and the cold of the water had raised the skin of her neck into little bumps where it was exposed above her wet suit, like the tiny nodules on a sea urchin. He closed his eyes and inhaled. Just for a moment, he could taste her—her skin rinsed with sea water, the salt in her hair . . .

'You haven't washed the squid properly, Bruno,' Tommaso said, tossing the shapeless polyp into his lap. 'You'd better take it down to the water and clean it again.'

The squid, of course, was fine. 'Sure,' Bruno said, getting up.

'What are you cooking us, Tommaso?' Judith asked.

'Sea bass stuffed with shellfish, and a mixed grill of marinated *frutti di mare*,' Tommaso said proudly. 'It's very simple, but I promise you, you'll never have eaten anything like this before. Pass me that knife, would you?'

Bruno had spent an hour or so back at the apartment teaching Tommaso how to open clams. By the time he returned from the sea with the squid, Tommaso was in full flow, explaining how he had been preparing this recipe since he was a child, giving orders, tossing shells in all directions, and generally making an exhibition of himself while Bruno quietly got on with the real work.

'*Ueh*, Bruno, you need to put some more flavours in that fish. Chop some garlic, would you?'

'Certainly.' The garlic was for the potatoes, not the fish, which would be annihilated by its pungent flavour. Bruno made a show of smashing some garlic on a stone, then quietly put it to one side. His hands twitched helplessly as he watched Tommaso clumsily stuffing the shellfish into the sea bass.

'Now we simply put the fish in the dish . . .' Tommaso was saying. Bruno quickly passed him the bottle of wine, a cold, white Orvieto.

'Thank you, my friend,' Tommaso said, taking a long swig.

'The fish,' Bruno muttered. 'It's for the fish.'

'And the fish needs a drink too,' Tommaso said smoothly, upending the bottle into the fish's jaws.

When at last it was time to eat, Bruno watched Laura intently as she pulled the shellfish apart, cramming them into her mouth with noisy expressions of delight, the buttery juices running down her chin, giving her skin a glossy sheen in the fading light. He loved the way she ate: without inhibition or guilt, sucking the oil from her fingers with gusto, revelling in every new taste and unfamiliar flavour. She ate with genuine pleasure, and the pleasure she felt was echoed in his own heart.

'You eat like an Italian,' he said to her sincerely.

'Is that good?' she asked with her mouth full.

'*Si*. It's the only way to eat.'

'Actually, I eat like a pig. My mother despairs of me.'

'What are the herbs in this, Tommaso?' Judith wanted to know.

'Er,' Tommaso said anxiously, looking at Bruno.

'I can taste fennel and oregano,' Laura said, screwing up her face. 'And something else. Ginger?'

Bruno nodded surreptitiously at Tommaso.

'Well done,' Tommaso declared. 'Fennel, oregano and ginger. Laura, you are exactly right.'

Bruno's heart swelled with pride. There had been only the faintest whisper of ginger in the sea bass. Even a professional chef would have been hard-pressed to identify it. Laura's palate was untrained and untutored, but she had the taste buds of a true aficionado.

When the last *cicala* had been pulled from the embers and devoured, and the discarded shells lay hissing in the fire, Tommaso passed round a joint. Soon the only light came from the glowing embers. For a long time nobody spoke.

Laura leaned back against Tommaso. 'I'm stuffed,' she said dreamily.

'*Sono pieno come un uovo*,' Bruno murmured.

She smiled at him. For a moment his eyes smiled back, then his gaze slid away shyly. 'What does that mean?' she asked.

'It means "I'm as full as an egg".'

'Italian is such a beautiful language.'

'American sounds pretty good too.' He wanted to add, 'when *you* speak it', but he couldn't. Tommaso could say it—not just because she was his girlfriend: Tommaso could pay anyone a compliment and make it sound, if not sincere, then at least charming and funny. Only if he, Bruno, said it would it sound like a corny, desperate pick-up line.

'*Sono pieno come un uovo*,' Laura repeated.

Tommaso put his arm round her shoulder. It was the signal Bruno had been waiting for.

'I'm going for a walk.' He got to his feet, his heart heavy.

'I'll come with you,' Judith said quickly. She reached out a hand to him. 'Pull me up?'

As Bruno pulled her upright, Judith came a little further into his arms than he had been expecting. He suddenly realised that, while he had been thinking about Laura, her room-mate had evidently been considering the possibility of a romantic encounter with him. He glanced at Tommaso for support but his friend was already entwined with Laura, their lips glued together.

'OK, let's walk over there,' he said. He looked down at the lovers. 'I expect we'll be gone some time,' he added reluctantly.

THE FOOD OF LOVE

Soon after they had left the others, Judith put her arm through Bruno's. She's waiting for me to kiss her, he thought awkwardly. They reached the water's edge and she leaned into him meaningfully.

'Judith,' he began apologetically, 'there's something I should tell you.'

'What?'

'Well—there's someone else.'

'A girlfriend?'

'Not exactly.'

'A boyfriend?'

'No, no, not that.'

'What then?'

'The usual thing. Just a girl who isn't in love with me.'

Judith thought about this. 'Well, there's not much point in being faithful to her if she isn't in love with you,' she pointed out.

'I know, but—I can't help thinking about her.'

'Suit yourself. But I need to cool down,' she said decisively. 'I'm going to swim. Want to come?'

'Why not?'

As they plunged together into the creamy white spume, he called, 'Now surf!'

'But the boards are back at the van.'

'Who needs a board?' He waited for a wave, then threw himself into it, letting it carry him towards the beach.

Eventually they all piled into the van for the long drive back. Unfortunately Tommaso's driving, while perfectly adapted to weaving a scooter in and out of endless Roman traffic, was hardly conducive to sleep. Bruno stared out at the darkness. In his imagination he was cooking meals for Laura, presenting her with dish after dish, simply for the pleasure of watching her eat.

For his first dinner he had cooked her the countryside. For his second he had cooked her the sea. For his third, he decided, he would cook her the city—the rich, dark, intense city, in all its pungent history. If he was right, it would awaken something in her. If he wasn't—well, at least he would have cooked her a real Roman meal.

As they walked to their first lecture of the day, Judith told Laura about Bruno's curious behaviour on the beach.

'So he basically said that he was too much in love with this mystery woman to fool around with me,' she explained.

'Ahh. That's so romantic.'

'Just my luck. I thought Italian men were supposed to be fickle, faithless horndogs, and I get one who doesn't want to play.'

'I didn't realise you liked him that much.'

'After a meal that good, I would have done it with the Pope,' Judith said, with some feeling.

Bruno was building a house of cards. Or so it felt. In fact he was cooking a fruit *millefeuille*—layers of delicate pastry leaves, crushed fruit and cream. This being Templi, however, the dish had been adapted by Alain so that it was a bravura display of technical virtuosity. First, the layers of pastry were cooked between heavy weights to make them flaky and crisp. Then they were sprinkled with icing sugar and caramelised with a blowtorch. Between each of the three layers was a filling of the lightest, most delicate fruit soufflé. Because it looked exactly like pastry cream, the diner would only realise it was a soufflé when he took a mouthful. But there were a frightening number of things that could go wrong with this concoction. Each soufflé had to rise with a smooth, hydraulic motion, lifting its delicate ceiling of caramelised pastry without tilting it, so that it could provide a level floor for the next layer up. The slightest sticking or swelling would mean that the whole assembly would lean sideways like the tower of Pisa. Again, each soufflé had to be just a little smaller than the one below, so that the weight of the top layers did not crush those underneath. And finally, the very top layer had to accept a spoonful of *coulis* without breaking or sagging.

Bruno had taken an order for two *millefeuilles* and had cooked three, just in case. He had not been thinking about pastry, though. In some part of his mind he was thinking about offal—about dark, sticky sauces of braised calves' liver, about combinations of mushrooms and kidneys, sweetbreads and artichokes, turning over and over in his mind the various possibilities of his next meal for Laura. Back in the real world, his timing faltered. Two of the soufflés collapsed and he was obliged to halt the delivery of the dishes to the table while he started again from scratch. To save time, he didn't make a spare. His arm went numb as he frantically folded the sieved fruit into the egg white, which meant that he couldn't tell from feel alone whether it was just stiff enough to produce the light, airy consistency Alain required. There was no time to wait and check. He eased the second batch of soufflés into the oven and turned immediately to make the *coulis*.

A few moments later there was a faint popping sound from the oven as an air bubble in one of his imperfectly folded soufflés exploded, sending shreds of half-cooked egg mixture in all directions.

'*Un ce pozzo credere*,' Bruno cursed. On the other side of the kitchen, Alain raised his head. Knowing that he was now being watched made it even harder for Bruno. He also knew that the one soufflé that hadn't exploded would be past its best by the time the other one was ready. He started again from the beginning on two more soufflés. Sweat was trickling down the small of his back as he whipped and folded and sieved. Eventually the replacements were ready, and this time he was lucky. They weren't the best *millefeuilles* he had ever made, but they were acceptable—or so he thought. When he finally carried them, with shaking hands, over to the pass, he had to suffer the humiliation of having the *sous-chef* inspect them, wordlessly, for several long moments, as if Bruno were a *commis* on his first job. To make matters worse, Alain himself came over to take a look. For another agonising moment both the *chef de cuisine* and the *sous* peered at his dessert like doctors examining an open wound. Then Alain glanced at the clock, and Bruno's cheeks flushed with shame. Alain was communicating to the whole kitchen, as clearly as if he had said it aloud, that he would have liked to redo the dishes completely but Bruno had taken up so much time that it was not possible. At last he nodded reluctantly, and the waiter quickly placed the substandard dishes onto a tray.

A subtle shift had taken place in the pecking order of the kitchen. Bruno could sense it. He hadn't thought he cared about being Alain's favourite, but he realised now that was only because he was so accustomed to it. He saw that, in fact, Alain's approval could come and go as quickly as the heat on a hob, and that most of the young chefs had to compete desperately for their share. There was only one person whose work Alain seemed consistently pleased with: Hugo Kass, the newly appointed *saucier*. A handsome young Frenchman with a sleek mane of floppy black hair. He was only twenty-two years old and already people were talking about him as a future Michelin winner. Alain treated Hugo almost as an equal, and once that afternoon even asked his advice on a marinade, holding up a spoon for the younger man to taste. Bruno was too far away to hear what Hugo said, but he saw Alain nod vigorously.

Laura, sitting in Dr Fellowes's seminar room, hums to herself as she writes notes about *torsione* and *contrapposto*. On the whiteboard there is a large projection of a Michelangelo drawing, a male nude. His buttocks flit across Dr Fellowes's face as *il dottore* paces back and forth, explaining in well-rounded sentences the nobility of the ideals that lie behind them.

On her notepad, Laura doodles buttocks. Her humming becomes audible, until her neighbour gives her a surreptitious nudge.

The hush of the restaurant was broken suddenly by a loud crash. In the kitchen, everyone jumped. There was the sound of shouting from the direction of the dining room.

The kitchen emptied as the staff went to see what was going on. It seemed that a delivery man had been carrying a box of eels through the foyer when the bottom of the box had burst open. About half a dozen eels were now zigzagging across the carpet in search of freedom.

Franciscus clicked his fingers as he snapped out orders. 'Pieter, Stephanie, move the customers to the bar. The rest of you, deal with this.'

But it was easier said than done. The eels were small, agile and determined, and the staff were hampered by having to crouch down to apprehend them. The customers, ushered to the bar and initially distracted by glasses of free Dom Pérignon, were soon crowding back into the restaurant with their glasses in their hands, cheering a successful catch or groaning as yet another eel slipped through its captor's grasp. Alain stood watching from the side, his face like thunder.

It took five minutes before two eels were back in the box, and another five before the next one joined them. The staff, exhausted, paused for rest.

Tommaso nudged Bruno. 'Where's the delivery man gone?' he muttered in an undertone.

Bruno looked around. It was true that whoever had caused the mayhem had disappeared.

'And how come he didn't bring them to the kitchen door?' Tommaso continued. 'Everyone who delivers to Templi knows to use the kitchen entrance. There's something strange about this.'

'You two,' Franciscus snapped. 'Talk later, when you've caught them all.'

Obediently, Tommaso went and prodded an eel from under the table where it had taken refuge, only for it to slither beneath a nearby chair before he could grab it.

It was Hugo who eventually broke the stalemate. He turned on his heel, went into the kitchen and returned a few moments later with two huge knives, one in each hand. He advanced on one of the eels and, rather than trying to catch it, simply stabbed it behind the head with the point of his knife, spearing it on the steel blade.

The watchers fell silent. Without pausing to remove the writhing *anguilla* from his knife, Hugo moved on. Again the point of the knife stabbed down. Now there were two eels wriggling and twisting on the bloody blade. The third and final eel was making a break for freedom across the floor. Calmly, Hugo took three paces towards it and, crouching down in one fluid movement, speared it behind the gills with his second knife. Without a word he went back into the kitchen.

'Back to your places, all of you,' Alain ordered. 'And thank God some-one around here has some sense.'

When the kitchen brigade returned to their stations, the eels were gone and Hugo was calmly preparing sauces.

It was Tommaso, clearing away bits of the broken box from which the eels had escaped, who found the words written on a piece: *Be careful who you throw out of your restaurant. They may have slippery friends.*

Finally it was Bruno's day off and he could go in search of ingredients for his next feast. The old municipal slaughterhouse in Testaccio was long closed, turned into stabling for the horses that pulled tourists round the city in little traps, but there were still several smaller places nearby that took delivery of carcasses and butchered them on site. One of these was Elodi, a butcher's shop hollowed out of the base of Monte Testaccio—an ancient rubbish mound some thirty-five metres high that dated back to Roman times, formed from an orderly heap of broken amphorae. Elodi was gloomy, but the quality of the meat was second to none.

Bruno spent twenty minutes talking to the owner, Iaco. With offal, you were working on trust, and the consequences of being sold some dubious meat were far worse than with ordinary cuts. He let the other man know he was a chef, and discussed various recipes with him until the butcher was as excited as Bruno himself was about the meal he was preparing. Iaco impressed upon Bruno that he was not to make the dishes too fanci-ful. 'Stick to the simple recipes and you won't go wrong,' he insisted.

In the event, Bruno's menu largely reflected the old man's advice. His *antipasto* was the classic Roman *fritto misto*—tiny morsels of mixed offal, including slivers of poached brains, along with snails, artichokes, apples, pears, and bread dipped in milk, all deep-fried in a crisp batter. This was to be followed by a *primo* of *rigatoni alla pajata*—pasta served with calf's intestines, simmered with onions, white wine, tomatoes, cloves and garlic. For the *secondo* they would have *milza in umido*—lamb's spleen stewed with sage, anchovies and pepper. A salad of *puntarelle al' acciuga*—chicory sprouts with anchovy—would cleanse the palate, to be followed by a simple *dolce* of *fragole in aceto*—Gorella strawberries in vinegar. To finish the meal off with a theatrical flourish, he had tracked down a tiny amount of *kopi luwak*, a rare coffee bean from Indonesia.

In his heart happiness and sadness were now inextricably mixed, like the yolk and white of an egg when they are whisked together in an omelette. The pain of not having Laura himself was exactly balanced by the pleasure that it gave him to cook for her, until he no longer knew where the sadness ended and the happiness began.

Even before she got to Tommaso's apartment Laura could smell the rich, earthy miasma that wafted down the little street. She stopped, closed her eyes and inhaled deeply. Her nostrils flared and her mouth watered. Pushing open the door into the courtyard, she hurried up the stairs.

The door to the apartment was opened by Tommaso's room-mate. 'Hi,' she said. 'Is Tommaso here?' She smiled at Bruno, whom she liked.

'He's putting the finishing touches to dinner,' Bruno said. 'Come in.'

The door to the kitchen was closed and from behind it came the sound of various Roman oaths and curses.

'I wouldn't go in there if I were you,' Bruno advised shyly. 'He's a bit obsessive when he's cooking—he likes everything to be perfect.' A crash, and the sound of shattering crockery, served to underline his words.

'I guess it's hard work, following a recipe.'

'Sometimes, yes, but there's much more to being a chef than just assembling ingredients.'

'Really? Like what?'

'It's like the difference between a pianist and a composer,' Bruno said hesitantly. 'The pianist is creative, certainly, but he is only the mouth-piece of the person who dreamed the tunes into life. To be a cook, it's enough to be a pianist—a performer of other people's ideas. But to be a chef you have to be a composer as well. For example, the recipes you are going to eat tonight are all traditional dishes from old Rome—but if all we do is simply re-create the past, without trying to add to it, it stops being a living tradition and becomes history, something dead. Those dishes were refined over centuries, but only through people trying dif-ferent things, different combinations, rejecting what didn't work and passing on what did. So we owe it to the chefs of the past to continue doing as they did and experiment, even when we are dealing with the most hallowed traditions.'

Laura nodded, fascinated, and he plunged on, 'Take one of the dishes you will be eating tonight: *fritto misto*. The old butcher who sold me the meat was most insistent that it should be cooked the old way—so brains, for example, are always poached in vegetables, then left to cool before being sliced and deep-fried in batter. But then you think, this batter is not so different to Japanese tempura, and tempura can be served with a sweet chilli and soy dipping sauce, so why not make an Italian version of that, perhaps with balsamic vinegar from Modena instead of soy, and see what happens—' He stopped, suddenly aware that he was getting carried away. He thought back rapidly. Had he said anything stupid?

But Laura had other concerns. 'Tommaso's cooking me *brains*?'

'Among many other things that you won't have tasted before,' Bruno said gently. 'Brains, liver, intestine. You just have to trust'—he wanted to say *me*; with an effort he swallowed and went on—'trust Tommaso. He knows what he's doing, and there is nothing that you won't think is delicious once you've tried it. You may surprise yourself.'

'Maybe.' Laura felt a little uncomfortable. Bruno was looking at her in a weird way, and his conversation was full of awkward pauses during which he glanced at her and then shyly moved his gaze away again.

She noticed, though, that when he was talking about food he wasn't shy at all. Then he looked her straight in the eye, his own eyes blazing with passion. To try to get him back onto the subject, she said, 'So it was you who bought the food, not Tommaso?'

'What?'

'You said an old man sold you the ingredients.'

'Did I?'

Laura gave up. After a minute Bruno mumbled something about going out. He got up and dashed for the door.

There was a triumphant yell from the kitchen. The door opened and Tommaso appeared, holding a salad bowl in both hands at shoulder height as if it were a race winner's cup. '*Puntarelle al' acciuga, alla Tommaso.*' He stopped dead. 'Oh, Laura. I didn't hear you arrive.'

'Bruno let me in.'

'Is he still here?'

'No, he's gone out.'

'Oh. OK.' Tommaso became aware that he was still cradling the salad bowl. 'It's a very difficult salad,' he explained. 'First you have to slice the chicory just so. And the anchovies—the anchovies need chopping too. Salt, pepper, oil . . . it's tricky to get it just right.'

'It doesn't sound all *that* hard. Not compared to some of the other things you've cooked me.'

Tommaso's face took on a serious expression. 'Ah, but in cooking, the simplest things are the hardest. It's a Zen thing.'

'Now you sound like Bruno.'

'Bruno? Yes, I call him the philosopher of food. Not that he knows much about it,' Tommaso added quickly. 'But he's picked up the odd bit of knowledge here and there. Crumbs from the master's table.'

'Is the master going to give me a kiss?' Laura asked prettily.

Tommaso put the bowl down and kissed her upturned mouth, followed by her neck, her chin and her eyes. 'Hey, forget supper,' he whispered into her ear as he bit at her ear lobe. 'Let's just go to bed instead, hmm?'

383

'You must be kidding,' Laura breathed. 'It smells fantastic.'

'We can have it later. It'll keep.'

Tommaso's hands were expertly undoing buttons all over her body. She felt her trousers loosen as the button on her waist was popped. At almost the same time her bra was being undone. For a moment she was in two minds, then she pulled away. 'So will I. Please, Tommaso?'

He shrugged. 'OK. Food first, then we'll go to bed.'

Laura felt a flash of irritation. It wasn't that she didn't want to go to bed with him, just that she didn't want him to assume that she would, or that the meal was just courtship. She opened her mouth to explain, then closed it again. For all his charm, she didn't think Tommaso under-stood the complications and contradictions of the way her body worked. She wasn't altogether sure she understood them herself.

Once they had started to eat, though, she had to revise her opinion. Anyone who could cook *antipasto* like that—who could put what must have been hours of work into a few delectable mouthfuls of crisp, light batter, each one concealing a single morsel of tender meat or sharp crunchy fruit, each individual flavour as precise and decisive as the sound of different instruments in an orchestra—must surely have depths of complexity and feeling, even if he kept them well hidden.

'It's like a lucky dip,' Laura sighed happily. 'I just have no idea what I'm putting in my mouth. What about this? What is it?'

'That is a sweetbread. A piece of the thymus.'

'And what's a thymus?'

Tommaso had absolutely no idea. 'It's a part of the thyme, which is inside the animal, just here.' He pointed to his chest, somewhat vaguely.

'Oh. Well, it's good, anyway. How about this?'

'That, I think, is a *testicòlo d'abbacchio*. A lamb's—well, testicle.'

'A testicle? Let's try it.' She put it in her mouth. 'Mmm. It's crunchier than I expected.'

'Yes,' Tommaso said faintly. 'I wasn't sure you'd like it, actually.'

'Oh, it's wonderful,' she assured him. 'Are there any more in there?' She stabbed the bowl of *fritto misto* with her fork.

Tommaso put his own fork down. Suddenly he wasn't feeling hungry. 'I'm sure there are. You help yourself while I get the pasta.'

Like most Romans, Tommaso had been brought up eating offal, but for that very reason he had never really stopped to think about it. It was just there, something your mother put in front of you that you ate appreciatively while talking loudly across everyone else. He had never considered the origins of the various dishes he had been served. Now, under the glare of Laura's curiosity, he started to do so, with the result that he was soon feeling a little squeamish.

Laura ate everything he put in front of her, and Tommaso consoled himself with the thought that Bruno had succeeded in pulverising any shred of inhibition Laura might have had. So long as he could get through dinner, what happened afterwards was going to be fantastic.

Eventually they got to the strawberries, the sweetness of the fruit colliding with the sharp tang of vinegar in an explosive conjunction of flavours. Laura exclaimed softly with pleasure each time she put one in her mouth. 'Oh—oh—*wow*—that's *so* good.'

Tommaso smiled modestly and shrugged. She hasn't made those noises yet with me, he thought a little jealously, only with Bruno's cooking. Then he stopped himself. It was he, Tommaso, who was going to go to bed with Laura. What did it matter if she liked to put Bruno's food in her mouth first?

'I'll make the coffee,' he said.

When he came back from the kitchen with the espresso pot and two tiny cups, Laura had turned the lights down and was lying on the floor, leaning against the sofa. She smiled up at him invitingly. This is more like it, he thought. He poured two cups and sat down next to her.

She sniffed appreciatively. 'Interesting. What kind of coffee is it?'

'*Kopi luwak*.' He tried to remember what Bruno had told him about it. 'From Indonesia.' He tried some. It had a slightly musty, smoky taste.

'*Kopi luwak*—wow.' Laura took an experimental sip. 'I've heard of this stuff but I never thought I'd actually drink it.'

'No? Why not?'

She looked at his face. 'You do know how it's produced, don't you?' When he didn't say anything, she explained, 'In the coffee plantation, there's a kind of rodent called a *luwak* which eats coffee berries—and because there are so many, it chooses only the very ripest, reddest berries it can find. The coffee bean, which is the seed in the centre of the fruit, passes right though the *luwak* and is excreted. It's considered a great delicacy, and the young men who work in the coffee fields give it to their sweethearts, so it's not usually exported. I love coffee, but I've never come across any of this stuff before.'

Unobtrusively, Tommaso put his cup down. He couldn't believe it. Bruno had given them coffee made from rat crap.

'How about a *distillato*?' he suggested. Anything to take away the taste of that coffee.

'You go ahead.'

He poured himself a *sambuca* and put his arm round her. That was better. She turned her head towards him and leaned in close, her eyes closing as her lips found his.

That damned coffee. He could taste it in her mouth, and behind that a faint ghost-taste of all the other dishes they had eaten that evening. The word 'thymus' popped back into his brain. As her tongue explored his mouth and her teeth nipped at his lower lip, Tommaso found himself wondering exactly where in the body the thymus was. For all he knew, it was the same as a prostate, and a prostate was . . . He closed his own eyes and tried to think of nice, simple things—pizza, meatballs, *spaghetti alla carbonara* . . .

Tommaso felt Laura's hand slide inside his trousers and he drew in his breath. Now that was more like it. She was doing things with her long, delicate fingers that he certainly hadn't expected. There was no doubt about it, she was a dark horse. He slipped his own hand under her T-shirt and expertly unclipped her bra. She took his hand away for a moment, then pulled her T-shirt over her head for him before going back to what she had been doing.

He peeled her remaining clothes off her, kissing each area of exposed skin. Then she was doing the same to him. He had been right: the meal had shattered any inhibitions she had left. He took a strawberry from the bowl and stroked it down her breasts, before going in with his tongue to lick up the trail of vinegary sweetness it left behind.

Bruno was dismayed to find that Hugo Kass had been assigned to work alongside him on the *pâtissier's* station. Even more worryingly, and against all the normal etiquette of a three-star kitchen, it had been left vague as to which of them would be in charge. Ostensibly the move was because Alain had been developing some new *dolci*, but Bruno knew that it was really because the chef wanted to play a little mind game with Bruno, to punish him for his recent lack of performance.

It did not take him long to realise that Hugo was intent on seizing any opportunity to demonstrate his own superiority. As the orders came in and were called aloud, Hugo claimed them as his own. Hugo even took on orders that required him to work on two dishes simultaneously, while Bruno was left fuming and twiddling his thumbs.

Tommaso, passing with a tray of dirty dishes, saw what was happening. 'Why aren't you doing anything about this?' he hissed.

'There's nothing I can do,' Bruno hissed back, watching Hugo build an intricate terrine of fruits in layers of alcohol-soaked sponge.

'Your problem, Bruno, is that you're a nice guy. Too nice. If you want something, you have to fight for it.'

'OK, OK. Point taken.'

The next time Karl called out an order, Bruno had rapped out a '*Oui, chef*' before Hugo could open his mouth. It was an order for *bananes en papillote*. Even in the sophisticated version served at Templi—cooked in a parcel, with vanilla pod and a passion-fruit *coulis*—it was a dish Bruno could have cooked to perfection in his sleep. Hugo stood back, his face expressionless, as Bruno brushed grease-proof paper with egg white.

'Table fourteen, one *tarte fine aux pommes*,' Karl called.

'*Oui, chef*,' Hugo said instantly, turning to his station.

'One *gratin de fruits*—'

'*Oui, chef*,' Bruno snapped. Even before Karl had finished speaking, he was reaching for the eggs.

A waiter handed another order to Karl, who scanned it quickly and added, 'Table eight, another *gratin*.'

Bruno was about to respond but this time Hugo beat him to it. '*Oui, chef*,' Hugo said quickly, reaching for some eggs himself.

So now they were cooking the same dish, *gratin de fruits*, in parallel. It was a deceptively simple recipe: fresh fruit in a *sabayon* sauce, lightly caramelised. *Sabayon* is the sophisticated French cousin of the Italian *zabaione*. The difficulty of the dish came in the way it had to be cooked, which required precise timing. Egg yolks were whisked in an electric mixer at the highest speed until they had tripled in volume. Meanwhile, rhubarb was cooked with sugar and lemon juice and strained through a sieve to make a syrup. Then the mixer was reduced to its lowest speed and the hot syrup poured drop by drop into the *sabayon*. This hot mixture both cooked the egg yolks and stabilised them. If the syrup hit the cold sides of the bowl it would solidify into thick lumps.

Like choreographed dancers, the two chefs reached in unison for lemons and halved them. Their knives, as they chopped the rhubarb, were as perfectly synchronised as a drummer's sticks. They both hurled the husks of their juiced lemons into the bin, where the two fruits collided as they fell. They both turned to the big gas stoves at the same moment, and the two coronets of blue flame appeared on both their burners at exactly the same time.

The other chefs had realised by now that something was happening. They watched, surreptitiously at first and then with open-mouthed amazement, as the two young men battled it out. As he whisked the egg yolks, Bruno plated the *bananes en papillote* with his left hand and slid them down the counter towards a *commis* to go to the pass. Hugo, though, had neglected his *tarte*. With an oath he had to break off from the *sabayon* and lower the heat before the apples burned.

Now Bruno was precious seconds ahead. Calmly he lowered the mixer speed and prepared to add the hot syrup, drop by drop.

'*Soufflé aux fruits de la passiflore*,' Karl called.

Neither chef responded. Neither wanted the burden of yet another dish to prepare until the battle of the *sabayon* was resolved.

'*Soufflé aux fruits*,' the head chef repeated.

Bruno didn't want to do the order. But this was his station. It was his responsibility to make sure the customer wasn't kept waiting.

'*Oui, chef*,' he muttered. Opposite him Hugo smiled wolfishly.

Bruno reached for another mixing bowl with his left hand. He poured in equal amounts of passion fruit purée and pastry cream for the soufflé and flicked the second mixer on. Luckily he had kept the egg whites left over from the *sabayon*. Still with his left hand, he started to whisk them in a bowl, at the same time adding a thin trickle of hot syrup to the *sabayon* with his right.

Bruno placed the fruits on a plate, poured the *sabayon* on top and reached for his blowtorch. While his left hand still folded egg white into the soufflé mixture, with his right he began to glaze the surface of his *sabayon* with the naked flame.

His attention on the food, it was only the sudden intake of breath from the onlookers that alerted him. He leapt back just as a foot-long flame lanced out of Hugo's blowtorch, missing him by inches.

'I beg your pardon, Bruno,' Hugo said calmly, adjusting the nozzle.

Bruno said nothing. The surface of his *sabayon* was webbed with caramel now, crisp and brown. It was finished. Wiping the sides of the plate carefully with the end of his cloth, he called a *commis* to take it to the pass. One or two of the other chefs broke into applause.

'Quiet,' Alain snapped. He had been watching silently from the other side of the kitchen and came over to where the two men were working.

'If I ever see the pair of you doing anything like that again,' he said quietly, 'you will both be out of here. Do you understand?'

'Yes, chef,' they muttered.

'This isn't a racetrack. It's a kitchen.' He stalked off.

Bruno turned back to the oven, pulled out the soufflé and cursed. The top had burned. Then he saw why. He had set the oven to 190°C. Now it was at 210°. Someone had changed the setting while he'd been distracted. He glanced at Hugo, but the Frenchman's head was bent over his counter and it was impossible to tell what kind of expression he had on his face. Bruno chucked the soufflé in the bin and started again. He might have won this battle, but he was prepared to bet that the war had only just begun.

'We come now to the difficult notion of harmony,' Dr Fellowes was saying. 'Harmony was not just an aesthetic ideal for the great men of the Renaissance but a spiritual one also. It is the point at which conception and creation mesh, the painter's skill reflecting and celebrating the greater harmony of the Divine.' He plucked a piece of fluff from his shirt, which was of a colour best described as grape.

Laura smiled at him dreamily. She had been smiling at everyone today. He coughed and continued: 'The grace of the human figure, the delicacy of forms, the precise symbolism of colour and placement— these are all elements of harmony.'

As Laura bent her head over her notebook, Dr Fellowes admired the *quattrocentro* profile of her neck, both delicate and harmonious. For a moment he faltered. He thought how amazing it was that Italy could do that, could bring out the beauty in the most ordinary people.

'Harmony,' Kim repeated, favouring Laura with a smile.

Bruno and Tommaso were at Gennaro's, savouring the first *ristretti* of the day. Bruno felt a little light-headed. He wasn't sure if it was because he was in love, or because Gennaro had now turbocharged his Gaggia by fitting to it a vast pump from an industrial pressure washer. The *caffè* was now so potent that even die-hard regulars sometimes found themselves staggering to a table and sitting down.

'I have to tell you that a slight complication has arisen,' said Tommaso.

'It can hardly be any more complicated than it already is,' Bruno pointed out.

'Perhaps complication is the wrong word. You see, Laura has a friend, Carlotta, who works in Milan. Carlotta's parents live here, in Rome, and she has told them about me. The result is that they want me to go and cook for all of them at the parents' house, where Carlotta and her boyfriend will be staying. So of course I had to say that would be fine.'

Bruno stared at him. 'Are you crazy?'

'What's crazy?' Tommaso shrugged. 'I'll go and commandeer the kitchen, throw the mother out and find a way to get you inside.'

'So let me get this clear. You're expecting me to break into this house—'

'Apartment.'

'Apartment. Even better. I suppose it's on the sixteenth floor?'

'Uh—second, I believe.'

'To break into this apartment, which is on the second floor, conceal myself in the kitchen, and then, without being spotted, cook a meal?'

'Exactly. Bruno, your grasp of the situation is masterly and shows that you are clearly the man to formulate a plan to carry us through.'

'Sooner or later, Tommaso, we're going to be found out. Have you thought of that?'

'Of course. And then we'll run like hell, before we have a good laugh about it all. *Meglio un giorno da leone che cento da pecora*, as my father used to say, God rest his soul.'

Bruno decided that the only way Tommaso could possibly pass off a meal cooked in Carlotta's parents' apartment as his own was to assemble and cook everything beforehand. He would make something simple but impressive that could be smuggled into the other kitchen for Tommaso to heat up. And there was nothing simpler or more impressive than really good fresh pasta.

He had placed a large wooden board on top of his work surface. Handmade pasta is never prepared on marble; its coldness stiffens the dough and prevents the breakdown of glutens. A pile of Tipo 00, the finest grade of flour, stood to one side, its top gently flattened to make a small crater. Into this he poured some beaten eggs. Drawing flour over the egg mixture with the tines of a fork, he worked the two together a little at a time. Then he put the fork aside and started to use his fingers. Gradually, the sliminess of the eggs and the dryness of the flour became one smooth, muscular mass, worked and reworked until there was no trace of stickiness. After Bruno had washed and dried his hands, he was able to press his thumb into the mixture and pull it out again without the dough clinging to his skin at all.

Using the heel of his palm, he pushed the dough away from him, then folded it over. A quick half-turn and then he did the same again, slowly breaking down its inner resistance. Push, fold, turn. Push, fold, turn. Bruno kept up his kneading for exactly eight minutes. It was hard, physical work and he was soon perspiring freely, but slowly the dough became elastic, its surface as smooth as Laura's skin.

While the dough was resting, Bruno prepared his *secondo*, which was to be *saltimbocca*, the classic Roman sandwich of veal beaten paper-thin and folded over a slice of *prosciutto* and a couple of sage leaves. Once prepared, the *saltimbocca* could be flash-fried in minutes, something even Tommaso couldn't mess up.

After about ten minutes Bruno returned to his dough, squashed it down a little and picked up his pasta-rolling pin. The pin was as long as a sword—eighty centimetres, to be precise—and thinner than a conventional rolling pin, so that it would spin faster between his hands as he pushed it over the pasta.

When the rolled dough was the size of a pizza base he changed the movements of his hands, letting them slide sideways along the pin as he worked it, distributing pressure evenly along its length. This was the hardest part. Bruno knew he was not as good at this as a housewife who did it every day of her life, but there was no time to be cautious. If he went too slowly, the pasta would lose its moisture and crack before he was done. He felt his way into the dough, stretching it little by little until it became as thin and filmy as silk, fluttering a few centimetres off the table each time he rolled it. It was time to stop and cut the pasta into *tortellini*.

'Signora, do you have a colander?' Tommaso called through the kitchen door. Carlotta's mother bustled in to open a cupboard and show him where the implement was kept, passing a critical eye as she did so over the array of ingredients he had assembled on the work surface.

'You are making fresh pasta?' she said in surprise, looking at the pile of flour and the eggs that he had ostentatiously placed to the fore.

'Of course.'

'Do you want to borrow a rolling machine?'

Tommaso looked down his nose haughtily. 'I never use them. I prefer to do everything by hand.'

'But do you have a rolling pin?'

Tommaso waved his hand airily. 'I'll improvise.'

Carlotta's mother looked sceptical. 'How can you possibly improvise a rolling pin for pasta?'

Tommaso decided it was time to change the subject. 'I'll need a large jug, please, *signora*, ceramic not glass. Oh, and a bottle of good Marsala.' That should keep them distracted, he thought, watching her scurrying off to do as he had asked. He hoped Bruno wasn't going to be long. This was turning out to be harder than he'd expected.

'How's it going?' Carlotta asked her mother. The would-be diners had been banished to the dining room to await Tommaso's masterpiece, and everyone was getting impatient.

'He hasn't started the pasta yet, and he's been chopping the same stick of celery for twenty minutes. Now he wants a bottle of Marsala.'

'I'll get it,' Dr Ferrara said quickly, getting to his feet. He still wasn't quite sure how it had come about that a stranger had commandeered his wife's kitchen, but after years of living with her he knew a potentially explosive situation when he encountered one. Costanza Ferrara's mouth was set in a thin line, and she had pulled her hair back so tightly that her scalp had gone white.

'I promise you it'll be worth it in the end,' Laura said loyally.

The Piazza Agnelli was in the middle of a grid of identical streets, each containing dozens of identical white apartment blocks. After scouring the area on Tommaso's scooter for half an hour, Bruno finally located the right place and sounded his horn twice. Above him, on the second floor, a window flew open.

'*Pe' ventinove e trenta*,' Tommaso said urgently. '*Tengo certi cazzi che mi abballano per 'a capo.* You're just in time: this is doing my head in.'

'Sorry. I got lost.'

Tommaso was already lowering a bucket on a string. The bucket contained a mess of flour and eggs hurriedly scraped off the work surface. When it reached the street below, Bruno carefully replaced it with a pan containing his parcels of pasta, which Tommaso rapidly hauled up again.

'These are the *tortellini*, si?' he called.

'Yes. The sauce is in the jar.'

'Where are the *saltimbocche*?'

'Coming up next. Send down the ingredients.'

Tommaso sent down the raw veal and loose sage leaves, and Bruno sent up the meat he had prepared earlier.

'You'll remember what to do?' he called anxiously.

'Of course. Years of remembering orders. It'll be fine.'

Bruno didn't have Tommaso's confidence that this would work, but it was out of his hands now.

Tommaso burst out of the kitchen with a dish of *tortellini* and set it down on the table with a flourish. 'Here, everybody. Time to eat.'

Carlotta's mother's face was a picture of surprise. 'It's ready?'

'Of course.' Tommaso served them all with a flourish. 'While you eat that, I'll get back to the kitchen and make the *secondo*.'

'It smells amazing,' Carlotta said.

'It tastes pretty good,' confirmed Andrea, Carlotta's boyfriend, who had already started eating.

Costanza sniffed. Men might call themselves chefs, but that was a very different thing from being able to cook. She had rarely eaten in a restaurant that in her opinion served food as good as that which she herself prepared at home. She speared one of the *tortellini* on her fork and held it up.

'It's not a good shape,' she commented critically. She put it in her mouth. Everyone looked at her, waiting for her verdict.

'Hmm,' she said at last, spearing another. That was all she said until the end of the *primo*, but it was not lost on those around the table that she finished every single scrap of pasta on her plate.

As the meal wore on, Laura, who was seated to Dr Ferrara's left, couldn't help noticing two things. First, he seemed remarkably eager to engage her in conversation; and second, during those conversations he seemed to be looking at her breasts rather than her face.

On the other side of the table, Carlotta was making eyes at Andrea. She slipped her shoe off and worked her foot up his leg, laughing at the effect this had on his attempts to make conversation with her mother.

The *dolce* was *tartufo*, a chocolate *gelato* dusted with cocoa. Around 85 per cent of the world's chocolate is made from the common-or-garden Forastero cocoa bean. About 10 per cent is made from the finer, subtler Trinitario bean. And less than 5 per cent is made from the rare, aromatic Criollo bean, found only in the remotest regions of Colombia and Venezuela. These beans are so sought-after that, kilo for kilo, they command prices many times higher than the other local cash crop, cocaine.

A *tartufo* is shaped to look like a truffle, but it is an appropriate name for other reasons too. Made from egg yolk, sugar, a little milk and plenty of the finest Criollo chocolate, with a buried kick of chilli, Bruno's *tartufo* was as richly sensual and overpowering as the *funghi* from which it took its name—and even more aphrodisiac.

The arrival of the *tartufo* at the table finally persuaded the diners to return their attentions to the food. For a few minutes there was a stunned silence as they spooned the rich ice cream into their mouths, each of them lost in a private reverie of sensation.

It was Costanza Ferrara who finally broke the silence. 'That was remarkable,' she said. Around the table, heads nodded vigorously. Tommaso smiled modestly. 'After such a meal,' she continued, 'we must certainly all have a siesta.' She rose majestically from her seat. 'Come, Aldo.'

Startled, Dr Ferrara hauled himself upright. His eyes had suddenly acquired the thousand-yard stare of a soldier walking out of the safety of his trench into no-man's-land.

'I'm rather tired too,' Andrea announced when they had gone, with a meaningful glance at Carlotta. 'Tommaso, a fantastic meal. I feel as if my trousers are suddenly much too tight.'

'Let's hope so,' Carlotta murmured. 'Laura, there's a spare room through there if you and Tommaso want to take a nap as well.'

Fifteen minutes later the apartment echoed to muffled grunts and gasps as the three couples succumbed in different ways to the passions engendered by their lunch. Dr Ferrara, who had not made love with his wife for many months, was gasping for breath as she bounced on top of him, making the legs of the bed splay alarmingly every time she did so.

Carlotta and Andrea were enjoying a more relaxed coupling. And Tommaso and Laura were in the spare bedroom, their clothes strewn across the floor, when Laura broke away from Tommaso and whispered, 'I've got an idea. Wait here.'

Pulling on a T-shirt in case she met anybody, she crept to the kitchen where the remains of the chocolate *tartufo* sat in the icebox of the refrigerator, and took it back with her to the bedroom.

'Now close your eyes,' she told Tommaso as she climbed back onto the bed. 'And lie very, very still.'

Obediently he closed his eyes. She took a spoonful of the cold ice cream and carefully placed it over his left nipple.

'Ow,' Tommaso said. 'It's cold.'

'It'll soon warm up.' She spooned a second mound on the other nipple. He gasped again.

'Good?'

'Um,' he said, shivering a little.

'And one *here*,' she said, putting a third on his belly, just below the navel. 'Now, which one shall I eat first?' She looked at him, trying to choose. The *gelato* was already starting to melt. Rivulets of dark ice cream were running down his sculptured chest. She bent to the little mound of *tartufo* in his navel and slipped it into her mouth. She sighed ecstatically. *Oh . . .*

Bending back to his supine body, she followed one of the streams of melted chocolate up his chest with her tongue. *Oh . . .*

She felt dizzy, unable to tell where her taste buds ended and her nerve endings began. Switching the other way, she began to nibble down towards the crumbs of half-melted chocolate around his hips. He squirmed with relief as she licked the last morsels of icy chocolate off him with her warm tongue, like licking a cone. Then she could wait no longer.

While Andrea snored gently beside her, Carlotta lay awake. An idea had occurred to her, one so irresistible that she couldn't get it out of her mind.

Carlotta was thinking that, even now, as her boyfriend slept, there was a dish in the refrigerator in her mother's kitchen containing the remains of that delectable *tartufo*.

Throwing back the covers, Carlotta pulled on a robe, crept into the kitchen—and stopped. Her mother, also wearing a robe, was just walking through the other door.

Mother and daughter looked at each other, both immediately guessing why the other was there. The fridge was exactly halfway between them. Casually, as if she were just going to the sink to get a glass of water, Carlotta sidled towards it. On the other side of the kitchen, her mother also moved nonchalantly in the direction of the fridge.

Carlotta moved a little faster. Across the room, her mother picked up momentum too. Throwing dignity to the wind, Carlotta broke into a run. But her mother could move surprisingly fast for such a small, stout person. As Carlotta reached the fridge and yanked on the handle of the icebox, she found her mother's thick arm blocking the way. They stopped, glaring at each other. Then, as if by unspoken agreement, they both pulled on the handle together.

The icebox was quite empty.

At that moment Laura walked in bearing the empty *tartufo* dish, which she carefully carried over to the sink before greeting them with a smile.

While the three women did the dishes in silence, the cause of their discord was discovering a common bond with Carlotta's father, who had put on one of his old CDs.

'Ah, "Return to Fantasy",' Tommaso said, listening. 'One of the greatest album tracks ever.'

'I'm amazed you recognise it. I was a young man when this came out.'

'Oh, I'm a big Uriah Heep fan.'

'You're a pretty good cook too,' Dr Ferrara said over the music.

Tommaso shrugged modestly.

'The thing is, I have some money to invest,' Dr Ferrara said. 'And I don't want to put it in the stock market; the government just takes whatever you make. I want to put it into a cash business, something small and local where I can take the profits straight out of the till when times are good and shout at the staff when they're not. Like a restaurant, for example. And it seems to me that people would pay good money to eat like I did today. What's more, I have the perfect place. Old Christophe has a little *osteria* right in the centre of Rome and I know for a fact he wants to sell up. What do you say?'

'Oh, I'm very happy where I am,' Tommaso assured him.

'I'd make you a partner, naturally. Well, not an equal partner, but you'd have a share of the profits.'

For a moment Tommaso was almost tempted. 'No, really,' he said. 'I love to cook, but I don't think I'm ready for my own restaurant.'

'He's amazing,' Carlotta said to Laura later. 'Your Tommaso is simply *amazing*. What an artist!'

'Isn't he?' Laura agreed.

'You know my father wants to back him in a restaurant of his own?'

'No, he didn't tell me that.' It occurred to Laura for the first time that Tommaso didn't actually tell her very much. In fact, when she thought about it, she could barely remember one proper conversation they had had. There was the food, of course, which was fantastic, and the sex, and the jokes, and there were the sweet Italian endearments he murmured when they were either about to eat or about to have sex, but she very rarely knew what was really going on in Tommaso's head.

But then, as Carlotta said, he was an artist, and food, not words, was the medium through which he expressed himself.

'Dr Ferrara wants me to open a restaurant with him,' Tommaso said. He laughed. 'Can you imagine? He even offered me a share of the profits. If I hadn't known what your reaction would be, I might almost have said yes.'

They were in Gennaro's. Bruno drank his *caffè* with a thoughtful expression on his face, but said nothing.

'Of course,' Tommaso continued, 'I told him it was impossible. We have enough complications without trying to set up a restaurant as well.'

Bruno still didn't say anything. Erotic images of Laura kept erupting into his head. He was imagining what the different parts of her body might taste like. The sensation was so real that his mouth watered.

'I've been thinking,' he said as they left the bar. 'Next time, I'd like to cook Laura something a bit different. Some old country recipes, perhaps.'

'But why?' Tommaso said, puzzled.

'Well—I think she'd enjoy it.'

'No—I meant why does there need to be a next time?'

'Well,' Bruno struggled, 'for Laura, of course.'

'But your cooking has done all that I asked of it, and more. *I* can take over from here.'

'You can?' Bruno said doubtfully.

'Of course. I'm getting bored with all this rich food, in any case.'

'But what will you cook her?'

'Simple stuff. Simple, but wholesome.' Tommaso waved his hand dismissively. 'Pasta, for example. Salads. Risotto.'

'Risotto is harder than it looks.'

'Nonsense. My mother used to make it when I was a child. There's nothing to it. A little rice, a little wine, a little Parmesan . . .'

'She's used to the best,' Bruno warned. He felt sick. Not even to be allowed to cook for her! It was as if his tongue had been ripped from his throat and he was to be left mute, unable to express his feelings. But Tommaso was adamant.

'She'll soon get used to it. When all's said and done, it's only food.'

Tommaso opened a bottle of wine and set about preparing his first solo dinner for Laura. It was good wine, he thought as he poured himself a glass to try it, and with risotto that was really all that mattered. He put the rice in a pan with some butter and started to chop an onion into chunks. What else did he need? Some oil, some garlic. And herbs. He couldn't remember precisely which herbs his mother had used, so he cut a generous selection at random from Bruno's window boxes.

When he had finished adding the herbs, his risotto still looked a little sparse. He opened the fridge and peered inside. Ah yes, some cream—cream always made things better. In a cupboard he also found some dried *porcini*, which he chopped up and threw into the mix as well.

A ring at the door heralded Laura's arrival. As usual, she came straight into the kitchen to see what was cooking.

'Uh-uh,' Tommaso said. 'Tonight it's a surprise.' He replaced the lid on the pot she'd been trying to smell and gently pushed her out of the kitchen.

'Then for the time being I'll just have to make do with the chef,' she said, lifting her head up for a kiss.

Five minutes later she said breathlessly, 'How long until it's ready?'

'Don't worry. We've got ages,' Tommaso said, continuing with what he had been doing.

Five minutes after that they were entwined on the sofa, half-naked, when Tommaso suddenly smelt burning.

The risotto! Dashing into the kitchen, he lifted the lid on the pan. Instead of a creamy liquid soup of wine and rice, what stared back at him was a stinking, sulphuric crater of blackened grains.

'Fuck,' he said with feeling.

'Is everything OK?' Laura called from the other room.

'It's fine. Everything's fine.' He thought rapidly. Bruno had said he'd be in Gennaro's. Perhaps his friend could still salvage this.

'I'm just popping out for ingredients,' he called. 'I'll only be a moment.'

Bruno listened to his friend's explanation and guessed what must have happened. 'Did you soak the *porcini* before you used them?' he asked.

'Soak them?'

'Never mind. Let's go upstairs and we'll see what we can do.'

'But we have to stop Laura seeing you,' Tommaso said. 'I know—I'll go first and blindfold her.'

'*Blindfold* her?'

'Sure. She'll think it's a game. Girls love that kind of thing.'

'They do?' Bruno said doubtfully.

'Just leave it to me.'

Bruno waited outside the apartment. After a few minutes Tommaso slipped out. 'Done it,' he whispered. 'She doesn't suspect a thing.'

'Well . . . if you're sure . . .'

'Don't worry. Now, what do you want me to do?'

'Run down to the store and get another bottle of red wine. As fast as you can.'

'OK.' A quick thumbs up and Tommaso was gone.

Bruno pushed open the door and crept cautiously into the apartment. It was silent. Then there was a dirty giggle from the direction of the sofa.

Laura was lying on it, half undressed. A thick woollen scarf was tied round her head, covering her eyes. 'Tommaso?' she said.

Bruno froze.

'I know you're watching me because I can't hear you cooking.' She turned her head this way and that, trying to detect his whereabouts with her ears alone. 'And if we're going to play this game, I want a kiss,' she announced. 'A kiss for every five minutes you keep me waiting for my meal. So that's at least two you owe me already.'

Bruno stood stock-still, not daring to move.

'Or else I take the blindfold off.'

Unsure what to do, he took a step towards her. He must have made some sound because she said, 'Aha,' and lifted her head up, waiting.

He couldn't help it. He bent his head. He touched his lips to hers, briefly. The lightest of kisses, so brief and fleeting that it barely counted. Then a second . . . His stomach felt as if he were falling through space.

'Hmm,' was all Laura said, and he thought in his guilt that she sounded a little puzzled.

He went into the kitchen and tried to pull himself together. A risotto would take at least twenty minutes, but he didn't have the ingredients for anything else. He put the rice on and started frying up the other ingredients. While they were cooking he quickly assembled some *antipasti* from the bits and pieces in the fridge: olives into which he stuffed some capers and sage; breadsticks wrapped in slices of *prosciutto*.

'Time's up,' Laura called from the other room.

He tiptoed out and, when she lifted her mouth for a kiss, carefully pushed one of the olives inside it.

'Mmmm,' she said. 'Very nice. But I want a kiss as well.'

Bruno hesitated, then quickly dipped his head and kissed her, briefly. The taste of the olive mingled with the sweeter taste of her own mouth. He gasped, and took a step backwards.

'More,' Laura murmured. 'Tommaso, stop teasing me.'

The sound of his friend's name shattered Bruno's reverie. What on earth am I doing? he thought, aghast. He went into the kitchen and leaned against the door, trembling.

At last Bruno heard Tommaso coming up the stairs. When he slipped into the apartment, holding his bottle of wine, Bruno quickly left his friend to take care of the rest of the evening.

He wandered the tiny cobbled streets of Trastevere for hours, trying not to imagine what Laura and his friend were doing now. He had a *distillato* at a late-night bar to calm himself.

He was shaking as he contemplated how close he had been to disaster. If the blindfold had slipped . . . it didn't bear thinking about. He could imagine all too readily the horror and disgust in Laura's eyes. Not to mention, of course, Tommaso's red-blooded rage. What had he been thinking of?

You have to get a grip on yourself, Bruno told himself. You've just got to exercise more self-control. She's Tommaso's girl, and that's an end of it.

Bruno let himself into the apartment and listened. All was quiet. He went into the kitchen. There was only one remedy when he was feeling like this. Trying not to clatter the pans, which would wake the others, he poured some olive oil into a frying pan and added some slices of chilli and a crushed clove of garlic. In another pan he heated up some stock for *pasta in brodo*. Lost in what he was doing, he didn't notice the face at the window, watching him, until he was taking the stock off the heat. Caught by surprise, his hand shook and some of the boiling liquid slopped onto his bare arm. He gasped in pain.

Laura, unable to sleep, had climbed out onto the roof to sit and look at the view—that incredible chaos of medieval rooftops tumbling down to the river, with the palaces and domed churches beyond. Hearing noises coming from the kitchen, she had assumed at first that it was Tommaso. Then she'd seen that it was Bruno, cooking. But what made no sense was that he was so good at it, even better than Tommaso. She had never seen anyone who could prepare food like that. Then he saw her watching him, and spilt the boiling liquid on himself.

'I'm sorry,' she said quickly, 'I didn't mean to frighten you.' Bruno had already thrust his arm under the cold tap. 'Wait, I'll come round.'

By the time she got to the kitchen he was trying to wrap a dressing round his arm one-handed, tightening it with his teeth.

'Here, let me.' A patch of skin on his forearm was starting to blister.

He looked down at her hair as she tied the bandage for him. Automatically he began to separate the various ingredients of her scent.

Bergamot, citrus, cinnamon . . . and something else: a faint, sweet top note that was the smell of her skin. He tried to capture it in his memory.

'All done,' she said, stepping back to admire her handiwork.

'It's tight,' he said, trying to flex his arm.

'It needs to be.'

'But I need to finish the soup.'

'I can do it.' She put the saucepan back on the stove for him. 'Just tell me what to do.'

'There's a spoon on your right to stir it,' he said. 'And the chilli needs to go in now.'

'Like this?'

'Perfect.' He watched her. 'It will be about ten minutes before it's ready,' he said. 'You don't have to wait.'

'No, I'd like to. Least I can do.'

There was a long silence. Laura said, 'When I was watching you through the window, do you know what you looked like?'

'No, what?'

'A wizard. Stirring your cauldron. Eye of newt and wing of bat.'

'Eye of newt?' He screwed up his face. 'That would taste of very little,' he said thoughtfully. 'Too small.'

She smiled. 'It's just an expression.'

'Oh. I see. Well, I suppose cooking is like magic, in a way. Spells are just recipes, after all.'

'Imagine if you could really cast a spell on someone just by cooking. That would be freaky, wouldn't it?'

'Yes,' he said, avoiding her eye. 'Imagine.'

She pointed at the soup. 'Should we taste this?'

'If you like.' He already knew exactly what it would taste like.

She took a spoon and tasted some of the broth. 'That's really good,' she said, surprised. 'I mean—really, really good.'

'It needs two pinches of salt and a little olive oil.'

'You haven't tasted it.'

He shrugged. 'That's still what it needs.'

'OK, mister wizard. You're in charge.' She added the salt, then picked up the bottle of oil. 'How much?'

'Two glugs.'

'Could we possibly translate that into imperial measures?'

'Put your thumb over the top of the bottle and tip it up. When you let your thumb off, the olive oil will glug twice as it comes out. Then you've put in just the right amount.'

'Neat.' She put the bottle down and sucked the last drops of oil off her thumb. Bruno felt his heart lurch. 'So how come you aren't a chef?' she said, not noticing. 'You've obviously got the talent.'

'Well—maybe one day.'

'Tommaso's teaching you, I suppose?'

'Something like that.'

'He's a very talented cook.'

'He's talented at lots of things,' Bruno said loyally.

'I guess he's always been a big hit with women,' she said casually.

'I suppose so.'

'Was there ever anyone—you know—special?'

'No,' he said truthfully.

'But there must have been other women he's cooked for?'

Bruno hesitated. How he longed to tell her the truth! But it was too late now. Too many lies had been told.

'No,' he said. 'I can promise you: Tommaso has never cooked like this for any girl before.'

He saw the happiness flood into her eyes and had to turn away.

In the kitchen at Templi, quiet reigned. The first diners were sending in their selections, Karl was calling each item, and all around the room chefs were quietly acknowledging their orders as they began to execute their allotted tasks. Surveying the scene, Alain Dufrais allowed himself a tiny nod of satisfaction.

Over in the *pâtissier*'s corner, Bruno was also feeling better. A shortage in the *garde-manger* station meant that Hugo Kass had been temporarily removed from desserts, and Bruno was able to get on with his preparations undisturbed.

Suddenly he heard a '*Pssst*'. Looking around, he could not at first identify the source. Then he saw Tommaso crouching behind the stove.

'Hey, Tommaso. What's up?'

'We have to swap places. Carlotta's parents are here.'

'Why?' Bruno asked, puzzled.

'I don't know. Because they think I cook here, I suppose. Dr Ferrara must want to get laid again.'

'I meant, why do we have to swap?'

'Because if they see me they'll know I'm only a waiter. I need to hide in here, and you need to put on my uniform and look after their table.'

Bruno sighed. For a moment, he was tempted to tell Tommaso to forget it. But the memory of those stolen kisses was still on his conscience. 'All right. But I'll have to be back at my station before the first orders for *dolci* come in.'

At that very moment, four men were sauntering through the front doors of the restaurant. Although they were expensively dressed, there was something about the rough-and-ready way they walked that suggested these were not the sort of customers Templi usually dealt with. Their leader was a tiny man, barely five foot tall, whose well-cut suit had clearly been specially tailored to fit his diminutive frame.

A waiter hurried forward. Before he could open his mouth, the small man said, 'We have a reservation. Four people, in the name of Norca.'

The waiter looked at the list. Sure enough, there was a reservation. He was not to know that the real Signor Norca, the businessman who had originally made the booking, had that very morning been persuaded to relinquish it in favour of some well-connected friends.

As they walked through the bar, one of the men casually helped himself to a bottle of whisky. The waiter pretended not to notice.

The news that there was a group of *mafiosi* in the restaurant went round the waiting staff like wildfire, and from them permeated into the kitchen. Alain Dufrais stiffened and reached for his hat. As he marched rigidly towards the doors into the dining room, however, the maître d' headed him off. Franciscus was an Italian and knew how these things worked. He whispered urgently in the chef's ear.

For a moment it looked as though Alain was going to ignore him. Then, with a mighty effort, he turned and went back to the pass.

It was a long time since Bruno had been a waiter. Moreover, each table at Templi bore a bewildering assembly of cutlery and utensils, and it was up to the waiter to pour the wine into the right glass and ensure that the correct implement was positioned next to each plate. Soon Bruno was horribly confused. Luckily Dr Ferrara and his wife were cooing like a couple of teenagers and didn't seem to notice.

Then Dr Ferrara called him over. 'Am I right in thinking you have a chef called Tommaso Massi working here?'

'Yes, of course.'

'Can you tell me which dishes he would have prepared?'

'The *dolci*,' Bruno replied.

'In that case,' Dr Ferrara said, turning to his wife, 'we shall just have a *primo* and then one of Tommaso's desserts.'

Franciscus himself served Teodoro's table. He started off by saying that the meal would of course be on the house. In addition, he murmured, the chef's signature dish, the *confit* of lamb *en persillade*, was particularly good at the moment.

'I'll have *pasta carbonara* and a steak,' the first man said firmly.

'I'll have the same,' his neighbour said.

'We don't actually . . .' Franciscus began, then stopped.

'Since it's Thursday, I'll have *gnocchi*,' the next man added.

'And I'll have *gnocchi* and a *piccata Milanese*, followed by *tiramisù*,' Teodoro said benevolently. He handed the menus, which none of them had opened, back to Franciscus. 'I'll leave the choice of wine up to you, since you're paying for it.'

'Of course,' Franciscus said with a slight bow, hoping that the Château Petrus was still in the cellar, and in good condition.

'Two *pasta carbonara*. Two *gnocchi*. Two steaks, well done. One *piccata Milanese*.' Karl called the order in an appalled whisper, as if by lowering his voice the words were less likely to sully the rarefied air of Monsieur Dufrais's kitchen. In equally hushed tones, various chefs acknowledged that they had heard.

There was a brief pause after Karl called the *tiramisù*. If there was something a little strange about the *pâtissier*'s voice when he eventually did respond, nobody noticed. They were too busy wondering how on earth they were going to cook the unfamiliar Roman dishes that had just been ordered.

Tommaso stared at the contents of the fridge. A *tiramisù*, he knew, was just *biscotti* soaked in espresso and brandy, topped with beaten egg and mascarpone. But in what proportions? Desperately, Tommaso pulled out some ingredients and prepared to improvise.

Bruno made it back to the *pâtissier*'s station just in time to stop him. Fortunately, the head chef's attention was elsewhere.

'Is there no one who knows how to cook these peasant dishes?' Karl roared. 'For God's sake, one of you Italians must have some clue.'

'He's talking about *gnocchi*,' Tommaso whispered, pulling off his whites and grabbing his own jacket from Bruno. 'And *piccata Milanese*.'

'I do,' Bruno called. For a moment there was silence, then with a collective sigh of relief the whole kitchen turned towards the *pâtissier*.

Roman *gnocchi* are a completely different dish from the light, fluffy *gnocchi* that are found in the rest of Italy. For one thing, they are made not from potatoes but from semolina, the coarse-ground flour of the durum wheat. Essentially they are a kind of pancake.

'You mix the milk and the semolina in a saucepan,' Bruno was explaining as he cooked. 'Beat in an egg and leave it for a few minutes to cool. Then just cut it into circles, sprinkle the cheese on top, and bake them in the oven.' While he talked he was also assembling a *tiramisù*. He had already explained to Karl how to make a *piccata Milanese*, and the head chef was busy chopping parsley and strips of Parma ham.

'Add some pork rind to that, if you can find any,' Bruno called over.

Meanwhile, another chef was making the sauce for the pasta. Other orders were forgotten as the whole kitchen mobilised to cook the unfamiliar menu.

To everyone's surprise, the *mafiosi* were reduced to silence by the unexpected excellence of the cooking, and the atmosphere at Templi slowly returned to normal. After the meal, Teodoro and his companions sent a message via Franciscus, summoning the chef to their table.

Whatever Alain was, he was certainly no coward. He glanced at the clock and curtly told the maître d' to inform table four that he would be out in a quarter of an hour, when service was finished.

Franciscus, who *was* a coward, was a little free with his translation of this message. 'Monsieur Dufrais has just popped out and will be with you as soon as he is back,' he told Teodoro.

When at last Alain did deign to visit the dining room, he made a point of touring all the tables in his customary clockwise direction, coming to the Italians' table last. But the *mafiosi*, soothed by large cigars and a hundred-year-old cognac, were too relaxed to care.

'Your restaurant is a little fancy for my tastes, my friend,' Teodoro told Alain, 'but your cooking is first-rate. Just make sure you're hospitable to any colleagues of mine and you'll do well.'

'And how will I know who your colleagues are?' Alain asked coldly.

Teodoro thought for a moment. 'You won't,' he said. 'Better be nice to all Romans, just to be on the safe side.'

'Get those plates out of my sight,' Alain ordered, marching back into the kitchen. 'Wipe the surfaces. And get rid of all that peasant food, too.' He swept the leftover pieces of *gnocchi* into the bin and glared at Bruno. 'Chef, your station is unmanned.'

'Did they like their meal?' Bruno asked.

'Apparently.'

'You see, I was thinking. It might be nice, for local people, if some of those dishes were available on the menu.'

Alain stared at him. A vein throbbed on his forehead. 'Last time I looked, I was the *chef de cuisine* in this restaurant,' he said icily.

'Of course,' Bruno said quietly. 'Sorry, chef.'

'I want to do it.'

'Do what?'

'Open a restaurant with Dr Ferrara. I think it's a good idea.'

'Are you serious?'

'Why not?' Bruno shrugged. 'It's not so complicated, not compared to what we've been doing already. I'll do the cooking and you can help me.'

'Is this to do with all the trouble at Templi?' Tommaso said quietly.

His friend avoided his eyes. 'Perhaps.'

'You're really going to let those talentless bastards drive you out?'

'I don't know. Yes, perhaps. But it's more than that. These other dishes I've been cooking recently, for Laura—they're not Alain's, or Hugo's, or anyone else's. They're mine. And if I don't leave Templi and start cooking on my own somewhere, they'll just be lost. Don't you see, Tommaso? I have to give them the chance to exist. I can't explain it. It's like a woman wanting to have children, or something.'

'Except you want your children to be eaten.'

Bruno said helplessly, 'I told you I couldn't explain it.'

'Then there's the fact that we'd be trying to fool everybody. Customers, critics, suppliers, staff—this is serious stuff, Bruno. It's not like a little joke to get a girl into bed. If we're caught—*when* we're caught—there'll be hell to pay. We'd never work in this industry again.'

'*Meglio un giorno da leone che cento da pecora*, as your father used to say, God rest his soul.'

'Ah, Bruno, did I ever tell you how my father died?' Tommaso asked.

'I don't think you did, no. And I didn't like to pry.'

'He ignored a stop sign and drove straight out in front of a truck. He assumed the truck would slow down for him. It didn't.'

'Ah.'

'Sometimes lions get killed. Particularly when they pull out in front of trucks.'

'It's a good thing we're only opening a restaurant, then, and not a transport company.'

Tommaso sighed. Something about this conversation told him that Bruno wasn't really listening. He knew from experience that his friend, normally the most easy-going of people, was also extraordinarily stubborn about anything to do with food. 'Wouldn't it bother you that Dr Ferrara would think it was me, not you, who was the head chef?'

'Not in the least. In fact, it could be a great partnership. You could do all the shit that chefs have to do these days—talking to customers, flattering reviewers, dealing with Dr Ferrara and so on—while I get on with the part I really enjoy.'

Tommaso and Bruno made a trip to inspect the restaurant in which Carlotta's father was proposing to invest. As might be expected, since the existing owner was nearing retirement, it was a run-down *trattoria* with no airs or graces and an all-pervading atmosphere of neglect.

Christophe showed them round with an air of apologetic resignation. 'We have our regulars,' he confided to the two young men. 'But there are too many restaurants round here, and people don't eat out as much as they used to. It's a struggle to pay my staff and sometimes we lose money, even in the good years.'

'How many people do you employ?' Tommaso asked.

'Two. Johann helps me in the kitchen, and Marie is our waitress.' He called to a young woman who was sorting cutlery on the other side of the room, 'Marie, come and say hello.'

The young woman turned round. Marie was raven-haired, dark-skinned, full-mouthed and full-breasted, and, as her curvaceous body squeezed between the tightly packed tables and chairs, Tommaso muttered '*Fosse a' Madonna!*' under his breath. Automatically he broke into his most winning smile. She scowled back at him, but he didn't take any notice. For a girl like her, a little scowling was only to be expected.

'Pleased to meet you,' Bruno said, shaking her hand. 'Tell me, Christophe, how often do you have the ovens serviced?'

'Every six months.' It was Marie who answered, not Christophe. 'At least, since I've been here. Before that,' she shrugged, 'who knows? The paperwork was a bit of a mess.'

'Marie helps with the administration, too,' Christophe explained.

'Sweet-talking creditors, mostly,' Marie said.

'I'm sure you're very good at it,' Tommaso said knowingly. Marie ignored him. 'Of course, we hope you'll stay on,' he continued.

'I may do,' she shrugged. 'It'll depend on what plans you have. If I like them, I'll stay for a bit, see how things work out.'

'Our plan is simple,' Bruno said. 'We're going to serve the finest food in Rome. Proper Roman food, the same dishes your grandmother made, but brought up to date—a bit simpler, a little lighter, and given a small twist here and there.'

'Hmm,' Marie said suspiciously.

'Marie's nice,' Tommaso said casually as Bruno and he took a coffee together after their visit.

'She seems very organised. Which, to be honest, could be a godsend, since neither of us are.' He looked his friend in the eye. 'So. Are we going to do this or not?'

'Absolutely,' Tommaso said, his earlier misgivings forgotten.

'Good. We'll need to call it something different, so people know it's under new management.'

Tommaso thought for a moment. 'What about Il Cuoco?'

'"The Cook". Hmm. Meaning you, or me?'

'A bit of both.'

'Il Cuoco it is then.' Bruno raised his espresso cup. 'To the best restaurant in Rome.'

It was one thing to create a few meals. To create a whole menu, Bruno soon discovered, was another thing altogether, and required much more work. But his inspiration remained the same: Laura.

From the little kitchen in their apartment emerged dish after dish. Bruno was trying to re-create the traditional dishes of Rome, but he was also trying to impose a little of his own personality on them, and to bring to them some of the quality he loved in Laura—the same mixture of complexity and simplicity, freshness and acidity, innocence and experience. In some way, every dish he created had to taste of her.

Laura had decided to show Tommaso some of her favourite paintings.

'Caravaggio was famously excitable,' she told him as they stood in front of *Boy Bitten by a Lizard*. 'And he loved his food. He once asked a waiter which artichokes were cooked in butter and which in oil. The waiter told him that if he couldn't tell by smelling them he certainly wouldn't be able to taste the difference. So Caravaggio hit him.'

Tommaso nodded unenthusiastically. 'It's tough being a waiter.'

'His big obsession was realism,' she continued. 'He wanted his paintings to show ordinary Romans, not idealised figures from the Bible.'

But Tommaso had already moved on. His idea of a tour round a gallery was a brisk stroll, glancing at whatever took his fancy, but certainly never stopping, the sooner to reach the exit.

Eventually Laura gave up. What did it matter if Tommaso didn't share her appreciation of art? He clearly had a lot on his mind at the moment.

Something *was* troubling Tommaso, in fact, and that was the cost of refurbishing Il Cuoco. The redecoration was proving incredibly expensive. And Bruno was hiring staff and ordering state-of-the-art kitchen equipment with no regard to compromise or cost. When Tommaso asked his friend if a twenty-speed mixer or a wood-fired oven was really necessary, Bruno simply gave him a puzzled look.

There was only one thing for it, Tommaso decided: Bruno would have the equipment he wanted, but the rest of what was needed they would obtain in the same way Tommaso had stocked his larder when he was an impoverished waiter, just starting out. Night after night, therefore, Tommaso and Bruno left Templi with their pockets full of silver cutlery. Clanking audibly, they trudged back down the hill, before finally emptying their haul into a box at the apartment.

'At this rate it'll take us a year to get enough,' Tommaso said, inspecting the contents of the box one night. 'I'm going to put the word out.'

From then on, petty theft at Templi escalated to epidemic proportions. Franciscus would pull open the silverware drawer to discover that there were no teaspoons left at all, while bowls, platters, side plates and even lead crystal glasses kept vanishing.

'It's the Mafia,' Franciscus said despairingly to Alain. 'Once those thieving bastards have their eye on you, there's nothing you can do.'

Alain had no wish to see Teodoro and his pasta-eating companions again. 'We'll just have to live with it then. Order some replacements, and put the prices up by another ten per cent.'

There was no money to employ decorators, so Bruno and Tommaso did most of it themselves before they went to work. They were painting the walls one day when they heard an unfamiliar sound coming from under the dustsheets. It turned out to be an ancient telephone.

'*Pronto*,' Tommaso said into the receiver.

'Is that Il Cuoco?'

'*Si*, but we're not open yet.'

'Well, when will you be?' the voice said impatiently.

Tommaso plucked a date from the air. 'Two weeks on Saturday.'

'Good. I want to make a reservation.'

'Our first customer,' Tommaso said wonderingly as he replaced the receiver. 'It looks as if this is really going to happen.'

Laura decided to wear a pair of white linen shorts she hadn't worn for a while. When she came to do them up, however, she discovered they no longer fitted. She tried on a pair of trousers instead and found that they, too, were a little tight around the hips.

'Never mind,' Judith said. 'I've got plenty of looser stuff you can borrow. And it's got to be worth it for all that fantastic sex, right?'

Laura hesitated. She hadn't yet told her friend that sex with Tommaso actually wasn't that fantastic. Oh, he was beautiful, for sure, and the food he cooked made all her senses tingle in anticipation, but when it came to the act itself she was slowly coming to the conclusion that Tommaso was just a bit too—well, perfunctory. Slow and painstaking in his cooking, it seemed as if in bed he sometimes reverted to that other Tommaso, the impatient, exuberant Italian who drove at ninety miles an hour, swallowed espressos in a single gulp and toured art galleries at breakneck speed. But when everything else was so perfect, it seemed a small price to have to pay.

When Bruno finally plucked up the courage to tell Alain he was leaving, the *chef de cuisine* took him to one side.

'And where are you going?' he asked calmly.

'I'm going to open my own place.'

'In Rome?'

'*Si*, in Rome.'

Alain sighed. 'Listen,' he said kindly, 'you're a good chef. If I'm hard on you sometimes, it's only because I can see that you have potential. But can you honestly tell me that you know everything?'

'Of course I don't. No one does.'

'Then why are you in such a hurry to stop learning? If you really want to leave here, let me make some calls for you. I can get you a job with someone good, someone who'll teach you properly. Don't you want to work with the best? I can call Bras, Martin, Ducasse . . . even Adrià, if you fancy going to Spain. A word from me and any one of them would create a job for you.'

Bruno hesitated. The names Alain was dangling in front of him were the names of his heroes. A few months ago he would have given his right arm to be told that he was good enough to work with Guy Martin or Michel Bras.

But a few months ago, many things had been different. In some way, his feelings for Laura had also changed the way he felt about food, and the dishes he had been cooking for her had been part of a voyage of discovery for him, too; one from which there was no turning back.

'It's kind of you, chef, and I will always be grateful,' he said. 'But my mind's made up.'

'Wily old bastard,' Tommaso commented later when he heard what Alain had said. 'The only reason he wants you out of Rome is because he doesn't want Il Cuoco stealing his customers.'

There is not a great abundance of gyms in Rome. The average Italian male, when faced with the evidence of his increasing stomach in the mirror, will tend either to invest in a more generously cut pair of trousers or to buy a new mirror, while his female counterpart seems to be genetically programmed to slenderness, at least until her wedding day. It was perhaps not surprising, therefore, that when Laura went along for her first session at the grandly named Gymnasia de San Giovanni, she found several other Americans of her acquaintance among the clientele, including Kim Fellowes. Dressed in faded sweats emblazoned with the logo of his East Coast alma mater, he was pulling a steady stroke rate of twenty-eight on the ergometer.

'Hi, Dr Fellowes,' she called as she mounted a treadmill.

'Good morning,' he called back. 'I haven't seen you here before.'

'I just joined today,' she explained.

He watched Laura as she began to run. Her skin was soon flushed with perspiration, and a sweet, almost imperceptible odour began to suffuse the air around her. It was the smell of summer herbs, and honey, and olive oil, and salt—the tastes of Bruno's cooking, released into the air for a second time, mingled now with the delicate scent of her skin.

According to the rowing machine's read-out, Kim had reached his daily one thousand-metre mark, but he kept on rowing for the pleasure of watching Laura. She had tied her hair back in a ponytail and the fine hairs on the back of her neck were now beaded with sweat, like the beads of moisture on a glass of cold white wine.

There was something undeniably fine about her, Dr Fellowes thought to himself. One could almost fall in love with a girl like that. Of course, relationships between staff and faculty were, strictly speaking, against the rules, but they were in Italy, where rules were a little more flexible.

After Laura had showered, she came out of the changing room to find Dr Fellowes waiting by the notice board, a sweater draped elegantly over his shoulders.

'I thought you might like to come with me on a little tour,' he said diffidently.

'What sort of tour?'

'A tour of my own personal Rome. There are some wonderful collections that aren't open to the public. And after that'—he shrugged—'perhaps we could have a little lunch somewhere?'

'That sounds wonderful,' she said.

He took her to places she didn't even know existed—to tiny *palazzi*, where archivists and curators unlocked dark rooms containing priceless masterpieces. He ushered her past the security guards into the Farnese palace, now the French embassy, its fabulous Carracci ceilings long since closed to the vulgar hordes. They visited tiny, jewel-like chapels, grand salons with majestic ceilings, dimly lit churches where at the flick of a switch vast frescoes of unimaginable beauty leapt out of the darkness.

'Enough,' he said at last. 'We mustn't cram you too full of art on an empty stomach.' He escorted her to a restaurant in a little square where the owner greeted him by name. A bottle of cold Orvieto and some *grissini* arrived on the table a few moments after they sat down.

'I'm afraid my diet doesn't allow me much in the way of carbohydrate,' he said apologetically. 'I'm just going to have a salad. But please, order anything you want.'

'I'll have a salad too,' she said. 'I've been eating way too much, and I don't want to undo all that running at the gym.'

'Is Laura coming to the opening night?' Bruno asked Tommaso.

Tommaso screwed up his face. 'To be honest, I hadn't thought about it.'

'She should,' Bruno said emphatically. 'I'm planning something special for her. An authentic Renaissance menu, in honour of her studies.'

'You don't have to do that,' Tommaso said. 'Let's face it, on the opening night the place will be full of important customers—maybe even some reviewers. We should be concentrating on them, not Laura. Why create more dishes just for her?'

For a moment Bruno felt a terrible compulsion to tell Tommaso everything. Because to me she's the only person who matters, he wanted to say. Because I'd swap all the good reviews in the world for a smile from her. Because I love her in a way that I don't think you, Tommaso, fine and noble friend that you are, are actually capable of.

But he swallowed those words before he spoke them. He said, 'But think how it will look to the reviewers and all those important people to know that certain dishes have been created in honour of one particular woman. People will talk about it, and perhaps they'll bring their own girlfriends and wives to try it out.'

'Hmm,' Tommaso said. 'Yes, I like that. The grand passion of the chef, reflected in his creation of a dish of love. That's a great idea. I wish I'd thought of it myself.'

For inspiration, Bruno went to art galleries and studied the paintings, making sketches of the meals they showed. Luckily there were plenty of portraits that showed people eating. He was in the Galleria Borghese one afternoon, studying the paintings, when he suddenly heard a familiar voice calling his name. He turned round. It was Laura.

'Hello,' she said, surprised to see him. 'What brings you here, Bruno?'

Putting away his notebook, he mumbled something about looking at a new display.

'Well, since you're here, let me show you my favourite painter,' she said, slipping an arm through his.

'Caravaggio, you mean?'

'How did you know that?' she said.

He shrugged. 'Tommaso must have told me.'

They stopped in front of Caravaggio's *Boy with a Basket of Fruit*.

'You like the light,' Bruno said. 'The way it falls from one side, putting half the face in shadow.'

'That's right. I *do* like that.'

'Whereas Tommaso'—he gestured at the paintings—'sees all of these in terms of food.'

'He does?'

'Oh yes. He told me so. He told me that you could see what each painter ate, by the way he painted. So Michelangelo there'—he nodded—'could only have been a Florentine. He would have liked simple grills, the plainer the better.' He pointed across the room. 'Raffaelo, on the other hand—he's all grace and lightness, like the cooking of his native Urbino. But Caravaggio was a Roman, with a Roman's hearty appetite. When he paints a Last Supper, it's a painting of a proper Roman dinner, with a real roast bird just out of the oven and a plate of *contorni* beside it, just as he himself would have been served at the *osteria* he was lodging at.'

'Tommaso said all that?'

He glanced at her, wondering if she was teasing him, but she seemed entirely serious.

'Actually, I think he may be right,' she said, as they continued through the gallery. 'Raphael fell in love with a baker's daughter, and started putting little pastries into his paintings in her honour. And Caravaggio was broke most of the time, so he was probably thinking about his next meal while he painted. I'll have to tell my teacher what Tommaso said. I think he'll be really interested.'

Laura lies in Tommaso's bed and stretches luxuriously. Tommaso himself has already left to supervise last-minute preparations at Il Cuoco. Today, finally, is the grand opening, and there are a million and one things he still hasn't done.

She gets out of bed and starts to dress. Last night they ate baby artichokes, flattened into stars and deep-fried in oil, and she sees to her consternation that there's a streak of olive oil on her shirt. She opens Tommaso's cupboard to find a clean one, and takes a step back.

The inside of the cupboard is covered with photographs. Photographs of girls. There are brunettes, redheads, a few black-haired Italians, but overwhelmingly the cupboard is filled with blondes. There's a picture of herself, and she remembers now the occasion when Tommaso took it, in this very room, right after they had slept together for the first time.

Oh, she says out loud, as the implications of that sink in.

She looks again at the other girls. Now that she examines them more closely, she sees that the photos were also taken here, just as hers was.

At the thought of all those women sharing a bed with Tommaso—the same bed that she now shares—the tears spring to her eyes.

As the restaurant filled up with customers, Bruno kept a careful eye on the table in the corner that had been reserved for Laura and her room-mate. But it stayed empty.

By one thirty the orders were coming in thick and fast. They had done well to attract so many people to their opening. Carlotta's contacts in the magazine world had helped: the little dining room was full of people who would certainly never have visited the restaurant under its previous ownership.

For Bruno it was a new experience to be running an entire kitchen, and he had his work cut out making sure all the food was absolutely perfect. Eventually, though, during a brief lull, he had time to pause. Tommaso was looking as miserable as a dog that had lost its bone.

'Where's Laura?' Bruno asked, suddenly fearful.

'Not coming,' his friend said tersely. 'We had a row.'

'What about?'

'Nothing. Well, something, obviously. But nothing I could make any sense of. What do women ever pick fights about?'

Tommaso looked so crestfallen that Bruno put his arm round him. 'Tommaso, I'm so sorry. I can tell how upset you are,' he said gently.

'What are you talking about? It's just a row. I'm upset because I'm stuck in *here*'—he indicated the kitchen—'while it's all happening out *there*.'

As he spoke, Marie whirled in with another fistful of orders, slapped them into Bruno's hands and picked up half a dozen plates from the pass before rushing out again.

'I can feel it! It's alive out there. Whereas in here'—he looked around and shrugged—'you're just cooking.'

'This is the bit that really matters,' Bruno pointed out gently.

'But it's *your* bit. I'm just hanging about. Can't you give me something to do?'

'Sure. We need some fish filleted for table four.'

'Great. And where's the fun in filleting a fish if there's no one to see you do it?' Tommaso demanded miserably as he moved off.

Bruno had no answer. It occurred to him that if this venture was going to be a success, he'd need to find Tommaso some proper work to do.

Eventually everyone had eaten their fill, and the roar of noise from the dining room lessened to a contented hum.

Tommaso was outside, talking to a pleased Dr Ferrara. Bruno was alone in the kitchen. He saw Tommaso's phone lying on a counter, and saw that Tommaso had been composing a text message to Laura.

He picked it up and read it. It said:

Hi Laura. Sorry about all that. CU tomorrow? Regards, Tommaso.

It hadn't been sent yet. Bruno picked it up and, with one eye on the door in case Tommaso came back, began to change it.

By the time he had finished it read:

There was something I wanted to cook tonight—

The recipe of love

Take one American girl with honey-coloured skin and freckles like orange-red flakes of chilli on her shoulders.

Fill her with flavours, with basil and tomatoes and pine nuts and parsley.

Warm her gently with your hands for several hours, turning occasionally, and serve with wine and laughter, straight from the dish.

—but sadly 'one' of the ingredients was missing. Maybe tomorrow?

He pressed SEND, and waited for a long, agonising minute before the phone beeped with a reply.

That's lovely. Why wait till tomorrow? I'll come round later. Hope it went well, love L x.

When Tommaso returned, he picked up the phone and said, 'Oh.'
'What is it?'
'I must have sent my text without meaning to. Still, it looks like Laura's forgiven me.'
'That's good,' Bruno said, his face buried in the pan he was cleaning.

From *Stozzi* magazine:

Cucina Romana becomes Cucina Romantica

Six weeks ago I ate one of the best meals I have ever had. The location was Rome, in the apartment of my parents, where a talented young chef, Tommaso Massi, had volunteered to cook us some of the dishes of our native city. The menu was a simple one, such as might be found in any one of the hundreds of *ristoranti* that crowd the city centre: *pinzimonio*; fresh *tortellini al pomodoro*; *saltimbocca*; a chocolate *tartufo* for dessert. What elevated this meal to the level of high art was, first, the quality of the ingredients and, second, the skill of the chef, whose passion is to re-create such traditional dishes and reveal them in their true glory.

What was most remarkable about this meal, however, was the effect it had on me—and I do not just mean my palate. How can I put this? As the meal was consumed, I too found myself being consumed by passion of a different kind. Massi's intense, sensual flavours and deft handiwork in the kitchen seemed to have awoken appetites that could only be fully satisfied in the bedroom.

Massi is perfect casting for a god of love, being both handsome and charming. He is also winningly modest. When asked about any of his recipes, he struggles to explain what makes them work. 'It's just food,' he says with a shrug. 'You buy it, you cook it, you serve it. At the end of the day, the cook is no more important than the waiter. A really good waiter, now, has a skill that is often underestimated.'

The good news is that this remarkable chef is now cooking in his own establishment, Il Cuoco in Viale Ostenze. I was fortunate enough to eat there soon after the opening, and was delighted to find that his talents have survived the transition to a bigger stage intact. The women of Rome are in for a treat—and so are their boyfriends.

From *Time Out Roma*:

Fellini meets foodie in hip young *überchef* Tommaso Massi's take on the traditional Roman trat. The crowd is young, the ambiance dark, the music fashionably retro and the word-of-mouth impressive, but the food lives up to expectations. The buzz is that this is a chef who understands women; when Massi came out of his kitchen to tour the tables the reaction was more like that afforded to a rock star than a restaurateur. Book ahead.

From RomeBuddyBoard.com:

Posted by Alessandro Bonaguidi:
> Have you heard the rumour about Il Cuoco? Apparently women go wild for the food there.
Posted by Miko Trenti:
> Yeah, I went there with my girlfriend. It worked for us.

From *Il Messaggero*:

The tradition and inspiration of the cultural imperative that is Rome can nevertheless be explored gastronomically through the fantasy of a chef. At Ristorante Il Cuoco, greedy pilgrims may entrust Tommaso Massi with the creation of an *abbacchio all cacciatora* or a *coda alla vaccinara*, as well as more mythical dishes according to his alimentary philosophy. Roman tradition is a reference point. Flavours are in harmony with the past and the present also, and thus the expression of a civilisation that is rigorously passionate and creatively orientated. Approximately 80 euros for two, with wine.

From *Roma'ce*:

Some of the best food this reviewer has ever had. Each dish tasted distinctly of its ingredients, which were of the highest possible quality. Simple, precise, imaginative reinterpretations of the classics. Chef Tommaso Massi is a wonder. Reservations essential.

It was full. Not just at weekends, either; every evening and every lunchtime the little dining room was packed to capacity. Two by two they came, for the reputation of Il Cuoco rested partly on the wonderful flavours of the food and partly on the wonderful effect that eating the food had on the female libido. Husbands discovered that their wives forgave them their domestic shortcomings; young men on a first date found that picking up the bill at Il Cuoco was more persuasive than any number of whispered compliments; and lazy boyfriends realised that the subtle seductions of a five-course dinner were a congenial alternative to foreplay.

They had taken on a couple of extra *commis* to help with the prepping, but even so Bruno was busier than he had ever been in his life. His day started soon after dawn, when he arrived at the restaurant to check the deliveries. By ten he was making desserts, and by eleven he was preparing lunch. This being Italy, lunch started late. It was not unusual to have people turn up at three, and—this being Italy—these same diners, who had been tearing about and cursing each other and generally rushing around all day, suddenly lost any desire to hurry the moment they sat down at the table, and would be mortally offended if, say, their *secondo* arrived less than half an hour after the end of their *primo*. Thus the last lunchers would still be finishing their *distillati* at five or even six o'clock, barely two hours before the first evening customers were due. Bruno would be lucky to leave the restaurant by midnight to catch a few hours' sleep before it all began again.

But he was cooking, and that was all that mattered. For the first time in his life it was *his* signature on the plates that were going out of the little kitchen. The dishes were an exact expression of his personality, his influences: Roman, just as he was Roman; virtuoso, just as he was a virtuoso; sensual, passionate and physical, because that was part of his nature too. And if his own yearnings were unfulfilled, if his love for Laura was unreciprocated and unconsummated, perhaps that only gave his dishes an extra piquancy, a tantalising sense of urgency mixed with regret.

Tommaso, meanwhile, still had very little to do. In the kitchen he could help Bruno a little, but once service got under way his friend functioned on some kind of mystical autopilot, and didn't want assistance from an amateur. Marie, though rushed off her feet, was so competent that front-of-house ran perfectly. Tommaso liked to watch her working. He liked the way she had to go up on tiptoe to squeeze her bottom through the gaps between chairs, the fluidity of her bosom when she leaned down to clear a table. Occasionally he tried to flirt with her, but although he used all his considerable charm, she maintained a professional detachment. Tommaso wasn't used to this. He found himself thinking about her wistfully.

They were clearing up one evening, after all the customers had gone, when Marie said, 'I think you'd better tell me what the deal is here.'

'Deal?' Tommaso asked innocently.

'You're supposed to be the chef, but *he* does all the cooking.' She pointed at Bruno.

'Ah,' Tommaso said. He paused. 'You see, there was a girl, and she wanted to go out with someone who could cook, and I wanted to go out with *her*, so I told her I could. Cook, that is. And I couldn't. But Bruno could, and—and—it just all started from there,' he said helplessly.

'So you've started a restaurant because you didn't want to tell a girl you can't cook?' Marie said in disbelief.

'Um, yes, I suppose so.' Hearing it put like that, Tommaso experienced a feeling he got more and more these days—a feeling that he couldn't quite work out how or why things had got as complicated as they had. 'You see, if she thinks I'm only a waiter, she'll dump me.'

'And what's wrong with being a waiter?' Marie wanted to know, tapping her foot dangerously.

'Oh, nothing,' he assured her. There was something about Marie that made him not want to argue with her.

'That's the stupidest story I ever heard,' Marie decided.

'It's pretty stupid, yes,' Tommaso agreed.

'So when are you going to tell her the truth?'

'Soon,' he said. A thought was forming in his mind. If Laura found out the truth, she would dump him. Life would go back to the way it had been before, and actually Tommaso wasn't averse to that at all.

Ever since Bruno had started creating the menu for Il Cuoco, he had been struggling with the impossibility of creating the dish he had spoken of to Tommaso that first night, walking back from Templi, when the two of them had discussed the difference between aphrodisiacs and the food of love itself.

Bruno remembered very well what he had said on that occasion: 'If you want someone to fall in love with you, you cook them something that shows you understand their very soul.'

'Such as?' his friend had asked.

And Bruno remembered, too, every word of the answer he had given: 'You'd have to really know the person concerned: their history, their background. You would have to have tasted them, to know whether their own flesh is sweet or savoury, salty or bland. In short, you would have to love them, and even then you might not truly know them well enough to cook a dish that would capture their heart.'

But even though he knew he loved Laura, he found it far, far harder than he had expected to create a recipe that would do justice to her. He knew that it would have to be something sweet, and so insubstantial that it was barely more than a morsel, leaving the palate gasping for more. But it would also have to be perfect, and perfection remained elusive. Bruno tried everything, but there was always something missing.

And then, one afternoon, Laura herself came round to Il Cuoco. She was looking for Tommaso, who wasn't in, and she came into the little kitchen before Bruno was aware of her presence. He was muttering to himself as he spun barefoot from stove to fridge to prep surface, trying different combinations of tastes and textures, half demented with his lack of success.

Laura had been drawn into the kitchen by the most extraordinary smell. She had expected to find Tommaso, and her surprise at discovering Bruno was matched only by her shock at the intensity of the aroma.

It smelt of baking cakes, which took her back to the kitchen of her childhood, coming home from school to find her mother making her cookies . . . but it also smelt medicinal, and that made her think of being ill and being looked after when she was tucked up in bed. Then there were spices, and a faint hint of Christmas: nutmeg, perhaps, and cloves . . . But underneath all of those was something else, something insidiously smooth and emollient, like vanilla or eucalyptus. She had a sudden memory of touching her father's cheek as he gave her a kiss good night—the rasp of his eight o'clock shadow, and that smell . . .

'What is that?' she breathed.

Bruno spun round and stared at her like a madman. 'I'm making apple pie,' he said.

Apple pie . . . Laura hadn't had apple pie for years. Suddenly she felt thousands of miles from home, and a tear welled into her eye. 'I'm sorry,' she gasped.

'Here. It's ready.' Without bothering to use gloves, Bruno pulled open the oven door and brought the pie dish out. She noticed that it was extraordinarily tiny, like something made for a doll. He put it on the counter. She buried her face in the steam and inhaled deeply.

'Can I have some?'

'Of course,' he said. 'I made it for you. It just needs a little cream . . . here.' He took out a spoon and thrust it into the pie, releasing more vapour. The whole creation was barely more than a single spoonful big. He poured a little cream on top and held it up to her lips. 'Don't worry. It's not too hot.'

She opened her mouth and he slid the morsel inside. She closed her eyes and chewed ecstatically, unwilling even to swallow lest she make the experience a moment shorter than it had to be.

'Bruno,' she said, when she was capable of speaking, 'it's fantastic.'

He kissed her.

Shocked, she pulled away. Bruno was looking at her with an expression of such intensity that she was almost frightened.

'I'm sorry,' he said quickly. 'It's an Italian thing. We—we kiss each other all the time. It really doesn't mean anything.'

'No, of course,' she said, recovering. 'I know it doesn't. I was just a bit surprised. Americans don't do that, you see.'

'No.'

'And I don't think we should mention it to Tommaso.' She looked him in the eye. 'I think he would misunderstand too.'

'Of course,' he said. 'And I promise you, it won't happen again.'

Tommaso, returning from a pleasant morning arguing with friends over coffee, was surprised to see Laura's textbooks on the kitchen counter.

'Laura's here?' he asked Bruno, who was busy washing up.

'She was, earlier.' Bruno kept his eyes on the sink, afraid that he wouldn't be able to meet his friend's gaze.

Tommaso put his finger in the little pie dish, licked it and made a face. 'Actually, I'm glad she's not around. I want to talk to you about her.'

'You do?'

'Si. I think this thing I've been having with her has run its course. It's been fantastic and everything, but the truth is—well, I'm getting itchy feet. Actually,' he added, for he was always honest with Bruno, 'maybe it's not my feet, you know?'

'You're going to dump her?' Bruno said, stunned.

'Yes, but that's the problem. This is sort of new territory for me. I've never been in a proper relationship before, so I really don't know how it's done.'

'I'm probably not the right person to ask,' Bruno said. 'Since I've never been in a proper relationship either.'

'But you know things, like how to let her down gently.' An idea occurred to him. 'Maybe you could say something to her for me. Kind of preparing the way.'

'I really don't think that's a good idea,' Bruno muttered. 'This is something that's got to come from you.'

'But you could help soften the blow. You know—explain what an idiot I am, how I'm always messing around with other women . . .'

'Tommaso, there's something I've got to tell you.'

'Yes? What?'

Bruno kept his eyes on the sink. 'I'm fond of Laura.'

'Ah.' Tommaso nodded. 'You don't want to see her hurt.'

'No—not that. I'm not making myself clear.' Bruno struggled to find the words. 'I think I'm in love with her.'

'Oh,' Tommaso said. He thought for a moment. 'When you say "in love", you don't actually mean—'

'I mean I think about her every single moment of every single day. I think about her when I sleep, when I wake up, when I'm doing other things. I even think about her when I cook—especially when I cook. I think about her smile, about her frown, about her mouth, about the little orange-brown freckles on her shoulders. I have imaginary conversations with her. I dream of catching a glimpse of her. Then, when she turns up, I can barely look at her.'

'Oh. Ah. I see.'

'Are you angry with me?'

'Of course not. I mean, it's not your fault. You've done nothing wrong.'

'That's not—' Bruno was about to say 'That's not quite true', but then he realised that he couldn't. He had promised Laura that the kiss would remain a secret.

'Listen, it happens.' Tommaso slapped Bruno on the back. 'I'll tell you something I've never told anyone else. I fancy Lucia, Vincent's girl. See?'

'But you're not in love with Lucia.'

'True,' Tommaso conceded. He began to pack coffee grounds into an espresso pot. 'That's weird, isn't it? All the time I've been going out with Laura, you're the one who's in love with her.'

'Yes. It's weird all right.'

'So after I finish with her, are you going to ask her out?'

'I can't.'

'Of course you can.'

'Trust me, Tommaso, I can't. She'd never have me.'

Tommaso tried to steer the conversation round to the subject of breaking up. 'Laura, there's something I want to talk to you about,' he began, then stopped. How was he going to put this? 'The thing is, it's like a meal. When you've had beef every day for two months, you're ready for some lamb. Which is not to say,' he added hurriedly, 'that there was anything wrong with the beef. The beef was perfect. Unforgettable, in fact. But eventually the time for beef is over.'

'You mean, like the seasons?' Laura asked, not understanding.

'Exactly. Beef season is followed by lamb season. Well, actually there isn't a beef season, but there is a season for lamb and it's over, and soon it'll be time for something different. Game, for example.'

'So you'll take lamb off the menu, and put game on.'

'Exactly.'

'And how will you cook game at the restaurant?'

'Ah.' He saw the difficulty now. 'I'm not talking about the restaurant,' he said helpfully. 'I'm talking about us.'

'Us?'

'Yes.' He struggled again. 'Let me put it another way. Sometimes, when two people linger over a long meal, it takes them a while to realise they've reached the end. They have a *grappa*, perhaps some *biscotti*, then they order some coffee, but really it's time to call for the bill. To say good night, and goodbye, and of course to tip the waiter. But instead they linger until the last possible moment.'

'And when that happens, the staff can't go home. They have to wait.'

'Yes. Exactly.'

'I understand. Sometimes you have to stay late. It's not a problem.'

'It isn't?'

'No. It's your job, and I love the fact that you're a chef. Even if it does mean that you sometimes fall asleep during sex.'

'I do not!' he said, offended.

'But it's all right, Tommaso,' she assured him. 'I don't want to change you. You've got your cooking, I've got art history. That's why we're great together. We've both got other interests.'

'Talking of other interests—'

'I love you,' Laura said happily. 'And I love it when we talk about food like this. What's on the menu at the restaurant tomorrow?'

Tommaso walked to the restaurant with a heavy heart. He had tried to spell it out to Laura, but it was so hard to say the blunt words that would break her heart. Everyone was going to be cross with him. There was Laura, of course, but there was also Dr Ferrara, his backer, who was the father of Laura's best friend. The atmosphere at Il Cuoco was difficult enough already. Ever since he had revealed that he wasn't actually a chef, Marie had begun treating him with apparent disdain, while deferring with exaggerated respect to Bruno. Bruno, meanwhile, had fallen into a huge, inexplicable depression and barely spoke.

'*Scusi?*'

Tommaso looked up. It was a girl who had spoken to him. She was blonde and pretty, and she was wearing shorts. There was a rucksack on her back and she was holding a guidebook.

'*Si?*' he said.

'Can you tell me how to get to the Piazza Navona?'

A tourist. Tommaso had forgotten how much he liked tourists. 'Of course,' he said. 'In fact, I'm going that way myself. But I'm afraid'—he dropped his voice gravely—'that there has to be a fee for guiding you there. It's a city regulation.'

'And how much is this fee?'

'The fee is that, when we get there, you allow me to buy you a *grappa*.'

The girl laughed. 'And if I don't want to pay that fee?'

'Then you have to give me a kiss.'

'I'll settle for the *grappa*. For the moment.'

'Excellent. What's your name?'

'Heidi. I'm from Munich,' she said.

'Hello, Heidi. My name is Tommaso and I'm—' He hesitated. He had almost said, 'I'm a chef,' but at the last moment he stopped. 'I'm a waiter.' As he said it he felt a wonderful sense of liberation, as if a great weight was lifting from his shoulders.

Laura runs up the stairs to Tommaso's apartment. Her diet, and the exercise she's doing at the gym, are *definitely* starting to have an effect.

'Tommaso?' she calls. 'Bruno?'

There's no answer. But Tommaso has been here recently. The CD player is playing one of his favourite songs, 'The Boys of Summer'.

Then she hears the shower hissing. He must be in the bathroom. She smiles and goes through to his bedroom to wait.

The printer by Tommaso's computer is whirring. Idly she goes to see what he's printing. And watches, dumbstruck, as a picture of a pretty blonde girl, taken in this very room, scrolls out, line by line.

She hears footsteps on the stairs. The door of the apartment crashes open. '*Due cappuccini*,' Tommaso's voice calls triumphantly. 'Heidi, I persuaded the crazy old barman to serve us cappuccino in the afternoon!'

The shower is turned off. The only noise now is the whirring of the printer and the pounding in Laura's head. Tommaso comes into the bedroom and sees her there, and for a moment everything is suspended in time, like a film that has been frozen—

And then she pushes past him, desperate to get out of there before the bathroom door opens, before the other girl comes out. She spills the coffees and does not stop, runs down the stairs, out into the street, with Tommaso calling her name somewhere behind her.

He catches her up but she won't listen. He tries to talk to her as he walks alongside her, dodging cars and pedestrians while she pushes forward, refusing to give way for anyone or anything.

'Laura, listen, I didn't mean for it to be like this, I wanted to break it to you gently—'

'Get away from me,' she hisses. 'Leave me alone. Go back to your cappuccino-drinking Heidi.'

'I tried to tell you I was fed up,' he cries.

She searches for the most hurtful thing, the very worst thing she can say to him, and she finds it. 'You're as bad as Bruno, you know that?'

'What do you mean?'

'Your friend Bruno. Kissing me. Staring at me all the time. Making my skin crawl. You're a pair of perverts, both of you.'

She breaks into a run again, and this time he doesn't try to follow her.

When Bruno got back from Il Cuoco it was after midnight. Tommaso was waiting in the apartment, his face dark.

'You told Laura?' Bruno asked gently.

Tommaso shrugged.

'You seem pretty upset.'

'Yes.'

'I hadn't realised it was going to be so hard for you.'

'It wasn't,' Tommaso said curtly. 'Not that part, at any rate. Laura told me you kissed her.'

Bruno froze. 'Ah.'

Tommaso got to his feet. 'How many times?' he said threateningly.

'Once,' Bruno said. 'Maybe twice. Three times. Tommaso, I'm sorry. I told you how I felt about her—'

'You tried to steal her,' Tommaso snarled. 'You're my friend—*supposed* to be my friend—and you made a pass at my girl.'

'It was just a kiss.'

'Only because that's all she'd let you do. If she'd been willing, would you have stopped there?'

Bruno couldn't answer that.

'If it was anyone else, I'd beat you to a pulp,' Tommaso said. 'As it is . . .' He slammed his fist into his palm. 'We're not friends any more, Bruno.'

'What about the restaurant?' Bruno heard himself say.

'I don't give a shit about the restaurant. It was a stupid idea in the first place.' He pointed to the door. 'Now get out of here.'

Bruno stumbled out of the apartment, followed by Tommaso's shouts. A final '*Vaffanculo!*' issued from the window above his head as he staggered blindly down the street.

He wasn't surprised that Tommaso was angry. The knowledge that another man has made a pass at your girlfriend would still, in some parts of Italy, be considered grounds for pulling a knife. The fact that he had been on the verge of finishing with her was no excuse.

Bruno started running. He had to find Laura. Perhaps if he could just explain how it had happened, how he had only gone along with Tommaso's crazy scheme as a favour to his friend . . .

At last he reached the Residencia Magdalena. There was an entryphone, and he buzzed the bell marked Patterson until a voice answered.

'Judith?' he panted. 'It's Bruno. I need to speak to Laura.'

'She doesn't want to talk to you. Just go away.'

'Please,' he begged. 'Just get her to come to the intercom.'

'She doesn't—'

Then Laura's voice, brittle and hoarse, interrupted her. 'What do you want, Bruno?'

'I can't let you walk out of my life without telling you how I feel about you,' he said.

'Oh, sure. You and Tommaso both. Why—?' Bruno had to stand back to let a group of people into the building, and by the time he got back to the speaker she was just finishing. '. . . thought you were my friends. I actually liked hanging out with you both. What an idiot you must have thought I was. When I was just another tourist to warm up your beds.'

'No,' he said quickly. 'Laura, listen to me. I love you. I love you more than I've ever loved anyone.'

There was a moment's silence from the entryphone, and just for a second he thought he might have got through to her, but her voice, when she answered, was thick with tears and disgust.

'Just get away from me, you creep. Don't you know how repulsive that is? Go away and leave me alone.'

When Gennaro came to open up the coffee bar the next morning, he found Bruno slumped in the doorway.

'I need a favour,' the young man said as he hauled himself to his feet.

'By the look of you, you need a coffee.'

'That too. Look, Gennaro, you know that van of yours?'

'You want to borrow that old rust bucket again? It's in pretty bad shape at the moment. I'm not sure how far you'll get in it.'

'I was wondering if you'd sell it to me.'

'Oh.' Gennaro thought for a moment. 'It's a fine vehicle, structurally. I mean, when I call it a rust bucket, that's just my affectionate name for it—for her.'

'How much do you want for it?' Bruno said wearily.

Gennaro gave it some more thought. 'Well,' he admitted, 'the truth is that she may need a few minor mechanical upgrades. I've been cannibalising her, you see, for the coffee pump.' He pointed proudly to where his Gaggia stood, now almost invisible inside an elaborate cage of auxiliary pipes, stopcocks, valves, conduits and fans. 'So I'll accept five hundred.'

'I have two hundred. But I'll throw in these.' Bruno pulled something out of his jacket, a rolled-up bundle of cloth that he proceeded to open.

'*Uanema!*' Gennaro breathed. 'These are your cooking knives!'

'They were. I don't need them any more. What do you say?'

'It's a deal,' Gennaro said, picking up one of the knives.

'Can I have the keys then?'

'No point,' Gennaro said cheerfully. He pointed to where the ignition lock of a Fiat van was now built into his Gaggia.

'So how do I start it?'

'Here.' Gennaro handed him a spoon. 'This should do it.'

Insalata

'L'insalata is served invariably after the second course to signal the approaching end of the meal. It releases the palate from the grip of the cook's fabrications, leading it to cool, fresh sensations . . .'

MARCELLA HAZAN,
The Essentials of Classic Italian Cooking

THE YOUNG WOMAN seated across the room at table twelve is familiar to us. As the crowd of attentive waiters finally steps back, leaving the couple to enjoy their *persillades* of wreck-caught salmon, celeriac purée, jasmine sauce and roasted fennel, not to mention their glasses of chilled Puligny-Montrachet, we can see that she is indeed Laura, though a rather different

Laura from the one we left three months ago in Trastevere. For one thing, she looks fantastic. Gone are the extra pounds she put on when she was gorging herself on Bruno's extravagant pasta and rich desserts. Her newly sleek and almost muscular torso is a testament to the many hours she has put in at the gym. Her hair is different, too: shorter and tied back in a fetching little ponytail. We cannot see her eyes, because they are hidden behind a pair of elegant dark glasses which reflect the image of her companion, who is equally smartly dressed, for this is a special occasion.

'Potatoes, madam?' the waiter enquires, his spoon hovering over the silver dish of vegetables.

'Not for me.'

'Sir?'

'Just one, please.' Kim Fellowes adds to Laura, as an aside: 'The great thing about this kind of food is that the portions aren't too big. I still have twenty grams of carbohydrate left.'

'You're going to stick to the diet today?'

'Of course. Especially today. It isn't a diet if you throw it out of the window every time you walk into a good restaurant. It's places like this that separate those with self-control from the rest.' He reaches for the wine, nestling in its silver cooler, and a waiter's hand immediately completes the action for him, filling their glasses to the exact halfway mark. 'A toast,' Kim says, raising his own glass to his lips. 'To us.'

Laura drinks. 'To us.' Dabbing her lips with a crisp white napkin, she adds, 'You know, I thought this place was going to be different.'

'Why so?'

'That guy I—' She pauses, as if there is something in her throat, then continues: 'That guy I went out with worked here. I thought it would be—well, more like the stuff he cooked. You know, Italian food.'

'Aren't you glad it isn't?' He tastes his wreck-caught salmon, one of Templi's specialities. 'One gets a bit fed up with pasta, to tell the truth.'

In another restaurant, just a few miles down the road, Tommaso is cooking. The dish is a simple one, but the presence of several cookery books, their pages liberally encrusted with scabs of dried meat-juice and calcified egg yolk, would suggest that he is having trouble.

'Two *saltimbocche*, one *tagliatelle*, one *insalata*,' Marie says, coming into the kitchen with an order on her notepad.

Tommaso doesn't reply.

'Did you hear me? I said—'

'*Me ne sbatto il cazzo*,' Tommaso fumes. 'Can't you see I'm busy fucking up the orders I already have? Just leave it on the side.'

After Bruno had left Rome, Tommaso's anger had evaporated as quickly as it had come. In fact, he soon started to feel a little guilty. What he had said to Bruno was certainly true—Bruno *had* kissed his girl behind his back—but given that he himself had been unfaithful to the same girl-friend with a pretty blonde backpacker from Munich, he was hardly entitled to claim the moral high ground. Besides, Tommaso loved Bruno, and the harsh words had been as much from a sense of hurt that he hadn't been told the whole story as from any real injured pride.

As the realisation dawned that Bruno wasn't coming back, Tommaso had sunk into gloom, along with the fortunes of Il Cuoco. Had the restaurant not by now owed money to everyone, he might have tried to walk away from it. But gradually he realised that there was another reason why he couldn't leave. It was to do with the look on Marie's face when she'd discovered that he wasn't a real chef. He was determined to show her that he was just as capable of running a restaurant as Bruno had been. But the truth, at this moment, seemed to be that he wasn't.

Bruno had simply driven north after leaving Rome. Quickly growing tired of the *autostrada*, and unable in any case to tease more than sixty or seventy kilometres an hour out of the rickety vehicle, he had turned onto the smaller roads. Near Florence he camped for the night in a tiny olive grove, next to a 500-year-old tree as fat and short as a Tuscan grand-mother. In the morning he found a tiny stream, where he caught a small trout which he cooked over a fire of fragrant dry olive wood. The trout would have been delicious, he knew, but on this occasion it might as well have been made of cardboard. He had completely lost his sense of taste.

From Tuscany he continued to head north, hugging the Ligurian coastline as far as Genoa. Here he ate *minestrone con pesto*, soup with fresh basil, and *farinata*, the staple street food of the seaport: a batter made with chickpea flour, mixed with extra-virgin olive oil, water and salt, spread out on a two-foot platter and cooked quickly in a wood-fired oven. It was properly *croccante sopra e morbida sotto*—crisp on the top, soft underneath—but it gave him no pleasure.

The way north left the coast for the very different landscape of Piedmont. Here long, straight roads built at the command of imperial Caesars ran across smooth plains filled with flooded rice paddies, for this part of Italy is the largest producer of rice in the Western world. When he ate it was usually a simple, soupy *risotto* from a roadside *osteria*: rice cooked with chicken or the ubiquitous frogs' legs, flavoured with cinna-mon and made liquid with the heavy wine of the region. Eventually, though, there was no more paddy plain left, and the bristling foothills of

the Alps rose up ahead of him. Now when he stopped the van the locals
spoke a harsh dialect, their speech a strange intermingling of Italian,
German and French, and the roadside cafés served boiled meats, *sauer-
kraut* and Austrian-style pastries. He knew the van would never survive
up in the mountains, so he reluctantly turned east towards the Adriatic
coast. Here he picked up another Roman road, the Via Emilia, now
known more prosaically as the N90 but still running straight and true
for hundreds of miles across Emilia-Romagna to the sea.

This was the gastronomic heartland of Italy, where every inch of the
fertile soil was cultivated. In Parma he visited shops festooned with
hams, each one postmarked with the stamps of a dozen inspectors—
only a handful of towns between the Enza and the Stirone rivers are
allowed to designate themselves producers of *prosciutto di Parma*. In a
valley to the north of Parma, Bruno sampled *culatello di zibello*, perhaps
the greatest of all Parma's pork products and for that reason almost
never exported, even to other parts of Italy: a pig's rump marinated in
salt and spices, then sewn inside a pig's bladder and aged for eighteen
months in the humid air of the flat river basin. It is a process so delicate
that almost half the hams are spoilt before they are ready, but those that
survive are incomparably delicious. There had been a time when the
almost creamy texture and sweet, intense flavour of the meat would have
made Bruno laugh out loud for sheer joy. Now, although he still found it
curious, he was like someone who eats with a bad cold. It was as if his
palate, usually so exact, had become no more sensitive than that of any
ordinary person.

As Bruno neared the sea the little road became crowded with tourists
spilling off the *autostrada*, heading for the fashionable resorts around
Rimini. It was time to change direction again. This time Bruno set the
van's nose southwest, once more heading inland.

He had been driving for weeks, but he had never experienced such an
empty, rural landscape as the one in which he now found himself. This
was Le Marche: the Marches. There were few major towns here. For mile
after mile the only signs of life were tiny hamlets and villages dotted
between wild limestone gorges, where peasant farmers scratched a living
tending a few pigs, a few cows and a few sheep on a couple of steep
fields. The roads tended to be winding, following the contours of the
land and the serpentine rivers, and Bruno made slow progress.

That suited him fine, though. It was becoming apparent that unless he
stopped somewhere, and perhaps got himself a job as a labourer, he was
eventually going to end up back in Rome again, where all roads led, and
that was the last place he wanted to be.

Bruno picked up another Roman road, the Via Flaminia, which took him through the dramatic Furlo gorge. As he climbed higher above Acqualagna the van began first to breathe heavily and then to wheeze, all the time going more and more slowly, until finally, with a coughing fit worthy of a forty-a-day smoker, it came to a complete stop.

Bruno got out and contemplated the silent engine. He was about 300 feet above the valley floor, somewhere between the little towns of Cagli and Città di Castello. He could not, however, see a single house or farm. The sound of goat bells clattering in the distance indicated, however, that there was some sort of settlement nearby.

He tried in vain to coax the engine back to life. Once he thought he had it, but the van seemed to splutter apologetically and then lapse back into its coma. Sighing, Bruno pulled his backpack from the passenger seat and prepared to walk. Since he knew there was nothing for miles the way he had come, he walked uphill, hoping that the woods that obscured his view were also concealing the presence of a village.

The nights had been the worst. That was when Laura had found herself thinking that she actually couldn't stand the pain, that she would do anything, anything at all, if only Tommaso would take her back, that she would even share him with all the tourists in Rome if it meant she could be with him again. On nights like those she would sit numbly on her bed, leaning against the wall, and wait for the morning, her cheeks burning with humiliation and her eyes stinging with wretchedness.

She had cried all the time. She had cried all over Judith, and on the phone to Carlotta. She had come within a whisker of abandoning her course and going back to America. She had cried over Kim Fellowes. He had been sympathetic, arranging to see her privately to help her catch up, at which kindness, of course, she had simply cried some more. He did not seem to be in the least repelled by her tears; if anything, the more she cried, the more attentive he became, and she soon got used to the familiar comforting smell of the cologne on his elegant linen hand-kerchiefs. Gradually the pain receded, and when, finally, he had escorted her to his bed, she realised how lucky she was to be loved at last by someone who genuinely cared for her.

Bruno walked uphill for over an hour. Although the sun was setting it was still hot, and only dogged determination, and the knowledge that if he didn't find somewhere to stay he was going to have to sleep out in the open, kept him going.

Eventually he saw houses in the distance. There was a plume of smoke beyond them, as straight and upright in the windless air as the cypress trees that dotted the hillside. As he climbed higher he saw that it was indeed a tiny village, consisting of no more than a dozen stone houses. On one of the buildings there was an ancient advertisement for Fernet-Branca, painted directly onto the crumbling plaster. That was a good omen: it meant there was probably some kind of *osteria*.

As he walked into the village a couple of dogs on chains barked at him, but otherwise the place seemed deserted. He could, however, smell something coming from the direction of the smoke he'd seen from the road. He recognised the aromatic smell of burning beech wood immediately, but it was the scent of roasting pork that made his mouth water and his pace quicken. Someone was barbecuing a pig, and Bruno suddenly realised that he had not eaten for days.

He rounded the corner of the piazza—which was hardly a piazza at all, but an open space round which the houses and a church were grouped. Its surface was unpaved and it contained little apart from a few lime trees and a vast Fascist-era war memorial representing Victory as a naked woman being held aloft by half a dozen soldiers. It did, however, contain the source of that wonderful smell. Outside a tiny bar, someone had set up a makeshift spit over a fire. A few people were milling around it, tending to the golden-brown piglet that was slowly rotating above the hot embers. Chairs and tables had been dragged out into the evening sun, someone was fingering an accordion, and one or two elderly people were dancing. Half a dozen pairs of eyes turned to watch Bruno as he approached, although no one spoke to him.

Bruno hardly noticed. I can smell it, he thought. Really, properly smell it. Somehow, the smell of that *porchetta* had done what all of Emilia-Romagna's finest produce had failed to do. His extrasensory perceptions of taste and smell, which had all but disappeared, were flickering back into life.

Stuffed whole suckling pig is a feast-day speciality everywhere in Italy, although each region cooks it slightly differently. In Rome the piglet would be stuffed with its own fried organs; in Sardinia, with a mixture of lemons and minced meat. Here, evidently, the stuffing was made with breadcrumbs and herbs. He could make out each individual component of the mixture: wild fennel, garlic, rosemary and olives.

'Hello,' Bruno said politely to the person nearest to him. 'My van has broken down and I'm looking for somewhere to stay the night.'

The man scratched his ancient brown suit while he considered this. '*Ueh*, Gusta,' he called at last.

One of the people near the fire turned round. It was a woman, her face weather-beaten and leathery from the sun. Bruno surmised that this was the owner of the bar and repeated his request.

The woman stared. 'We don't rent rooms, usually. You can use the telephone, if you like, to get someone out to your van. Where are you trying to get to?'

Where was he trying to get to? It was a good question, and one that Bruno had no answer for. He shrugged.

Someone spoke from the group round the fire. Although the speaker didn't turn round, Bruno heard a female voice, murmuring something.

Gusta shrugged. 'My daughter says it's too late to get anyone out from Acqualagna, and Hanni, who usually deals with the breakdowns, has gone to Belsaro to help his brother build a roof. We can make up a room, if you really have to stay, though as you can see, we're cooking *porchetta*, so don't expect any choice for dinner.'

Bruno assured her that he would be delighted to eat *porchetta*, and that he would try to be no trouble as he could see that they were busy. He sat down at one of the tables with his backpack at his feet and tried to make himself as inconspicuous as possible. The villagers, for their part, pretended to ignore him. The only one who looked directly at him was Gusta's daughter. She stood up and stepped back from the fire, wiping her hot forehead with her sleeve, and glanced at him for a moment with dark, unreadable eyes.

Someone put a glass of wine in front of him, and a plate containing a few squares of crispy pork skin. He ate them gratefully, by now very hungry indeed. Eventually, after much discussion, the *porchetta* was ready, and was lifted away from the heat to rest. But first, of course, there was pasta—great bowls of fresh green *tagliatelle*, made with spinach and a hint of nutmeg, served with *fagiole*—fresh beans—and a little goose broth. No, not spinach after all, Bruno decided after a second taste; the green in the *tagliatelle* was actually from young stinging nettles. Rather to his surprise, it was excellent.

He was by now squashed between two large women, their accents so thick he could barely understand what they were saying. He asked what they were celebrating and they launched into a long explanation, the gist of which seemed to be that someone had borrowed a tractor from someone else, but the brakes didn't work properly, and then it had hit this poor three-legged piglet and killed it, so of course it had to be eaten straight away. Had Bruno not noticed that the *porchetta* had only three legs? Bruno confessed he hadn't, a comment that prompted much hilarity from those around him. He was asked where he came from. Rome, he answered. His companions nodded thoughtfully, as if that explained everything.

The *porchetta* was delicious. It was handed round not on plates, but wrapped in myrtle leaves, so that the bitter flavour permeated the meat. Everyone else had fallen silent too, and the only sounds were the satisfied sighs of the diners. Finally bowls of fresh peaches were brought out, served sliced and covered in sweet wine. Then the accordion struck up again. The large lady on Bruno's left, who must have consumed at least a dozen glasses of wine during the meal, immediately asked him to dance, much to the amusement of their neighbours. Feeling that part of his payment for their hospitality was to provide them with entertainment, Bruno agreed. He happily made a fool of himself for a few minutes before excusing himself and sitting down again.

Someone sat down in the large lady's place, and he turned to find that it was Gusta's daughter. She had changed out of her cooking clothes immediately before dinner was served and was now wearing a long, dark dress—a patchwork of silks and other shimmering materials. Her hair was dark, as dark as the night behind it.

'I've made up your room,' she told him. 'When you get tired, just tell Mother or me and we'll show you where it is. Though I'm afraid you may not sleep very well. Once this lot get started, they'll be drinking and dancing all night.' There was an affection in her voice, he noticed, that belied the curtness of her words.

'Thank you. But I'm enjoying myself, really. And that was a remarkable meal.'

She shrugged. 'Just a pig. It doesn't take much to cook a pig.'

'That pasta, too,' he said gently. 'The nettles and the nutmeg—fantastic. Who made that?'

'My mother,' she said. She looked up.

A huge young man with sandy blond hair and the broadest shoulders Bruno had ever seen was standing on the other side of the table. 'Time to dance, *bella di casa*,' he said. Though he spoke to the girl, his eyes were on Bruno. He leaned across the table and placed a large, muscular hand in Bruno's. 'I'm Javier,' he said. 'Pleased to meet you . . .'

'Bruno,' Bruno said. He felt his hand being crushed for a moment, then released. 'My van broke down.'

'Yes, I know.' Javier turned back to the girl. 'Come on then.'

She got up, her dress shimmering. She said to Bruno, 'But I added the nettles. And the nutmeg. It makes people . . . happy.'

He watched her dancing, his eyes straining in the dark for the shimmer of her dress as she spun. Then he realised what he was doing. Laura was right. I am a pervert, he thought wearily. Always watching, never doing. He got to his feet and went to find Gusta and directions to his room.

When Bruno got up the next morning, the little piazza was deserted. He assumed they were all sleeping off their hangovers—the music had gone on late into the night, just as Gusta's daughter had predicted. Then the doors of the church opened and a stream of villagers poured straight down the steps and across to the bar, where Gusta, still in her church clothes, immediately got to work dispensing *distillati* from unmarked bottles while her daughter took round a tray of pastries. Bruno accepted both. The drink was a fiery peach alcohol, not unlike schnapps, while the pastries were soft and sweet, dusted with almond flour.

He was introduced to Giorgio, a dishevelled-looking young man who was happily having third helpings of the liqueur. Giorgio, he was told, had brought his tractor to church and would soon take Bruno to pick up his van. 'Soon' turned out to be a relative concept. It was another hour, and several more schnapps, before Giorgio finally took Bruno behind the piazza, where the tiniest tractor Bruno had ever seen was parked. Giorgio shooed a mongrel off the seat and settled himself at the controls. He pressed a button and the engine belched black smoke. An elderly man, walking in the opposite direction, laughed and shouted something over the noise of the engine. It sounded like 'Nice pig, Giorgio'. Giorgio scowled. It occurred to Bruno that this must be the tractor responsible for running down last night's meal. It seemed unlikely; surely even a three-legged piglet could outrun this relic.

Bruno and the dog walked behind as the tractor putted slowly down the road. Rather to Bruno's surprise, however, the dwarf tractor turned out to be easily capable of towing the defunct van up to the village, and his vehicle was eventually uncoupled and pushed into a small barn, which contained a reassuring number of wrecked, half-cannibalised cars, all awaiting the return of Hanni the mechanic from his brother's roof.

'Hanni has a piece of everything here,' Giorgio commented. 'He'll sort you out.'

There was nothing to do now but wait. Bruno went back to the piazza, where the smells of lunch were already wafting out of Gusta's kitchen. Plates of *antipasti* were placed on the tables in the square, which magically filled with people—whole families, still in their church suits, and the priest himself with a paper towel tucked into his cassock. Bruno took a piece of chicory and dipped it into a saucer containing a tiny black yolk of *aceto balsamico* floating in olive oil. He was amazed to find that both the oil and vinegar were among the very best he had ever tasted.

The pasta was *taglierini*, thinner and longer than *tagliatelle*, sparsely flavoured with garlic and *porcini* mushrooms. Again, Bruno was surprised:

the season for *funghi* was many months off. But these were undoubtedly fresh. He commented on this to the family whose table he was sharing, and they nodded.

'It's all a matter of knowing where to look,' the man told him. 'And there's not much the Galtenesi don't know about *funghi*.'

The Galtenesi, it turned out, was the collective name for those who lived in these hills.

'You see those two?' the man continued, nodding at a mongrel scratching itself in the dust, not far from where a weather-beaten old man was polishing off an enormous bowl of *taglierini*. 'That's Alberto, and his dog Pippino. He's one of the best *trifolai* in all Italy.'

Bruno looked at the old man with new respect. If there were truffles here, that explained why the locals ate so well. A good *trifolau*, or truffle hunter, could make thousands of pounds in a single night during the winter season. Then, for the rest of the year, he could relax.

A sudden shout came from the direction of the bar. A little terrier was scurrying from the door, carrying off a huge joint of meat in its jaws, hotly pursued by a red-faced Gusta, yelling profanities. The chuckles of the villagers rapidly turned to alarm when it became clear that the animal had just made off with the *capretto*, the joint of kid that had been going to be the *secondo*.

There was a long wait, punctuated by occasional bursts of shouting from inside the house. Tensions in the kitchen were clearly running high.

Bruno got to his feet. 'Excuse me,' he said politely to his companions, 'I think I should go and offer to help.'

He made his way into the tiny bar, and from there to the kitchen behind it. It wasn't much bigger than the bar and it contained both Gusta and her daughter, who were staring fiercely at each other across the kitchen table. Evidently he had walked into the middle of a row.

'Excuse me,' Bruno said mildly, 'I came to see if you'd like some help.'

'Everything's fine,' yelled Gusta, flapping her apron at him. 'Go and sit outside.' She glared at her daughter. 'And take Benedetta with you.'

'For example,' Bruno continued, 'perhaps I could turn the leftover *porchetta* from last night into meatballs, while your daughter makes a tomato and olive sauce, and you, *signora*, prepare some *finocchio fritto*.'

There was a brief silence while the two women thought about this.

'For that matter,' Benedetta said at last, 'we have some sheets of pasta left over from making the *taglierini*. We could make a *vincisgrassi*.'

'We don't have a food processor,' Gusta said dismissively. 'If we have to dice all that *porchetta* by hand, we still won't have fed everyone by the time evening Mass starts.'

'With respect, *signora*, I am a very fast worker,' Bruno said. He reached for a knife, a chopping board and, since no one stopped him, opened the meat safe to remove the platter that held the remains of the *porchetta*. There was rather less than he had remembered; even if he flayed every ounce of meat from the bones, it was going to be hard to make it stretch to feeding the thirty hungry villagers who were waiting outside.

'We'll need some stale bread,' he decided. 'We can soak it in oil and use it for bulk. And some herbs, of course. What do you have in your garden, *signora*?'

'Sage, thyme, marjoram, oregano, bay, basil—'

'And what vegetables?'

'Celery, courgettes, peas, tomatoes—'

'Bring in as much as you've got,' Bruno said, 'particularly the celery and the *zucchini*.' As he spoke, his knife, almost without his thinking about it, was dancing over the carcass of the pig, stripping it of meat. He saw Benedetta glance down at his hands, her eyes widening a little, although she said nothing. She reached for a length of tomatoes, still attached to their vine, and with her own knife began to chop them without even bothering to strip them from the stem.

Bruno started to dice the strips of pork into tiny pieces. Not needing to look at what his own hands were doing, he looked instead at Benedetta's. She was good, he thought; she must have been cooking for years. Her knife was a blur as she worked her way along a celery stalk. He realised that Benedetta, too, wasn't looking at her own hands but at his. Then, at the same moment, they both looked up at each other's face and their eyes met.

Bruno's knife didn't miss a beat, but he felt a shock of recognition. It was like looking in a mirror.

'You're left-handed,' he said, noticing.

'And you're a chef,' she said drily.

'Yes.'

'So what are you doing in Galtena?'

'Just passing through.'

'Really? The road up here doesn't go anywhere else.'

He opened his mouth, and a moment later felt a sharp pain on his knuckle as the knife sliced deep into the skin. 'Shit!'

'There are plasters by the sink,' Benedetta said, sounding amused.

He rinsed the cut and wrapped the plaster round it before picking up the knife again. 'I'm a little out of practice,' he muttered.

'So I see. Never mind, we need all the meat we can get, even if it comes from your fingers.'

ANTHONY CAPELLA

Angry with himself for making such an elementary mistake, Bruno chopped even faster, as Gusta returned with the vegetables.

In half an hour the three of them prepared a meal that would normally have taken four or five hours. It was not the best dish he had ever cooked, Bruno admitted to himself as he sent the first plates out of the door, but it was one he would always remember. In particular, he would remember the way that he and Benedetta had worked together, in silence but in perfect accord.

Finally there were just three plates left.

'These are for us,' Gusta said, taking off her apron. 'Let's go outside.'

If the customers had minded the wait, they didn't show it. The accordion was out again and the children were being allowed to run around, teasing the dogs and each other into a frenzy of excitement. There were places left at the main table, but Javier was sitting there, his food untouched, waiting for Benedetta with a scowl on his face. Bruno thought it was probably tactful to go back to the table he'd been sitting at before.

'Did you make this?' the man he'd been talking to earlier wanted to know.

Bruno shrugged. 'Well, I helped.'

'It's not bad,' the man commented, 'though there's a touch too much marjoram for my taste.'

Damn, Bruno thought as he ate his own plateful, he's probably right at that. These country people had more sophisticated palates than any he'd come across at Templi. To change the subject, he said, 'What happened to Signor Gusta?'

'Ah. He ran away. Years ago, when Bene was just a little girl. People say that's why his daughter learned to cook so well, because she had to help her mother instead of going to school. Now,' he sighed, 'we're going to lose her anyway.'

'Oh? Why's that?'

'Are you crazy? She's twenty-one, she's beautiful and she cooks like an angel. Every young man in the Galteni wants to come home to her.'

Bruno looked across to where Benedetta was sitting next to Javier. 'So is Javier the one she'll marry?'

The man shrugged. 'Who knows? It's the dog who howls at the moon but the fox who eats the chicken. Just because he's following her around like an idiot doesn't mean that he's getting anywhere. In fact, he's probably doing it as much to impress his rivals as anything.'

Looking at Javier's vast frame as he silently shovelled food into his mouth, Bruno could see how that would work. But it was nothing to do with him. He was just passing through.

436

Back in Rome, Tommaso was looking at the empty walls of his apartment. He had already sold all of Bruno's kitchen appliances, his own watch and his digital camera. The restaurant had been picked clean of its wine—he was down to just half a dozen bottles and there was barely a corkscrew left to open them with. Yet still the bills kept coming. Now there was nothing left but to sell his prized CD collection, and when the money from that was gone, he would have to fire Marie.

Sighing, he packed the CDs into boxes and lugged them downstairs to where the vast Porta Portese street market stretched from the Tiber right up to the Viale Glorioso. There was a record dealer just across the street. Tommaso put the box down on his stall.

'How much for all of them?'

The stallholder flicked through the collection, which was full of Japanese imports and rare bootlegs. 'Five hundred,' he said at last. It was worth double, but he recognised a fire sale when he saw one.

'Done,' Tommaso said wearily. The stallholder pushed some notes into his hand quickly, as if afraid Tommaso might change his mind.

As he was going home, Tommaso heard a voice whispering from a doorway: 'Grass, speed, pills, coke . . .' It was an ageing Scottish hippie who hung around the markets, doing a little dealing to fund his own habit. Tommaso stopped. A desperate idea had just begun to form in his mind.

That evening, the menu at Il Cuoco was reduced to a choice of just one pasta, followed by a single *secondo*.

Unknown to the four couples who comprised the restaurant's only customers, their *spaghetti carbonara* had been dusted not with *pecorino romano* but with a highly idiosyncratic and frankly unpredictable mixture of cheese and ecstasy. What Bruno had achieved with his culinary skills, Tommaso was hoping to replicate with simple pharmacology.

Bruno, meanwhile, had finally made the acquaintance of Hanni the mechanic, who was examining his old van with a portable lantern and an expression of dismay.

'You're looking at about four weeks,' Hanni informed him. 'More if I can't get a gearbox.'

'Four weeks? But that's impossible. Nothing takes four weeks.'

'The problem is, they don't make these any more.' Hanni shrugged. 'It's like waiting for a heart transplant. Some other vehicle has to die and give up its parts before yours can be repaired.'

With a sense of dread Bruno asked, 'And how much will it cost?'

Hanni shrugged again. 'Who knows? Could be a hundred, could be five hundred. We'll just have to see what's available.'

'This is how we cook rabbit in Rome,' Bruno said. 'A little sage, a little rosemary, then we leave it to simmer in the wine.'

'Interesting,' Benedetta said. 'But incorrect. In Le Marche we stuff the rabbit with peppers, *pancetta* and liver before cooking. And when we simmer it we leave the lid off, like *this*.' She pushed the lid of Bruno's pan askew. 'That way it reduces while it cooks.' She glared at him.

Bruno sighed. His plan to ask Gusta for a job in exchange for board while he waited for Hanni to get the spare parts he needed was proving trickier than he'd expected. Gusta had insisted on giving him a trial run, and Benedetta in turn had demanded that he use it to demonstrate that he could cook the local dishes in the local way—which, of course, meant *her* way.

'Well,' he suggested, 'we could be a little creative.'

'What do you mean, creative?' Benedetta asked suspiciously.

'Instead of stuffing the rabbit with the peppers, we could stuff the peppers with the rabbit.'

Gusta laughed. 'Are you joking? Our customers would riot if you tried to pull a crazy trick like that.'

Bruno said nothing. He was looking at Benedetta.

'It's an interesting idea,' she said slowly. 'You could grill the peppers first, and then you could put some lemon zest in with the rabbit—'

Gusta looked horrified. 'Now why in God's name would you want to do that?'

'To balance the sweetness of the roasted peppers,' Bruno explained.

'Oh, you young people cook what you like,' Gusta said impatiently, throwing up her hands. 'I've got customers to attend to.'

While Bruno cooked the stuffed peppers, Benedetta made pasta. But they were both watching each other surreptitiously.

'Do you have some cloves?' Bruno asked politely.

'Yes. In the cupboard. But don't use them.'

Bruno sighed. 'May I be permitted some nutmeg, then?'

There was a pause. 'A pinch, no more.'

She watched suspiciously as he grated a little nutmeg over the rabbit meat. The message was clear: this was her kitchen and she was in charge. He sighed again. Not since he worked for Alain Dufrais had he encountered anyone quite so opinionated about cooking.

'When you said that nutmeg makes people happy, why was that?' he asked, hoping some conversation would break the ice.

'Because it does,' she said tersely. 'Just as fennel relaxes people, and cardamom is good for the digestion, nutmeg makes people dance.'

'I've never heard that before,' he muttered.

'Oh well, in that case it can't be true, can it?' she said icily. She pounded the pasta dough with her fists, a quick one-two that left deep depressions in the mixture. It occurred to Bruno that, skinny as she was, it wouldn't do to get on the wrong side of Benedetta. He got on with his cooking in silence.

He had to admit, though, that he had never seen anyone make pasta as well as this. When she rolled out the *sfoglia*, the sheet of fresh dough, she barely glanced at it, but it was so thin and so even that he could see the grain of the wooden table through it.

He couldn't help himself. 'How do you get it so thin?' he asked.

'Practice.' Then, relenting, she added, 'And I have the right hands.'

'What sort of hands would that be?'

'Here.' She held out her hands to him. They were warm, almost hot. 'You can't make good pasta with cold hands,' she explained. 'That's the secret. So I eat a lot of *peperoncino*. It keeps my hands warm.'

Bruno opened his mouth to point out that this was unlikely to be the cause of her warm hands, but closed it again. They were just about talking to each other, and there was no point in starting another fight.

Benedetta was looking pointedly at her hands. With a start Bruno realised that he was still holding them. Abruptly, he let go.

Benedetta turned back to her pasta. But just for a moment, a ghost of a smile flitted across her face.

When she had finished making the pasta, Benedetta cut it roughly into *maltagliati*, random shapes that were traditionally made from leftover scraps. Then she pressed each piece against a strange implement with long, stiff wires, like a comb.

'What's that?' Bruno asked.

'That's the *pettine*.'

'What's it for?'

'Don't you have these in Rome?' she said, surprised. 'I don't know. I suppose it gives the pasta more grip.'

He nodded. He could see how that would work: the grooves left by the comb would give the thin pasta more surface area, which would hold a creamy sauce better.

'What sort of pasta are you making?' he asked.

'*Pasta con funghi.*'

He watched as she took a bowl of reddish-brown mushrooms out of the larder. The air was immediately filled with their rich, earthy scent. 'How many kinds of *funghi* do you cook with?' he asked.

'Oh—hundreds. It just depends on what I find in the woods.'

'You pick these yourself?'

'Of course.'

As the smell of *funghi* combined with the scent of hot butter and garlic in the frying pan, Bruno felt his nostrils flare. And not just his nostrils. The aroma was stirring up his blood, awakening sensation in a part of him that had been quiescent for a long time.

'They say these are an aphrodisiac,' Benedetta said, as if reading his thoughts. 'Of course, it's just a kind of superstition that the old grand-mothers like to talk about.'

'Of course,' he said stiffly.

Laura, in Rome, does not spend the nights crying any more. She attends concerts with Kim—small gatherings for a select few, held in the salons of baroque palaces. But sometimes, in the intervals, she surrepti-tiously takes out her mobile phone and scrolls through the text mes-sages until she finds one that she rereads for the hundredth time:

There was something I wanted to cook tonight—

The recipe of love

Take one American girl with honey-coloured skin and freckles like orange-red flakes of chilli on her shoulders.

Fill her with flavours, with basil and tomatoes and pine nuts and parsley.

Warm her gently with your hands for several hours, turning occasionally, and serve with wine and laughter, straight from the dish.

—but sadly 'one' of the ingredients was missing. Maybe tomorrow?

Then she allows a tear to roll silently down her cheek until it reaches the corner of her lip, where she licks it off absent-mindedly, salty and insubstantial on her tongue.

Bruno woke up with a start, certain he had heard Benedetta's voice. He listened. It was still dark. He must have dreamt it.

'Bruno?'

It *was* her. She was standing in the doorway of his little room. Just for a moment a crazy notion popped into his mind.

'Do you want to come and pick *funghi*?' she whispered.

So that was why she was here. He pushed the crazy notion away. 'Sure.'

'Come on then. I'll see you downstairs in ten minutes.'

A little while later they set off uphill in the darkness, both carrying the shallow wicker baskets in which they would bring home their haul.

'Are you sure there'll be any? At this time of year, I mean?' Bruno asked.

'Of course. Perhaps not so many now as autumn. But there'll be *coprini*, and *orecchiette*, and *piopparelli*, and *ceppatelli* if we're lucky—'

'OK,' he said hastily, 'I get the idea. And none of these is poisonous?'

'Some of them are very similar to poisonous mushrooms. But don't worry. I know what we're looking for.'

By the time they reached the woods it was starting to get light. She led Bruno to where, in the long, lush grass at the edge of the trees, a dark green circle twenty feet across stained the paler green of the pasture.

'*Gambe secche*. A fairy ring. This one is quite old—it gets a little bigger each year as the mycelium spreads out.'

'It's edible?'

'No, but once the fairy ring's established, the *prugnolo* comes and shares the circle.' As she spoke she rummaged in the wet grass, pushing it apart with her fingers. 'See?' She twisted the mushroom deftly from its stalk and put it into her basket. 'There'll be more, if you take a look.'

When they had harvested a dozen mushrooms from the fairy ring they went into the woods, each plucking a hazel stick on the way to push aside the undergrowth. After a few minutes Benedetta stopped and sniffed the air. 'Can you smell it?'

Bruno sniffed too, but all he could smell was the dank, mouldy scent of the woods.

'Over here.' She pushed a little way off the path and there, like a tiny Neolithic henge in the forest floor, stood a cluster of squat mushrooms. 'These are good,' Benedetta confirmed. 'Make sure you snap them off without pulling them or you'll damage the roots.'

'What are they?'

'*Ceppatelli*. Like *porcini*, but they fruit earlier in the year.'

Bruno plucked one. It was lighter than the chocolate-brown *porcini* he was used to in Rome, but it had the same heady, pungent smell.

'And tap the spores onto the ground,' Benedetta added. 'That way you'll make sure it grows again.'

After the *ceppatelli* they followed a tiny trail left by a deer, pushing deeper and deeper into the woods.

'There's one,' Bruno said, pointing with his stick to where a tall, pale mushroom with a spotted cap stood at the base of a beech tree. It seemed to glow faintly with phosphorescence in the dim light.

'Now that *is* poisonous. It's an *Amanita phalloides*. You can guess why it's called that from the shape.' She had crouched down beside the mushroom and was plucking it carefully, her hand wrapped in a tissue to avoid touching the mushroom's flesh.

'Why are you taking it?'

'Oh, poisonous ones are useful too. We use these to kill mice.'

By midmorning it was hot. Both baskets were full, though Bruno was frustrated to find that he was still unable to follow the scent trails Benedetta was tracking so easily.

'We may as well give up now,' she said at last, sitting down in a little clearing on a bank of moss and thyme. 'The smell of the *funghi* isn't so strong any more.'

Bruno sat down next to her. Below them, the village basked in the sun. Trails of smoke and the distant sound of chain saws reached them. Benedetta stretched and lay back.

'It's so quiet up here,' he said.

'Yes. No one from the village ever comes up this high.'

The weight of their bodies was crushing the thyme, releasing wafts of warm scent that mingled with the dank smell of the *funghi* in their baskets. Benedetta began unbuttoning her shirt. His surprise must have shown on his face, because she explained, 'I'm going to sunbathe.'

'Oh. Right. Go ahead, I won't look,' he said, averting his gaze. Out of the corner of his eye he could still see her, though; a flesh-coloured shape lying back on the warm moss. Was he blushing? And if so, how could he have so much blood in him, that it was rushing to his cheeks and his groin at the same time? He lay back and closed his eyes.

There was the rustle of cloth on skin. A few moments later, Benedetta rolled over and slipped her hand under his T-shirt.

'Oh,' Bruno said, his eyes opening again. There was a pert nipple dangling inches from his face, as ripe as a fruit, and that warm pasta-making hand was stroking his stomach in slow, circular movements. 'Benedetta,' he said. His voice came out hoarse. 'You should know—I'm just—just—'

'Passing through? Of course. That's why I can sleep with you.'

'What do you mean?' He gasped as her fingers slid under the waistband of his jeans.

'Isn't it obvious? If I sleep with Javier, I'll have to marry him. If I sleep with one of the other men from the village, they'll tell each other and I'll be labelled a *puttana* and a witch. Whereas you'—she stood up and pulled off the remainder of her clothes, before lying down again and easing herself against him, skin against skin—'aren't going to tell a soul.'

The next day they went to pick *fragole di bosco*, wild strawberries, and made love in a deserted old barn above the pastures, their lips still smeared with the pulp of the fruit. The next day it was *misticanza*, wild leaves for salad. Benedetta insisted that they always pick first. If anyone

THE FOOD OF LOVE

saw them walking home with empty baskets, she warned, tongues would start wagging instantly. So they filled their baskets with rocket, wild fennel, dandelion and lamb's lettuce before temptation overcame them and they collapsed into a quiet corner of a field, hidden only by the tall fronds of the *finocchio* stalks.

The next morning she woke him very early again, while it was still dark, and took him to a dense wood they had never visited before. She wouldn't tell him what they were after, but when they were deep inside the trees she told him to smell the air. He sniffed obediently.

'Can you smell it?' she whispered.

'No. Can you?'

'Yes. Over here.'

He followed her into the dense undergrowth. She was turning her head this way and that, sniffing like a dog. He understood that whatever scent she had caught, it was elusive and precious, so he kept quiet, not wanting to disturb her concentration.

She tracked backwards and forwards between the trees, her nose close to the ground. Abruptly she stopped, and began to lever up the earth carefully with the end of her stick. Then, suddenly, Benedetta was pulling a knobbly object like a tiny misshapen potato from the roots of the tree—a *tartufo*, quite small, still caked with earth, its reek filling the air.

'Alberto would kill us if he knew,' she whispered. 'We shouldn't really pick them at this time of the year.'

She broke the truffle open and pressed it to his nose. The scent was almost overpowering: sex and old socks and musk. He felt himself becoming aroused, and saw by her eyes that she was too. He reached for her, pulling her towards him.

Tiny as it was, the truffle lent its intoxicating flavour to enough dishes to feed the whole village. *Taglierini*, sautéed in a frying pan with lesser *funghi* such as *cardoncelli* and *orecchiette*, had some truffle shaved over them before they were served. Then a leg of kid was served from a giant casserole into which the rest of the truffle had been diced, along with tomatoes, marjoram and rosemary. There was a noticeable air of excitement in the little piazza that evening during dinner. Laughter was louder, flirting more obvious, more wine was consumed, and afterwards the accordion came out. Bruno had no idea how much Gusta charged for the food—there was nothing so straightforward as a price list, let alone a menu, and the electronic cash register, as required by the tax authorities for every retail business, sat untouched in a corner, gathering dust. However, he saw her folding up a great wad of banknotes and tucking it away carefully in a pocket, so presumably she was doing quite well out of the truffle too.

Javier was sitting with a group of his friends. They were drinking beer rather than wine, and vast quantities of it at that. Benedetta and Bruno helped Gusta wait tables by carrying plates outside when the food was ready, and Bruno noticed that there was much ribald laughter and joshing between Javier and his friends whenever Benedetta went out.

Suddenly he heard a yelp. He looked up. It was instantly clear what had happened. The young farmer had just grabbed Benedetta's behind. The two of them were frozen in a tableau: she had jumped away from him, her eyes blazing, and he was laughing at her. Bruno took a step towards them, his fists clenched. Benedetta's eyes swivelled towards Bruno and saw what he was about to do. Instantly she took the plate she was holding and smashed it down over Javier's head, breaking it in two. There was a moment of stunned silence, then his friends started applauding and whistling. Bruno stepped back, his fists unclenching.

At first Javier sheepishly joined in the applause. Then his eyes followed Benedetta's own gaze, over to where Bruno stood, and his face darkened.

She came to his room after Gusta was asleep and slipped into bed beside him. 'That was quick thinking earlier,' he whispered.

'I only did it because I thought you were going to hit him.'

'I probably would have done,' he admitted.

'But you mustn't. Promise me, Bruno. As soon as you do something like that, he'll think he has to fight you. And let's face it, he'll beat you to a pulp.'

'Don't you think he's guessed about us anyway?'

'He may suspect. But so long as it isn't obvious—so long as there's nothing public—he'll tell himself that it's just gossip.'

'But if Javier knew, it might stop him making a nuisance of himself.'

'No, it wouldn't,' she said firmly. 'I've known him all my life. Besides, I don't think I want Javier to lose any sleep over you. I may want to marry him one day.'

'What! Are you serious?'

'Of course.' She put her hand on his chest. 'You won't be here for ever, and I don't intend to be an old maid. Javier is a good man. Any woman would be lucky to have him.'

'I—' Bruno felt awkward. He knew he ought to tell her that he loved her, that he wanted to stay here with her for ever. But he couldn't, because it wasn't true. He thought she was the warmest, most generous person he had ever met; he adored her; she was beautiful and sexy, and she was a soul mate and a friend. But his heart had already been given to someone else. So he said instead, 'You're wonderful, Benedetta.'

'I know.' She wriggled on top of him and opened his lips with her tongue, the way a fisherman opens an oyster with a knife. 'So let's enjoy it while we can.'

He had thought they were being discreet, but the next afternoon he had a strange conversation with her mother.

It was the quiet part of the day, the siesta between lunch and starting to prepare dinner. Bruno was reading. He had asked Benedetta if there were any local recipes written down and she had shown him where the family notebooks were kept—ancient, handwritten cook books, row upon row of them, the oldest on yellowing paper as fragile as tissue.

Just as practised musicians can read an orchestral score and hear the music in their heads, Bruno could read a recipe and taste the result in his mind. He was turning the pages slowly, garnering ideas, when Gusta came into the room. She was holding a tiny jug.

'Ah, there you are,' she said. 'Benedetta said you were going through the old books. Where have you got to?'

'Goose stewed in red wine.'

'Oh, yes. *Oca in potacchio*—my grandmother's recipe. You cut the goose into pieces and stew it in *peperoncini* and wine, very slowly. Then, just before you serve it, you add a little vinegar to offset the richness of the goose fat.' She hesitated. 'That reminds me. Have you got a moment? There's something I've been meaning to show you, up in the attics.'

Intrigued, Bruno followed her up the stairs to the very top of the house. Producing an old key the size of a spoon from her pocket, she unlocked a dark wooden door and ushered him through.

The moment he smelt the air he knew what the attic contained. The sight of a dozen or more wooden barrels, all of different sizes, confirmed it, and the smell of balsamic vinegar was overwhelming.

'Here.' Gusta had crossed to the largest barrel and put down her jug. 'Look at this.' She pointed to a date carved roughly into the wood.

Bruno crouched down next to her. 'My God,' he breathed, '1903.'

She nodded. 'And it still isn't empty. It was my great-grandmother's dowry, the same one who wrote that recipe for goose. This barrel was started by my great-great-grandfather when she was just a baby.' She tapped each of the barrels in turn with her fingers. 'This one's oak, but this small one is beech . . . and that's juniper . . . and chestnut . . . and cherry. After the vinegar drips out of one barrel, it gets put into the next, and then the next, getting a little thicker each time, taking a little of the

ANTHONY CAPELLA

flavour of each different wood. Then some of it goes back into the first barrel, along with a little new wine to keep it going.'

Around the bung there was a tiny ooze, as thick as toffee, straining to fall into the bucket beneath. As Bruno watched, it fell, making hardly a ripple in the viscous liquid.

Gusta said softly, 'When I married, this was my dowry too. And when Benedetta marries, it will go with her. Go on, try it.' She reached for his hand and lifted it, pressing his finger into the thick, sticky liquid.

Bruno put his finger to his lips and felt his mouth flooded with the taste of it—old wine, and honey, and wood sap, and the almost citrus sharpness of the vinegar itself, flowing like warmth through his stomach.

'It's good, isn't it?' she said.

Unable to speak, Bruno nodded.

'Do you know why they call it *balsamico*? They used to believe it was a balm that was able to cure anything. Any illness you had.' She reached to the smallest barrel and carefully opened the tap, allowing a tiny amount into the little jug. 'Even a broken heart.'

Bruno didn't tell Benedetta what her mother had said. Gusta had evidently had a similar conversation with her daughter, though, because Benedetta no longer confined their lovemaking to the outdoors. Most nights she slept in his room now, and although they never referred to it in her mother's presence, it became, like so many things in Italian life, *pubbliche bugie e verità private*; something that was accepted but never spoken of.

Even between the two of them they did not discuss the implication behind Gusta's tacit acceptance of the situation: that she approved of him as a prospective son-in-law. Perhaps if Bruno had been absolutely certain that he did not want to marry Benedetta, he would have said something. But the truth was that he wasn't so sure any more. I could be happy here, he found himself thinking as he trailed through the fields behind her, or watched her rolling pasta on the kitchen table. I've never found anyone before who shares my gift, let alone a woman. I'd be crazy not to marry her. Together we'd build up the *osteria* into a famous restaurant, one that people would come to from right across Italy, and we'd make love every day and have babies and do all the things that happy people do.

If only it was Laura.

If only it was Laura who was sharing her bed with him, who was cooking with him, and yes, whose family owned a beautiful little restaurant in the middle of nowhere. Because no matter how wonderful a time he shared with Benedetta, the truth was that his heart had already been given to a girl with orange-red freckles on her shoulders.

Tommaso's restaurant was full again, though the clientele had changed somewhat. The food might have the desired effect on the passions, but it tasted awful, and now the couples chewing their way with grim determination through his *saltimbocca* or *padellata di pollo* were jaded businessmen, dripping with jewellery and chest hair, lunching their perma-tanned young mistresses, or groups of drunk students looking for the quickest route to another high. Even foreigners had started turning up—a sure sign that Il Cuoco had dropped off the culinary map.

What was more, he had failed to stem the financial haemorrhage. The restaurant might be booked out, but he had been forced to buy huge amounts of drugs and the costs were ruinous.

'I can't believe we're losing so much money,' Dr Ferrara shouted at him when he saw the monthly audit.

'Look, we've turned the corner,' Tommaso said desperately. 'Just stick with it for a few more weeks. There'll be more tourists then.'

'I'll have to go to the bank and arrange a bigger overdraft. This is my pension on the line, you know.'

'Just a few more weeks,' Tommaso promised.

There was no option but to sack Marie. Tommaso was dreading it, but he couldn't think of an alternative.

She seemed to take it quite well, he thought. She listened to him in silence, nodding occasionally as he explained that there was simply no other way for Il Cuoco to survive.

'So what you're saying is, there's no money to pay me,' she said when he had finished.

'That's it, in a nutshell.'

'And you're not paying yourself?'

'No. I haven't been for months.'

Marie seemed to make a decision. 'Right. I'll work for nothing too.'

'You mean that?' He stared at her.

'I said so, didn't I? But there are conditions. I want a share of the profits when we do make money. And I want to go through the books to see why we're losing so much. I may want to make some changes.'

The car that made its way up the winding road from the valley was hired, and its occupants clearly tourists: they stopped several times to admire the views, and when they finally parked in the piazza and folded up their map they went off to take a look round the church, the war memorial and the rest of the sights. But even the most determined sightseer could not find much to detain them in Galtena, and it was inevitable that, come lunchtime, they would settle themselves at a table for two and wait for Gusta to come and tell them what was on offer that day.

Gusta's face, when she came into the kitchen with their order, bore the studiously blank expression she put on whenever she was confronted by the oddness of strangers.

'One truffle salad, *to share*,' she said pointedly.

'And?' Benedetta asked, not looking up from the stove.

'And nothing. No pasta. No *secondo*. A *glass* of wine each. And they want to know what kinds of mineral water we have.' She shrugged. 'They're foreigners, of course.'

Since Gusta used the word foreigners to describe anyone from beyond the valley, Bruno didn't pay much attention. 'I'll make the salad a large one then. No point in sending them away hungry.' He began to arrange the ingredients in a dish.

Then he heard her voice.

The small kitchen window overlooked the square where the tables were and conversation often drifted in—so much so that Benedetta and Gusta would sometimes join in, shouting their contributions over the crash of pans. Benedetta was searing meat now, and the hiss made it hard for him to hear. Bruno put a hand on her arm to stop her and listened.

'Probably about another hour or two from here to Urbino,' a man's voice was saying, in American.

'So there'll be plenty of time to go right up to the top,' his companion agreed. The hairs on the back of Bruno's neck tingled.

Benedetta looked at his face. 'What's wrong?'

'Nothing. I thought—nothing.'

Through the window, they heard the voices again.

'. . . can't believe how much cooler it is up here than Rome,' the man was saying.

'And so beautiful. And that food smells *fantastic*.'

When he heard her say that, Bruno was sure. He put down his knife and went through to the tiny bar, from where he could see all the tables.

She was thinner than when he'd last seen her, but there was no mistaking the sweep of her neck. He felt dizzy.

'It's her, isn't it?' Benedetta said softly beside him.

He nodded, unable to speak.

'Do you want to speak to her?'

He shook his head and made his way back to the kitchen. There was a dish of snails to prepare, ordered by the Luchetta family, and he tried to force his mind to concentrate as he cleaned them. But his hands were shaking and the slippery shells clattered all over the floor.

Benedetta grabbed a board and began chopping livers. *Thwick—thwick—thwick* went the knife, just a little harder than was necessary.

'I'm sorry,' Bruno said at last.

'For what?' Benedetta's reply was even sharper than the knife.

'For being upset, I suppose.'

Benedetta tipped the chopping board against the pan and scraped the livers into the bubbling oil. 'You can't help the way you feel.'

He opened his mouth to speak, then closed it again.

'She's pretty,' Benedetta said, taking an onion and slicing it in a dozen deft movements before reaching for another.

'Yes.'

'Prettier than me.'

'No,' he protested. 'Just—different.'

'And you love her.'

It wasn't said as a question, but it was a question nevertheless, and Bruno knew he had to try to answer it. 'Well,' he began, 'it's complicated. I fell in love with her but she didn't love me back, and I'm not sure whether—I mean, they say you can't really be in love with someone unless they love you too, don't they?'

'That's what they say.'

He looked at her but she was concentrating on what she was doing. Her voice was a little thick, but that might just have been the onions.

'So you told her that you loved her, and she told you she wasn't interested,' Benedetta went on. 'What happened next?'

'It was a bit more complicated than that,' Bruno confessed. 'She was in love with my best friend, and—well, it all spiralled from there.'

Benedetta wiped her hands and poured two glasses of wine from the bottle that stood open by the stove.

'I think you'd better tell me exactly what happened,' she said gently.

So Bruno talked, and Benedetta listened and nodded, cooking while she did so, and Gusta, coming in and out of the kitchen with empty plates, pretended she wasn't eavesdropping.

'And that's why I don't want to go and speak to her,' Bruno said finally. 'She thinks I'm a complete pervert and I don't blame her.'

'Nor do I.'

'Thanks,' he said wearily.

At that moment there was the sound of shouting from outside, followed shortly afterwards by the unmistakable sound of someone retching. Bruno heard Laura's voice in the bar. She sounded panicked. '*Scusi, signora*, is there a doctor? My friend has been taken ill.'

Bruno glanced at Benedetta but her face betrayed nothing. They heard Gusta's voice saying that she would call for the doctor straight away. In the meantime, they would make her friend comfortable on a bed. Benedetta went to see if she could help.

'What's all that about?' Bruno asked when all was quiet and Benedetta was back in the kitchen.

'It must have been the *funghi*.'

'In what way?'

'Some people have an allergic reaction to *coprini*. Particularly if they mix them with alcohol. He must be one of those.' She gave him a blank look. 'He'll be laid up for at least two hours. There's nothing the doctor can do, but he'll have to wait for him anyway, and my mother will give him some *aceto balsamico* to settle his stomach.'

'Benedetta, we don't have any *coprini*.'

'No, but that's because I used them all.'

He gave up. It seemed to him more likely that Laura's companion was suffering from a small amount of one of those poisonous mushrooms that Benedetta insisted on collecting during their forays into the woods. But the important thing now was what he was going to do about Laura.

'I can't talk to her,' he decided. 'She thinks we've given her boyfriend food poisoning, for God's sake. I can't go out there and start talking to her as if nothing's happened.'

'No,' Benedetta agreed. 'But my mother's already told her about the effects of *coprini*, and we're not going to charge her for her meal, so . . .'

'. . . so I could cook her a *dolce* on the house, by way of apology.' As he spoke his hands were already reaching for ingredients. Figs, yes, and cream, and nuts. Some sort of cake?

He was not thinking now, but improvising. No, improvising wasn't the right word, Benedetta thought as she watched him juggle candied fruits and pastry cream, and pound hazelnuts into a paste. Bruno was composing. Occasionally Benedetta made a comment, or a quiet suggestion, but he could barely hear her, so focused was he on what was in his hands.

Eventually it was done. He blinked, and there in front of him was a kind of trifle cake, a many-layered mousse that was sweet and bitter, smooth and sharp, cold on the outside and warm underneath: a dessert, he thought, that was as rich and as simple as life itself.

'Well done,' Benedetta commented. 'Although it has to be said, it might be better prepared in advance next time.'

He stared at her. How long had he been cooking? He had no idea. Then he heard the church bells striking four. Four o'clock! He had been making this dessert for over an hour.

'I'll take it to her,' Benedetta said beside him.

'Are you sure?'

'I said so, didn't I? She should taste it before she knows who it's from.'

He knew what an extraordinary thing it was that she was offering to do. He watched as Benedetta picked up the little plate. She touched her finger to the side of the cake, picked up a crumb and tasted it. For a moment her eyes met his, and there was something in them he didn't quite understand. Then she took his *dolce* outside.

Laura had been terrified when Kim started having convulsions at the table, but now the doctor had confirmed that it was just an allergic reaction to a particular type of mushroom, and that he would be right as rain in a few hours if he was left to sleep quietly. The other customers and the lady who ran the place were sympathetic and helpful, and now, with the sun filtering through the trees and the amazing view beyond the war memorial to entertain her, and a bottle of the restaurant's best wine open in front of her, she was feeling quite mellow. She helped herself to another glass, a little guiltily. Poor Kim. On the other hand, if he were here he would almost certainly be reminding her of the one-glass-a-day rule, and it was really rather nice to be able to indulge herself a little.

Heavens. Here was one of the kitchen staff coming towards her, a strikingly pretty girl in a white jacket, her black hair cascading over her shoulders in defiance of all normal kitchen regulations. She was bearing a plate on which a dessert sat, an island in a little lake of sauce. The girl put it down in front of her and said, 'Here. This is for you. Cooked specially by our chef, with his compliments.'

Was it her imagination, Laura wondered, or did the other girl's eyes search her face with a quizzical look while she spoke?

'Oh, thank you,' Laura began. 'But I don't eat desserts.'

'And a *vin santo*,' the girl said, ignoring her and placing a glass of golden liquid on the table.

'No, really,' Laura said firmly. 'Please take it away.' But the girl had already gone.

Laura told herself she didn't want to appear rude. She would have a couple of mouthfuls, and she could always slip the rest to the dogs that lay panting in the shade of the church wall. She pushed the teaspoon into the top of the pudding, through the layer of sauce, and tried a little.

The sauce. Memories flooded into her brain. It was *zabaione*. She had a sudden vision of herself, that first night in Tommaso's apartment, licking sauce from her fingers.

Coffee. The next taste was coffee. Memories of Gennaro's espressos, and mornings in bed with a cup of cappuccino . . . but what was this? Bread soaked in sweet wine. And nuts—a thin layer of hazelnut paste—and then fresh white peaches, sweet as sex itself, and then a layer of black chocolate so strong and bitter she almost stopped dead. There was more sweetness beyond it, though: a layer of pastry flavoured with blackberries; and, right at the centre, a single tiny fig.

She put down the spoon, amazed. It was all gone. She had eaten it without being aware of eating, her mind in a reverie.

'Did you like it?'

She looked up. Somehow, she wasn't surprised. 'What was it?'

'It doesn't have a name,' Bruno said. 'It's just . . . it's just the food of love.'

She was silent, remembering the apology that Tommaso had texted her once, still stored on her phone. It seemed so long ago.

As if reading her thoughts, Bruno said: 'Take one American girl . . .'

She looked at him, surprised.

'With honey-coloured skin,' Bruno continued softly, 'and freckles like orange-red flakes of chilli on her shoulders. Fill her with flavours, with basil and tomatoes and pine nuts and parsley. Warm her gently with your hands—'

'It was *you*,' she said, realising at last.

'Yes,' he agreed. 'It was always me.'

'You're the cook. And Tommaso . . .'

'Tommaso is a fine person in many ways. But not a chef.'

She closed her eyes. 'Why?'

'As a favour to Tommaso, originally. And then—I really did love you, and I loved to see you eat. And it all got horribly complicated, but I was too stupid to see that it would end the way it did, and before I knew it everyone was shouting at everyone else.'

'There *was* a lot of shouting, wasn't there?' she agreed with the faintest of smiles.

There was a sudden commotion at the door of the *osteria*. Gusta's voice could be heard, and it was clear that she was arguing with someone. A moment later Kim appeared, looking pale and angry, with Gusta and Benedetta just behind him.

'Sweetheart,' he said icily, stopping at Laura's table. 'When we ordered, do you recall seeing anything like a menu?' There was a note of petulance in his voice that Laura hadn't heard before.

'I guess not,' she said.

'And do you remember reading, on this non-existent menu, a non-existent warning to the effect that dangerous mushrooms were being served at this restaurant which might precipitate an allergic reaction?'

He waited. Laura was clearly meant to play her part in his tirade. With an apologetic glance at Bruno, she muttered, 'No.'

'Was there any verbal warning, explanation or other rider to the effect that this meal was actually life-threatening?'

'Not that I heard,' she said, looking at the ground.

He turned to Gusta, who was standing with her arms folded and a face like a dog that has just swallowed a wasp. 'And *that's* why I want the name of your lawyer. So that I can sue your fat ass into the ground.'

Laura flinched visibly, though Gusta herself didn't blink.

'It might have been the wine,' Benedetta said. She shrugged. 'Everyone knows you have to be careful if you drink white wine with mushrooms.'

'Everyone except *me*,' Kim said firmly. 'And who served me this wine?' He pointed at Gusta. 'She did. Did she tell me to be careful? She did not.'

'I prepared the food,' Bruno said calmly. 'If anyone's going to be sued, it's me. I'll happily give you my name and address, though I'm afraid I don't have a lawyer.'

There was a brief silence as the two men stared at each other; Kim still flushed with rage, Bruno apparently unconcerned.

'Oh, forget it,' Kim snapped at last. 'Come on, Laura. We're going.' He stalked off to their car, leaving Laura to follow.

'I'm so sorry,' she said awkwardly to Gusta. 'He doesn't like being made to look stupid, that's all. It was . . .' She hesitated. 'It was really good to see you, Bruno.'

'When do you go back?'

'To Rome? Right away.'

'I meant to America.'

'Next week.'

He nodded. She was flying away, like the skylarks. He watched the two of them buckle themselves into the car, and then the car itself move off rapidly down the hill, towards the *autostrada*, and Rome.

They went back into the kitchen to finish clearing up. For a long time nobody spoke. After a while Benedetta announced that she was going up to her room to rest. Bruno tried her door later, but it was locked.

He had to wait until much later, when the evening service was over and the house was quiet, before he was able to speak to her. There was no answer when he knocked, but this time the door opened.

She was sitting at her dressing table, brushing her long black hair. 'Go away,' she said without turning round.

He sat down on the end of the bed. 'I wanted to say thank you,' he began. 'What you did earlier—that was unbelievably generous.'

'Too generous. If I really cared that much about you, I wouldn't have helped you go after someone else.'

'You cared as my friend,' he said gently. 'You're my mirror image, Benedetta. We understand each other. We even have the same gift. If I'd never met Laura I'd want to be with you, but I did meet her.'

'So why didn't you go after her today?'

He shrugged. 'I did my best.'

'Oh, sure. You offered to let her boyfriend sue you. Nice work.'

'What was I meant to do?'

'You were meant to hit him!' She stamped her foot. 'I went to a lot of trouble to arrange things so that you and he were out there, with every-one shouting, and you didn't even hit him! What sort of an Italian are you?'

'Not a very good one, evidently,' he muttered.

'You know your problem, Bruno? You don't really give a shit about any-thing or anyone apart from your cooking. Not her, and certainly not me.'

'That's not true,' he protested.

'Isn't it? Did you even *ask* Laura to choose you over that idiot today?'

'No,' he admitted.

'And why not?'

'Because she would have chosen him.'

'How would you know, if you haven't asked her?'

'Look at me,' he said hopelessly.

'What do you mean?'

'Just—look at me.' He gestured at his own face in the mirror. 'That guy she was with—he's good-looking. Tommaso—he's good-looking. Laura's beautiful. Why should she choose a guy like me?'

Benedetta regarded him with narrowed eyes.

'You're beautiful, too, of course,' he added belatedly.

'Thank you. So why did *I* sleep with you?'

'I've no idea,' he confessed. 'I'm glad you did, but it's a mystery to me.'

'*Santa Cielo!*' Benedetta cried in exasperation. She held up a comb from her table. 'This is a magic wand. Now pay attention, because I am going to offer you the chance to make one wish. Understand?'

'I think so.'

'If you want, you can wish that you become as good-looking as Tommaso—but at the same time, you will become like Tommaso in every other way as well, with Tommaso's talent for cooking.'

He stared at her. 'No! If it meant I couldn't cook, I wouldn't want to be like anyone else. Cooking is who I am.'

'Exactly,' Benedetta said quietly. 'That's who you are. So stop regret-ting that God has made you exactly the way you actually want to be.'

She tossed the comb back onto the dressing table. 'And if you want to be with Laura, go to Rome and tell her so. Tell her so, and keep telling her until she understands.'

He kissed her, wrapping his arms round her and hugging her until she gasped. 'Thank you,' he whispered. 'Thank you for everything.'

The next morning he was up early, battering at the door of Hanni's barn and shouting that he needed his van back.

'Come in,' Hanni said, opening the barn door. 'And don't worry. I got the message yesterday.'

Bruno had no time to wonder exactly what he meant. 'It's mended? You've finally got the parts?'

'More or less. Of course, I had to improvise a little.' He led the way to where, in the middle of the barn, a strange vehicle now stood. It had the body of Bruno's van, the front wheels of a tractor, and the pop-up head-lamps of a very old Alfa Romeo. Inside, Bruno could see that where the steering wheel had once been there was now a pair of scooter handlebars. 'It may not look much,' Hanni added unnecessarily, 'but I reckon it'll get you as far as Rome. After all, it's downhill most of the way, isn't it?'

Dolci

'In the relationship of its parts, the pattern of a complete Italian meal is very like that of a civilised life. No dish overwhelms another, either in quantity or in flavour, each leaves room for new appeals to the eye and palate; each fresh sensation of taste, colour and texture interlaces with a lingering recollection of the last. To make time to eat as Italians still do is to share in their inexhaustible gift for making art out of life.'

MARCELLA HAZAN,
The Essentials of Classic Italian Cooking

LAURA HAD ARRANGED to meet Judith for lunch at one of her favourite restaurants, Cecchino's. It was not, Judith thought as she entered the long, low, tunnel-like room, the sort of place she would have chosen herself. It was distinctly lacking in what the guidebooks would call 'ambiance'. The tables were plain and functional; the lights, which hung directly overhead, were relentlessly bright; and the waiters, who all seemed to be at least sixty, could barely manage a token smile, even for beautiful young women dining without male company. But the food, Laura had assured her, would more than make up for these shortcomings.

Judith paused by the door. On a trolley, displayed as proudly as any array of desserts, were the specialities of the day: a dozen or so calves' feet, neatly laid out in rows, along with several mounds of a white, gristle-like substance whose function in the body Judith could only guess at. She made a face and looked around for her friend.

Laura had been seated right at the back, a bottle of wine already open on the table. Her lunches with Judith were a chance to abandon Kim's dietary strictures and restricted intake of alcohol, and Laura had already made inroads into her first glass of Sangiovese.

'Hey, girl,' Judith said, kissing her friend before taking the other seat. 'How was your trip?'

'Great. But a bit shorter than we planned. Kim got sick. A touch of mushroom poisoning.'

Judith sensed there was something she wasn't being told. But the waiter had arrived at their table, flipping open his order pad with a bored expression that suggested he knew already what they were going to eat.

He had clearly not expected to be interrogated fiercely, in Italian, about the day's specials. The trolley by the door was wheeled over and a long discussion ensued, during which the waiter began to look at Laura in a different light. To discuss gristle with knowledge and passion in Cecchino's is to command instant respect.

Eventually the girls ordered—*rigatoni con la pagliata* and *zampetti* for Laura, *bucatini all'amatriciana* and *scottadito* for Judith—and Judith was able to tease some of the details of Kim's misadventure out of her friend. Eventually Laura got to the part where she had met Bruno unexpectedly in Le Marche. Judith gasped. Knowing how much Laura hated even to hear Bruno or Tommaso's name, she could see how meeting him by chance must have been an unsettling experience. As yet more details tumbled out of Laura's mouth, Judith became increasingly horrified.

'So they were lying to you? All that *time*? That's—' She wanted to say 'humiliating', but she settled for the milder 'weird'.

'Yes,' Laura said. 'All the time I thought it was Tommaso doing the cooking, it was actually Bruno.'

'But why?'

Laura shrugged. 'I suppose—' She stopped. 'I suppose because he was in love with me.'

'Tommaso?'

'No. I think Tommaso—well, if it hadn't been for the food it would only ever have been a quick fling. Of course, I thought that because he was cooking for me like that, it must be something more he wanted. Whereas Bruno . . .' She hesitated. 'Bruno was probably someone I'd never have looked at twice, to be honest. And I think he knew that. So he went on cooking for me because it was all he could do.'

'You're well shot of both of them,' Judith said. 'And all's well that ends well—if it hadn't been for Bruno and Tommaso, you'd never have got together with Kim.'

'Absolutely,' Laura said. But there was a note of doubt in her voice that her friend immediately picked up on.

'Things *are* all right with Kim?'

'Oh, of course,' Laura assured her. 'Things with Kim are great.' Because although she knew Judith very well by now, there were some things—some niggling doubts—that you couldn't say even to your best friends without seeming—well, a bit disloyal.

Hanni had been partly right: the way to Rome lay downhill as far as the Furlo gorge, but after that there were more mountains to cross—the fearsomely high Sibylline peaks, snowcapped even at this time of year. The van gasped for breath, and Bruno gasped with cold, since a heater was not one of the luxuries Hanni had thought worth installing. His maximum speed was barely more than a tractor's, thanks to the various modifications, and it was an exhausting day and a half's drive before signs to familiar towns such as Frascati, Nemi and Marino came into view. Before leaving, Gusta had given him a basket of food: some *piadina* and *salume* to eat on the way, and other culinary treasures for the task ahead: two large white truffles, the finest they had, prised from the roots of a nut tree, now wrapped separately in foil; a sheep's cheese matured in the cool limestone caves beneath the village; and a tiny flagon of the family's precious *aceto balsamico*. At the very bottom of the basket, wrapped in a piece of old brown canvas, he found four ancient chef's knives, their blades discoloured but their cutting edges newly honed.

When he finally entered Rome, Bruno's first task was not to find Laura but to repair another fractured relationship. He drove slowly through the outskirts, oblivious to the whistles and honks of his fellow motorists, and finally drew up outside the little building that had once housed Il Cuoco. With a heavy heart he pushed open the door.

He stopped, amazed. It was full. More than full: there were people waiting patiently at the bar for tables. The long cellar where once bottles of wine had gathered dust had been opened up to make more space, the wall between the kitchen and the main dining room knocked through, and there was Tommaso, cheerfully cooking away to the accompaniment of deafening rock music—

Pizza. At every table, Bruno now saw, they were eating pizza. He laughed out loud. Of course! As he watched, his old friend flung a huge ball of dough into the air, spinning it nonchalantly above his head to aerate it before slamming it down onto the counter again and grabbing a pair of rolling pins to bang it flat in a blur of movement, like a drummer. There was a burst of whistling and applause from the waiting customers, which Tommaso acknowledged with a huge grin and a roll of his shoulders, before flicking the pizza across the kitchen into the wood-fired oven as casually as if it were a Frisbee. Now that Bruno looked more carefully, he realised that many of the adoring customers were young women, and that they were not so much hanging round the bar as hanging round the kitchen.

Another familiar figure rushed past. It was Marie. If Tommaso was drawing plenty of female admiration, Marie was getting the same from the men in the room. Her top was the shortest Bruno had ever seen, exposing a swath of brown midriff, and instead of an order pad she had been writing orders directly onto her arms, legs and even her stomach, which were covered in scribbles of different colours. Together with her newly pierced eyebrow, low-slung hipster jeans and cowboy boots, she looked more like a rock chick than a waitress.

He made his way over to the kitchen, squeezing through the crowd. There was a pizza on the counter in front of him and he broke off a piece to try it. It was really very good—a thin Roman crust, a slather of fresh tomato pulp, some chunks of creamy buffalo mozzarella, sea salt and two fresh basil leaves, nothing else. As he watched, Tommaso added a looping signature of olive oil to the one he was making. The oil, Bruno was pleased to note, was from the same estate he had used himself when cooking here—though he had never been able to pour it from over his head, like a bartender making a cocktail, the way Tommaso was doing now.

'Tommaso,' he yelled over the din.

Tommaso saw him and froze for a moment. Then he wiped his hands on his apron and clapped Bruno on the shoulder. 'How are you? I didn't expect to see you here, old friend.'

'Neither did I. Tommaso, I'm sorry I went off like that.'

'My fault. I overreacted about that girl.' A worried look crossed his face. 'I suppose you want your job back. But I should warn you, our new clientele doesn't go a bundle on calves' intestines and all that shit.'

'It's all right, I don't want a job,' Bruno assured him. 'I've come to look for Laura.' He noted the way Tommaso was able to keep track of half a dozen pizzas even while they were talking: pounding the dough on one, dragging another out of the oven, sliding a third down the counter for collection by a waitress, and still finding time to play air guitar on his rolling pin to Status Quo's 'Caroline'.

Bruno gave up. 'Listen, I'll see you later. Oh, and this is for you.' He took one of the foil packages out of his pocket.

'We don't do that stuff any more,' Tommaso yelled.

'It's a truffle. Just grate it on the pizzas.' He gestured at the crowds. 'It'll be the best pizza they've ever had.'

He drove to the Residencia Magdalena. But Laura's name was not on any of the doorbells. Eventually he stopped someone coming out and asked if they knew which apartment was hers.

'I don't think she's here,' the man explained. 'This is a summer school course on Etruscan history. I guess the regular students had to leave.'

'Do you know where she's gone?'

'Sorry.' The man shrugged. 'You could try the university office. They may have an address for her.'

He drove round the streets of Trastevere, searching for her. He knew it was hopeless but he couldn't bear to do nothing. Eventually, well after midnight, he went back to the little side street that snaked down the hill from the Viale Glorioso. It occurred to him that he hadn't actually asked Tommaso if he would mind him sleeping there; it was perfectly possible his friend had a new room-mate now.

He climbed the stairs to the top floor and let himself in. It was quiet and dark. Then, from the direction of Tommaso's room, he heard a familiar sound.

'Oh—ah—oh—*oh*—'

Laura.

He heard Tommaso laughing throatily in response. His blood boiled. Kicking open the bedroom door, he flicked the lights on.

'*Scusi*,' he said apologetically as Tommaso and Marie stopped what they were doing and stared at him. 'I thought—that is—I'll just go now.'

'Nice to have you back,' Tommaso called as Bruno beat a hasty retreat.

Gennaro was so delighted to see his van again, he offered to take it back for what Bruno had paid for it, plus free espresso and *cornetti*, a deal that Bruno thought remarkably generous.

'I'm impressed by these modifications you've added,' Gennaro explained. 'Not to mention the old girl's homing instinct, of course.'

If only I had a homing instinct for Laura, Bruno thought gloomily. He had already phoned the university office and got a recorded announcement saying it was shut until term started the following week.

'But a week's not long to wait, is it?' Marie asked, her arm looped casually through Tommaso's as they drank their coffees.

'No, but in a week's time, she'll have gone back home.' He sighed, then a thought occurred to him. 'Tommaso—her mobile phone number. It's programmed into your phone!'

'Ah. It was, yes. But Marie has wiped all my old numbers from my card.'

Marie shrugged. 'An accident,' she said.

'Damn. So what do I do?'

A girl roared past them on a scooter, helmetless, her dark hair flowing out in her own slip-stream like a cape. Automatically, Tommaso turned his head to look. When his gaze returned to the others, Marie slapped his face, once, very hard.

Tommaso continued, as if this were barely worth remarking on, 'I guess Carlotta could tell you her number.'

'It's like training a dog,' Marie explained under her breath to Bruno, seeing his puzzled expression.

'I see,' Bruno said. 'Tell me, do you know about the cupboard?'

'I'm the only girl in the cupboard now.'

'Nice work, Marie,' he said, impressed.

'Will you two listen to me?' Tommaso complained. 'It's a good idea. We phone Carlotta; she tells us where Laura is.'

'Except we don't have Carlotta's number.'

'Maybe not, but we know a man who does.'

Bruno looked at him quizzically.

'Dr Ferrara,' Tommaso explained. 'Remember? My backer, who just happens to think the sun shines out of my *culo*.'

But when they called Dr Ferrara, they discovered he was out of town.

'We'll just have to look for her ourselves,' Marie decided. 'Where does she like to hang out, Bruno?'

He shrugged. 'Art galleries, mostly.'

'Then that's where we'll look.'

'Art galleries?' Tommaso looked pained.

Marie poked him in the ribs. 'Yes, art galleries. And don't think you're not helping, because you are.'

There are over 500 art galleries in Rome. By the end of the day the three of them had succeeded in visiting twenty-five.

'This is hopeless,' Tommaso groaned. 'I have to work this evening and I'm already exhausted.'

'I'll help in the restaurant,' Bruno offered. 'It's the least I can do.'

Tommaso looked stern. 'OK—but remember, my customers have come for pizza, not fancy cooking.'

Bruno would have laughed if he hadn't been so worried about finding Laura. 'So what are you telling me? That I mustn't get too creative?'

'Exactly. We do Margherita, Marinara, Romana and Funghi. Our motto is: you want anything else, you eat somewhere else.'

'That's fine by me. I'll just do what you tell me,' Bruno promised.

While Tommaso delighted his female fans by kneading the dough in swooping, flamboyant gestures, spinning it like a lasso or tossing it from hand to hand, Bruno concentrated on quietly adding the toppings. It was undemanding work and he was able to let his mind return to the problem of finding Laura. He knew she went to a gym but he couldn't remember which one. What was left? Bars, he supposed. He realised he had absolutely no idea where Americans hung out in Rome. He lifted his head, thinking that there were bound to be some Americans in the crowd waiting for pizza. He would ask them where he should search.

He looked up, straight into Laura's eyes.

There was a group drinking beers near the entrance. Laura was standing with a bottle in her hand, blowing across the top of it absent-mindedly as she listened to something one of her companions was saying. Then she looked up, saw Bruno staring at her, with Tommaso standing next to him, and her face darkened. She said something to the person next to her and turned towards the door.

She's going, Bruno thought. She's going and I'll never see her again.

He leapt onto the counter. The crowd, thinking this was part of the show, roared their approval. Bruno jumped down the other side and tried to force his way through. It was impossible. They were packed too closely. He pushed and shoved but it was like trying to swim through treacle, and he made no headway.

He had an idea. Turning back to the bar, he got up on the counter again. This time when the crowd roared he simply fell forwards onto their hands as if he were stage-diving.

For one awful moment he thought they were going to let him fall, then he felt himself bouncing back up again, carried aloft towards the back of the room on a moving conveyor belt of hands. Of Laura, though, he could see no sign.

Running out into the street, he thought he saw a figure hurrying round the corner. He ran after it. Yes, it was her; she was walking fast, her head down. He shouted but she didn't hear him. Then a taxi with its light on came towards her and slowed as she waved at it, and she was climbing into it, and though he sprinted after her as fast as he could, he was just one more yelling Italian in the driver's rearview mirror.

He had lost her.

Wearily he trudged back to Il Cuoco. My one chance, he thought, and I blew it. And even worse than that thought was the knowledge that she had seen him and turned away. She hadn't even wanted to talk to him.

'Bruno?'

He looked up. 'Oh. Judith.'

'It *is* you. I thought it must be.'

'When you saw Laura run away, you mean?' he muttered. 'Yes, I think I'm the only person who has that sort of effect on her.'

She was silent for a moment, then she said, 'I wouldn't be too sure.'

'You mean there are others? That's some consolation.'

'I probably shouldn't say this,' Judith said slowly, 'but she's been talking about you a lot since they came back from their trip.'

'Saying what?'

'Nothing in particular. Just talking. But a bit too much, if you know what I mean. I think that's why she doesn't want to see you, Bruno. Because it's too late to turn the clock back. Why make everyone miserable by talking about how much better things could have been if you hadn't been such a dickhead?'

'I've got to find her, Judith, please. You've got to tell me where she is.'

'I don't know where she is right now. But I know where she'll be tomorrow. There's a restaurant called Templi—'

'I know it.'

'There's a big dinner there tomorrow night. Everyone who's still here from the course is going, and all the faculty as well. To celebrate our last night in Italy.'

The next morning Bruno made his way to the restaurant at the top of Montespaccato and asked to see Alain Dufrais. When he was taken to the great chef's office, he asked for his old job back.

Alain smirked. 'I knew you'd be back. Your own establishment is making pizza now, I hear.'

'Yes,' Bruno said meekly. He didn't tell Alain that he hadn't been working there for some time.

'Well, I'll think about it. Come back in a week or so.'

'I need the job immediately.'

Alain raised an eyebrow. 'You haven't got any more reasonable while you've been away, have you? I can't just take on another chef at the drop of a hat.'

Instead of replying, Bruno reached into his pocket and took out a little flask and a small package wrapped in foil. He unstoppered the flask. Silently he held it towards the other chef's nose.

Alain's nostrils flared. He took the tiny container, dabbed a few drops of the hundred-year-old *aceto balsamico* onto the end of his finger and touched it to his tongue. His eyes closed, and for a few moments he seemed incapable of speech. Then he said, 'Remarkable.'

Bruno unwrapped the one remaining white truffle. There was no need for Alain to hold it to his nose. The smell gushed into the little office, flooding every corner and cranny, saturating both men's brains with pleasure, like bread soaking up oil.

'How much do you want for it?' Alain said hoarsely.

'Nothing—so long as I can cook with it, here, this evening.'

'Done,' Alain agreed. 'But you can't be a *chef de partie*—I already have every station covered. You'll come back as a junior, or not at all.'

Like Alain, the other chefs assumed that Bruno had returned to Templi with his tail between his legs. Hugo Kass, in particular, lost no time in putting him in his place.

'Go and chop those chillis, chef.'

'Yes, chef.'

'Now dice those onions.'

'Yes, chef.'

Somebody laughed. They understood what Hugo was doing: if Bruno wiped his eyes while he was dicing onions, the chilli would get in them.

Bruno chopped the chillis and the onions, then washed his hands and walked over to where Hugo was preparing a ferociously complicated *gratin* of crab meat and pink grapefruit. Without a word, Bruno picked up a crab and began to copy the other chef's movements.

'What are you doing?' Hugo Kass enquired icily.

Bruno didn't answer. He simply worked faster. By the time Hugo had finished his first crab, Bruno had already moved on to his second. Hugo snarled and concentrated on what he was doing. But Bruno had already finished his second crab and was reaching for a third. Unlike the duel the two of them had fought the last time Bruno had worked here, this was a hopelessly uneven contest. Beads of sweat popped from Hugo's forehead as the heat of the burners combined with the humiliation of being shown up. With an oath he reached for a sharper knife, and in doing so dropped his crab on the floor.

There was silence in the kitchen. Bruno calmly walked away from the counter and made himself a space to work between two of the other chefs. He knew that Hugo would not be troubling him again. But Bruno had more important things to think about now, such as what he was going to cook for Laura.

Like Bruno, Kim Fellowes and Laura were getting ready for their big meal at Templi. But while Bruno was chopping, peeling and sifting, Kim and Laura were washing and dressing.

It was a particular ritual of Kim's that he liked to dress Laura himself. She stood naked in his apartment in front of the mirror as he pulled a red chenille dress over her head.

'This dress is kind of heavy,' she murmured.

'But it makes you look like a Botticelli *principessa*,' Kim said. 'Besides, this evening is going to be special. You'll want to have looked your best.'

'I know. I've been looking forward to it.'

'That's not what I mean, Laura.'

'And of course, it's the last night. Last time either of us will see all the guys.' For Kim was leaving Rome, too, off to take up a plum appointment at his old college.

'I didn't mean that either.'

She shot him a puzzled glance.

He closed his eyes for a moment, then said, 'In my pocket is a ring.' He touched the side of his dinner jacket. 'An exact copy of the one in Caravaggio's portrait of Mary Magdalene. I had it made up specially by the head jeweller at Bulgari. I thought you'd like to know now, so that when I say something later you'll be prepared. I know you'd hate to be so overcome that you'd spoil the perfection of the moment.'

'Kim, what are you saying?'

'I simply want you to be prepared for something special to happen tonight, Laura. But when I do say a few words, later, will you do me a favour? I'll speak in Italian, and I'd appreciate it if you'd do the same. It will sound so much better, and I want everything, every tiny detail, to be just right.' The doorbell buzzed. 'There. That'll be our transport.'

'You ordered a taxi?'

'Not exactly. Like I said, everything about tonight is going to be special.'

He had booked a horse and trap; waiting in the back of the trap was a bucket of ice and a half-bottle of champagne. As he helped her onto the seat it was still sinking in: her last night in Rome was also going to be the night that Kim proposed to her. She felt completely stunned.

As the sunset turned the church towers orange, a flock of doves wheeled over Santa Maria de Trastevere.

'Next week it'll be back to stressed-out Americans, psychotic panhandlers and DON'T WALK signs,' Laura said.

'How ghastly. Let's not think about it.' Ghastly: that was a word he was using a lot these days.

Suddenly the trap lurched and came to a stop. A tiny Fiat van had reversed into the road without looking and was now blocking the street as it tried to straighten out. The driver of the trap shouted something: the Fiat's window was wound down and the young man at the wheel retorted that he would only be a moment, and in any case the trap-driver might like to use the time to make love to the horse, who was probably also his mother. Laura laughed.

Kim took her hand. 'Thank you for not minding,' he said quietly.

'Mind? Why should I mind? It's—' She had been about to say, 'It's the best bit,' but thought better of it. 'It's just one of those things,' she said.

The trap-driver had obviously come up with a suitably inventive response, because the Fiat-driver had abandoned any attempt to unblock the road and was now telling the trap-driver what he had previously done to the trap-driver's sister.

'You know what?' Laura said. 'This might take a while. Let's walk to the end, then get a taxi.'

Kim's mood was quickly restored when the taxi deposited them at the door of Templi. Alain's establishment had lost none of its graciousness, and from the moment the man whose sole job it was to open the door to them opened the door to them, Kim was in heaven. Nor was the cosseting provided by Templi the only soothing influence. Kim had pulled out all the stops. As they greeted their friends in the bar, a barbershop quartet dressed in dinner jackets sang Puccini arias, their mellifluous voices mingling with the quiet hum of conversation.

Laura suddenly had the sensation that she was waking from a dream. The dream had been quite pleasant, but like a sleepwalker who suddenly wakes up and knows where they are but not how they got there, it was a complete mystery to her how her life had come to this point.

'Kim,' Laura said carefully. 'There's something I've got to tell you.'

'What is it, *cara*?'

'What you're going to ask me later—if it's what I think it is—I'm so flattered and pleased, and you really are special to me, but—well, I need much more time before I'm ready for something like that . . .'

Kim's eyes flashed, but he said mildly, 'I've told you before, Laura:

you've got to learn to be more spontaneous. Don't be so American. Just go with your heart.'

'Yes, but—'

'It's your last night in the Eternal City. What better place to pledge eternal love? Ah, here are the flowers I ordered.'

A waiter was bringing over the largest bunch of roses Laura had ever seen. They were, she noted, the exact same shade as her dress. The other diners, having realised by now that something special was happening this evening, started nudging each other and looking expectant. Laura, who had gone as red as the roses, tried to accept the flowers in a way that looked grateful but not engaged. Definitely not engaged.

It is hard to carry a bunch of thirty-six long-stemmed red roses and maintain a conversation at the same time. By the time the students and staff moved to their table, Laura felt like the statue of Daphne in the Villa Borghese, caught at the very moment she turned into a tree. Finally, she managed to persuade a friendly waiter to take the flowers away on the pretext of putting them in some water. By this time Kim and some of the others were having earnest discussions about which wine to choose, and she was able to look around.

'I guess tonight's a big night for you,' said the man on her right conspiratorially. 'Kim's a lucky guy.'

It dawned on Laura that Kim had already told some of his colleagues what he was intending to do. He must have been planning it for days, weeks even, without saying anything to her. If she turned him down in front of all these people his vanity—never inconsiderable—was going to be horribly punctured. He would, in fact, be totally humiliated. Did she really want to do that to him? Or was there some third option, such as saying she'd think about it, or saying yes but then changing her mind a few days further down the line?

She sat there, sick with nerves, trying to think of a way out of this. As a result, she was the only one not to eat any of the *amuse-gueules* that were being passed round the table and loudly exclaimed over.

In the kitchen, a second plate of *amuse-gueules* was waiting at the pass when Alain suddenly strode over to take a closer look.

'What are these?' he demanded. No one answered him.

Bending down, he tasted one. For a long moment, as he ate it, his face took on the distant look of a man who has seen beyond the mortal world and witnessed seraphim. He turned towards Bruno. There was no need for either of them to say anything. There was only one person in the kitchen who could have been responsible for what was on that plate.

Alain stared at Bruno. Then he took the plate and tipped it into the bin. 'Do these again,' he said quietly. 'No, not you,' he added quickly as Bruno reached for his pastry knife. 'You.' He nodded at Hugo, who shrugged and prepared to do as he had been told.

'Orders for table twelve,' Karl called. 'One salmon . . .'

Table twelve. That was the Americans' table. '. . . one scallops, one velouté, one caviar—'

'*Oui, chef, oui, chef, oui, chef,*' Bruno was calling as he scrambled to claim all the orders for himself.

With two long strides Alain was standing in front of him. 'What in God's name are you doing now?' he snapped.

'Cooking,' said Bruno, to whom the answer was obvious.

'Not in my kitchen, you're not. Get out.'

'But you said—'

'—nothing at all about you coming in here and destroying the discipline of my brigade. Get out, before I have someone throw you out.'

Stunned, Bruno picked up his knives and went. He couldn't believe it. Just when he'd got everything organised, it had all gone horribly wrong.

He blundered out of the back door and straight into a waiter. '*Scusi,*' he mumbled, his head still down.

'What's up, Bruno?'

He looked back. It was Tommaso, dressed in his old Templi uniform.

'See? Still fits,' his friend said. 'Though not as well as hers.'

He pointed to where Marie was emerging from the changing room, trying to make the uniform she was squeezed into look like it belonged to her instead of to a short Italian man several sizes smaller.

'What are you two doing here?' Bruno said.

'We thought you might need some help,' Tommaso answered.

Bruno sighed. 'Thanks, but it's no use. I've been thrown out of the kitchen.' He explained briefly what had happened with Alain.

'And where is the head prick now?'

'In the kitchen, supervising the service.'

'Any way we can get him out of there?'

'Absolutely not. He never leaves the kitchen during service. Not for anything.' A thought occurred to Bruno. 'Apart from when he throws people out, that is.'

'Excellent.' Tommaso delved into the pocket of his waiter's jacket and came up with an order pad. He scribbled something on it. 'You two wait here, and get ready to lock him in the coat cupboard as soon as he comes out.'

Tommaso walked up to the pass and handed the slip to Karl, who glanced at it and froze.

'What is it?' Alain snapped.

'Table twelve. One of the Americans has asked for,' Karl lowered his voice, 'steak with ketchup.'

'Has he indeed?' Alain said icily. 'Hugo, come with me. The rest of you, get on with your work. And cancel all the orders for table twelve,' he called over his shoulder as he walked towards the doors.

Seconds later, Alain and Hugo were safely incarcerated in the coat cupboard. 'Now what?' Tommaso asked.

'Now I have to talk to the others.' Bruno walked back into the kitchen. 'Listen to me, everyone,' he called.

Instantly he had the attention of the room. But now that all their eyes were on him, he wasn't sure what to say.

'It's like this,' he began. 'There's a girl here tonight, on table twelve, and I want to cook her the best meal she's ever had. It means changing the menu, because the kind of food this girl really loves isn't Alain's food, good though that is. It's Roman food, the kind of food I like to cook. But I can't do it on my own, not at this level. We'll have to prep an entire menu from scratch, right now, which means I need all of you to say you'll help.'

There was a long pause. Then Karl said, 'Where's chef?'

'Locked in the coat cupboard.'

There was another long pause. 'He'll fire us,' someone said nervously.

Bruno shook his head. 'No, he won't. If you *all* agree to help, how can he pick on any one of you? And if he fires all of you, he wouldn't be able to open tomorrow. The truth is, he needs you more than you need him.'

Karl said, 'I liked that Roman dish you showed me how to cook when the Mafia turned up. And I've been calling out that idiot's orders long enough anyway. It's time we had some fun around here. I'll help you.'

'What about the rest of you?' Bruno said, looking around.

One by one, with various degrees of enthusiasm or reluctance, the kitchen brigade nodded.

'Right,' Bruno said. 'Let's get to work. You,' he pointed at the *sous* nearest to him, 'get me some whites.'

'Yes, chef.'

'The rest of you, listen carefully.'

'Hi,' Marie said brightly to table twelve. 'Has anyone told you guys the specials?'

'We've already ordered,' someone pointed out.

'I'm afraid what you ordered is off.'

'All of it?'

'Pretty much. But we do have, uh, *carpaccio* of pan-fried *capretto* with a sleepy margherita jus and line-caught *radicchio*,' she said, rattling off the ingredients very fast since she actually had no idea at all what Bruno planned to cook.

'Sounds good to me,' said the young man nearest to Marie's breasts.

'Me too,' said the girl next to him, who couldn't remember what she'd ordered in the first place.

'Good. Chef's specials all round. And let me get you some more of that wine,' Marie said quickly, bending low over the table to pour the last of the bottle into Kim Fellowes's glass.

'Does the chef's special have carbohydrate in it?' he asked.

'Absolutely not,' she assured him. 'It's one hundred per cent organic.'

She was gone before he could ask her to explain. At the next table, Tommaso was also busy explaining that the menu had been unavoidably changed at short notice.

The kitchen staff at Templi had never worked so hard under Alain's dictatorial rule as they did now for Bruno. Dishes that should have taken hours to prepare were being turned out in a matter of minutes.

'It's going great,' Tommaso confirmed when he came back for more plates. 'Just keep the food coming.'

'I'm doing my best,' Bruno muttered.

'I need your best, but faster. There are people in there who'll start to get hungry in about ten minutes.'

Bruno cooked faster. Soon a stream of dishes was being carried out to the dining room, but he had no time to rest. He immediately got the kitchen to work on the *secondi*.

Something strange was happening in the dining room. The kitchen staff became aware of an unfamiliar hum, like the buzzing of a swarm of bees, coming from beyond the swing doors. One or two of them, who had been present during the night of the eels, looked up apprehensively. Then a waiter pushed through the doors and the sound, previously muffled, suddenly came into focus. It was the hum of animated conversation. And not just conversation. Mingled with it was the sound of laughter, laughter of every sort—amused, bawdy, raucous, jovial.

At table twelve, only two people remained immune to the changing mood. Laura, sick with nerves, wasn't eating a thing. And Kim, rigidly adhering to his diet, was looking increasingly puzzled as all around him his fellow diners appeared to be intoxicated. They weren't even staying in their seats, he saw to his horror: people were walking around, chatting to complete strangers, laughing and joking. He made a decision. Better to do this now, before these noisy Italians ruined the perfect atmosphere he had worked so hard to engineer.

Kim stood up. One by one the other diners stopped whatever they were doing and turned to see what was going on. Kim nodded to his barbershop quartet, who began to sing. The hum of laughter died, replaced by the quiet, solemn harmonies of Allegri's *Miserere*.

'Laura, my darling,' Kim began in Italian. 'It was in this very city that Petrarch wrote some of his most beautiful poems about a girl called Laura. Now, five centuries later, I too have fallen in love with her . . .'

It's happening, Laura thought as forty-eight pairs of eyes swivelled to look at her. What on earth am I going to do?

'It's a disaster,' Tommaso shouted to Bruno as he rushed into the kitchen. 'The American's proposing to her.'

'*What?*'

'*Si.* You'd better come quickly.'

Bruno looked at the mess of ingredients on his board. 'But it's not ready.'

'Too bad. By the time you *are* ready, it'll be too late.'

Kim was reaching the end of his speech. It was fine and noble and deeply moving: men as well as women were brushing away tears as Kim finally went down on one knee, pulled out a small box and flipped it open. There was a collective gasp as the ring flashed in the evening sunlight.

'Laura—*bellissima*—will you be my wife?' he said, just as the singers drew to a close.

All around the room, people lifted their hands expectantly, ready to clap. There was just the little matter of Laura's response—which would undoubtedly be equally as beautiful and equally as moving—and then they could all go wild.

Laura took a deep breath.

'Kim, you've asked me this question in front of all these people, so it's in front of all these people that I have to respond. You're a wonderful, intelligent, sensitive person, and I've really enjoyed our time together. But the answer's no. You can ask me to explain now, or I can explain later, but I'm sorry, my mind's made up.'

You could have cut the silence with a knife.

Kim said quickly, 'Laura, it's a lot to take in. Yes, let's talk about it. Of course we must talk about it. You've drunk a little wine, you've eaten well—you know how stupefied carbohydrate makes you feel—so I'll take that as a maybe, and you can have all the time you need—'

'You're not listening,' she interrupted. 'No isn't a negotiating position, Kim. You've taught me a lot, but you were only ever my rebound from—from something before that went horribly wrong. I don't want to spend the rest of my life being told what to do by you, and I don't want to be told that I have to marry you.'

At the back of the room, Tommaso pushed Bruno forward. 'It's now or never, my friend,' he whispered.

Bruno was holding a plate on which there were some pieces of pear and a small amount of *zabaione* sauce—all he had had time to prepare. As he walked towards Laura, the other diners, sensing that the entertainment wasn't over yet, swivelled to watch him. Bruno felt his cheeks go red.

At last he was standing in front of her. In her eyes there was nothing he could read, no expression from which he could take either comfort or despair.

'This is for you,' he began, putting the plate in front of her.

Laura looked at the pear in its little island of *zabaione*. Suddenly Bruno knew that it wasn't enough. There was a long, terrible silence.

'I was going to tell you that it expresses what I feel better than I ever could,' he said helplessly. 'But that isn't true, is it? It doesn't express anything. Sometimes food is just—food.' He glanced at Kim, who was staring at him with an expression of fierce disdain. 'At least *he* had the guts to tell you what he wanted. Whereas I always thought that my silence, and my cooking, would somehow be enough.'

Laura nodded slowly.

'When I think back to all the meals I made for you,' he said, 'I remember meals that were meant to impress you, meals that were meant to dazzle you, to excite you, to comfort you, even to seduce you. But there was never a single dish that was designed to tell you the simple truth.'

She said nothing.

'The truth is,' he began. He stopped, aware that every single person in the room was staring at him, their expressions varying from amusement to incomprehension. The silence stretched on for ever. He could taste it.

'The truth is that I love you,' he said softly. 'I've always loved you. I always will love you. And what I want, more than anything else in the world, is to go on loving you.'

'I'm going home tomorrow,' Laura said.

'I know,' he said simply. 'But we've got tonight.'

As she stood up, she took one of the pieces of pear and slid it into his mouth. 'In that case,' she said, 'let's not spend it here.'

471

ANTHONY CAPELLA

In a little bar in a side street off the Viale Glorioso, Gennaro had finished the modifications to his Gaggia, created from the tractor parts he had found on his van. Having packed the barrels with coffee grounds, he turned on the ignition and stood back.

For a moment nothing happened. Then, with a great clanking throb, the vast engine caught and began to build the pressure.

Across the street, on the top floor, Bruno and Laura did not hear the chugging of Gennaro's coffee machine. Finally, they were oblivious to everything except the sweet, long-awaited taste of each other's body.

As the needle on the pressure gauge climbed towards the maximum, Gennaro exhaled a sigh of satisfaction. It was working. He had achieved his life's ambition—the perfect cup of coffee. He reached for the valve that would release the pent-up water into the coffee grounds. But he reached for it a moment too late.

There was an explosion that was heard on the other side of the Tiber, and the sky above Trastevere lit up briefly.

'What was that?' Bruno said, pausing for a moment. Then, because Laura didn't answer, he went back to what he had been doing before.

Ricette

'The taste [these recipes] have been devised to achieve wants not to astonish but to reassure. It issues from the cultural memory, the enduring world of Italian cooks, each generation setting a place at table where the next one will feel at ease and at home.'

MARCELLA HAZAN,
The Essentials of Classic Italian Cooking

To: Bruno
From: Laura
Re: Well, here I am.

And there you are. A long way away. This place seems very big and stressed-out after Rome. College, though, is exactly the same. Weird, when I've done so much, to come back and find the same people doing exactly the same stuff as before I went away.

In ten weeks it'll be the holidays, and then I'll be straight back to see you. (Thank God for cheap flights.) In the meantime . . . this afternoon I went down

472

to Little Italy and found a deli. OK, it isn't Gigliemi, but it's got lots of stuff you'd recognise. And guess what? There's a cooking class I can sign up for. You'd better watch your laurels, boy.

love,

L

PS Where should I start?

**To: Laura
From: Bruno
Re: re: Well, here I am.**

Spaghetti ajo e ojo.

This is about as simple as it gets . . .

Actually, spaghettini—the thin stuff—probably holds the oil better than spaghetti. If you can't get that, try linguine or even vermicelli.

Slice a clove of garlic as thinly as you can and fry it in some good oil until it goes soft (not brown). Add some dried chilli flakes. Remove the garlic. Meanwhile, boil the pasta in salted water, drain, and tip it into the frying pan to fry for a minute. Serve with salt, pepper and a lot of grated pecorino romano.

Alternatively: *Tagliatelle con ragù bolognese*

Fry some chopped vegetables—onion, carrot, celery, maybe a couple of mushrooms. You'll need about 100g of pancetta or chopped bacon for 300g of minced meat. (Pork is best.) Fry until the meat goes grey, then add a little wine; wait till it evaporates, then add four tablespoons of tomato paste and season. A dash of chilli helps too. Gradually add the rest of the bottle and half a pint of stock. Traditionally you should cook this 'from sunrise to sunset', but actually a couple of hours will do. Then stir in some cream and cook, uncovered, until it goes thick and sticky.

Or, if you're feeling a little braver: *Pappardelle con sugo di lepre*

Fry some chopped bacon or pancetta, add your hare in (fairly small) pieces & brown it all over, remove and keep warm. Fry a chopped onion and some garlic gently until soft but definitely not brown. Stir in a handful of flour (gradually), then add three-quarters of a bottle of wine. Drink the rest. Put the hare back in, season, add a clove and plenty of thyme (not the stalks) and a dash of pepper sauce. Simmer for two hours, then strip the meat off the bones and shred it before returning it to the sauce. Turn the heat up to reduce it further. (If you have the hare's liver, fry it and blend it with the sauce to thicken it.) Serve with pappardelle and grated Parmesan.

Did I tell you I love you?

B

To: Bruno
From: Laura
Re:re:re: Well, here I am.

Yes, several times.

Tried the ragù last night on my new room-mate, Lucy. Which led, of course, to the whole story coming out, bit by bit, over dinner . . . She actually cried. So, to cut a long story short, she's appointed herself your official representative, keeping me from temptation, singles bars and middle-aged lecturers. I think I may be able to give her the slip, though. (Joke.)

Tomorrow I have my first cooking lesson. Apparently we will be learning how to chop. Ha! I shall soon be a mean hand with a sharp knife, so don't mess with me, lover boy.

Laura

PS If you really think we can get hares over here . . .

To: Bruno
From: Laura
Re:re:re:re: Well, here I am.

Thanks for the hare. You're very sweet. The man from FedEx looked a bit puzzled, though.

According to Martha, my cooking teacher, I have nimble fingers!

To: Laura
From: Bruno
Re:re:re:re:re: Well, here I am.

Actually, I remember those nimble fingers very well . . .

To: Bruno
From: Laura
Re:re:re:re:re:re: Well, here I am.

Speaking of which . . . phone sex, tonight, about ten p.m. my time?

To: Laura
From: Bruno
Re:re:re:re:re:re:re: Well, here I am.

Mmmmmm. That was nice. Sleep well.

To: Bruno
From: Laura
Re:re:re:re:re:re:re:re: Well, here I am.

Wasn't it? & I will. What's for breakfast?

To: Laura
From: Bruno
Re:re:re:re:re:re:re:re:re: Well, here I am.

Zabaglione—eaten as a breakfast dish in the countryside here, I'll have you know.

Beat 6 fresh egg yolks with 3 tablespoons caster sugar until pale, then stir in a glass of dry white wine. Pour into a bowl which you have placed in a saucepan of gently simmering water, and whisk. It will swell to a thick foam. Lovely.

To: Bruno
From: Laura
Re:re:re:re:re:re:re:re:re:re: Well, here I am.

That zabaglione . . . pure heaven. Lucy says: if I am ever unfaithful, can she have you please?

I can now make béchamel sauce! Martha says I have a knack.

And today she told us to buy our first Italian cookery book, a massive tome written I'm sure by a real *nonnina*. I'm determined to learn how to make pasta by hand. Then I'll be a real Italian housewife.

PS What are you going to cook me the first night I come back to Rome?

To: Laura
From: Bruno
Re: Coming back?

Now that is a tricky one. Perhaps we could cook it together?
  B

To: Bruno
From: Laura
Re:re: Coming back?

Oh no, maestro—don't forget, I've only been doing this stuff for about two minutes. And I know what you chefs are like. You'll shout at me if I get it wrong, won't you? You'll probably make me cry.
  L

To: Laura
From: Bruno
Re:re:re: Coming back?

Shout at you? I'd rather cut out my own heart and fry it. And sharing a kitchen with you would be just the most wonderful thing I could imagine . . . which reminds me, there was something—someone—before we got together that I probably need to tell you about. Call me later—but not before you've closed your eyes and thought about:

Porchetta

You can get suckling pig any time of year. (Well, maybe not where you are.)

There are many ways of doing this. I had some once that was stuffed with sage and wild fennel, which was amazing. But I prefer this recipe, which is more Roman:

Take the pig's offal—heart, lungs, liver etc—slice finely and sauté in lard or oil. Add rosemary, garlic and sage. Bone the pig and stuff with the mixture before sewing it together again, scoring the skin, and roasting for five hours over a wood fire. If no wood fire is available, a wood-fired pizza oven would do.

Let's talk later,

B

To: Bruno
From: Laura
Re: That conversation last night

Well, I suppose I should thank her. She obviously taught you a lot. (I'm talking about cooking here, of course.)

To: Laura
From: Bruno
Re:re: That conversation last night

Of course.

Winter's almost here now. I only noticed it at first because there were chestnuts in the market, and in the restaurants they've put Monte Bianco on the menu . . .

Monte Bianco. A seasonal dessert from the north.

Before you start, put a mixing bowl in the freezer. Soak 500g fresh chestnuts in water, then cut around the shells to loosen them—your cookery book will show you how to do this. Boil for 25 minutes and peel while warm.

Put in a pan and cover with milk. Simmer. After about 15 minutes the milk will have been absorbed. Purée in a food processor. Add 200g chocolate, melted in a double boiler, and a little rum. Cover with Cling Film and refrigerate for one hour. Use a food mill or a pierced piping bag to turn the mixture into little worm-sized pieces, like mince. Pile up on a plate. Mix 300ml cold whipping cream with a teaspoon of caster sugar, whisk until it stiffens and pour it over the dessert so that it looks like Mont Blanc—which we call Monte Bianco—covered in snow.

Now that it's getting cold my bed seems very empty.

B

To: Bruno
From: Laura
Re: Cold

Cold? In Rome? You must be joking. It's −10 degrees here.

How's the new season's oil? According to my Italian lady's cook book: 'On those brisk days that bridge the passage from autumn to winter and signal the release of this year's freshly pressed olive oil, toasting bread over a smoky fire and soaking it with spicy, laser-green newly minted oil is a practice probably as old as Rome itself . . .'

To: Laura
From: Bruno
Re:re: Cold

Yes—she's describing bruschetta. Just grill some good Italian bread, preferably on a flame (a naked gas flame would do). Rub it with a mashed garlic clove and pour on a thin stream of the new season's olive oil your faraway lover has just sent you by FedEx. Sprinkle with salt. For a more filling antipasto, top with diced tomatoes and fresh basil.
   Love you,
   B

To: Bruno
From: Laura
Re: That recipe for bruschetta

Thing is, I just don't seem to be able to get that one right. It's simple but difficult, as Tommaso would probably have said. Every time I try to do it, something goes wrong. Tell you what—I think I need someone to show me how to do it . . .

To: Laura
From: Bruno
Re:re: That recipe for bruschetta

??????????? I'm not with you.

To: Bruno
From: Laura
Re:re:re: That recipe for bruschetta

Aha! No, you're not. And that's my whole point.

To: Laura
From: Bruno
Re:re:re:re: That recipe for bruschetta

I mean, I don't understand. How can you not be able to cook bruschetta, when you can do all those other things? And what do you mean about needing some-body to show you?

To: Bruno
From: Laura
Re:re:re:re:re: That recipe for bruschetta

Well, it's like this . . .

I was talking to my cooking teacher the other day. She says she knows of at least a dozen Italian restaurants over here where someone who's cooked at Templi could get a job . . .

What do you think?

To: Laura
From: Bruno
Re:re:re:re:re:re: That recipe for bruschetta

I think I'm on my way.

Want to send me a shopping list?

ANTHONY CAPELLA

After all the wonderful, mouth-watering descriptions of Roman dishes in *The Food of Love*, I was rather worried about where to meet Anthony Capella for lunch, so I took the coward's way out by asking him to name his favourite Italian restaurants. 'I love Locanda Locatelli,' he replied by email, 'or Passione, or any branch of Zizzi's or Spiga.' We settled for Passione, where we chatted about his first novel.

'I had the idea quite some time ago,' Anthony told me. 'But it sat in my bottom drawer because there always seemed to be a reason not to write it.' Anthony Capella and his wife were busy running a free-range pig farm in Oxfordshire, but sadly the venture failed when their pigs contracted a disease called blue ear. 'This disease stops the sows from having litters and for us, as breeders, it was disastrous.' With a family to support, Anthony had to take on a variety of jobs but they all came to nothing. 'Then, one weekend, I thought about my languishing novel and decided that the time had come to write it. Unfortunately, I was looking after my youngest son that weekend, and I had to follow him round the house with my laptop! But, luckily, the pages kept flowing and after a week or so I sent the first few chapters to an agent I had used before when I had tried—and failed—to write screenplays. The agent took it to the Frankfurt Book Fair and called to tell me that I had to keep writing because I had been offered a lucrative publishing deal. I was stunned, especially when the film rights were also sold.'

To help capture the Italian atmosphere, Anthony Capella returned to Rome, a city in which he had spent his gap year before reading English at Oxford University, and where he had fallen in love with Roman food. 'Researching the novel meant that I had to do a lot of eating,' Anthony said with a smile, as he tucked into octopus salad. 'And I've acquired a strong stomach as a result!'

So, is Anthony Capella a self-taught chef? 'God, no,' he laughed. 'I can cook a bit and I like to muck around, try different ingredients, mix different cultures. But I've never worked in a kitchen or anything.' What he did do was read lots of Italian cookery books. 'When Italians write about food, they are also writing about life. And that's what I wanted to do too.

'I had a kind of eureka moment,' Anthony continued, 'when I thought it would be fun to make comparisons with Edmond Rostand's *Cyrano de Bergerac*. Cyrano is an accomplished swordsman, for example, and so I emphasised Bruno's dexterity with a chopping knife. Then there were the duels in the kitchen, the large nose versus a Roman nose, the phone text message instead of the lyrical letter . . .'

Anthony Capella works part-time in advertising and is busy working on ideas for his second novel. 'My only concern is that, without the impetus of a large overdraft, it will be much harder to write than *The Food of Love!*'

Jane Eastgate

601-027-1